*The*

# LADY BREWER
*of* LONDON

# *The* LADY BREWER *of* LONDON

### A NOVEL

# KAREN BROOKS

**WM**
WILLIAM MORROW
*An Imprint of* HarperCollins*Publishers*

HarperCollins books may be purchased for educational, business, or sales promotional use. For information, please email the Special Markets Department at SPsales@harpercollins.com.

Originally published as *The Brewer's Tale* in Australia in 2014 by Harlequin MIRA.

FIRST U.S. EDITION

*Designed by Diahann Sturge*
*Title page illustration © Istry Istry / Shutterstock, Inc.*

Library of Congress Cataloging-in-Publication Data has been applied for.

ISBN 978-0-06-300824-3

20 21 22 23 24  LSC  10 9 8 7 6 5 4 3 2 1

*This tale is for my wonderful agent and friend,
Selwa Anthony, who is quite simply the best.*

*It's also, like all my books, for Stephen, without
whom my life would be a very different story.*

*Twenty thousand years ago, it was a goddess who gave
life and abundance and it was the goddess who, out of a
mother's love and pity for her fallen children, gave the gift
of brew to the women of mankind. The cup of bliss, the
gourd of temporary forgetfulness was filled with beer . . .*

*In all the ancient societies, in the religious mythologies
of all ancient cultures, beer was a gift to women from
a goddess, never a male god, and women remained
bonded in complex religious relationships with
feminine deities who blessed the brew vessels . . .*

—Alan Eames, quoted in Stephen Harrod Buhner,
*Sacred and Herbal Healing Beers:
The Secrets of Ancient Fermentation*

*If a venture prospers, women fade from the scene.*

—Joan Thirsk, quoted in Judith M. Bennett,
*Ale, Beer, and Brewsters in England:
Women's Work in a Changing World, 1300–1600*

# PART ONE
# The Brewer of Elmham Lenn

*SEPTEMBER 1405–JUNE 1406*

*A man that hath a sign at his door,*
*And keeps good Ale to sell,*
*A comely wife to please his guests,*
*May thrive exceedingly well . . .*

—From "Choice of Inventions," quoted in Judith M.
Bennett, *Ale, Beer, and Brewsters in England: Women's*
*Work in a Changing World, 1300–1600*

# ONE

ELMHAM LENN

Dawn, the day after Michaelmas

*The year of Our Lord 1405 in the sixth*

*year of the reign of Henry IV*

*A* sharp wind slapped the sodden hem against my ankles. Clutching the cloak beneath my chin with one hand, I held the other over my brow as a shield from the stinging ocean spray and squinted to see past the curtain of angry gray mizzle drawn across the entry to the harbor. I tried to transport myself beyond the heads, imagine what lay out there; see with my mind's eye what my physical one could not.

Just as they had for the last three days, land and water conspired against me.

With a protracted sigh, I turned and walked back along the dock, my mantle damp and heavy across my shoulders. Brine made the wood slick and the receding tide had strewn seaweed and other flotsam across the worn planks. Barnacles and ancient gull droppings clung to the thick timbers, resisting the endless waves. I marveled at their tenacity.

On one side of the pier, a number of boats protested against their moorings, rocking wildly from side to side, abandoned by their crews till the weather passed. Along the pebbled shores of the bay, smaller vessels were drawn high, overturned on the grassy dunes, their owners hunkered near the harbormaster's office at the other end of the dock, drinking ale and complaining about the unnatural weather that stole their livelihood, pretending not to be worried about those who hadn't yet come home. I waved to them as I drew closer and a couple of the old salts raised their arms in return.

They knew what dragged me from my warm bed and down to the harbor before the servants stirred. It was what brought any of us who dared to draw a living from the seas.

I continued, lifting my skirts and jumping a puddle that had collected where the dock ended and the dirt track that followed the estuary into town began.

To the toll of morning bells, I joined the procession of carts, horses, and vendors trundling into market as the sky lightened to a pearlescent hue. The rain that hovered out to sea remained both threat and promise. Ships that plied their trade across the Channel were anchored mid-river, their sails furled or taken down for repairs; their wooden decks gleaming, their ropes beautifully knotted as captains sought to keep their crews busy while the weather refused them access to the open water. Some had hired barges to transport their cargo to London, while others sold what they could to local shopkeepers or went to Norwich. Closer to the town, abutting the riverbanks, were the warehouses belonging to the Hanseatic League, their wide doors open. Bales of wool, wooden barrels, swollen sacks of grain and salt were stacked waiting to be loaded onto ships that were already overdue—ours being one of them. The workers lingered near the entry hoping to snatch some news. Like us, these men, so far from their homeland, longed to hear that their compatriots were safe. Apart from the whinny of horses, the grunt of oxen, and the grind of cartwheels, silence accompanied us for the remainder of the trip into town.

As our procession spilled through the old wooden gates, dirty-faced urchins leaped onto the path, offering rooms, food, and other less savory fare, tugging at cloaks, pulling at mantles. Avoiding the children, I steered around the visiting merchants and traveling hawkers who paused to pay tolls and slipped past the packhorses and carts to head toward the town center. Jostled by the farmers with their corn and livestock, apprentices wearing leather aprons and earnest expressions, the way was slow. Before I'd passed the well, the bells of St. Stephen's began to toll, announcing the official opening of the market. Around me, shop shutters sprang open, their bleary-eyed owners waving customers forth. "Hot pottage," "Baked sheep's cheek," "Venetian silk," "Copper pans going cheap"; their cries mingled and were soon drowned in the discordant symphony of market day. Catching a glimpse of our housekeeper, Saskia, among the crowd, I darted down the lane near St. Nichols and increased my pace. It wasn't that I didn't like Saskia—on the contrary, as one of my mother's countrywomen, a constant presence since I was a baby, I loved her dearly. I just wanted to enjoy a few more minutes of my own company, without questions or making decisions or, what I was really avoiding, the suffocating weight of the unspoken. I also wanted to make it home before Hiske knew where I'd been or the twins escaped the nursery. If she spied me, Saskia, with the familiarity of a valued servant, would suborn me to her will. I needed to dry myself and change my gown. More importantly, I had to erase the worry from my face and voice. Why I insisted on doing this, going to the seaside these last few days, I was uncertain. It was a compulsion I couldn't resist. It gave me purpose, prevented me from feeling quite so helpless. I thought about what I'd tell the twins today, how I would distract them. I rounded the corner back onto Market Street, the main road that led to the gate at the other end of town. Walking against the tide of people, I drew my hood, quickened my step, and entered the alley that ran beside my home. I unlatched the garden gate and squeezed through.

Passing our scant vegetable patch, I hugged the outside wall of the old stables, plucking at the laces at my throat and pulling my cloak off my shoulders and my hood from my head, still hoping I wouldn't be spotted from upstairs. I was relieved to note Patroclus and Achilles, our two wolfhounds, were absent. Adam Barfoot, the steward, must be walking them—a task he'd performed for years now, ever since we'd let go of the servants Hiske persuaded Father we no longer needed. I tossed the two bones I'd carried in my pockets as a bribe for their peace toward the kennels. The dogs could enjoy them on their return. Perhaps my early-morning vigil would go undetected after all.

Folding my cloak and hood over my arm and adopting nonchalance, as if it was always my custom to stroll in the gardens at dawn, I crossed the courtyard, passing the disused brewhouse.

"God give you good day, Mistress Sheldrake."

My hand flew to my breast.

The chambermaid, Doreen, appeared carrying a basket of eggs

over her arm. "About early again?" Her sharp eyes looked me up and down, taking in my windswept hair, damp clothes, and muddy boots. "And alone, I see." She sniffed her disapproval.

With a sinking heart, I knew she'd report me to Hiske. If Hiske knew, so too would Father. I sighed. There was no point denying what her eyes, the state of my clothes, and my chest, heaving from rushing, clearly told her.

"As you can see, Doreen, I am. *Again*," I added defiantly, my cheeks flaming, then swept past her, almost knocking the basket from her forearm.

I entered the kitchen with as much equanimity as I could muster. The heat of the stove and the smell of baking bread made me aware of how chilled I was—and hungry. My mouth watered as I greeted the cook, Blanche, who stopped what she was doing and studied me, eyebrows arched.

"Mistress Anneke, you haven't been," she began, but paused as Doreen appeared behind me, "enjoying the fresh air and rain again?" she asked with false gaiety. "I'll have some hot water and a tray sent to your room, shall I? We don't want you catching your death."

"Mistress Jabben is expecting Mistress Sheldrake to join her in the hall, Mistress Blanche—" Doreen was getting bolder by the day.

Ignoring Doreen, I turned to the cook. "Thank you, Blanche." My gratitude was in my smile. "That would be perfect." Avoiding Doreen's pursed lips and cold stare, I scurried through the hall before Hiske, who was sitting at the far end, close to the hearth, saw me. Thrusting aside my dignity, I bunched my tunic and shot up the stairs two at a time.

Walking through Tobias's old room, I threw aside the curtain that divided our chambers and flung my cloak and hood across the chest that held my clothes and other belongings. Though I could have taken down the curtain and adopted my brother's room as my own, giving myself more space, I'd chosen to maintain what I'd always had and keep Tobias's bedroom as it was. Hiske disapproved, saying shrines were for God only and I was making a false idol of my brother. I wasn't so foolish. Content with what I had, I was also happy knowing that Tobias had a place to lay his head should he ever require one.

I opened the shutters, and ashen light poured in, along with a cold draft tinted with more rain. Stripping off my tunic and kirtle, I stood shivering in my underclothes and undid my braid. Lifting a used drying sheet from the small table abutting my bed, I quickly toweled my body and then focused on my hair, ears pricked for sound—for Hiske. How ridiculous that, at my age, I snuck about the house like a thief in the night.

Blanche was true to her promise, and the kitchen maid, Iris, arrived with a bowl of steaming water and a fresh drying sheet, taking away my used one. Minutes later, she reappeared with a tray holding a trencher of bread, a lump of yellow cheese, and a small beaker of ale. Curtsying, she left me to tend myself as was my wont.

Washed and dressed in a clean, dry kirtle and tunic, my hair tidied, I was picking at the cheese when I heard the clatter of boots and loud whispers. Karel and Betje burst through the curtain, followed by their apologetic nurse, Louisa.

"Anneke!" they squealed, as if they hadn't seen me the night before. Dropping to my knees, I hugged them fiercely, inhaling scents of rosewater and lavender. Holding first Betje, then Karel, at arm's length, admiring their sturdy arms and legs, pink cheeks, and gapped teeth, I released them and stood, laughing. How could anyone be gloomy with these two around? Sinking onto the window seat, I watched them taunt Louisa, who tried and failed to prevent Karel jumping on the bed. Giving up, she attempted to tame Betje's hair. A riot of silvery curls, it refused to remain in the plaits Louisa insisted upon weaving.

"Anneke, tell Betje," said Karel, almost falling off the bed, waving his arms in circles to regain his balance. "Tell Betje . . ." he tried again, then gave up trying to talk and bounce at the same time and instead sat heavily on the end of the mattress, swinging his legs. His energy was something palpable, infectious. "Papa's coming home today, isn't he?"

"And Tobias," added Betje, twisting toward her brother, exclaiming when her hair was pulled. "Don't forget him. You always leave him out."

"I do not!"

"You do so. Just because he doesn't live here doesn't mean we shouldn't worry about him as well." Betje glared at Karel then spun back, rubbing her head. "Is it today, Anneke?" Betje's large gray eyes alighted on mine, her little brow puckered. "Will Papa be coming home?"

Louisa and I exchanged a look.

"Perhaps," I answered cautiously. "Now remain still and let Louisa finish," I admonished gently, cupping her cheeks briefly.

"Perhaps! You said that yesterday." Karel pouted.

"And the day before," added Betje.

"And *perhaps* I will say it tomorrow." They both groaned. "The fact is, I don't know." I shrugged, affecting a lightness I didn't feel. "No one does." I sat back down and looked outside. A squall rattled the panes. The trees in the churchyard next

door were buffeted by winds, stubborn autumn leaves clinging to the branches. They looked like hungry fingers reaching,
grasping . . . I stared beyond the garden wall, past the church,
the road, toward the wide, white-capped bay and into the vast
ashen void. Somewhere across that raging sea were the Netherlands, Flanders, Rotterdam, Ghent, and my mother's home,
Maastricht, and all the places Father sailed, as did Tobias with
his master. I imagined Father looking back at me, frowning, his
thin lips disappearing as he prepared to scold me for allowing
emotions to govern common sense. They voyaged in this kind
of weather all the time, a trader's life was built on risk, he would
remind me—and not only those offered by the oceans.

*But this time is different . . . They should be home by now . . .*
*Papa, at least . . .* I bit my lip. As for Tobias, he belonged to another family now, called another place home. It didn't stop me
claiming him still or, as Betje said, any of us worrying.

Betje climbed onto my lap. I shifted to accommodate her and
wrapped my arms around her tightly.

Snuggling against my breast, she tilted her head back. "We
won't be able to do this anymore once Papa is home, will we?"

"We'll have to stay in the nursery again, won't we?" said Karel
quietly from the bed, staring at the toe of his boot.

"We won't, my sweetlings, and," I said softly to Karel, "you
will. Papa is a very busy man. He doesn't like to be disturbed."

"But we want to disturb *you*, not him," said Karel.

I bit back a smile.

"Papa doesn't like a lot of things," said Betje, with the innocence of childish observation. She stared out the window.

No one replied.

"The sky is angry," she said in an awed voice. "That means God is as well, doesn't it?"

I followed her gaze and it struck me, as the rain fell, steady enough to form rivulets on the thick glass, that if God was expressing any emotion, it was sadness. I kissed the top of Betje's head, preparing a reassurance, when something attracted my attention.

Betje saw it too. "Look!" She sat up and pointed. "There's a rider."

The messenger tore by the church walls, his slender mare churning the road. With a lurch, I recognized the livery and wondered what was so important he should be abroad on such a day.

Karel bolted from the bed and squeezed beside us. "Where?" he demanded, his head swiveling until he spotted him. "Look, there's someone else with him as well. They're stopping. Right outside our house!" He pressed his face against the window, the glass turning opaque where his breath struck.

"Let me see," complained Betje, trying to shove her brother out of the way.

Karel was right. The men talked urgently, walking their horses toward the front of the house.

"Oh my," added Louisa from behind. "Mistress—" Apprehension inflected her tone.

I rose, lifting Betje from my lap, eyes fixed on the figure tethering his horse, waiting for the black-robed gentleman beside him to dismount before they strode out of sight. "Louisa, take the children back to the nursery, would you?"

"But Anneke . . ." they chorused.

"Come now," said Louisa, authoritarian. "You heard what your sister said. Out with you."

Once I heard the nursery door close, I checked my hair, straightened my tunic, and, taking a deep breath, went back downstairs.

⟨≈×≈⟩

As I reached the bottommost stair, I almost collided with Will, the footman. "M . . . Mistress Sheldrake," he said. "I was just coming to get you." He stepped back and bowed, his face hot.

"Thank you, Will," I said. "The office?"

"Aye, mistress. Master Makejoy's here . . ." he hesitated. "Mistress Jabben's there as well."

Will opened the door and stepped aside.

My father's office always roused mixed emotions. It was a forbidden, hallowed space, long and narrow, like a tomb. Sepulchre-like, a lone candle flickered on the desk. Though he wasn't there, my father's presence lingered in every corner, in the ebony wood of his desk, in the stools against the walls, the folios, vellum scrolls, maps, star charts, and ledgers stacked on the shelves, the metal safe under the table, even in the cracked sill of the small, shuttered window that opened onto the shop.

"Mistress Sheldrake." Leonard Makejoy handled Lord Rainford's business affairs and, by default, my father's as well. As I entered, he clambered to his feet, and in that action banished the ghost of my father. With what passed for a smile, he came forward, one arm held out to clasp my waist, the other to take my hand, as if I were an invalid in need of assistance. "God give you good day. Come, sit down."

Attempting not to recoil at his touch, I raised a hand. "If it's all right with you, Master Makejoy, I would rather stand." His attenuated fingers retreated and instead discovered each other. Wringing them, he nodded gravely, his eyes traveling to the piece of paper unfurled on the desk.

"Very well. But with your permission, I'll resume my seat."

I nodded and he sat erect in Father's hard-backed chair, passing a hand over his brow as though fevered. I too felt unnaturally hot. Yet the room was cold. Bitterly so. It had been over three months since a fire had been lit in here.

"What is it, Master Makejoy? What brings you to our home so early on this chill autumn day?" I stepped closer, trying to read what it was he'd carried with him. The Rainford seal occupied the lower left corner, bold black strokes the rest of the missive. I could see our name—Sheldrake. "Is this for me?"

"It is, Mistress Sheldrake. It's from the most honorable and worthy Lord Hardred Rainford." Master Makejoy glanced toward a corner. "I've taken the liberty of informing Mistress Jabben of the contents."

A quiet murmur located Hiske behind me. I looked to where she sat and acknowledged her with the barest inclination of my head. "Cousin Hiske." Emboldened, I pressed on. "What brings *you* to Father's office?"

Hiske rose slowly, smoothing her russet tunic, and approached the desk. The flickering light transformed her face into a foreign landscape of gulfs and ravines.

"Curiosity. I too heard the commotion Master Makejoy's unexpected but most welcome arrival made, and wished to know the reason. Anyhow, it's my right to be here, as you well know."

I pursed my lips, uncertain how to reply. While I wanted to send her away, she was correct. She had the right. Turning back to Master Makejoy, I saw a look pass between them. A flash of . . . what was it? Triumph? Understanding? A shudder ran through me.

"Mistress Sheldrake"—he cleared his throat—"I'm afraid I'm the bearer of terrible tidings . . ."

A frigid wave rolled in my chest. I held out my hand.

With a look I only understood later, Master Makejoy passed me the missive. I read it slowly and, while I registered what was written, another part of me began to resist. The words swam on the page, re-forming to say something completely different. My body endured all seasons in the time it took to process the words. I stared and stared and yet nothing I did changed what was stated in stark, ebony ink.

Raising his rheumy eyes to mine, I saw the future foretold in Master Makejoy's miserable regard.

"This says the *Cathaline* is lost at sea." Though I whispered, my words seemed to echo.

I felt Hiske's shoulder brush mine. She thought to stand by me now, of all times.

"Aye." Master Makejoy waited for me to say more, but nothing came. His confirmation pitched around in my head before I tasted its salty bitterness, then allowed it to meet my heart, which was beating frantically in my ears.

"Father?" My voice was dry, scratchy.

Master Makejoy stood unsteadily and I saw the empty mazer of ale and the jug beside the letter; Hiske had attended quickly to our guest.

"I'm afraid, like the rest of the crew and cargo, he too is unaccounted for. Lord Rainford"—he gestured to the parchment—

"as you have read, presumes him drowned. No one could have survived such a storm, the wreckage . . ."

Darkness collected at the edge of my vision and then sped to steal my sight. I swayed. Master Makejoy said something and Hiske's fingers gripped my arm. A stool was dragged over the floor. I was pushed none too gently onto it. There was a gurgle and splash of liquid.

"Here, drink this," said Hiske, shoving the mazer into my hands. I refused. "Drink it," she insisted.

Ignoring her, I turned to Master Makejoy. Melancholy etched his features, the lines of his long years forming deep furrows. "What about Tobias?"

"There's no word, yet," sighed Master Makejoy. "But thank the good Lord, he's with Sir Leander Rainford, on the *Sealhope*."

"It survived?"

"Along with the rest of Lord Rainford's fleet, it never left Bruges. Sir Leander is . . . more cautious . . ." He held up his hands as if to ward off my protests, though I made none. "You know your father. He would have taken the weather warnings as a personal challenge." Reaching over, he removed the mazer and, placing it gently on the desk, took my fingers. His flesh was papery, dry, his eyes moist and cloudy.

"Father is dead." I said it like a vow.

In reply, he squeezed my hands tighter.

I sat there, lumpen, solid, waiting for the tears, the grief I knew should overcome me. Instead there was silence. Silence broken only by the spit of the candle, the wheeze of Hiske's breathing, Master Makejoy's swallowed belch, and the stench of burning tallow. My head was bowed, my eyes fixed on the floor.

*Father is dead.*

The past telescoped until all that remained were these last few seconds where I was propped in Father's room, a lifeless doll holding the hand of this husk of a man, one who knew the world only in terms of debits and credits and had announced what was to be my lot today: loss.

I thought of all the other ways this description fitted—my father would be spoken of as *lost* at sea, his children as *losing* their father, as if we'd carelessly misplaced him. There would be condolences offered for our *loss*, prayers, sorrow, tears.

A thud above forced my thoughts to fly upstairs. *The twins! Oh dear Lord, the twins.* How would I tell them? They loved their father, in spite of everything . . .

My heart became a thick, swollen mass that pinned me to the seat. It had finally filled, and the pain was indescribable, at once exquisite and deadly. Tears spilled, rolling down my cheeks, dripping onto my hands, onto Master Makejoy's. A sob tore from my throat, a bark that would have done our hounds proud.

With a click of pity, Master Makejoy stood and brought me to my feet. Unpracticed, awkward, he folded his arms around me, pinning my head against his bony shoulder. As the rain beat against the house, the invisible waves beyond surged and hungered, and the heavy clouds slumped above us, God help me, I cried my own torrent—not so much for Father, but for what I knew in my heart his loss augured.

# TWO

ELMHAM LENN
The day after Michaelmas
*The year of Our Lord 1405 in the sixth
year of the reign of Henry IV*

Sorrow, guilt, and, if I searched deeply enough, a sense of relief warred within me in equal measure, prolonging my weeping until Hiske's next words abruptly checked it.

"Tell her the rest, Master Makejoy."

*The rest? What else was there?*

A handkerchief was thrust into my palm. Master Makejoy's
arms withdrew and, once more, I sank onto the stool.

There was the brush of material against my thigh. Cousin
Hiske pressed closer to me. "She must needs know. After all, it
changes everything."

As if Father's death didn't . . . I raised my swollen face.

"Despite his lordship's instructions, it's too soon," said Master Makejoy, examining the lip of the beaker before downing

a good swallow. "Let the poor girl, the family, mourn. They need time."

"That's a luxury they can ill afford," said Hiske, gesturing at the parchment. "Mourning isn't helped by time or tears, Master Makejoy. It only makes sorrow grow. Grief needs to be checked as soon as possible lest we overindulge in it." She sniffed. I twisted and saw in her eyes a peculiar glimmer. "Anyway," she said, flashing her teeth in what passed for a smile, "there are decisions to be made. You must not be seen to thwart his lordship's intentions."

Impatient to be away from them, to get to the twins, I blew my nose in a most unladylike manner. "Too soon or not"—I struggled not to glare at Hiske—"I'd best know what is being referred to, good sir. What does his lordship want?"

Master Makejoy sighed. His eyes lingered on me before he glanced at Hiske and shrugged.

"Very well." Dragging the candle closer, he rolled out another, larger piece of parchment. This was not offered to me. It looked like a deed. Clearing his throat, Master Makejoy used the beaker to hold the parchment flat. "Lord Rainford asked that"—he gave Hiske a reproachful glance—"in due time, I draw your attention to this. I'm not sure how much you know of your father's affairs, Mistress Sheldrake, but over the years, in order to consolidate his business, Master Sheldrake entered into an arrangement with his lordship, one that saw Lord Rainford underwrite all your father's ventures."

"I was aware of that." Not because of Father, but because of Adam Barfoot and Tobias. Master Makejoy didn't need to know that detail.

Master Makejoy arched a bushy brow. "Really?" He cleared

his throat again. "Well, what you may not know is that upon your father's death, any business dealings with Lord Rainford are revoked."

Frowning, I stared at Master Makejoy. "Revoked? What does that mean?"

Master Makejoy gave me the sort of indulgent smile one does a very young child. "Dear Mistress Sheldrake. Your father's death, never mind the sinking of the *Cathaline*, means that any agreements your father had are now invalid; they no longer apply." His tone changed, became businesslike. "You can thank our Maker for Lord Rainford's generosity in appointing Tobias his youngest son's squire. Thus his future is assured. One less Sheldrake to worry about. But as for everything else . . . well . . ." He waved a hand in the air.

"Well, what? To what agreements are you referring?" Darkness made a slow passage from the back of my mind, tarnishing my ability to think clearly.

Master Makejoy leaned back in Father's chair and laced his hands together, the index fingers forming a pyramid that pointed toward the ceiling. "Quite simply, your father's interests in the fleet, his dealings with the Hanseatic League, any merchandise awaiting export and import. Concern for all this now passes back to Lord Rainford, who, of course, will find someone else to manage his mercantile affairs. The good news is that this includes any debts, and believe me when I tell you, the sinking of the *Cathaline* will incur a great many. The business agreement struck between your father and Lord Rainford spares you this at least—these debts are not your responsibility. The bad news is"—he hesitated—"while you don't have any debts to discharge, you no longer possess any assets either."

"None?" I forced my hands still. "But . . . I don't understand."
"It's very simple, Mistress Sheldrake. You have . . . nothing."
I stared at Master Makejoy, aghast. "But how is this possible? Father is . . . was a man of means. We have wanted for very little." I looked to Hiske for confirmation. She regarded me steadily, no inkling of her thoughts evident in those cold eyes. "The shop," I continued, gesturing toward it. "We have a business. Yesterday, there were customers. And the warehouse"—my arm indicated the opposite end of the house, where the goods Father traded, *had traded*, were stored—"there are bales of fabric, wool, spices, some wine—not much, I know, we were awaiting Father's return to replenish . . . but surely they're ours to sell and—"

"Not anymore, I'm afraid. Neither are"—he leaned over and referred to the parchment, his finger trailing down the page— "the control of the remaining ships for which your father bore responsibility. Including the *Cathaline*, there were four in total. There are also the lands abutting this house, which incorporates three holdings, the orchard, and other interests. These were all managed by your father on his lordship's behalf, and for this, your father was paid a fee. Naturally, they now return to the original owner: Lord Rainford." Master Makejoy frowned and his eyes drifted back to the page. "Once they're sold or leased again, there's always the possibility they'll not come anywhere near compensating Lord Rainford for his original investment." He wasn't addressing me but indulging in some imminent conversation with his employer.

"But I always thought that his lordship and Father were business *partners*. What you're saying implies that their relationship was unequal, that Father was akin to a . . . bondsman . . ." My voice petered out.

"Indeed, that's an apt analogy, Mistress Sheldrake. The original contract was signed over sixteen years ago, and both your father and Lord Rainford have enjoyed many successes, have profited in all sorts of ways from their joint ventures." Master Makejoy pushed back the chair and rose, his fingers dusting the metal astrolabe sitting on the desk. "But this doesn't concern you any longer and, in legal terms, a contract is a contract." Reaching over the desk, he opened the shutters, allowing air and light to spill into the room. From where I was sitting, I could see a portion of the shop and, past the large, battered sea chest that I knew contained spools of fabric and lace from Venice and Bruges, as well as dyed rolls of wool from Florence, the outside window admitted views of the street. It was still early, the rain falling more heavily now, and, with the shutters open, I could hear the howl of the wind.

"In an effort to try and recoup previous losses and to compensate for the steady decline in trade that these endless wars with France and Wales have brought about, your father risked everything on this voyage. Some might say too much." Master Makejoy's eyes flickered to Hiske. "It was, he said, to be the making of him."

I looked around the bleak space of the office, stared into the shop. I saw it through different eyes. The empty shelves, the lonely jars and barrels, a sad reel of ribbon, a bolt of ruby cloth, the spaces where nothing sat but flattened rushes. "Is there nothing left for us?" My voice was too quiet, too small.

"For you and your siblings?" Master Makejoy shook his head. "I'm sorry, Mistress Sheldrake, apart from a meager sum, there's not."

No one spoke. The wind whistled and the trees across the

road danced. Adam Barfoot came into view, his head bowed against the wind. His hood had fallen back and he held his cloak together at his throat. Achilles and Patroclus bounded past, their great shaggy coats pressed against their lean frames. At the sight of them, my throat tightened and I felt the prick of tears. I blinked them back.

"There is not," I repeated.

"Not even the house," added Hiske, so softly I almost didn't hear.

"I beg your pardon?" I swung toward her.

"Not even the house." She slowly enunciated every word.

"Is that true?" I asked Master Makejoy, almost rising to my feet. I could hear Achilles and Patroclus barking as they ran down the alley and toward the back gate. *Our back gate.*

Master Makejoy frowned at Hiske. "It is. I was going to get to that, but since Mistress Jabben has seen fit to raise it . . ." Disapproval tinged his tone as he swept the second piece of parchment into his hand. "His lordship granted your father a life-interest in this house and its commercial premises. It was very generous. It included the servants, wages, food, and drink in return for Master Sheldrake's services as master of the fleet, his connections with the Hanseatic League, and those he developed throughout the Low Countries and Germany."

I struggled to get my thoughts together. I tried to understand what it was Master Makejoy was saying. "In other words, Papa doesn't own this house . . . he never has. Like everything else, it belongs to Lord Rainford."

"That's correct."

An image of my father—his stern face, iron eyes, and unsmiling mouth—came into my head. I heard his stentorian tone as he questioned me over dinner in the hall about my day's lessons, what the nuns had taught me. I'd always thought him hard, demanding, implacable, and, worse, cold. Later, I thought I knew why. But I couldn't forgive him for his inflexibility, his lack of affection—not so much toward me or Tobias, but the twins . . . This new knowledge made me see him in a different light, as a man anxious about his prospects, his family; about his obligations. Tears welled as a sense of injustice and contrition rose.

Pushing back my sorrow to examine it later, I looked from Master Makejoy to Hiske. "But, surely, now that Papa's dead, Lord Rainford wouldn't force us onto the street, would he? Not after everything my father has done for him? We have some time to make alternative arrangements?"

"What your father has done?" snapped Hiske. "Child! Haven't you been listening? He's incurred a massive debt, one that would ruin a lesser man. Lord Rainford is simply staking his rightful claim; recouping his losses."

"*His* losses? How can you defend him? You live here too. Papa's death affects you as well." Indignation propelled me to my feet. I was gratified to see Hiske step back.

"*Ja*, it does, Cousin Anneke. And you would do well to remember that."

"What's that supposed to mean?"

Hiske laughed. Her teeth were small, yellow, her gums pale. Her eyes were the color of the pewter jug, flat, depthless. "Just like you, I'm affected by my *dear* cousin's loss. Only, I have options. I always knew my time here was limited, so I've been considering my choices. Whereas, from now on, you're on your own. Your father's death means you've lost everything—your house, your lifestyle, and"—her eyes narrowed and her lips thinned—"your position. You've lost your position."

In my swift accounting, I hadn't considered that—the loss of social status. I didn't want to—I couldn't.

Eyes fixed to my face, Hiske continued. "You'll have to learn to appreciate what others can do for you."

"Are you referring to yourself, Cousin?"

"I am."

"And what is it that you might do?"

Hiske drew herself up to her full height. She looked at Master Makejoy, who smiled and nodded.

"You'll be pleased to know, Cousin Anneke, that though this is a time of great sorrow, on its heels follows great happiness. Master Makejoy and I have an understanding." I looked from one to the other and was astonished to see Hiske redden and Master Makejoy appear coy. "Soon," continued Hiske in a softer voice, "I'll be in a position to be able to offer you, and your brother and sister, a roof over *your* heads."

"*You* would offer me, us, a home?" I couldn't keep the surprise from my voice.

"I didn't say a home, I said a roof." She bent until I was forced to meet that gelid gaze. She might be my mother's blood, but her eyes were like my father's. "Up until a few hours ago, you had a dowry, prospects. Your father and I would have found someone in town who'd be pleased to call you wife, mayhap even one of those brokenhearted souls you've rejected over the years. Now you're a liability. That's the word you used, isn't it, Master Makejoy?"

Master Makejoy mumbled into his chest, shuffling the parchment on the desk.

Hiske laughed. "You've no prospects, Cousin. Not anymore. Why, you're less than a crofter or villein's daughter, and who in their right mind would want the burden of a penniless wife encumbered with two extra mouths to feed?" She paused as if expecting me to respond. "Exactly," she replied, snapping the silence. "That's why, though my responsibilities have, with your father's demise, formally ended, out of the goodness of my heart, and Master Makejoy's, I'm prepared to have you come and live with me—"

It was my turn to look startled.

"As my housekeeper."

I swallowed. "And the twins?"

"I would clothe and feed them until they were of age and then, of course, they would be put to work. Master Makejoy is sure he could find a position for Karel. Betje, well, one can always do with an extra kitchen hand or chambermaid. I'm sure Blanche, or Doreen for that matter, would be happy to teach her. If not, the nuns would take her."

Doreen's growing impudence suddenly made sense. Hiske had been planning to leave, to set up her own house, for some time.

Taken aback at her boldness, her certainty that such an opportunity would be grasped, I gathered my thoughts before speaking. Hiske was right. Not only was I on my own, an orphan, so were my brothers and sister. Whereas Tobias, thank the dear Lord, was assured a future, nothing was certain for the twins or me anymore. As an unmarried and penniless nineteen-year-old woman, I was indeed a liability. My situation had been

cruelly defined, and it was brutally reduced. As for the twins . . .
I recalled the fate of other, less fortunate children whose parents
had been taken from them while they were still young. Monasteries were filled with these souls. Now, here I was, along with
the twins, to be counted among the unfortunate, an object of
pity. My chest burned.

I could hear Will in the corridor outside, Iris too. It wasn't
just me and the twins who stood to lose each other, our house,
our world. Our servants, most of whom had been with us since
before I was born, relied upon us. They too were family. *My
family*. And my family would not live with Hiske.

No matter what.

That Lord Rainford could set out the family's obligations at
such a time, define the extent of our losses; that Hiske and Master Makejoy resolved between themselves to announce our plight
so soon after the news of my father's death, reflected poorly on
all of them. It made me furious and more than a little afraid.
Our destiny had never been mine to control—that was for Father to manage—and he'd neglected that responsibility. Though
I thought I knew why, I couldn't forgive him. For just a brief
moment, when I'd learned of Father's death, I was disconsolate,
but, in the furthest recesses of my heart, I'd also caught a glimpse
of liberty and extraordinary possibility. I wasn't prepared to relinquish that and hand over my future to someone else—especially
not to Hiske. I looked at her now, the narrow mouth, the almost
nonexistent eyebrows arched in superiority, her long neck with
its horizontal lines. Master Makejoy refused to look at either of
us and pretended to reread the contents of the deed.

I could hardly believe that we'd be thrown out of the house,
that this dark, sometimes joyless place, where there'd been life,

terrible secrets, dreadful pain, some joy and too much death, could be taken away—and why? Because an agreement had come to an end. Because of business.

I needed time to think, to find a solution to this new problem. Moving quickly, I forced Hiske to jump to one side. "Cousin Hiske, Master Makejoy, I wish to thank you for your unexpected offer. I would like some time to consider it."

"But, Mistress Sheldrake"—Master Makejoy rose and, with what he thought was a benevolent smile, addressed me—"I don't think you understand the position you're in. How precarious it is."

"Master Makejoy, I understand all too well. And as a consequence, I intend to take as much time as I'm able before I make any decisions."

"There's only one to make, Cousin." Hiske folded her arms beneath her breasts.

I met her gloating gaze without flinching. "Perhaps," I said and, with a small nod to Master Makejoy and a last glance at Hiske, I kept my despair contained and left the room.

# THREE

*I*'d barely time to think about our circumstances as the news spread of Papa's death and the loss of the *Cathaline*. After leaving our house, Master Makejoy rode into town and delivered an account to the Merchants' Guild, and to the Kontor or offices of the Hanseatic League. As it was market day, it didn't take long for word to circulate. From warehouse worker to landlocked sailor, vendor to customer, innkeeper to delivery boy, the usual moaning about taxes and the king's wars and the price of wool was momentarily suspended—Elmham Lenn was suddenly the center of its own tragedy. Swept up in an emotional maelstrom, I accepted commiserations and outpourings of sympathy as neighbors and strangers arrived at our door. I also offered consolation—for we were not the only family to be affected by the ship's sinking. Over forty men had been lost to the sea; other families also felt the loss of a provider, of a husband, son, or brother, of relatives and friends, with a profound yet numbing sorrow, and I ached for these people as well.

Above all, the twins' welfare was my first consideration, and every spare moment was spent with them. While I expected tears and outbursts, both Karel and Betje displayed the pragmatism of the very young, accepting the news with quiet grace and sadness, before looking to Louisa and me to provide their next distraction. Their faith in the patterns of the everyday would have been amusing if it weren't so simultaneously heart-wrenching and comforting. Denied first their mother and now their father, I promised myself I would serve as both for as long as the good Lord allowed, no matter what Hiske threatened.

My next priority was the servants. They already knew what had occurred before I told them. Will, of course, had learned the nature of Lord Rainford's missive—having fetched me to the office, he pressed his ear to the door before racing straight to the kitchen and telling whoever was there. I knew it would only be a matter of time before the servants also knew of Lord Rainford's intention to reclaim the house, and I wanted to be sure they heard it from me first. My reassurances that I would find work, so they were neither thrown to the mercy of the street nor Cousin Hiske, were grasped as a drowning man does driftwood. But the smiles that broke through the weeping and anxiety failed to conceal their doubt. What could a woman, an eldest daughter *with no prospects* do? Their ambivalence simply steeled my resolve.

I sent Will to fetch Father Clement from St. Bartholomew's next door. The man who was both our parish priest and friend should know what had befallen us. He would provide a measure of solace for the servants and, if I was frank, myself as well. I wasn't disappointed. Moments later, Father Clement strode through the gate. I watched him cross the yard, talking to Will, his cassock swinging as he clutched the cross hanging from the cord about his waist, and my heart lifted. Stepping into the kitchen, he sheltered my hands within his own and his hazel eyes said more than words. As he murmured a quiet prayer, Blanche, Adam, Iris, Doreen, Will, and Saskia lowered their heads, the women with handkerchiefs screwed in their fists, the men pale as they slowly took stock of what this change meant.

I recalled an earlier time and a similar tableau. A balmy summer's evening just over six years ago. The sky was leaden, poised to rain, the heat moist. Mother had been listless all day, but it wasn't till her waters broke in the afternoon that we understood the baby had decided to ignore nature's course and arrive early. That it was two months before its time formed a patina of worry that overlaid the excitement. Father was in Ypres—as usual, worlds away from his wife and his expanding family. The midwife and her assistant were sent for and, in a gesture that announced my entrée into the adult world, I was given the role of attending to my mother's needs and helping Saskia in whatever way I could.

Terrified of what was happening, I'd nonetheless obeyed every instruction: wiped the sweat from Mother's brow, held her hand, rubbed her back, propped beside her as she squatted over the freshly laid rushes, teeth clenched, eyes screwed shut, clots of blood dropping from her body, more coating her inner thighs. Hours later, after I'd slept and woken, not once, but twice, first one babe and then another were drawn from her womb. We were jubilant. Two babes! And alive. Cords were cut and they were tenderly swaddled, their squawks softening to whimpers as they were brought to her breast. The afterbirths were examined the moment they were expelled and removed, the stained rushes with them. Once it was over, I felt a rejoicing in my heart. After all the babies Mother had tried and failed to bring into the world—five, at last reckoning—this time she'd managed a pair: a beautiful, red-faced boy and girl. Father would be thrilled; this would make him smile, this would transform him back into the man of my earliest recollections. I couldn't understand why the midwife wasn't radiating joy, why her eyes when they slid from mine to my mother were brimming with sadness. At Mother's insistence, the babes were lifted from her and placed in my old crib. The midwife's young assistant stepped away from the pallet upon which my mother lay, leaving her pale, sweat-drenched, and alone.

Calling me in a voice I no longer knew, Mother took my hand and pulled me to her side, requesting we be left alone. I was scared of the blood, of the strange odor exuding from the woman who always smelled so sweet. Her violet lips and shadowed eyes made her a stranger. Tears began to spill and my nose began to run, even though I couldn't have told you why. Drying my eyes with kisses, stroking my face with trembling, loving fingers, she made me promise that I would obey my father and, in a broken, weary voice, she revealed a terrible, shameful secret. A secret that even now, so many years later, I wanted to erase, to forget, to doubt. Yet it explained so much . . .

I hadn't questioned her, I was shocked into silence. When she had finished, she sank back against the pillow and wrapped her arms around me. Lying across her swollen breasts, I felt her lips and hands against my hair, her hot breath on my head, the slow, ponderous beat of her heart, until, suddenly, I didn't.

It was Father Clement, newly arrived in the parish, who gently coaxed me from Mother's side, performed extreme unction, and held me as I wept. It was the good Father who allowed me to see Mother at peace, her body cleaned and wrapped, her face stripped of color and life, her lips and eyelids forever closed. He'd been so calm, so capable that night. I knew if ever there were a crisis, he would be the one to have by my side. Once the body had been carried to the church, the servants and Father Clement had sat across from each other in the kitchen; the servants quietly weeping, the Father praying. I had stood out of sight in the corner, unable to cry, unable to think or speak. I was like the shadows into which I'd shrunk. Crossing himself, Father Clement raised his head and I was stunned to see tears staining his cheeks; I'd never seen a man cry before. He looked at Saskia and said: "Death too often chases birth and triumphs." His mouth trembled, but he lifted his eyes to the ceiling. "God forgive me," he whispered, but we all heard. "Why does our dear Lord make even good women pay for the sins of Eve? Surely"—he dropped his chin and stared into a space over my shoulder—"surely, the debt has been repaid in full?"

I'd never thought about God in terms of debits or credits before. If I had, I'd have believed my gentle, kind mother would have earned, over and over, a place on earth and an eternal one in heaven. I once would have sworn that God owed her, not the other way around. But not anymore. With Mother's whispered words my eyes had been opened. My mother was as brazen as Adam's wife and as great a sinner. Reproach colored my cheeks but also pride that she'd trusted me with the darkest of confidences. I loved my mother with all my heart and I didn't know how to reconcile what she'd told me with the woman who raised me, the woman I thought I knew. And what about the twins? Were they stained with her sin as well? Blessed Mother Mary knew Tobias was. What did these sweet little babes owe to God? Were they to continue to pay Mother's debt by being denied her? What had I done to suffer such a loss?

That night, I burned with hate for God and Eve, the original sinner. I imagined setting fire to the Garden of Eden and watching the Tree of Knowledge flame, wishing what I'd learned could be reduced to ashes and blow away on the winds. Instead, I pushed what I knew into the recesses of my mind and determined that one day, when the time was right, I would seek the truth. Till then, I would keep what I knew as close to my heart as my mother had.

All this crawled through the maze of my mind as I listened to Father Clement's prayer for my father. When he finished, he reluctantly released my hand and administered what succor he could to the household. Cousin Hiske didn't interfere but quietly thanked him. Later that day, he sat vigil in the church for those whose loved ones had died on the *Cathaline*. I attended briefly, offering words of consolation and receiving them. This wasn't just our loss, but the entire town's. That the ship bore my mother's name made it all the more painful. Guilt attended my every word as if, somehow, I was responsible for these good people's pain. But it was my father who'd christened the ship. Returning home after Mother died to find he had two more mouths to feed (as he put it) and no wife, he'd spoken to Lord Rainford and, within months, another ship was added to Father's

small fleet. Father chose to name it after his dead wife. If anyone thought the gesture ill-omened, they hadn't spoken out . . .
not then.

In my mind, life was divided into two parts: before Mother
died and after. There was another schism too, but I would only
admit it in moments of weakness: before the secret and after.
Between both was a threshold over which I'd been pushed and,
at first, floundered. After Mother died, Father came home to
absorb the news and, I thought, to comfort his children. Within
twenty-four hours of Mother's burial, after grunting at the twins
as Louisa held Karel and I held Betje, Father left—for what port
I did not know. Subsequently, he transformed into little more
than an unpleasant presence that I tried to replace with older,
happier versions until they too faded from memory.

Four months later, bearing a curt explanatory note from Father, Cousin Hiske arrived and promptly took over. Within the
household she'd become my guardian, my torment. I regarded
her now, trying not to feel resentful that the freedom I believed
Father's death would accord me was to be Hiske's instead.

Within a few hours of learning Father's fate, the head of the
Merchants' Guild and the mayor of Elmham Lenn, Master
Dickon Fortescue, arrived with his daughter and my childhood
friend, Betrix. Master Fortescue clumsily offered his sympathies
before informing me that because my father had alienated himself from the guild by joining forces with Lord Rainford and
therefore wasn't obligated to pay tithes, he was unable to offer
me the usual financial and other support provided to merchant
families at these times. Betrix simply held my hand while her
father stuttered and stammered, relieved when he'd done his

duty and was able to leave the solar and join the other callers in the hall downstairs.

"I'm sorry, Anneke," said Betrix after I recounted for her as calmly as I could Master Makejoy's visit. "Papa would do something if he could . . . you do know that, don't you? The other merchants . . . they won't allow him . . . it's just, your father didn't—" She paused, hesitating to speak ill of the dead.

"Have many friends." *I* would say it. The truth cost nothing. Not anymore. Nor did Papa hold any title or office in town. Once, he'd been an alderman and a juror, but those positions had been relinquished before Tobias was born. All my father had was his family and the sea. He turned his back upon one and the other claimed him. I extracted my hand from Betrix's and stood, staring out the window at the procession of people continuing to arrive at the house. I would need to hear their platitudes as well. "Father made his choices and now—"

"You have to suffer them," Betrix finished, and placed an arm around my shoulders.

Had anyone else said those words, I may have denied them. But I'd known Betrix for years. When Father refused to heed the guild and became independent (or so I'd thought) by going into business with Lord Rainford, Betrix's mother, Else, and mine managed to ensure their friendship, and that of their daughters, survived. Up until Mother died, we'd shared so much—silly secrets and the frivolous dreams of the very young; our blooming attraction to various visiting knights or the sons of lords or wealthy merchants. The kind one has when the future is all rosy promise and a press of lips both harmless and pregnant with meaning. Once Hiske was ensconced within the house, taking control of Mother's duties and many others as well, sacking servants and allocating their tasks to me and those who remained ("Idleness is the devil's playground," she'd say), she rejected Mistress Else Fortescue's attempts at friendship, literally closing the door upon her. That meant Betrix was also denied. Though we'd exchanged furtive and even passionate letters of indignation and endless reassurances of sisterly love, and managed to meet in the woods and even at the market once or twice, Hiske's snubbing of Mistress Fortescue (who, as far as she was concerned, as the daughter of a laundress, had married far above her station) meant our friendship eventually cooled. I'd been allowed to attend Betrix's wedding, and I'd even squeezed in a visit after her son, Henry, was born. But I'd seen her stepping out with other girls, girls we'd once laughed at for their foolish antics and lack of learning. The truth was, I'd thought Betrix lost to me and mourned her long ago. Father's death proved me wrong and for that I was very grateful. I learned that some things weren't altered by time, not in an irreparable way anyhow.

Betrix left the house promising to return when things settled. I would hold her to that—Hiske or no Hiske.

I'd half expected the head of the Kontor, the foreign trading post set up by the Hanseatic League in Elmham Lenn, Captain Hatto Stoyan, to call. Amid all the other visitors, I felt his absence acutely. Though Mother's death had put a strain on his relationship with Father (he'd known Mother's family for years and would deliver news from Maastricht whenever he returned from there), I'd thought he'd make the effort. Despite Father, he'd always had a kind word for me and made a point of bringing the odd cask of wine or two from Bordeaux, cheeses from Ghent, and ribbons or lace from Italy for our pleasure. Excuses to visit they may have been, but I always enjoyed the captain's presence and Mother's spirits were visibly buoyant after he'd visited. Though I'd barely seen him since Mother died, I regarded Captain Stoyan, possibly unrealistically, as a link to her. Puzzled and hurt by his absence at first, I later discovered he was in London. I considered writing to him; I wanted him to know about Father, about us. But there were others who needed to be told first.

Bad news is bold, a jackanapes, spreading faster than a plague, whereas good news is like a freshly hired hand, circumspect, afraid to overstep the mark. Just as I'd told the twins, I wanted to be the one to let Tobias know. Even though I was sure Lord Rainford would have dispatched a messenger to his son, I wrote briefly but, I hoped, lovingly. Tobias may have let correspondence between us falter, but I'd never done so. Though, since Mother died, I'd not had to deliver such bad tidings.

After organizing the making of mourning clothes, a task readily undertaken by Mistress Taylor in town, I pulled Adam aside and shared with him the rest of what Master Makejoy had told me. Adam listened respectfully as I explained my situation (*ours*, he gruffly corrected, and I wanted to throw my arms around his neck as I had as a child), his strong jaw clenching and unclenching, his hand occasionally rising to run through his thick, gray hair or graze the fine stubble on his cheeks. I finished by asking him to elucidate where we stood as a household and business. I thought maybe I could throw myself on Lord Rainford's mercy, but in order to do that I needed to understand the costs of running a house our size. If Lord Rainford was, as Master Makejoy inferred, to offer the lease to someone else, why could it not be me?

For the next three nights, Adam and I waited until everyone was abed, then equipped with candles and cresset lamp, retired to the office. There was nothing surreptitious in our action; it was just that I preferred Hiske remain, for the time being at least, ignorant of what I was doing. On the first night, Adam made a fire and, as the kindling took, he opened a big ledger on the table. Inviting me to take Father's chair, he sat beside me. Moving through the columns of neat figures and annotations he'd made over the weeks and months, I learned, to my dismay, that the day-to-day costs of running the house were more than I anticipated. While the tenant farmers paid reasonable tithes and supplied a variety of meat, grain, and dairy produce, like most of the town we were beholden to the Friary of St. Jude's for our ale and purchased wood and coal from the respective merchants. Cloth and other sundries were bought when needed. Occasionally, small amounts went to the thatcher, farrier, cooper, cobbler, and all other manner of trades for repairs to and replacements of objects I had taken for granted. Then there was the servants' wages . . .

To ensure we maintained the household, even at the most basic of levels, more income was required. If we reestablished the vegetable garden, planted some more trees in the orchard, and started making our own ale again, we could make some savings. Wood could be collected from the forest, coal we'd have to ration. Mother's and Father's clothes could be recut for Karel and Betje and shoes patched; apart from mourning clothes, I could make do. I drank in all this information like a thirsty pilgrim. There was still some produce awaiting sale in the shop, but I no longer had the rights to it.

I closed the pages we'd been studying, and tied the boards

protecting them together. We sat companionably, staring at the flames. The office looked quite welcoming in its cheerful light, the halo of the candle we'd lit possessing an unearthly quality, the lamp aglow.

"I feel most foolish. I'd no idea the house cost so much to run. And please don't even think it." I shook a finger in his direction. "No one will be asked to leave. Not yet. Not ever if I can help it." I sighed and threw my hands up in the air. "What do we do now, Adam?"

He looked at me sadly. "Pray for a miracle, Mistress Anneke. Pray."

"Well, then," I said, slapping my thighs and rising. "Let's make a start on that, shall we?"

# FOUR

ELMHAM LENN
After the Nones of October
*The year of Our Lord 1405 in the sixth
year of the reign of Henry IV*

*O*ver the next few days, Hiske took every opportunity to remind me of my situation and to refresh her offer of employment. Doreen had taken to putting on airs, earning a scolding
from Saskia and Blanche. Unperturbed, the cocky girl raised her
chin and strode off with the confidence of one who knew her
place would soon be higher than those to whom she currently
answered. From the looks that were exchanged, so did Blanche
and Saskia.

To make matters worse, five days after the news of Father's
death and our changed circumstances, Master Makejoy returned with another letter from Lord Rainford. Passing it to
me, Master Makejoy waited while I read the contents. Quite
simply, it was a notice to quit the premises. We'd four weeks.
The housekeeper, steward, and cook were invited to remain for

the new tenant, while the rest of the servants would be paid a small sum and given "goodly references as they deserve" from his lordship. There was no mention of the twins or me. It was as if we didn't exist.

I sat staring at the letter, arms loose by my sides. My mind refused to still as a thousand thoughts flew around like caged birds. I could not capture one. My stomach churned. *Four weeks.*

Master Makejoy rested a hand on my shoulder. "Our offer still stands, Mistress Sheldrake. Myself and Mistress Jabben, soon to be Mistress Makejoy, would make you most welcome."

I gave a deep sigh. "I'm sure that *you* would treat your servants very nicely, Master Makejoy—"

Puzzled by my tone and words, Master Makejoy shook his head. "You'd be no servant."

I didn't correct him but continued. "Only, it's difficult for me to consider such a reduction in circumstances when I've been accustomed to a very different life. You can understand that, can you not?"

"I do understand, Mistress Sheldrake, I do indeed. You've also enjoyed the help of your good cousin for many years, so it wouldn't be so strange, surely, if this was to continue longer? Is it not time for you to repay your debt to her?" When I didn't reply, he coughed into his fist. "Forgive me for saying so, but those who have no choice cannot be so fussy, can they? You can't change what the good Lord intends." He gave a crooked smile to lighten the severity of his words. It only succeeded in rendering them cruel.

As I escorted him to the door, I wondered, *What* could *I do?* Even as I tried to think of ways of earning an income, of supporting the household, I knew I would have to inform Saskia and the others about Lord Rainford's generous terms, that they didn't have to leave the house or Elmham Lenn. It was the one bit of bright news. Was that what bothered me? The idea that educated as I was, trained to be a good wife and mother for some impoverished noble or wealthy merchant, I would suddenly be relegated to the status of servant? Surely, we were all servants in God's eyes? Was it that or was it the idea of working for Cousin Hiske and Master Makejoy that perturbed me, indeed, made me rebel with every fiber of my being?

God help me, I was proud. I would keep my own house, my own family. But how could this happen? I'd no means, no prospects . . .

Was I being punished for my sins? Or for Mother's?

I could feel Will's eyes upon me as I walked down the hall and knew my distress would carry the conversation in the kitchen tonight. I was beyond caring. I needed to find an answer and fast. But what? *Oh, Papa, Papa . . . Mother . . . Moeder . . .*

That night a storm raged, shaking the shutters while rain lashed the roof and lightning tore the sky. Instead of remaining in the solar with Hiske, I endured her disapproval and wandered downstairs to the main hall. Taking her role of chaperone seriously, Hiske followed. The trestle table and benches had been cleared, the floor swept. Unlike many houses, with the exception of the shop, we eschewed rushes in the lower rooms, adopting the style of my mother's homeland, laying timber floors. The hounds bounded over to greet me, their claws clicking and sliding, their tongues wet, their breath steaming. Thrusting their great shaggy heads beneath my arms and onto my lap as I knelt, they whimpered when a low, long growl of thunder shook the

house and their hackles rose. I laughed that two such huge creatures were rendered helpless by the weather, then remembered
how treacherous and deadly it could be and my laughter died.

Joining the servants by the hearth, they welcomed me and
Hiske, the women returning to their sewing; Saskia, her spinning. Sitting down close to a cresset lamp, I unpicked some
embroidery Betje had attempted. Hiske sat on a stool beside
me, back erect, hands in her lap, not speaking. Even the silence between us was laden with meaning, with pressure and
inevitability. I felt it with every sigh my relative issued, every
look cast upon me with all the grace of a seagull. The low chatter of Saskia and Blanche, and occasional comment from Doreen, Iris, and Will, was a blessed relief.

After the first candle expired in a molten pool of wax and the
lamps dimmed, I excused myself to go to bed. But first I looked
in on the twins, who slept soundly, Louisa stretched on a
pallet at the foot of their bed. In my room, I slowly undressed
and, placing my nightgown near the fire to warm it, wrapped
a shawl tightly to cover my nakedness and sat at the window,
watching and listening to the storm. How terrifying it must
have been for those on the *Cathaline*, trapped upon the sea in a
creaking, shuddering wooden vessel, the waves arching over the
deck, pounding them into the fathoms below. My reflections
were dark. I wondered if Father suffered. What had been his
last thoughts? Were they of Mother? He'd never shed a tear for
her, not that I'd seen. Did he weep for himself when he realized
all was lost? Or, as I now suspected, had everything he valued
vanished years earlier? But if that was the case, why had he ever
entered into such a one-sided agreement with the man who was

the cause of such grief? Did he no longer care? How could he
make himself so beholden to the noble who'd been party to such
a great betrayal? I would never know. Not now.

Retreating from the gasps of cold that crept through the
cracks, I threw on my nightshirt and snuggled under the furs.
Despite the comfort and warmth, sleep eluded me. I tossed and
turned, adopting the wild rhythms of the weather. Sometime
toward dawn, I drifted into that in-between space where the
waking world and that of apparitions and spirits collide. Mother
came to me, drawn across a nimbus of memories. There she was,
a younger, more colorful woman, holding my hand steady as
I practiced my letters; then she was beside me; then opposite,
a book open in her lap, reading to me. Her gentle brow was
drawn, her white-gold hair framing her face, her voice earnest.
Next, we were conversing, our hands as much a part of the
conversation as our tongues. I couldn't tell if we were speaking
German, Dutch, or Spanish, languages Mother insisted I should
be fluent in, but we were laughing between words. Father listened, hands behind his back, a bemused look on his face as his
women chattered in foreign tongues. His stern voice demanded
we speak French or English and, with a look of regret, we did,
Mother promising me with her eyes that as soon as Father departed again, our language lessons would resume. We could set
the patterns of our days when Father was gone. Read, talk, explore, garden, brew, ride. My soul began to lighten as I relived
the times I'd shared with Mother until I found myself thinking
of those last frenzied words she'd uttered, after she'd revealed
the terrible truth . . .

"I tell you not to torment you or taint your memory of me,
but so that you will understand. Do not blame your father. He

is faultless in this. I tell you so that one day, my darling, you will have the power to help yourself, Tobias, and the twins should the need arise, should Father be unable or"—she coughed, her breathing labored—"choose not to . . . What happened . . . it hurt him deeply. Scarred him in ways I can only imagine. If you cannot see it in yourself to forgive me, then please, my sweetling, at least forgive him."

I rolled over. *What did you mean, Mother? I don't understand . . . I don't know what to do . . .* I was three again, wailing in my sleep, crying for my mother.

As when I was little, she came to me just as I'd given up hope, standing at the end of the bed, regarding me in a manner I knew all too well. Her soft smile, tilted head, exuding faith in her eldest; it was brimming from her eyes. "You will make it work, Anneke. You always do." It's what she would say to me whether it was a napkin I couldn't fold correctly, a stitch I hadn't mastered, or a word I couldn't translate. I reached out and her image dissolved. I fell into sleep then—the kind from which there is no rest. All the while, her words echoed: *You will make it work, work, work.*

The sky had begun to transform, its oyster dullness just creeping into the room when I woke and sat bolt upright, my heart pounding. I threw back the covers and went to the window. Wrenching open the panes, I gazed upon the new day. Following the boundary of the property, I took stock of what it contained: the storage rooms at the rear, the kitchen below, the stables with the rooms above, the bakehouse, the brewhouse . . . the brewhouse with the small room attached at the back. The silhouette of the buildings blurred before forming something more solid, something upon which my mind could alight and hold fast. As I stared, an idea plucked at the edges of my imagination, teasing me with its incompleteness, its fragments refusing to cohere, until . . .

I knew what it was I had to do—what I had to try.

*You will make it work, Anneke. You always do.*

In order to do this, there was one person to whom I could turn, if not to learn the truth, then to test its veracity and possibly change everything.

Wrapping a shawl around my shoulders, I flew down the stairs. Outside, the cocks crowed and the rattle of the henhouse doors reverberated causing the dogs to bark, telling me the house was astir. I slipped into the office and, shivering in its icy darkness, lit the remnants of a candle. I quickly found what I was looking for and while I still felt my mother's presence, wrote a letter.

Reading it over, I sanded the paper and, using Father's seal, closed it. I sat for a moment; the cold had fled my body to be replaced by unnatural warmth. I wiped my brow, my chest tight, my throat ashes. *I can make this work. I can.*

"Mistress Sheldrake!"

"Will!"

"I saw the light beneath the door." Will's face flamed. "I wondered if someone had left a candle burning. But you're here. Sorry, mistress . . . Is there anything I can fetch you?"

I stared at him, at his sleep-patterned face, at the way his uniform was not yet laced properly. "Nay. Thank you." He bowed and went to leave.

*Make it work.*

"Wait. Actually, there is." I rose. "I need you to saddle Shelby and deliver this." I handed him the letter, my hand closing over his for just a second, imparting significance, urgency. "You're to wait until there's an answer and return at once."

He took the folded parchment, noted the seal, and frowned. "But, Mistress Sheldrake, Mistress Blanche and Mistress Saskia have work for me. They will—"

"Understand when I inform them I've sent you on an errand."

Will stared at the letter. "Where am I to deliver it, mistress?"

I hesitated. If I asked Will to take it to Lord Rainford's house in town, then chances were Master Makejoy and Hiske would learn of my intentions. That would not do. Not yet. I made up my mind. "To Scales Hall, Will."

"Lord Rainford's residence on the Gayfleet?"

"The same. I want you to do whatever you can to ensure this reaches his lordship. Am I clear?"

"But what if he's in town or at court, mistress?"

The thought had occurred to me. The king had retreated to Hereford after his efforts to subdue the Welsh failed, so chances were Lord Rainford would be by his side. Regardless, I had to try. "I'm praying it's not so but, if he's not in residence, return and I will find another way to reach him."

Will's eyes widened and his chest puffed at being trusted with such an important task. "You can count on me." He turned and almost ran from the room.

From the office, I heard his boots echo across the hall. I smiled wistfully. "I am, Will Heymonger. I'm counting on you and a man all my instincts tell me not to."

# FIVE

SCALES HALL
The following day
*The year of Our Lord 1405 in the sixth
year of the reign of Henry IV*

*E*arly the next morning, I set out for Scales Hall. Lord Rainford's reply had been swift and precise:

> *His Right, Worshipful, Lord Rainford, will meet with Mistress Anneke Sheldrake on the morrow, no later than sext. May the blessed Trinity keep you.*

Hiske's response to my request for an audience with Lord Rainford was mocking, her confidence that my plans would fail unshakable, but that only reinforced my determination.

The Rainford estate lay just over two hours away, toward Norwich. Ensuring we had plenty of time, we left just after the bells for tierce sounded. Dressed in my new kirtle and black tunic, with a clean woolen cloak, gloves, and my long hair tied neatly at the nape, a modest scarf wrapped around my head to prevent the wind making my locks too disheveled, I perched beside Adam on the cart and waved farewell to the twins, Saskia, Blanche, Iris, and Louisa, trying not to laugh as Will restrained the hounds, who barked their indignation that they weren't accompanying us, almost pulling him off his feet. Of Hiske and Doreen there was no sign.

The gray, storm-tossed days that had dominated the past month had finally surrendered. The sea, for weeks a churning mass that would have made Aeneas balk, was a sparkling viridian platter, dotted with fishing vessels and, beyond the heads, the occasional cog and caravel, their sails brighter than angels' wings. Trade had resumed. Crisp and cool, it was a glorious autumn day. The sky arced above us in a never-ending palette of blues and dusty white clouds. Gulls winged overhead, their cheeky caws echoing as they swooped toward the waters.

Exiting through the city gates, we crossed the bridge where the Gayfleet flowed into the sea, turning our backs on the coast and following the river. Adam began to whistle. As far as memory stretched, there was Adam. A mellow soul, I'd known him since I was a babe. It was Adam who, when I should have been in the nursery, would take me with him to visit the tenants, walking through the woods, pointing out not just the names and properties of various plants, but the real nature of the sea-blown trees in which, he would whisper, dwelt beautiful dryads. He would hoist me onto his shoulders as we trekked along the river so my boots wouldn't muddy. There he would tell of the wild naiads who swam in the watery depths and had weed and moss for hair, and dulcet voices that could lure men and women to their deaths with silvery singsong promises.

It was Adam who, after Mother died, brought home Achilles and Patroclus, determined a ray of joy would pierce the pall of sadness hanging over our lives.

In many ways, he came to replace Father, who was absent so often, and whose name in the years after Tobias's birth instilled a fear that had the power to command obedience from my brother and me. There was no doubt that whenever Father returned after being away for months at sea, the mood of the house changed. It was as if the very fabric of the building altered—the wood, stone, and rushes darkened, retreated into themselves, much as the servants did. There was no talking at meals, no walks with Adam, no bedtime stories or reading by the fire during the day. The servants were banished from the hall, my brother to the nursery and me to the nuns for lessons, and Mother would withdraw either to the solar to read or to the brewhouse to make ale.

One week after Tobias's seventh birthday, Father sent him away. Instead of being assigned as one of Father's apprentices, destined for a merchant's life and the sea, he was squired to Lord Rainford's youngest son, Leander Rainford. We'd barely time to register that Tobias was leaving, let alone to say goodbye, when he was gone. Images of Tobias's brave little face as he mounted the horse in front of a strange man dressed in the Rainford livery haunted my every waking moment. Mother tried to ease my sorrow by reassuring me that becoming the squire of someone as important as the son of Lord Rainford was an honor, that our family was viewed as favored and fortunate by the townsfolk. I didn't care. Not when all the Rainford name conjured was the bereft face of my mother as she stood in the yard, touching Tobias as if to imprint him on her memory. The indifferent visage of my father, who offered no final word of advice or farewell, but spun on his heel and returned to business before Tobias had even left the yard, remained with me.

I missed Tobias so much at first. After a while, however, I barely remembered what it was like to have him about. His letters were few and news of his progress scarce. He was alive, well, and, if he served the Rainfords valiantly and became adept at the longbow he now used and attended to his other lessons, on the brink of opportunity. According to Father, that was all that mattered. He rarely spoke Tobias's name again.

The distant strains of monks chanting ended my reverie. The Gayfleet widened at this point and laden barges appeared upon its swift-flowing surface, both going to and coming from Norwich. Trees lined the banks, and through their spindly branches I was able to see the Friary of St. Jude. Above the high stone walls the twin spires of the church rose, and I could spy the thatched roof of the huge buildings in which the Benedictine monks lived, and the topmost boughs of their orchard.

It took us a good while to ride past the friary, so large were the grounds, like a miniature city itself with merchants, farmers, knights, travelers, and pilgrims arriving by river, road, and foot.

We rode for another hour, until finally the walls of the Rainford manor house came into view, and the small town that had grown up before it. Smoke curled from chimneys, the local bakers' ovens roared, and a malty smell filled the air, reminding me of not just freshly baked bread but of the hours Mother and I spent in the brewhouse making ale. The smell was almost the same—it had that rich, loamy quality that made me think of Yuletide, sunshine, Blanche's apron, and Adam's laughter all at once.

That ended when Mother died. The moment Cousin Hiske crossed our threshold, she stopped me making ale, declaring it to be the work of a sloven, not the daughter of a high-ranked merchant. I'd argued, of course I had, but as with all the other debates I fruitlessly entered into with Hiske, I lost that one as well. When Father returned home after one of his voyages, I complained, but he upheld Hiske's order, as he did any new rules my mother's cousin introduced. After that, like most of the townsfolk, we purchased our ale from the friary. Occasionally, if the monks were slow to deliver or the road to the friary impassable, we'd buy from one of the brewsters in town. None of it ever tasted as good as Mother's ale.

The gates to the manor house were open and we entered slowly, Shelby's hooves crunching across the gravel that covered the large open space between the outer walls and the entrance to the house. I'd been here once before, when I was much younger, but there was little I recalled. More like a castle than a house, it rose three stories and had turrets at the north and south ends, a battlement with crenellations and arrow loops joining them. Liveried servants ran forward to take Shelby's head.

The massive front door stood open and a tall, smoke-haired man with a fine dark tunic, bright hose, and pointed shoes stepped forward. Helped from the cart by one of the younger men, I waited as the older one descended the steps. Behind me, Adam was given directions for the cart and invited to dine in the servant's hall. Glancing over my shoulder, I gave him a reassuring smile. He nodded slowly, his eyes reminding me he was only a short distance away should I need him.

"God bid you welcome. Are you Mistress Anneke Sheldrake?" said the older man with a bow.

"I am."

"I'm Evan Underwood, his lordship's seneschal. If you would follow me, Mistress Sheldrake, his lordship attends you in the solar." Without waiting for a reply, Master Underwood turned and strode into the house.

Taking a deep breath, I followed, trying not to let the grand facade with its gray stone blocks, towering chimneys, long mullioned windows, and knotted wooden doors intimidate me the way they must surely have done when I was a child. Nonetheless, my heart was racing as I stepped inside the imposing entrance.

Master Underwood waited for me at the base of a large staircase and I fell into step behind him as we ascended. The air grew warmer as we climbed, and the scent of lemon and honey enveloped us.

The door to the solar was open and Master Underwood announced my presence as he stepped aside and, with a half-bow and sweep of his arm, invited me to enter.

I gulped, my throat dry. I walked into the solar.

Two things struck me. The first was how big the room was compared to our humble solar at home, and how richly yet tastefully decorated. There were rugs on the walls and wooden floors, and chests and cabinets displayed objects both familiar and strange—ornate boxes, jeweled bowls, shining handled daggers in decorated sheaths, as well as instruments better suited to a ship or guild master's office. I recognized a brass astrolabe. Servants stood around the room, awaiting their master's whim. In the center, facing the windows, were three huge chairs and two beautifully carved stools. From the largest chair rose Lord Rainford.

Tall and lean, he had a head of thick, dark brown hair streaked with silver. As I drew closer, he made no attempt to hide his attention and I felt my face burn. I raised my chin and, while I knew I should have lowered it modestly, decided to offer his person the same sort of examination. His doublet was a deep blue with a high white collar and was inlaid with pearls. His legs were encased in vermilion hose and his boots were of soft brown leather. Altogether, he gave the appearance of wealth and artlessness, but I knew the trouble, let alone expense, that would have gone into his ensemble.

As I studied his lordship's face, a second realization occurred. If ever I'd held any doubts about what my mother had told me the night she died, they were instantly dismissed. In Lord Rainford's dark gray eyes, high cheekbones, and prominent nose, I saw my brother forty years hence. Even in the way his hair grew from his forehead. Anger flooded my body as I thought how this man had so callously discarded our family—especially now I knew for certain that the connection between us was more intimate and complicated than business alone.

Standing before him, I curtsied, making sure I showed due respect. Apart from the servants, we were alone. Unconventional, but then, my chaperone was in the kitchens and Lord Rainford either didn't think to supply one or thought it unnecessary. I knew he was a widower, the third Lady Rainford having died, like my mother, in childbirth. Provided with three sons from his previous two wives, his succession was assured.

Taking my hand as I straightened, his eyes narrowed. "Mistress Sheldrake. I must say, apart from the hair, you're very like your mother. You have her eyes . . ."

I drew my breath in sharply and resisted the urge to touch my face. "Many who knew her make a similar observation, your lordship."

Releasing my hand, he grunted and indicated I should take the chair next to his. He waved a footman over and offered me a goblet of wine. I thought to refuse, simply because I wanted a clear head, but knew it might be construed badly, so took it reluctantly.

His lordship gestured, his many rings catching the light. "It's watered."

I took a sip. It was sweet, soothing on my throat. I felt his lordship's eyes upon me again.

"I confess, Mistress Sheldrake, that your letter aroused my curiosity, something that has not been stirred for a very long time." A finger stroked the rim of his wine cup absentmindedly. "But before we get to the reason for your visit, let me offer you my sincere condolences for your loss. Your father was a hard-working man and it will be very difficult to replace him."

The lack of compassion in his tone took me aback, but I remembered my manners. "Thank you," I said, feeling tears prick the back of my eyes. They came from a place of injustice, not grief, and I worked hard not to let them fall. How dare this man acknowledge my father's value yet be so swift to leave us destitute?

"You said in your missive that you wished to discuss a business proposition with me," said his lordship. "I'm trusting your note wasn't simply a ruse to get in the door and throw yourself on my tender mercies. Because that will not work with me, Mistress Sheldrake. Others have tried and they always fail."

I drew in my breath. This man did not waste time. Neither would I. "I've not come here under false pretenses, your lordship. Master Makejoy has made clear the nature of your business relationship with my father." My tone was cold, distant. I'd the distinct feeling that if I showed my emotions, my proposition would be rejected outright. "I wish to talk to you about Holcroft House and its lands, which, I understand, along with his—I mean *your*—ships, Papa leased as part of your agreement." I reached over and set down the heavy goblet. I needed my wits about me.

"He did. It's a long-standing arrangement, Mistress Sheldrake, one that goes back over sixteen years. It protected me and ensured that your family was comfortable and your father's . . . compliance. Since he is now dead, I no longer need to assure myself of that, do I?"

I drew my breath in sharply. *Compliance?* So much for suppressing my agitation.

"But I do need to acquit the losses your father's"—he searched for the right word—"*recklessness* has caused. I cannot afford to be charitable. Business is business, and one cannot manage estates the extent of mine, nor fulfill obligations to king and country, if we allow the passing of a worker, even a valued one, to impact upon processes. Your father agreed to these terms. I'm simply abiding by them as well. Do you understand?"

"I wouldn't be my father's daughter if I didn't," I lied. I wanted to clench my fists, protest, use the heat of my fury to melt his coldness. I forced my breathing into a slow rhythm.

"Good. We understand each other then." He drained his cup

and indicated the footman should refill it. I wasn't offered any more and understood I'd but a short time left to present my suit. He waved his hand, prompting me to continue.

"My proposition is very simple, your lordship. What I ask is that you lease Holcroft House to me."

Lord Rainford slowly took the goblet away from his mouth. "I beg your pardon?" Laughter infused his tone.

"I ask, my lord, that you lease the home you leased to my father, Holcroft House, to me."

Lord Rainford held out his goblet for the footman to take. "I thought that's what you said." He shook his head. "You certainly have my attention now." He leaned back in his chair and crossed his legs, resting his elbow on its wooden arm and holding his chin between thumb and fingers. "It's not common practice to lease to a woman, certainly not an unmarried one; someone so untutored in life, in business." In any other context, his look would be an insult. That his words rang with truth did not salve my feelings. "Pray, how do you intend to meet the obligations that come with such a lease? It does not come cheaply."

"Of that I am aware. Along with my steward, Adam Barfoot, I've studied the ledgers and I believe that, given time, I can meet the costs—at least, I would like the opportunity to attempt to do so."

"Ah." Lord Rainford nodded. "There it is."

"Your lordship?"

"The flaw in your proposal." He released his chin. "You're simply clutching at straws and have found one with 'time' etched onto its stalk. You piqued my interest, Mistress Sheldrake—for a moment. As it is, you're the same as any number of the villeins and laborers who come to see me. What you really want is a loan. After all, time costs money but since you have none, it's me who will be bearing the expense of your suggestion. It's me who will be paying for this time you're requesting."

"That's true, my lord. But what if I said to you that I'm not asking for it for nothing. I intend to buy this time from you." Lord Rainford opened his mouth, but I continued. "I know I've no funds with which to pay you *now*, but given the chance, I'll not only repay in full, but with interest."

"You think I've not had these kinds of promises made to me before?" He took another drink and deposited his goblet heavily on the table. "How do you intend to do that?" His voice was flat, disinterested.

I took a deep breath. "By starting a business myself."

That he did not laugh in my face went some way to mollifying my anger. "Really? What sort?" There was something in his tone that made me color again.

"I intend to brew ale, my lord."

Lord Rainford studied me in silence. I endured his scrutiny, refusing to look away. So much depended on him believing me capable.

"I've been told by a reliable source that your future was assured, that you and your younger brother and sister were to be taken care of," he said quietly. "That leaving the house would not be a hardship."

*An unasked question answered.*

I dipped my chin. "In one sense, this is true. Mistress Jabben and Master Makejoy have offered me a position in their household after they wed. Me and my siblings."

Lord Rainford reclined further. "And you don't wish to avail yourself of this generous"—his mouth twitched—"offer?"

"Not unless I'm left with no choice."

He uncrossed his legs. I noticed the elegant buckles that decorated his boots. "I see. And that, I assume, now depends on me."

I inclined my head.

"You would rather try your hand at being a brewster than live with your cousin and my clerk in respectability?"

I choked back a laugh. "You mean as a servant. At least as a brewster I've a chance to make my own way."

Lord Rainford threw back his head and guffawed. I cast a look at the servants to see what they made of their master's outburst, but they remained as unmoved as the portrait staring at me from the opposite wall. "But you won't be attempting this on your own. Let's be frank with each other, Mistress Sheldrake, your plan requires my complicity. You need my cooperation in order to even make an attempt. To be blunt, you need my money."

"I need to *borrow* your money. As I said, I intend to pay it back."

Lord Rainford examined his fingernails. "Why should I give to you what I wouldn't offer to anyone else, Mistress Sheldrake, not even my sons? Why should I make an exception for you?"

It was time to play my final card. I licked my lips and squared my shoulders. "Because of Tobias."

This time, his laughter went for a long time. My cheeks blazed. I desired nothing more than to flee the room. Only Mother's voice in my head and an image of the twins kept me seated.

When he'd finished being amused, he dashed a hand beneath his eyes and, taking a kerchief from within his doublet, blew his nose. "I understand now that you sought to use leverage over me. Clever. May I ask, how long have you known about your brother?"

"Mother told me on her deathbed."

"I see," said Lord Rainford. He held my eyes for a moment then swiftly stood, tapping his fingers on top of the chair before stepping to the window. "Pray, what did she tell you?"

Speaking to his back, I answered. "She said that Tobias was a Rainford. That . . . she erred in her judgment and fell pregnant. She told me that if ever I needed anything, I was to seek you out, that you would understand and make amends for what you did"—I cleared my throat—"what you did to her, to Father." My voice hardened toward the end.

"Did you ever raise this . . . this matter with your father?" He turned.

"I . . . that is . . . The time was never right and now . . . well . . ." I folded my hands in my lap. "But I'm raising it with you in the hope you see fit to make redress by helping me."

Only the rise and fall of Lord Rainford's chest, the slight narrowing of his eyes, suggested any humanity. I could hear my breath in my ears. Wanting to move, I dared not. What was he thinking behind that impenetrable face?

When he swung back into his seat, the move was so swift and unexpected, I jumped. "I want to make something very clear, Mistress Sheldrake. Despite what your mother may have said, I owe you and your family nothing. I owe your father nothing. On the contrary . . ." He paused. "I more than compensated him for what happened. I gave him the house, the land, the lifestyle to which you've grown accustomed. Beyond that, I've made certain Tobias is taken care of and, as far as I am concerned, always will be. I paid what was due. It was more than he deserved." His eyes narrowed. "Frankly, Mistress Sheldrake, you and the twins are not my concern."

How I managed to speak, I don't know. Fury overtook me, making me tremble. Fury that he could be so dismissive, and rage at my impotence. I brought it under control. "And yet, here I am."

"Indeed."

"If I may be so bold, my lord, why would Mother have said you have amends to make if you do not?"

"Because women always want more."

Tossing back the last of his wine, he studied the sky. The sun had commenced its descent and the bells for sext had sounded some time ago. Springing to his feet, he wandered over to a nearby cabinet and poured himself another wine before the footman could.

"You've spirit, young lady, I'll grant you that." Turning around, he raised the goblet to me and drank. "Beauty does strange things to men, Mistress Sheldrake, very strange things . . ." His voice lowered and his eyes remained fixed on me. "Things for which, if we're not careful, we'll pay for the rest of our lives."

I turned away, finding the waning day preferable.

"Delightful as this has been, Mistress Sheldrake, I really cannot spare you any more time. Tempting as your offer is, I have to decline. As I've made clear, I owe you—and your family—nothing. My debt is paid." He offered me his hand. I stared at it, and tears threatened. I blinked them back furiously. "Take Mistress Jabben and Master Makejoy's offer. It's the best you'll receive . . . for now. I'm sure a woman like you will be courting all kinds in the near future." About to say something more, he changed his mind. "Master Underwood will show you to the door. James," he alerted one of the footmen, "Mistress Sheldrake is leaving."

"Wait," I said, rising to my feet, ignoring his hand, which was rapidly withdrawn. My heart was thundering, my palms began to sweat. "I'm not finished."

Aggravated, Lord Rainford clicked his tongue. "What now?"

"Despite what you say, you do have an obligation to me, Lord Rainford. You say you're a man of business—well, I'm here to collect *my* debt."

"I'm beholden to *you*? How? In what possible way?" Impatience clipped his voice. Anger flickered in his eyes.

"You've not compensated me for what I was forced to endure as a consequence of your liaison with my mother."

"*My* liaison? That's what you think?" His words rang. He shook his head. "I see." His voice was quieter, calmer. "Tell me then, how could what happened with your mother have affected you?"

"In every conceivable way, your lordship. My father worked hard to ensure you profited while, in the meantime, as his daughter and eldest child, I can record only losses." I used my fingers to count them off. "The love and attention of my father, the presence of my brother, the death of my mother—"

"You cannot blame me for your mother's death!"

I stepped closer to him. "Perhaps not. But I can blame you for my father, for what he became, a hollow version of his former self. I can blame you, my lord, for how everything between my mother and father was irrevocably altered from the moment Tobias was conceived. From that day forward, I lost one if not both parents. I certainly lost a father and the woman my mother once was. Tell me, if not you, then to whom do I attribute these losses?"

He failed to hold my gaze.

I continued. "Then there are the twins. They lost a father long before he ever died and that was due to you, your lordship." My breasts were heaving; a trickle of perspiration traveled between my shoulder blades. My head was buzzing. I didn't know where this rush of courage came from, but I used it. "For those losses, your lordship, I call you to account. For all of this, I demand compensation. As you said earlier, this is business." I lowered my voice. "I ask that your debt to *me* be repaid in time and thus money—in the form of a loan. If, by the end of a period upon which we'll agree today, I cannot meet my liability, then I'll leave Holcroft House and you'll never hear from me again."

I stood before the window, the sunlight warming my spine. My nerves were strung tight.

One arm folded behind his back, Lord Rainford walked to the next window and stared out.

Over his shoulder, I could see the large courtyard below. Maids carried pails from the washhouse to the kitchen. Chickens scratched in the gravel, dogs chased each other toward the stables, where a beautiful black destrier pranced. My eyes grazed his lordship's velvet spine and I willed him not only to consider my offer, but to agree to it. His shoulders were broad; his fingers, stroking each other against the small of his back, were long. In his youth, he would have been a handsome, if somewhat inflexible, man. The resemblance Tobias bore to him was astonishing. How hard must it have been for Father to see them together, to be reminded every time he looked into Tobias's face of Mother's . . . No wonder he sent Tobias away so soon. I marveled that my mother had . . . with this man.

Lord Rainford turned. Embarrassed by the direction my

thoughts had taken, I brushed an imaginary stray hair behind one ear.

"You're even lovelier than your mother," said Lord Rainford quietly.

There was a movement in the doorway. "Ah. Master Underwood." My heart sank. I was to be escorted from the estate after all. "Is Master Makejoy still on the grounds? He is? Good. Fetch him immediately. Tell him to bring parchment and inks."

I didn't dare breathe.

Lord Rainford closed the distance between us, standing so near I could feel the heat of his body, feel the penetrating intensity of his gaze. I could smell wool, leather, horseflesh, and sweat. "I'll give you the time you ask for, Mistress Sheldrake."

Joy filled my chest, expanding out to my limbs. I felt light, weightless almost.

"A contract will be drawn up today."

I released a long, quiet breath.

His lordship continued. "I confess, I'm more than a little interested in how, given the circumstances, you will fare. You have until Hocktide to meet the fees required for the leasing of Holcroft House. That gives you around six months. That should be more than adequate."

My heart soared. Six months! It was more than I'd dreamed. I just hoped it was more than I needed.

"If you fail to meet the terms of our contract," continued Lord Rainford, "then, as was originally intended, you'll leave the house. If, however, you succeed, then perhaps we will speak again."

"Thank you, my lord." I offered a curtsy. "I won't disappoint you."

"Disappoint me? I don't think you could. But you can fail and, Mistress Sheldrake, while I've gone against my better judgment in this instance, I'll not be so easily persuaded by a pair of beautiful green eyes or"—his eyes traveled my body—"anything else."

I didn't know what to say. Like a startled fawn, I couldn't move.

"But trust me when I say, I can be ruthless, Mistress Sheldrake." He smiled, but there was no warmth behind it. "I keep a close eye on all my investments. So, while I have to return to the king's side, I'll ask my son"—he gestured to the portrait I'd noticed earlier—"to . . . let's say, keep abreast of your progress. When he returns from France, he can confer with Makejoy, examine the accounts, and keep me advised. And, when the time comes"—he chuckled at his little joke—"he'll see that the terms of the contract we're about to sign are met in full. Are you prepared to meet my conditions?"

My mind was whirling. I wanted to fling open the window and shout my small victory to the shire. I'd taken the first step in my independence and, no matter what happened from here on in, I wasn't going to fall.

"I am, your lordship."

"No matter what they entail?"

"Whatever they entail, your lordship," I said, smiling as Master Makejoy entered, his portable desk strapped to his hips, parchment and quills under his arms. "I'll gladly sign."

And with that cavalier dismissal, I made my first mistake.

# SIX

BETWEEN SCALES HALL AND
HOLCROFT HOUSE, ELMHAM LENN
The same day in October
*The year of Our Lord 1405 in the sixth
year of the reign of Henry IV*

As Adam and I left Scales Hall, the chapel bells sounded, their chimes echoing around the valley and following us through the village, a joyous song that matched the one resounding in my heart. I'd been granted the time I needed to earn a living, to keep the house and thus prevent us from becoming little more than Cousin Hiske's servants. That this came at such a cost, being beholden to the man I'd come to regard as the source of all our woes, that I was placing myself in a situation akin to that which Father had, was not something I wanted to consider. Not until it was forced upon me. In the meantime, I'd plans to make and work to do. In order to achieve any of this, I needed the help of the servants.

We rode in silence, but my thoughts were so loud and busy

I wouldn't have been surprised if Adam had begun answering the conundrums I posed myself. We left the village and traveled along the muddy road that ran beside the river, careful to avoid the deeper grooves so as not to bog our vehicle. Swaying from side to side, I replayed the conversation with his lordship, still not quite able to believe I'd managed to reverse his initial refusal. Sending a swift prayer of thanks to the Holy Mother and my own, the thing that struck me most was Lord Rainford's reluctant acknowledgment of his affair with Mother, that he'd used her so disgracefully. I hadn't expected that and, I confess, it hurt. I'd half-hoped he'd scoff at my accusation and demand I leave his house. But one would only have to see Tobias next to him to know any denial of paternity would be moot. My stomach lurched. Others must realize what to me was now so apparent: the resemblance was uncanny. I glanced at Adam, his concentration fixed on the road, on guiding Shelby onto the slightly higher ground. Was it possible Adam knew? That he'd known all along? That Saskia, Blanche, and the entire household knew what I'd only just confirmed? That Tobias was a Rainford? I chided myself. My brother was only partly a Rainford. He was also a de Winter—just like me.

No wonder Papa not only kept away as much as he could but also sent Tobias from his sight at the first opportunity. That must be why he'd resigned all his offices, withdrawn from public service, and taken to the oceans; his pride wouldn't allow him to do otherwise.

Bringing Cousin Hiske into the household simply gave him less reason to come home and face his shame. Torn between pity for my father and angry disappointment that he could treat us in such a fashion, I was conflicted. Did Cousin Hiske know?

She'd never met Lord Rainford as far as I knew . . . My chest went cold and I gripped the cloak at my throat, the parchment of the contract rustling as it was crushed.

*But Master Makejoy would know . . .*

The idea that Mother's dreadful secret had never really been one made me feel peculiar. It was a mixture of both release and acute humiliation. But what about Tobias? Was he yet to discover the truth of his birth? And what about Leander Rainford, Tobias's master and his lordship's youngest son? He must know. How did he feel? Did he even care? If Sir Leander was anything like his father, it would make not one iota of difference to him; men of his rank sired bastards everywhere and he no doubt had a brood of his own being raised around the countryside.

Or was I creating drama where there was none? If the truth of Tobias's birth *was* known, why had no one come forward before? Of all those in my small circle of acquaintance, Hiske wouldn't have remained silent. I could just imagine how she'd deploy such knowledge. Saskia would have intimated something before now as well. I glanced at Adam. Perhaps no one knew after all—and, really, what difference did it make? Mother was dead, so was Father. Tobias was secure and, just as Mother intended by confessing to me, it had given me an advantage and I'd been able to attempt to shore up a future.

The lilac hues of approaching evening began to transform the blues of the sky into something softer. Knowing we still had a while before vespers and spying the friary wall looming in the distance, I asked Adam if we might stop for refreshment. The friary ran a guesthouse that offered passing travelers cheap ale and some nourishment. I needed to order my thoughts before we arrived home and Adam deserved to know what had happened in Scales Hall. He wouldn't ask me because he was far too circumspect and aware of the differences in our station—a situation Father's death had made more apparent as overnight I changed from being the master's daughter to mistress in my own right. I started to piece together what I would tell my steward about the contract I'd made, knowing that portions of what Lord Rainford and I'd discussed, the leverage I'd used to persuade him to aid me, would never be revealed—not by me. Not until there was no choice.

Adam touched his cap in response to my suggestion. "Good idea, Mistress Anneke. It will give the road a chance to clear."

It wasn't long before we were inside the walls of the friary. An ostler took Shelby's head and, after tying him to a post, provided a nosebag. Dismounting, Adam tossed him a coin as another servant ushered us toward the guesthouse. Sat at table, we were swiftly brought beakers of watery ale and asked if we wanted something to eat. We both declined. Through the smoke haze filling the room, others enjoying a rest from the road could be discerned. An older couple sat next to each other on a bench, a trencher and pints of ale between them. Nearby, a group of merchants, wool from the color of their hoods and insignia, gathered around a table arguing, their brows furrowed, their greasy fingers stabbing the air. Remnants of a meal sat on the table, hardening in the heat of the fire. A mangy dog lay by the hearth, its head resting on its paws, its eyes fixed on an old man sitting on a stool, his chin lowered to his chest as he slumbered. Apart from the merchants, conversation was low, the room stuffy, and the atmosphere constrained. I waited until a servant carrying a tray passed us, then brought my stool closer to Adam.

I quickly filled him in on my meeting, mentioning Lord

Rainford's initial reticence, but omitting anything to do with Mother or Tobias. "In the end, Lord Rainford agreed to give me until Hocktide to find the monies needed to pay the lease."

"He will underwrite the costs of the house until then?"

I nodded. "He will. And providing we manage the crofts, we can continue to take a percentage of the rents as well."

Adam eyed me carefully before drinking from the beaker. Pulling a face at the sour taste, he put it down. "Six months give or take a few days," he said slowly, swiping a hand across his lips. "I didn't expect such generosity from his lordship. It's more than he'd do for your mother or father."

What did Adam mean by that? Before I could ask, he continued.

"It's a goodly time . . . depending on how you intend to find those monies."

It was time to announce my plan and pray that Adam didn't laugh in my face or walk out the door.

I wrapped my hands around the beaker, staring into its yellow depths. The scant foam that had sat upon the surface had already dissolved. "I intend to become a brewer, Adam." I lifted my chin and met his steady gaze. "I'm going to make and sell ale."

Adam flicked his vessel with his fingers. "Well, you've not much competition, I'll say that." His eyes twinkled.

My mouth twitched, then I chuckled. "You, Saskia, and Blanche always said that if Mother sold her ale, we'd run the friary and all the other brewsters in town out of business."

"Aye, we did and she would have. But Mistress Anneke, that wasn't said in any seriousness . . ."

"Are you telling me that Mother's ale wasn't any good?"

"Good?" Adam sighed and licked his lips. "It was the best I've ever drunk, lass, and believe me, I've had my fair share." He rested his arms on the table. "It was said because we knew it would never happen. Mistress Sheldrake made the ale for the household and gave the leftovers to Father Clement to distribute as he saw fit. She never sold it. Doing something like that was beneath her . . . It's beneath you too, Mistress Anneke, if you'll forgive me for saying."

I'd hoped I wouldn't have to justify, let alone defend, my decision, that Adam would understand, offer to help. How was being a brewer worse than being a servant? How could I even pose that question to Adam without causing offense? My heart plummeted into my boots. I'd managed to persuade Lord Rainford; I hadn't really expected resistance from Adam. He had to understand, he just had to.

"This is different, Adam, and you know it. Everything's changed." I pushed back my hood and pulled off my scarf. Anything to keep my hands busy. "Mother had a choice, that's true. But I don't, not anymore. I have to do something. I have to find a way to earn enough money to keep Holcroft House, to keep the twins and Saskia, Blanche, all of you, all of *us*, together. If I don't . . ." I waved my scarf through the thick air, allowing him to imagine the consequences. "I have to try, Adam. I have to. It may have been above Mother to become a brewer, but it's not above me. I'm no longer worthy of being considered a wife, at least not without a dowry, and frankly I won't subject the twins, myself, or any of you to Cousin Hiske. My only option is to find work. Good, honest work. Brewing is a respectable trade. Look at Mistress Amwell and Mistress Scot—why, they're both brewsters and they're very respected in Elmham Lenn."

——"They're also married."

"Mistress Scot's a widow. Master Anthony died last summer—remember? Anyhow," I said, my tone becoming sharp as I felt Adam withdrawing, "I know it's something I can do and, with your help, Adam Barfoot, do well."

Beneath fine brows Adam watched me retie the scarf. I could see a muscle working in his cheek. He didn't say a word. In the silence I didn't realize how much I needed his approval.

"Prior to Cousin Hiske's arrival, we always made our own brew. What about all the offers to buy it that we declined? Mother wouldn't sell. She thought Father wouldn't endorse such a thing or it would upset the local brewsters or worse, Abbot Hubbard and the friary." I looked over my shoulder and lowered my voice. "But that's what I have to do—become a rival. A serious one. I need to attract customers, take them if I must—even from the good monks here." I leaned across the table, aware the sleeve of my tunic was sitting in something sticky. "Oh, Adam, I've thought of very little else since I wrote to Lord Rainford. Everything is in place already. All we have to do is tidy up the old brewhouse and we can start. The mash tun is fine, I'm sure. We already know the water from the Nene is easily accessible and it's pure. We'll buy bigger quantities of barley from Master Bondfield and, if he can't supply enough, we can ask Master Hamerton. If I talk to Perkyn Miller, I'm certain he'll grind it for us. The quern stones we have are too small for the amount I intend to malt and dry. And, I was thinking, if I speak to Master Proudfellow at the Gull's Rise, I'm sure he'd purchase some of our ale. He was always urging Mother to sell to him. Once he does, the other innkeepers might also follow . . ."

Adam did something he'd never done before. As I was speak-

ing, he lifted my hand from the table and took it in both of his.
I was so astonished by the gesture, I fell silent. My eyes became
glassy, partly from the fire, but also from the emotions I held
in check, that I'd stifled for so long. I hadn't expected to meet
resistance. Not from Adam.

I was a fool.

"Mistress Anneke," he said finally, his voice harsh, scratchy.
"It breaks my heart to hear you talking like this. To know that
you've put such thought into what no lady of your station, your
birth, should ever have to." He stared at our conjoined hands.
"It would break your mother's heart as well."

My shoulders slumped.

"You might not believe it, but it would rend your father's
in two."

A tear escaped and trickled down my cheek. I let it fall.

He gripped my hands more tightly. "I understand you've no
choice but to do *something*, you'll get no argument from me in
that regard. But it's the choice you make that will define your
life from this point. Do you understand that, child?"

I flashed him a smile through my tears. "I'm not a child,
Adam."

"To me you are. Do you understand?" he repeated more
firmly. "That if you choose this path, then it will be nigh on impossible to turn back. Once you begin it, you must keep going.
Are you prepared to do that, no matter what obstacles you face?
Resistance and misunderstandings, even from folk you think
good and reasonable?"

I sniffed. Loudly. "Of course I am."

"People will judge you. They'll make assumptions—about
you, the twins—and they won't be . . . nice."

I gave a wistful smile. "I know to what you refer."

Adam gave a derisive snort and shook his head. "Only as rumors about others, gossip in the marketplace and halls. You don't know them as one day you will. It's like a sackcloth you can never shuck. Once you step in this direction, you can never go back."

Taking a deep breath, I released it slowly. "This *is* the right choice, Adam. I know it."

"A brewster, Mistress Anneke?" I almost didn't hear him, so quiet were his words.

Dropping my forehead onto our linked hands, I whispered, "I really don't have a choice." I dropped a light kiss on his fingers as I pulled away and released him, staring as he sat across the table from me, doubt on his features.

He leaned back, his arms outstretched, regarding me with a look I couldn't fathom. Drumming his fingers on the table, he stopped, picked up his beaker and drained it, slamming it back down. "Forget Master Hamerton—he carries too many fines for my liking. Bondfield's the one we want. As for Perkyn Miller, I'll speak to him. And, regarding the mash tun, if we can convince Mistress Saskia to release Will from his duties for a couple of days, I'll see to its repair as well. But you're right; they're in good condition considering they haven't been used in nigh on six years." He rubbed his chin. "We'll need to look to getting some barrels to transport the water. The skins we once used will never do for the quantities you need. And as for old Proudfellow—let Iris have a word with him. He's her uncle, did you know? He's a sweet spot for her—"

Adam talked for ages, organizing the staff, assigning duties to each member of the household. I sat there like a coney struck by a stone, unable to move, think, or speak. I saw Adam's mouth moving, but I could no longer hear the words; the wave of happiness that enveloped me prevented it.

"Are you listening, lass?" asked Adam after a while.

I blinked. I nodded, my throat tight. My eyes welled and overflowed.

"Ah, don't do that," said Adam, reaching into his jerkin for a kerchief. He dabbed my cheeks until I took the scrap of fabric from him and tended myself. "I thought you'd be happy?"

I choked back a laugh. "I am, Adam. I am. It's just that I thought you weren't going to help, that you didn't approve."

Adam shook his head, a grin splitting his face. "I don't. But that's all the more reason to help. To stop you getting into trouble—well, more than I think you will anyhow."

Drying my eyes, I smiled at him. "Shall we go, then? Tell the others what our new life's to be?"

Adam looked into his beaker, pushed it away with a grimace, and rose. "Aye, let's be on our way."

He waited for me to stand and then, depositing a few coins on the counter, led us out of the friary's taproom and into the busy yard.

As we rode out the gates and back into the glorious sunset, Adam turned to me. "You don't ever have to doubt me, Mistress Anneke. Not ever. For as long as you need me, for as long as you want me there, it's by your side I'll be."

It was some moments before I was able to respond. "I'm sorry, Adam. It won't happen again."

# SEVEN

HOLCROFT HOUSE

That evening

*The year of Our Lord 1405 in the sixth*

*year of the reign of Henry IV*

*A*dam and I returned to Holcroft House that evening to find the entire household crammed into the kitchen. Even the twins were there, one each upon Saskia's and Blanche's knees. Iris held an inconsolable Louise, while Will looked on, one eye obscured by the cloth he pressed against his face, his mouth twisted by violent words. I stood in the doorway, my body gripped by an invisible vise that squeezed the very breath from my lungs. My heart pounded painfully as my imagination tried to come to terms with what I saw. Clearly, bad news had once again touched the house. My only thoughts were for Tobias. I tried to speak, when Karel looked up.

"Anneke!" He bounded from Blanche's arms. Betje wriggled out of Saskia's and I barely had time to kneel before they flung themselves against me, howling.

The rest of the staff clambered to their feet; Adam finally managed to hold and silence the hounds.

"Thank the good Lord you're home, Mistress Anneke!"

"Master Adam, it's so good to see you!"

"Oh, Adam, if only you'd been here . . ."

"The wickedness of people . . ."

"Evil, pure evil . . ."

"If I get my hands on them, I won't be responsible . . ."

The cacophony of voices was more than I could stand. "Quiet! Please, all of you!" I shouted from the floor. The voices ceased. One of the dogs whined. Saskia stood wringing her hands; Blanche screwed her apron into a ball while Will glowered at a spot on the wall. Louisa looked up and Iris shook her head in sorrow. The twins huddled closer.

Words stuck in my throat. I was aware of everyone staring at me, concern shaping their features.

"Saskia," I gasped. "Tobias? Is he . . . What have you heard . . . ?"

"Tobias?" said Saskia, puzzled. "Oh, you poor lamb." She swooped and raised me to my feet, pulling me against her breast before holding me at arm's length. "*Nee*, Mistress Anneke, *nee*. It's not Tobias. God love you. It's *her*."

"Her?"

"Mistress Jabben," said Blanche sourly.

I moved out of Saskia's embrace. The twins clutched my skirts. "What's wrong with her?" My heart began to beat strangely.

"Wrong?" spat Saskia. "Where do I begin?"

Adam stepped forward. "Enough. What's happened?"

Saskia pushed her hair, which was in disarray, from her

forehead. "To her? Nothing. Though, may the good Lord forgive me, I wish it had."

Will made a noise of agreement.

"I'm sorry, Mistress Anneke." Saskia's face was drawn, old. "We couldn't stop her. We tried, but she said it was her right and that we were to do nothing. We thought about fetching you, or the sheriff, but you were too far away and mayhap the sheriff would've prevaricated . . ."

Fear was swiftly replaced by a cold, hard shell. "For goodness sakes, Saskia, what *are* you talking about?"

It was Blanche who answered, sinking back onto her stool. "Mistress Jabben has left the house. Normally, we'd be celebrating our good fortune—oh, don't look at me like that, Adam Barfoot, you know we would. Mistress Anneke here too, if I'm not mistaken." The twins exchanged a look. I frowned in warning. "It's true," Blanche added with a defiant huff of air.

"Please, just tell me what she's done." I sat on the bench and pulled the twins closer.

"What she's done," said Saskia, coming forward to stand in front of me, "is rob you blind, Mistress Anneke. She's taken everything she could lay her hands on—all the merchandise from the shop, what was left in the warehouse and more. A cart came this morning, not long after you and Master Adam left. There were two men, hired by Master Makejoy, I've no doubt. Marched through here like they owned the place and began loading up under Mistress Jabben's directions."

"We tried to stop them," said Will. "But they threatened us. Said they were working within the law. And when I said I wanted to see something in writing, one of the men punched me." He removed the cloth he'd pressed against his face to reveal a very swollen, half-closed eye. "Said I'd find it harder to read with only one . . . Fool didn't know it'd make no difference, can't read nohow."

"But that's not all," continued Blanche. "The evil chicken-necked cow took as many rugs, goblets, linen, and clothes she could lay her greedy hands on. You name it, she claimed it. Said it was her due, that the Sheldrakes owed her, and she was going to take what was rightfully hers."

My heart began to pound. *The chest in my room . . .* My stomach lurched and nausea rose in my throat. The irony that, after all, Hiske may yet have ruined my plans was not lost on me. A bitter laugh escaped, earning me surprised glances.

"When we realized what was happening, that it wasn't just Master Joseph's and thus Lord Rainford's unsold merchandise she was claiming, we whipped through the house and brought as much as we could in here—" Saskia's arm swept the kitchen.

Searching the room with new, frantic eyes, I noticed how crowded it was—not just with people, but objects. There was the rug from the solar and some of the tapestries that had adorned its walls were rolled next to the door. There were the instruments from Father's office, a small table and some Venetian glass by the stove. Near the door to the main part of the house stood the chest containing the twins' clothes. There were furs, blankets, and decorative plates, a brush and mirror and so many other things piled on benches or on the floor. Even the table was groaning under the weight of dishes and implements. I studied the earnest, indignant, and furious faces of those around me and imagined them rushing through the house, trying to snatch things before Hiske could and racing with them down here to protect them. I could see Hiske's face when she understood her intention to strip the house was thwarted. But of my chest, there was no sign. Prying the twins from my side, I stood hastily and began to push things out of the way, lifting bundles, ignoring the mess as they tumbled on top of each other and struck the floor.

"Whatever we could salvage from her clutches, we did." Saskia lifted a stack of scrolls into her arms as I tried to shove them off a counter. "We figured she wouldn't dare touch a thing with all of us to guard them, and we were right."

"I rescued that," said Karel, pointing to one of Father's old sextants on top of a box.

"I took that!" said Betje, indicating Father's rather crumpled star chart. Blanche moved it out of my way.

"We did what we could, Mistress Anneke," said Saskia softly, watching me sadly as I sorted through the chaos, not understanding my purpose.

I searched the mounds and muddles of cloth, uncovering what I could, each discovery fueling my growing sense that all was lost.

Then I saw it.

Over by the milk pail, peeping from under the furs that had been stripped from a bed, was my chest. Wading toward it like one possessed, I knelt and hefted the furs to one side. I was aware of Saskia and Blanche trading glances. Will's mouth was hanging open; Iris backed away, confused and alarmed. Louisa sought Karel. Only Adam was unperturbed by my behavior, and Betje, who clambered over things to join me.

"What's wrong, Anneke? Why are you messing everything up?" asked Betje quietly.

Everyone waited for me answer.

Slowly, I raised the lid of the chest. Lifting the tunics, kirtles, undergarments, scarves, and hoods out of the way, I rummaged around, brushing against some leather shoes, a tightly wound curl of ribbon, and a couple of books. Then, my fingers found what I so desperately sought. Lifting it out carefully, I brought the bound pages into the light. With a sigh of relief, I sank onto my heels and sent a swift prayer to the Holy Mother that this had been spared.

Within the yellowing pages I clutched so tightly were the recipes my mother used to make her special ale. Though I was sure I remembered how, knowing I had these was the closest I would ever come to having Mother beside me. They'd been passed down through generations of de Winter women, all of whom had made ale and other brews to delight their kin and neighbors. All the quantities, additions, timing, and measures that my Dutch ancestors had used for centuries. Upon these pages, painstakingly recorded by Mother and hers before her and so on, were the recipes I believed would be my salvation; what would make our ale more desirable and sought after than any other brewed in town. The moment Hiske banned me from brewing, I'd hidden this book, knowing that if she found the recipes, she would have had them destroyed. Never believing I was shoring up our futures, I'd thought I was preserving a beloved keepsake.

Relief flooded me. I pressed the pages to my chest and bowed my head. The scent of marigolds, lavender, sunshine, laughter, and love seemed all around me. "Mother," I whispered. It was a moment before I was able to face the others, but when I did, it was to hold the pages aloft triumphantly.

"Nothing's wrong, Betje. Nothing." Adam smiled and nodded at my little sister. She grinned at him.

"Not anymore," I agreed and swept Betje into my arms and carried her to the table and perched her upon it. She wriggled till she cleared a space.

"But Mistress Anneke . . . the house . . ." said Saskia, only now daring to release what was in her arms. Parchment, linen, and a goblet tumbled onto the table.

"It doesn't matter." I laughed. "I was likely going to have to sell most things anyway. We will make do. All that matters is that I have this." I clutched the small book. "And that we have each other." Looking at their faces, I beamed.

"Not Doreen," said Will. "She went with Mistress Jabben."

"She even had the gall to offer me and Blanche a position in her house—Mistress Jabben, that is." Saskia sniffed and raised her chin.

I studied them, my loyal servants, my family, and my heart filled. I looked at the table, scattered with odds and ends. Karel was twirling an iron object. Will was watching me with his one good eye, his other closed completely now. Louisa's tears had ceased and she reached for Betje and encouraged her off the table and onto her lap. Saskia appeared resigned, Blanche and Iris perplexed. All of them were looking to me, bewildered by my sudden composure after my frantic search amid what they perceived as another disaster. But this was nothing to me . . . if anything, it was cause for celebration.

Hiske was gone—the last obstacle to my plans—or so I thought.

Crossing to one of the cabinets in the corner, I shoved the books and blankets aside with my foot, opened the door, and peered inside. I could sense the glances and frowns behind me, the slight apprehension that had started to fill the room.

"What are you looking for?" asked Blanche finally. She didn't like anyone prying in her cupboards—not even me.

"Ah, here it is," I said, and removed a jug of wine. Setting it on the table, I looked around. "Pass some goblets and mazers, would you, Iris?"

Checking with Blanche first, who nodded brusquely, Iris made some space and lined them up.

"Adam, if you would be so kind?" I gestured to the jug. Adam took his knife out of its sheath and knocked the wax and cork off the top.

"Shall I pour?" he asked. I nodded.

"Mistress Anneke, begging your pardon," said Saskia as Adam handed her a brimming goblet, waiting until she took it before passing a mazer to Blanche. "But have you heard a word we've said?"

"Every single one, Saskia."

"Are you sure?" she examined my face. "On top of losing the house, you've been robbed blind and instead of demanding restitution or sending Will for the watch, you stand there with some bits of paper, flashing those dimples of yours and offering drinks around like it's the Last Supper!"

I smiled. "Not the last. On the contrary, it's the first. The first supper in *our* house. You see, something very important happened today and I want to share it with you." I quickly explained what eventuated at Scales Hall and my plans. Adam, as I'd hoped, filled in the gaps and informed everyone what their duties would be over the coming weeks. As he spoke, I watched their faces. There was surprise, confusion, a little nervousness— all of which I shared. But, most of all, there was excitement and determination. Bless them, they wanted my venture to succeed as much as I did.

Adam finished and I lifted my goblet. "So, let's raise our drinks, shall we? For, as of tomorrow, we're no longer Holcroft House, traders of fine goods. When day breaks and the cock crows, we begin our transformation."

"Into what?" asked Saskia.

I rested my eyes upon each of them in turn. "Into Holcroft House, the home of Sheldrake brewers—makers of the finest ale in all of Norfolk."

There was a beat before everyone raised their vessels and in voices ringing with excitement, chorused: "To Sheldrake brewers, makers of the finest ale in all of Norfolk."

"Nay!" cried Will, spluttering as he swallowed his wine too quickly. "Not Norfolk. Why stop there? As God is my witness, Mistress Sheldrake will be the finest brewer in all of England."

As the servants cheered and Karel and Betje clapped, I met Adam's eyes across the room. *In England,* he mouthed and raised his mazer.

"In England," I echoed.

With the love and support of these people, that night I believed anything was possible.

# EIGHT

HOLCROFT HOUSE
October
*The year of Our Lord 1405 in the sixth
year of the reign of Henry IV*

The next few days passed in a blur. After returning what had
been salvaged from Hiske back to where it belonged, I was
faced with the bleak reality of how empty, how hollow, the
house seemed. The night I'd returned from Lord Rainford's,
drunk on excitement that my bid to secure us time had succeeded, it had been easy to be indifferent to what my cousin
had done, but in the gaps and spaces in every room, I was
forced to confront Hiske's avarice and spite. Almost all of Tobias's possessions—from a knife and sheath to a Lancastrian
pennant his lord had given him to commemorate his first battle
at Shrewsbury that he'd sent home for safekeeping, to clothes
he'd worn as a child that were being kept for Karel, as well as
a book that belonged to Mother—all had been seized. The old
sea chest and carved stool in his room were gone. The furs from

his bed, the curtains that surrounded his mattress as well. In the solar, apart from a couple of stools, the rug, and two tapestries, Hiske had claimed everything—the cabinets, the two chairs, and the cushions that adorned them. The tables filled with curios Father had collected on his travels, the mementos Mother had brought with her when she came to England as Father's bride were no longer there. Even the main hall and Father's office hadn't been spared. The shop and storeroom at the rear of the house, which had held what were now Lord Rainford's goods, were completely empty. As far as I could tell, only the contents of my room, the nursery, and the kitchen had been saved in their entirety and for that I was grateful. Trying not to be despondent, the starkness of the rooms simply gave me another reason to make my enterprise work.

Though part of me wished to seek justice, it was easier to surrender a few possessions and believe I'd never see Hiske again than have her charged and deal with the very public consequences of that. A court would cause a scandal none of us could afford. And, I told myself, as much as I may not like it, she was family. I couldn't bring the law down upon one of my own. Mother wouldn't want that.

A few days later, we heard through Master Jacobsen that Hiske and Master Makejoy had married and were staying in rooms above an inn near the law courts until they could lease their own premises.

With the house returned to some sort of order, Saskia and Blanche tended to the gardens. Though it was late in the year to plant, there would be some vegetables that would yield in early spring and they set about ensuring we'd reap that small harvest. In the meantime, Adam, Will, and I set to restoring the brewhouse.

Entering it for the first time in six years was not the joyous moment I'd imagined. As we pushed open the old door, snatching it swiftly as it almost came away from the hinges, the smell of dust, bird droppings, and the odor of stale wort assailed us. A stream of light filtered through the filthy windows, striking the aged mash tun, exposing the garlands of cobwebs suspended from the wood. Colonies of dust spiraled into the sunlight like tiny moths chasing a flame. In the far corner, a huge kiln loomed. Under the windows, two shallow troughs sat, dark and empty. A row of barrels squatted between them and the kiln. The good news was their wood appeared sound and the metal hoops that girthed them weren't rusted. I might yet be spared the cost of a cooper.

Leaning against one of the barrels was the mash stirrer. Hefting it off the floor, I upended it so I could examine the laddered paddle for any splintering or rot. Mother had brought this with her when she came from Holland and, though it was a deceptively simple piece of equipment I'd seen deployed in other brewhouses, she insisted on using this stick to stir the mash and wort. She claimed it carried within it her family's talent for brewing. I didn't doubt it and proposed to use it as well. Satisfied it was intact, I set it down and continued my survey.

Gathering dust on the table in the middle of the room were bungs for the barrels, a copper hand cup, spigots, and a mallet that, when I picked it up, was lighter than I recalled. Putting it down carefully beside a dull funnel, I flexed my fingers.

As I crossed the room rats scurried before me, and from the

shadows and dark corners came the sound of small feet and high-pitched squeals. I opened the door at the far end that led to the small shed Mother had used as a malthouse. The hinges were stiff, and I used my shoulder to thrust the door open, almost tumbling down the steps. It was too dark to see clearly— not even the small window admitted much light. Propping the door open, I descended the few steps and bent down to touch the floor. It was, thankfully, dry, but filthy with grit and dirt. I shuddered and, not for the first time, doubt engulfed me. I went back up the steps and stood in the doorway, hands on my hips, facing Will and Adam.

Will shook his head, arms folded. He didn't believe we could do it. I took a deep breath and the disturbed dust made me cough. I resolved then and there that I would prove Will wrong. I swung to Adam and, to my great relief, saw only calculation on his face.

"How's the malthouse?" he asked, putting down the old tundish.

"Dry." I clapped my hands together to rid them of debris. "For now."

Adam nodded. "That's a start." He turned slowly. "Well, at least all the equipment appears to be here."

"Aye. But the truth is, it will take more work than I first thought . . ."

"More work, Mistress Anneke?" griped Will. "It'll take the king's army."

"Rubbish," said Adam. Propping the outside door wide open so more light flooded the space, he knocked his fist against the mash tun. The sound reverberated. "This merely needs a good clean." He bent down and examined it from below. "There's a piece of wood wants replacing, but nothing Jasper Cooper won't be able to tend quickly. I'll go and see him shortly, ask him to have a look."

I wasn't to be spared a cooper after all.

Adam strolled to the troughs and inspected them as well. "You weren't a part of this household when the brewhouse was used almost every day, Will. It was a sight to behold and one we'll see again." He smiled. "Just as the equipment is coated in dirt, disguising its value, you're allowing first impressions to blind you to what's before your eyes." Wiping away a cobweb, he used his jerkin to clean part of the metal. Mimicking Adam, I went to the kiln, passing a hand across its surface and rubbing it on the apron I'd thankfully thought to don. My hand left a dark gray streak on the fabric.

"This is the same, I think." I opened the door and was enveloped by a cloud of ashes and soot. Caught unawares, I fell backward, coughing and spluttering. I began to laugh. Adam hauled me to my feet, chuckling, his eyes studying my face.

"Nothing a good scrub won't fix."

Self-consciously, I raised my hands to my face.

I chortled and coughed again. "I'm sure." I applied my apron to my cheeks. "I'll ask Iris to help me clean this and the oven," I added, noting the grime and rodent droppings across its surface as well. "We'll fetch a couple of buckets and brushes and tend to them immediately. Perhaps I can persuade Blanche, if she's not too busy, to help scrub out the troughs." I ran my hands along their solid edges and then, leaning over, tried to clear the thick glass above with the end of my sleeve, leaving a greasy smudge. "These windows too." I sighed as the amount of work began to add up. I pressed my back against the trough and reexamined the room. It was hard to imagine it free of all the filth, let alone functioning. With a deep breath that ended in a volley of coughs, I began to recite all that was needed, counting chores off on my fingers. "Oh," I added, looking toward the stove and kiln and the crooked chimney breast in which they sat. "We'll need a sweep as well, Adam. And someone needs to scrub the malthouse. I'm not laying grain until the floor is spotless."

With good humor that owed nothing to false bravado, Adam slapped his hands together. "Let's be about it then," he said.

Setting Will to clean the mash tun and the barrels, Adam left to organize their repair with Master Cooper, commission a chimney sweep and the other trades we'd need, as well as purchase supplies of coal and collect enough wood to get the brewery in working order again. Hauling pails of hot water from the kitchen, Iris and I set to cleaning out the kiln and stove. Outfitting the twins in leggings and shirts that had seen better days, Louisa led Betje and Karel to attack the cobwebs before sweeping and scrubbing both the brewery floor and the malthouse. It wasn't long before Betje and Karel looked more like coal merchants than trader's children.

Breaking before sext sounded, we sat on the garden walls outside and savored fresh-baked bread, wedges of cheese, and crisp apples, as well as some cold rabbit. We were joined by Jasper Cooper, who, after replacing the rotten wood on two barrels, much to my delight, gave a good report on the state of the mash tun. Adam passed around a jug of small ale and mazers and, from the grimaces on everyone's faces as they drank, I knew the beverage had come from the friary.

"How the ale-conners let Abbot Hubbard sell this pig swill is beyond me," said Master Jasper before he remembered the company he was in. "Forgive me, Mistress Sheldrake," he said. "But it riles me that they pay the same tax as the folks in town and churn out what I wouldn't give my dogs to drink."

"You're not the only one dissatisfied, Jasper," said Adam, placing his mazer on the ground. "The good news is, as soon as Mistress Sheldrake has her brew ready, you won't have to tolerate the abbot's ale any longer."

"I'll look forward to that," said Master Jasper, raising his beaker toward me. "There's many of us will. It's not much to ask, surely? All we want is food in our gullets, something decent to wet the throat, and a warm place to rest our weary heads at night." With a wink, he drained his vessel, shaking his head and pursing his lips as he finished. "Proudfellow always said you and your ma, I mean, Mistress Cathaline, didn't just make ale, you made magic. I'm looking forward to tasting me some of that." With a loud belch and a quick apology, Master Jasper went as red as a beet.

We all laughed and my spirits, which had flagged a little as, despite our hours of work, very little impression was made on the brewhouse, were lifted. I liked the idea that, together, Mother and I "made magic." The good Lord knew, I needed some of that now.

Laboring throughout the afternoon we stopped only when the light was so dim, shadows engulfed the interior. By then, not only had Master Jasper ensured the mash tun was ready for use, the copper had been brushed out, scrubbed, and was shining. Will, the twins, and Louisa had thoroughly swept the drying floor in the malthouse, and the barrels, which had been rolled out into the yard, were cleaned, checked for leaks, the new wood sealed then brought back inside and stood next to the troughs.

Instead of looking like remnants of a forgotten past, they were poised to be filled.

My fingers kneaded the small of my back as I examined the fruits of our work. I was more than pleased. It was with great cheer tempered only by the exhaustion of a good day's work that we retreated to the kitchen. The smells drifting through the open door had been tantalizing us all afternoon. Blanche not only ensured there was warm water in which we could wash, but she'd excelled herself by roasting a capon, fish, and potatoes, and she'd bought some almond-paste sweetmeats from the market as a treat. She'd also baked apples infused with cloves and some cinnamon, steeping them in almond milk. My mouth watered and my stomach clenched in hunger. From the wide eyes and moist lips of the others, I knew I wasn't the only one. Shooing us away with orders to tidy ourselves, Blanche finished preparing our feast.

Louisa took control of the twins while I ascended to the bedroom to use the waiting water. Crossing through the hall, I noted that while it was no longer decorated with tapestries and scattered with benches, the chair from my father's study had been placed by the blazing hearth and a tattered cushion I couldn't recall left on the seat. In place of the usual stools, Blanche and Saskia had lugged in some tree stumps. Topped with patched pillows, they gave the hall a rather jovial, informal air and I was deeply touched by their efforts. Upstairs, apart from the rug and a couple of wall hangings, the solar was bare. Only a few objects remained. I resolved then and there to take these downstairs to adorn the hall. The solar would remain unused for the time being.

Pulling off my tunic and kirtle and throwing them to one

side, I stood before the crackling fire and removed my under-clothes, dipped the washing cloth in the hot water, rubbed the soap into it, and scrubbed myself from head to foot. The water turned dark quickly.

Wrapped in a drying sheet, I sank onto the bed and began to undo my hair, disentangling the plaits and letting it flow over my shoulders. I reached for a comb and teased it through the thick strands. Lord Rainford had commented on my hair, how different it was to my mother's. Many people did. Whereas To-bias, I'd always believed, inherited Father's dark curls and the twins Mother's flaxen hair, I was the paintbox in which the colors had been mixed—at least, that's what Mother always told me. When I'd been tormented by other children for my autum-nal hair, even cursed as unlucky, Mother would tell me that only special children were graced with such a color. That Blessed Mary too had possessed fiery hair, akin to dragon's breath, and she'd been beloved by Jesus. I'd always thought she meant the Virgin Mary—until Hiske set me straight.

Not long after Cousin Hiske arrived, she'd taken offense at my tresses, what she claimed was my vanity, and threatened to cut them. Distressed that she would consider such a thing and give the other children yet another reason to mock me, I'd pleaded with her, saying that she couldn't cut hair that was like the Virgin's.

"Like the Virgin's?" she'd scorned. "Who told you such non-sense?"

"Why . . . Moeder told me." My bottom lip started to trem-ble. I'd not yet learned to hide from Hiske the power her words had to hurt me.

Hiske had thrown back her head, opened her lipless mouth,

and laughed. Cowering, my hair gripped in one hand, I'd waited for her to finish.

"The Virgin? You stupid child! The Virgin's hair is as untainted as yours is stained by sin. Hers is golden, like the twins', like your silly mother's. *Nee*, Cathaline meant the whore Mary. The one who was to be stoned." Hiske dried her eyes and then appraised me. She pulled her eating knife from the folds of her tunic and came toward me. "Your hair is nothing but a reminder of women's wanton ways. It needs to come off. It's shameful."

I cried out, and the sound drew my father from his study and up the stairs. Thank the Lord, it was one of the few times he'd been home. By then, the servants had gathered too. Hiske explained her intention, confident she would have Father's support. I began to weep. God forgive my conceitedness, I imagined strands of hair falling around my ankles and the mortification of facing the townsfolk.

Father folded his arms across his chest and regarded me. As the seconds passed in silence, I raised my tear-stained face. His expression was one I'd not seen before. Even trying to recall it now, it was inscrutable. Not quite distaste, not quite sorrow.

"Put your knife away," he said to Hiske, then spun on his heel and went back to his office.

Four days later, as he departed on another voyage, he gave me a perfunctory kiss on the cheek. "Be good for your cousin," he ordered and, after bestowing his blessing, rested his hand against my hair a fraction longer, pulling a stray tendril with his fingers. As soon as I was aware of it, the gesture ceased and I wondered if I'd imagined it.

Cousin Hiske had been particularly vindictive after he left, so I knew I had not.

Reaching down to my hips, my hair was an unruly curtain. I pulled the comb through it, the drying sheet falling from my shoulders and onto the bed. For just a moment, cursed by the self-admiration Hiske perceived, I felt like a goddess, one of Adam's dryads or a naiad. My breasts burst through my hair, the nipples taut from the cold air that turned my flesh into that of a goose. I ignored the drafts, staring at my pale legs and thighs, at the coiled, coarser hair at their juncture—a sinner's body, Hiske had said, warning me to disguise it. "No good will ever come of possessing a body like that," she'd say.

Putting down the comb, I wondered if she was right. Mother had the same physical shape, and look where that had led. Beautiful, the object of men's desires, she'd made a good marriage and then destroyed it by succumbing to lust. Pleasure and happiness—my mother had, for the last years of her life, been denied both. Nothing could convince me that Father had enjoyed much of either, not for a long, long time. Had Mother ever loved Father? What about Lord Rainford? I couldn't imagine anyone loving him—not even Mother. So what had driven her into his bed?

Was I to ever know love? Oh, I'd had fancies, Betrix and I had shared many a girlish daydream, and I knew some of the young men in town (and older ones) looked at me with more than passing interest, but that wasn't love. Nor was it likely to lead to offers of wedlock. As Hiske and Master Makejoy said, not only was I more than old enough to enter a first marriage, I'd no prospects. Did that include being loved? While I understood that love and marriage didn't necessarily follow, I harbored hope. Or was I to be denied that too?

With a long sigh at how melancholy my thoughts had

become, I roused and dressed quickly, tying back my hair. I didn't have time to feel sorry for myself. I'd work to do, people dependent upon me and the fulfillment of my plans. Forcing a smile to my lips, I went to the nursery to see how Louisa was faring, before finally, with the twins in tow, making my way downstairs for supper.

⋗⋈⋘

Three days later, with the brewhouse almost ready, Adam and I went to see the local miller, a jolly-faced fellow called Perkyn Miller. I'd known Master Perkyn for as long as I remembered. His wife had died of fever a few years earlier, leaving him to raise their daughter, Olive, on his own. Olive was a gentle, perpetually happy soul who, though she possessed the body of a grown woman, had a mind trapped forever in the nursery.

On our arrival, Olive, who was very tall and well-rounded, with pale blue eyes and honey-colored hair that was never combed or dressed, bolted out of the mill, three little spaniels cavorting at her heels. Flinging her arms around me, she planted a wet kiss on my cheek, before doing the same to Adam. The dogs leaped upon us, refusing to calm until they received attention.

"My Lady Anneke, Master Adam!" Olive's sweet face was shining. "It's been a long, long time since you've visited Olive." She looped her arms through ours and dragged us forward. "Papa! Look who Olive found! My Lady Anneke and Master Adam."

Accustomed to Olive and her ways, we smiled at Master Perkyn as he appeared in the doorway, wiping his hands on a towel. "Olive, I've told you, you need to be saying *Mistress Sheldrake*—"

"It's all right, Master Perkyn, really," I assured him. Ever since Olive's mother had told her a story about a dragon and a princess with long auburn hair, Olive had decided I was the heroine in a fairy tale. I didn't mind. Olive had nicknames for most of the townsfolk—some less generous than others. She referred to Cousin Hiske as "the chicken neck"; there was nothing we could do to deter her either.

Drawing us inside, Master Perkyn poured some small ale and invited us to sit.

Olive latched herself to my side, her head on my shoulder.

"I just want to say, Mistress Sheldrake, I'm very sorry for your loss," began Master Perkyn, staring at me earnestly. "Your father was a man who . . . who wasn't inclined to go the ways of others. He trod his own path." He looked down at his drink, searching for more to say. Honesty prevailed and he gave me a small, sympathetic smile instead.

"Thank you," I said.

"My mother died once," said Olive sadly.

"I know," I replied softly. "Mine too."

"We heard what your cousin did," said Master Perkyn. "Shameful, that was."

My eyebrows rose.

Master Perkyn cleared his throat. "Excuse me liberties, Mistress Sheldrake, but the whole town knows. Not much escapes notice, as you can imagine and, with Mistress Jabben being a foreigner and marrying that Master Makejoy, well, it was the talk for many a day. As was you not calling the sheriff. There was a few wished you had and then some." He took a gulp of his ale. "Let's just say, I don't think she should show her face around here for a while."

Olive started making little clucking noises and bobbing her head. I had to repress a smile.

"It hadn't occurred to me others would know . . ." I appealed to Adam. I didn't really want to discuss it; Hiske's actions still upset me.

Sitting up straight, Adam cleared his throat. "Look, Perkyn, the reason we're here is that Mistress Sheldrake's reopening the brewhouse at Holcroft House, only this time with the intention to make larger quantities of ale for sale in town. I've spoken to Master Bondfield, and he's able to give us a regular supply of barley, but we also need someone to grind the grain once it's malted and dried. Do you think you can help?"

I had to force my hands to remain still.

Perkyn Miller lowered his beaker to the crude table. "Do the monks out St. Jude's know 'bout your plans?"

I shook my head. "Apart from a few people in town, no one does—" I saw the look on Master Perkyn's face and remembered Hiske. "Oh . . . which is the same as saying everyone."

Master Perkyn gave a sympathetic half-smile and nodded. "'Fraid so, Mistress Sheldrake. Even me. But I just wonder how the monks will feel 'bout it considering they've practically tied up the business in Elmham Lenn and, if rumors be true, Bishop's Lynn, Cromer, and beyond. They're not inclined to welcome competition."

"Competition? As much as I would like to be, I'm hardly that. If they sell their ale so widely, why would they worry about a small business like mine?"

Master Perkyn exchanged a concerned look with Adam. "You don't know much 'bout the abbot, do you?"

"Abbot Hubbard?" I took a sip of the ale. Master Perkyn

made his own. Though it was a small ale, from a second press, it was still rich, foamy, and quite dark. "Not really. Just . . . rumors . . ."

"You don't want to get on the wrong side of him, mistress," said Master Perkyn.

"I've no plans in that direction, Master Perkyn, but thank you for your concern. I don't think he'll even notice I'm trading."

"Oh, he'll notice, all right." He studied me. "He has eyes and ears everywhere. Just when you think you've got away with something, one of his brothers will be around to lecture you and ask for coin in penance. And that's for a minor sin. Not sure how he'll take to you brewing. He barely tolerates the goodwives producing for their families and neighbors. Why, only a month back, old Peckman and his missus who live out near the east gate—you know them, don't you? Well, their little brewhouse was burned to the ground—and when we had all those rains. Then there was Goodwife Doyle and the incident with the ale-conners."

I looked at Adam, who shrugged.

"I don't think Mistress Sheldrake needs to hear all this."

Shaking his head, Master Perkyn stared at Adam, then me, and then into his beaker. "Mayhap you're right. But mayhap she does as well. Needs to know who she's up against by starting trade. He might be God's man, but that abbot's slimier than a Gayfleet eel. Has his ways, and I don't think they always accord with what the good Lord would do, if you know what I mean . . ." He touched the side of his nose and glanced over his shoulder.

"I'm afraid I don't." I followed the direction of his gaze. All I could see was the great wheel of the mill turning against the sky.

Master Perkyn leaned closer. "And hopefully, you never will." He pushed himself away from the table. "Can I ask why you're doing this, Mistress Sheldrake?" His voice was gentle. Olive tightened her hold on my arm.

"Because I've no choice, Master Perkyn. Not if I want my family to stay together." I reached over and patted Adam's hand, which was resting on the tabletop.

Master Perkyn noted my gesture and his eyes traveled to Olive. "Aye, well, there's no better reason, is there. I'd be happy to help. As it happens, Abbot Hubbard no longer uses my services or Bondfield's—now, he'll be glad you went a-calling. For a few years now the friary has been growing its own barley and milling it on site, so it's no longer any of the abbot's business who we supply or grind for, despite what he might think."

Adam looked at him in surprise. "He makes it his business to know who the farmers and millers supply as well?"

"Oh, aye. I told you. He knows everything. The friary has a pretty enterprise going with the ale. Turns a tidy profit, despite the fact it tastes like laundress's piss."

Olive burst into peals of laughter and snorted. I stifled a giggle and felt my cheeks color, but not as much as Master Perkyn's. He stared at me in horror.

"Oh, Mistress Sheldrake," he said, climbing to his feet and bowing. "Forgive my crude ways, my fast tongue. I wasn't thinking. I don't see many ladies and . . ." He began to mumble.

"Please, Master Perkyn, sit down. All is forgiven." I waved him back to his stool.

Adam frowned at the abashed miller as the poor man slowly retook his seat. "Olive, that's enough," her father said sharply.

Olive stopped laughing and, snuggling into my side, shoved her thumb in her mouth.

"What were you saying?" I asked.

Master Perkyn brightened. "Oh, aye, well, not only does the abbot know who's supplying who and with what grain, it's rumored he's put the ale-conners on a wage so they turn a blind eye when it comes to tasting the quality of the brew. I mean, how else can that filthy pond water be explained?" Master Perkyn lowered his voice, forcing Adam and me to lean toward him to hear. "It's said he's paying 'em, the ale-conners that is, to claim the brewsters in town's ale isn't to standard. Forcing everyone, from Proudfellow to the other innkeepers and even the hucksters in the market, to buy their ale from the friary. When they told Goodwife Doyle her ale wasn't fit to sell, she made a scene and said she'd go to the sheriff, further if necessary. The next day, the brothers came to talk her out of it. They couldn't. The day after, she found her cat—he'd his neck broken. The next time she sold a brew, her horse was nobbled." He paused long enough to let his words sink in. "We all know who did it."

"That's a serious accusation, Perkyn," said Adam.

"Aye, it is. But I only tell you to warn you. You don't want to get on the wrong side of the abbot. Goody Doyle understood. She withdrew her complaint. Ask Mistress Amwell if you don't believe me; Mistress Scot too. They've all but stopped producing and won't think of selling to the taverns or inns again, not since the brothers or their hired hands visited them."

Master Perkyn grunted and folded his arms across his chest. "The first thing his grace will do when he finds out you're intending to sell is get in the ears of the ale-conners and force 'em to say your brew's soured or make you destroy it like he did those women. If that don't work, mayhap he'll have 'em fine you for your measures, even if they're exact. Or he might appeal to a guild. If that fails, then he'll do whatever it takes. He doesn't like being thwarted and especially by a woman."

My heart sank. This was an obstacle I hadn't thought to reckon with.

Wiping his mouth with the back of his hand, Master Perkyn became thoughtful. "It's a pity you don't have someone to vouch for you, someone the ale-conners and guild, never mind the abbot, would be concerned about crossing . . ."

Master Perkyn was right. If there was someone I could ask to help, someone with status . . . Then it occurred to me. Of course. There was someone, someone from an organization who wielded such great influence that I knew the abbot didn't have the power to touch him.

While Adam and Master Perkyn discussed the quantities of barley we'd need and debated prices, some of which would be paid in ale (if it passed the ale-conners' standards), I thought about how I'd approach Captain Stoyan. I'd had a brief note from him in response to mine telling him of Father's death. Short, but no less warm for its brevity, he'd written that if I needed anything to let him know.

These sorts of platitudes were often uttered in times of tragedy, I was sensible enough to know that. But Hatto Stoyan was different. And I would test his statement at first light tomorrow.

From Master Perkyn's warnings, if I was to have even a chance of succeeding, I needed all the friends I could muster.

# NINE

ELMHAM LENN AND HOLCROFT HOUSE
The following day
*The year of Our Lord 1405 in the sixth
year of the reign of Henry IV*

*A*dam and I stayed in earnest discussion well into the evening, locked away in the office. Master Perkyn's words had affected us both deeply. While they made Adam want to dissuade me from proceeding, they had the opposite effect upon me. If anything, they strengthened my resolve. Perhaps it was foolish, but the injustices Master Perkyn described fired me. Somewhere, in the back of my mind, I thought I could change everything, that if I defied the abbot and sold my ale, then others, like Mistress Amwell, would be able to as well.

Mollifying Adam's worries about my stubborn refusal to relinquish my plans by agreeing to be chaperoned when I went to the Hanse was no hardship, and Will was delighted to escape his usual tasks.

The next morning, Adam harnessed Shelby to the cart, so

instead of walking through town and along the estuary to the bay, Will and I rode, joining other folk on their way to market and going about their daily business.

The mornings were getting colder, tacit reminders of the winter fast approaching. Though the sun was climbing over the horizon, it battled its way through a thick mist, beams of tepid light striking the damp road and gently melting the frost. Grateful for my fur-lined coat and woolen gloves, I nonetheless enjoyed the crispness of the air and noted how it turned Will's cheeks and the end of his nose bright pink. I imagined mine looked the same.

Merchants and market vendors doffed their caps to me as we passed. Those who'd also lost loved ones aboard the *Cathaline* met my eyes sadly. It was distressing to see the depth of anguish among the townsfolk, the constant reminders of loss. Melancholy, I stared out to sea, surprised I felt no resentment, no anger toward the element that had claimed so many.

Both the bay and the river were filled with traffic. Now the storms had called a truce, ships that had been confined to the North and Baltic Seas were able to make their way into port and unload men and cargoes before reloading and returning to the Cinque Ports, Calais, Germany, and Flanders. The Wash was crammed with galleys and barges navigating the inland waterways. Even at this time of the morning, the air rang with shouts, whistles, and the hum of activity. A few ships were in dry dock, held tightly in wooden scaffolding so their hulls could be caulked. The smells of tar and pitch joined those of fish, smoke, spices, and cooking, all mingling with the ever-present tang of the sea and the musty odor of old seagull nests.

Leaving Will and the cart at the end of the track before it

surrendered to the pier, I gave him coin so he could purchase some breakfast from one of the vendors that catered to sailors and shipwrights.

My step quickened as I passed warehouses filled with salt, wool, silks, yarns, tin, and other produce. Up ahead, a familiar figure stepped onto the dock. Captain Hatto Stoyan stood outside the Kontor, arms folded, legs apart, as if he was riding a canting deck, and watched me approach. Short and stout with the broadest of shoulders, he had an unruly thatch of graying chestnut hair, a neat, trimmed beard, and the face of a man who'd spent most of his life squinting into the sun. Lines crisscrossed his darkened skin, which only threw the clarity of his pale blue eyes into stark relief. They were the kind of eyes dishonest men could not hold for long.

"*Guten Morgen, Fräulein Sheldrake,*" he said as I joined him, giving me a small bow. "*Es tut mir leid um ihren Vater.*"

Unlike the words proffered by Lord Rainford and others, the captain's sympathy sounded sincere. Captain Stoyan may not have liked my father, but he had respected him—at one time, at least.

"*Danke schön,*" I replied.

Glancing pointedly at the smaller boats and barges floating in the water outside the warehouse and the crews working on them, the captain lowered his voice. "*Wir unterhalten uns später in Ruhe.*"

It suited me to wait till we were inside to talk. I didn't want what I was about to say overheard. Indicating I should go ahead, Captain Stoyan shouted some orders then followed me into the Kontor.

It took a moment for my eyes to adjust to the dark interior.

Beneath the pitched roof and wooden walls of the warehouse men rolled huge barrels, clambered over enormous bales of wool, sorted crates of metal, hammered nails into chests, and, using ropes and pulleys, moved enormous loads in and out of the building. Spools of fabric were checked by well-dressed merchants, while clerks stood nearby with counting boards and portable desks, ready to record any transactions that might take place. Livestock was quarantined to one side: chickens, sheep, and cattle. In one corner, the floor was being swept vigorously by two lads with straw brooms. In another, crates were being stacked on top of each other. There was a sense of order in the work around me. As I walked beside Captain Stoyan, I caught snatches of conversation in different languages, including the singsong purr of Flemish and my mother's native Dutch, as familiar to me as English.

The captain and I entered a large quiet room at the back of the warehouse. It had been years since I'd been inside this room, and yet, it was as if time had stood still. The aging map featuring England, Scotland, and Wales was nailed to a wall. France, the Netherlands, the German Empire, the kingdoms of Denmark, Sweden, and all the small countries, duchies, and provinces that lined the North and Baltic Seas were captured in pastels. I used to stare at this map for hours when I came to Father's meetings with the captain, imagining traveling to such marvelously named and shaped places. The rusting iron holders still clutched their melting pillar candles, which the captain lit as I waited. Everything was exactly as I remembered. Boxes were still stacked against one wall; the tattered rug from Persia, with its ruby and sapphire boldness, was the same. Even the cobwebs appeared unchanged, shimmering in the corners. A fire burned in the grate, making the place warm enough for me to ask permission to remove my cloak.

"Of course," said the captain, and he came to take it from my shoulders. "I ask that we speak in English, Mistress Anneke. If we're overheard, we're less likely to be understood. My men are many things, but fluent in that, they're not."

"Very well."

Hanging my cloak on a hook that jutted out of the wall behind his desk, he gestured to the comfortable chair opposite his own. Gathering my skirts, I sat.

"It's been too long," he said, and, going to a huge old sea chest in the corner, pulled out a jug and two silver mazers. Knocking the top off the jug, he first poured a drink for me, then himself, and sat, pushing aside the clutter on his desk with his forearm. His voice was almost a growl. "The last time I saw you, you were but a *kind*, a child. Now, you're a woman grown and, if I may be so bold, a very lovely one."

My cheeks reddened as I thanked him.

"I'm sorry about your father. His loss will be felt by many in very different ways."

I didn't know what to say.

"To old acquaintances," he said and raised his drink.

"Old acquaintances." I sipped the ale slowly, noting the foam on top and the rich honey color of the fluid. It had a mild, slightly bitter taste. "Where's this from?" I knew the captain imported wines and ales from across Europe.

"That's from Bruges. I thought you might like it. Reminds me of what you and your mother used to brew."

It was a perfect introduction to what I wanted to discuss, but before I could say anything, he resumed. "Forgive me, Mistress

Anneke, but when I heard the news of your father's death and received your note, I made some quick inquiries." He drained his mazer. "*Mein Gott!*" He thumped the table hard, the empty mazer tipping over. "What was your father thinking? To not look to his children's future, to leave you in such a position?"

*He wasn't thinking. He was hurting.*

I examined my hands, twisted together for strength.

"Do you know the story of when I first met your mother?" the captain said softly.

My head flew up. "Please, tell it to me."

Righting his mazer, he refilled it and sank back into his chair, legs stretched before him, his face taking on a dreamy, faraway look. "I first met your mother when she was but a child. As the daughter of Herr Gottfried de Winter, the great merchant and official of the Hanseatic League, she was precious, not just to her parents, but to all who served Herr de Winter, myself included."

I knew my grandfather had been an important man, but to hear Captain Stoyan speak of him in such tones imbued him with a significance I'd never gleaned from Mother's or Father's conversations. It filled me with a combination of excitement and sadness. I'd never met any of my German or Dutch relatives, except through Mother's tales . . . apart from Hiske, and she'd spun her own, less favorable stories to counter Mother's. Listening to Captain Stoyan was an unexpected boon.

"Herr de Winter was not always able to return to his home in Maastricht to see his family. Too often he was called upon to attend to Hanse matters in other ports, other countries. He would ask those of us he trusted to visit in his stead, to take gifts and letters to his wife and daughter on his behalf. I was one of the first to be given the duty. That was how I met your mother."

I placed my elbow on the table and rested my chin in my hand. "What was she like?"

Captain Stoyan chuckled softly. "An angel. I still recall disembarking from the small barge I'd hired to sail up the River Maas. I was all of seventeen, a callow youth, and how I'd resented this task your grandfather had forced upon me!" He chuckled and shook his head. "I was determined that I would simply drop the parcels and notes and leave immediately, believing I'd much more important things to occupy me. I even told the boatman not to weigh anchor, but to tie the craft and wait. Stupid, when I think of the currents in the Maas. As it was, I leaped onto the bank and, in my haste, landed heavily, twisting my ankle. I fell over, rolling and yelping like an injured pup. And when I stopped, there was this vision with silver hair and the greenest eyes I'd ever beheld"—he focused on me briefly—"your eyes—standing over me. God bless her, she placed her tiny hand in mine and tried to help me to my feet. 'You'll be all right,' she said. 'I'll make sure of it.' I'll never forget that. This sweet child helping me." He paused, savoring the recollection.

"After that, I volunteered to make the trip, going back many times over the years. Each visit, Cathaline would seek me out, talk to me. I used to bring her not only Herr de Winter's gifts, but treats I'd found to delight her. There was nothing I would not give to see her smile." He rubbed his beard.

"Then I was given my own ship to command and sent to the Mediterranean. Years later, I returned, only this time your mother was no child. She was a woman and so comely to behold, she left me speechless. By then, she was already engaged to your father—the *Englischer* bastard, we'd call him, so envious were we. We couldn't understand why Herr de Winter was giving her to an Englishman, this prize! We should have known; everything Herr de Winter did was costed and measured and your mother's husband was no different. She was given to Sheldrake because of what he promised he could do for the Hanse—dominance of the ports along this part of the English coast.

"Your father persuaded Herr de Winter that there was great wealth to be had through importing salt, ale, and wool and exporting beer, cloth, and spices, especially with prices rising so high here and crops failing. That he'd ensure, using his legal skills and connections with a great English lord, that exclusive contracts were granted, shoring up the Hanse's profits." He gave a dry laugh and paused to drink. I did as well. Questions burned inside me.

"Over the years, in fact, quite quickly, your father did well; he expanded trade, negotiated excellent tithes in ports, and overall made profit. What I don't understand is the nature of the agreement he had with Lord Rainford. I never knew . . . It wasn't until I looked into matters after he died that I discovered the truth . . . that while he lived, Joseph Sheldrake earned an excellent living, but upon his death, everything reverted back to Lord Rainford." The captain threw his hands up in the air. "It's perplexing and seems out of character with the man I knew. With the man to whom Herr de Winter gave his daughter."

A wave of heat swept my body and took my voice away momentarily. I cleared my throat. "I didn't know about any of this until after Father died either."

*Not about the debts . . . the fact that Father effectively signed over all his rights to any profit . . .*

Unaware of my disquiet, Captain Stoyan continued. "Part of me can forgive your father placing his trust in Lord Rainford—

what I cannot forgive is that he placed *your* trust"—he jabbed a thick finger on the desk—"*your* future, there as well and, in doing so, denied you one. You and Cathaline's twins."

What could I say? Captain Stoyan was right, but I knew why. Outside, a dog barked and seagulls cawed.

"So," said the captain finally. "In your note you mention seeking my help. What can I do for you?"

Gratitude flooded my body. At last, I could steer this ship into what I hoped were less troubled waters. "I have a request to make—"

# TEN

## OFFICES OF THE KONTOR, ELMHAM LENN

The same day

*The year of Our Lord 1405 in the sixth*

*year of the reign of Henry IV*

*I* told Captain Stoyan my plans. I told him about my meeting with Lord Rainford, his assurances that I would be granted till Hocktide to try and earn enough funds to keep the house. I told him about the brewhouse, Mother's recipes, the arrangement with Master Bondfield and Master Perkyn, my desire to enter the brewing trade. Then I told him what I'd learned from Master Perkyn about the abbot and the city ale-conners. I also told him my fears that, somehow, the guild, which I'd first thought to seek help from, might also be receiving bribes, that in Abbot Hubbard and the Friary of St. Jude's lay potential danger.

"And yet, despite telling you this, this miller, he will still grind your malt?"

"He's a friend."

"That he might be, but he's also foolhardy. Not that this is necessarily a bad trait." The captain gave me a crooked smile.

I placed my forearm on the desk and leaned forward. "All I want, all I need, is the chance to sell my ale, to make enough to pay the lease, maintain the house, keep my family and our servants together. But I'm concerned I may not get that opportunity. And that's where I need your help, Captain Stoyan." I sat up, businesslike. "Firstly, I need to know: Is Master Perkyn right? Are the ale-conners in the abbot's pocket? Is the guild? Because if they are, and the abbot learns what I'm doing, he may ask them to sabotage my business as he has others—accuse me of using incorrect measures, declare my ale unsuitable for drinking whether it is or not, and apportion a fine. If that should happen . . ." I left Captain Stoyan to draw his own conclusions.

I omitted to tell him what else Master Perkyn shared with Adam and me—about the fire, the brutal killing of a pet, and injury to livestock.

Instead, I waited for the arguments as to why I shouldn't brew: that it was unsuitable, that I would never succeed.

Captain Stoyan straightened, his brow furrowed. "If that should happen, you would be ruined before you even started." He tapped his fingers on the desk a few times. "It's common knowledge around here that the abbot pays the ale-conners to pass his ale for sale. The mayor doesn't care so long as the friary pays its most generous tax, the Merchants' Guild turns a blind eye because they still get paid to sell it around the county. And the Mystery of Brewers? Well, how often does a representative from London get to Elmham Lenn?"

I shrugged. I knew not.

"Exactly. As for the ale-conners, well, they're simple folk tempted by extra coin. Of course they accept the abbot's bribes—all they have to do is pass as acceptable what any decent alewife would tip in the dirt and call draff. To them, it's not a great sin and I'm sure the abbot, or whoever he sends to deal with them in his stead, grants them indulgences, or for a groat they get one from a pardoner." He inhaled sharply. "In other words, Mistress Anneke, you're right to be concerned." Rising to his feet, Captain Stoyan circled the room. "We all know what's going on—the mayor, the aldermen, the Hanse. Frankly, I didn't care. If the *Englischer* were stupid enough to drink the friary's rubbish, let them. Here we have access to some of the finest ales and beers in Europe." His hand swept toward the jug on the table. "Why would we drink the abbot's?" Rubbing his chin, he regarded Anneke carefully. "But it's different now. I'll not let him or any of those crooks hurt you."

Hope fluttered in my breast. "You'll help me?"

A wicked grin split his face. "Sweet *fräulein*, I can and I will." Sitting back down, he propped his elbows on the desk and lowered his voice. "You see, Abbot Badon Hubbard has been in control of the friary for a long time; he's forgotten that he's simply a spoke in a big wheel that will turn with or without him. I think he just needs a little reminder about what his order owes the Hanse. We not only control the trade routes throughout Europe, but the pilgrim passages as well. Like most religious orders, the Benedictines need access through the Rhine in order to make their holy treks and, for that to happen, they need the cooperation of the Hanseatic League.

"All it would take for that to become . . . let's say, most troublesome, for the passes to become impossible, for ships to become unavailable, rivers and oceans unnavigable, roads too dangerous, is a word from me to my colleagues in the Stilliard in London or, better still, Cologne. From there, every port between Lübeck and Harfleur, Hamburg and Venice, Danzig and Ypres, and the entire Rhine, never mind passage through the Alps, would be closed to the Benedictines. Once word gets out that the Friary of St. Jude has caused this . . . well . . . you can imagine. Every Catholic between here, Rome, and even those who follow the Antipope in Avignon would be calling God's wrath upon them and, ultimately, his grace. I don't think Abbot Hubbard would want to risk that, do you?"

My eyes widened. "You would threaten the abbot?"

"For you, Anneke, I would do that and more."

"You're not going to try and talk me out of it? Out of brewing?"

Captain Stoyan snorted. "What? Like your mother when she had her heart set on something? Like I tried to talk her out of marrying your father?"

Failing to notice my surprise, he shook his head, his bushy hair thrown back and forth. "*Nein, liebchen.* Not me. I'll not try to dissuade you. I will see you're given every chance to succeed."

My face grew warm, my heart light until the shadow looming over me reappeared. "My impression is that Abbot Hubbard is someone who wouldn't take kindly to being threatened . . ."

Captain Stoyan laughed. It was dry, bitter. "I don't threaten. I'm doing him the courtesy of issuing a warning. He leaves you alone. Him and his *verdammt* ale-conners."

I repressed a smile. "You think that will work?"

"Unless the abbot is a very stupid, or very cunning man—"

"He's a man of God."

"Then he is both." Captain Stoyan pushed back his chair

and stood, striding over to the map on the wall. He traced a finger along the lower part. "If the throne of England bows to the might of the Hanse"—he drew a huge circle that encompassed all of France, Burgundy, the kingdom of Poland, Sweden, and beyond—"then your abbot will too—he will, or he'll be crushed."

Smiling at Captain Stoyan through blurry vision, I blinked the tears back rapidly.

"Don't cry, *liebchen*." Stepping toward me, he suddenly halted and struck his forehead. "Of course," he exclaimed. Swinging toward the chest, he flung the lid back with a resounding bang. "Since you're entering the brewing trade, I've something here that you may be interested in. Something that may give you an advantage." Pulling out a small sack, he untied the opening. "Hold out your hands."

Wiping my eyes quickly, I dried my palms on my dress and then held them up obediently. Captain Stoyan poured some herbs into them. They were a light green. I bent my head and inhaled. They smelled of a freshly plowed field or an aromatic spice I couldn't place.

"What's this?"

"Something that's been used in Germany and your mother's home as long as I can remember. You will have heard of it—it's called hops." He dragged his finger through the hops, tickling my palm. "We use it all the time. Few of you *Englischer* appreciate it, but that is slowly changing. When added to the ale at the right time, it makes a drink we call beer. It's what you're enjoying with me now."

I breathed in the scent again and then, as the captain had

done, rolled the herb between my fingertips. It was quite fresh, oily almost.

"I have heard of it and, of course, Mother spoke if it. But I'd never seen it before, or used it. There're many recipes among the ones she left. If I remember correctly, she said the reason the English didn't like it was because it gave the ale a very bitter taste."

"It does, but it also preserves it. Hence, the Hanse can export all over Europe, not like your ale that sometimes sours in mere days. Not much beer comes to England . . . not yet—but once a taste has been developed . . . Well, why import what you can make and purchase at home?" He paused. "Perhaps this is something you can do?" Propping himself on the edge of his desk, he folded his arms and regarded me seriously. "If you learn to use this properly and make beer, you might be able not only to educate the English palate, but to look at exporting. Apart from a couple of brewers in Winchelsea, there are one or two in London who are using hops, but they haven't perfected their recipes yet. Haven't quite managed to get the taste right, and they're working on a small scale."

I looked from the hops back to the captain. "Maybe I could experiment . . ."

"*Ja,*" he said. "You should." Returning to his seat, the captain drained the last of his drink. "Take that." He waved at the sack on his desk. "I've more. It's only a small amount. I will give you some beer to take with you as well. You can taste it, do some tests with the hops. If you wish, I can bring more back from Germany when I return in late December. But trust me when I say, if you learn to brew with hops"—he opened his palm to reveal what was nestled in there—"make a beer that the English will like and which you can sell beyond your shores, you won't only be able to provide for your family, you'll become a wealthy woman."

My heart filled with hope and my fingers closed around the herbs, the fragile pieces of green that could represent my future, my fortune. Then doubt hit me. "And if I can't?"

Captain Stoyan gave me a stern look. "Your name may be Sheldrake, but the blood of the de Winters, of your Dutch and German ancestors, flows strong in you. There is no such thing as 'can't.'"

I rose to my feet. "You're right, Captain. If my mother was alive, she would tell me the same thing."

"But she is not," said Captain Stoyan, his face downcast. "And it's left to me to remind you."

I held out my hand and he came around the desk and took it. "And for that, Captain, I'm beyond grateful."

Arm in arm, the captain and I left his office a short time later, he carrying the sack and two jugs of beer. The men glanced at us as he escorted me through the warehouse, along the dock, and back to where Will and Shelby waited. Helping me mount the cart, he placed the sack in my lap and the jugs at my feet. If my presence at the pier was the source of gossip, I was oblivious. My mind was filled with what lay ahead, with the potential of Captain Stoyan's gift—not merely the hops, but what he would say to the abbot.

For now, I would push thoughts of the abbot to the back of my mind. I'd work to do, ale to perfect, and, when I was ready, a small sack of hops with which to experiment.

# ELEVEN

## HOLCROFT HOUSE
### One week later
*The year of Our Lord 1405 in the sixth*
*year of the reign of Henry IV*

A week after I had been to see Captain Stoyan, he came to Holcroft House. I'd finished work in the brewery for the day and was in the office with Adam, tallying up the accounts. Though I was delighted to see him, I knew the reason for his visit. I'd been expecting to hear from him. What I hadn't anticipated was that he'd come in person, nor so late. It was as though a little pulley was tugging at my heart, causing me simultaneous pain and excitement. I welcomed him and waited in nervous silence as Iris brought a tray. Disheveled and thirsty from being on the road, the captain took the proffered ale and sat opposite me, looking about with interest.

"You've made some changes," he said as Iris, in a flurry of skirts and curtsies, scurried out, closing the door with a last glance toward us. The kitchen would be full of surmise.

I followed the direction of the captain's gaze. For certes, I'd rearranged Father's things, but since Hiske had also taken some, I'd found other objects to fill the gaps—a few books, my favorite quill, and a small painting Mother had given me for my fifth birthday. In a flight of fancy, I'd placed a row of silver-banded mazers atop the mantelpiece. Saskia had seen to it the room was polished to shiny perfection now it was being used regularly. I'd also opened the shutters and lit a number of candles to admit more light. The fire in the hearth added its own special glow. It was a different space.

"A few." I smiled.

Pretending to fuss over the captain's cloak and hood, but really giving me respectability by acting as a chaperone, Adam first loitered then gave up all pretense and stood by the fire, arms crossed. The way the muscle in his cheek pulsed, I knew he was keen to hear the captain's news.

"I took a ride out to St. Jude's today," said Captain Stoyan finally.

Closing the ledger slowly, I sucked in my breath. "And?"

"Let us say, neither the ale-conners nor the guild will trouble you for now."

"*For now.* The abbot said that."

"In not so many words. It was more what he implied." He ran fingers through his windswept hair, taming it into submission. "To be frank, Mistress Anneke, Master Barfoot"—he turned slightly to include Adam—"I may have underestimated him. He's not what I anticipated. Not at all. Where some men issue orders in loud voices, deliver threats of God's punishment and their own, this man ensures compliance with smiles and silence—smiles that never reach his eyes and silences more deep and deadly than the Baltic in winter." Reaching for his drink, he swirled it a couple of times. When he'd taken a long swallow, pulling a face, he continued. "He offered me wine, Rhenish no less. It was poured into a goblet with so many jewels decorating the stem it would fund a voyage to Muscovy and back. It was just one of many in the room. So much wealth and all very deliberately on display. There were gold platters, silver chalices, a bejeweled cross gleaming on the wall behind his velvet-and-ermine-clad shoulders." He shook his head. "His room reeked of money. *Ja*, I answered the wrong calling when I chose the sea." With a half-laugh, he drank again. I exchanged a glance with Adam, whose frown had deepened.

The fire crackled. Outside, the sounds of a cart rumbling past and the conversations of passersby formed a faint counterpoint to our conversation.

"Anyway, I told him in no uncertain terms what would happen should he interfere with your business."

"What did he say?"

"Say? Everything and, thus, nothing. He's a shrewd man, with more cunning than a hawker, and more canny than a Venetian moneylender."

"How can one say everything and nothing?"

"It happens all the time, *liebchen*. Oh, he gave me the assurances I asked for, said the right things, made the right noises. When I first began, he acted as if I'd delivered some terrible blow to his pride, to the friary's. When I mentioned the aleconners and the guild, the well-known interference with ale production in Elmham Lenn and farther, he blanched, he couldn't hide that. But he quickly recovered. Where I expected wrath and denial, he quietly played the role of the injured party."

I glanced at Adam. "But he didn't deny it?"

"Deny? *Nein*. He said it was a terrible misunderstanding. He said the friary was the victim of slander, no more, no less. He spoke of the sins of those who sought to denigrate and defame and how God would be their judge. He told me how the brothers prayed for the souls of these trespassers daily. It was quite a sermon. Practiced, assured."

"Oh, the abbot is that," I added, remembering the times I'd heard him deliver mass in town.

"I can't help but feel he's had to say these things before, to others." The captain shrugged. "I might be wrong, but the man was prepared. After a drink or two, whereby he shared with me the history of the friary and the changes that had been wrought under his watch, he told me there was no need to worry, let alone alert the Hanse. He was most insistent on that last point. For just a moment, his guard slipped and I saw that he was genuinely worried, that he'd never anticipated our interest." Captain Stoyan grinned. "Other than that, he smiled, nodded, performed benevolence with ease. If I didn't know any better, I'd swear he was innocent. That in good faith, the friary makes its ale and everyone purchases it because that's what they desire to drink."

Adam made a noise.

"Do you believe him?" I asked.

The captain looked at me as if I'd suggested he dine on parchment. "I may be thought reckless, but I'm no fool. Would you buy this"—he lifted his mazer—"if you had a choice? Exactly. The man is not to be trusted. Especially not when he said he welcomed competition, a new brewer in town. He even went so far as to say he would like to try your ale when it's ready."

Adam made a scoffing noise. "Try and copy it."

"*Ja.* This was my thought too." The captain rubbed his chin. "The entire time I was in his presence, his obedientiaries, his office-bearers, four of them, interchangeable in their black robes, two with their faces disguised by heavy cowls, the others with their tonsured heads, stood to one side murmuring, tut-tutting, coughing and gasping like a chorus of consumptive angels. If they hadn't been so caught in this man's spell, blinded by his loquaciousness and manner, they would have been funny. As it was, they too are dangerous. They will do whatever this man bids."

"You think he's dangerous?"

"*Nein.* I know he is. I've seen his sort before. He comes from the wrong side of the blanket, a noble's bastard who feels the world owes him something and he'll claim it whatever it takes. He is a greedy man. The friary is his empire, his world, and he will take down anyone who threatens it."

"Even me?"

"You're a woman; as far as he's concerned, you're no threat to him or any man. But the Hanse . . . Well, we're another matter altogether. I've invoked their specter—worse, you have, and he doesn't like that."

"Are you concerned?"

"For me? What can he do to the Hanseatic League? He'll be furious, his pride will be hurt, and I've no doubt someone will pay, but it won't be us." He regarded me steadily.

"Well, then, I'd best get my first batch of ale ready for sale, hadn't I?" My cheer rang as false as my bravado.

"I think you should reconsider your plans, Mistress Anneke," said Adam, taking a step toward the desk, placing his hand upon the wood. "I don't like the sound of this abbot."

I stared at him in dismay; fear darkened his eyes. *Not now, Adam. Please, I need you to stand by me as you did over a week ago.*

"What's the alternative, Adam?" My tone was sharper than I intended. "Working for Hiske? Watching Karel become an apprentice somewhere and Betje little more than a servant to do her bidding? That is, until she's sent to a nunnery for the rest of her life." I shook my head. "I can't allow that. Brewing has been in my family for centuries. It's what de Winters do; it's how my grandfather earned and kept his office with the Hanse. It's how we made our living and, God willing, it's how I am going to as well."

"But is God willing?"

"God is. It's Abbot Hubbard who's not."

"She's right, Master Barfoot." The captain rose, draining his mazer as he did. "Anyway, this isn't about God, this is about something and someone much more earthbound, no matter how he styles himself. This is about the abbot, and while he won't like it, he won't be able to stop Anneke either."

I could have kissed the captain there and then.

Placing the cup down on the desk, the captain gestured for Adam to pass his cloak and hood.

I rose, running my hands down the sides of my tunic. "Thank you, Captain Stoyan. Thank you. Now I can throw myself into this business without worrying about being sabotaged every step of the way."

With Adam's help, the captain shrugged on his cloak.

"Forgive me, sir, but Mistress Anneke, I wouldn't be so quick to thank the captain." Adam smoothed Captain Stoyan's cloak, then stepped to one side to face us both. "Hasn't it occurred to either of you that until the captain went to the friary and spoke to the abbot, he'd never heard of Anneke Sheldrake? Now, despite his assurances, which you yourself admit, Captain, are fairly meaningless, he'll be watching you like a hawk, waiting until he can strike."

Adam was right. I hadn't thought of that. I cast a look of concern at the captain.

"*Ja*, Master Barfoot is right." He tugged his hood into place. "But consider this: until I went to the friary, the abbot didn't know how great the might of the Hanse was either. He might watch you, Mistress Anneke, but I'll be watching him—wherever I am in the world, I'll be watching him . . ."

"Until he moves out of sight." Adam's tone was dry, skeptical.

Captain Stoyan poked him in the chest with a thick finger. "Then it will be up to you, Master Barfoot, to keep Mistress Anneke under observation. Ensure she's safe."

Adam nodded. "Very well. So be it."

Eager to put an end to this discussion and banish the demons plaguing my plans, I thanked the captain again and escorted him to the door. He was about to mount his horse when, as an afterthought, he turned.

"By the way"—he placed a hand on my shoulder—"I've spoken to Master Bondfield. Whatever barley you require will be paid for by me."

Rendered speechless by this unexpected act of generosity, I froze, my hand resting on the horse's smooth withers.

"It's my investment," he muttered, embarrassed, fiddling with the bridle. "I expect a share of the profits—in ale, and later beer, of course."

A light rain began to fall, mingling with the ribbons of mist that slowly descended. Casting propriety aside, I threw my arms around him and kissed him soundly on the cheek. Red-faced, he returned my embrace and patted my back. When I drew away, I could see he was enormously pleased with my reaction.

"It will be all right, *liebchen*. Forget the abbot, forget the friary, and go make some liquid magic."

"I will," I said. But as I waved farewell, I knew that for the next few days, if not weeks, I would be looking over my shoulder. Despite the captain's reassurances, I couldn't forget the abbot so easily.

# TWELVE

*M*aking sure the haircloth that lined the bottom of the kiln was in place before loading more coal, Adam stood back and wiped his hands on his apron. "Perforce, this is hot work," he said, grinning to indicate he took no displeasure in the task. It was a cold, dreary day and the brewhouse, with its raging kiln and crackling stove, was a most agreeable space.

I flashed him a smile, my eyes fixed on glowing coals and the newly sprouted barley we'd painstakingly collected off the malthouse floor, laid upon large perforated trays, and slid into the kiln so they could be dried. Over the past few days, tray after tray of moist grain had been slowly and carefully fired. The latest sat upon a table nearby, golden, divested of its little green shoots, the steamy haze surrounding it dissolving as the cool air grabbed the heat and swallowed it. Tasting the grain to ensure it was cured correctly, I found the buttery, nutty flavor lingered pleasantly in my mouth. Before long it would be cool enough to pour into sacks to go to the mill for grinding.

Louisa and Blanche had collected heather from the moors behind the church, and I picked some up. First shaking the white powder from the fronds onto a piece of fabric so I could save it to use as an additive later, I threw it in the flames. The kiln smoked fiercely for a few seconds, forcing Adam and me to back away. Fast consumed, the dry heather released a sharp smell that caught in the back of the throat. Turning slightly to cough into my fist, it struck me how the brewhouse, now a veritable hive of activity, was unrecognizable from the bleak space it had been only weeks earlier.

Adam, Will, Iris when she could be spared, Saskia, and I, and even Louisa and the twins, had done nothing but work from dawn until dusk for days. Making larger quantities of ale required more hands than had once made the household's supply. What I also discovered was that six years is a long time between brews. Unpracticed with the stages, determined to follow my mother's recipes lest I make a mistake, I commenced slowly. Flopping into bed at night exhausted and filled with self-doubt, I prayed to not only the Virgin and my Lord Jesus Christ, but also (may God forgive me) to the Sumerian goddess of brewing, Ninkasi.

Ninkasi was a beautiful goddess from ancient times, and Mother had taught me the hymn brewsters in the Low Countries, Germany, and other parts of the continent sang to her to ensure the ale became yeasty and rich. Sometimes we'd even call upon Hathor, the Egyptian goddess of drunkenness, but Mother warned we were only to invoke her for very special occasions. I wondered if our first ale would warrant Hathor's help and decided it would, so, when the opportunity presented itself, I summoned her presence as well.

Barely stopping for meals, throwing down a piece of bread, some cold rabbit or eel, depending on the day of the week, the entire household committed fully. We had to—our livelihoods and the roof over our heads depended on it. There was an undertow of desperation to all we did, an unspoken fear of failure.

By the end of the first two weeks, when the first batch of grain was dried and ready to go to the mill, we had found a rhythm. Preparing the malt became a matter, over ten days, of tossing the grain across the now-clean and better-lit floor of the malthouse and watching it fall like a brief shower of rain. Soaking the barley in the crystal waters we'd drawn from the nearby stream, the Nene, it spread over the floor, a slow-moving marsh settling against its earthen banks. Bare-footed engineers, we'd lean on our tools and watch our muddy demesne form around our ankles. As the hours and days passed, we used the rakes and shovels to prevent the roots from fastening to the floor and each other, our backs and shoulders aching. Keeping the kiln and stove burning constantly, within days a fresh field of tiny green shoots sprouted and we became farmers rejoicing in our crop. Scooping up the new life, we layered it onto the large trays that went into the kiln. This was the point at which the previous hard work could easily come undone. If the temperature was too high and the grains burned, the ale was ruined before it was made. Likewise if the heat was too low. Mother had taught me how to ensure the fire burned slowly but consistently, waiting until the grains transformed into a mixture of amber or the color of the sandstone rocks that swept the bay, before swiftly removing them.

After the cooled grain was poured into sacks, it was sent to the mill to be ground. The following day, it was returned—a coarse flour littered with chits and husks ready for the next stage.

The milled grain was tipped into the mash tun and hot water added. As with the heat from the fire, if the water was too hot or not hot enough, the brew would be spoiled. Many brewsters destroyed their ale during this process—Mistress Margery Kempe from Bishop's Lynn was as famous for her piety as she was for ruining brew after brew. It was hard to gauge the heat. It required experience and what Mother used to call "the touch." Her trick was to allow the water to boil, cool it slightly, and then place her elbow just below the surface. If she could tolerate the conditions and, more importantly, the steam had dispersed enough so she could catch a glimpse of her face upon the now-still surface of the water, it was time to add the milled barley.

Rolling up my sleeve, I did exactly as she'd always done. The water was hot but not boiling, and gazing back at me, as if about to emerge from the dark liquid, was my wide-eyed visage, tendrils of hair glued to my forehead and cheeks, as if I too were an ingredient. Mayhap I was. Using old drying sheets, Adam and Will hoisted the huge copper off the stove and slowly poured the contents into the mash tun, where the grain drank it thirstily. Grabbing the long-handled ladle, my mother's mash paddle, I stood over the tun and worked clockwise then counterclockwise, moving around and blending the ingredients to prevent clumps of grist forming. Saskia took over when my arms grew tired. Following one of Mother's recipes, I added cloves, some sweet gale, and bog myrtle to the mixture, sprinkling them onto the surface. Saskia stirred and I watched them whirl and settle and listened to the plashing of the liquid wort as it drained through the natural sieve of broken husks and grain into the copper underneath the tun.

We now had the beginnings of our ale. Tomorrow, before dawn, when the house was still abed and I was certain no one could bear witness, I would perform the step I believed made my mother's brew unique. A process no one, not Saskia, Father, or, God forbid, Hiske, knew about. It had been Mother's secret and mine, one passed down through the de Winter women for generations. I would ensure it was kept that way, until I was ready to pass it on to Betje and my children, and she to hers.

The thought of children of my own, let alone little Betje having any, gave me pause. Would my womb ever quicken? In order to have a child, I first had to find a husband, and that was unlikely to happen any time soon.

Sending Will out to chop wood, Adam and I turned our attention to straining the last of the wort away from the mash. This would be done twice—the first time created a rich, full-tasting ale. The second, after we poured more water upon the mash, made a weaker small ale that would mostly be kept for the household to drink. Some brewers, including the friary, would not only add more water to their first press in order to create more volume, they would also do a second and even a third pass, producing a very thin drink, unfit, by most folk's reckoning, for consumption. I refused to do this. I wanted to sell only my first, unless taste and demand said different, and let my reputation and fortune stand on that. Watching the honey-colored broth move through the remnants of the mash and splash into the huge copper pots that sat beneath the tun did much to elevate my spirits. We were so close.

When Will returned, the wort-filled coppers were heaved onto the stove. It was this part that went a long way to making the ale my mother used to make different from everybody else's. Few bothered to boil the wort—not the brewsters in Elmham Lenn nor the monks at the friary. It wasn't economical or, many believed, necessary. Maybe not. But it did add flavor to the ale and, for some reason I didn't understand, preserved it for longer as well. The trick was to bring it to the point where the wort roiled around the pot and then create a whirlpool with the special ladle. One hour was all that was needed. Using a marked candle, I ordered Will to light it as soon as I detected signs that the boiling point had been reached. Standing on a stool by the pot, I placed the ladle in and stirred, imagining, as I used to years ago, I was bringing the great whirlpool Charybdis, she who tried to confound the hero Odysseus, to life. Tiny ships filled with terrified sailors were tossed upon my waves . . . just like those on board the *Cathaline* . . .

I withdrew the ladle in shock. How callous of me. My face burned with shame. I'd become lost in the joy of creation and wasn't thinking, allowing the stories of old to sweep me into another world. Thank the good Lord Adam and Will seemed oblivious. I quickly replaced the paddle, my daydreaming tempered. After a while, the brewhouse walls ran with rivulets from the steam, and they seemed like tears of happiness.

That night the boiled wort was left to cool in the troughs beneath the windows, which I left open. Sacks of grain sat by the door, the tun was gleaming, awaiting a new mash, and the malthouse floor was full of sprouting barley. Production could now begin in earnest. I tossed and turned, unable to rest despite fatigue so great it made my head throb. Anxious lest I'd lost my touch, failed both my mother's instructions and her memory, I gave up trying to seek the oblivion of sleep and rose before the sun, throwing on some clothes and creeping downstairs, across the garden, and into the brewery.

There were final steps to complete. One, an essential part of the process; the other, a de Winter tradition. The ale could not be drunk, let alone sold, without this arcane undertaking that made Mother's ale distinctive and had folk returning for more. This made the "magic" of which Perkyn Miller and Captain Stoyan spoke, though they were ignorant of its origin.

I shut the door. No one must know. No one could see. I couldn't leave anything to chance.

With a flaming candle resting atop an empty barrel, I examined the contents of the trough. The window above revealed the pre-dawn sky. Angry red streaks punctured the gray, promising a day of sorry weather. My breath misted as I studied the coat of soft white spume dressing the ale. The smell was overpowering. Images of rolling hills, days of sunshine, freshly turned earth, and baking bread filled my vision. My headache began to abate and a smile tugged the corners of my mouth. I could detect the wild notes of pine and winter. Shutting my eyes briefly, I also saw Mother's sweet face. *You will make it work*, she whispered.

Uncorking one of the jugs of beer Captain Stoyan had given me, I slowly tipped it into the wort, relishing the splash and gurgle as it tumbled from the spout into the trough. Until I'd been given this, I'd believed myself doomed to use the friary ale in order to add the vital ingredient, the godisgoode, the element all brewers needed, to my brew. Using the Low Countries beer, the "son of ale" as I'd heard it called, meant I not only brought some of my mother's homeland to my recipe, but I avoided what I felt was contamination—the friary.

Lowering my arm into the trough, I slipped through the flocculent, luscious froth. Transformed into a fleshy paddle, I divided the cool liquid, caressing it, murmuring, allowing the love I felt for my family, the hope I clung to for our future, to flow from me into the ale. I thought of the friends who supported this venture: Captain Stoyan; Masters Perkyn, Bondfield, and Proudfellow; not forgetting Adam, Saskia, Will, Blanche, Iris, Louisa, and, of course, the twins. Opaque, the now-golden water swirled as I carved a path through the creamy bubbles, back and forth, to and fro. Satisfied it parted so readily before my gentle intrusion, I began to sing, all the time my hand stroked the wort, calling the ale to life as Mother had taught me.

When I'd finished, I removed my hand and brought it to my mouth and licked it slowly. The earthiness of malt struck the roof of my mouth, the subtle sweetness of the fluids lathed my tongue. I shut my eyes in pleasure. A wild nectar clung to my teeth while cloves raced down my throat, nestling warmly in my chest. I sucked my fingers one by one and was rewarded with the bitterness of the bog myrtle and even the faint tang of the captain's beer. My head spun momentarily and the room expanded on itself before contracting, till there was only the beam of watery light passing through the window. Upon its shining span, I saw rows of tiny lights spinning toward me, toward the hand I held before my face. Lapping the last of the ale, reveling in the taste, the aroma, the effect, I wanted to giggle, dance, throw my arms out. I did all three, abandoning myself to the ale, to the magic created.

Once more, Mother's face manifested, laughing gaily, reaching for me—beyond me—with a look I hadn't seen before. Her cheeks were now pale, her eyes dark with disbelief, fear, even. Who was she regarding in such a way?

"*Moeder*," I called quietly, slipping into her native tongue, seeking to distract her. She turned toward me, the anguish gone, and with a sweet smile, met my eyes.

"The crones," she murmured. "Remember the crones." Her visage vanished and I was alone in the brewhouse as dawn broke over the county.

With a sigh that spoke of loss and longing, I dried my hand. From what I tasted, the brew exceeded my expectations. But the process was not complete, and if we were to be ready to sell by Martinmas, I'd one more thing left to do.

Reaching for the copper scoop that hung on a hook by the far wall, I dipped it into the trough. Collecting some wort, I went to each of the four corners of the brewhouse and tipped a portion onto the floor. Mother could be assured, I hadn't forgotten the crones. An old Low Countries custom, I offered our ale to the corner crones who dwelled in the brewery and asked that they bless what I made. The last dregs I deposited on the threshold of the malthouse and then, bowing to each of the spirits in turn, I thanked them from the bottom of my very full heart.

I'd just returned to the wort when Adam and Will entered, failing to notice the little wet patches in the corners or, as I imagined, the tiny old women, on hands and knees, lapping my offering up greedily.

❧❦❧

And so our days passed—malting, mashing, and preparing the wort. Now that I had my own godisgoode to make the brew froth, foam, and ferment, I was able to pass the goodness on to each fresh batch. Every day, I would conduct my secret ceremony—singing the ale into life and respecting the generations of women past, the goddesses and crones who'd granted to womenkind the joy and responsibility of brewing. Gradually, we filled our barrels and even a hogshead of small ale, and the day to summon the ale-conners to taste and pass the brew for sale drew closer. The day that would test the veracity or otherwise of the abbot's assurances to Captain Stoyan, and his to me.

# THIRTEEN

HOLCROFT HOUSE

Martinmas, Eleventh of November

*The year of Our Lord 1405 in the seventh*

*year of the reign of Henry IV*

*I*t was Martinmas, the day the last of the wheat and barley crops were planted. Livestock that couldn't be maintained over winter were slaughtered and a huge hiring fair was held in town. Tonight, there would be much gaiety and celebration as a feast with fires, mummers, jugglers, minstrels, and dancing was held in the main square. In previous years, though we hadn't been allowed to attend the dance (Hiske persuading Father that the strangers who poured into town at this time of year were not only dangerous, but posed a potential threat to our souls with their behavior), we'd enjoyed the fair and the festive foods, such as joints of beef, legs of mutton, and pottages full of bacon, wild onions, and herbs. Being conscious of spending this year, Blanche salted our beef and stored it away for winter, sold our mutton, and put goose on the menu for the evening instead.

But I'd much more to keep me occupied than thoughts of fine fare, the dubious company of strangers, or dancing. Up well before dawn, by the time the bells marking prime tolled, I'd been in the brewhouse for over an hour, my ancient rites completed and the fires stoked. Moments after I'd finished, Adam and Will, brushing crumbs from their mouths, stumbled through the still-dark skies and hoary frost to join me.

"We're doing well, Mistress Anneke. Almost five barrels full." Adam nodded toward where the ale was stored as he warmed his hands by the kiln.

While I didn't want to deflate his optimism, I also didn't want to create false hope. "It certainly appears we're doing well, but we won't really know until this afternoon."

"That's right," said Will, striding over to join us, slapping the side of the first barrel on his way past. It made a dull sound. "Not until we taste the brew!" He sidled in beside Adam, letting the heat strike his back. "Well, not until the ale-conners do."

We all regarded each other solemnly. Blanche always said the proof was in the tasting. So it would be with the ale. Confident that what I'd tried each morning was good, something the others had confirmed when they'd had a sip, I didn't want to say too much lest we'd grossly misjudged. After all, some of the brew had been fermenting in the barrels for well over a week now, and a great deal could go awry that had nothing to do with the ale-conners, bribes, or the abbot.

Though the day passed much like the others, this one carried the weight of expectation. It hovered over our activities and conversations like a threatening storm cloud. Today marked the threshold moment when our future as commercial brewers would be decided—not by our customers, not at first, but by the official town tasters, the supposedly impartial ale-conners. Required by law to test every fresh brew for sale, to assess the quality, check our measures, and set the price, nothing could be sold until the elected men approved it. Just as they could allow sales to proceed, they could equally order a brewer to tip the entire barrel into the earth and then fine them heavily for the privilege. According to gossip in the marketplace and generously passed on by those who knew what we were doing, including Betrix, that had been happening more than usual of late. Inspired by my efforts, women who'd previously lost brews or been fined because of the friary's intervention were making fresh ones. Whether they were too hasty in going to sale, didn't allow the ale to ferment long enough, or because the abbot still had his way, their efforts had been for naught.

Yet again, Mistress Amwell and Mistress Scot lost brews to the soil and received unusually hefty fines, Mistress Scot enduring a dunking for her efforts, making their continuance as independents in the trade all but impossible. They would now become hucksters, selling on ale from the friary like others before them. Two of the taverns in town and even more of the inns had been prevented from selling their own ale and forced to buy from the friary because what they produced didn't meet the ale-conners fickle standards. There was much discontent in town and murmurings about money changing hands, but no proof. Master Perkyn's warnings played on my mind. Whatever bribe the abbot offered, shouldn't quality speak for itself? All these other brewers failing—women and men—was more than a coincidence, surely? Captain Stoyan may have warned the abbot away from me, but were his words heeded? Would I be the exception to the brewing rule? Or had I made things worse for others by being so insistent I could do this?

"Is the ale-wand out, Will?" I asked finally when, by midday, there was still no sign of the ale-conners. The ale-wand or ale-stake was what announced a brew was ready to taste. Not that it was required—not the way rumor spread in Elmham Lenn. It was highly likely the conners would have known my brew was mature before I did. From what I'd heard, these men had an uncanny knack of arriving at a prospective brewer's house or inn before they'd even been summoned.

Though not, it appeared, today.

"Aye, mistress. I put it out first thing this morning. You'd have to be blind or drunk not to see it—or both. What with it being the fair, and all the people in town and us on a main road and all." Will frowned and craned his neck to peer out the window. "I would have thought they'd be here by now."

I followed the direction of his gaze. Long shadows crossed the courtyard; with winter almost upon us, the days grew shorter. A light rain struck the window. The ashen skies of the morning darkened until great bruised clouds sagged overhead. There was a mighty storm waiting to break.

"Me too," I said. "Perhaps they're busy with their other duties?"

"Mayhap," said Adam gruffly. "But I think a message is being sent and it might be one to which we're yet forced to listen. Captain Stoyan and Master Perkyn were right to be concerned about the friary. No one is able to go into competition with them—not anymore, the abbot won't allow it. Captain Stoyan may believe he's forced the abbot's hand, but he also told us he's cunning, and what's more cunning than the ale-conners failing to show? How can the abbot be held accountable for that?"

I paused over the mash tun, leaning against the stirrer, looking at Adam in horror. "Sweet Jesù, Adam. I fear you may be right." Wiping the back of my hand across my brow, I searched for reassurance. "Surely the conners wouldn't break their oath? It's not to be taken lightly. I've read it myself: 'So soon as you shall be required to taste any ale of a brewer or brewster, shall be ready to do the same . . .'" I released a huge sigh. "They're failing in their duties if they don't appear when summoned and can be charged."

All I wanted, all I needed, was a chance, but if the ale-conners didn't come, all our work would be for naught. My spirits began to flag, my shoulders drooped. I looked at the hogshead towering over its smaller wooden brethren. Orders from our neighbors had already arrived, and I was keen to sell what we didn't need; anything to make rent. But nothing could happen until officialdom gave permission.

"Come on," I said finally, leaving the paddle in the mash. "I can't stand around waiting. I've ale to sell. Let's move those barrels into the shop. If the ale-conners haven't come by the time we've shifted them, then Will, you go and fetch them."

Throwing some more coal into the kiln and stove, Adam brushed his hands against his jerkin and, with a nod to Will, cleared a space to roll the first of the barrels out.

The noise of the barrel on the gravel sent the chickens squawking and set the dogs barking. Thinking we were bringing out more of the spent mash, the draff, the pigs began to follow us and I had to shoo them out of the way.

Exclamations of glee, followed by the smacking of lips and clapping of hands met our entrance into the kitchen.

Blanche smiled so broadly, the gaps in her lower teeth were visible. "This is it then!" she cried. "Our first brew. Well done, mistress. You two as well," she added with a lift of her chin toward Adam and Will, who were out of breath and working up a sweat. Wonderful smells emanated from the feast Blanche was preparing. The plucked goose was trussed and basting in a big copper pan. Freshly baked pies sat on the table, steam still rising from the golden-brown pastry. Dough sat resting in bowls, its smell almost identical to that which permeated the brewhouse. Platters of late-autumn fruits and wedges of soft cheeses sat upon the table waiting our workday to end. Warming on the stovetop was some spiced mead and a huge saucepan of pottage.

Hearing my voice, the twins ran from the hall, twining their hands in mine.

"Is that it, Anneke? Is that our ale?" asked Karel, eyes fixed on the barrel Adam and Will leaned against while they gratefully gulped down a drink and tore at a piece of bread Iris thrust into their hands. I shook my head when she offered a piece to me. Karel pouted and was rewarded with some bread of his own. He bit into it hastily.

"Do we get to taste it too?" asked Betje, reaching out to stroke the metal bands that held the wood in place.

"Of course," I said, swinging their hands. "Not this barrel, but the hogshead of small ale, for certes. And soon."

Catching Adam's eye, I led the twins through the house, the barrel following. As they skipped beside me, I marveled that Karel and Betje had been so patient about what was happening. Not only had they suffered the loss of their father and the upheaval Hiske caused, but the last weeks had been even harder on them. Used to having me, if not at their beck and call, at least available, I was gone from dawn till dusk. When I came inside, I'd collapse in the hall each night. Waiting till I'd eaten, only then would they press me for a story. I always found one in my repertoire and, though my voice lacked its usual vigor and my imagination didn't quite spark, they never complained. Their resilience and good humor seemed boundless. I loved them all the more for it. How proud Mother and even Father would be of their children. The thought gave me pause. Would my parents be proud of me? Of what I was doing?

I pushed aside the idea they might not be and fixed a smile to my face. Tonight was for merrymaking; not just because of Martinmas, but because of what, together, we'd achieved—the ale. There were five barrels full of the heady liquid awaiting purchase and more lying in troughs in the brewhouse.

Adam and Will deposited the first barrel in a corner of the shop and returned for the second. The premises might have been bare, having been stripped by Hiske, but they were clean and stools had been found as well as a few wooden mazers for potential customers—most of whom I hoped would bring their own. Extra candles waited to be lit, and plates of flowers and late-season apples and some nuts had been discreetly tucked in corners, to give the place a festive feel. One of the women had even thought to leave parchment, a quill, and bottle of ink to record sales and a small tin in which to place coin. The shutters between the office and the shop had been opened and the fire blazing in the office had taken the chill off the room. I smiled at their thoughtfulness. We'd decided not to light the hearth in the shop, not to waste wood, not until we knew we would be allowed to trade.

"Market's finished," said Karel, his hands and face pressed against the window. Betje and I glanced up to see the train of carts and people ambling past. The wind whipped capes and the rain provided miserable company. Heads were bowed, cloaks swam heavily on shoulders, caps and headpieces were lowered and few words exchanged. Rain appeared to have put paid to the festivities in town. Pursing my lips, I looked at the long ale-stake jutting into the street, announcing to all and sundry that a brew awaited the tasters. Once permission to sell was given, we'd attach a bushel to the end of the sign, letting people know they could buy it as well. If only the ale-conners had come earlier and given permission, these disappointed passersby might have been my first customers. With wistful eyes, I watched potential business drift out of sight and wondered at these men that they were so busy they couldn't be prompt. A flash of anger toward the abbot and his machinations caught me off balance.

"Come," I said to Betje and Karel, ushering them into the corridor. Hunger and a heavy gloom gripped me at the same time. I thought to satisfy one and ignore the other by returning to the company in the kitchen. I also needed to wash and change, to look respectable in order to conduct business. If the ale-conners arrived soon, I still had a few precious hours before curfew.

The twins scampered ahead and I shut the hall door, only realizing as I did that it needed to be open for Adam and Will. Pushing it back, I was startled to see two cloaked shapes by the front door, huddled under the awning outside. The ale-conners. At last!

"Betje, Karel," I called to the two little shapes darting into the hall. "Tell Adam to make haste, the ale-conners have arrived."

Straightening my tunic and clicking at the stains on my

apron, which I removed swiftly and pushed under a stool, I went to greet them, when the door was flung wide open and upon a flurry of wind, rain, and leaves, the men stepped inside. The first was so tall he obscured the second, who struggled to close the door.

Shocked at their presumption, I froze, my hand rising to my throat. I was about to scold them when the first man pushed back his hat, revealing his face. Words caught in my throat. I knew the ale-conners, as they were long-standing citizens of Elmham Lenn, one was even an alderman. But I'd never seen this person before. I would remember him if I had. The gray light formed an aura behind him, giving his features an almost saintly glow. Long dark hair fell over his forehead, coming to rest against straight brows. Beneath these were eyes the color of midnight, of the deepest, darkest blue, like the Virgin's robe in the church window. Sparkling, as though fevered, they traveled over me leisurely and color rose in my cheeks. I did not, would not look away. Who was this ale-conner to appraise me so? My heart began to thud painfully. Just as I had with Lord Rainford, I returned the regard, with a deliberateness that was not in character but which something about this man spurred to life. Sweeping the rest of his face, I noted the long, dark lashes, high cheekbones, a full bottom lip and strong chin. It was a face that exuded strength and mastery and drew my gaze.

Aware of how I must look, my hair escaping from its binds, tumbling over my shoulders, my tunic streaked with charcoal, if not my face, and reeking of the brewery, I self-consciously pulled at my dress. That this man needed to shave drew my disapproval. He might be striking but he had no regard for his duties or those whose homes he visited—at least I had an excuse. Contempt began to control my study of his broad shoulders, wide chest, and long, shapely legs. I was staring at his boots, wondering that a man of his station should possess such quality when I noticed that one foot was turned slightly and he leaned against a stick— a polished piece of wood with a metal band at the top, upon which he had a white-knuckled grip. Sympathy rose within me. I was about to speak when the front door banged shut and a slightly shorter man joined him.

"Anneke!"

I blinked as I was pulled into the tightest of embraces and quickly released.

"Tobias?" I said weakly, not wanting to believe. I stared at the beloved face, matured and changed but still recognizably my brother. My heart soared and with a cry of joy I returned his hug, fiercely, protectively, showering his face with kisses, hearing laughter bubble inside him. "Tobias!"

Over Tobias's shoulder, my eyes flew to the other man. Amusement and something else, something that was neither polite nor warm but quizzical, shaped his expression.

Drawing me away slightly so he might consider me, my brother beamed. "Look at you! You'd be mistaken for a slattern in that dress. Is that an apron over there? What have you been up to?"

"You'll never guess." I smiled.

Tobias's eyes slid to the barrel. "Think I might." He held me again and I became aware that he was broader, harder, taller. This time, I pushed him away and studied him, gripping his forearms to hold him in place. Over two years had passed since I last saw him and the boy had become a man. Taller than me, he had dark curls, gray-blue eyes, and a windburned face. His teeth looked so white against his skin. His body had filled out, grown where it needed and diminished in other parts as well. Gone were the chubby cheeks, the childlike stomach. I smiled at him, tears blurring my vision, and drew him back to my breast.

"Oh, Tobias, I've missed you so . . ."

Then I remembered.

"Tobias . . ." I wrenched out of his arms, but kept one hand upon him. "You know about . . . Father?" I could have kicked myself for hesitating over the word.

A dark look flashed across Tobias's face, and in that second I saw and felt pain, anger, and quickly stifled resentment. Tobias may appear a man, but like a child, he'd not yet learned to guard his emotions.

"Of course. I'm sorry, Anneke, sorry I wasn't here for you, the twins. I came as soon as I could."

"Don't apologize. I'm just so glad you're here." I took a deep breath and noticed for the first time the state of his clothes. "What am I thinking? You're soaked. You've traveled to get here. From London? The docks? Don't answer. Come through to the hall, please. There's a fire and food. We have to get this sodden cloak off you, dry your hat, get you some wine and—"

The other man cleared his throat and I swung back to him in horror. Here I was daring to be critical of his manners when my own were so lax. I'd completely forgotten about him.

"My humblest apologies, Master . . . ?" I released Tobias and turned to face the handsome stranger.

Tobias came to my rescue. "It's me who should be apologizing. In the excitement of seeing you again, I quite forgot. Anneke, allow me to introduce Sir Leander Rainford, son of Lord Hardred Rainford, and my master."

My eyes widened as I absorbed who it was that stood on my threshold. Not only the son of a man I'd learned to despise despite my sense of obligation, but Tobias's master. Of course. Who else would it have been? I just hadn't expected him to be so . . . so . . . My eyes slid from his rugged face to his foot. Disadvantaged. A memory arose unbidden of a young boy in breeches and a coat, moving along the corridors of Scales Hall . . . Even then, he'd possessed the same dark hair and those remarkable eyes. I'd chased after him in the hope of distraction, a friend with whom to explore the grounds, the house, on a long, lonely day while my mother kept his pregnant stepmother company. I vaguely remembered catching up with him. His affliction made it difficult for him to move swiftly, though walking was not a problem. He'd frowned at my chatter, pulled a face, and then shut the door on me . . . It was his other brother . . . Symond, who, older and less embarrassed at entertaining a child, found me in a crying heap outside the door. Picking me up, he'd looked to my amusement that day. For the youngest son of Lord Rainford, I'd been beneath contempt.

I'd not thought about that moment for a long time, not since Tobias left to be his squire and I'd prayed that the dour young man of recollection had changed—for my brother's sake. And indeed he had, apart from the forbidding expression upon his face. But I'd not expected him to be so . . . so . . . comely. I looked from him to Tobias. Did he know what Tobias was to him? When they stood side by side, as they did now, the resemblance was there. Strong, once you knew what to look for.

Aware I'd remained mute beyond what was polite, I dropped a deep curtsy. "My lord, forgive me. Welcome to Holcroft House."

Sir Leander bowed and, reaching for my hand, pretended to kiss it, releasing it swiftly, as if touching my flesh burned him.

Puzzled, I gripped my hands together to cover my discomposure. "It's a pleasure to meet you again, my lord," I said and flashed my teeth.

"Again?" When he frowned, his eyes darkened.

"Aye, my lord. We met many years ago, at Scales Hall. I was but a child."

Raising his chin, he looked around the room, plucking at his gloves as he did so. "I don't recall." His tone suggested that even if he did, it was something he wanted to forget.

Arching a brow at Tobias, I chose to ignore his master's rudeness. "When did you arrive in Elmham Lenn? How?" I asked, peering outside, looking for horses.

"A few hours ago," said Tobias. "We're staying at Lord Hardred's house in town. Sir Leander insisted we walk, despite the weather." He shot his master a look of mock disapproval, and in the one Sir Leander returned I could see affection and even pride. I admit, that surprised and pleased me. "Trying to shed our sea legs," added Tobias, and did a little jig as if to prove it had worked. He froze suddenly mid-dance. Neither Tobias nor I looked at Sir Leander's leg. "I know I should have warned you, Anneke," Tobias continued quickly. "Sent a note, but"—he gestured to the barrel—"we heard about your plans—they're the talk of the town. Brewing? Really? Seems I'm back just in time. We've a great deal to discuss."

My heart sank at Tobias's tone and protests took shape in my head. And why was his master here anyway? If he wanted to become accustomed to land again, he could have walked anywhere. And who chose to walk in this weather? Before I could reassure Tobias, Adam and Will rolled the second barrel through the door and into the shop. We had to jump out of the way as the barrel hit the lip of the step and bounced against the floor, flattening the rushes. I found myself on the same side of the room as Sir Leander. Adam and Will maneuvered the barrel next to the first and righted it slowly. Delight creased their faces when they saw Tobias, and they stepped forward to greet him.

As they did so, Sir Leander leaned toward me. "When you discuss your plans with your brother, I ask that you not mention the arrangement you have with my father."

I looked up at him in surprise. "You know of this? Oh, of course you do. Forgive me, my lord, why on earth wouldn't I?" I spluttered before I could prevent myself.

Sir Leander's eyes were filled with repugnance. "Because I wouldn't want Tobias to discover that his sister's no better than a common whore."

My mouth fell open and I stood gasping like a market fish as Tobias introduced Will and Adam to his master and then, beckoning me to follow, led Sir Leander down the corridor and into the main hall, as if he hadn't left this house when he was seven. Tobias behaved like he was the master returned. Will scuttled after them.

Heat and then ice filled my veins. Tears threatened to spill as fury rose in my chest. Not at Tobias's actions—of those I was glad. I wanted him to treat this as his home. It was, after all. It was all any of us could claim, for now. It was Sir Leander Rainford who made me lose my equilibrium.

Pausing on the threshold before he followed Tobias, Adam looked at me inquiringly.

"Are you all right, Mistress Anneke?"

I didn't trust myself to speak. I fixed a grim smile, nodded, and waved my hand for him to go ahead. Adam hesitated, then strode down the hallway.

*How dare he. How dare he.*

It was only the delighted shouts of the twins and the joy in the servants' voices drifting down to the shop that enabled me to move again, to put on a public face and join them.

If I seemed stiff and formal, no one either noticed or cared, not even Sir Leander, who, as the afternoon wore on and the shadows darkened, acted as if I didn't even exist.

# FOURTEEN

HOLCROFT HOUSE
Martinmas
*The year of Our Lord 1405 in the seventh
year of the reign of Henry IV*

Squeezing themselves onto Tobias's lap, where he sat before the hearth, the twins were unable to believe that their brother, whom they barely knew except through infrequent visits, letters, and my tales, had returned. Unwilling to let him out of their sight, they begged him to regale them with his adventures since he'd last been in port. They bombarded him with questions, which they failed to give him adequate time to answer. Our best chair was found for Sir Leander and Adam poured him a drink of the finest wine we possessed. The fire was quickly stoked while Saskia procured a blanket for his lap. Blanche ordered Iris into the kitchen and they swiftly reappeared with a platter of food. I stood in a corner, my arms folded across my chest, and watched and listened, a mixture of bemusement, pride in my household, and anxiety about Sir Leander's words swirling within me.

Intending to leave the family with their noble guest, the servants began to retreat into the kitchen, but Tobias and, much to my surprise, Sir Leander quickly dispelled them of that notion and insisted they remain.

Uncomfortable at first, they looked to me for permission, which of course I gave and, joining Tobias and the twins by the fire, soon added their own questions to the children's. Stools and a bench were dragged closer, and we made a neat semicircle around the hearth. Struck dumb by fear and disbelief, the entire house was spellbound as Tobias told of the storms that claimed not just Father's life and the crew of the *Cathaline*, but of many other ships and men besides, wreaking destruction along the North and Baltic Seas. Entire fleets had been sunk, houses and businesses dragged into the raging waters, and even, along the coastline of Norway, a cliff collapsed, raining rocks and soil into the churning water. Cries of dismay accompanied Tobias's story, as did swift prayers. Unprecedented and therefore unexpected, no one had been prepared for the violence of the weather that early in autumn. Sir Leander's insistence they remain upriver till the weather calmed meant the crew of the *Sealhope* didn't meet the same fate as that of the *Cathaline*.

"Thank the good Lord for your prudence, Leander," Tobias said, sitting very still, staring into the distance.

"And providence," added Sir Leander modestly.

We fell quiet, acknowledging those who'd not been so fortunate, those who God willed would not find land again. The twins bowed their heads.

"Not that it was such a hardship to remain," said Tobias suddenly, breaking the somber mood. Betje and Karel raised their eyes cautiously.

"Why?" asked Karel.

Tobias grinned. "There're worse places than Bruges in which to be stranded. I'll take you both there one day, you wait." Karel and Betje's mouths dropped open and they stared at each other with wide shining eyes. Betje burrowed against Tobias, wrapping her arms as far around his waist as she could. Tobias turned toward me. "You should see the place, Anneke, you'd find much to please you. It's so pretty. Full of colorful houses with white shutters, huge stone churches inside the city walls, and perfectly arched bridges under which swans drift. Everyone seems to own a dog, cats meander along the cobbles, horses and carts jingle, and the women are so pretty. Why—"

Sir Leander coughed.

Tobias flashed him a look. "Um. They are. Very. And the entire place is laced with canals as well," he recovered. I buried a grin.

"They call it the Venice of the North," added Sir Leander, earning sighs of wonder from Louisa, who, sitting nearby with her chin resting on her hands, hadn't been able to tear her eyes away from our guest.

"What's a Venice?" asked Betje.

"Tell us!" demanded Karel, and Tobias complied.

My heart lurched, astonished at the desire his words aroused. Venice, Bruges, the Netherlands. The number of times I'd stood on the bay and imagined those worlds and places beyond Elmham Lenn . . . And here was Tobias describing them, revisiting his experiences for us to savor. I envied Tobias, but I didn't begrudge him. I knew life at sea was not a romantic adventure, but a dangerous and ofttimes unpleasant enterprise involving cramped quarters, sour ale and brackish water, spoiled food, illness, and even death—and that was before the elements or pirates were taken into account. Wanting to ask more, I was prevented as Blanche brought in a tray of cheeses and warm bread. Iris followed her, topping up mazers and goblets with the spiced wine made for Martinmas. I'd so wanted us to be imbibing the ale . . . At least Sir Leander appeared to find the wine agreeable; by my reckoning he was onto his third cup. I enjoyed the warmth it left in my throat, though it did nothing to settle the flutter in my stomach.

I still couldn't credit Sir Leander's words. What had I done to provoke such an insult?

Unable to relax with him in the room, I wasn't able to stop my eyes drifting in his direction either—neither were Saskia, Blanche, or Iris, who, like Louisa, were clearly struck by his appearance in our midst. My fixation came from a different source. Fury that the explanation I intended to insist upon must needs be delayed stoked my apprehension; my nerves were already frayed waiting for the officials to appear. Where on earth *were* they? The afternoon was dying. Evening would be upon us shortly. All around Elmham Lenn, Martinmas was being commemorated; people were buying and drinking ale— the friary's. Mine was sitting in barrels, unable to be consumed. Worse, unable to be sold.

Lost in a fugue of frustration, I tried to pretend that I wasn't preoccupied with anything other than Tobias's arrival. (*Whore! That . . . that . . . man called me a whore!*) I sipped my drink and tried to absorb the first real bit of happiness we'd had at Holcroft House in a long, long time. Contentment in which I too could have shared if not for Lord Rainford's arrogant son and his vicious words.

I glanced at him now and gave an internal hurrumph as the dogs sat at his feet, their tongues lolling. Putting his weight on his stick, he leaned over, scratched their necks and fondled their ears. How was it that even my animals betrayed me? Unable to watch any longer, I excused myself and went to my room to change my tunic and tidy myself in the forlorn expectation that the tardy ale-conners would indeed come. Truth be told, I also thought that a change of garment might alter Sir Leander's wretched opinion of me and thus took extra care with my toilet. Ale-conners be damned!

When I reappeared some time later and sat close to my brother, I saw the dogs had been dismissed to the yard and witnessed Sir Leander produce a box from his leather satchel, out of which he extracted a sweet each for the twins. Uncertain whether they should accept, they looked to me, their fingers twitching with excitement.

Tobias grinned at their antics. "It's called marchpane," he said over Betje's bobbing head. "It's from the kingdom of Denmark. It's delicious. Try some, Anneke," he said. Plucking a piece out of the box, he held out what looked like rose-colored dough. By now the twins were munching on theirs and exclaiming in raptures.

I shook my head. "Not now, Tobias, thank you. I will, later," I added when he appeared disheartened. With a shrug, he popped the piece in his mouth.

Sir Leander had enough for everyone to try. Looking at the servants' faces, his generosity was well received—even Adam was touched. This gesture didn't accord with my first impression. With an antipathy that depressed me further, I wondered what he'd expect in return and determined, despite what I'd said to Tobias, not to eat any.

Everyone was busy discussing the merits or otherwise of marchpane when Will, who'd left to see what was disturbing the dogs, scurried back into the hall, pale-faced. He raced to my side.

"It's the ale-conners, mistress, they're here!"

# FIFTEEN

My heart pounding, I rose slowly, placed my napkin on the stool, and brushed the front of my tunic. Adam and I exchanged looks. Excusing himself to Tobias and Sir Leander, he stood and ordered Will to remain in the hall. Tobias tried to remove the twins from his lap so he could accompany me, but I pushed him back, squeezing his shoulder in reassurance.

I whispered in his ear. "Please, I can handle this on my own. 'Tis but a formality. Take care of our guest," I said with a lightness I didn't feel.

As I strode into the shop, trying not to look too hasty, I was pleased to note the candles had been lit. I held my hands before me to steady their shaking and went to greet the man standing just inside the door. Adam stood to one side, waiting to receive his cloak.

As wide as he was short, Master Constable, the chief ale-conner and an alderman, came forward. Possessed of ruddy cheeks and, as he swept off his cap, strands of ginger hair that clung to the front of his freckled scalp, he wore the black and red livery of an ale-conner and a heavy scowl.

"We've been out there a goodly while, Mistress Sheldrake, being lashed with rain and wind, no less," he admonished me.

His hostility forced me back a step. "My sincere apologies, Master Constable, but we fail—"

"We almost walked away," he continued, talking over the top of me and shaking a stumpy finger in my direction. "It doesn't do any good to keep us waiting, you know." Refusing Adam's help, he lifted the strap of a satchel off his neck before dragging his wet cloak from his shoulders and throwing it at a stool, which promptly tipped over.

Beside me, Adam tensed. Before he could say anything, I dashed across and picked up the cloak, shook it, and lay it carefully across the stool, which I righted with my other hand. I gave a small curtsy.

"May God give you good day, and thank you for coming, Master Constable. Welcome to Holcroft House," I said sweetly. "Again, I apologize that you had to wait." It was hard to sound sincere; after all, the ale-conners had made us wait nearly all day. "We've unexpected visitors and didn't hear you arrive."

"I don't want your excuses. Let's get on with it, shall we?" Without waiting for an answer, he continued. "As you know, Emory Constable's my name. Head of the ale-conners of Elmham Lenn."

Master Constable was one of those men accustomed to

deference. Swallowing my pride, I determined to give him some and shot Adam a warning look to do the same.

I dropped another small curtsy.

"About your father . . ." He looked around the room, his face unreadable as outside the skies darkened. "May God assoil him." Master Constable rubbed the top of his head, making the few hairs rise. Proffering condolences was not within his remit; discomfort leaked from him. He held his bag over his generous stomach, staring at the floor.

"Thank you." I gestured to Adam. "This is my steward, Master Adam Barfoot."

"Aye," said Master Constable, his eyes narrowing as he studied Adam. "Me and Master Barfoot go back a long ways, don't we?" He tapped the side of his bulbous nose.

There was movement by the door and, to my astonishment, two other figures huddled outside. Master Constable was not referring to himself as "we" after all. There were a number of them. "Dear Lord! Hadn't we better get the rest of you inside?" I looked pointedly in their direction. "As you say, it's cold, wet, and you're pressed for time." I made a move for the door.

"Them?" Master Constable shook his head. "Nay, mistress, that's not the way it's done." My hand fell from the latch. "Since this is the first time *you've* hailed us with the ale-stake, let me explain. Until I've tested for quality and a decision's made as to whether or not we take it further, they can't step inside the premises. They must remain on the street—which is what they are doing. If you're worried about their well-being, I suggest we hurry up." He flapped his arms in front of him and stepped toward one of the trestle tables.

Shrugging apologetically to the men whose features I couldn't make out, their caps had been pulled down so low, I joined Master Constable.

"Let's proceed then." I gestured to the barrels, relieved to see my hands were steady now. "There are three more in the brewhouse."

"If they're all from the same batch, we've only to open one."

Fumbling inside his satchel, Master Constable drew out some bound pages and a slim wooden container in which lay a quill and inkwell. Placing the box carefully on the table, he uncorked the inkwell and dipped the feather inside. "And the measures by which you propose to sell?"

I motioned to his left.

Rummaging further in his bag, he drew out the official seals and a pair of leather pants that he laid to one side. Glancing at the measures, he picked them up one by one—the gallon, potel, quart, and gill—before examining first the copper then the harvester bottles we'd put aside. "Very good." He scratched some notes. "I've a few more questions." He rapidly fired queries about the grain used, how much we paid, the intended market, all of which would help the ale-conners set the price by which we could sell our ale, and the tax and fees I'd pay the town for the opportunity. Adam and I calculated the price we needed to sell per gallon to make a profit. Checking his notes, Master Constable rested his quill on the table, put down the pages, and slapped his hands together.

"Let the test proceed then." He indicated for Adam to tap a barrel and occupied himself with pulling the leather pants over his leggings.

Knocking the bung off, Adam drew ale into a jug and passed it to Master Constable.

Having never seen an ale-testing before, I was most curious.

Holding the jug steady with one hand, the ale-conner drew a wooden bench across the rushes with the other before, much to my astonishment, pouring a goodly portion of the ale onto the seat. Passing the jug back to Adam he promptly sat in the pool he'd created, his back straight, hands on knees, feet firmly planted on the floor.

"Would you like a drink?" I asked quietly after Master Constable failed to move or speak for some minutes.

"Nay, mistress," he said through tight lips, staring straight ahead. "That be for later. For now, I sit."

Casting a sympathetic look at the cold, wet men outside, I perched upon a stool near the barren hearth. Though I'd heard of the manner in which the quality of a brew was judged, seeing it for myself was quite an experience. Watching Master Constable, clad in his leather, immobile upon a spill of dripping ale, I wondered who invented this preposterous test to assess something that was drunk.

If he didn't stick to the bench, the ale would be deemed to have failed, so, while the wind howled and the rain struck the panes, I prayed that when the time came for Master Constable to rise, it would be with a bench glued to his hindquarters.

Just as I thought he must have dozed off, Master Constable cleared his throat and in one swift movement, rose to his feet. The bench followed.

Mirroring his action but sans the stool, I stifled an exclamation of relief and moved to the door as he pried the bench from his backside.

Registering my silent question, he placed the sticky seat on the rushes and then gave a click of exasperation. "All right then. Come on, gentlemen," he called. "Step inside. Be quick about it."

Equal parts uncomfortable and grateful, the two ale-tasters stood side by side just inside the door wringing water out of their caps while their cloaks dripped onto the rushes.

"That is Master Calvin Beecham," said Master Constable, wriggling out of his breeches and indicating the short, thin man on the left. Master Beecham mumbled something meant to be a greeting and glared at me from beneath bushy brows. "He is a clerk of the court."

I gave a slight nod.

"And this is Master Allistair Gretting." Master Constable pointed at the tall, broad-shouldered man with a thatch of dark hair. "He is the toll keeper."

"Will this take long?" grumbled Master Gretting. "My wife said she was cooking goose tonight, but it will be mine she'll be attending to if I'm late."

"Aye," grunted Master Beecham, folding his rangy arms across his chest and casting somber looks around the room. "Let's be tasting, not talking." He sniffed loudly.

"May I take your cloaks, gentlemen?" I asked.

"That won't be necessary, mistress," said Master Gretting, raising a huge hand. "This part won't take long. Being here is more or less a formality."

That was what I feared most—that the men wouldn't take long because their minds were already made up, whether or not the ale passed the quality test. But Captain Stoyan was certain his warning had been heeded . . . I watched Adam pour the rich foaming ale into mazers for the men to try.

"What's going on, Anneke?" With a catch in my breath, I spun around.

Tobias stood in the doorway flanked by Sir Leander.

My heart sank. "It's all right, Tobias." I shot him a look that he chose to ignore. "It's the ale-conners."

"S . . . Sir L . . . Leander," said Master Constable, his eyes widening and his face coloring as he saw the taller man. He gave a swift bow, shooting a look at the two other ale-conners who mumbled uncomfortably. They shuffled till their backs were against the wall. "We wasn't told—I mean, we didn't expect to see you here, my lord."

"I confess, I didn't expect to be here, Master Constable."

"Perhaps we can do this another time," said Master Constable, waving away the mazers Adam was holding.

"Please—" I began, raising my hands in protest.

"Don't let us stop you," said Sir Leander, leaning against the doorframe that led back inside the house. "Please, continue. Not only does my father have a vested interest in this, but I've always been curious to know on what basis ale-conners make their decisions, haven't you, Tobias?" He cocked his head toward my brother.

"I have, indeed. Often, my lord," lied Tobias.

The ale-conners shared another look, clearly ill at ease.

"Very well," said Master Constable finally. "Let's get on with it."

Adam solemnly passed mazers to the two men.

My heart was beating so violently, I was sure the front of my tunic must be quivering. While I wanted more than anything for the ale to be passed, I also wanted it to be because the ale had earned it, not because of Captain Stoyan's threats. But neither did I want to fail because an abbot said I must.

Master Gretting and Master Beecham stared at the contents of their mazers before rotating the wooden cups so the ale formed a gentle whirlpool. They held their noses over it and inhaled noisily. Neither revealed anything in their expressions. I glanced at Master Constable, who was busy scratching more notes; why, I was uncertain. I sent a swift prayer to the goddesses and the crones.

Holding the handles, first Master Gretting then Master Beecham tilted the cups and took a mouthful. Swilling the ale around in his cheeks a few times, Master Gretting's eyes widened, then he swallowed, before quickly taking another sip. Smacking his lips, he licked them slowly then pursed them tightly, nodding, but whether in approval or to confirm a doubt, I didn't know.

Master Beecham's cheeks bulged and he shut his eyes. Tipping back his head, he gargled and then gulped, his Adam's apple moving up and down the way a bird's did when it warbled. Then he bent his head until his nose disappeared into the vessel and drew in a breath deeply and noisily. Out of the corner of my eye I saw Tobias shove a fist against his mouth. Sir Leander coughed. I was too nervous to find anything funny. Too much was dependent on the outcome of this mummery.

"The verdict?" asked Master Constable shortly in a resigned voice, after the men had a few more mouthfuls and spent additional time sniffing and breathing in the fumes.

Both were frowning, their eyes hard. They looked at each other, shrugged, and then turned back to Master Constable.

There was nothing amusing about them now.

"I know what we've been told," began Master Beecham cautiously, his eyes sliding toward me. "And I know it passed the quality test, but I can't ignore me oath, nor me obligation to the town. I've never tasted anything like it before." He screwed up his face in what could only be read as displeasure.

"Me neither," said Master Gretting. "On the one hand, it's very different"—he looked meaningfully at Master Constable—"but on the other, that means it doesn't meet the standards to which we've grown accustomed either."

"Aye. It's too different, mayhap," added Master Beecham.

Master Constable put down his pages and rubbed his face. "That's your verdict then? It be less good than what's reasonable to pass?"

The two men looked into the mazers then shrugged again and nodded.

"If that be your *honest* opinion, then there's nothing more to be done." With a long, weary sigh, Master Constable began to pack up his quill and ink, his phlegmatic demeanor transformed into one of haste. "While some might be unhappy with this result, there are others who will find justice in it," he muttered, swinging around, urging his men to return their cups.

"Excuse me," I said, tugging gently at Master Constable's sleeve. "While 'others' might know what's just happened, I'm afraid I do not. 'Different' is not the same as 'less good'? Less good than what? Surely, it's not undrinkable?" I gestured to the two men draining their mazers.

Master Constable wouldn't meet my eyes. "I thought it was more than clear. The ale-conners have spoken, Mistress Sheldrake. The brew cannot be sold. It's so different there's nothing against which we can judge it."

Disappointment and fury rose, transforming into bitter tears that threatened to spill. All my plans and hopes unraveled before me. I tried to find the right words to reason with these men, to prevent them leaving and change their minds. This was a fine brew. Different, but with good reason.

I jutted out my chin and straightened my spine. I wouldn't let them see how much this upset . . . indeed, devastated, me. What could I do? What recourse did I have? I was one woman against not just these three men but, if the rumors were right, an entire friary and those they'd suborned. I took a step toward Master Constable, but before I could speak, Sir Leander's voice rang out.

"Let's not be so hasty, gentlemen," he said, binding them to the spot.

I swung around, my eyes ablaze, my cheeks red. "This has nothing to do with you," I hissed.

He ignored me. "If I may ask a question, Master Constable?"

Master Constable smirked at me. "For certes, my lord."

I spun around to glare at Tobias. He'd brought Leander Rainford here; he was responsible for this. What was the man up to? Why couldn't he just leave things be? Was he deliberately trying to make this harder? I wanted them all gone. Now. Tobias fumbled at my side, finding my hand and giving it a squeeze. I wanted to snatch it away. He didn't know how hard we'd toiled, what we'd sacrificed for this moment. And now his Godforsaken master was going to make everything worse.

"Watch," said Tobias so softly, I thought I'd misheard.

"Master Adam, can you pour another round for the aleconners, please?" asked Sir Leander.

"The decision's made, my lord, drinking more won't change that—" Master Constable shook his jowls.

"Fetch a drink for Master Constable too, would you, Adam?" added Sir Leander. Master Constable began to bluster. "This isn't an official tasting, Constable. This is merely something to wet your lips while we discuss why and how this decision was reached before you retire for the evening."

One didn't disobey a lord's son, especially not a Rainford. "So long as we're clear it's *not* official," said Master Constable gruffly.

Sir Leander's blue eyes twinkled. "Not *officially*. Though, I can't help but feel, since these two fine ale-conners concluded that they've never tasted anything like this brew before, that it's so different there's nothing against which to measure it, there's also the slight possibility that rather than 'less good,' as these fine gentlemen suppose, it might actually be 'more good.' But," he added hastily, before Master Constable could interrupt, "this would require someone with greater experience and knowledge to determine, with a more refined taste. In my humble opinion, there's only one person appropriate for that task—"

Everyone looked in Master Constable's direction. He opened his mouth to argue, then, realizing it would be to his detriment, shut it again. I swear his chest expanded. I returned Tobias's grip and waited.

Adam finished pouring fresh drinks.

"As far as I can recall," continued Sir Leander, "these fine ale-conners didn't even consider the possibility it might be more good. So, drink up, man, and tell us what you determine." Sir Leander struck his cane against a stool. "Let us hear the opinion of an expert."

Master Constable sniffed the contents of his beaker suspiciously. "This is not how a tasting is supposed to be conducted, my lord."

"But, as you pointed out, this isn't official, is it?" Sir Leander gave him what even I had to admit was a charming smile. "Indulge me, good sir."

"Smells strange." Master Constable hesitated.

"Drink," urged Sir Leander.

Master Constable did. All eyes were fixed upon him as he swallowed.

"Is it too sweet?" asked Sir Leander. "Or sour?"

The ale-conner considered what he'd just tasted. "Nay . . . nay . . . It's not too sweet . . ." Taking another swill he added, "Nor sour."

"What is it then?" asked Sir Leander.

Master Constable gulped some more. "It's like the lads said: different." Finishing the contents, Master Constable smacked his lips together. "Aye. There's something unusual about this brew, for certes."

"Unusual? Different? Is that grounds for failing it? Is the standard that's been set so pleasing that a new one can't be?" Sir Leander asked quietly, and I knew then he was familiar with the friary's ale. "Because I'd be reluctant to pronounce such a verdict if I wasn't confident it would hold up to scrutiny."

"What kind?" Master Constable puffed out his chest defensively.

"The Hanse kind," I added, finding my voice as I observed this masquerade.

The room fell silent. The ale-conners looked to Master Constable, who stared thoughtfully into his mazer. Outside, the rain became a light patter and the shriek of gulls could be heard overhead as they chased the evening light across the bay. In Father's office, a log shifted and the welcome crackle and snap produced a sudden flare of light. Shadows shuddered along the wall.

Master Constable let out a long sigh. "I know I'm going to regret this, but I wouldn't be doing my job if I didn't admit this is uncommonly good ale, Mistress Sheldrake."

Masters Gretting and Beecham glanced at each other and, with audible noises of relief, swung back to Master Constable, nodding. "Aye, that it is," they chorused. "Excellent," added Master Beecham, and asked Adam to pour him another.

"I think the word you're looking for is *incomparable*," added Sir Leander, and the men readily agreed.

It was only as the men's cups were being refilled that my success was brought home.

"You did it, Anneke." Tobias gave me a small smile and tightened his grip on my hand before releasing it.

Adam quickly found some decent tankards and, filling them with ale, handed them to Sir Leander, Tobias, and me. Only after he had one in his hand, did we raise our cups in a toast.

Over the next five minutes, the paperwork was finished and I paid my dues. The measures were marked with the official seal and the kegs stamped with the three *X*s that denoted their full flavor. Adam escorted Master Gretting to the brewhouse in order that the other barrels would also bear the sign and our hogshead the two *X*s for small ale. The price was set. It was better than I could have hoped, as was the tax levied on us. Flushed with accomplishment, my breathing came easier now.

Adam and Master Gretting returned, brushing the rain from their shoulders and stomping warmth back into their limbs. Emptying his cup, Master Constable found his cloak and tied it under his chin.

"For better or worse, our job here is done, gentlemen—time for us to return home before dark falls and the rain gets worse." He turned toward me. "You can put your bushel out now, Mistress Sheldrake."

Wrenching open the door and admitting a cold blast of air, Adam stood to one side, but before the ale-conners could leave, a body pushed past.

"About time, Emory Constable," cried a familiar voice. "It's freezing out here and we're thirstier than a pack of barking dogs!" It was Mervin Proudfellow, the local innkeeper. "Good evening, Mistress Sheldrake." He pulled off his cap and bowed. "Come to fetch a barrel as promised. I've the cart and some customers with me." He gestured to the street.

Beyond the small halo of light being cast from the shop, a line of lanterns could be discerned. Standing outside were at least a dozen people, skins, jugs, and mazers in their hands. Atop a cart, an old horse in its shafts, was Kip, Master Proudfellow's son. On spying me from beneath his sodden cape, he gave a jolly wave.

With muttered farewells and looks of surprise and concern on their faces, the ale-conners sidled past those entering. I wondered briefly what price they'd pay for honoring their oaths tonight.

Drawing the bushel out from under the trestle table, Adam quickly went outside and attached it to the end of the stake. We were now officially open for business. Cheers filtered into the shop.

"If you don't mind," said Master Proudfellow, "I've thirsty people waiting back at the inn for this." Between them, Adam and Master Proudfellow rolled a barrel outside and I had the pleasure of seeing our first coins drop into the small tin.

As soon as the barrel was out of the way, the customers (*customers!*) pushed their way inside. There was old Mistress Birkett, the widow of Sailor Errol; Simon Attenoke, one of the local fishermen; Brandon Franks, the old sea salt; Janekyn Shoemaker and his wife, Ruth; Velda Avison, the local midwife, and her son Phineas, also entered. More came in with their own mazers, placing coin down to not merely cart ale away, but drink on the premises—all brave souls who, for tonight at least, were prepared to defy the friary and support my venture. Adam was frantically tapping the barrel to fill orders; Tobias was catching up with townsfolk he hadn't seen in a long time. Sir Leander was caught between Master Attenoke and Phineas. I ran back into the house to fetch Saskia and Iris, so excited I could barely speak. They were waiting for me in the corridor; they couldn't remain in ignorance in the main hall and had been running back and forth reporting events to the others.

"You did it, Mistress Anneke," said Saskia, a huge smile upon her face.

I hugged her tightly. "*We* did it." I turned to face Louisa, Blanche, Iris, Will, and the twins, who'd all crept into the corridor, my eyes shining, my hands clasped in an attitude of prayer. Sensing my mood, the dogs barked and jumped around me. I rubbed their ears in the gesture I'd seen Sir Leander use earlier, and in that moment, it occurred to me the only reason my ale was selling tonight instead of being absorbed into the earth was because of him.

If that man hadn't intervened and persuaded Master Constable to try the ale, hadn't suggested that the process was not being done correctly, there would have been a very different outcome. While I'd perhaps helped Master Constable resolve his conscience by reminding him of the Hanse, it was Sir Leander who ensured I was in a position to do that. As much as I hated to admit it, I owed him gratitude, at least.

I had to thank him. The sooner the better. Then he could leave and I would make sure any future meetings were kept to a minimum. One Rainford in my life was more than enough. I made up my mind then and there that if I did naught else tonight, I would do my duty and express a proper and heartfelt thanks to Sir Leander Rainford, the man who, for reasons unbeknownst to me, called me whore.

# SIXTEEN

꧁꧂

HOLCROFT HOUSE

Martinmas evening

*The year of Our Lord 1405 in the seventh*
*year of the reign of Henry IV*

The last of the customers left and, after tidying up swiftly and securing the front door, we retreated to the warmth of the hall and to the repast that, according to Blanche as she flapped her apron, had already awaited us too long.

That was hours ago. Empty trenchers and bone-scattered platters covered the stained tablecloth. For just a moment, I considered the cost and then pushed such persnickety considerations to the back of my mind. It was Martinmas, my brew had passed. After weeks of accounting for every groat and penny, it was time to celebrate. I grasped the cup of brimming ale and drank again, sending a swift prayer of thanks to the Blessed Virgin and the goddess Ninkasi.

From the bench by the fire, I gazed around, filled with hazy thoughts. Peals of laughter and the warmth of conversation

washed over me. What a day—from the anxiety of awaiting
the ale-conners, to the unexpected arrival of Tobias, my emotions had been in turmoil. God forgive my vanity, but it was the
praise of my neighbors as they tasted the brew, even the small
ale, upon which I lingered; the astonishment writ upon their
features before words of delight and surprise—and orders for
more—spilled from their lips.

The only shadow was Leander Rainford. Try as I might, I
was unable to ignore him. As the ale sold and my neighbors
crammed into the shop with their empty firkins and skins to
be filled, I sought an opportunity to thank him for encouraging Master Constable to reconsider his original verdict, but the
chance never came. Keen to acknowledge their overlord's son,
either to make themselves known or renew acquaintance, the
townsfolk's interest didn't seem to trouble him. On the contrary, he appeared to enjoy it and, as twilight surrendered to
nightfall, even sought to detain some of them for further conversation. That I heard my name mentioned a couple of times
wasn't the only reason I found myself drawn to where he stood
again and again, nor was it the simple fact of his height, bearing, or the quality of his clothes. The man drew eyes the way the
ocean did the hungry gull.

Even Tobias, as he recounted his adventures, the places he'd
been, the people he'd met, allowed Leander Rainford's name to
pepper his conversation. Each time it was mentioned, I found
my cup at my lips, the ale helping me digest the admiration my
brother so clearly felt for his mentor and which, to Sir Leander's
credit, he bore with some embarrassment, his saturnine features
softening slightly. As soon as I could, I moved the conversation
to other subjects, like the scant letters Tobias wrote, scolding

him for the dearth of information in the few lines he would scrawl, which I always responded to with pleas for more.

Listening to Tobias explain his months away, it occurred to me how strange it was having him in the hall again. For all that I worried we would have so much to say that nothing would be, my fears appeared groundless. It was in what was not said as much as what was spoken that, after so many years apart, we found each other again. When he described his travels, his fingers underwent their own journey, while his darkening eyes sparkled with memories clearly not suited for his younger siblings' ears.

Vaguely aware of the bells tolling compline, night stole over us. The fire was fed and the rain eventually ceased. The twins were taken to bed, more ale and wine was poured, and a tired but satisfied sense of togetherness encompassed the room.

As far as I was concerned, the only sour note in an otherwise most satisfactory day was Sir Leander. His insult still rang in my ears and I couldn't relax knowing he had charmed not only my neighbors but my servants and, as I glanced up to see the dogs at his feet again, my treacherous pets as well. Inviting him to stay for supper, Tobias didn't seek permission first and before I could think of a reason to retract my brother's invitation, Saskia and Blanche had added their entreaties. I'd only a moment to hide my dismay before they recalled they had a mistress and I was left with no other option but to importune him to accept.

Which he did. Most graciously.

There he sat on the other side of the room, concentrating on Saskia, who sat chattering beside him. Her face glowed as she spoke of her beloved home, which she'd abandoned when she accompanied my mother to England twenty years earlier. Toward the passage that led to the kitchen, Blanche and Iris sat swaying on a bench as Adam sang an old song about gallant knights and Will quietly accompanied him on his flute. Music weaved its way around the rafters, drifting out into the passage, wrapping itself around the twins and Louisa as they slept upstairs, a harmony to pleasant dreams.

It was only when Tobias nudged me that I heard my name being called. Goblets and mazers were raised.

"To Mistress Anneke." Adam rose unsteadily to his feet. Tobias, Sir Leander, and Will hastily followed.

"Mistress Anneke," repeated the servants, their cheeks ruddy, their smiles almost too wide and bright. My eyes met Sir Leander's and, for the first time, his didn't slide away in disgust. Instead, he raised his goblet toward me and drank.

Heat traveled my face and while I wanted to turn away, I could not. Standing slowly, I raised my vessel in reply.

"None of this would have been possible without you. Thank you." I looked at each and every one of them, wanting them to know how much I meant what I said. It was the simple truth. They'd all enabled this to happen—even Sir Leander. Nonetheless, I reserved my warmest smile for Adam, who nodded in return, his grin wide. Draining his drink, he picked up his tabor and began beating a rhythm. Will picked up his flute. Iris tried to coax Blanche to her feet for a dance, hauling her upright under protest. Blanche laughed as Iris began to spin her around the hall.

Through the fogginess of ale, I watched the way candle and firelight gamboled across the room, flickering over faces, the manner in which it illuminated eyes, noses, and mouths while concealing other features. We hid so much from each other, presented a facade to the world upon which, fairly or unfairly, we were judged as either dark or light.

Unable to help myself, my eyes strayed once again to Sir Leander. What darkness had he seen when he looked at me?

Weary and more than a little head-sore from the earlier wine and the ale, which was stronger than I realized, I collapsed back on the bench. I tugged Tobias's surcoat and patted the space beside me. Tobias started to shake his head, shrugged, then sat heavily, his hands wrapped around his tankard, elbows on his knees, his head lowered as he stared into the foam. The pleasure that attended him earlier had transformed into something altogether different. His shoulders drooped and though there were inches separating us, it was as if a gulf had opened.

"What's wrong?" I asked him quietly, shifting closer and bumping him gently with my shoulder.

A long, slow sigh escaped his lips. For a while, he didn't answer. The music continued, slower now. Blanche and Iris resumed their seats, panting.

"Tobias? What is it?" I whispered.

Across the room, Saskia laughed. My head flew up and I saw Sir Leander smiling. "Is it your master?"

"What?" said Tobias, rousing from his abstraction. He followed the direction of my gaze. "Leander? Don't be silly."

"Is it Father's death . . . ?" my voice petered out.

"Not exactly."

"Well, what is it then?"

Tobias leaned back and rested his head against the wall. I studied him. The way his dark hair fell across his forehead; his hooded eyes; his wide, well-shaped mouth; cheeks that weren't stubbled but bore the blush of youth upon them. He wasn't yet a handsome man, Tobias, not like his master, *his brother*, but one day, he would be.

"This," said Tobias, lifting his goblet and waving it before him.

Frowning, I didn't understand. "The house? But I explained to you what Hiske did—"

"Not the house." Turning his head so his cheek rested against the white walls, he thrust his drink in my direction. "This. You."

"Oh."

"I'm so sorry, Anneke," said Tobias, staring at me but, I fear, not seeing me too well.

"What have you to be sorry for, my sweet brother?" I lifted the fist that rested against his thigh and untangled the taut fingers. "You're blameless in all of this."

"Mayhap. But that doesn't stop me being sorry that you, a Sheldrake, have been reduced to such circumstances." He lifted his goblet into my line of vision. "That for the time being, you bear the brunt of Father's foolishness. I can't help but feel we shouldn't be celebrating but rather, commiserating that my sister has been forced to take such measures." He put the vessel down on the bench between us. "I've been thinking about your plight ever since I found out about our financial situation. We need to find you a husband, Anneke. If you get married, it will solve everything."

Before I could summon a response, Tobias launched into his plan, ignoring my efforts to interrupt. Did he really think I hadn't considered all that he placed before me, including marriage? Failing to notice that my arms crossed my chest and I'd put distance between us upon the bench, he continued on. I stared at the wood of our seat, noting the grain, the scratches, the place where once Karel had hefted a hot poker, scarring it.

I traced the line, my nail burrowing deeper, wanting to leave my own mark. Listening to Tobias, I knew then that despite my earlier thoughts, there were some distances that could never be spanned. My brother didn't really know me at all.

Pondering this I only registered the words a moment after he finished. A smug, uneven smile upon his face, Tobias waited for me to respond.

I stared at him in disbelief. "Did you just say you spoke to Cousin Hiske?"

"Indeed, I did. She called upon us the moment we arrived at Lord Rainford's house in town."

"How did she know you'd be there? Oh. Master Makejoy."

"Indeed. He organized the house to be aired and the servants prepared for our arrival. Cousin Hiske was our first visitor. She wanted to offer me condolences and—" He paused.

"What?"

"To warn me what you were doing."

I pursed my lips.

"She also told me about the offer she made."

"Did she?" My eyes were cold, my chin thrust forward. "And did she tell you what I said?"

"She said you refused."

"Of course I did."

"Are you sure that's wise?"

Why was he being so obtuse? So difficult?

"*Wise?*" Heads swung in our direction. The mood had altered. Blanche danced a protesting Iris toward the kitchen. Will and Adam began locking up while Saskia and Sir Leander remained where they were, absorbed in their discussion. I lowered my voice. "She invited me to *work* for her, Tobias, to be a servant in her house. I don't know what she told you, but there was nothing to hope for in her offer. She's twisting her words to persuade you to her way of thinking. You don't know what it's been like living with that woman, what she's done. You can't really expect me to accept, you who's so worried about the Sheldrake reputation. What would being Hiske's servant do to our dear name?" Bitterness coated my tongue. I glanced at my cup, but it was empty. "Tell me. What kind of husband would I find then?"

"Servant? You misunderstood. Hiske said you did. She asked you to be her companion."

A bark of laughter escaped.

Tobias leveled a finger at me. "Don't mock. It's a perfectly acceptable position for someone your age and in your circumstances. It's better than being a brewster." When I didn't bother replying, he lowered his hand. "Think of the twins, Anneke. What about them?"

"I am thinking of them, Tobias. Them and the servants. I seem to be the only one."

"The servants will find other positions," said Tobias, waving his hand as if he were the king distributing Maundy coins. He brought his hand back to the bench, placing it over mine. It was warm and slightly damp. I tried to pull away but he increased pressure. "But you, Anneke, may not. Not if you keep up with this, this madness. Brewing's fine for a bit of sport, to keep the family in ale, but if you insist on being a brewer, of selling ale to all and sundry, it will be to your ruin."

I withdrew my hand out from under his slowly, my eyes boring into his. With great deliberation, I wiped the back of it across my skirt.

"You have the audacity to return home after all this time and

tell me what to do? I cannot credit that you sit here and rec-
ommend to me I should accept Hiske's offer."

"Anneke, as your brother and the head of this family, I insist
you take it."

So great was the anger that swelled my ribs and lifted me to
my feet, I swear, it was on the tip of my tongue to reveal the
truth. "*Insist?* Who do you think you are? Good King Henry?"

All other conversations in the room ceased. The noises coming from the kitchen slowly stopped as well. I didn't care. Let
them hear me. I fought to contain my thoughts, my sense of
betrayal.

"Sit down," said Tobias through gritted teeth. "Standing on
your dignity when you're only a brewster, for Godsakes, doesn't
work with me."

My hands clenched and unclenched by my side. A log dropped
in the fireplace, sending sparks into the room. Out of the corner
of my eye, one of the dogs yawned and stretched, rearranging
himself casually across his mate. The fever of my anger broke.
"Stop," I said softly. "Stop this before we say something we'll
both regret."

Behind me, talk resumed. Quiet. Careful.

Tobias rose on unsteady legs and I was forced to tilt my head
to meet his eyes. "Don't be stupid, Anneke." He brushed his hair
aside. "I'm not asking you to do it forever. All I'm saying is living
with Hiske—"

"Working, you mean. Being her servant. The woman who
stole from us."

"However you choose to see it. All I'm saying"—he placed a
heavy hand upon my forearm—"is that it has to be better than
brewing. If you continue to do this, then chances are a husband

won't be hard to find, he'll be impossible, and your life and that of our brother and sister will be ruined."

Tears filled my eyes, swam through my words. "You're wrong, Tobias. You're wrong about everything. You've conveniently overlooked that Mother's family, the de Winters, were respected brewers in their homeland. The women and men made ale and their fortunes at the same time. Mother is the daughter of a brewer, or have you so readily forgotten? A brewer who went on to lead the Hanse."

"The brewer's *daughter*, not the brewer herself." I opened my mouth to argue, but he swept on. "Anyhow, it's different over there. This is your home, Anneke, here"—his arm described an arc—"not the Low Countries, not Germany, but here. Elmham Lenn is not that big a place. And while you're here, it's not Mother's name you have to think about, but your own. You're not a de Winter but a Sheldrake, Anneke, like me."

I curled my hands into tight fists, my knuckles turning white, fingernails impressing my palm.

"We have to protect our name." He swallowed and had difficulty forming the next words. "I have to." What I mistook for solely the effects of ale, I now saw were tears toiling not to surface. "After what Father has done to us, it's all we have."

The last vestiges of anger fled. "Oh, Tobias, that's not true. Not all. We have each other too." I sank back onto the bench, pulling Tobias into my arms. He resisted at first, then held me tightly, his chin resting on top of my head. His chest heaved a few times; for all his height, his body felt vulnerable in my arms and I found myself remembering when he sheltered there the last time, after Father told him he was going to Scales Hall to become a squire. This time, it wasn't he who trembled, but me.

Shutting my eyes, I tried to think of how I could persuade Tobias that I knew what I was doing, that while I understood his concerns, he wasn't to worry. I pulled away slightly and attempted to meet his gaze.

"Tobias, listen to me. Everything you've said, all the fears you've given voice to, I share them—every single one. But, more than anything, I need to prove I can do this." I lifted my chin. "Please, give me the chance to do that. Don't stand in my way. For, if you do, you'll leave me no choice but to step away." I cupped his cheek briefly. "I would rather you're beside me."

Reaching up to sweep aside a wisp of hair that escaped my plait, he smiled and pushed it behind my ear. "Sometimes I forget you're older, that while I've been having adventures, traveling the seas, training with weapons, fighting battles, buying and selling the wealth of ten Elmham Lenns, you've been here, living a life too—a life I know so little about." His tone was wistful, faraway.

Alas, he was right. The luxury of danger and excitement was denied me. Yet I still bore the burden of responsibility—if not for Tobias, then for Karel and Betje.

"What I do know"—he stifled a hiccup—"is that you make a fine ale."

Had I heard him correctly?

Tobias chuckled. "I never really believed you'd be pliable, that you'd surrender to my wishes easily. God knows, I've deep unease about these plans of yours. I want more than anything to dissuade you, to demand you go to Hiske. But I have already lost so much—Mother, Father"—he hesitated as his thoughts tripped to darker corners—"and now you tell me if I seek to prevent you from brewing, then I will lose you too. You would walk away rather than comply. I couldn't bear that."

He waited for me to correct him, to say I would never allow such a thing to sever our relationship. God forgive me, I couldn't reassure him, for it would have been an untruth.

With a deep sigh that shuddered through his entire frame, he reached again for my hand. This time, I didn't resist.

"Anneke, you have to promise me: if this doesn't work, if you can't pay Lord Rainford, if anything should go wrong, you'll give away the brewing here in Elmham Lenn and go to Hiske— aye, aye, I know she's a damn thief, I know she's a gossip and a shrew, but she's family and she wouldn't dare to abuse that, no matter what you think. If needs be, you must put aside what she's said and done, your history with her, and swallow your pride—at least until such time as I can fetch you. If not for your own sake, then for me and the twins."

So, Tobias didn't know the full extent of my agreement with Lord Rainford. Relief washed over me, making me temporarily limp in his arms. And as I'd already concluded, what Hiske had done was inconsequential in the greater scheme of things.

I craned my neck and kissed his cheek. "Thank you, Tobias. From the bottom of my heart, thank you. You won't regret this. You have my word. If this venture does not provide, I won't brew in Elmham Lenn ever again."

And thus, my fate was sealed.

# SEVENTEEN

HOLCROFT HOUSE

The day after Martinmas

*The year of Our Lord 1405 in the seventh*

*year of the reign of Henry IV*

It was a dreary gray light that crept through my shutters and prodded me awake the following morning. With a groan I tumbled out of bed, washed, dressed, and, with the brittle air nipping at me, raced across the garden and into the brewery. My breath streamed in a nacreous mist as I honored the corner crones and, quickly prodding and blowing the glowing embers in the kiln into flames, sang the ale into life long before the rest of the house was astir.

Ignoring my pounding head and the lassitude that made it difficult to raise my arms, to drag one foot before the other, I found little pleasure in my tasks. Tobias's words of the night before came back to me. If I failed, then I would never brew again, but, if the brewing proved to be successful, well, perhaps I'd be doing it for a very long time . . .

Pushing aside my physical discomfort, I picked up the ale-stick and imagined the corner crones winking at me. If this was to be my destiny, then I'd best get on, regardless of how I was feeling. Christmastide was approaching and the demand for ale would grow tenfold over the period. I intended to take advantage of this by increasing production. Standing over the mash vat, pushing the ladle through the grain-tea, knowing there was still wort to boil and malt to dry, I finally conceded, as Adam and Will joined me, that I would need to employ extra people as soon as possible. It was too late to take advantage of the hiring fair, so I would have to spread the word through town. It would be hard to find someone now, as those who'd been unsuccessful finding employment would head to Norwich, London, Gloucester, and other centers to seek work before the winter set in.

Looking a little worse for wear, Tobias appeared mid-morning. Waiting for a ship from Exeter to arrive and take them to Rotterdam, he and Sir Leander were in town for at least a couple of days, and his master had allowed Tobias some free time till then. Quashing my surprise, I happily accepted Tobias's offer of help, and asked him to carry the sacks Master Perkyn had delivered earlier into the brewery. I also had him stoking the fire and even allowed him to stir the mash while Adam poured the heated water into the tun and, after he'd done that, to rake the grain. After a while, I wandered over to the malthouse door and, wiping my hands on the apron, leaned against the doorframe. Watching my brother in his bare feet with his sleeves rolled and his hose hitched, I noted his broad shoulders and flushed cheeks.

"Where's Sir Leander?"

Focused on hefting the sprouting grain, Tobias didn't answer immediately. "Not sure. We had some unexpected visitors early this morning and he left the house in a hurry. Didn't say where he was going, but I suspect it was to the docks."

Grateful the man hadn't thought to accompany his squire again, I threw myself into my tasks.

Before lunch, another three barrels of ale were filled and shifted to where the temperature was more constant. I was enjoying a drink of small ale, thinking how much having one set of additional hands helped, when Iris burst through the brewhouse door.

"Mistress, mistress, I'm sorry, I couldn't stop—" Before she had the rest out, she was pushed to one side. In her stead stood Hiske. Discarding the mourning attire we still wore, she was clothed in a dress of the highest fashion. A deep blue with long, cutaway sleeves and a matching hood, it shed years from her. A furred cape was tied under her chin and a small purse dangled from a gloved wrist. Married life evidently agreed with her; she looked better than I ever recalled.

"*Ja*," she said, her eyes sweeping the room, her face screwed up in displeasure as she took in my patched kirtle, stained apron, and unruly hair. "I always suspected you'd find your level."

Adam drew himself upright, looking to me for instructions. Anger radiated from him. Squatting in front of the kiln, Tobias was but a silhouette; Hiske hadn't spied him.

Stifling my dismay, I placed my cup down on the table and wiped my hands on the apron around my waist.

"Cousin Hiske," I said. I made no move to welcome her. "I didn't expect to see you."

"Well, I didn't expect to find myself here." With a loud sniff, she came down the steps and into the brewhouse, tut-tutting the entire way. "What would your father say, Anneke Sheldrake, if he could see the depths to which you've stooped? You, who dared turn up your nose at my offer and chose instead to become a common brewster. I can inform you now, your brother is most unhappy."

"There's nothing common about brewing, Cousin Hiske, as well you know. Not only did Mistress Margery Kempe from Bishop's Lynn run a brewery, but Mother's family have a long and respectable history—"

"*Respectable?*" She gave a mocking laugh. "You always had a way of coloring things in such favorable hues. I was only saying to your brother yesterday that I think you'll find your father was determined to erase that particular brand of *respectability* from your past. He was always so ashamed that your mother's roots were so . . . so . . ."

"Attached to yours?" finished Tobias, sauntering from the shadows.

Hiske recoiled. "M . . . Master Tobias . . . I didn't . . . I wasn't . . ."

"I can guarantee, Cousin," continued Tobias, ignoring her stammers, "that when Father sought your services, he neither believed he was sheltering a thief nor someone who would exploit my sister's grief for her own ends." He shook his head and stood, legs apart, studying our cousin. Pride filled my heart.

Hiske's eyes widened and she took a step back. "Master Tobias . . . Tobias . . . Forgive me. I didn't expect—"

"To see me here? That's evident." Tobias threw the rag upon which he was cleaning his hands to one side, narrowly missing the mash tun and came to stand by me. Together we faced the woman who'd been my torment ever since Mother died.

"Just as *I* didn't expect to see *you*, once I saw the state you left the house in, never mind my siblings. It's only my sister's sense of family obligation, an awareness of the humiliation your crime would bring upon the family, that prevented her calling the sheriff. Peculiar you didn't mention what occurred during our delightful chat yesterday."

Even in the dim light of the brewhouse, I could see Hiske's cheeks color. Her eyes shifted from side to side and she swallowed.

"I merely took what I was owed—" she began.

"You took whatever you wanted, Cousin Hiske," I corrected, emboldened. "Waiting until there was no one present who could call you to account."

Blustering, Hiske tried to find words and failed.

"And for the record, there's nothing common or otherwise about my sister, my mother, or our family," said Tobias. "Furthermore, Anneke has my support in this—as well as Lord Rainford's. I ask that if you can't respect the Sheldrake name, you at least respect that."

Something flickered across Hiske's face. Ribbons of ice unfurled in my stomach. Did she know about Tobias's parentage? Would she say something? Could Hiske be that cruel? I held my breath.

Regaining her composure, Cousin Hiske sniffed. "Whether or not someone is perceived as common is not something that you or I decide, Tobias Sheldrake. About the family or ourselves. That's a verdict the court of the townsfolk will proffer and which, as I warned your sister, you too may yet suffer."

I understood then, God be praised, Hiske didn't know.

Tired of her negativity, I wanted Hiske and her spiteful insinuations gone. "Why are you here, Cousin Hiske?"

Peering into the mash tun, Hiske chose her words. "I couldn't credit it when, at mass this morning, the talk outside St. Stephen's was not of Martinmas, but of the new brewer. They were saying how men flocked to her house like bees to pollen, how they remained drinking until well into the night, abandoning hearth, home, and families—and on Martinmas—unable to resist the unnatural temptations this flame-haired siren offered. I didn't need to be told. I knew exactly whom they were discussing. I simply couldn't believe you'd be so foolish as to destroy all your prospects; ruin your father's reputation as well as your own so readily. I had to come and see for myself." She looked me up and down with a calculated deliberateness, her upper lip curled. "The fruit doesn't fall far from the tree—"

"Don't!" I strode toward her, fury propelling me. Hiske butted up against the wall. "Don't you dare, Hiske Jabben." I glared at her, furious. "You'll not denigrate my mother's name ever again with your sly words and poisonous tongue. Thank the dear Lord I don't have to put up with them or you anymore."

"Oh, as much as I'm loathe to disappoint you, Cousin, I'm afraid that's not true," said Hiske. "And, for the record," she sneered, "it's *Mistress Makejoy.*"

"What do you mean?" My fingernails dug into my palm. Sweat trickled down my back.

"I mean that, you'd best get accustomed to my presence. Under orders from Lord Rainford"—she looked at Tobias— "my husband is checking your books as we speak, so both Master Makejoy and I will be frequent—"

"He's in the office? Alone?" Without waiting for further explanations, I pushed past Hiske, who stood sniggering, and ran through the garden into the kitchen. Deep in frantic conversation, Blanche and Iris broke apart as I entered. "I know, I know!" I said, holding up a hand. I darted down the passageway that joined the kitchen to the hall, bolted through the hall and into the corridor. I had a vague impression of laden sacks in the corner near the shop door, what looked like bolts of fabric, and other goods bulging from the opening, as well as some objects on the floor besides, but didn't pay too much attention. Not when there were raised voices coming from Father's office.

"—he's not here, but I am—and I'm ordering you to hand it over." There was a dull thump and a squeak. "Is *that* clear?" Sir Leander sounded like a man close to losing his temper.

Pushing the door slightly, a very gratifying scene met my gaze. Master Makejoy was pinned to the far wall of the room, the ledger that I'd been using to record our expenses and income dangling from one hand while the other was covering the top of Leander Rainford's, which was attached to his throat. A pot of ink had been knocked over; a quill snapped in two lay on the floor. I gasped and then opened the door wide, letting the men know there was a witness.

Tobias, Blanche, Iris, and Adam gathered behind me. Tobias inhaled sharply.

"Sir Leander, I beg you, please . . ." Master Makejoy's voice cracked. He raised the ledger. "Take it, dear sweet Lord, take it."

Snatching the ledger from his trembling hand, Sir Leander held it over his shoulder without looking around. "Mistress Sheldrake? If you please?" In two steps, I had it safe in my hands. I clutched it tightly.

"How dare you!" shrieked another voice and in swept Hiske. "Let Master Makejoy go!" Outrage made her skin blotchy and her eyes flashed.

Taking his time, Sir Leander released Master Makejoy, who

found his feet and, doubling over, coughed and then spat into the fireplace. He sank onto a stool, loosening his surcoat at the neck.

Hiske threw her arms around her husband, raising a furious face toward the nobleman. "You may be Lord Rainford's son, but you've no right to treat one of his employees that way! Wait till your father hears about this."

Her voice shook, but I admired her bravery. I didn't imagine many would confront Sir Leander, let alone threaten him. Looking at the tender way she held Master Makejoy, I wondered if she really did love this strange emaciated man.

"My mistake. I first thought your husband a thief and set about preventing him taking what I believed was Mistress Sheldrake's property," said Sir Leander with great calm.

Hiske's eyes became mere slits.

"The fruit doesn't fall far from the tree," said Tobias for my ears alone. I coughed.

"You attacked me!" Master Makejoy was hoarse. "My heart is pounding fit to burst."

Hiske made some soothing noises. Behind me, Iris stifled a noise of disgust.

"Well, it was an honest mistake." Sir Leander cocked an eyebrow at me, his meaning clear. "The room is dark and, hearing noises, I look in to spy a man I don't recognize sneaking about. Well, what was I to assume? Speaking of which, there's a mystery I'm hoping you can help me solve, Makejoy."

"My lord?" Master Makejoy rubbed his throat.

"Imagine my surprise when Tobias roused me from a very comfortable slumber this morning to inform me there were men outside the house waiting to pick up some property they'd been sold."

Hiske drew herself up, one hand still attached to Master Makejoy's shoulder. "I can explain, my lord."

"Oh, I'm sure you can, Mistress Makejoy, and I look forward to hearing what you have to say." Sir Leander rested his elbow upon the mantelpiece, poking the fire with the end of his cane. "Especially since the servants were at a loss as to clarify how my father's private house suddenly became the equivalent of a merchant's shop—selling everything from quite unique curios, I'm reliably informed, to larger objects such as rugs and tables."

I gasped. Behind me there were dark mutters.

"I can explain *that*, Sir Leander," said Master Makejoy weakly.

"And I would like to hear your account as well, Makejoy. Facts are, I told these men that what they sought to buy were in fact stolen goods and they'd better leave before I sent for the sheriff."

Master Makejoy groaned and buried his head in his hands. Hiske didn't move.

The smile left Leander Rainford's face. "What I want to hear from you, Makejoy, or your wife, is how you came to be in possession of such property."

Hiske flashed a look at me. "It's mine."

"Indeed? That's not what I've been led to believe, Mistress Makejoy. In fact, I was given to understand that it was taken unlawfully."

"Unlawfully?" said Hiske. "*Nee*. Not at all. I was merely ensuring I was paid in kind for services rendered. Isn't that right, Master Makejoy? Especially since it was clear that my cousin Joseph's estate could no longer guarantee my wages." I marveled that she could meet my eyes, let alone Leander Rainford's.

Master Makejoy rose unsteadily, tugging his shirtsleeves and faced Sir Leander. "That's right, my lord. Everything Mistress Jabben"—Hiske elbowed him in the ribs—"I mean, Mistress Makejoy, took was to compensate for wages owed while she lived under this roof and served as the Sheldrake children's guardian. You have to understand, Master Sheldrake promised Mistress J . . . Makejoy a great deal more than she ever received. So much so, one could argue she came to this country under false pretenses. We did nothing illegal."

"And one could also argue, Makejoy, that your wife has, how shall I say this? Overestimated her worth."

At the look on Hiske's face, I had to turn away. I knew well the false pretenses to which Master Makejoy alluded. There was a time when Hiske hoped she'd be the new Mistress Sheldrake. The day I learned this and confronted her, laughing at her temerity, was the day my torment began. Father only ever saw her as a guardian, not as replacement for Mother. His lack of desire to take the relationship further had nothing to do with me, despite what Hiske believed. Cruel as it was, she had overestimated her worth. Pity for the woman knocked against my heart. But not, God forgive me, for long.

"So," continued Sir Leander, "I've arranged a discharge on the difference as I see it."

Master Makejoy reached for Hiske's hand and gripped it. Her cheeks looked pinched; her lips had disappeared.

"At first, I thought of notifying Father and seeing what he wished to do. After all, some of it is his property. You might recall that on Master Sheldrake's death, the house reverted back to his ownership and thus responsibility, at least until new arrangements were made." He shot a glance at me. "The fact that we've now been implicated in a crime by becoming a storehouse for stolen goods will no doubt irritate him. He'll be more than displeased. Imagine if the sheriff should find out? I wonder who Father might see fit to punish?"

Master Makejoy fell back onto his seat. Hiske visibly paled. "Oh, there's no need to inform his lordship, Sir Leander, or the sheriff." He tightened his hold on his wife. "You're right. We could well have overestimated what my dear Mistress Makejoy was owed."

"What have you done with my . . . with the goods, my lord?" asked Hiske.

Sir Leander gestured to the door. "Some have already found their way back to their rightful home. Tobias, you'll find that pennant you coveted and some other items of interest in a sack in the hallway."

"My lord," said Tobias with a huge grin and a wink to me.

"Mistress Sheldrake, I believe there are some ewers, an unusual bronze mazer, candlesticks, rugs, tapestries, a Bible, a book of poems and even some cushions among what was retrieved."

"My lord." I curtsied.

So that was what I saw sitting against the wall. I took a deep breath, trying not to reassess Sir Leander. If actions and words maketh the man, as Father Clement preached, why was this one such a contradiction?

"The larger pieces will arrive later today," said Sir Leander, with a reassuring smile at Saskia, who clasped her hands together and smothered a whoop of joy. Behind me, she whispered orders to Iris and Blanche, who scurried down the corridor. From their muffled exclamations and the sound of dragging, the sacks were taken to the hall. I lowered my chin to hide my smile, shaking my head.

Hiske knew better than to speak. There was a moment of uncomfortable silence.

"I'm glad we've reached accord then," said Sir Leander finally, offering Hiske the most amiable of grins. "Once more, my humblest apologies for the error, Makejoy; Mistress Makejoy." He helped Master Makejoy to his feet, brushing down his jacket. "I swear by all that's holy, I didn't recognize you, what with this fine fabric, the white shirt—not a mark upon it. Not like the man I remember at all." He glanced at Hiske. "Your wife knows how to ensure a stain doesn't linger to cause comment or draw disapprobation, doesn't she?"

"Aye, she does," said Master Makejoy, a look of confusion upon his face. Ensuring his surcoat was straight, he smacked his hands together, casting Hiske urgent looks. "When your father instructed me to continue to look after the accounts at Holcroft House after Sheldrake's death, I was under the impression I'd be answering to your brother, that Sir Symond was responsible. I was clearly mistaken."

Sir Leander's eyes narrowed. "It's also my understanding that it's Symond's role, but since he's attending the king's daughter's betrothal at Westminster, I can substitute for the time being. In these circumstances, we'll have to agree, one Rainford is as good as the next." His lips tightened and a muscle in his cheek began to twitch.

"Of course, of course, my lord. When you're ready to depart Elmham Lenn," continued Master Makejoy, unaware of the effect his words had, "and if you wish me to check the books until your brother is able, you've only to ask and I'll arrange to inspect them—by appointment," he added hastily.

"How long do you think you'll be staying?" asked Hiske.

"Not long," I answered, at the same time as Sir Leander said, "As long as it takes," his gaze alighting on me briefly, a twinkle in those sapphire eyes.

I looked away.

Using his stick, Sir Leander lifted the cloak Master Makejoy had lost in their tussle and passed it to the factotum, who snatched it, wrapped it around his shoulders, and then, fitting his cap, mumbled a farewell.

"Good day to you, my lord. Master, Mistress Sheldrake. Come, Mistress Makejoy."

Cousin Hiske, quite unable to believe that she'd been so firmly reprimanded and made in some measure to account for what she'd done, was frozen in place. I couldn't help it, I felt a small flicker of pleasure and, I admit, gratitude toward Sir Leander that yet again, he had set something wrong to rights.

"Don't you look at me like that, Anneke Sheldrake," snapped Hiske, refusing to leave the room. "With that witch-gaze of yours."

Stepping back so she and Master Makejoy could pass, I didn't dignify her words with a response.

When she reached the doorway, Hiske turned and with a cold deliberateness examined me from top to toe. "You think you're better than me, Anneke Sheldrake, you always have. But you're not. Certainly not anymore. I'm a married woman and you're nothing but a . . . a . . . *brewster*."

She may as well have said slattern and we all knew it. Well, I'd been called worse and by so-called better people.

Tobias made a quiet noise that sounded like a growl. Hiske ignored him.

Master Makejoy tugged at his wife's sleeve. "Come, dear, there's no need for this—"

"No need?" she spat. "There's every need. Someone has to tell her!"

"Tell me what?"

"What they're saying in town."

"I suggest you leave, Mistress Makejoy." Sir Leander used his cane to indicate the door.

Hiske braced herself against the frame. "They're saying that it won't be long before you're selling more than ale here . . ." Her eyes flashed to Sir Leander. "But perhaps they're wrong, hey? Perhaps you've already started . . ."

With a swish of her skirts, Hiske fled. Master Makejoy trotted after her, casting a fearful and apologetic look over his shoulder.

Tobias followed. There was the chime of the shop door and heated words. Adam discreetly went after them.

Remaining in the cold, dark office beside me was Leander Rainford.

"Don't," I said, before he could open his mouth. "I know what you're thinking." Tying the boards, I slid the ledger back on the shelf.

"You might be surprised."

I could feel tears building—tears of rage and sorrow. But, God be damned, I wouldn't let them fall in front of this man. I needed to get out of the office before they did. "You've already made it clear what you think of me and I doubt what my cousin said will have changed your mind."

"They were just words," he said softly, stepping toward me, his stick slipping slightly on the wood.

I spun to face him. He was closer than I expected. "That's a fine jest coming from the man who wielded one with such venom upon our first meeting." Wetness struck my cheek and I swiped it away, all good intentions to thank him forgotten. "To you, maybe, they're just words, but to a woman, as Hiske so kindly pointed out, they're what her reputation is built upon."

I went to leave but, as I brushed past Sir Leander, he grabbed my arm.

I glanced at where he gripped me. He pulled me closer. By God he was strong. "Then make your cousin eat hers," he said quietly.

I held his eyes, my chest tight, my body burning, then shook myself free. "And you, my lord, what about you?"

"Me too," he said. "Make me eat mine."

I paused at the doorway, glancing back at him over my shoulder. "Not good enough. I want you to choke on yours."

Before he could respond, I took off down the corridor and into the main hall. My heart was pounding, my face flamed. Thank the good Lord no one was about. I leaned against the wall. I'd never spoken to anyone like that in my life. What was it about this man that he made my temper flare to the point that I forgot both caution and etiquette? What about the gratitude I owed him, owed his family?

Shutting my eyes, I took a deep breath and released it, opening the fists I'd formed and shaking my hands in an effort to ease the tension in my body.

No matter what Sir Leander made me feel, the dark humors he managed to unleash, as God was my Lord and Savior, I would offer him thanks.

By Ninkasi and the crones, I would.

Pushing away from the wall, I opened my eyes and headed to the brewhouse.

Just not today.

# EIGHTEEN

❧

HOLCROFT HOUSE

After the Ides of November to St. Catherine's Day

*The year of Our Lord 1405 in the seventh
year of the reign of Henry IV*

*T*hree days later, on a blustery autumn morning, Adam, Saskia, Captain Stoyan, the twins, and I waved farewell to Tobias and Sir Leander from the docks. Their cog, the *Lady Caragh*, a large vessel about eighty feet in length with cargo ranging from sheep and horses to wool and tin, cut across the placid waters of the harbor and into the churning seas beyond the heads. I confess my heart was in my throat as we watched their sails disappear over the horizon. They would be reunited with the *Sealhope* in London, and from there cross to Flanders.

On my return to the house, I was pleased to see Will and Blanche already looking after patrons in the shop. First ensuring the children started their lessons, I then went to the brewhouse.

By lunchtime, another batch of ale was cooling in the troughs, malted grain was spread across the trays ready to be dried in the kiln, and there were two brimming sacks to go to Perkyn Miller for grinding. As Adam strained finished ale into kegs, I thought how pleasant it had been having Tobias and, surprisingly, his master helping to make ale.

"Fancy such a fine gentleman offering his services and working so hard? And in here?" Adam shook his head in wonder. "He's not too proud, like some. That foot of his doesn't seem to be much of a liability either. Master Tobias boasted it's never been one—in battle, on horseback, or at sea. It's others who underestimate Sir Leander because all they see is an affliction. Yet my lord acquitted himself very well." As Adam praised Sir Leander, my mind drifted.

It was easy to underestimate my lord, but not only for the reasons Adam gave. Who'd have thought he'd be so willing to help indeed? Memories of Sir Leander toiling by my side were as fresh as the ale being poured behind me.

When Tobias first dragged his master to the brewery, I was angry and confused. Understanding that my mood would affect the ale, I pushed aside my misgivings and listened as Tobias justified their presence by arguing if I wanted his support, then he had the right to know exactly what I was doing. Interpreting Sir Leander's silence as complicity in Tobias's scheme, it also occurred to me that he was likely to report what I was doing back to his father, so I determined to demonstrate the seriousness of my intentions and the level of industry involved. I treated Sir Leander like the others, asking him to perform the same roles and to the same exacting standards. Convinced he wouldn't last the morning, I was astonished when, after breaking fast, he was the first to rejoin me in the brewhouse.

"If you could tend to the malthouse floor, my lord, I'd appreciate it," I said over my shoulder, loading wood into the kiln and blowing gently on the kindling.

"Certes," said Sir Leander, then hesitated.

Aware he hadn't moved, I turned around, my brows raised. "Just grab the rake over there, remove your footwear, and I'll show you what's needed in a moment. Adam will take over as soon as he's returned from Master Thatcher's."

I bent back to my task, feeling the first risings of antagonism that he should hesitate to do as I asked, when it occurred to me I'd been insensitive. The sprouting grain formed a mat of roots that became quite tangled and hard to separate, and he needed balance in order to heave the grain—how could he do that with his twisted foot, let alone a cane? I turned to retract my order only to find him almost upon me.

"Mistress Sheldrake, I feel I owe you an apology."

Sir Leander stepped even nearer and, all too aware of his closeness, of how large he was, I tried to resist the urge to create space between us. Was it the long-overdue thanks I'd finally and awkwardly proffered him the day our furniture was returned that prompted this? Steadying my breathing, I closed the metal door of the kiln just as the fire roared and rose slowly, dragging my sooty hands down my apron. Moisture dusted his dark cape, glistened in his black locks, a muscle in his jaw twitched. I don't think I'd noticed before the smooth, golden quality to his skin. There was a scent of warm velvet, musky cologne, and something else. My heart skipped. I prayed the heat in my cheeks would be attributed to the kiln.

"When we first met," he began, "I'm afraid my temper had the better of me. I allowed idle yet vicious gossip and my own assumptions about . . . well, I allowed my prejudices and, I admit, that of your cousin, to color my judgment of you. I called you an unforgivable name and for that, I'm deeply sorry. I do beg your forgiveness."

Unable to credit what I was hearing, I was caught unawares. Ready to trade barbs, the sincerity of his apology quite undid me. I grabbed the ale-stick. I needed to hold something, to be prepared for the distraction activity offered.

"I still find it difficult to credit, my lord, that you would think Tobias had such a sister as you assumed me to be."

Sir Leander made a soft noise that might have been a laugh. Resting his cane against the wall, he undid his cape, leaned against the trough, and folded his arms. "I didn't think. Tobias would only ever speak about you in the warmest and most respectable of terms over the years. When we arrived in Elmham Lenn and he learned what you were doing, never mind what your cousin told him, he was shocked; I was as well. On top of discovering what your father did; what mine . . ." He paused and studied the floor a moment. "I only sought to protect him, to lash out at those who I perceived had hurt him."

"You thought me capable of hurting my brother?" I regarded him incredulously.

"Your father did . . . It was not a huge stretch to assume another Sheldrake might as well."

*He was right. It wasn't.*

"I would never . . ." I began, then shut my mouth. Despite my best efforts, acrimony bloomed. I released the ale-stick and with one hand on my hip, directed a finger toward his chest. "That doesn't excuse what you said. That you thought to call me such a name."

Before I could prevent him, he swept my hand into one of

his. I tried to withdraw it, but he tightened his grip and stared, daring me to pull away. His touch was warm, strong. With his thumb, he gently stroked the back of my hand.

"I told you, I didn't think. That's my problem. When I discovered the terms of the contract you made with my father, that you agreed to work for him should this fail"—his gaze took in the brewhouse—"well, let's just say, when I then set eyes on you . . ." His thumb rested warmly against my flesh. I forgot to breathe. "I jumped to less-than-savory conclusions about the kind of work to which my father might put you, assuming your . . . complicity if not initiation of such an arrangement. It wouldn't be the first time Father has . . . taken advantage of a Sheldrake."

"You thought I— That he . . . Oh . . ." My hand went limp in his and I released my breath, unable to continue. I was shocked, ashamed. Sir Leander assumed I was like my mother, that I'd succumbed to his father's charms—worse, that I'd bargained my own away. My body was afire with indignation, humiliation, and emotions I couldn't understand. Part of me wanted to run from his sight, but another part wanted to defend both my character and my mother's. Only I didn't know how. And truth be told, while he caressed me in that absentminded way, I could barely think. My knees were weak, my resolve to confront him more so. What a sorry and unfair impression we must have made as a family. As far as he was concerned, my mother was a whore and my father, instead of punishing her as most husbands would, or seeking justice, had struck a devil's bargain with the man who'd cuckolded him, turning his shame into some kind of business arrangement that ensured the entire family was ruined. How could I expect Sir Leander to understand it when I did not?

The fire crackled, the kiln was hot against my back.

"Can you forgive me?" he asked softly, stooping slightly so our faces were level.

For a fleeting moment, I glimpsed a different man. The man who fearlessly strutted the timbers of a heaving ship despite his affliction, who, according to Tobias, was brave and foolhardy in battle, and accustomed to making quick decisions and being obeyed. This was the man who watched over my brother.

Sensing my hesitation, he raised my hand to his lips. Wide-eyed, I stared as they pressed against my skin, tender yet ever so firm. His lashes were long and dark, his hair shiny. I sucked in my breath; it was as if a spark ignited deep inside me. He kissed my hand again, this time, answering it with an insistent grip and turning his face ever so slightly so his cheek, for just a fleeting second, rested against the back of my hand. Shocked at such an intimate gesture, once more I tried to extract my hand. This time, he released it slowly, drawing out the moment, and looked at me with an expression I couldn't quite read. I brushed my other hand against where his lips had touched, where his cheek had momentarily lain. A flicker of a smile crossed his face. Ah, I understood. Sir Leander had used this ploy before.

Others may have accepted an admission of error, his heartfelt apology.

I was not others.

"I cannot," I said finally.

Sir Leander took a step back and blinked. If I hadn't been so serious, I would have laughed at the owlish expression on his face. Few denied this gentleman.

"I can't forgive you," I continued. "Not yet. It was a harsh, cruel word, my lord, callously and thoughtlessly delivered. It hurt me deeply. I cannot dismiss it from my memory simply because you bid me do so. I am not my mother, Sir Leander, neither am I my father to strike a poor bargain, and I perceive your apology to be one. You haven't yet paid the price of your rudeness, not according to my accounting." I raised my finger to prevent him speaking. "But, to prove I'm not completely without reason, there's something I can do—I can give you another chance."

He began to smile.

"Only one," I said, holding a finger steady to make my point.

"That's all I need," he said, and, with a toss of his head and a smile that creased his eyes and dimpled his cheeks, threw his cloak over the table, spun around, and headed to the malthouse. Shucking off his boots, he scooped up the rake with his cane, wielding it like a sword as he descended the steps.

It was some minutes before I resumed my work.

After that, things changed between us. As each hour passed, the tightness I felt between my shoulders, the hum of slow-burning anger that Sir Leander's presence generally presaged, transformed into something else.

Two days later, the ship from Exeter arrived and they were gone.

And so it was, in the days after we bade Tobias and Sir Leander farewell, Saskia, Adam, and I were doing the work that had for a short time at least been shared among five.

⋘⋙

For all the warnings about the friary, that townsfolk would be too afraid to purchase from me lest they offend the abbot, these past weeks had seen the ale walk out the shop door almost as soon as the bushel was hung. I'd begun to take orders as well.

Good as his word, Master Proudfellow not only sold my ale, but spoke to the other innkeepers in town, persuading them that if they all offered some of my brew as well as the friary's, then not only would they be unlikely to be punished, but they were helping everyone's business. I now brewed ale for the Gull's Rise, the Crown and Anchor, the Pickled Herring, and the Bull's Head, inns close to the docks. Master Proudfellow said there were more wanting to order, but they were being cautious, waiting to see if there were consequences for the others. I was relieved, for it was all I could do to keep up with demand.

It was St. Catherine's Day when Father Clement came to visit. I was on my way from the kitchen to the brewhouse when the hounds alerted me to a visitor. Waving with joy, I went to greet him, calling out reassurances to the dogs, only slowing my pace when I noted the two black-robed men accompanying him. What were they doing here? My heart began to hammer. I wiped my hands on the apron.

"God give you good day, Father Clement." I smiled, my expression quizzical.

"You too, Mistress Sheldrake," said the Father. "May the Lord shine blessings upon you." With a look I interpreted as apologetic, he introduced me to his companions. "This is Brother Osbert, the sub-prior of St. Jude's. Brother Marcus here is the cellarer." There was a slight quiver in his voice. For certes, the friary had sent some powerful men to me.

"Sirs, by God you are welcome," I said, granting them a curtsy, hoping I didn't sound as concerned as I felt.

"Mistress Sheldrake," said Brother Osbert, a portly man with a ruddy complexion and intelligent eyes. "Forgive this unexpected visit. His grace, Abbot Hubbard, has asked us to present a business proposition to you and, as we were in Elmham Lenn to oversee the St. Catherine's Day mass, we thought we'd take the opportunity. We pray this is a convenient time. Is there somewhere we can talk?"

Surely, my ears were deceived? "The abbot wants to do business with me?" The hairs on the back of my neck stood to attention.

"That he does." Brother Marcus nodded affably, a too-wide grin splitting his face, spoiled only by the fact he was missing many teeth and the smile didn't reach his eyes.

Before I could respond, Adam stepped out of the brewery, wiping his hands on a balled cloth. The dogs were still barking fit to bring down the heavens, and with a frown he shut them in the stables before joining me, his boots crunching in patches of remnant frost.

Introductions were made and with some reluctance, I led the brothers back to the house. As we passed the brewhouse, the door blew open and the rich aroma of mash and wort wafted over us.

"This is where you make your delicious ale?" asked Brother Osbert, stepping forward and peering inside.

Reaching past him, Adam wrenched the door closed and gave a curt nod. "It is."

"You've tasted it then?" I asked the brother.

"Ever since you first brewed, we've tasted every batch," said Brother Marcus with that fixed smile. "Marvelous how you manage to keep such consistency."

"Indeed," said Brother Osbert. "It's almost unnatural." His easy manner didn't deflect the sense of peril his words aroused. But all I could think about was that they'd tasted it and wanted to place a business proposal before me. Could Captain Stoyan be wrong? Was the friary not my enemy but, like Lord Rainford, a potential business partner?

"Please, come this way, brothers," I said quickly, trying not to let my growing excitement show. "Let me assure you, there's nothing unnatural about what I do. After all, this is ale we're talking about."

"Ah, but ale can lead to many interesting conversations, don't you find, Mistress Sheldrake?" Brother Osbert increased his pace so he walked beside me. "Just when you think you're discussing one thing, it becomes another matter altogether." He gave a laugh, an odd, high-pitched trill. "Who knows what we could end up considering?"

Brother Marcus chuckled. Adam, Father Clement, and I didn't join in.

I knew then I didn't want these men anywhere near the twins or my home, not until I could ascertain whether they were a threat or offering a flag of truce. Instead of leading them into the kitchen, I diverted by the vegetable garden and to the front of the house and the shop. As we passed the stables, the hounds' barking increased.

Will was in the shop finalizing a purchase with Master William Larkspur, owner of the Crown and Anchor.

"God's day to you, Mistress Shel—" began Master Larkspur, touching his hood. When he saw the brothers, his eyes widened. Turning back to Will, he quietly gave final instructions, and I steered the brothers toward a table near the hearth. The brothers made much of warming their hands and backs, pushing back their deep cowls, untying their mantles. Mixing his greetings and farewells, Master Larkspur practically ran out of the shop, his head low, his hood up. He didn't look back.

Asking Will to bring drinks, I invited the men to sit around the table. Adam sat next to me on one side, the brothers from St. Jude's with their backs to the fire on the other, while Father Clement sat at the head.

"See to it we're not disturbed, would you, Will?" I asked as he set down the pitcher with a terse nod. He went outside and took down the bushel, latching the door when he came back in.

Pouring the brothers some ale, I waited till they had the first drink before speaking. "I confess, I'm most honored to receive a visit from St. Jude's."

Brother Osbert put down his mazer and wiped the back of his hand across his mouth. "As well you should be, Mistress Sheldrake. It's not every day we take it upon ourselves to undertake such transactions in person. We have other ways of doing business . . ." His eyes remained fastened to mine for a second longer than was polite.

"So I have heard."

He was the first to look away.

Taking another drink, he studied the mazer. "Uncommonly good," he murmured.

Brother Marcus drained his and then gave a hearty belch. "May I?" he held up his empty mazer. I refilled it.

"I will get straight to the point," said Brother Osbert. "I detest those who prevaricate, play games and whatnot, and I hope you will extend the same courtesy to me."

I bowed my head.

"The reason we're here, Mistress Sheldrake—" he said, waiting until I'd topped his drink as well. A creamy foam wobbled prettily. Brother Osbert watched the motion, his tongue wetting his lips. "—is that we're very impressed with the quality of your ale. So, it seems, are many others. So much so, despite contracts whereby various businesses promise only to buy from the friary's brewery, some inns and taverns as well as hucksters are buying yours. Risking fines and much more, they're prepared to forgo the goodwill of those they've been dealing with for years—and for what? For this." And he lifted his drink.

All eyes were upon it.

"We've chosen not to pursue their bad faith through the sheriff or the courts. Instead, we wish to improve what *we* make. For that reason, we wish to buy your recipes. The ones you use to make this ale and any others besides."

I sat up. Whatever offer I'd been expecting them to make, it certainly wasn't this.

"My recipes?"

"Come now, Mistress Sheldrake, don't be coy. We know you follow a recipe or a number of them." Brother Osbert gave me the sort of smile you might give a contrary child. "There are quite a few people who can attest to this."

"You misunderstand, brother. I do not seek to hide the fact I follow recipes, from the Low Countries, no less; I'm just surprised you would wish to buy them."

"You call yourself a businesswoman"—he could have been discussing chamber pots—"and yet you express surprise that the major competitor in your trade wishes to reduce the effect your product is having on their profits by creating something similar? Why, this happens all the time! A dyer notes another's shade and how popular it's become and immediately emulates it. Tailors and cobblers spy the latest fashions and do likewise. Does trade stop for one or the other? On the contrary, they share in the profits. That's what we wish to do, share the profits that are coming your way."

I stared at Brother Osbert, unable to credit what I was hearing. Not only did I find it hard to believe that in just a few weeks of trade I was impacting on the friary's profits to such an extent they sought to copy what I did, but that they were so open about it. The idea they'd been following my progress made Master Perkyn and Captain Stoyan's warnings seem like clarions. These brothers took their brewing—and the consequent coin—very seriously.

Well, so did I.

"So, will you sell us your recipes? We're prepared to pay a fair price."

Aware of Adam and Father Clement's eyes upon me, I took my time answering.

"First of all, can I just say I'm honored to be so approached and by the greatest brewers in Norfolk." Brother Osbert's look said even he knew flattery when he heard it. "I feel humbled and blessed by the good Lord that you would make such a proposal." I drew my shoulders back and placed my hands flat on the table, my arms straight. "But, I'm afraid my recipes are not for sale."

Brother Osbert gave a bark of laughter. "I don't think I heard aright."

"Forgive me, brother, but you did. With all due respect, the recipes are not for sale."

"You have not even heard our offer."

"I do not need to. It won't change my response."

Standing in one swift movement, the brother rocked the table, spilling ale across the surface. Brother Marcus rose to his feet and so did I. Father Clement remained seated, his hands clenching his tankard like a lifeline.

"You would deny the friary? Abbot Hubbard?"

"You made the observation yourself, Brother Osbert; you wondered that I call myself a businesswoman. Well, I do. That and more besides. I'm responsible for my family, for their welfare, and for that, I need good coin. If I sell you my recipes, then not only will you be able to produce my ale, but you would also be able to make it in greater quantities and thus sell it at a cheaper price. Your comparison to dyers, tailors, and cobblers is a just one, good brother, but only if they are the same size business. We are not. You're a large producer, I'm simply a humble alewife seeking to gather loyal custom."

Brother Osbert's eyes narrowed. "Oh, you're attracting more custom than an alewife, Mistress Sheldrake, and it's disingenuous of you to pretend otherwise."

"Perhaps," I said with a small smile. "But it's disingenuous of you, good brother, to pretend that selling my recipes won't affect my trade. It will end it and I cannot afford that. However," I continued as his face reddened and a vein on his forehead pulsed, "the friary can afford to be magnanimous. There's room in Elmham Lenn for both of us and, if I may be so bold, more besides."

He drew back, a cat about to pounce, then stilled. Turning to Brother Marcus, he snapped, "Fetch our mantles, brother."

Snatching his from the smaller brother, Brother Osbert swung it across his shoulders, knocking his mazer over, nodding in satisfaction as what remained of his ale gurgled into the rushes. Gazing pointedly at the waste, he gave a crooked smile.

"Is that your final word, Mistress Sheldrake? Do I tell the abbot you refused his generosity? His effort to reconcile our competing businesses?"

Adam stood up, hands balled by his sides.

"It's my final word, Brother Osbert, but while I will not hand over my recipes, I do extend my goodwill and wishes for God's many blessings to the abbot and the brothers of St. Jude's."

Brother Osbert held my eyes for a long moment before striding out of the shop, striking the latch off the door as he did. Brother Marcus flashed a look of disgust mingled with regret.

"Don't bother following," he said to Father Clement. "It's evident where your loyalties lie," he spat.

"My loyalties are, first and foremost, with God," said Father Clement, stumbling to his feet. Brother Marcus sneered before he followed the sub-prior. The wind caught the door as they exited, slamming it against the frame.

We watched them storm off as snow began to fall. They looked like crows with their black capes and mantles flying out behind them.

I sank back onto the bench. Only now did I fill my mazer and drink.

Adam and Father Clement returned to their seats and tossed back what remained in their cups. Adam poured a generous amount for us all.

"You did well, Mistress Anneke, standing your ground against them."

"You're right, Adam," said Father Clement. "If you'd sold them the recipes, Mistress Anneke, it would have spelled the end of your brewing. They'd have undercut you."

I stared out the window, the image of the brothers' righteous indignation in my mind. It was clear they thought their proposal would be readily embraced, that they would not be denied. Yet like Peter the apostle, three times I'd denied them. My head sank into my hands. From where did such courage or foolhardiness come?

"Even if they had the recipes, they couldn't make the ale the way I do . . . they don't understand. But I couldn't give over Mother's recipes. I just couldn't. Not to them, not to anyone. They're for the family, no one else."

Adam touched the back of my hand gently. "It's all right, mistress, it will be all right."

"Will it?" I asked, raising my head. Again, my eyes followed their angry tracks in the muddy snow. "I'm not so sure. If I didn't have an enemy before, I do now."

# NINETEEN

*J*ust over a week later, we had another unexpected visit, this time from Master Perkyn and Olive. A soft snow was spiraling from the heavens, the pale morning light still trying to force its way through thick clouds. I was in the brewhouse and had only completed the ceremony to the goddess and crones moments before there was a knock on the door. When I saw the Millers and took in the expression on their faces and Olive's poor swollen eyes, I let out an exclamation and ushered them into the warm, bringing them close to the kiln.

"What is it? What's happened?" I asked. They didn't speak, but stared at the floor, the snowflakes on their capes melting in the heat.

"It's broken, Lady Anneke, it's all broken," wailed Olive finally, throwing an arm up over her eyes, resisting her father's efforts to comfort her.

I looked to Master Perkyn, confused and concerned as I untied Olive's cape and stroked her arms.

"Broken? What do you mean?" I quickly checked the young woman for injury.

"Aye," said her father with a heavy heart. "She's right, mistress. It's the mill. Some bastard's gone and taken an axe to it, ain't they? That and more besides."

*Oh dear God.*

"Forgive me, mistress," said Master Perkyn, "I didn't know where else to go."

"You did the right thing coming here. I'm glad you did." I threw Olive's cape over the table and scrambled for a kerchief, dabbing at her cheeks as best I could while her face remained buried in the crook of her elbow, immovable. "When did this happen? Thank the good Lord you're both all right. We'll get to the bottom of this." Words tumbled out of me. I felt at a loss to know how to comfort them. They needed to talk, but they also needed something to warm them, they were both shaking with cold and shock. "Do you want to come to the house with me or wait here? I'm going to fetch some warm wine and blankets."

Master Perkyn looked at Olive. "If it be all right with you, mistress, I'd as soon stay here. Olive, you see, it's been—" He couldn't finish.

I squeezed his arm in understanding and pushed the kerchief into Olive's fist. Her fingers tightened around it and she lowered her arm to peep at me.

"I'll be as quick as I can." Swinging my shawl around my

shoulders, I ran to the kitchen, set the servants to pouring drinks and finding blankets, and then searched for Adam. He was in the shop. I quickly told him what had happened. Dropping the paper on which he'd been recording our sales, he followed me back to the brewery.

A couple of hours and some wine, ale, and bread later, Saskia, Adam, and I had the story from the Millers. Huddled around the kiln, Olive snuggling into me like a cold cat before a fire, her father told us what happened.

During the night, the dogs had woken them, barking fit to wake the dead. Not able to see anything in the dark, and hearing nothing himself, Master Perkyn went back to bed. It was snowing heavily and bitterly cold outside and he could see no reason to venture out.

"But I should of, curse my lazy bones," he said. "For when I went to the mill this morning, it was to find the door shattered, my stone smashed, and the ropes cut. To add insult, some bastard pissed—and worse—in the grain that was stored there, and that includes yours, Mistress Sheldrake. I'm afraid your next crop of barley is ruined." He buried his head in his hands. "Ah, of all the boils on Satan's bony arse . . ."

Adam and I exchanged a long, level look. Saskia patted his back helplessly.

What would motivate someone to damage the mill? The Millers were not only popular in town, but hurting them affected so many other lives, not just mine . . .

My hand flew to my mouth. Could it be? Surely not. Was Abbot Hubbard behind this? The friary? After all, everyone knew Master Perkyn ground my malt. The monks wouldn't do this, would they? It was so . . . so ungodly. But then, Master

Perkyn himself had warned me about the abbot, Captain Stoyan too. Brother Osbert had intimated I'd regret denying him. Adam's face confirmed my suspicion.

After tierce, I left Saskia to manage the brewhouse while Adam and I returned to the Millers' to examine the damage. The door to the mill was a shredded mess. The odor of urine and excrement was overwhelming. The slashed sacks of grain, their insides spilling over the floor, evoked the aftermath of a battle or, more accurately, murder. A fine dust of flour floated in the air, coating everything, including us. But the worst by far was the sight of the great millstone hacked about until its shape was distorted so as to render it useless. The thick ropes that helped turn the waterwheel were severed. The spaniels, who'd been locked in the house, ran around sniffing in the corners, growling, their tails down. We watched them for a moment in silence. A cold draft blew around us.

"I think you'd better fetch the sheriff, Perkyn. See if he can locate the culprits—more than one person was involved, for certes." Adam paced around the stone, shaking his head, pointing at a set of footprints in the flour. "Someone wanted to make sure you were out of business."

"That they did and, if my suspicions be right," said Master Perkyn, sinking onto a stool, "they wanted to make sure you were too."

"You think this was the work of the friary?" I asked.

"Aye, and so do you, if I be reading those looks you've been exchanging with Adam here and the way you're worrying your lip. I believe the abbot paid someone to make sure you couldn't get your malt ground." He rubbed his hand across the stone and particles fell onto the dirt floor. "He may have promised your captain he wouldn't interfere with you direct, mistress, but I'm guessing that makes me and anyone else who associates with you fair game. After this, no one will dare touch your malt, no matter how much you offer to pay them. And without your malt, you can't brew."

"We'll do whatever we can to help you, Master Perkyn," I said. "It's the least we can do."

"I knew you would," said Olive, giving me one of her radiant smiles.

Master Perkyn wagged a finger at me. "I appreciate the offer, mistress, and I'm not too proud to accept. But this ain't your fault, and I won't have you taking blame for such vile deeds." He sighed. "I knew what I was getting into when I agreed to help you, and while this is a setback, I can't say I'm sorry."

"You can't?"

Master Perkyn turned to me, a twinkle in his eye. "Think about it." His arm described an arc. "This . . . this destruction means your ale is affecting the friary's sales; you're getting under their skin worse than a hairshirt and what with all that blustering, praying, and self-righteousness, things must be mighty uncomfortable over there."

I couldn't help it; I smiled. "Are you going to convey your suspicions to the sheriff?" I asked. "About the abbot?"

Master Perkyn gave a gruff laugh. "Nay, mistress. It wouldn't do any good if I did. Remember what I told you? Sir Grantham, well, he'd fuss around for a few days, maybe raise a hue and cry, but in the end, it'd be for naught. The friary is untouchable, isn't it? Sir Grantham and the abbot go back a-ways, don't they? Whatever we may wish, the brothers don't answer to the likes of you or me. They answer only to the highest authority."

He pointed toward the ceiling. He cast one more look around. The cheeky grin he'd worn briefly dissolved, replaced by a look of utter misery. The damage and the smell were more than he could bear. He lowered his head and studied the space between his boots. Olive stood next to him, swaying, one of the spaniels in her arms.

I found Master Perkyn's hands and clutched them in mine. "God is on our side too, you mustn't forget that."

Master Perkyn raised weary eyes to mine. "Is He, mistress? At the moment, it feels as if He's deserted us all."

❦

God didn't forget us, despite Master Perkyn's misgivings. Less than a week later, Master Perkyn appeared at the brewhouse door again, this time equipped with a huge smile and a cart.

"God give you good day, Master Perkyn." I emerged wiping my hands. The last few days, Adam had been working with him trying to source somewhere to mill our malted barley. Master Perkyn's suspicions had been correct: thus far, no matter how much we offered to pay, we'd been turned away. Down to the last of our milled grain and with sacks of malt ready to be ground, I was sick with worry. If it wasn't milled soon, I would be forced to sell it to someone else, and the only other brewer in the area who could afford to buy the quantities I possessed was the friary. Stubbornly, I refused to be beholden to them.

"What brings you here?" I asked, wiping my hands and waving to Olive, who ran toward me.

As she threw herself into my arms and planted a wet kiss on my cheek, I was delighted to note her radiance had returned. Not that it ever stayed away long.

"We have a stone, Lady Anneke! We have a new stone."

"Is this true?" I looked to Master Perkyn, who was tying the horse to the post outside the mews.

"Aye, mistress, it be true." He strode across the yard, his boots slicing through the newly fallen snow. His twinkling eyes and his gap-toothed grin lifted my heart. "I've come to pick up your malt and take it with me. You are the first of my customers. Actually, you are the last as well—you're the only one." He jerked a thumb back toward the cart. "The others won't deal with me. Won't say why, but I know. Can't say I blame 'em either."

"But a stone? How?"

"Perkyn," said a deep voice beside me, "I see you're back in business."

"Adam," said Master Perkyn, nodding. "I am indeed. Seems our talk with Master Baker wasn't a waste after all. After we left, Hugh had a think and came to see me after dark. Turns out, he had a spare. It's smaller than what I'm accustomed to, and has a few chips in it, but it'll do. We fitted it yesterday, on the quiet, like. And I managed to buy some ropes from your friend, the captain at the Hanse. They're not as thick as those we had, but again, they'll do until such times as I can replace everything properly."

Olive enfolded me in a huge hug that I returned. "Oh, Master Perkyn, this is wonderful." I turned a shining face to Adam. "See, I told you. If we all just work together, if we show we won't be defeated, work around the obstacles he throws at us, the abbot cannot quash us."

Adam and Master Perkyn looked at each other, then at me.

"Well, Mistress Sheldrake, it's nice to hear your optimism, but I'd still proceed with caution. Let the friary wonder how your ale is still reaching customers. Let's not be too hasty re-counting tales of triumph to further anger the abbot, hey? I promised Hugh no one but you would know where the stone came from."

I nodded. "Of course. You're right." I smiled at them uncer-tainly. "Come on then, let's get those sacks on the cart. If there's one thing I've learned over the last few days it's that no matter how hard I might wish, it doesn't mill itself."

⇜⇝

As if to affirm our triumph, sales of ale steadily increased as Christmastide grew near. We could barely keep up, limited as we were by the size of the brewhouse and our equipment, and how many of us were free to make it. Additional hands were now a priority. But just as more coin poured into the little tin, so too household expenses grew as the weather became colder and the days shorter. After he left us, I discovered Sir Leander had ordered and paid for enough wood to last us the entire winter, telling Adam that if he was to continue to enjoy our hospitality, then he too wanted to be warm. He also ensured we had a ready store of meat, fish, and grain, organizing supplies from Scales Hall to be delivered whenever possible.

But despite Sir Leander's generosity, wood became scarce and we were forced to buy extra quantities and scour the forest for fallen boughs. Then there were the coal, candles, blankets, and furs to replace worn ones and those that were never returned after Hiske's sweep of the house. Tools used in the brewhouse had to be replaced, new barrels made and old ones repaired, the children needed new clothes and boots, and the general up-keep of Holcroft House all severely dented profits. Pennies left our coffers as fast as we earned them and, not for the first or last time, I was grateful for the kind help Captain Stoyan and Sir Leander provided. Without their contributions to the ale-making and Holcroft House, any notion I had of making the lease payment would have been impossible. I'd less than four months left, and even though the brew was doing well, firkins, kilderkins, and barrels being sold weekly, it was at wholesale prices. The innkeepers and tavern owners were the ones who really profited from my ale. If I was to make this my occupation, draw enough money from it to support the family and keep the house, I needed to reconsider how to make brewing pay.

Just when I thought the friary might leave us in peace, Brother Osbert paid another visit. It was the Conception of the Blessed Virgin Mary and we'd not long returned from mass. This time, another monk accompanied him. Introduced as the Master of the Novices, Brother Francis was a stooped, wizened man with almost no hair and a badly scarred face. Like Brother Marcus, he allowed Brother Osbert to do all the talking, positioning himself near the fire in the office and latching his pale eyes onto mine. It was most disconcerting.

Once more, Brother Osbert offered to buy my recipes, only this time he proffered a sum of money that quite took my breath away.

"Twenty pounds?" I repeated, certain I hadn't heard aright.

The brother nodded.

Adam's eyes bulged and he cleared his throat. Why, it was more money than we could ever have imagined.

For as long as it took an angel to flap his wings, I was tempted.

Not only would I be able to meet the lease payment for this year and the next few besides, but I could pay our debtors and even put aside some money for the beginnings of a dowry for Betje. I could also ensure Karel was either squired or apprenticed. But then I thought of my mother's recipes in the monks' hands, in Brother Osbert's, which were twisted together in his lap, the knuckles white. I thought of those long pale fingers shuffling the papers, annotating the pages, fiddling with the ingredients. Then I thought of the ale itself and the corner crones. I could see them now, crouched in the brewery, frowns puckering their ancient brows as they grimly awaited my decision, ready to scold me before they vanished forever. I couldn't betray my mother, my family, my heritage by selling these recipes. Not to the monks. No money was worth that.

Ready to tell Brother Osbert my decision, I cast a glance at Brother Francis. Leaning forward, those gimlet eyes fixed upon me, there was a look on his face of such need, such desire—not for me, but for what they'd come fully expecting to walk away with—that I knew my decision was right. If the friary was prepared to pay so much for these recipes, then they expected to make a great deal of money from them. Well, so could I.

"I'm afraid my answer remains the same, good brothers."

"You refuse?" Brother Osbert fell back in his seat and blinked. "Twenty pounds is a fortune. Think what you could do with such a sum."

"I have, brother. Believe me, I have." I pushed myself away from the desk and stood. Brother Osbert also rose, his brow darkened. "But if they're worth so much to you, imagine what they are to me."

"We'll give you thirty," said Brother Francis quickly.

I inhaled sharply. "My answer is still no." Adam gave me the barest nod of approval. "They've been in my family for generations, brothers. They're part of a long-standing tradition. They're not something I can sell for others to use. I hope you understand."

"You foolish woman. So be it," said Brother Osbert and, before Adam could reach it, he wrenched open the door. With one long look at me, Brother Francis brushed past his superior and left. Brother Osbert hesitated.

"Denying the friary is akin to denying God, Mistress Sheldrake, and in my experience, those who don't obey the Holy Father are severely punished for their sins. I suggest you pray that He sees fit to forgive you before you too pay the price of denial." His look was unmistakable. Releasing the handle, he exited, his boots loud on the floorboards.

Propelled by fury and a sense of indignation, I followed him into the corridor.

"Forgive *me*?" I called after their backs as they entered the shop. "My conscience is clear, brothers, but what about yours? God knows the truth, He sees what's in our hearts, in our words and actions, even when we try and abjure them."

Before he reached the front door, Brother Osbert spun around. "Are there no bounds to your sins, woman? First, you deliberately challenge the might and right of the friary with your Low Countries ales, then you deny us the recipes, even when, in good faith, we offer far more than they're worth. But now, now"—he drew himself up to his full height, his black gown and broad shoulders blocking the door—"now you presume to lecture *me*, God's emissary on earth, about spiritual matters." He shook his head and pointed at me. "Hubris is a sin and by your very existence, you have made it a mortal one. Your day of reckoning will come, mistress. You'll not see where or when, but it will."

Lowering his arm, his chest heaving, he departed.

The anger left me as fast as it came. I swung to Adam, who stood close behind me.

"You made an enemy today."

"They were already that. But now I see through the mask they wear; I see my enemy for who and what they are."

Adam cocked his head. "God's emissaries have many faces, Mistress Anneke."

"And so do the devil's," I whispered. "Sometimes, I fear, they're one and the same and telling them apart is nigh impossible."

# TWENTY

HOLCROFT HOUSE
Early to mid-December
*The year of Our Lord 1405 in the seventh
year of the reign of Henry IV*

*W*ork in the brewhouse all but enabled me to push Brother Osbert's visit and the friary's threats to the back of my mind. Even so, I kept the recipe book close and, as the need to refer to it decreased, I took the precaution of hiding it in the chest in my room again. I couldn't say why—it was instinctive. Fortunately, I didn't have time to dwell on the repercussions of my refusal of the brothers' offer. There were orders to fill and thirsty customers to serve. The days passed in a flurry of activity, not even the icy winds and constant snows of winter slowing us.

Though I'd made up my mind we'd need additional hands, I hadn't had time to locate anyone suitable. What brought Master Westel Calkin into my orbit, I did not know. It was not God. God could not be so cruel or unforgiving. All I know is that if Westel could speak, it would be to deplore that he ever set eyes

on Holcroft House, let alone on Anneke Sheldrake. But whatever he'd bemoan, it would be nothing to the regret I live with
to this very day.

For everything that happened, the memory of Westel rests
heavily on my soul . . .

Iris brought him to the brewhouse mid-morning on a Friday,
not long after I'd returned from listening to a very long sermon.
Aware valuable time had been lost, even if it was in service to
the good Lord, I was more than a little annoyed at being interrupted. Rather surly and red-cheeked from kneeling by the
kiln, I stepped out into the crisp air, dusting palms on my apron.

"What is it, Iris, this is not a good time," I rebuked, and then
saw the unfamiliar face. "Oh, can I help you?"

Iris bobbed a curtsy. "I'm sorry, mistress, but this gentleman
here is looking for work."

Discommoded that the one thing I needed but had procras-
tinated over was suddenly forced upon me, I didn't respond
straightaway. I studied the person before me. Perhaps a year or
so older than me, the man was cleanly if simply dressed; his coat
patched, his cap worn, and his boots scuffed. Carrying a sack
that I imagined contained his possessions over his square shoulders, he regarded me with large blue eyes, eyes that brought to
mind the frailty of a bird's eggs and bleached summer skies.
Ashen-skinned, he had an unmarked complexion, a chiseled
chin, and a full but firm mouth. Clean-shaven, his fingernails,
which I noticed as he pushed his cap back on his head to reveal
thick white-gold hair that reminded me of Mother's, were nicely

shaped but stained black. Was that ink? Certainly, his hands did not look like those of a laborer.

"God give you good morning, Mistress Sheldrake," he said, with a little bow. "May the Lord bless and keep you well." His voice was deep, melodic, like the angels'. "My name is Westel Calkin." He gave me a big smile, flashing creamy, even teeth, and it felt as if the sun had sprung into the sky and chased away the clouds. Reaching for the wall of the brewery, I steadied myself, wondering at my momentary dizziness. "I've been traveling awhile, seeking work, and I heard from the father next door"—he jerked his head in the direction of St. Bartholomew's—"that there may be some going here."

"There might," I said cautiously, unable to prevent the smile that tugged at my lips. "What kind of work do you do?"

"Anything, mistress. I am strong and willing."

"You can't ask for much more than that," said Iris.

I silenced her with a look. She mumbled something and buried her chin in her chest.

"What I need is quite specific . . ."

"I've a reference," he said, fumbling in his pockets. "I know my letters and can read passably well too." Pulling out a piece of parchment, he handed it to me and I noticed his hands were shaking slightly. My heart went out to him. It was a bitterly cold day and his garments appeared thin.

"Come, there's no need to do this outside. Iris, how about you take Master Calkin to the kitchen and let him warm himself before the stove? I'm sure Blanche can find a hot drink and some bread to spare? I'll join you in a moment. May I keep this till then?" I asked, holding the reference.

Master Calkin smiled even more brightly and a look crossed his face that I failed to fathom. "For certes, mistress."

Iris didn't need to be told twice. Chattering away as if Master Calkin were already employed, she led him through the garden to the kitchen, shoving the pigs out of the way with her boot, pointing out the various buildings as she did so.

I went back inside the brewhouse. "Well," I said to Adam and Saskia, who looked up at my entrance, "it seems God may have provided."

"In what way, Mistress Anneke?" asked Saskia.

Standing near the window, I unfurled the parchment and scanned it. The writing was very fine, the ink nice and dark.

"In a practical one," I said slowly, reading what turned out to be a reference from the second sub-prior at the Priory of St. Rebecca's in Norwich, one Brother Roland le Bold. "He has seen fit to bring us those extra hands we needed."

Adam came and read over my shoulder. "The lad is seeking work, is he? Educated by monks, is he?"

I glanced up at him. "I know what you're thinking, but he hails from Norwich, St. Rebecca's, Adam, not St. Jude's."

"That's run by Benedictines too," said Saskia, frowning. "You don't think—"

Adam shook his head. "I'm not sure what to think anymore."

I sighed. "I think I can't afford *not* to hire someone. Christmas is almost upon us and if I don't do something now, well—" I waved the reference in the air.

"What if he's been sent by the abbot to undermine you?" asked Saskia.

"Or worse," added Adam.

I thought of Master Calkin's beaming smile and his spun-gold haïr. "He doesn't look like the kind who would stoop to such measures."

"You of all people should know you can't judge a person by their looks," said Saskia.

"I know, I know. But this"—I flapped the paper—"appears genuine. It has a seal and all." I put the reference on the table and leaned on my elbows, staring at the words. "I can't let fear of the friary and the abbot cloud my judgment or affect my business decisions. If I do that, then they've defeated me already." I straightened and looked around. The kiln was roaring, the mash tun was full, the malthouse floor had a new crop ready to be dried and the trays were laden with cooling barley. Rows of barrels sat, some empty, others waiting to be taken to the shop, to be moved to the warehouse for storage, or picked up by customers. "We need a pair of willing hands, and that's just to start. Master Calkin's here and able. Anyhow," I added quickly, as Adam opened his mouth to speak, "what if everything he says is true? Certainly, this testimony is glowing. If I don't take him on, then he's being punished as well and that doesn't seem fair."

"It's probably not. But it's sensible." Adam picked up the reference and reread the contents. "Says here he has excellent skills with figures."

"Mentions how trustworthy he is as well," I muttered.

"You could give him a trial." Saskia went to the tun and proceeded to stir the wort. "Mistress, that tray needs to come out of the kiln." She nodded toward it.

I raced over, grabbing the cloths off the table as I did, wrapping them around my hands.

"Aye, a trial. We could all watch him," said Adam. "First sign of anything suspicious, he goes."

Lifting the smoking tray out, I heaved it onto the table, waving the steam out of my eyes, peering at the golden grains. "Shall I hire him then?"

"*Ja*," said Saskia, stirring the wort earnestly, her face red.

Adam nodded brusquely. "I'm not happy about it, but I don't think we have a choice."

"We don't," I said and went to rescue the second tray from the kiln before my barley was burned. "After I've moved these, I'll go to the house and tell him the good news."

❧❧❧

In exchange for a shared room with Will on the topmost floor, meals, and a small wage of a penny a week, Master Calkin fast became the most valued member of my brewing team. Whereas Adam, Will, Saskia, and the other servants who would occasionally help had other duties that would take them from my side, Master Calkin was dedicated to helping me alone.

From cock's crow to first stars, he labored, doing whatever I asked of him—even running errands in town. In only a matter of days, if the twins needed me, or Betrix paid a visit, I felt confident enough to leave him in the brewhouse, knowing it was in good hands. Sunday was his day off, but he left the house only to attend services next door before returning and begging to be given something to do. When he'd been with us six days, I decided to test the veracity of his reference and make use of his gift for figures.

Each week, Adam and I would calculate the cost of the grain so the ale-conners could set the price at which we would sell each brew. Deducting the cost of the tax and the other debts we had to pay, including a seller's fee, we were still managing a profit,

albeit one that didn't go very far. Nonetheless, I wasn't ashamed
to let anyone see my books. Still a long way from covering the
rent for the months leading up to Hocktide, I either had to raise
the level of production or seek other ways of selling my ale to
widen distribution. That my ale was of a quality unfamiliar to
those in town was without question. Many were keen to try it
but were reluctant to buy their household supplies from me instead of the friary. Rather than purchase a barrel, a hogshead, or
more, they risked only a flask here, a firkin there, perhaps a few
jugs, even though, as they would whisper to Adam or Will, they
longed to buy more. Some would choose to drink mine in the
inns and taverns, rather than buying it from me and risking the
wrath of God and the abbot. Master Proudfellow and the other
innkeepers attracted so many patrons they could sell both the
friary's ale and mine. "But it's yours they ask for, Mistress Sheldrake," Master Proudfellow would reassure me when he came
for more stock. "St. Jude's is only drunk after yours has gone."
The reports from Master Larkspur were the same.

The only exception was the Millers, who, since their millstone was destroyed, continued to drink small quantities at the
shop—Master Perkyn explaining that it was best he kept to old
habits and thus allay suspicions. So, though I paid them in kind
for grinding our malt, giving them a firkin every week, they
would make an almost daily pilgrimage for a jug or two. Olive
would enter the shop, squealing with delight, twining her hair
around her fingers, flirting with Westel and Will and, in her
unabashed way, remonstrating with customers that they didn't
purchase more of my ale, calling them fools and toadies. Not
even her father's threats or my entreaties could silence her. As
for the patrons, they weren't offended, they simply indulged

her. After all, as Simon Attenoke noted, you shouldn't punish someone for speaking God's truth.

If I could sell my ale directly to more people, even in smaller quantities, then I might be able to meet my debt to Lord Rainford. In the end it was Master Calkin who voiced the solution staring me in the face.

He was in the office, checking my calculations and jotting down sums, adding to the stains that already coated his fingers. These, he told me, were the result of years of copying manuscripts. I watched him scratching away with the quill, muttering to himself, and exchanged a look with Adam, who was clearly impressed. Behind me, the fire crackled; outside, the snow fell silently.

Westel raised his head. "I know you're concerned about your figures, Mistress Sheldrake, and, at the rate you're going, you'll be hard-pressed to meet the lease payment. But I think I know a way around this."

"You do?" I placed my elbows on the desk. "What's that, Westel?"

"Well, I've been talking to Master Proudfellow and the other gentleman who owns the tavern down around the square—"

"Master Peter Goddard of the Thistle and Whey?" said Adam, joining me at the desk.

"That's him. And it seems to me, you've only one choice if you want to make real money from brewing."

I knew what he was going to say. The same idea had been going around and around in my head for weeks.

"You must turn the shop into an alehouse."

A warm, not unpleasant feeling sped through my body. "An

alehouse." There. I'd said it. I could hear Tobias's protests; the disapproval of Hiske, Father, Mother—admonishments that beat against my fevered mind. I brushed them aside. "Go on . . ." I said, my heart pounding.

Sitting opposite, Westel began outlining what we needed to purchase, how much extra ale would be needed to meet demand and how the household could be arranged to accommodate the new business, referring to his notes as he did.

"Iris could serve, as could I. And while I'd be loathe to ask you to perform such a common task, Mistress Sheldrake, until folk know about it and we can afford to hire someone else, it could work in our favor."

"How do you know so much about this?" I asked.

"The monks who raised me also brewed." He shrugged. "All us orphans had to help sell what they made. Brother Roland, my mentor and friend, supervised. He taught me everything I know." He gave me his incorrigible grin and I found myself responding.

Adam frowned and shook his head but, caught up in the excitement that my debt to Lord Rainford might be extinguished so quickly, I ignored his doubts and, drawing closer to Westel, began to make plans. God forgive me, but pride and more blinded me that night. *See*, my eyes and mind sang, *we trusted this man, refused to let the friary crush us, and this is how we're rewarded for that faith. Faith in God and faith in ourselves.*

"An alehouse is very different to a brewhouse, Mistress Anneke. So is how it's perceived—how *you* will be," warned Adam. "You need to think of your reputation . . ." I shooed him away. I didn't want to hear, not that I would have listened anyway, not once I saw what kind of profit and security such a venture could bring. Reputations, especially my own, were the least of my worries.

Turning away to tend the fire, Adam didn't join in the conversation, but he listened. We would open an alehouse in the new year, after Twelfth Night. I committed myself to brewing enough ale to satisfy the customers I hoped our new premises would attract. Organizing expenses for the next few weeks, a small part of me dwelled on Adam's words. I was glad neither Tobias nor his master were there to make me heed my steward.

# TWENTY-ONE

HOLCROFT HOUSE
The week before Christmas
*The year of Our Lord 1405 in the seventh
year of the reign of Henry IV*

Christmastide was less than a week away. Learning that Captain Stoyan was back in town, I invited him to join us for supper. Not only did he bring ale from Germany, but also a large sack of hops.

"Straight off the ship," he said. "If you store it in a cool place, which you'll have no trouble doing at this time of year," he added, brushing the snow off his shoulders as he entered the house, "it will keep for months. In fact, providing it's dried properly, sometimes the longer you leave it, the better it tastes." He lifted the jugs of beer and placed them in Will's arms. "But you'll see for yourself."

I didn't admit that I hadn't yet had the chance to try the smaller sack of hops he'd given me, but was determined to try both, and soon.

Retiring to the solar after the twins were put to bed, Captain Stoyan and I tasted the hopped brew of the Germans, and while at first I found it bitter and quite dry, after a few mouthfuls, I enjoyed it very much. The recipe would have to be adjusted for local palates, accustomed to much sweeter beverages. Captain Stoyan said beer was all that was drunk throughout the continent and, he added, was slowly growing in popularity in London.

"Even your king enjoys a beer. Developed a taste for it when he did the reyse, that crusade of his to Lithuania." My ears pricked up. If the king enjoyed beer . . . "But your brewers' Mystery are fools," continued the captain. "They insist if a brewer makes hopped ale, that must be all they produce. If they make ale, they're limited to that as well. They want no mixing, no confusion." He gave a spurt of mocking laughter. "No one is confused but them. After all, why can a brewer not make both?"

"That makes no sense to me either," I said. "Surely, offering customers choice and quality is what we should be concerned with. Why would the Mystery even worry themselves over such trifles?"

Captain Stoyan rubbed the tips of his fingers together. "There's only one reason—the same reason parliament became involved in the concerns of ale-makers in the first place. Money."

The captain was right. Though I'd only been brewing a few months, I was shocked at how much of our profits went to pay this tax and that official. Restricting what someone could brew so charges could be levied was just another way for pockets to be lined—the pockets of anyone but the brewers. Leaning back in the chair, I stared into my mazer, swirling the amber ale around.

"It would be so easy to make both—to sell both."

"Why don't you?" said Captain Stoyan, leaning forward, the

candlelight making his eyes glimmer. "At least, until the Mystery find out what you're doing."

I stared at him thoughtfully, ignoring the creasing of Adam's brow. The captain had a point: Why didn't I? As an unmarried woman, let alone a small producer, no guild would admit me. They'd take my hard-earned coin in taxes and other tithes, send the ale-conners and monitor my sales, but they would never acknowledge me as an official member. What obligation did I carry to follow their rules? Sitting up straight, my heart beating hard, my fingers became restless. I put down the mazer. Why didn't I sell ale *and* beer? At least that way, if the beer failed to appeal to customers, I still had the ale to fall back on. I didn't need to make too much to start with, just a firkin or two. Opening an alehouse provided the perfect opportunity to test the beer, introduce it to customers, allow word to spread. Plans began to form in my head. Nothing was stopping me doing this—not directly . . . not yet.

Staring out the window into the blustery night, watching the snow strike the pane and stick to the glass like thin little hands, I determined to revisit my mother's recipes and, as soon as possible, learn how and in what quantities to add hops to the wort.

"You're right, Captain Stoyan." I raised my cup to him. "There's no reason not to—no good one, anyhow. So, here's to hops . . ."

"To fine ale *and* beer," added Captain Stoyan.

Reluctantly, Adam lifted his cup.

With excitement and some nerves on my part, the very next day, as the wort was boiling, I added hops to the mixture. The sharp aroma of mint fused with sour notes of wild grass enveloped me. It was heady, strong, wild. My mother also recommended, as a way of offsetting the bitterness, that honey be included. I added some dried elecampane as well. While I knew apothecaries recommended it to assist with eyesight, Mother always said there was something wholesome and honest about the plant and the flavor it released was sweet and pleasing.

Watching me from the doorway of the malthouse was Westel. I sensed he was annoyed that I hadn't asked him to help make the beer. Bombarding me with questions when he discovered I intended to use hops, his interest was at first gratifying, but, after the umpteenth inquiry, grew tiresome. Preferring to keep my experiments to myself, I set him a task that would remove him from the brewery for a time. It wasn't that I didn't trust him, not exactly; it was simply that there were some aspects of making ale I wasn't yet ready to share with anyone, not even Adam. Having finished fetching wood, Westel, barefoot from wading through the malt, now loitered nearby.

Passing me the elecampane, Adam hesitated. "Are you sure you want this, Mistress Anneke? Legend says this only grows where tears fall."

My hand paused. "Tears don't only mean sorrow, Adam. They can also fall for joy."

Westel made a noise, but whether of agreement or dissent I was uncertain, and when I turned to ask him, he was back in the malthouse, bent over the rake.

Before I could change my mind, I took the elecampane, broke it between my fingers and threw it in.

"Let's hope you're right," muttered Adam.

A few days before Christmas, we tapped the troughs and

filled two firkins and, much to my surprise and delight, a hogs-head with beer. Adding hops meant that we didn't need to use as much malt as we did when making ale, and so produced more than twice as much for less grain. Though we used more wood, this was more than offset by the saving in malt. Due to lack of storage space, we were forced to place the barrels atop the central table. I couldn't go past them without stroking the aging wood, sending a swift prayer to the goddesses that they bless this new enterprise.

Whether it was my imagination or the peculiar mist that hovered about the yard, wrapping the brewhouse in spectral fingers as I entered before dawn each day, I thought I heard and felt something respond. Raising my head to peer through the window at the gray skies and watching the flurries of snow strike the panes, I smiled and shut my eyes before thoughts of the abbot and an image of Brother Osbert intruded: *Hubris is a sin, and by your very existence, you have made it a mortal one. Your day of reckoning will come, mistress.*

"Mistress Anneke, are you all right?"

My eyes flew open and in my fright, I slipped on some liquid spilled near the trough. If Westel hadn't caught me, I would have fallen. Waiting for me to find my balance, he kept his arms around me. I became aware of him in a way I hadn't before. The hardness of his body, the way his mouth curved, making two lines on either side of his cheeks; I noticed how straight his teeth were, how clear his eyes, eyes that revealed, even as they bore into mine, so very little. If they were mirrors to the soul, why could I not fathom Westel's?

"I . . . I'm fine, thank you, Westel," I said and found my feet, unsettled by his cold gaze, his warm flesh.

He released me slowly, his smile broadening, and I hoped that he couldn't tell how fast my heart beat or how uneasy I suddenly felt.

"You startled me. I lost my footing," I said, my voice weak.

"I know."

We stared at each other a moment longer.

"What needs doing?" he asked.

Studying his hands where they rested against the brewhouse wall, I hadn't noticed before how feminine they were. Long, tapered fingers, a narrow palm. The ink that had stained them when he first came had long been washed away. Yet they were also deceptively strong; he'd held me as if I weighed no more than a mazer. His arms were sinewy, more rugged than I realized, dusted with that ice-white hair, so different to Sir Leander's. They reminded me of the silvery beech by the river, the one in which a highwayman had been hanged years earlier and left to the carrion birds until he was only bones and sinew.

A shiver ran through me.

Westel was watching me, his mouth curled in a question. My cheeks flamed and I pushed past him to hide my discomfort. Something akin to foreboding shot through my chest and made me catch my breath. The vision of the dead robber had made me giddy. Foolish thoughts were bobbing in my head.

Westel followed. I didn't turn, but I was aware.

Saskia chose that moment to enter. Sensing something at odds, she began talking as if we were mid-conversation.

"I think Westel should attend to customers this afternoon, Mistress Anneke. He can take Iris if Blanche has finished with her by then. It looks like everything is under control in here." She gave Westel a curt nod.

I scanned the brewhouse. Saskia was right. Everything was under control—so much so, I'd be able to send Adam to town to purchase extra mazers, despite the ale-stake being hoisted to ensure the ale-conners knew to be here before the bells tolled none.

I turned to Westel, driving my earlier dread deep inside. Westel was such a boon, I was lucky to have him. *Think where you'd be if he hadn't missed the hiring fair or hadn't possessed the wherewithal to ask Father Clement if he knew of work . . . or if you'd dismissed him believing him to be in service to Abbot Hubbard . . .*

"You can make sure the tables are clean and there's enough stools, and that the barrels are tapped and ready for pouring." Westel nodded and went to leave. "Oh, and fetch the tin from the office. We'll need coin."

"Very good, Mistress Sheldrake." Westel bowed and, with one last look around, strode off, patting his head to ensure his cap was in place. The cap, a worn woolen accessory of faded blue, rarely left his head. I began checking the malting trays.

Saskia rested her elbow on the ladle. "Do you think you might be placing too much faith in him, Mistress Anneke?"

"Too much?" I relieved Saskia of the ladle and began to stir the mash. "What do you mean?"

"I don't know . . . He hasn't been here very long and here you are, letting him wander into the office without supervision, giving him free rein in here . . . allowing him to plant ideas in your head . . ." Like Adam, Saskia was of two minds about the alehouse and, while I assured her it was a notion I'd been toying with for some time, she credited the decision to Westel. "Have you forgotten? He's meant to be on trial."

"That he is. So, what's he done to deserve such suspicions?

He's been reliable, hardworking, and, thus far, has done everything to earn our trust."

Saskia frowned. "*Ja.* True. So far . . ."

"Then surely it's better to have faith than deny it without proof?" Was I reminding Saskia or myself?

Saskia stared at the spot where Westel had just been standing. "Of course . . . you're right, mistress. It's just . . ."

A thread of anticipation tugged the base of my neck. "What is it, Saskia?" I stopped stirring. "Tell me."

Saskia dashed a hand across her forehead. "Nothing, really. I don't know . . . I shouldn't be saying this, but there's something about him that unsettles me—"

"What?" I released the ladle and drew closer.

"You'll think me foolish, but have you noticed the way the hounds never go near him, except to growl?"

I cast my mind back to the times I'd seen Westel near the dogs. Saskia was right, they would circle him like wolves before retreating, snarling, their tails between their legs. Both Adam and I had thrown them out of the hall so their grumblings didn't disturb us.

"That's nothing," I reasoned. "He's still a stranger. Give them time. How can we trust their judgment? They adored Cousin Hiske."

Saskia guffawed. "You're right," she said. "I'm being silly. But he does smile too much. I don't trust anyone who's always smiling. It's not natural."

I snorted. "That's hardly fair. I would rather someone who smiles too much than otherwise." *But when that smile doesn't reach their eyes . . .* An image of Sir Leander drifted across my mind, the way his deep blue eyes sparkled when he was amused, the warmth that could infuse them when he forgot to guard his expression . . . The way he stroked my hand . . .

Together we gazed into the gray-cream sludge in the mash tun. The smell was pungent, smoky. I slipped an arm around Saskia's waist and rested my head on her shoulder. Still preoccupied, I murmured, "Louisa says he can't take his eyes off me."

"For that, I don't blame Westel."

I grew very still. I hadn't meant Westel . . .

Saskia dropped a kiss on top of my head. "Louisa's right. He stares at you all the time. But that's another thing. It's the *way* he looks at you that makes me uneasy."

"How's that?" I asked, relieved she wasn't aware of my slip, enjoying the roundness of her shoulder, the malty smell that emanated from her tunic and apron.

She paused, then whispered, "Like a hungry animal. Like he wants to devour you."

I raised my head and stared at her as a shudder wracked my body—but whether it was of excitement or foreboding, I couldn't tell. I recalled his grip, the vise-like fingers, the hard frame; the way he exuded . . . what was it? Power?

I levered myself away from her. "You're exaggerating, Saskia. Anyway, he was raised among monks. He's not used to women, that's all." *That was it.*

Saskia looked at me as if I'd grown scales. "If you think monks aren't used to women, then you're more naive than one your age has a right to be."

Coloring, I turned and stooped to add kindling to the fire. She was right. The number of bastards Abbot Hubbard sired, let alone those of half the monks at St. Jude's, was local legend. Why would the men of St. Rebecca's be any different? Westel admitted he'd no calling to the priesthood. Could women have been his downfall? It wouldn't be the first time, only most monks chose penance and kept wearing the cassock, enjoying the influence and privileges that came with being part of God's work on earth. If that was his reason, at least Westel had had the strength to admit it. Could that explain the hungry, lingering looks?

As I threw more wood into the kiln, all I knew was that Sir Leander was banished from my thoughts and in his place was Westel Calkin, smiling, hovering, watching . . .

# TWENTY-TWO

### ❧

## HOLCROFT HOUSE
Adam and Eve's Day, the day before Christmas
*The year of Our Lord 1405 in the seventh
year of the reign of Henry IV*

*B*efore we knew it, Advent was over and preparations for Christmastide began in earnest. The remnants of last year's Yule log was found and placed on the hearth beside the new one Adam had cut in the woods; holly and ivy were hung from the beams and draped across the chests and cabinets. Iris fashioned some extra candles, while Blanche began making humble pies and collecting the ingredients for frumenty. Each day brought new smells, sounds, and sights into the house. Blanche outdid herself.

While I had some misgivings about Westel, mostly brought about by what occurred with the monks long before he arrived, as the days rolled by, they diminished. Though he'd only been with us a short time, it was hard to remember the period before he came, we'd become so reliant upon him. Or rather, I'd become reliant. So reliant, I was able to make excuses for him if Will, Saskia, or the twins complained. There were even times, despite his tendency to stare, when I enjoyed his company. He didn't feel the need to fill the silence with endless chatter, nor did he need me to direct him in his tasks, not after the first few weeks. While he still asked questions about brewing or sought my permission before doing something, I felt it was done out of respect and genuine desire to demonstrate interest, to prove his worth. Sometimes, when the wort was settling or the mash had been stirred and the grain tossed, we'd sit before the kiln and share a small ale and talk; it was at these moments I learned a little of the man upon whom I was coming to depend.

Born a bastard, Westel never knew his father and only vaguely remembered his mother, the daughter of a Norwich alderman. She died young, in childbed. Westel was reared and educated by monks, taught to read, write, and more besides, the priory the only home he knew, those within it his family. Believing his destiny lay within St. Rebecca's, a friary known for its hospitality, ale, and wine, it wasn't until Westel had become a novice and was confronted with the reality of making his solemn vows that he confessed to being denied a calling. He was sent away. Cast adrift, but with an excellent reference from Brother Roland le Bold (of whom Westel could not speak highly enough), but little else, he sought his way in the world, following the pilgrim trail from Norwich to Attlebridge, intending to go to London. One day, he decided to let God direct his course and, after spending hours in prayer, deviated to the coast and Elmham Lenn. Arriving far too late for the hiring fair, he instead found work with us. "God provided, as He always does." Westel crossed himself. With the flickering flames of the kiln making his hair and eyes glimmer, he reminded me of the statue of the Archangel Gabriel in St. Stephen's. It too wore a look that spoke of both elation and vigilance.

Knowing what it was like to have expectations dashed only to have them renewed, and feeling great sorrow that he had no one to whom he could turn, his story stirred my pity. Yet he never complained, nor did he judge the monks and find them wanting. "It's God's will," he said, and guilt consumed me that I could so easily question the Almighty when Westel could embrace all His intentions with such grace and goodwill. When I expressed surprise that he felt no calling after being raised within the cloisters, he shrugged.

"I may not have had a calling in the strict sense of the word, not as a brother, but God looks out for me nonetheless. He intends a higher purpose. Of that I've no doubt." He smiled. "He must, Mistress Sheldrake, He brought me to you."

Smiling in return, I shook my head. Watching him later as he whistled over the grain, I believed I should take heart from such convictions.

Apart from the twins and Adam, I'd never spent so much time with another person. From the time the sun rose until it set, Westel and I were together in the brewery. Along with the rest of the household, we shared most meals as well.

I fell into a familiar pattern with Westel. He didn't judge or find me wanting, and after living with Hiske, never mind Father, it was refreshing. When he entered the brewery each morning, only barely disguising his surprise that once more I was at work before him, I would greet him warmly, enjoying the way color flooded his cheeks, how his lips curled and his eyes flashed. If Iris brought food, or if Will or Adam came to report the carter had delivered water, when they left, Westel would raise an eyebrow in my direction and bend back to his task. More and more, I found my eyes drifting toward him and, more and more, I caught him watching me, swiftly turning aside to disguise a look I understood all too well.

A not unpleasant feeling would lodge beneath my breastbone.

There was a lot to be said for intrepid, dependable men who didn't call you a whore upon first acquaintance and who respected your decisions.

Nonetheless, my thoughts would often stroll in the direction of Sir Leander and, in unguarded moments, usually as I was drifting off into an exhausted sleep, I would recall conversations we'd shared or relive evenings spent around the hearth in the main hall. Then I'd remember his apology and my entire body would quicken.

These recollections would force me into wakefulness. Pressing my hands to my burning cheeks, I would sometimes indulge in whimsy, like a younger and more foolish woman—one who believed in knights who rescued damsels from burning castles, or launched a thousand ships to save them from brazen princes dwelling in walled cities; one who believed in love . . .

I would doze off to sleep, a lump of sadness in my throat that fortunately would dissolve by morning.

Westel and I brewed continually, just keeping up with the growing demands of our customers. The extra production meant more coin and thus I was able to employ two extra girls. Delyth and Awel Parry were the daughters of the best farrier in town. Keen to earn a wage, they'd heard I was hiring over Christmastide and found Saskia at the market one day. With their dark, twinkling eyes and smiling mouths they were persuasive. Every morning except Sunday they'd arrive as the sun rose and leave before it set each night, Will or Westel escorting them home. Throughout the day, they chatted nonstop and flirted outrageously with Westel, who would lower his head and focus on his work, answering them with few words and wary smiles. Both were a boon and additional female company. Their presence meant Saskia was freed to supervise the running of the house and monitor sales throughout the day. Thus Adam was able to leave the shop to Saskia and focus solely on the upkeep of Holcroft House and care of our tenant farmers. Will was also able to perform his regular tasks—assisting Adam, chopping wood, managing the pigs and chickens, changing the rushes in the shop, running errands for Saskia and Blanche. I still used him to fetch the water carter when Westel couldn't be spared and to deliver malt to Master Perkyn—Shelby was used to him and Will enjoyed taking the cart out.

Overall, we relaxed into an arrangement that meant each day was much the same as the next. After all the upheavals we'd experienced, I drew comfort from this. Betje and Karel were happily distracted with Louisa and, as Christmas drew closer, she'd take them into town to watch the troupes of players who came from all over, most on their way to either London or Norwich for the season. They'd return before evensong, full of stories about King Herod's treachery, the Three Wise Men, fire-eaters, jugglers, and humming unfamiliar but catchy refrains.

With Tobias and Sir Leander gone, Master Makejoy maintained a weekly check on business so he could provide a monthly report to Lord Rainford and his son, Sir Symond.

Arriving after tierce on Adam and Eve's Day, Master Makejoy didn't even remove his cloak, but promptly checked the figures and scribbled some notes. I sat near the fire as he worked, lost in my own world, enjoying the all-too-brief reprieve from the brewhouse. Adam waited patiently, ready to answer any queries Master Makejoy might have.

"Everything seems to be in order," said the clerk after a few minutes. Keen to leave, he placed his cap back on his head and packed up his few belongings. "I won't be required to do those for a while, Mistress Sheldrake," he said, jerking his head toward the ledgers. "I received a note from Sir Leander. He'll be back for Christmastide, so no doubt he'll wish to check the figures himself next time."

God help me, but my heart kindled.

Westel appeared and I asked him to escort Master Makejoy to the door, Will being on an errand for Blanche. Exchanging blessings for Christmas, I suppose it was unchristian of me not to ask these be extended to Hiske. Master Makejoy made no sign he was offended, bestowing very warm felicitations upon me, and Adam, indeed. Feeling the tiniest bit guilty as he departed, I went to the desk and turned the ledger toward me to see if Master Makejoy had made many annotations. I was about to ask Adam to explain a note in one column, when Westel reappeared.

"Did I hear that Sir Leander will be joining us, mistress?" he asked, peering around the door, his smile very bright. "Lord Rainford's youngest son?"

A hand stole to my cheek and wrapped itself around the back of my neck. My face was warm. The figures on the page momentarily blurred. Without looking up, I answered, "I believe Master Makejoy did make mention." I glanced at Adam. "That means Tobias might be home for Christmas!"

Adam smiled at me. "Indeed he might. Your mother would be pleased to have you all together for this time of year."

My eyes softened. "She would, wouldn't she?" Memories of past Christmases, of Mother making sure Tobias found the bean in the pie so he was king for the day, of singing carols in Dutch, German, and English with Saskia, handing out presents to us all on St. Stephen's and New Year's Day, the delight on her face when she recorded our happiness. Westel cleared his throat. Immersed in reverie, I'd quite forgotten him. "Oh, Westel. Forgive me. Did you want me?"

An odd expression flashed across his face before it was gone again. "You asked me to let you know when the wort came to the boil. It would have been for a few minutes now."

"Thank you. If you could ensure it remains that way, I'll come shortly."

Westel gave a small bow and left. Waiting till I could no longer hear him, I swung to Adam. "And?" I asked, looking pointedly toward the books. "What's the verdict?"

Adam glanced at the figures. The frown that drew his brows together disappeared and his eyes sparkled. "Let's just say, Mistress Anneke, the Lord's blessed us with a fine Christmas."

I threw my arms around him and planted a kiss on his cheek. "We're in profit?"

"That we are." He laughed. "Just. Sales are slowly rising, but we're still a way off meeting costs once wages are paid and we subtract any lease monies. The good news is, we've almost doubled what we were making from last month. That's what Makejoy noted." Closing the book, a finger rested on the cover. He sighed. "It's a good result. Mayhap you might rethink the alehouse?"

Folding my arms under my breasts, I frowned. "Adam, we've discussed this. I'm going ahead. After all, it's not like I have a reputation to protect—just ask Cousin Hiske."

Adam took my chin in his hand and peered at me earnestly. "Anytime Makejoy appears, his wife's words trail after him, don't they?"

I lowered my gaze. "I'm most cross with myself that I allow them to bother me still . . ."

"Don't let that harridan disturb you so, Mistress Anneke," said Adam, aware of my thoughts. "Your mother and, may God assoil him, your father, would be proud of you, alehouse or naught. You've made something from nothing and achieved what many of us, including me, thought you could not."

"What's that, Adam?"

"Kept us together, and for that, Mistress Anneke, I'll be forever grateful." His hand fell away. "Only . . ." He looked aside, releasing me at the same time.

"What?" I asked softly.

"Be careful, Mistress Anneke." He bit his lower lip. "We're so worried about the friary, we forget those much closer can cause a different sort of harm. There are people in town prepared to believe the worst, ready to accept lies even when the truth is standing before them."

I knew what was being said about me throughout Elmham Lenn. My intention to open an alehouse had reached the farthest parts of town, attracting the kind of talk I'd been warned to expect. Anticipating it was not the same as experiencing it, and I found the cruel assumptions of those who'd once regarded me very differently hurt deeply. Whispers followed me at the market like an unwelcome shadow. The servants heard a great deal as well, friendly warnings, jibes, and unkind observations from hawkers and other servants as well, and while they were at pains never to repeat anything lest it cause me injury, I would hear them discussing it.

That Hiske was behind a great deal of the rumormongering was certain. The woman took pride in drawing attention to my shortcomings and let all who came into her sphere know about them.

"Aye, well . . ." I stroked the ledger's cover, my fingertip resting on the calfskin. "I don't know what to do about it, Adam. Worse, I don't think there's anything I *can* do. There are always going to be detractors, especially when we're talking about ale and alehouses. On top of everything, I'm an unmarried woman who has chosen not to seek a union, or take up the position of *companion*"—I grunted—"with my cousin, but to tie herself to a business that's perceived as less than worthy—more so, because I'm female." Adam opened his mouth to argue, but I lay a hand on top of his. "It's all right. You warned me of this and you were right. My choices mean I'll always attract this sort of gossip. I have to learn to live with it." I applied pressure to his hand. "You know what makes it easier to bear? You. You, the twins, Saskia, Blanche, and everyone else." The sweep of my arm encompassed the entire house. "You know the truth. You know me. And that's all that matters."

*It has to be.*

Adam's eyes looked glassy in the firelight. "That we do. And I thank the Lord for it. Every day."

Ignoring the tear that trickled down Adam's cheek, I blinked back my own. I *was* blessed. Despite what Hiske said, what the townsfolk wanted to think, I knew differently. In my heart, in my soul—and God did too. Surely, that's all that counted? Westel believed that; I must as well, despite Brother Osbert's threats. Let Him be my judge, not some wretched idle women or greedy monks.

"Come then"—I gave Adam's hand a final squeeze—"let's go and tell Saskia and Blanche the good news."

"About the profits?" Adam was most perplexed I'd discuss these openly.

"About Tobias. Let them know there'll be an extra mouth to feed."

Dragging him forward, I doused the cresset lamp and extinguished the candles on the way out. "Come along, I can't dally, I've beer to make."

"Two mouths," he added as we entered the hall.

"What?" Using the doorframe as a pivot, I spun around. "What did you say?"

"You can't forget Sir Leander," said Adam.

I held his gaze a moment longer, before walking slowly down the passage to the kitchen, the spring gone from my step.

Adam was right. As much as I might try. Damn him, I could not.

# TWENTY-THREE

The day that followed was one of great joy and perplexity. After attending mass at St. Bartholomew's and making sure the tenant farmers received their allotted fish, meat, and vegetables for their table, we spent the rest of the morning preparing for our Christmastide feast, one which we would all, including Father Clement and Captain Stoyan, share. For years, Father Clement had joined our family in celebrating Christ's birth and I didn't want this year to be any different.

At midday, we left Blanche in the kitchen and walked into town to St. Stephen's to hear Abbot Hubbard give the mass. The church was so full many had to stand in the snow outside. Westel and Will ran ahead and reserved us places, so we were able to squeeze our way through the crowd and between the columns toward the area allocated to wealthier townsfolk. Curt nods and

frowns greeted our arrival, followed by murmurs of disapproval
and some louder-than-necessary sniffs. My cheeks grew hot and
Betje's grip on my hand tightened. Not far ahead of us, I saw Betrix with her parents. The mayor stood with a gentleman I recognized as Master Underwood, Lord Rainford's seneschal. Lord
Rainford was spending Christmas with the king at Westminster.

As the abbot ascended the pulpit, the crowd grew quiet. The
chandeliers smoked, as did the censors swinging from the rafters,
dusting us all with their opaque scent, though it was not enough
to completely mask the other odors so many people huddled together produced. Above me, the stone pillars disappeared into the
vaulted ceiling, and I imagined colonies of cherubs sitting in the
corners, chuckling at the humans compressed so tightly together
to worship their Father on this bitterly cold day. Muffled coughs
and a wave of movement that pushed me forward brought my
thoughts back to earth. Behind me someone sneezed. A child
giggled and was quickly hushed. In front of the parishioners, the
altar glowed in the flickering lights of candles and cresset lamps:
golden goblets, crosses, the bejeweled container carrying the host,
and the huge open Bible sat upon the white linen. The deacons
and other brothers from St. Jude's and surrounding parishes took
up their positions. Among them were Brothers Osbert and Marcus, their benign spiritual roles belying my previous encounters
with them. Outside, the snow fell steadily; the uneven gray light
coming through the stained glass refracted into tiny, precious
rainbows of color, which fell upon the heads of those around me.

As Abbot Hubbard's dulcet tones took wing among the soar-
ing columns and curving arches, I found myself curious about
this tall, well-fed man with pale, almost silver hair who spoke
with both authority and barely repressed indifference about the

birth of our Lord Jesus Christ. Chopping the air with his hand, Abbot Hubbard stared through one of the stained-glass windows, his mind seeming to drift away from us. Once, he might have been described as handsome; remnants of his beauty were evident in his fine nose and high cheekbones, but age and good living had added jowls and heavily pouched eyes. As the choir sang and he broke the bread and supped upon Christ's blood, I prayed to my Lord to forgive me what the abbot could not.

A sudden movement from behind jolted me. Thrust forward, I collided with Will.

"I thought it was you," hissed a voice in my ear.

"Tobias!" I tempered my voice just in time, but my heart leapt. Spinning around at his name, the twins, who were on either side of me, squealed and were immediately hushed.

Tobias lifted Betje into his arms, and she strangled his neck. Karel hugged his legs and if it hadn't been for Sir Leander's timely arrival at his back, he would have toppled.

"God's good day and a merry Christmas, Mistress Sheldrake," said Sir Leander softly, sliding between Tobias and me. As he bent down to whisper, his mouth brushed my earlobe.

A wave of heat that had nothing to do with the crush of people swept over me.

"Merry Christmas, my lord," I replied, my voice foreign, twisting my head slightly, only to find his lips inches from my own. My eyes dropped to that mouth, so full, so firm. Blushing, I raised my eyes to find his locked onto mine.

Time contracted in the tiny space in which we were trapped. I was no longer aware of the crowd, of the sermon, or even of the twins or Tobias. All that existed was Sir Leander and those cerulean eyes and that mouth. Unable to move, to think, it was only another push, this time from Saskia, that brought me to my senses.

"Thank the Lord that's over," said Saskia, a little too loudly. Frowns and some laughter washed over us.

Caught in the tide of people leaving the cathedral, it wasn't until we were outside, the cold nipping our flesh, that we were able to find one another again, and it occurred to me that I hadn't seen Westel since we entered.

Just as I was about to ask Adam where he was, Westel rounded the corner of the building, his cheeks red, his cap askew. Before I could ask where he'd been, the twins tugged at my arms.

"Come on, Anneke. Hurry up." Karel jumped up and down.

"I'm getting cold." Betje's teeth started to chatter.

The contrast between the church and outside was harsh. Questions flew out of my mind as the twins led me away, though I did remember to introduce Westel to my brother and his master. Overwhelmed, he kept his face down, his cap low, and mumbled greetings.

To the ringing of bells and the joyful strains of carols, we walked home quickly, the wind blowing flakes of snow into flurries around our ankles, catching our cloaks and whipping them aside, allowing the air to grip like an iron vise. Increasing our pace, we laughed at nature's attempts to cool our excited spirits.

If there weren't as many calling out greetings as last year, or if those who turned aside before I could offer good cheer left me a little deflated, I chose not to dwell upon it. Not today. Tobias was here. No one and nothing could spoil Christmas. I linked arms with my brother and, with Westel leading the way, the twins skipping at our heels and Sir Leander escorting Saskia while Adam accompanied Iris and Louisa, I chose to thank the good Lord for sending me this day and everything that came with it.

"Hope you don't mind," whispered Tobias. "But I told Sir Leander he was welcome to join us. His father and brother are with the king at Westminster, so . . ."

"Of course," I said quickly, the tinder in my heart catching fire.

Twenty minutes later, divested of coats, hoods, and gloves, we entered Holcroft House, the servants scattering at once to their tasks. It was left to me to escort our guests inside.

Draped with ivy and other greenery that Adam and Will had cut from the forests, the hall looked festive. A huge fire roared in the hearth with the logs we'd added before mass. Trestle tables covered with white linen ran down one side of the room, the stools and benches tucked beneath. A pearly daylight streamed through the windows, but even so, we lowered the chandelier by its rope, lit the candles and then hoisted it up again. Around the room, more candles were lit, including the large Yule one that sat in the center of the table. The scents of pine and cloves made the smoky air sharp and alive. As Sir Leander entered, Blanche clapped her hands in delight and, before I could prevent it, grabbed a stool, put it in the center of the room and urged him to stand upon it.

"I need the tallest man here, my lord. And that's you," she said. "If you're able," she added, glancing uncertainly at his leg.

"If I can fight for king and country and sail the oceans, I can surely attend to this." He laughed.

With goodwill, he mounted carefully, handing his walking stick to Saskia as Blanche passed him the mistletoe. The twins chased the hounds around the table, testing Will, who was trying to place the goblets, mazers, and spoons. Iris and Louisa

narrowly avoided Karel as they carried in trays replete with trenchers of bread, tureens of rich gravy, and bowls of hot fruity
sauces, while Blanche followed with a plate upon which reclined
a huge steamed sturgeon. When Iris and Blanche returned with
a large bowl brimming with wassail, cups were quickly found
and the rich, heated spiced wine was passed around. With a
heave-ho, Westel and Adam added another huge log to the fire,
sending sparks flying up the chimney and into the room as they
leaped out of the way, laughing and brushing their hands together. The dogs began barking at Westel, Achilles's teeth bared.
Westel froze while Adam tried to restrain them. Father Clement
chose that moment to arrive, beaming at us all and bestowing
blessings upon the house. A cheer was raised, and, Westel forgotten, the dogs raced toward the good father, Adam capturing them before they could pounce. Dragging them outside, he
tossed them a bone and shut the door.

The bell to the shop rang loudly and Will darted down the
corridor, reappearing with Captain Stoyan, who clutched two
large jugs of what I guessed was beer and a flagon of Gascony
wine. More greetings were given and happy chatter flowed.

Tobias took my fingers in his and called everyone to the table.
Seating me in the center, he sat to my right and invited Sir Leander to sit on my left, Captain Stoyan beside him and Father
Clement next to Tobias. Delighted that Tobias surrendered his
rightful position to me, in what I recognized was both an apology and affirmation, I beamed at everyone, conscious mainly
of Sir Leander and the way his shoulder kept brushing against
mine. Once Will and Blanche ensured everyone had a fresh
drink, the twins included, Tobias struck his knife against the

side of a gilt bowl, calling for silence. Holding his vessel aloft, he offered the first of what would be many wassails.

We drank and, taking our seats, clapped as Blanche brought in the goose. Steam wafted from its golden skin and the smell of its tender flesh made my mouth water. A suckling pig, basted in spiced apple and wine sauce was followed by mortrews— crumbed chicken and pork dusted with saffron, sugar, and salt. There was roasted venison, salted herring, baked mackerel, and so many other delicious dishes of meat, fish, and sauces, I lost count and instead unlatched my eating knife and prepared to feast.

The sadness that had hung like a pall over our house ever since Mother died, and which was renewed with Father's passing, was finally lifting. Studying the faces of those who sat at the table as they filled their trenchers, first offering their neighbor the finest cuts of meat or fish, wiping their shared goblets with such consideration, I felt a sense of contentment, of being among family and friends, and satisfaction with what we'd achieved thus far washed over me.

Hours passed as we ate, laughed, and drank, and shadows grew. The bells for vespers tolled and yet none made any effort to move, choosing to nurse our drinks and pick at the remaining food. Outside, the snow fell, cocooning us within the hall. When the little rectangular mince or humble pies, made from the innards of game, were passed around, there was hesitation as everyone considered what they would wish for before they took the first bite. Having prepared my wish some days ago, I was about to sink my teeth into the tawny crust when I caught Sir Leander staring at me with the most peculiar expression on his face. Pausing, I tipped my head toward him. What was he thinking to regard me so?

"I know what I'm wishing for," announced Karel, kneeling on the bench, trying to shove the entire pie into his mouth.

"Karel!" squealed Betje. "You'll spoil it that way." She tried to prevent him, tugging at his arm so only a portion went into his mouth. The remainder of the pie fell on the floor and, with a hoarse bark, Patroclus, who'd been readmitted some time ago, fell upon it, Achilles being too slow. A squabble broke out and I was forced to set my pie down, rise to my feet, and separate the twins. Adam jumped up and ordered the dogs back to their place by the fire. Will and Iris laughed while Blanche took it as a cue to start collecting empty platters.

The threat of missing the dancing was enough to quieten the twins. While Blanche and Westel cleared the tables and organized what leftovers would provide alms for the poor who would gather soon at the church door, Will and Adam took up their instruments—this time, a gittern and flute. Tobias led Betje into the center of the room, while Sir Leander, leaving his cane, took Louisa's hand. Saskia grabbed Father Clement; Iris, Captain Stoyan. Sitting on a stool, with Karel upon my lap, we clapped in time, watching them spin, stamp their heels, and weave around each other. The pace slowly increased, until they were a whir of color, hair, wool, linens, and boots. Testimony to tiredness, Betje was unable to maintain the pace and tripped. Tobias fell over. He landed on his rump next to the hounds, who promptly jumped upon his chest, forcing him to the floor and licking his face. Betje also climbed atop her brother. Karel as well.

The laughter was loud and contagious, and it was a while before we recovered.

Even then, amongst all the gaiety, I noted the way the hounds slinked around Westel, their hackles raised; how they maintained a distance from him and he them.

Later, another, slower tune was played and I forgot about the hounds, Westel, the way the people in the church had snubbed me, I forgot about everything . . . Saskia and Tobias swayed in time with the music, as did Westel, holding a blushing Iris. Solemnly, Karel led Louisa to the floor. I was astonished to find Sir Leander standing in front of my stool, his hand held out.

"Go on, Anneke," said Betje, nudging me. Captain Stoyan and Father Clement added their entreaties.

Staring into those sapphire eyes, I wanted to refuse, but didn't want to appear churlish. It was Christmas. What would one dance matter? Anyhow, I had offered him a chance. My cheeks pinked as thoughts of what happened in church took off in a series of complicated steps.

In less time than it took to say "Ave Maria," my hand was clasped in his. As our fingers touched, my heart became a juggler's ball and heat traveled from my center to, God forgive me, lower regions, causing my mind to reel.

Drawing me to my feet, Sir Leander moved me into position. The dance required us to come together and then part. Whereas a civil distance was generally maintained, Sir Leander abided by no such rules, pulling me so close to him, I could smell the sweet scent of cloves on his breath, catch that musky, warm smell that was his own. Refusing to meet his eyes, I was all too aware that his never left my face. His palm was warm, hard, his long fingers twined possessively through mine. As we stepped toward each other, his hip brushed against me and a violent jolt ran through my body, causing me to gasp. Spinning me around so my hair, already tumbling from its bindings, flew out, he grinned. With a gentle tug, he drew me back toward him, remaining still while I whirled around him, a star locked in his orbit. Refusing to release me to my next partner, Sir Leander laughed. Westel, understanding that my lord had no intention of surrendering me, took Iris back with a frown.

Thinking this was a game, the twins giggled and clapped their hands in appreciation. Saskia called encouragement.

"You can't follow the rules, can you, my lord?" I said as we came together.

He smiled. His teeth were so white. His skin, even in the dead of winter, darker than most, especially against the creamy collar of his shirt, carried lines of experience and laughter. I could see some bristles where Tobias's razor had missed.

"I find that amusing, coming from a woman who creates her own."

I shook my head, glancing down at my feet so I didn't have to look at him any longer. The warmth that suffused my body was fast becoming a furnace and I felt everyone watching us. I wanted to escape his hold, return to the safety of my stool, but I let the music and Sir Leander carry me forward toward the center of the room.

"Mistress Sheldrake," he said softly. "Anneke . . ."

My head shot up. Not so much at the use of my name, but at the tenderness in his tone.

"There's something I've not told y—"

"Look where you are!" Betje leapt to her feet, pointing.

"You have to kiss her!" shouted Karel.

I glanced toward the twins to see what Betje was madly indicating when a pair of lips captured my own.

It was as if a thousand butterflies were released inside me. My heart hammered, my head spun. Tingling sensations that began where his mouth held mine escaped to travel to every single part of my body, suffusing it with white-hot heat.

His kiss deepened as the roaring in my ears, in my chest, in my heart, grew. An ache such as I'd never known rose from deep within me to radiate out to the tips of my fingers, to the ends of my feet. God forgive me, I groaned into his mouth as our tongues twined. I so desperately wanted to draw him closer, feel the entire length of his firm body against mine. My hands explored his back, inching upward and longing to coil his silky black locks around my fingers. The hand that held me tight crept lower until it rested against the curve at the base of my spine, his fingers burning through the wool of my tunic . . .

The surging in my ears increased, warning me.

My eyes fluttered open and with all my strength, I shoved Sir Leander away. He staggered back a step or two, tossed that dark head, and laughed. Without his stick, he almost lost his footing.

The twins were crying out in glee; the servants were open-mouthed, laughing and cheering. Father Clement crossed himself; the captain clapped. Tobias shook his head, what I thought was an uncertain smile hovering on his lips. Only Westel, who'd abandoned Iris to watch, was grim-faced. I stared at them all and then Sir Leander, chagrined, perplexed. I pressed my fingers to my swollen mouth and then swiped the back of my hand across it. My cheeks were flaming, my eyes glassy.

It was not that he'd kissed me that distressed me so much as how I'd responded. Oh, sweet Mother Mary, with every fiber of my being I'd answered his Christmas kiss with a wantonness that shocked me.

Frozen in the moment, the movement around me didn't register until the swirl of skirts and flicker of hands could no longer be ignored. Already the kiss was forgotten and the dance had resumed. After all, what else did one do beneath mistletoe? It was custom. First Saskia and Captain Stoyan, then Iris and Blanche, Tobias and Louisa also kissed, cheeks, mouths, fingers, as they moved around and beneath the greenery.

I wandered unsteadily back to my stool, to the twins who both sought my lap as soon as I sat down, Karel winning, Betje taking second place by my side.

In a daze, my thoughts and flesh afire, I watched the dancing, refusing to look at Sir Leander, even though I knew exactly where he was in the hall and with whom he chose to dance and for how long.

Tobias staggered over, looking as if he wished to say something, but, as he drew closer, he changed his mind and led the twins away instead.

"Last dance before bed," I called, grateful for the distraction.

"Not till we've had frumenty!" cried Karel as Tobias swept him into his arms and spun him around. Finding his feet again, Karel planted his hands on his hips and stared at me, waiting for a reply, determined not to miss any of the fruity pudding he loved.

"Very well," I agreed, "but then straight to the nursery."

Leaning back against the wall, I sighed and ran my fingers through my hair. It had come completely loose and fell over my shoulders, forming tangled tendrils around my face. I tried to make it neater. It was a lost cause. Addle-headed, I left my hair undone and sighed again.

"Are you all right, Mistress Sheldrake?"

It was Westel. Standing next to me, on the other side of Betje, who'd fled the dance, he passed me a fresh cup of wassail. I blinked and gratefully took it, swallowing it too quickly. I spluttered and wiped my mouth, aware again of my lips, of Sir Leander's. I saw the flash of his dark green doublet out of the corner of my eye.

"Shall I get you some water?" Westel pushed Betje aside gently and knelt down. Our eyes were level. He had such a sweet face. No wrong could come from someone who looked like that, could it? He didn't steal kisses, call me whore, retract it, and then confuse me with his ways.

"I'm fine," I said slowly. "Just very warm." I fanned myself with my hand. "Thank you for the drink."

"Thank you, Mistress Sheldrake."

Betje tried to grab my attention. Karel ran over, a bowl of frumenty in his hand.

"Are you all right, Anneke?" he said between swallows.

"I think it's time for you two to go to bed," I said.

They began to argue, but hearing me, Louisa came at once. "Come on," she said softly. "It's well past bedtime. Bring the frumenty with you. Tomorrow's St. Stephen's Day and you want to be awake early to receive your gifts, don't you?"

The reminder of the presents we would exchange was enough to still any arguments the twins were ready to muster. With hugs and kisses, bows and goodbyes, they bid us all good night.

Once they'd left the hall and the dancing resumed, I turned my attention to Westel again.

"For what do you thank me, Westel? The way I see it, I owe you a great deal. Life has been very different since you arrived at Holcroft House. The success of the ale, the quantity we produce, is in large part due to your hard work."

Squatting, his elbows on his thighs, his fingers pointing toward the floor, Westel considered his response. For all that he appeared open, Westel was a closed book to me. Aware of my thoughts, he flashed a grin. "Aye, and for that I'll reap my own rewards. But you've been so kind to me. You've not only given me a job, but you've welcomed me into your family and given me a home." He looked around the room. "I don't recall ever experiencing merrymaking like this. Christmas past was spent in prayer, in cloisters, and then tending the poor."

"I don't imagine you would have spent the day this way where you came from. It must feel strange . . . wrong?"

"Not wrong. Not exactly." Westel gazed at the floor. "It's not what I'm accustomed to, that's all."

Interpreting that as another thanks, I patted the back of his hand where it dangled above the floor. "You're very welcome." I smiled. "I hope you're with us for a long time, and that you will always enjoy the fruits of your labor."

"Oh, I intend to, Mistress Sheldrake. Always. No matter how hard or long I've to work."

There was something in his tone that gave me pause, but then he flashed that smile. I nodded and returned it. "May God bless you!" I lifted my cup toward him, inviting him to touch it with his own.

Our cups clicked and for a fleeting second, I saw something in his eyes that reminded me of the icicles that formed over the lintel to the shop. I shrugged the notion off and, in companionable silence, Westel and I watched the dancing.

Little did I know as the music played, the floor thrummed, and my mind settled into a comfortable haze, that this would be the last time I would know real happiness.

# TWENTY-FOUR

HOLCROFT HOUSE

St. Stephen's Day

*The year of Our Lord 1405 in the seventh*
*year of the reign of Henry IV*

*T*ipping his comb so the wattle beneath was exposed, the rooster stood atop the stone wall and crowed as I crossed the yard. Wrapping my shawl tightly and striding quickly, my breath was a stream of pearlescence against the coming dawn. The ground crunched, each footstep loud in the still air. As I neared the coop, the soft clucks of the chickens disturbed the peace, followed by snuffling pigs who began to trail my path, searching for something edible where my heel cracked the white mantle of snow. I missed the hounds' enthusiastic welcome, but assumed Adam must have risen early to walk them.

Pushing open the brewery door and inhaling the rich malty scent that clung to the place the way woodsmoke does clothes, I lit the candles, stoked the kiln, and, as I did every time a brew was ready to be barreled, sang the ale to life.

Lowering my arm into the cold mixture, I sucked the air in through my teeth. Before long, I'd shucked off my tiredness and relished the way the liquid caressed my flesh, adhered to my arm, covering me in a protective layer. Perhaps it was my imagination, but I fancied the fluid grew warm with each verse. Out the window, the sky slowly transformed, the gray swallowed by a whispering palette of rosy pinks and soft yellows before a band of gold fired the horizon. Lost in reverie as I sang, my mind drifted back to last night and the moment Sir Leander kissed me.

It had been so unexpected, and yet, as his lips touched mine, it was as if I too had been sung into life.

A sweet feeling blossomed in my core, my song deepening as I relived the sensations summoned from my body. I remembered the taste of cloves and wine upon his warm, firm lips, his liquid tongue . . . Oh dear Lord, his tongue . . . The scent of pine, the comforting odor of velvet, and something that I couldn't identify, something that belonged just to him clinging to his doublet. I recalled the silky feel of his hair sweeping my cheek as we closed the distance between us and, earlier, as we moved across the floor, united in our dance in a way that we could never be in life. A tremble shook me. Shutting my eyes, I allowed one arm to drift in the now-tepid ale, while the other tightened around my middle, imagining that it was Sir Leander holding me once more.

A shout brought me back to my senses. My eyes flew open and, finishing the song as quickly as I dared, I withdrew my arm, studying the pale ale, fancying that it wasn't the sunlight stealing through the window alone making it glow, but the heat and ridiculous hope roiling in my soul.

If my offering to the corner crones and goddess was not as

measured as usual, I knew they'd forgive me. The house was astir and the call I'd heard earlier now echoed about the yard. Frowning, I wiped my arm and hands on a cloth and went to the door. I was about to pull it open when it was wrenched from my hands.

"Morning, Mistress Sheldrake." Sleep-tousled and rather heavy-eyed, Westel flashed me his customary grin, touched his ever-present cap, and, tucking in his shirt, staggered down the stairs and wended past the tuns and troughs to the malthouse.

"Good morning, Westel." I peered around the door. Dressed in cloaks, Adam, Saskia, and Iris were shouting for the hounds. "Is everything all right?"

Westel shrugged. "It's the dogs, mistress. They're missing. Adam thinks something's happened to them." He scratched his head. "They probably became fed up with waiting and took themselves for a walk; it's well after prime."

Frowning at Westel, who shrugged, heaved off his boots, picked up the shovel, and descended to the malthouse, I glanced back outside. There was an urgency to Adam's stride as he marched around the yard, to the way he cupped his hands about his mouth and shouted.

"I'll be back shortly," I said to Westel. "Can you stir the mash as well, please?" I ran outside.

There was no sign of Iris, and Adam slipped out the church gate before I could reach him. Spinning around helplessly, I saw Saskia. She was ignoring the pigs grunting at her feet, her eyes screwed up against the sun, her mouth grim.

"Oh, Mistress Anneke." She wrung her hands. "The hounds have gone. Normally, that wouldn't be such a worry, but their rope's been cut and the gate's open." She pointed toward the alley.

I half-ran to the stables where the dogs were secured each night and bent down to inspect their bindings. Saskia followed.

"See?" She pointed at the neatly severed ends of rope. "That's been done by a knife, and a sharp one at that." I glanced over my shoulder toward the gates. One was ajar—just wide enough for the dogs to slip through. "Someone's taken them . . ."

"But they wouldn't go with just anyone," I protested. "The gate's been left open plenty of times and the dogs have slipped their rope before. Someone had to have lured them out of the yard." I studied the ground. Fresh snow had fallen overnight. There were no prints except for the scuffed marks of boots— ours. "Or forced them out . . ."

"That's what Adam thinks," said Saskia. "He's taken Will and they've gone into the woods. He said they'll come back along the bay. Iris is combing the nearby streets."

In the distance, I could hear their voices. Images of my two great shaggy hounds, their wiry coats, their gentle brown eyes and lolling tongues, rose in my mind. Please, God, don't let anything have happened to them. But hounds like Patroclus and Achilles were valuable—good hunting dogs, they'd sell in a market. Not here in Elmham Lenn, where everyone knew who owned them, but the markets at Bishop's Lynn and Norwich were not out of the question.

"If Adam returns, tell him I've gone to search as well—only, I'll go into town. You never know. Someone may have seen them." *Or who took them.* "I'll head straight for the square and then come back past St. Nichols and up Gold Street. If he finds them, please send someone to fetch me; I'll send word should I be so fortunate."

Saskia held my arm. "Mistress Anneke, leave it to Adam and Will. What if—" She left the thought unsaid.

"I have to, Saskia. They were Adam's gift after Mother's death. They too are family."

Saskia nodded. Though she'd often complain about the beasts, their noise and smell, I knew she loved them. With a sigh, she released me.

"When the twins wake, don't tell them what's happened." Replaiting my hair, I tucked it firmly beneath my kerchief. "Once we find them, they'll be none the wiser."

Saskia bit her lip.

I clutched her hands and then turned to leave.

"Wait! You can't go on your own," she called as I raced toward the house to grab extra layers.

"I'll take Westel," I shouted back. "He'll need a cloak and gloves. Tell him he'll find me out front on Market Street."

With a brisk nod, Saskia raced to the brewery.

⊰⊱

We never found a trace of the hounds that day or in the ones that followed. It was as if they'd melted away like spring snow. Westel and I searched until nightfall, our voices hoarse, our steps ragged, the brewhouse forgotten as I grew more distraught with each passing hour. If it hadn't been for Westel, I would have given up long before, but he encouraged me to keep searching, to hope. Fetching a drink when I thirsted, buying a pie from a street vendor that he insisted I share with him, he was a good and loyal companion that day and I would not easily forget that.

Finding me in town, Tobias and Sir Leander joined the hunt as well, entering darker alleys, questioning the women and men who lolled in corners and on stoops, but to no avail.

We were a subdued household that night. Not even the twins' delighted squeals as they received and gave gifts could penetrate the mantle of gloom that settled over my heart. My eyes continued to stray to where the dogs used to lie, close to Adam, and the way his hand dropped to his side, his caress meeting only empty air, was a cruel reminder our hounds were gone.

Deep in my heart, I knew who was to blame. Brother Osbert's warning echoed through me.

After the twins went to bed, I found it hard to settle. The false jollity of Louisa, Iris, and Westel, even the efforts of Tobias and Sir Leander, both of whom had tirelessly searched and were now simply attempting to divert the rest of us with their songs and stories, irritated me. Rather than spoil their kindness, I excused myself and went to the office. I was in no mood for music or even food. My appetite had fled along with my goodwill toward men. I needed a diversion, something upon which to focus, something I could control. Prodding the fire back to life and illuming a couple of rushlights, I pulled out the piece of paper upon which I had calculated how much ale and beer needed to be sold to ensure a profit when I opened the alehouse.

But I wasn't in the right frame of mind for figures and facts either. Pushing the document away, I opened the shutters between the office and the shop, leaning on the lintel. As my eyes grew accustomed to the darkness, I began to picture the space as an alehouse. To imagine how it would look and feel when it was filled with people buying and drinking not only my ale, but beer as well. I knew I was playing with the laws, that like London brewers, I should be choosing to sell one or the other but, until my patrons decided whether they'd like beer, until I knew whether it was worth my while, there was no point trying to sell it alone in Elmham Lenn. A tankard or mazer, even a jug in an alehouse, however, was viable. When it came to new products, caution was a sound business partner.

Already there were two low tables and a few stools in the middle of the room, and a long bench tucked under the large table I used to conduct transactions. I would only need a few more seats and tables to create the right kind of atmosphere. The logs we'd used as stools after Hiske left would suffice until I had the funds to purchase proper ones. Likewise, we could move a couple of the small tables from the hall into the tavern. Sconces were screwed into the walls and, once torches burned in these, a good light would be cast. The hearth on the north wall was usable again since the chimney sweep had cleared it of the gulls' nests and rodents. Altogether, it wasn't a big room, but it was adequate for my purposes. I began to plan how I would notify folk that an alehouse was in operation. A poster in the square on market days, a word in a few traders' ears, and, of course, a sign. Master Proudfellow would let his patrons know, especially as I intended to give him additional ale for the service, while a couple of the nearby inns might also point some customers in our direction, for the right price. Dipping the quill in the ink, I began to design how I would arrange the tables, exactly how many more I would need. I drew benches, stools, and a service area behind which the drinks would be poured and mazers, tankards, and wooden trenchers for basic food could be stored. I began to tally up how many trenchers I would need, how much, if any, wine I would purchase, the number of goblets, napkins, and spoons I'd require. Delyth and Awel had already expressed an interest in serving; Will and Iris as well. Westel would do anything I asked. The thought made me smile. Able to push aside my misery, I wasn't aware the office door had opened until Tobias leaned over my shoulder.

"What's this?" he asked.

I leapt in fright, my hand gripping my chest. The wisp of rushlight flickered and almost went out. "Tobias!"

He gave a laugh and placed a reassuring hand on my shoulder. "Sorry. I didn't mean to startle you. I was worried. You looked so melancholy back there." He jerked his head toward the hall. "I guessed you wanted time alone, but I wanted to say goodbye. Leander does as well. We sail to Gascony tomorrow." He glanced through the open shutters. "It's dark outside and no doubt we'll be accosted by the night's watch and asked to explain why we're abroad."

"Let me fetch you a lantern," I said, not moving. Without intending to, I released a long sigh.

"What's bothering you, Anneke? It's not only the dogs, is it? I don't have to be on my way just yet . . ." Slipping onto the stool opposite me, he rested his elbows on the desk, regarding me earnestly.

"Oh, Tobias. It's just—" I shrugged, then shook my head, staring into the flames. "I know to some people they're only dogs, but they're more than that—in so many ways." I searched for the right way to explain. "It's what their absence means that's affecting me most of all. They're another loss, aren't they?" I used my fingers as a tally. "Mother loses all those babies, then she dies. Father is lost at sea, we lose the rights to his business, and, just when I'm getting to know you all over again, I'm about to lose you too . . . Oh, I know I'm being silly, that you have a life, you're a squire to a merchant knight, you travel all the time. It's just . . . well"—my eyes flickered to the corridor—"who knows when I'll see you again?" I dropped my hands into my lap, blinking fast. "I sometimes wonder if that's to be our destiny, or, at least, my fate. To always lose things . . . people . . ."

Tobias knelt at my feet and took my hands into his own. "How can you think such a thing?"

I raised miserable eyes to his. "If truth be told, with small effort, Tobias. The proof is all around me." I choked back a sob.

He tightened his fingers around mine, rose and placed an arm about my shoulders. "But, Anneke," he said, his chin resting on top of my head, "you've also gained so much. Look at your business, it's doing very well. You managed to secure a loan from Lord Rainford and, to hear Leander talk, that's nigh on a miracle." I bit back a laugh. "That's more like it! And you've won the respect of the locals—why, Father Clement can't say enough good things about you, neither can Captain Stoyan, Hugh Baker, Peter Goddard, Master Larkspur, and Master Proudfellow, never mind Master Miller and Olive." He lowered his lips to my hair. "Even Sir Leander thinks you're worthy of esteem and that's no small concession coming from him."

I raised watery eyes to my brother. "Sir Leander?" I made a harrumphing noise. "I doubt that."

"Aye, the very one. He speaks very highly of you and that's rare, Anneke. He's not one to engage in flattery."

"Oh, I know." I twisted so Tobias was forced to drop his arm, release my hands. "Do you know the first time he met me, he called me a whore?"

"He *what*?" Tobias's mouth fell open. He leaned back. "Well, that explains . . . Never!"

"He did."

Tobias ran his fingers through his dark hair. "I believe you, it's just . . . well, unfair." There was a false note in his rather glib response. I tried to meet his eyes, but he was evasive. I felt his weight shift where his body still touched mine. "So, what is this you're doing?" He dragged the drawing I'd been working on toward the light.

"Oh." I glanced over. "Some ideas for the alehouse."

It wasn't the cold silence that followed my statement that warned me, rather it was as if the air both chilled and contracted.

"The *what*?" Tobias's words reverberated like the toll of a bell.

*Oh dear Lord.* I laughed nervously. "The alehouse. Remember? I told you last night. In order to make enough money to pay Lord Rainford, I've decided to—"

"Are you completely mad?" Tobias's voice was a whip that cracked between us. He pushed the parchment away, placed one arm on the back of my chair and the other on the desk, trapping me. He lowered his head so his face was only inches from mine. "Through the fug of wine and ale, I thought you were jesting. But you're serious, aren't you? You can't open an alehouse, Anneke! What on God's earth are you thinking? Has brewing gone to your head?"

"Of course not. It's just we're not making enough money to cover the wages and the lease. If I was able to sell direct to customers as well as distribute larger quantities, I've worked out I will make more than enough to cover expenses and increase profits at least fivefold."

Tobias shook his head, repugnance transforming his features. Pinning the paper to the desk with a heavy finger, he frowned. "Brewing is one thing, but turning this house, our home"—he waved his arms—"into an alehouse that any knave can enter is something altogether different. I won't have it, Anneke. You're to discard this foolish notion. I tolerated the brewing; after all, Mother used to do it. It's not entirely disreputable, despite what Cousin Hiske says. But an alehouse? That's completely different."

Standing abruptly, I knocked his arms away, pushed past him, and stood before the fire. I'd expected resistance, but not another assertion of brotherly authority. Bitterness and injustice warred within me. I knew I should remind him of his promise to trust my judgment, to support me, but fury wouldn't allow for compromise.

"I'm not turning *my* home into anything. I'm simply using the commercial part to trade in a different business. You of all people should understand that. As for worrying about who might frequent an alehouse, you've been listening to too many stories, or the wrong sort. Master Proudfellow, not to mention his wife, Jocelyn, have no such complaints and they've been running a tavern for years. And what about Mistress Amwell and Mistress Scot? They've had no cause—"

"It's not the same for them, and you know it."

"In what way?"

"Proudfellow aside, the others are married. Those women have husbands."

"Had," I corrected. "Mistress Scot is a widow."

"Don't be deliberately obtuse. My point stands. They've a man or men behind them. You don't—if you did, you wouldn't be contemplating such a mad scheme. As you've had pointed out to you, you're unmarried. A woman entering this type of venture on her own . . . well . . . you're vulnerable. It's dangerous."

"I've Adam, Will, and Westel, I'm not on my own. I've men behind me. Men who at least respect my decisions."

Tobias's eyes narrowed and his lips thinned. "*Respect?* Is that what you call it? They're besotted with you, Anneke, the lot of them. The fact you pay them to hang around and do your bidding is just a bonus."

I closed the distance between us swiftly. Once again, I was the angry big sister chastising my younger brother.

"Don't you ever speak about Adam, Will, or Westel in that way again, do you hear?"

"Fine. I won't. I won't ever speak about them again if you like." His voice grew louder, reverberating around the office. "But someone has to tell you what you're risking because they damn well won't!"

"And what am I risking, Tobias? Go on, say it." I wanted to hear it from his lips.

"Your reputation, Anneke. If you open an alehouse then any chance you have of finding a husband is dashed. All the tales being woven about you in town, they'll not be restricted to a few bitter women or unhappy, jealous men. On the contrary, they'll spread faster than Greek fire and you'll be the one to burn. It won't just be my master calling you a whore either."

Thunder roared in my ears. Darkness flickered at the edges of my vision. I couldn't recall ever being so angry. That he might be right infuriated me even more. I flexed my fingers by my side.

"You dare to say such a thing to me?"

"I'll say whatever it takes to talk you out of this foolery! And, if I can't, then you better get used to having it said about you. After all, you know what they say about women and alehouses?"

"Why don't you tell me?" I said in a voice that suggested the opposite.

Tobias took a deep breath. The throbbing vein at his temple revealed the depth of his rage.

"When a woman opens an alehouse, she may as well open her legs."

Unable to bear the reproach in his eyes, the superior tone in his voice, and, if I'm candid, the truth in what he said, I didn't respond. Returning to the desk, I collected up my papers, running my eyes over the diagrams, the figures, though I didn't really see them.

"Good God, Anneke." He ripped the papers away from me. "You can't seriously be considering this? If you go ahead, it will just be a matter of time before you and the family are dragged into the mire."

"What else am I supposed to do, Tobias?" I took the sheet back, tearing it slightly as I did.

"Anything would be better than what you're proposing."

"Anything? What, even working for Cousin Hiske?"

"Aye, if it would save you from this." He snatched the papers back and flapped them in my face. His eyes were flashing, and there were high spots of color on his cheeks.

I no longer knew my brother, and he certainly didn't know me. The accord I'd felt between us was simply a product of my desperate imagination.

"Anyway, this is moot. I've made my decision." Tobias slammed his fist into the palm of his other hand. "I forbid you."

"You *what*?" My eyes narrowed. Incandescent fury began to

unfurl, a great black sail in my gut. "*Forbid me?* Since when do you tell me what to do?"

Tobias lifted his chin. "I'm your brother and head of this family. I can tell you whatever I damn well please. You'll not do this and that's my final word." He began to tear the paper into pieces. Flinging them into the fire, he slapped his hands together. "This conversation is over."

I stared at him in shock. He may have had the Rainford blood running in his veins, but at that moment, he reminded me of Father.

Without thinking, I raised my hand and with all my strength struck Tobias across the face. His head snapped back. Blood poured from his lip. Staring at me in wide-eyed disbelief, he tentatively touched the area and his fingers came away carmine.

"You're right, Tobias," I said slowly and carefully, my hand burning, the jolt of drawing blood not yet registering. "We'll not speak of this again. In fact, once you leave here, we won't speak. Now, I suggest you go." I pointed to the door, my arm quivering, my eyes glassy. Part of me wanted to stop this now, to run to my brother and fold him in my arms, take back everything. This wasn't us; this wasn't how it should be. I hesitated. May the dear Lord forgive me, I was too angry to apologize, too enraged to be the first to concede . . .

"I can't believe you did that." Tobias shook his head and gave a bitter laugh, wincing as his lip pulled. Dabbing his mouth with a kerchief, Tobias held up a hand to prevent me coming closer. "What was I thinking? Perhaps Sir Leander was right, perhaps he saw something that I've failed to note."

"What's that?" I asked.

Tobias pushed his face into mine. "You're a whore after all."

Inhaling sharply, I stepped back. "Mind your next words, Tobias. By all that's sacred and holy . . ."

I could see the battle taking place behind his eyes. I prayed we would make things right between us. But the devil was in Tobias tonight as well. "Sometimes people deserve the names we bestow."

A shudder ran through me. There was no return from this. "Get out. Now."

"Oh, I'll leave." He wiped his mouth with the back of his hand. "But let me say one last thing. If you go ahead with this, then understand, I won't be here to protect you—not from gossip or rumor, not from the unwelcome attentions of your guests, or from yourself. If you proceed then you're on your own."

"What you've shown me tonight, *brother*, is that I always have been."

Without another word, Tobias strode from the office, slamming the door so hard the windows in the shop shook. I stood staring at the fire, without moving. Slowly, I sank into the chair, my entire body atremble, my throat dry, my mind numb.

*Oh God, what just happened?*

Like my parents, the hounds, and my reputation, it was evident I'd lost my brother as well. My head dropped and I wept as only one with a broken heart can.

# TWENTY-FIVE

HOLCROFT HOUSE

After the Feast of the Epiphany to the Ides of February

*The year of Our Lord 1406 in the seventh*

*year of the reign of Henry IV*

.

*I* heard through Captain Stoyan that Tobias and Sir Leander arrived safely in Gascony and, after taking on cargo, sailed to the Mediterranean. Neither would be in English seas for at least another six months. In front of Adam and Saskia, Sir Leander bade me a solemn farewell; the way he pressed my hand and searched my eyes led me to surmise he knew that Tobias and I had argued. That my brother had stormed from the house before I rejoined everyone in the hall made our falling-out obvious, but I was too angry to explain or apologize. Promising to keep my brother safe, Sir Leander kissed my hand slowly and warmly, his eyes lingering on my lips as he raised his head. When he didn't relinquish my hand but squeezed it involuntarily a few times, I gave him a pretty curtsy, despite my shaking knees. Too tense and anxious to understand that this leave-taking was for a goodly time, I said goodbye. Who was Sir Leander but my brother's master, anyway? And hadn't he been the one to bestow on me the awful name that Tobias used in the first place? I was glad to see the last of him, I told myself.

Was I a poor sister if I confessed to feeling relieved that Tobias had left? That I did not have to endure another moment in his company? Well, I was, and I stubbornly refused to accept any blame for our disagreement and pursued my plan to open an alehouse with renewed determination. Not only did I need to pay Lord Rainford, I also had to prove my brother wrong. If I was to earn any reputation, I would tell myself as I scrubbed the soon-to-open alehouse, polished spoons, and cleaned tankards and mazers alongside Iris and Westel, it would be as the efficient and generous manager of an excellent establishment that sold fine ale, beer, and fare.

I didn't confide in anyone about my fight with Tobias. To tell the truth, as Christmastide drew to a close and we celebrated the Feast of Epiphany with prayer and carousing, I was embarrassed and saddened beyond measure. Then I would remember Tobias's words. It was tantamount to betrayal. Most of all, I felt utter indignation that he saw fit to forbid me.

While the twins were oblivious to the schism, Adam, Saskia, and Blanche at least knew exactly what had gone on. They didn't say anything; they didn't need to—their respectful silence, the additional attention paid to the meals sent to me in the brewery or the way they drew their stools closer at night in the hall spoke of how they felt. I basked in their support, knowing that the alehouse would be the saving of Holcroft House.

Westel was more than usually attentive in the days following the argument. So much so, I became convinced he must have been privy to the words exchanged. This proved to be right when, in an innocent comment, Karel revealed that Westel had followed Tobias out of the hall on St. Stephen's night.

"He was supposed to be fetching Tobias's cloak, but he was gone so long, we thought you must have kept him in the office."

I didn't explain that I'd neither kept Westel nor been aware of his presence. That little piece of information went a long way to explaining the willing way Westel went about his tasks and more. In what used to be the shopfront and which was slowly transforming into my alehouse, Westel would entertain me by describing the customers we'd have, their manner, their dress, and inventing ways in which they'd laud our ale. He gave me hope, just when I thought there was so little as the pressures of furnishing the alehouse, promoting its forthcoming opening, not to mention increasing the amount of ale and now beer we produced, were taking their toll. Without Westel, Awel, and Delyth, and the quiet cooperation of the twins and the servants, I never would have accomplished it.

I was grateful to them all—but most especially Westel.

Our original intention to open on Twelfth Night was delayed by over a month. Instead, on a bitterly cold Saturday, just on the ides of February, I announced the Cathaline Alehouse open for business. The name was my choice—I knew it would arouse Tobias's ire and possibly that of my patron, Lord Rainford, but I wanted to honor my mother. I drew strength from her name.

The morning of our opening, I emerged from the brewery as the sun began to peep through the leaden mist. The smell of moisture clung to everything; the tang of salt was there too, if you dared breathe the cold air deeply enough. Crossing through the snow to the kitchen, my heart contracted as, once again, I missed my hounds. Chickens and pigs did not arouse the same degree of affection, and though the slender church cat would wend its way along the wall, sometimes jumping down to weave between my legs, she belonged to Father Clement.

Spying my approach, the twins raced outside, took my hands and pulled me into the warmth of the kitchen. Inside, Blanche and Iris were preparing small loaves of bread to serve in the alehouse while a huge pottage bubbled away on the stove. The smell was comforting, as were the children's bodies, pressed close to mine we sat on the bench and drank some almond milk.

Blanche and Iris chatted. They were anxious and excited about the alehouse opening. Adam and Saskia had gone to the market to fetch some last-minute supplies; Louisa was busy in the scullery, pressing tablecloths and attending to the dress I was determined to wear that afternoon to greet my first customers, while Will was laying a fire so the room would be warm. I'd left Westel and the Parry sisters in the brewhouse. I admit to enjoying the guilty pleasure of a pause in my otherwise busy day.

"Can we come to the alehouse too?" asked Betje, leaning over the table with a wet finger, daubing the salt that had spilled on the table and bringing it to her mouth. It was satisfying to me that she defined the alehouse as a separate space that required permission to enter. I'd worked hard to maintain the division between commercial and domestic parts of the building as we'd always done.

"Oh, please say aye, Anneke!" begged Karel, widening those big blue eyes.

Ruffling his curls, I shook my head. "I'm afraid my answer today is the same as it's been every other day you've asked that question."

"*Nay, my darlings, you cannot,*" said Betje in a perfect imitation of my voice, grinning at me.

I threw back my head and laughed and the others joined in. Karel jumped off the bench and began to strut around the kitchen, giving orders to imaginary staff, adopting my walk and stance with remarkable accuracy.

"I do not look like that," I objected, as he placed one hand on his hip and shook a finger.

"You do," said Betje, applauding her brother.

I was about to join the mummery, when Will entered waving a letter.

"Mistress Sheldrake. This just arrived."

I didn't recognize the handwriting or the frank. "Thank you, Will."

"Open it," said Karel, clambering back up next to me.

"Read it to us," said Betje, looping her arm through mine, making it difficult for me to break the seal. It was very good quality paper, the ebony ink pronounced against the creamy surface.

"*Right Honorable Mistress Sheldrake.*"

"Who's it from?" chimed Karel.

My eyes dropped to the signature at the bottom. My stomach fluttered. It was from Leander Rainford. My cheeks began to pinken.

"Sir Leander," I said quietly.

Beside me, Blanche and Iris stopped talking. My heart thundering, I slowly rose to my feet. Why would Tobias's master write to me? I scanned the contents quickly.

*I commend myself to you and trust this missive finds you well. I pray you do not think this presumptuous, but I wanted to reassure you about Tobias.*

My veins turned to ice. Oh dear God, what's happened?

"What is it, Anneke? What's wrong?" asked Betje, crawling along the bench to reach me. She touched my cheek. I pressed her hand against my face. It was warm, solid.

"Nothing, nothing," I lied and kept reading Sir Leander's bold, tidy script:

*Though Tobias has not been forthcoming about the manner in which he departed Holcroft House the night of St. Stephen's, I gather there has been a disturbance in your good relations and I wanted to express my sorrow and hope that my unforgivable behavior on first making your acquaintance, never mind the deplorable liberties I took on Christmas Day, have not been in any way responsible.*

I burrowed my cheek into Betje's hand, a small smile tugging the corners of my mouth. If only Sir Leander knew . . .

*I further pray that one day, you will find it in your heart to forgive me.*

Looking up from the letter, I pulled Betje's hand away and kissed her palm warmly.

"What's that for?" She extracted her hand and wiped it on her dress.

"No reason," I said, and tugged her plait before continuing with the letter.

*Above all, I wanted to reassure you that I will continue to look to Tobias's health and well-being as I have always done so that you need not cast your mind in our direction but focus on what needs be done at Holcroft House.*

There were a few lines about the ports they would be calling upon and the weather they were anticipating before he signed off.

*I wish you every good fortune in what is a brave venture for a woman, more so one on her own. With that in mind, I invite you to call upon me for assistance or advice at anytime. May the Holy Trinity have you and your family in their keeping always, yours in blessed Christ's name, Leander Rainford.*

Aware of everyone's eyes upon me, I folded the letter quickly and tucked it against my breast.

"Anneke! You said you were going to read it to us." Karel folded his arms and pouted.

"I said no such thing."

"Is Sir Leander well, mistress?" asked Will, who'd lingered in the hope of news.

"Very, Will."

"What does he say?" said Betje, her voice demanding.

I spun on the bench and stood, taking a crust of bread from the trencher. "That all is well with him and he sends his best to you."

"That's it? What about Tobias?"

A shadow flitted across my mind. "He's well too."

I glanced at Blanche and Iris, who both found the dough and pottage very interesting.

The bells for sext sounded. Midday. Adam and Saskia entered, creating a welcome diversion. Flushed from walking quickly, Saskia heaved her basket onto the table, pulling off her mantle, hood, and gloves, brushing bits of snow from the fabric.

"Well, that should be everything," she said, using the ends of her scarf to wipe her face. Adam hefted two laden sacks onto the table.

"I placed a poster up near the pillory, Mistress Anneke." He removed his cap and ran his fingers through his hair. "As you can imagine, there're a few people in the stocks with it approaching Lent, so I figured they would draw a crowd."

"I told him we didn't want that sort coming here," chided Saskia, shaking her head. "But would he listen?"

"All sorts stroll by the pillory, Saskia." I laughed. "It's those locked into it whose custom we'd decline, not those who choose to mock or study folk foolish enough to break the law."

"*Ja*, well, I hadn't thought of it like that." Saskia wrapped an apron around her waist and shot Adam a smile. He winked at me. Saskia began unpacking her basket, while Adam unwrapped the additional candles and haunch of mutton he'd bought.

I stayed a moment longer before deciding it was time to prepare myself. Running up the stairs, I looked at the freshly washed kirtle and tunic draped over my bed. They'd once been Mother's. One could not serve patrons in the color of death; it was time to cast off our mourning attire. Emerald green and sapphire blue, the latter recalled to me the color of Leander

Rainford's eyes. I reached over and stroked the material. Fancy him writing to me like that. I hadn't imagined it—he *was* sorry for what he called me. Recalling the pressure of his fingers, the feel of his lips, was it possible, could it be that . . . I dared to hope again.

Extracting the letter from where I'd folded it against my bosom, I pressed it in my palm then against my mouth, before opening my chest and tucking it beneath my undergarments.

If I could prove to Sir Leander, a man of firm convictions, I was no whore, then how hard would it be to demonstrate the same to others, alehouse or naught?

Dipping a cloth in the water Iris had delivered to the room, I began to wash, pushing thoughts of Tobias and our angry, cruel words aside, my head filled with ocean-blue eyes and a dazzling smile.

⤜⧓⤛

Reluctant though I was to call our first evening as the Cathaline Alehouse an unbridled success, all the evidence confirmed it: the number of customers pouring through the door, their gaiety and goodwill, praise for the ale—and even the beer, which was eagerly tried, though only a few chose to drink it exclusively, preferring the taste of the familiar—never mind the coin that now rattled in the tin. Music, food, laughter, and conversation flowed along with the amber liquid from the moment we officially opened our doors until the last patron left before curfew sounded. Not only did regular buyers of our ale attend, but many curious new customers as well as travelers who had entered through the city gates from the south and encountered us as the first establishment. Pilgrims, monks, hawkers, a troupe of traveling players making their way along the east coast before heading to York, a couple of knights and their squires, even some bargemen and their wives popped in and remained a goodly while. Sitting at the tables or on the window seats, leaning against the wall, or simply standing, it didn't take long for the room to feel crowded. The strange thing about groups of people is that they attract more, so even when some left, others quickly replaced them. Amidst them were Master Perkyn and Olive, who enveloped me in a huge hug; Hugh the baker; Simon Attenoke; Master Larkspur, briefly; and, much to my surprise, Master Allistair Gretting, the ale-conner. Of Betrix and Master Fortescue there was no sign, but I didn't expect Betrix to come to an alehouse, even if it was run by me. Master Fortescue couldn't endorse what the friary did not, so his absence was regrettable but understandable.

I could barely keep up with demand, and every time I checked on the servants, either Iris and Awel were bringing more food from the kitchen or Westel was tapping another barrel. Will served drinks with great cheer and, when able, Westel roamed the tables with a brimming jug, encouraging customers to drink up. When Will brought out his flute and Adam appeared with his gittern, there was clapping, stamping, and calls for songs to be sung, poems to be recited. Lost in the atmosphere, I stood near the table from which we served the drinks, swaying to the melodies.

By the time we closed and tidied, collecting the crushed and dirty rushes and throwing them into the ditch outside, turning over the tablecloths that couldn't be salvaged for use another night, and taking the dirty mazers, tankards, and goblets (though many patrons had, as was usual, brought their own) to

the scullery to be cleaned, I left Westel and Iris to lock the door,
staunch the fire, and snuff out the candles. Will was checking
the gates, while Adam was ensuring no patrons hovered outside
before putting Shelby to bed and ensuring the pigs and chickens were safe. First thanking Saskia and Blanche, the Parry sisters having been escorted home before dark, I then climbed the
stairs to look in on the twins. Exhausted, I was also filled with a
glow of excitement, the heat of success. The alehouse had operated more smoothly and more successfully than I dreamed. *Oh,
Tobias, I wish you could have been here.* Holding a candle aloft, I
entered the nursery.

The rise and fall of the twins' chests told me they were asleep
before their quiet breaths and sweet, dream-sent smell did. I
pulled aside the curtain and sat gingerly on the edge of the
mattress. Betje rolled toward me and I lifted her back into the
center. Snuggling into her brother, they slept face to face, their
full, pink mouths slightly open, their silver curls peeping from
beneath their sleeping caps. I tugged the furs higher and tucked
them around their throats, leaving soft kisses on their cheeks.
They stirred briefly, settling back into slumber. I felt the surge
of protectiveness that their innocence and trust in me always
aroused. It brought tears to my eyes and prayers to my lips.

"How was it, mistress?" asked a sleepy voice from the foot of
the bed. Bleary-eyed, Louisa sat up, the ends of her cap falling
over one shoulder.

"Sorry to disturb you," I whispered, rising swiftly. "It went
very well. Now, go back to sleep."

"God bless you, mistress. I'm so happy for you," said Louisa,
beaming at me as she lay back down. "You deserve happiness.
As Mary is the Holy Mother, you do."

With a full heart, I took the candle and tiptoed out. As I shut the nursery door, a hand touched my shoulder. I spun around. It was Will.

"Mis—Mistress Sheldrake! I'm so sorry, I didn't mean to startle you."

"It's all right, Will," I said, waiting for my heart to return to normal. "I was . . . lost in imaginings. What is it?" I asked. Will didn't often come to this part of the house.

"I was wondering, Mistress Sheldrake, may I've a word? In private?"

More startled by this than his sudden appearance, I gestured for Will to lead the way. "Let's go to the solar. There's no fire, but we won't be disturbed."

"Thank you, mistress."

The solar was cold and dark. Taking a rug from the back of one of the chairs, I first put the candle between us and threw the blanket to Will, urging him to cover himself. Hesitating, he sat in the seat opposite, tucked the blanket around his lap and plucked at his lower lip. I found another cover and wrapped it around my legs.

Waiting for him to speak, I rested my hands on the arms of the chair, remembering how, for a few weeks, I'd believed these pieces of furniture gone for good until Sir Leander organized their return. The thought made me smile and it was with this expression that I gave my attention to Will, even as I absent-mindedly stroked the wood.

"Now, what is it you want to speak to me about?"

In the candlelight, Will's sandy hair glistened and the freckles that dotted his face blurred into a golden perfection the daylight hours disallowed. "Well, mistress, I don't like to tell tales, and this may be nothing, but when it happened again, I felt you should know."

"When what happened?"

Will's eyes flashed to the door. He wrung his hands together then leaned closer and lowered his voice. "Westel passing notes."

I stared at him confused. "What do you mean?"

"I first saw it before Christmas. Westel was in the shop, helping sell ale, when a couple of men I've never seen before came in. They waited until Westel was free. I was busy fixing Master Larkspur with his ale and Westel was chatting to Olive. I asked him to tap a barrel, and that was when they pulled him aside."

"That's not unusual, is it?"

"It ain't usual either, mistress, not for strangers to take such an interest. I mean, what could they be saying that couldn't be spoken in front of me? They were whispering and waving their arms about. Anyhow, I didn't think too much about it until, first, I heard your name mentioned—"

"But I'm the brewster, Will."

"Nay, not by Westel, by one of these men. Then I saw Westel pass a note. He thought I didn't see, he waited till I left the room, but I stopped in the corridor, hoping to discover what they were talking about and he did it then."

"I still don't see why this is important. I mean, perhaps they were people Westel knew?"

"Oh, he knew 'em, all right. But that's not why I'm here, not the sole reason. I mentioned it to Adam and he said I was to keep an eye on Westel, and I have been. Until tonight, I saw nothing untoward, unless I count those letters he received . . ."

I let that slide. All the servants received correspondence. With the exception of Adam and Westel, the others required me to read it to them. It vexed Will that Westel didn't need my services and that his letters remained private. He saw it as a personal slight.

"Did you see those brothers what come in, mistress?"

"I did." It was hard to miss them with their black robes and heavy crosses. "Well, Awel was serving them when, lo and behold, just as the music starts, I see Westel pass another note. Not in an open way either. He held it beneath the trencher. I wouldn't have seen it except the monk he gave it to had had too much to drink and it slipped from his fingers. He bent down to pick it up and I saw it clear as the ears on Father Clement's head." He tweaked a lobe to emphasize his point.

I wanted to reassure Will there was nothing to be concerned about, but passing a note to monks—especially Benedictines— didn't sit comfortably with me. What possible reason would Westel have to do that? Having them in my establishment was cause enough for concern and I'd been careful to ensure they were served swiftly. I'd no doubt they were there to spy on me. So why would Westel be passing notes? Mayhap they weren't from St. Jude's but were old friends from the friary in Norwich. That must be it.

Will was watching me with wary eyes. "Sometimes, mistress, he also wanders the house at night. I wake and he's not in our room. I don't always hear him come back, but when I do, I know he's been gone a while." I wasn't sure what to say. There could be a perfectly reasonable explanation for that as well.

"I didn't want to worry you, but I thought you should know."

"Thank you, Will, thank you. I appreciate it."

"What will you do?"

"Do?" I stood up, folding the blanket and placing it on the

seat. "What any rational person does in these situations—seek the truth."

Will neatly folded his rug and laid it across the stool.

"I'll ask Westel."

The expression on Will's face caught me unawares. There was a flash of what I can only describe as concern before it changed into a mask of obedience.

"Aye, mistress," he said and, with a small bow, went to leave. As he reached the door, he turned, one hand on the frame. "Only, be careful, won't you? I don't think Westel is what you think he is."

"What do you think he is, Will?"

The darkness between us tightened.

"Dangerous."

# TWENTY-SIX

*O*ver a week passed before I'd a chance to speak to Westel and, when I did, it was in the brewery, where we were both occupied, as the mash tun, malt, and wort took precedence. Nonetheless, Westel wasn't upset by my question.

"It was a chance for me to let Brother Roland know I'm in fine hands," he said, pausing over a tray of dried malt, the steam from the hot grain moistening his face. Pushing his hair off his forehead, his eyes crinkled at the corners.

"I'm happy you think so, Westel." I paused. "So, you wrote a message to Brother Roland?"

"Aye, and asked the monks to carry it. Is there a problem, Mistress Sheldrake?"

I'd never spoken to Westel about the brothers, Abbot Hubbard, or his threats to undermine my efforts. Talk among the servants and in the town would mean he wasn't completely ignorant. I decided it was time to tell him. Briefly, I spoke of what happened—Brother Osbert's visits, his offers and my refusal to sell, the damage done to Master Perkyn's place, and even my misgivings about the dogs' disappearance, that it too was an attempt to warn me away from ale-making. Westel listened, his large eyes growing rounder.

"How dare they," he said between clamped teeth. "As God is my witness, the monks of St. Rebecca's would never condone such practices, such tactics. Oh, mistress, no wonder you were worried about the notes. I'm so very sorry. If it will reassure you, I'll never speak to them again."

I looked at his earnest face. "Nay. Nay, Westel, there's no problem." The man was entitled to speak and write to whom he wanted. I'd allowed my prejudice and Will's to gnaw at me.

Holding my gaze a moment, he gave a nod and returned to work. I watched him a little longer. Hefting the tray to the table to cool, he went about his tasks, picking up the shovel and entering the malthouse. His relaxed manner and readiness to explain banished the last of any suspicions I'd been harboring.

Turning back to the mash, I didn't raise the issue of wandering about the house; after all, there was probably a perfectly reasonable and private explanation for this as well. And what did it matter anyway? In my own mind, I put Will's concern down to jealousy. There was no doubt that since Westel's arrival, the attention Will once received from the female servants, and probably me as well, had been reduced. No longer was he the only young man in the house. Furthermore, they shared a room. I hadn't considered it before today, but the more deeply I thought, I could see the jealousy—the disdainful glances Will would flash, how he'd roll his eyes or mutter under his breath if Westel spoke, often exchanging a meaningful look with Adam. I didn't have time to pander to Will's pride and thought that learning to live and work with another man would teach Will some valuable lessons in both cooperation and humility. I determined to speak to Adam about this and enlist his support. I did not want my servants at loggerheads.

First days, then weeks went by in a flurry of activity and, before I knew it, it was spring and Lent with all its strict observances arrived—observances that were occasionally overlooked within the confines of the alehouse. From dawn until the alehouse closed just before curfew, I was consumed by all things brewing. And when I wasn't preoccupied with boiling wort; making sure the right quantities of additives, including hops, were placed in the vat; or getting to the brewhouse before anyone stirred so I could sing the ale and now beer to life; or serving what I'd made, I was toting up figures, paying creditors, ordering barley, making certain requisitions were filled and customers satisfied.

The only interruption to my otherwise steady routine occurred in the mornings. For some time, I'd been unable to shake the impression I was being observed. Rising early and going to the brewery had become such a solitary and accustomed habit, it took me a while to pay attention to my feelings. Without the dogs to warn me if someone was coming, I was more conscious of listening out for Westel or the Parry sisters' arrival. I pricked my ears but not, initially, my other senses. When I did, I felt as if I was wading in cobwebs; as if invisible fingers were caressing my flesh, tugging at the roots of my hair. I was certain I was being spied upon.

Yet, though I kept the doors closed and one eye on the window when performing the ancient rites, the feeling remained. The displeasure of the corner crones, who didn't like our customs to be seen, was palpable. I worked hard to appease them and yet . . . no matter what precautions I took, no matter how careful I was to check no one else was about, I couldn't shake the notion I was being watched.

But if I was, why could I see no one?

When Westel stumbled in some time after the sun rose, rubbing his face and stifling yawns, I'd ask him if anyone was about.

"Nay, Mistress Sheldrake," he'd say, scratching his head. "It's just you and me." Then he'd flash that broad smile and I'd try to dismiss my worries.

After a while, it became a game to him. "Feel any eyes upon you this morning, Mistress Sheldrake?" he'd ask as he entered the brewery.

With a hollow laugh, I would shrug and feel more than a little foolish and, after a time, the sensation dulled or, as I suspected, I became accustomed to it. Nonetheless, though the days lengthened, I took to rising even earlier and satisfying the crones and the needs of the ale while it was still dark.

Whenever possible, I'd spend time with the twins. Often, in the middle of the day, I'd leave the brewery and alehouse to the others and accompany Louisa and the children on a walk along the bay or in the woods behind the church. Sometimes, Father Clement would join us and it was on these occasions I could put aside my concerns and lose myself in the joy of the children as they kicked rivulets in the melting snow, chased a daring rabbit, spied a robin or lark, and, as springtime blossomed, happened upon birds' nests and eggs. If we strolled by the ocean, we'd cast pebbles into the water, pass the time counting the number of caravels drifting in the harbor, or collect shells to bring home.

While Tobias's prediction that the alehouse would become a den of vice didn't eventuate, I could no longer ignore how my reputation in town had suffered as a consequence. Though we'd only been open a few months, there was a distinct shift in the manner of the vendors in town. Where once the men would treat me with a deference due to my position as a Sheldrake, some took to gazing at me boldly as I handed over coin or argued about the price of a coney, halibut, or spices. It was as if they wanted to say something else but didn't yet dare. Whether it was the presence of Adam or Westel by my side, I never knew, but I sensed the change, and though I continued to behave as I'd always done, something important had been lost.

Women were more obvious. Some whom I'd known well when my mother was alive, and who, in the past, had visited our solar, sat at our table, or invited us to theirs, turned away on sighting me. But it wasn't until Betrix and her mother made a point of changing direction when they saw me as I was leaving Master Proudfellow's one day that I knew for certain those small differences I'd detected in people's behavior were real. Betrix didn't even look over her shoulder; there was no reassuring glance or smile, just the back of her ruby mantle and the kick of her hem as her leather boots scurried out of sight. After that, I searched for excuses to avoid going to town, sending a servant in my stead.

Saskia didn't say anything, but she knew. I heard her talking with Adam late into the night as I sat in the office, the murmur of their voices offering both comfort and a painful reminder that my rapid social descent affected them as well. Accumulating enough to pay Lord Rainford came at a cost and, for the first time, I wondered if it had been worth it.

After the last of the patrons departed—many now foreign sailors who were keen to drink the beer—and we'd tidied the alehouse, the servants left me in peace. Instead of retreating to the hall for supper and a tale or two before bed, I pulled a stool toward the fireplace, sinking gratefully upon it. That's how Saskia found me some time later, staring despondently into the flames. She stood beside me and, without saying a word, pressed my head against her thigh, stroking my face, wiping away tears I didn't know I'd begun to shed.

"*Mijn zoete kind,*" she whispered. It had been years since she'd used that endearment, *my sweet child*. I cried harder. "What is it? Tell me."

Words tumbled out. "Tobias . . . he . . . he warned me. So did Adam, Captain Stoyan, and even Sir Leander. But would I listen? Nay. And now . . . now . . ." I raised my arms in a clumsy gesture before they flopped back into my lap.

"They knew they could never talk you out of the alehouse, my *zoete*. They told you this, gave you such warnings as they could to prepare you. They knew what people would be like. How narrow and judgmental they can be." She smoothed my hair. "Folk don't cope well with change; they're threatened by it, fear it."

"As God is my witness, Saskia"—my voice was fragile, quavering, and I hated it—"I haven't changed. I'm the same person I always was. Why can't people see that? I'm still Anneke Sheldrake who used to be welcomed with smiles and encouraging words. I'm still the Anneke Sheldrake they paid their respects to after Father died. All that's changed is I serve ale to people . . . nothing else." I buried my face in my hands and wept.

"Hush, hush, my lamb, *mijn zoete*." Saskia bent down and took my face in her calloused hands, her smile so sweet, so gentle. "Listen to me." She forced my chin up so I had to look upon her. There was a hard glint in the amber depths of her eyes. "Anneke. You're not the same person. You've changed and praise be to God that you have."

I sniffed loudly. "But—"

"How can you be the same after all you've endured?" Pushing strands of hair off my cheeks, she continued. "You're stronger. More determined." She took one of my hands in her own. "You've a family to raise, bills to pay, a household and business to run. You refuse to be influenced by what others say, think, or do. Those people out there"—she waved her hand toward the street—"they don't like that they can't control you anymore— the shrews with their gossip and rumors, the men because you're proving a woman can be without a husband and survive. That she can run a business." She laughed. "You're not a servant, you're not a wife, you're not a mother. You're queen of your own realm, your own woman, and they don't know what to make of you anymore."

I choked back a sob. "What if I don't want to be my own woman?" I wiped my nose on the end of my apron and stared at her.

"Whose would you want to be?" she asked softly.

I opened my mouth . . .

"Excuse me, Mistress Sheldrake."

Saskia released my hand with one last tightening of her fingers and rose slowly, her joints creaking. I quickly brushed the tears away and straightened my scarf.

"Aye, Westel?"

"I put the tin on your desk. I also took the liberty of leaving a goblet of wine there for you." He hesitated. "You look like you need it."

I lifted my hand to prevent Saskia rebuking him for his familiarity. "Thank you, Westel." He bowed and left.

Rising, I turned and gave Saskia a hug. "Thank you too."

Returning my embrace, she held me at arm's length and beamed. "You're always welcome, Mistress Anneke. Always. You know, if God had ever seen fit to bless me with a daughter, I'd have wanted her to be just like you."

I almost bumped into a table, so thick were the tears that welled in my eyes.

"But," she continued, drawing close to me and lowering her voice, "if I may give you one piece of advice"—she didn't pause long enough for me to answer—"be careful with that lad, Mistress Anneke, with Westel. You indulge him. He thinks because he works beside you, he can hover all over the house and say what he likes. He's getting a bit too big for his boots. As far as I'm concerned, he's still on trial and if you won't watch him, I will."

I sighed. First Will and now Saskia. "You do that, Saskia," I said and kissed her soundly on the cheek. "It's a great solace knowing you're looking out for me."

# TWENTY-SEVEN

HOLCROFT HOUSE

Lent

*The year of Our Lord 1406 in the seventh*
*year of the reign of Henry IV*

*W*e opened our doors as the bells for sext chimed. People poured out of St. Bartholomew's into the cold, and while many headed home, more than I expected entered the Cathaline Alehouse. In no time at all, the fireside was crowded. Orders were placed quickly and drinks were downed with enthusiasm. Delyth, Awel, and Westel wandered around the tables, squeezing past strangers and locals alike as they deposited brimming tankards, foaming mazers, and set down jugs and vessels. Will and Adam tended the barrels, while I supervised between the kitchen and alehouse, making sure the limited food we were allowed by law to serve was readily available. Perhaps because it was Lent and yesterday had been an Ember Day, where fasting and penance was observed, people were tired of all the restrictions and looking to ease their long period of denial. There were more unfamiliar faces than usual and while I wasn't initially alarmed, as the afternoon wore on and the place grew rowdy, a sense of unease overtook me.

A granite sky made the shadows appear early and, when it began to drizzle, a few men took the chance to leave. But as they did more came to take their place. The smell of damp wool, horseflesh, sweat, and the sweet odor of ale and fire smoke lingered. In one corner, an old man I'd never seen before but who'd asked to bring his three-legged dog inside, pulled out a set of pipes and began to play a mournful tune. When his dog started to howl, some men sitting nearby complained. Amused by the dog's antics and the men's protests at first, when one of the men, tall, wearing a liripipe—a long, pointed hood that fell down his back— staggered to his feet and took a swipe at the dog, I called Adam.

Bearing the great wooden staff we kept hidden, Adam made his way through the crowd. Simon Attenoke stood ready to lend assistance. Before Adam could call for peace, another man, even bigger than the first, with thick, short hair and the build of a knight, grabbed the first man and, lest he attempt another strike at the dog, threw him backward. The man wearing the liripipe fell against a table, knocking it over and spilling drinks. After that, mayhem ensued.

There were grunts and shouts. Fists flew, bodies doubled over. Tankards smashed, ale spilled, and the dog barked. Backed up against a wall, shouting at Awel and Delyth to flee, I was trying to stay out of the way when someone grabbed me from behind, their hands kneading my breasts, pulling at my skirts. Shock stilled me before rage took over and, as the hands fumbled over my body, I grabbed hold of one of them and sank my teeth into it. There was a scream of pain and, as I spat blood on the floor, I was released. Swinging around to identify the rogue, I was again grabbed and lifted off my feet. Kicking, I tried to pry the fingers from my waist.

"It's me, Mistress Sheldrake." *Westel.* "You need to get out of here."

I ceased struggling at once.

Westel carried me from the room, using his back and shoulders to thrust people out of the way. Putting me down in the corridor just outside, he pushed the tin into my hands. I clutched it gratefully. Will brought Awel over, Delyth following, tears streaming down her face.

"Stay here," ordered Will, and he was about to return, the light of battle in his eyes, when I grabbed ahold of him. "Nay, Will. Run, fetch the sheriff. Tell him to bring his men. Hurry."

Will glanced at Westel.

"Don't worry. I'll look after them," he said.

Will opened his mouth, shut it again, then nodded. Pushing past us, he grabbed his coat and raced down the corridor, leaving through the kitchen. Standing beside Westel, I placed myself between the girls and doorway, using my boots and arms to push anyone who came too close away again. Westel delivered a few hard punches, breaking the skin of his knuckles, wincing in pain. I couldn't help but be grateful for his presence, his determination to protect us.

In dismay I watched as tables broke, mazers were dented, crockery smashed, and my ale and beer spilled over the rushes. Adam was trying to separate two men, one of whom was bleeding profusely from the nose, when another crept up behind, a stool raised above his head.

"Adam!" I shouted in warning. Adam ducked as the stool

swept through the air, striking another man with a resounding crack, lifting him off his feet. Westel left my side and ran to Adam's defense, but by then the fight was so thick, the roiling bodies so tight-knit, I couldn't keep track. Above the din, the bell over the door clanged as men fled. Running past the windows, their shirts torn, their heads bare as they churned up mud with their heels. One paused to tear down the sign that was swinging wildly in the wind.

"Oy!" cried out Westel, his voice so loud I jumped. "Nay, you rogue," he exclaimed and, before Adam could prevent him, tore off after the men.

"Westel! Leave it . . ." It was no use. He sprinted up the street.

"He's a brave one, mistress," said Awel, her eyes wide.

"Aye, or very foolish," I said wryly.

There were still too many writhing, grunting bodies left inside. Fists connected, arms swung. Cheeks were torn, teeth lost, and bodies crumpled. Atop the last remaining table, the old man's dog howled, scampering from side to side like a wounded squire at a joust. Slumped against the wall was the old man. I wondered if he was even alive.

Once the sheriff arrived, worse for drink himself, and ordered the watchmen haul away those offenders who refused to concede defeat, bellowing they be locked in the stocks to cool their tempers, the remainder understood it was over. Above the sheriff's slurred threats and warnings, the men collected their coats and looked around in bewilderment at the remains of the Cathaline Alehouse. Subdued by the enormity of what they'd done, the sheriff asked for descriptions of those who'd bolted, strangers to Elmham Lenn who were already being blamed for starting what happened.

The shadows lengthened and the rain was falling steadily by the time the last man left, escorted by two of the watchmen, cross their afternoon was spoiled. They pulled him forward, uncaring that his coat slipped from his shoulder or that his cap came off and was trampled in the mud.

Picking up one of the stools, I sank onto it and stared at the room, the tin resting in my lap. Piles of rushes flecked with blood, shattered utensils, and pieces of what had once been benches, toppled tables, and too many pieces of broken jugs, tankards, and split mazers were scattered everywhere. The only things unaffected were the three barrels behind the serving table and the fireplace.

The sheriff, Sir Grantham, asked me questions and I know I answered, but I don't remember what I said. In the midst of all this, Westel returned, his shirt torn, a bloody streak across the front, but he had our sign and held it aloft triumphantly. "I couldn't let them steal that too, Mistress Sheldrake," he said.

I shook my head wearily.

The sheriff fired questions at Westel; I didn't hear his responses. My mind was too busy trying to work out how the fight started, whether I could have done anything to prevent it. Everything was such a blur. It was only as Sir Grantham was leaving, promising to return the following day after I'd rested, that I thought of Delyth and Awel and asked him to escort them home. I looked at their pale faces and their large, frightened eyes and wondered if they'd have the courage to return. Delighted he'd enjoy the company of two such pretty girls, Sir Grantham bade farewell with more goodwill than he arrived.

As the door closed, Tobias's words rang in my ears. *"Turning this house, our home into an alehouse that any knave can enter is something altogether different . . ."* Just how different, I'd not known. Until today.

Before long, Saskia came and pressed a mazer of mulled wine in my hand. Grateful for its warmth, I sipped it slowly, smiling weakly as Blanche, Westel, and Adam, who held a wad of cloth over his left eye, gathered around me.

"Where are the twins?" I asked quietly.

"Iris and Louisa took them to the nursery the moment the fighting started. They're fine," said Saskia, gripping my shoulder. I reached up and closed my hand over hers.

"Thank you."

Using a piece of tinder from the fire, Blanche went around and relit the candles. Their bright flames were at odds with the ruins.

The faces of my servants told me they were as dazed as I felt. Blanche had to touch everything, pick up a stool here, a crumpled tablecloth there. She found shards of pottery and glass and piled them neatly on a table, walked in circles pushing the rushes back down with her boots. We watched her in silence. Adam seemed resigned. Only Westel, his eyes neutral, dwelled upon me.

"Where's Will?" I asked suddenly.

Blanche stopped and glared at the rushes, hands on hips, as if expecting him to rise from beneath them.

"I last saw him when he went to fetch the sheriff," said Westel, scratching his head through his cap.

"He should be back well and truly by now." Adam nodded at Westel. "Go and see if he's in the kitchen."

Westel darted off.

"This is a right mess, Mistress Anneke," said Blanche, finding another shard of pottery.

"Nothing we can't fix," said Adam quickly, as if Blanche's observation was somehow critical of me.

"Aye," I agreed, "but should we?" Resting my elbows on my knees, I looked at Adam and Blanche. Neither answered. Saskia rubbed my back. They knew it was not their decision to make.

Westel reappeared. "He's not there, Mistress Sheldrake. Nor's he in our room, the solar, or the brewery." He hesitated. "Do you want me to lock up the chickens and pigs? They're still out."

"Will wouldn't overlook his duties," said Adam, slapping his thighs and standing, raising his voice to be heard above the rain that was now coming down in torrents. He stared out into the sodden gloom. "Where's that lad disappeared to?"

"Could he have stopped at another tavern on the way home?" asked Westel.

"He wouldn't be foolish enough to give chase to those strangers, would he?" asked Saskia, giving Westel a pointed look.

"Nay," I said quickly. "Please, God, nay."

"Maybe he went to warn Master Proudfellow?" added Blanche hopefully.

"It's possible, I suppose." Adam sighed and reached for his cloak and hat. "I'll go and find him. Westel, look to the animals." He turned to me. "Mistress Anneke, if I may be so bold, I suggest you go to the twins and reassure yourself as to their well-being. I'll return soon enough and we can discuss what we do about"—he shook his head as he studied the room—"this."

Standing, I straightened my tunic. "As you say, Adam."

"Don't worry, mistress," he added quietly. "We'll sort this out."

The bell above the alehouse door couldn't be heard above the rain as Adam left. The wind was so strong, he was almost bent double as he passed the window. I shivered, whether in empathy or foreboding, I wasn't sure. I ordered Saskia to take the tin to the office and Blanche to prepare hot water for Will and Adam for when they returned and to warm some drying sheets for Westel. I didn't have to tell Saskia to heat some additional wine. We'd all be needing it before this night was over.

Turning my back on the wreckage of the afternoon, I ascended to the nursery, quickly tidying myself before the children saw me. As Saskia said, the twins were unaffected by what had occurred, and for that, at least, I was grateful. Louisa was telling them a story, Iris by her side. Wide-eyed, Iris started to ask what had happened, but I sent her downstairs to help Blanche and, casting a warning look at Louisa, sat quietly while she finished her tale.

Insisting I also regale them, the twins had their way. Exhausted, I was also filled with a nervous energy that found some comfort from an old fable Mother used to tell about a beautiful woman, an oracle, who was so desired by a god, he promised to give her anything she wanted if only she would succumb to his charms. When she asked for everlasting life, he readily granted it, but when she reneged on her part of the agreement, that they be lovers, he altered his gift so she could live forever, but would continue aging.

"How long did she live?" asked Betje, breathlessly.

"For eternity," I said.

"Forever? But if she lived forever . . ." Betje tried to absorb what that meant.

"What did she look like?" asked Karel. "Worse than Good-wife Barrett?"

Goodwife Barrett was the oldest woman in Elmham Lenn. Rumor had it that she was one hundred and five years old, but I knew she was four score years and two, a fine age, but to the twins and others, ancient. Karel and Betje were fascinated by her sunken, lined cheeks, her toothless mouth, the wattle that hung from her neck, and the fact one of her eyes had turned white.

"Much, much worse," I said. They oohed in delighted horror.

"That just proves, you should always keep your promise, doesn't it?" said Karel.

My throat seized and a fire licked the inside of my ribs. I hadn't ever thought of the tale as carrying that meaning. To me it had always been about being cautious when making commitments, ensuring all the terms were clear. I stared at Karel.

"It does," I said as panic rose in my chest and I wondered how I would keep mine now. All of them. I'd promised not only to keep the family together, but to find the means to pay the lease. I'd also promised Tobias that if my efforts failed, I would never brew again. I stood up quickly. The room began to spin and my arms flew out.

"Are you all right, mistress?" asked Louisa, reaching out to help me.

"Fine. I'm fine." I had a desperate urge to count coin, check the ledgers.

When the room stopped turning, I kissed the twins, wished them sweet dreams and God's love, and crept out of the nursery and ran downstairs.

A fire was blazing in the office hearth and I blessed Saskia's foresight. Wine awaited me, no longer warm but no less welcome.

The battered tin glowed in the light. Opening the lid, I looked at the small pile of coin in dismay. I'd thought there'd be more. Few of the patrons had paid before the melee broke out. I struck my forehead with the heel of my hand. "Damn, damn."

I pushed the tin away and picked up the goblet.

Draining it, I heard voices.

"Mistress Anneke, Mistress Anneke!" I recognized that tone. Ice crawled into my heart. I ran to meet whoever it was summoning me in such a way.

It was Adam. Dripping wet, his face leached of color, his lips were trembling, but not from cold.

"What is it, Adam? Tell me." I stood in front of him, staring, afraid.

"It's Will. Oh God, Anneke." It wasn't just the rain streaking his cheeks, there were tears and . . . blood.

*Blood.*

"What?" I whispered, dreading to hear.

"He's been murdered."

# TWENTY-EIGHT

HOLCROFT HOUSE

Lent to Easter Monday

*The year of Our Lord 1406 in the seventh*

*year of the reign of Henry IV*

*W*ill's death plunged us into an ocean of grief. Our love for him was a garment we held in common and, instead of wearing it in turn, we donned it together. Yet, for all the succor this offered, it was also a hairshirt that I for one did not wish to remove.

Never before had I felt so utterly responsible for something. Will was only fifteen, on the cusp of manhood. Born and raised in Elmham Lenn, the third son of a tanner, he'd come to us when he was eight years old; a mixture of shyness and cockiness tempered by a desire to please and do his family proud. Adam had taken him under his wing, as had Saskia. Not even Hiske's sharp tongue or Father's curt demands had managed to staunch his pride in his position or his gregariousness. I would miss his bright eyes, his freckled nose, his crooked grin. The way his face infused with color when he was caught off-guard; how his hair would never sit flat but always stand to attention. In quiet moments, I found myself reflecting on the last time we really spoke. He'd told me about Westel; the passing of notes, his inclination to wander. I'd dismissed his concerns as jealousy. Feeling I owed Will something, I found myself watching Westel more closely and I began to ponder, if he did indeed leave his room regularly, as Will said, where he went.

After some consideration, the sheriff concluded the assailants were strangers who, affected by drink, angry at being forced to leave, and holding little value upon life, treated Will as a scapegoat. To them, he said, knocking a youth unconscious with a cowardly blow and then slitting a throat was as simple as lacing a boot. With his callous rendering of the crime, the guilt I'd carried with me the moment I caught sight of Will's limp body— with its wide, unseeing eyes cast toward the harsh heavens, the livid gash and bruising on his forehead, the ghastly wound on his neck—found voice. If I hadn't opened the alehouse, if I hadn't invited strangers into Holcroft House, if I hadn't asked Will to serve them, none of this would have happened. He would still be alive, his parents would still have a son, his two older brothers and younger sister their sibling, and none of them would be plunged into mourning. Words tumbled out and, beyond caring how I sounded, I railed at Adam, Sir Grantham, Westel, Blanche, and Saskia, who tried to silence me. I would have none of it. Sweeping aside her reassurances, I accused myself, took responsibility for Will's murder, until the burden was so great, I could no longer bear its weight.

Striding out of the hall, ignoring the stunned faces of my servants, Westel's foiled attempt to follow, and the cries of the twins, who, hearing raised voices, had run down from the nursery, I fled to the brewhouse, tears flowing freely.

Adam found me a while later, staring into the mash tun, the ale-stick unmoving in my hand. I didn't acknowledge his presence but remained inert, numb with guilt and sorrow and, I admit, self-pity.

"Mistress Anneke," Adam said softly, his voice a sigh that carried with it overtones of such kindness, my tears began anew. Prying my fingers from the stick, he gently lowered my hand. "Here, let me." He lifted the paddle over the edge of the tun, slowly steeping it into the thick, creamy sludge, and then began to stir. At first I ignored him and the soporific movements he was making, but gradually my eyes latched onto the spirals of his actions. Slowly, my other senses became aware: the soft splodge of the mash folding upon itself, the little burps and exhalations the mixture made, familiar companions who, just as I sang them to life each day, now sought to return the favor, chasing the specter of brutal death from my mind. Beneath my fingers, the firmness of the tun I was gripping took shape. Sniffing loudly, I caught the malty smell that characterized the brewhouse. Will would always comment on the odor. "Why, it smells good enough to eat, not drink," he'd say.

"Oh, Adam." His name shuddered on my lips.

"It's too late to tell you not to do something you've already accomplished, Mistress Anneke, but blaming yourself achieves nothing. Will's death is God's will."

"God's will?" My head snapped up, eyes narrowing, chin jutting defiantly. "*God's* will?" I repeated more loudly, dashing the tears from my face. "God didn't will this, Adam. This was man's doing and man's alone. Wicked, terrible men with murder in their hearts and blood on their hands. You heard the sheriff. They care not a jot for God's will."

"Exactly," said Adam and, letting go of the ladle, gripped my shoulders, forcing me to look at him. "It's *man's* doing. If you're going to take responsibility, then you have to allow me to take some as well." He leveled a finger to stop my retort. "After all, I urged him to protect you, to fight. Then he went for the sheriff and into the path of the cutthroats. How am I any less responsible than you? Stop condemning yourself for something you didn't contrive. If you don't, then you may as well include me and everyone else there among the guilty."

"But if there was no alehouse—"

"Mayhap Will would still be alive. But why stop there? If there was no Holcroft House, if there were no Sheldrakes, Barfoots, people entering Elmham Lenn. We can play that game till the oceans dry and the clouds cease to gather. What will it accomplish? What-ifs, whys, and wherefores are like capturing mist—empty of purpose. Facts are, Mistress Anneke, nothing you or I do or say will change what's happened. Even if the watchmen find who's responsible and hang him from the gallows, it won't bring Will back. Blaming yourself won't either, but it will hinder everything you do from here on in." He paused and tilted my chin till I was forced to look at him. "And God's truth, Mistress Anneke, our Will wouldn't want that."

Letting me go, Adam opened his arms. I fell into them, burying my head in his chest. "Who would do such a thing, Adam?"

I could feel Adam's chin against the top of my head. "Someone with no conscience, Anneke; someone who feels they don't have to answer to God or man."

I shut my eyes and tried to block out the terrifying image Adam's words conveyed. The notion that someone so ready to embrace sin existed was hard to bear. That Will should have encountered such a one.

"You don't think it was the abbot, do you? You don't think he was behind this?"

Adam stiffened. "I don't know what to think, mistress."

Weeping until my throat was sore, my ribs aching, and the front of Adam's shirt wringing wet, I remained in the comfort of his embrace until the afternoon bells sounded. Only then did I break away, feeling suddenly awkward, vulnerable.

Before I could say another word, the door opened. I broke away from Adam's arms.

It was Westel.

"Sorry, Mistress Sheldrake, Master Adam, but Mistress Saskia asked me to fetch you. Father Clement's here to discuss the burial."

"Thank you, Westel." I dabbed my eyes with a cloth and took a deep breath before smoothing my skirts. Though I wasn't ready for this, I'd no choice, not if I wanted to spare Will's parents the heartache. I glanced at Westel, who remained in the doorway looking from me to Adam. He was very pale. Dark crescents circled his eyes. None of us were sleeping well, for certes.

Following Adam and Westel back into the house, I pushed the murmurs of misgiving aside. I would deal with them later.

⋖≈×≋⋗

Will's funeral was held the next day. A small, private affair consisting of his immediate family; all of Holcroft House; the Millers; Master Proudfellow, Kip, and his mother, Jocelyn; Simon

Attenoke and Widow Atwell; Sir Grantham and his squire; and a few others—we gathered first in the church, and later in the pouring rain outside. Delyth and Awel Parry came, escorted by their father, but they only stayed long enough to see Will put in the ground and they didn't exchange a word or glance with me.

Through tears, I muttered responses hopelessly, taking small comfort from the twins, who wrapped their arms about me, their faces puffy from crying, their little mouths downturned. Not even the usually reassuring presence of Captain Stoyan helped.

A procession of bedraggled black, we doggedly followed his bound corpse, rain pounding our coats and hoods, drowning out Father Clement's prayers, quenching the censor. Buried alongside his grandmother, Will was finally laid to rest and, as clods of heavy soil were tossed upon him, every shovelful was a blow that struck us all. I turned away, unable to bear the sobs of his sister or the quiet, blanched stoicism of his mother and brothers any longer.

Afterward, we retired to the hall. Eschewing the formalities, we ate together. Bread, ale, cheese, Blanche's pottage, and, though it was Lent, pork, chicken, and even some venison were served. Will's family, the Heymongers, sat quietly, eyes widening as dish after dish was brought out. Unaccustomed to such extravagance, they didn't understand that this feast was my way of honoring their son and, if I'm honest, assuaging the responsibility Adam argued I shouldn't feel. Not even bearing the expense of the funeral achieved that. Nothing did.

For a long time after, I was listless, agitated, and unable to work with my usual enthusiasm. Habits are hard to break, though, and after tossing and turning most nights, I'd rise and make my way to the brewery before cockcrow, sing to the ale and honor the corner crones, but my heart wasn't in it. It was Westel who saw to all the little but important things, and though I was grateful for his determination not to let the ale spoil, I was beyond caring. I also began to find his incessant need to make sure everything was right jarring. Whereas I'd once enjoyed his smiles, like Saskia I now found his constant grin rang false, his observations about the ale, beer, the weather, and the household irritating, and longed for the silence of my thoughts. Once, when I brought the recipe book to the brewhouse in order to try something new, anything to detract from my usual ruminations, he asked if he might see it. He'd never made such a request and, I confess, as I refused him—and quite sharply—his eager curiosity about the contents added to his perceived sins. Pondering what Will said, what Saskia had added, I began to view Westel with different eyes. Doubt began to color my appreciation. Instead of seeing him as helpful, I saw him as interfering; instead of inquiring, his questions were suddenly prying. I began to shut off to him. I was too heartsore to make an effort, to get to the bottom of this change. Was it him or me? I didn't care to find out. Courteous, I offered very little else. In response, Westel sought even harder to bridge the widening distance.

The day after the funeral, I'd written to Tobias and Sir Leander, informing them of what had happened. God knows, I didn't want to, but it had to be done. I entrusted the letters to Captain Stoyan, who left for Ypres the following day. When a letter of sympathy arrived from Sir Leander weeks later, I felt strangely relieved, as if sharing the burden beyond our walls made it easier to carry.

Clutching his letter to me, I memorized the words:

*The horror of what occurred must color life at Holcroft House in the darkest of hues. You have my deepest sympathies. I will pray for you, for young Will's soul, and for the twins and servants. Mostly, I will ask God that he attend most swiftly to the recovery of your spirit, which must be sorely battered by such a terrible ordeal. Please, Mistress Anneke, if there is anything I can do to aid you in your time of grief, do not hesitate to ask. Oceans can be sailed, distance closed. I am yours to command. All it would take is your expressed need.*

With Sir Leander's words, I found a modicum of peace.

*I am yours to command. All it would take is your expressed need.*

The day after his letter arrived, to which I swiftly replied, another was delivered. I'd hoped it was from Tobias but, alas, there was no word from my brother, just a telling and, I felt, righteous silence. The letter was from an entirely different and quite surprising source.

The bells for none had not long rung. I'd finished in the brewery and was in the office brooding over the ledgers when Adam rapped smartly on the door. He'd quietly assumed Will's duties as well as his own.

"This just came, Mistress Anneke. The messenger didn't wait for a reply."

Moving to stand by the window to read, I was afforded a view of the alehouse as well. Saskia, Blanche, Iris, and Adam had worked hard to remove all signs of damage and, though we had two less tables, too few stools, and more cracks in the walls, the rushes had been replaced, the fire re-laid, and the room was ready to serve customers again.

The last step was the most difficult to take—it was a chasm I could not yet cross. For the moment, the alehouse remained closed, though the shop still traded.

Failing to recognize the seal, I broke it and, unfurling the parchment, caught my breath when I saw the familiar script. The few harsh lines took only moments to scan.

*If only you'd listened to those who knew from the outset how such outrageous plans, such ungodly behavior would conclude. You have no one to blame but yourself, Anneke Sheldrake, for the shame and ignominy you've brought upon your family. You forget your place in every regard and so God has seen fit to punish you, as you so justly deserve. That He chose to strike one in your care for sins you've committed lies upon your conscience alone. I am writing to inform you that from this day forth, you are no longer my cousin, nor of my blood. I formally and irrevocably sever all ties with the Sheldrakes. Any offers made to you in the past are rescinded. You, your brother, and your sister must needs fend for yourselves because you will receive nothing more from this quarter. May God see fit to forgive you, because no one else will.*

Sinking onto the chair, I felt Hiske's accusations leap from the paper, full of invective. They were also the truth. How could anyone forgive me when I couldn't forgive myself?

Shame and regret swamped me. Tears pricked my eyes. I shut them to prevent them falling, but my thoughts forced them open again. I wanted to be furious with Hiske but she only stated what others were thinking—what I was thinking. I'd no doubt my name, which was already questionable in town, was now a byword. *And whose fault was that? Why, yours, Anneke Sheldrake.* I'd brought this all on myself.

Only, the twins would now suffer for my schemes; and Will . . . Will paid the ultimate price. Who else might?

Folding the letter and its bitter contents away, I rose. Moving back to the window, I stared at my small demesne—the Cathaline Alehouse.

Two choices lay before me: I could either forget the alehouse and brewing and throw myself upon Lord Rainford's mercy, or, with less than a month to acquire the monies to make the lease, reopen and do everything I could to ensure that not only my business survived, but Holcroft House and all who remained here did as well.

Beyond the shop window, a cart rolled past. Two boys ran after it, beating sticks against the sides, dogs cavorting at their heels. Some peddlers laden with pots, sacks flung over their shoulders, headed in the direction of the square. A gray palfrey cantered along the street, its hooves flinging up mud, earning the rider a scolding from an old woman with a child who tried unsuccessfully to avoid the muck. A couple of dark-robed monks strode by, looking up at the last minute to peer into the windows. I was unable to make out their features, their cowls were so deep, but felt the intensity of their stare . . . *as if they knew I was looking out upon them . . .*

I made up my mind.

If I didn't continue with the alehouse then Will's death would have been for nothing. It would mean that whoever killed him had taken more victims; it would mean they'd also

murdered my ambitions. If I conceded Hiske was right, that
I should have listened to her, to Tobias and those who disapproved of my attempts at independence, that I should have
heeded the abbot's warnings, sold my recipes to Brother Osbert
and washed my hands of brewing, then it wasn't just Will's life
that would be meaningless, but mine, the twins', and the lives
of everyone who supported me. I would be like the oracle who
spurned Apollo and broke her promise, locked in an eternity of
regret and maybes, aging into an already withered future.

"Goddamn it, Hiske Makejoy." I gave a bark of laughter at
the irony of her new name and screwed the letter into a ball.
"You've unwittingly earned my gratitude. Without this"—I
threw it into the cold grate—"I would have given up, surrendered
to fate. No more. I'll take it into my own hands, thank you."

If no one would forgive me, then I had nothing to lose.

⋘⋙

We reopened the alehouse, but it was subdued. Though there
was plenty of ale to sell and barrels of beer, custom was slow,
patrons few, and coins sparse. As each day passed with only
a handful of pennies and groats trickling in, I grew increasingly anxious. Lord Rainford's monies were due in less than a
month.

With just over a week to go till Easter, I pressed Master Proudfellow for any reasons (apart from the obvious) as to why folk
were avoiding us. Standing outside the brewhouse, we watched
Westel and Kip roll a barrel of ale out to Master Proudfellow's
cart. I was grateful for his continued support at least.

Reluctant to answer at first, Master Proudfellow finally
confessed. "There be two reasons as far as I can tell, Mistress

Sheldrake." He waited till the men were out of earshot. Taking his cap off, he scratched his tufted head, squinting in the spring sunshine. It was a glorious day, the first really sunny one we'd had in weeks. Above us, the sky was a soft blue, the clouds mere wisps that garlanded the endless dome. Our chickens roosted beneath the shade of the old wych-elm, the sun, as it broke through the foliage, dappling their feathers. The pigs quietly foraged in the spent mash. Birds wheeled above us and bees hummed among the flowerbeds. With all the color and new life around, I felt better equipped to handle unpleasant news, though Master Proudfellow clearly didn't want to be the one to deliver it. Looking around, he drank in our surroundings, as if to draw strength from their beauty.

"First, Will's death, may God assoil him"—he crossed himself and I followed suit—"it scared many. His killer or killers not being caught simply adds to the misfortune that some say haunts the place." He waved his cap in circles.

"The alehouse?"

"Nay, Mistress Sheldrake." He twisted his cap into a knot. "I mean yourself." He stared meaningfully. "They swear that fortune is not your friend. They believe God has abandoned you."

"I see."

"It's not fair, I know, but then, these things aren't, are they? Feelings, I mean. We're a superstitious lot at the best of times and, once the rumor starts that God's forsaken you, well, even those who don't normally abide by such nonsense start to consider mayhap they should as well."

I took a deep breath. Though not surprised, his words were hard to hear. "And what's the other reason? You said there were two."

"Eh? Oh. Aye, well . . . while I don't like to speak ill of any of your family, there be one not helping matters."

I cocked my head. "And who might that be, Master Proudfellow?" The way I asked indicated I knew already.

"Aye, it be Mistress Makejoy. She's let it be known that she's cut all ties with you—"

"Cut? She's denied me, Master Proudfellow, just as Peter denied the good Lord. So, don't concern yourself, you're not speaking ill of anyone related to me."

Master Proudfellow examined the toe of his boot. "If that's the way the wind blows . . ." He paused. "She's also said—" He pulled his top lip a couple of times.

"What? I would rather know than remain in ignorance. After all, if I'm to run a business, I need to know what my customers think or what they're being told to."

"Forgive me for repeating this, but she says you're a stain that will spread and mark any who come into contact with you. That your ale and that sour drink—her words, Mistress Sheldrake, not mine, I've grown quite partial to the beer—you make is contaminated. She tells everyone who will listen and, in Elmham Lenn, there're many."

We fell into silence, the only sound the rumble of the wood on gravel and the grunts of the men as they hefted the barrel into the cart. A lone bird circled high above.

"There, I told you. I feel no better for having done so." He replaced his cap, giving it a tug for good measure. "You're not to listen to that rubbish, Mistress Sheldrake. That Mistress Makejoy's poison—one draft and all who taste it will suffer blight." With a huff of indignation, Master Proudfellow folded his arms.

I began to laugh.

"Begging your pardon, mistress, but I hardly see the funny side."

"Don't you? Oh, Master Proudfellow, according to the town, I'm a stain, and to hear you tell, my cousin is poison. Seems to me that between us, we're an affliction worse than the pestilence."

Master Proudfellow's lips twitched, then he too began to chuckle. "I doubt she'd see it like that. But I know which disease I'd rather catch." We both laughed then and I rested a hand briefly on his forearm, grateful for his frankness. No matter how much I pressed Saskia and Adam whenever they returned from town, they wouldn't tell me what was being said. When Louisa stopped taking the children to see the troupes of actors passing through on their way up the coast for Eastertide, I knew things were worse than I'd feared. Hiske and her twisted tongue I could live with—I was accustomed to her ways—but not her influence. As for superstition, I could hardly blame folk for feeling that way. Even before Father died, ill fortune dogged our family—it wasn't until he'd passed that I understood how much.

With a sigh, I pocketed the pennies Master Proudfellow paid and, saying my farewells, set Westel to stirring the mash. I went to the office to deposit the coin in the tin and, for the umpteenth time that week, added up the ledgers.

Not even Good Friday and Easter Sunday broke what had become a daily habit: tallying up the coin, adding up the columns, hoping and praying for an increase in sales that would allay my growing fear. The figures barely changed from day to day, but so long as there was something to place into the credit column, I could persuade myself that our goal of paying the lease was coming closer, even as I knew the only person I was fooling was myself.

Just before sext on Easter Monday, I left Westel tending the boiling wort and went to the house. Saskia met me at the door to the kitchen.

"There's a gentleman to see you."

"Who?" I wasn't expecting anyone.

"Sir Rainford."

"Sir Rainford?" My hand flew to my mouth. "Why didn't you say?" I quickly undid my apron and threw it on the bench. "Does he have refreshment? Where is he?"

"Adam is with him and, *ja*, he and his squire have drinks."

Bending in front of a large upturned pot, I tried to see my reflection, straighten my kerchief, tidy my hair. My heart was beating and my throat dry. It took a moment to register Saskia's words. "His squire? Is Tobias here too?" I swung around.

"Mistress Anneke," said Saskia, shooing Blanche and Iris, who, seeing me so flustered, had paused in their tasks. "Anneke"—she laid her fingers against my wrist—"it's not Sir Leander Rainford who's here. It's the other one."

"The other?" I stared at her. "Who?"

"The elder brother, I believe, Sir Symond. He says he's here on behalf of his father. Mistress"—she lowered her voice—"he told Adam he's here to collect the lease monies. That it's time to honor the contract."

I stared at her in horror. "Today? But he's at least a week early."

Saskia bit her lip.

The blood fled from my face. "If that's the case," I said, my shoulders slumping, "we're doomed."

# TWENTY-NINE

*E*rasing the despair from my face, I took a deep breath and entered the office. A tall man with dark hair, gray eyes, and a grossly misshapen nose rose languorously out of my father's chair. Across his hips he wore a thick belt, and from it hung a huge scabbard from which an ornate and bejeweled hilt protruded. The size and evident seriousness of the weapon was at odds with the fashionable, almost frivolous, garments he wore. I noted the open ledger before him, the half-drunk mazer of ale. This man had made himself comfortable indeed.

In the corner stood another well-dressed, younger man.

"Sir Symond?" I asked, and bobbed a curtsy. "My lord, you are very welcome."

"Indeed," said Sir Symond, giving me a small bow and looking me up and down in the invasive manner particular to his family. "Sir Symond Rainford. This is my squire, Michael de Montefort." I nodded to Master de Montefort, who barely acknowledged me, a look of disdain on his features. Shocked at such contempt from someone who was, at the least, my social equal, I turned back to Sir Symond. "And you must be Anneke Sheldrake."

"My lord." I lowered my head. I gestured to Adam, who stood to one side. "You've met Adam Barfoot, my steward."

"I have."

Before I could invite him, Sir Symond sat back down. I perched on the stool opposite, rearranging my tunic to cover my uncase. Behind me, Adam and Master Michael stood at either end of the cold hearth. "How can I help you?" I asked.

"Come, come. I think you know why I'm here, Mistress Sheldrake." Tipping his head to one side, he smiled, but it never reached his eyes.

"Even so, to avoid confusion, I'd be very grateful if you would inform me, my lord."

Sir Symond appraised me as I imagined he would a horse or fatted calf. I wanted to rub my arms, my neck, but I forced my hands quiescent in my lap.

"Very well. I'm here on my father's behalf to collect the annual dues for Holcroft House and lands. It's my understanding that you"—he dwelled upon my décolletage, which I resisted covering—"and my father have a contract which expires at Hocktide."

I willed him to look upon my face. When he did, I answered. "This is true, my lord. However, if I may be so bold, you're a few days early. I assumed that collection would not take place until *the day itself* and so have not prepared my dues." It was hard to keep the remonstration from my tone. "I was expecting to make payment on Hocktide. By my calculation, I still have eight more days."

"You're mistaken, Mistress Sheldrake."

"I do not think so, my lord. Your father—"

"Entrusted *me* to examine your books and collect all monies owing and that's what I'm here to do. You have too much to say for yourself, Mistress Sheldrake. He warned me as much." He struck the desk with the flat of his hand, the noise loud and violent in the small space. I almost leaped off my seat. A vein in Sir Symond's temple began to throb. It was then I noticed the scar that ran down the side of his face and across the upper part of his cheek. It was white and jagged, pulling the flesh into a ravine. I wondered if he'd received it in battle or from being struck across the face for want of manners. Certainly, he didn't possess the charm of his younger brother or, for that matter, the polish of his father. What he did possess was an awareness of his social status and an ability to make me acutely aware of where I stood.

"Good," he said, his lips, which were also ravaged by a deep split, curving into what might have passed for a smile. "Now that you're listening, I will say this one more time only: I'm here to collect the rent."

"My lord." Adam stepped from the hearth.

"Was I addressing you?" snapped Sir Symond.

"Why, no, but my lord, I—"

"Will mind your place." Sir Symond glowered at Adam. "As much as it disturbs me to do business with a woman, I'll not discuss these matters with a servant."

I inhaled sharply. Anger flooded every part of my body and it took all my control not to order this man from the room. I needed his cooperation, not his irritation. I could ill afford to give offense.

Half-twisting in my chair, I gave Adam a reassuring smile, even as I burned. "It's all right, Adam, thank you. I'm sure Sir Symond and I can settle this."

"There's nothing to settle." He drawled the last word and stood. "Michael, take Master Barfoot and conduct an inspection of the premises, would you? Father wants a report on the condition of the house." The lie was as evident as his nose, but Sir Symond didn't care.

Adam hesitated. Propriety demanded he didn't leave me unchaperoned. Sir Symond clearly didn't see it as a problem. To him, I was a mere tenant and due no such courtesy.

With a slight brush against my shoulder, which Sir Symond observed with an arch of his brow, Adam ushered Michael de Montefort from the office.

Waiting till his squire closed the door behind him, Sir Symond sank back into the chair and drank. "Where were we?" He smacked his lips together. "This is uncommonly good," he muttered. "Oh, aye, the lease."

Taking my time, I rose from my seat and moved to the hearth. I wanted distance between us. "The facts are, my lord, I cannot pay the lease in full today. I'm short by a small amount. However, I hope that by Hocktide I'll have the requisite monies."

Putting down the mazer, Sir Symond rested his elbows on the table and pressed his palms together in an attitude of prayer. He possessed long, thick fingers with calluses across the palm— the hands of someone used to wielding a sword. Famous for his bravery across Elmham Lenn and beyond—how he'd ridden at the king's side at Shrewsbury, masqueraded as our monarch to confuse the enemy, single-handedly saving him when an arrow struck him in the face—stories of how Sir Symond earned his knighthood were well known. It was rumored he was about to be endowed with a greater honor as well, reward for his courage against the Welsh and his loyalty to the House of Lancaster. This was a man accustomed to victory.

I swallowed, feigning indifference to his bold gaze.

"Despite what Father and Leander told me"—his voice was quiet, amused—"you're not what I expected."

*Leander had spoken of me to his brother?* I knotted my fingers together. "I'm sorry to disappoint."

"Disappoint?" Pushing back his chair, he stood and came around to the other side of the desk, the mazer small in his huge hand. "On the contrary, that's not the word I'd have used. You're nothing like your mother, not really . . ."

*He knew my mother?* His eyes were the color of the sea as it lapped the ships in port. I lowered mine. The conversation was heading down a dangerous path.

"The facts are, my lord"—I took a step toward the door, keeping my voice businesslike, trying not to let this man see how much he unnerved me—"as I wrote to your father and brother, we had an . . . an incident here. A tragedy, actually. One of my servants, Will Heymonger, was—"

"Murdered," finished Sir Symond. "I was informed. I'm not sure why you see fit to raise it, Mistress Sheldrake, or why you wasted time appraising Father or Leander. It's irrelevant. A contract is a contract and must be honored regardless of any inconvenience."

My cheeks grew hot.

"Aye, my servant's death was most *inconvenient*." I spat the word and was rewarded with a flicker of those hard eyes. "It's meant that not only have we been a hand short, but due to superstition and fear, custom has all but dried up and the monies I'd anticipated receiving have failed to materialize. In light of what's happened, I'd hoped . . . rather, I'd intended to ask your father if I might change the terms of our contract."

I'd never considered this. I was simply clutching at straws, thinking on the wing.

"*Change* them? Mistress Sheldrake, you're clearly unfamiliar with—"

I swept on as if he hadn't spoken.

"I intended to ask if I might pay Lord Rainford for the months already owed now and the months I owe in advance at a later date." I ducked behind the desk and swung the ledger around to underline my point.

Sir Symond turned slowly, his face suffused with color. I pretended not to see.

"If you will look here, my lord, you will see that I can readily pay—"

"I'm afraid that will not do, Mistress Sheldrake. The terms of the contract are clear." Placing down the drink, he reached into a coat pocket and produced a copy of the original, tossing it upon the desk and gesturing for me to read. "I suggest you familiarize yourself with what you and my father agreed upon once more." One side of his mouth curled, the contract becoming something vile.

I quickly unfurled and reread the parchment, glancing at my signature, thinking how foolish I'd been not to bargain harder, insist on more time. But then, I'd been in no position to ask for anything. *Just as I wasn't now . . .*

Leaning over the desk, Sir Symond brought his face to within inches of mine. I could smell the ale on his breath, the sweat of his body, see the fine weave of his amber coat. "This states it's all or nothing." He jabbed the parchment. "It's clear. As is your signature." He ground my name into the vellum.

The terms were unambiguous. My heart sank until something caught my eye.

"You're right, my lord." I straightened, taking my hands away from the parchment and watching it twirl into a cylinder again. "We must abide by that upon which we sign our name. A contract is binding, is it not?"

"It is . . ." His words propelled him to the other side of the desk. Too late, I was trapped between the wall and Sir Symond. The only way to escape was to go over or under the desk. I was a fox cornered by a large, unpredictable hound. I determined not to show fear.

He put his thick, hot hand over mine where it rested on the desk and ran it up my arm, spreading his fingers so his thumb brushed against my breast. "You agreed to serve my father should you fail to make lease, serve him and his family at Scales Hall, the Rainford home that, in the very near future, will be mine . . ." Every part of me rebelled. I wanted to push him away, swipe his fingers from my body, leave his presence and never return. But I had one last card left to play.

I stopped his hand at my shoulder, lifting it away. "Aye, I did. And, should it come to that, I will honor my agreement. After all, as you say, we cannot change a contract to suit ourselves, not once it's signed." Pushing past him, I twisted his arm so he could not grab me, shoving him away, bumping the desk hard in my eagerness to be free.

Panting, one hand on the door, I faced him. He leaned against the wall, rubbing his wrist, unconcerned by my actions.

"Just as I cannot change the terms, neither can you. Lord Rainford and I agreed that rent would be due at Hocktide. That, my lord, means Tuesday next week. By my reckoning, and by the terms of the contract, I have just over a week in which to pay." I grasped the door handle, staring at him defiantly.

"Listen, you slattern, you don't dictate terms to me. I'm the lord here, I'm the one who gives orders."

"Ah, my lord, you misunderstand. I'm not dictating terms. I'm merely following the ones that you've been at great pains to point out to me your father insisted you reinforce and I follow. If anything, I'm being your most humble and obedient servant."

Pure fury swept over his face. "Why, you little bitch," he began, raising his hand.

Wrenching open the door as fast as I could, I all but fell into the hall, heart pounding.

"Mistress Anneke." Adam ran toward me. Following him at a more leisurely pace was Michael de Montefort, boredom personified. Relief swept over me. "Adam. Please escort Sir Symond to the door. Our business is concluded."

"For today," said a slow, deep voice behind me. "But understand this, Mistress Sheldrake. I'll be back in a week and, if you want to keep this place, I will take what's due. In one form"— his eyes slid over me—"or another."

Along with his squire, he left through the shop.

I followed cautiously, remaining out of sight. As he mounted his large destrier, all I could think was that I had one week, one week before Holcroft House and what remained of my independence and my dignity were lost to me for good.

# THIRTY

HOLCROFT HOUSE

The week following Eastertide

*The year of Our Lord 1406 in the seventh*

*year of the reign of Henry IV*

Over the next week, we worked relentlessly, even, God forgive me, eschewing mass in an effort to claw back time. But it didn't seem to matter how much ale or beer we made or how low I dropped the prices in the alehouse, except for our stalwart regulars, a few pilgrims, sailors, and a couple of passing merchants, trade barely resumed. Adam went to the Saturday market to spread the word that our ale was half its usual price and the beer even less. Prepared to be inundated, nothing changed.

Determined not to let the others see how desperate the situation had become, I decided that on the morrow, taking Adam with me, I would load up the cart and head into Bishop's Lynn. The bigger alehouses and taverns would open their doors on Sunday, the most sacred of days; folk still drank and would be searching for a cheap supply. As an unknown huckster, if I avoided the authorities, I could trade. It was a madcap scheme, but choices were diminishing.

With the bells marking the closing of the city gates about to ring, Simon Attenoke and the Millers dragged themselves off their stools and out into the setting sun. Once they left, there was no one remaining in the alehouse for whom I had to stay cheerful. It was all I could do not to sink into despair and wallow. Turning to mundane tasks to keep my mind busy, I insisted on sweeping the hearth and collecting the few used mazers, one eye on the door in the hope that custom might still come our way before curfew. Adam and Iris attended to the tables and floor. Taking the vessels from me, Iris followed Adam back to the kitchen. About to open the door and check the streets for signs of passersby, I was startled when Captain Stoyan entered.

"Good evening, Mistress Anneke," he said, crossing the threshold and whipping off his cap. "Forgive me for coming so late, but I was trying to hire a cart until it occurred to me that you have one."

"Good evening, Captain." I closed the door behind him and, accepting no one else would follow, secured the latch. "I don't mind how late you arrive, you're always welcome."

The captain smiled and, taking my hands, kissed my cheek. His brow furrowed. "You're looking pale, *liebchen*." He looked me up and down. "You're fading away before my eyes."

"I doubt that." I released his fingers, but not before giving them a squeeze, and went to pour him a drink. "Beer or ale?"

He rubbed his chin. "What have you ready?"

A sigh escaped before I could prevent it. "Both. And lots of it. Which would you prefer?"

The captain slid onto one of the stools. "To drink now, ale. But, to take with me to Flanders, I'd like beer—not even your ale keeps for as long as I'd wish. I want as much beer as you can spare."

Attending to his drink, I didn't comprehend his meaning immediately, but continued to pour. "Excuse me?" I ceased what I was doing and turned as calmly as I was able, taking in his grin, the twinkle in those gray eyes. Placing a beaker of foaming ale before him, I sat down opposite, my eyes never leaving his face. "Did I hear you aright? You wish to take beer to Flanders? *My* beer?"

"*Ja.* To Flanders, Ypres, and in the months to come, farther afield again—wherever the ships of my Kontor sail. Four barrels for the time being, if you have that. The sailors in the fleet gain a mighty thirst at sea and it seems they've developed a preference for your beer."

Unable to believe my ears, my mouth opened and shut so often I could have been sold for a fish.

"Why else did you think I needed a cart?" added the captain, raising his beaker toward me.

I did what any woman in my situation would at that point. I launched myself over the table, into his arms, and promptly burst into tears.

⋖⋟⋗

Insisting Captain Stoyan sup with us, my intended venture to Bishop's Lynn was canceled and Adam, the captain, and I organized the barrels to be delivered to the Kontor as soon as the town gates opened Monday morn. Leaving for Flanders with the dawn tides Tuesday gave the captain plenty of time to load them on his ship. When the captain decided to head back to his rooms, Adam insisted on escorting him, taking a lamp.

"The nightwatch know me," said Adam, silencing Captain Stoyan's protests. "Anyway, it's the least I can do. It's the first time in weeks I've seen Mistress Anneke relax, let alone smile."

"I *do* smile." I forced one to my face as proof.

"Aye, with your mouth," said Adam, "but it hasn't reached here"—he touched a place below his eye—"or here"—he rested a hand over his heart—"for weeks."

He was right.

Bidding Captain Stoyan farewell, I first checked on the twins and then fell into bed, exhausted in the way someone who uses excessive labor and seeks aching limbs to hasten forgetfulness would, something we'd all done these last weeks since Will died. But it was only as I pondered Adam's words that I finally understood that while I'd kept my body occupied, my spirit had been neglected. Something Sir Leander had prayed wouldn't happen . . .

Lying back on the pillow, my arms folded behind my head, I listened to the evening trill of crickets and frogs in full song, watched the play of changing light upon my walls as darkness descended and wondered at my sudden good fortune, daring for the first time to imagine what it would be like to hand over the full amount of rent, knowing we were secure for another six months.

Gratitude toward the captain filled my veins. Though I'd believed his act to be prompted by charity, he'd reassured me it wasn't.

"I cannot afford to be charitable," he said. When I reminded him about the barley he regularly supplied and his other gestures of kindness, he demurred. "Have you so swiftly forgotten? This is a business arrangement, Mistress Anneke. I'll be as demanding as Sir Symond and Lord Rainford if required." He grinned to soften his threat. "I expect a percentage—held over until such time as you can afford it," he added quickly. "I'd be failing as a captain if I didn't provide my men with the best on offer and I'd be useless as a merchant trader if I didn't take this opportunity to introduce the fine beer you've made to the continent. I once told you there were opportunities there for a good English supplier. Well, I've finally found her."

For some reason, Will's words from months ago echoed in my mind.

*"As God is my witness,"* he'd said, *"Mistress Sheldrake will be the finest brewer in all of England."*

Around me, the house settled, its regular conversation between timber and thatch comforting. Karel coughed once or twice and I heard Louisa rise to him. The door to the barn squeaked. Adam had returned and was ascending to his bed in the loft. The great oak brushed the sides of the house, its leaves rustling in the gentle winds.

Daring to hope, I curled under my furs and shut my eyes. Before I knew it, a dreamless sleep claimed me.

# THIRTY-ONE

HOLCROFT HOUSE
The day before Hocktide
*The year of Our Lord 1406 in the seventh
year of the reign of Henry IV*

As a household, we attended the early mass, stifling yawns. Entering the coolness of St. Bartholomew's as the cock crowed, Father Clement's welcoming smile and the rhythmic chanting of the novices warmed us from within.

Returning to the house before tierce, I downed a small ale and headed into the brewhouse when Adam caught up with me, announcing we had guests.

It was Sir Symond Rainford and his squire.

Astounded the man had the gall to come to the house so early, I was more shocked to discover he was here to demand payment of the rent. Why, he was still a day early. Flustered, I scurried across the garden, untying my apron and dumping it unceremoniously on the kitchen table. It wasn't until I stood outside the office, forcing myself to take deep breaths and collect my thoughts, that it occurred to me this was quite deliberate. Sir Symond had done this with the intention to teach me a lesson. Unable to stomach that I'd managed to outwit him at our first meeting by making him adhere to the original terms of the contract, he sought to turn the tables. He thought to catch me unprepared.

Well, he was about to be disappointed.

Entering the office, Adam on my heels, I found Sir Symond seated behind the desk, his squire and, to my surprise, Master Makejoy hovering on the other side. Sir Symond rose as I came in and, in what was intended to appear an act of gallantry, bowed and kissed my hand. I resisted the urge to wipe it on my tunic.

Pleasantries were stiffly exchanged, poor Master Makejoy having been dragged away from church, clearly wanting to be anywhere but Holcroft House this fine morning. I could hear him uttering prayers under his breath and the cross he carried in his pocket was transferred to his palm.

"Forgive our intrusion so early," said Sir Symond, towering over me, "but a contract, as you pointed out the last time we met, is a contract."

"It is, my lord. And you are a day early."

"It isn't convenient for me to attend on Hocktide. It has to be today."

"I see. And is it also inconvenient for Master Makejoy, who's obliged to collect rents from Lord Rainford's other tenants on Hocktide?"

The look on Master Makejoy's face revealed he'd made the same argument.

Sir Symond gave a dismissive flick of his wrist. "I'm making an exception for you."

*Of me*, I thought, but did not express this aloud. "Then it's just as well I'm exceptional, is it not, my lord?"

Without further ado, I opened the cupboard by the hearth and from a small safe within, extracted a hessian bag, placing it before him on the desk. "Consider the terms of my contract met." I gave a small curtsy.

Sporting an expression of disbelief, Sir Symond nudged the bag toward Master Makejoy. Taking a seat, Master Makejoy sighed and, untying the knot I'd securely fastened only the evening before, tipped the coins onto the wood. A few rolled away, Master Makejoy's long fingers grasping them before they collided with Sir Symond's silk-clad elbow or fell on the floor. Taking his time, Master Makejoy counted them, stacking them one atop the other in small piles. Once he'd finished, he gestured the squire over to check his calculations. I couldn't conceal my smile when, finally, Master de Montefort announced, "It's all here, my lord."

"All?" said Sir Symond, looking down his misshapen nose at the crooked towers of coins, coins that represented over five months of our endeavors, months of heartache and grief as well. Barely able to conceal his astonishment, he simply stared.

"Every last noble and groat," said Master Makejoy, recording the amount in the book he'd brought. Pulling a piece of parchment out of his satchel, with a wink he handed me a quill and pointed to a space on the bottom for me to sign. It was a receipt.

I looked at Adam in triumph, returning the quill to Master Makejoy, who quickly made a copy. Adam folded his arms and flashed me a grin.

Sir Symond gestured toward the money. Master de Montefort scraped the coins back into the pouch. "Well, well, well, Mistress Sheldrake. There's more to you than meets the eye, as delightful as that might be."

"There's enough, my lord." I deliberately misunderstood him, concentrating on folding the receipt and tucking it in a pocket. I would put it with my other documents later. "What is owed—no more, no less." I fixed a bright smile. "Now, if you'll forgive me, I've work to do. Adam will escort you to the door." I dropped another curtsy.

"Before you leave, Mistress Sheldrake." Sir Symond was on his feet and in two strides blocked the doorway.

"My lord?"

Leaning so his mouth was close to my face, he tipped his head slightly. "I'm not certain how you managed to do this, but I've an idea. You won't always be so lucky. If you find yourself unable to meet the Michaelmas rents, I want you to know there's always a bargain to be made with another Rainford." He moved closer. The odor of sour wine enveloped me. "That way, we keep it in the family." His eyes glinted, his meaning unmistakable.

Adam gasped and Master Makejoy cleared his throat.

"A bargain? With you?" I stepped away, my back against the door. Really, this man was insufferable.

"You'll find me much more agreeable than my father or my cripple of a brother."

I drew my breath in sharply and, fumbling for the handle, swung the door open, making it a barrier that came between us. "I would rather deal with the devil." With that, I swept from the room.

Making the rent monies as well as what I owed in arrears had a remarkably liberating effect—not just upon me, but the entire house. We went from despair to exhilaration, from anxiety to confidence, the latter helped by Captain Stoyan placing additional orders, meaning I was now to supply any of his fleet leaving from Elmham Lenn with beer. He also sent me a note announcing my beer had been well received in Flanders and that he would require more barrels to take on his next voyage there. I was ecstatic. Though business had slowly picked up in the Cathaline Alehouse, I'd no longer any need to rely on it exclusively for income. Freed from the urgency to bring in custom, it's a rich irony that patrons then came. As it was wont to do, word spread that not only were the foreign sailors swallowing my beer like drowning men do the sea, but I was exporting the drink as well. Not wanting to miss out on what those on the other side of the sea, "the damn Dutch," were clearly enjoying meant that not only the curious but also the indignant chose to frequent my establishment.

The weeks flew by and as the tragedy of Will's death became less immediately painful, my visits to his gravesite became more an act of honor and remembering than a desperate desire to seek atonement. The entire house fell back into old rhythms that suggested normalcy had once more taken roost in Holcroft House. The only discord in an otherwise peaceful time involved the office and the brewery. Just as the feeling of being watched as I performed the ancient rites would not leave me, so too when I entered the office each afternoon, the sense that the ledgers and books had been disturbed grew daily. There was nothing obvious—a sheet of paper askew, the ink bottle moved, a book placed where I was sure it hadn't been a day earlier. When I asked Adam about it, he shook his head. "Perhaps you should lock the door?" Loathe to do this because of the lack of trust it suggested between me and the servants, I waited for the right moment to ask the others if they'd entered. They all denied it.

Only Saskia, when I mentioned it to her, studied me over the hem she was lowering. "Strange that you should notice such a thing after Will mentioned Westel's habit of sneaking about the house when we're abed."

"Why on earth would Westel slink into the office? For what purpose? He sees the ledgers weekly. He enters the office regularly. I oft request he fetch something for me. Secrecy isn't necessary."

Saskia shrugged. "I don't know. The same reason he's always sneaked about. I've heard him too. I told you, you allow him too much leeway, Mistress Anneke. You have from the moment he came into this house. I just hope you don't live to regret it."

"You've never liked him. Why, you even said he smiles too much."

"He does." She paused. "I don't like him. Nay, that's not right. It's that I don't trust him. And to make matters worse, he's replaced all that smiling with prayers. Have you noticed? Always muttering and asking the Lord for this and that God forgive him that. There's something wrong with Westel. That behavior isn't normal for a layperson."

I had noticed. How could I not? "A commoner raised in a priory." Yet again, I defended him.

Saskia sighed.

"What do you suggest I do about it?"

"Do? If it were up to me, I'd pay him for his services and send him on his way. I know, I know, you can ill afford to do that. He's a good worker and God knows, with the Parry girls gone and others too scared to work here, we need all the hands we can get. But if I were you, I'd keep a closer eye on him than ever. He's up to something, mark my words."

"Perhaps he's a spy." I scoffed at the notion.

"I thought they were supposed to fit in, not draw attention to themselves by flashing their teeth all the time and calling upon God. If he's a spy, I'm the Queen of the Muscovites," she said, and chuckled at the very thought.

For a couple of days, I found myself watching Westel and indeed he did frown and mutter prayers a great deal, crossing himself, smiling and then muttering some more. It was as if he were conversing with the Holy Spirit or debating with his conscience. But when he caught me looking at him, he'd always give me a huge grin. I took to locking the office door but, as the days grew longer and other thoughts occupied me, I forgot and I didn't notice anything out of the ordinary again.

Though within the brewhouse it was another matter . . .

The twins thrived as the weather grew warmer, and Louisa would take them for walks along the Nene, down to the bay and to visit Master Perkyn and Olive. Karel underwent a growth spurt and I sent Saskia to the mercers for cloth for trousers and a new shirt, acutely aware the time for both the twins to leave the nursery was fast approaching. Pushing those thoughts to the back of my mind, it was Master Makejoy who forced me to consider the implications of having two growing children under my roof.

Not long after Whitsunday, one day late in May, he was preparing to leave after checking the books when Karel, with nary a knock or by your leave, burst into the office.

"There you are, Anneke!" he exclaimed. "You should see the harbor; why, it's full of—" He stopped when he caught sight of Master Makejoy. "Forgive me, sir," he said quickly and, doffing his cap, bowed. "I didn't know we had a guest. God give you good welcome."

Master Makejoy nodded agreeably. Though his wife abjured the family he was forced to reckon with, he was always pleasant, especially since the incident with Sir Symond. "That's all right, lad. Master Karel, isn't it? My, you've grown, haven't you?"

Karel puffed out his chest, the laces on his shirt pulled to their ends. "I'm seven now," said Karel.

"Seven! We'll have to put you to work then, won't we?" Master Makejoy leaned over and ruffled his hair.

Taken aback, I stared at Karel as if with fresh eyes. Tobias had been squired at seven; all the tenant farmers' children were out in the fields by this age. Master Makejoy was right, it was time to consider Karel's future. But surely, I thought, looking at the way he smoothed down the hair Master Makejoy had disturbed, noting the dimples on the backs of his hands where his knuckles would one day protrude, not yet. There was time for Karel and Betje to just be children, surely? Ushering him out with promises I would come and see what delighted him so—a fleet of caravels, as it turned out—I closed the door upon him, just as I did the disturbing thoughts Master Makejoy's observations aroused.

Two days later I was obliged to muse over them again when a note arrived from Master Makejoy offering to negotiate an apprenticeship for Karel as a clerk with a Master Muire. Master Muire was a law clerk who had an excellent reputation and worked with the Justice of the Peace, which meant the likelihood of him one day securing that role for himself was very high indeed. Looking at the neat script, the care taken with the writing, the offer itself, my immediate instinct to burn it was checked. Master Makejoy meant only kindness, and it was evident from the terms and conditions he outlined that he was serious. I wondered if his wife knew. Was he trying to make amends for the damage Hiske's vicious tongue had caused?

An apprentice clerk may not have been what Mother or Father intended for him, nor I, but it was not something I could readily cast aside, not anymore. Karel was quick and clever, and as Master Muire's apprentice, he could not only remain living at Holcroft House, but the possibility of a sound career in London was not out of reach either.

Pondering what to do, the following day saw another letter from Sir Leander arrive. It had come all the way from Venice. Lingering over Leander's long missive, I laughed at his description of the boats the Venetians used—long, sleek craft called gondolas. In great detail he described Tobias's efforts to stand in one like a native. From Tobias, there was not a word. He'd not yet forgiven me. Saddened, Sir Leander's letters went some way to compensating and I grew to anticipate these missives that arrived almost weekly. That Sir Leander made the effort to write touched me deeply, stirring feelings I pretended didn't exist. A tale of how Tobias managed, after bartering at a market, to walk away not with bolts of cloth as he'd intended but two pet monkeys, had me falling about in helpless giggles, wondering how the animals would settle into sea life and whether I'd ever see them.

Alone in the office, I held his letter under my nose. The paper smelled of other places, other times. Imagining Sir Leander sitting at a table aboard ship or in a foreign inn, the paper laid before him, drawing the candle near, dipping his quill, his face a study in the flickering light, I closed my eyes to contemplate the picture. I saw his broad shoulders, the dark, disorderly hair, and his leg stretched out to one side to alleviate discomfort. His cane was resting against the edge of the table, a mere handspan away, his scabbard unbuckled and lying on the other side of the tabletop. His shirt was open at the neck, his coat discarded. I wondered if he thought of me reading his words as he wrote, choosing what to relay and what to omit, knowing I would want to learn of Tobias but including the information in a way that was sensitive to our siblings dispute. Settling back in the chair, I became conscious of the beat of my heart, how the mere idea of Sir Leander made it quicken so. What was this I felt? Dare I name it? It was affection, no more . . . *no less either* . . . I laughed at myself and quickly quashed the other memories that surfaced when I indulged this daydream—his firm, warm lips capturing mine, the scour of his unshaven cheek against my flesh, the way the tip of his tongue explored my lips and teeth as I opened them to receive more . . .

Sitting up, eyes open, I admonished myself, using the paper to fan away the heat flooding my cheeks and making my bodice suddenly very tight. Resting the paper against my bosom, allowing the uneven edges to stroke the exposed skin, I began to compose a reply in my head, thinking how to respond to Sir Leander's questions, but what to include to amuse him as well. I would relay his brother's visit (how unalike they were!), Westel's odd behavior, and my growing disquiet for certes. I would also tell him of our success with the Hanse in Elmham Lenn and in Flanders and Germany. I decided I would also ask his advice on Karel's future. My purpose, I confess, was twofold. In announcing Master Makejoy's offer and expressing my doubts, Sir Leander would be able to either reassure me or, as I hoped, counter with a better offer for my little brother.

A response would take a while, so in the meantime, I wrote to Master Makejoy as well, asking him to give me some time to consider his most generous offer. A gracious reply arrived the following day, inviting me to take all the time I needed.

And so I did. May segued into June and preparations for midsummer began in earnest. Beyond the town gates, farmers sheared sheep and kept anxious eyes upon the weather. They weren't the only ones. For a few years now, unseasonal rain had ruined crops and driven up prices. The days grew longer; our little hatchlings developed into strutting chickens and the piglets doubled in size every week. So, it seemed, did the twins, but, while the brewery kept me busy, I refused to make a decision about Karel, indulging both him and Betje, allowing them to spend at least this summer together before the world of work tore them apart.

The twins were not the only ones changing, nor were they the only members of the house to preoccupy me. Ever since Saskia and I spoke of Westel, I noticed differences in him. Gone was the ebullient man who strolled into the yard seeking work last year. In his place was someone I often caught gazing into space or praying almost obsessively under his breath. His quick smile and eagerness to please were no longer so apparent, though they surfaced occasionally. Nonetheless, his work was always done and without complaint. Whereas once he sought tasks even on his day off, ever since Will died he would leave the premises every Sunday, satchel slung over his shoulder, cap upon those pale locks, and not return until curfew. I knew from Father Clement that he often attended more than one service at St. Bartholomew's, but where he chose to spend the rest of the day, I did not know. I imagined him wandering through the woods or down to the harbor, seeking the solitude the shared space of Holcroft House mostly denied him.

As the weeks went by, he grew quieter, more intense. We all grieved for Will in our own way, but Westel, who had found the body, appeared to have been unhinged. Not even the passage of time could appease his sorrow.

I didn't know what to do about it and decided to seek the advice of Sir Leander, who I was becoming increasingly reliant upon as a sounding board for my troubles. I wrote to him that night.

⸎⸎⸎

The church cat surprised us one day after an absence of a few weeks by introducing us to her litter of kittens. Scrappy bundles of fur, the children went into paroxysms of ecstasy when they saw them, calling me from the brewhouse to meet the little creatures.

"Can we keep one?" asked Betje, her eyes wide and hopeful.

"Each?" begged Karel, clutching a tiny ginger life to his cheek. How could this lad be ready for work?

"You'll have to ask Father Clement," I said, surrendering to the twins' pleas rather than my better judgment. They tore off to find the priest, Louisa chasing after them.

I watched them disappear through the gate, shaking my head.

"I like cats."

"Westel." I swung around. I hadn't heard him approach.

Nodding toward the rest of the kittens, their mother trailing after those the twins had taken, Westel wiped his hands on his apron. "Aye, they're creatures who serve no one, not really. They only appear to."

"What an odd thing to say." I frowned, noting that his eyes seemed colorless, like the puddles of rain that collected on the roadway or clouds that presaged a storm. I gave a half-laugh and the day seemed to dim. "Cats are like most of us," I added. "Happy to be fed, have a roof over their heads, and someone to pay them attention."

Westel met my eyes. "We don't ask for much, do we?"

"We don't need much. Not really." I studied him a moment longer, trying to ignore the unease that crept up my spine. "Come, we've two more barrels to fill before sext." I let him precede me into the brewery and, as I watched his slump-shouldered walk, made up my mind that before the summer was over, I would ask him to leave. Saskia was right. There was something not right about him. Will's death had affected him badly and it was cruel to have him stay. I would broach it with him shortly and give him plenty of time to become accustomed to the idea. I would ensure he had good references and enough coin to tide him over until he found employment.

I followed him inside, my mood and body lighter than it had been for a while.

That night, I asked Westel to accompany me to the office and told him of my decision that he would leave before the end of summer.

At first, he said nothing, just stared at the floor.

"Are you all right, Westel? I hope you understand, I'm very happy with you and your work and it will be hard to let you go, but I think that, in light of what's happened, it's for the best, don't you?"

Surprising me with a dazzling smile, Westel nodded. "Oh, aye, mistress. It's for the best. In fact, you took a difficult decision out of my hands and for that, the good Lord knows, I'm very grateful."

# THIRTY-TWO

HOLCROFT HOUSE

Midsummer's Eve

*The year of Our Lord 1406 in the seventh*
*year of the reign of Henry IV*

*M*uch to my delight, the steady seas and Midsummer's Eve brought a reply to my letter to Sir Leander and, to my shock, one from Tobias as well. Too busy to read them at first, I tucked them in my bodice, intending to read Tobias's later and, like a fine repast, savor every word his master had written.

Midsummer's Eve was a time for celebration and yet, as was our wont of late, we eschewed the town's festivities to create our own. Even so, all day long people arrived at the church to set the bonfire that would blaze long into the night. Minstrels, jesters, and other mummers who would perform appeared in the neighboring yard, their colorful costumes, loud hails and cheers, as well as music, adding jollity to our day. There would be food, dancing, and much merrymaking, all of which meant the alehouse was extraordinarily busy.

Perhaps to make up for missing the public festivities, Blanche outdid herself, preparing venison pie, baked sturgeon, cheese tarts, lamprey, and custard swimming with almond milk, as well as beautifully shaped marchpane for us to relish. We ate late in the afternoon, around none, Father Clement briefly joining us, his efforts to persuade us next door unsuccessful. We took it in turns to tend the alehouse. Conversation flowed, and laughter. It wasn't until Father Clement left to honor vespers, the servants closed the alehouse and began to clear away dinner, and Louisa took the twins to the nursery that I had the opportunity to retire to the solar and read my letters undisturbed.

Outside, the flames from the bonfire licked the sky, the smoke spiraling into the evening. Laughter, song, and good cheer accompanied me as, tempering the tiny thrills that raced through my chest, I broke the seal on Sir Leander's missive carefully.

I cannot say what happened to alter the attachment I felt growing between myself and Sir Leander, but as I read the first few lines of his letter, the light of anticipation burning inside me all day was swiftly doused. The brevity of his note merely enhanced this. With a sinking heart, I read.

*I send my greetings and God's blessing and mine to you, Mistress Sheldrake* (Why the formality when I believed us exempt from such things?). *I've given some thought to young Karel's situation and feel it would be in everyone's best interests if you accepted Muire's most generous offer. If Karel should excel as a clerk, which I'm in no doubt he will, then being apprenticed to the likes of Muire, with his connection to the Justiciars, means a career in law is not out of the ques-*

*tion. Tobias informs me your father began in law before turn-*
*ing to a merchant's life, so legal blood may yet be proven to*
*flow in Karel's veins. While this might go against your better*
*judgment, to take help from the husband of someone who has*
*caused you grievous injury, it's to the future that you must*
*look no matter what the past may have seemed to promise.*

*May God have you in his keeping and give you the grace to*
*do as well as you know I would want.*

*Leander Rainford.*

I froze, my back straight, my face unmoving, the letter utterly
still in my rigid fingers. What was this? Where was the warmth?
Our mutual understanding? Our mutual admiration? Or had
that been a figment of my colorful imaginings? What happened
to "I am yours to command"? Or, "All it would take is your
expressed need"? It was as if the friendship I believed we'd nur-
tured had somehow wasted away. What had I done? My chest
became heavy, solid. I know it was unreasonable, but until that
exact moment, I didn't know how much I depended on Sir Leander to offer me hope—and not just over Karel. I confess, I'd
secretly longed for another solution to Karel's situation, one that
Sir Leander would provide and for which I'd be most grateful.
But instead, he pushed me toward a course that filled me with
despair, as it announced to the world that our standing had
forever changed. Allowing Karel to become an apprentice to
one of Master Makejoy's acquaintances confirmed how far we'd
fallen on the social scale.

I put Sir Leander's letter aside and opened Tobias's. It was
a few pages and my eyes flew across the untidy words.

*Greetings, dear sister,*

*I trust this finds you and the twins well and in God's good graces. Sir Leander told me of Will Heymonger's death and you have my deepest sympathy. It would be remiss of me, Anneke, if I did not remind you that I warned of what might happen if you ignored the advice of those who know better and proceeded with the alehouse. It is therefore God's judgment that you now bear the consequences of your willful sins and foolish decisions, and I hope you're doing this with good grace and many prayers. I expect that if you've not already relocated to Cousin Hiske's that you will have done so by the time we next meet. Understand, Anneke, there's no shame in companionship, not even to one such as our cousin and, over time, memories of what you did and what your poor choices led to will be forgotten. For certes, if from this day forth you demonstrate the good sense and modesty that I know resides within you, they will be forgotten by me.*

If Tobias had been before me at this moment, I think, God forgive me, I would have slapped him again. The self-righteousness, the smugness, was more than I could bear. I scanned the rest of the letter quickly. He wrote about his travels along the Dalmatian Coast, the islands they encountered, the people. Lacking Sir Leander's playfulness and eye for detail, his tales didn't hold my interest, not when he held such a poor opinion of me.

Disheartened and about to toss it aside, the last few paragraphs caught my eye.

*I also write to inform you that though we'd hoped to return to Elmham Lenn before the end of summer, another pleasure has been afforded us. Sir Leander and I will be docking in London, where, in the first week of August, my master will fulfill long-held plans of marrying his betrothed, the Lady Cecilia, widow of the former Chancellor of the Exchequer, Sir Walter Barnham . . .*

My vision became distorted. The roaring in my ears grew. *Marrying? Cecilia Barnham? Long-held plans?* I tried to place the name, conjure a face. Why, she was a very wealthy widow, but old . . . so old . . . My eyes dropped back to the letter.

*Good King Henry arranged this excellent match as a favor to Sir Leander's father for, as you can imagine, being the youngest son and carrying an affliction as my lord does, a suitable union was difficult to arrange. But, typical of my master, who does not let that which would defeat a lesser man discommode him, he manages not only to find an heiress, but a noble one as well.*

*While Sir Leander wished to bear these good tidings to you and does intend to do so, I would not be fulfilling my brotherly duties if I did not inform you first. Perforce, I am also using this opportunity to call you to task once more. This gives me no pleasure, Anneke, but it must be said. It is apparent to me, and no doubt others, that you harbor improper feelings for my master, ones unbecoming of your station, as your shameless display Christmas Day and frequent missives to him attest. It is my solemn wish that upon learning of his forthcoming*

*nuptials you will banish whatever foolish fancies or impru-*
*dent desires you may have accommodated, for such are the*
*vagaries of females I do not doubt that you imagined some*
*romantic attachment between yourself and my lord. Sir Le-*
*ander was always destined to make a fine marriage and you*
*were prideful to think otherwise. I hope this news reminds you*
*of your place and duties. For now, you must set your sights on*
*restoring your reputation and the name of the family in the*
*hope that one day I can secure for you a match worthy of a*
*Sheldrake.*

   *I know you will add your felicitations to those I've already*
*expressed to Sir Leander and I will be sure to pass these on.*
   *May God have you, Karel, and Betje in his keeping,*
   *Written in haste, Trinity Sunday,*
   *Your loving brother,*
   *Tobias Sheldrake*

Waves of emotion washed over me. A mixture of disbelief,
outrage that Tobias could presume to second-guess my feelings
and address me so brutally, and frustration I couldn't defend
myself raged within. Most of all, I felt sadness. Sadness that my
brother could write to me thus and sadness that Sir Leander
hadn't seen fit to tell me himself about his pending nuptials. I
now understood the coldness in his letter. He'd already begun
the process of distancing himself, of placing me at arm's length.

   *Cecilia Barnham. Cecilia Rainford. Lady Cecilia Rainford.*
*Why hadn't he told me?*

   There'd never been so much as a hint of it. But why would
there be? Sir Leander was under no obligation to confide in me,
to discuss his private affairs . . . I knew so little about him. Only

that, whatever I may have thought at our first encounter, I was wrong, hasty . . . *Just as he confessed he'd been about me.*

The way he kissed me . . . I thought . . . I hoped . . . I shut my eyes and inhaled deeply. I'd no right to hurt so.

I could hear my heart beating in my ears, feel it hammering against my ribs. It was hard to breathe. Tears pricked my eyes, and I fought them back. The noises from the churchyard next door were more subdued but no less joyous. They simply compounded my growing misery.

Opening my eyes minutes later, the room was darkened, the melting candles throwing only the faintest of lights as the velvet hues of evening and the crackle of the church's bonfire closed around me. I glanced at the letter again and, though it was too dim to make out the words, they were burned into my memory. I wanted to deny Tobias's accusations, point out to him how ludicrous, how priggish . . . Only . . . I did have feelings for Sir Leander. But they weren't improper. How could they be, when they sprang from deep affection, friendship, and trust?

As for my shameless display at Christmas, why, Sir Leander had initiated that kiss.

*Aye, but you did answer his passion with your own . . .*

*Oh God. And I would do it again—over and over . . .*

Holding Tobias's letter at arm's length, I stared at it, the words beginning to blur. Leander Rainford was getting married. Soon. He was my confidant, a friend, nothing more. Nothing more . . . I wasn't a fool. I wasn't.

*Except in your wildest and most secret imaginings . . .*

Perhaps there, but only there, where dreams could run free . . .

"You're wrong about my feelings for Sir Leander Rainford, Tobias Sheldrake," I spoke to the empty room, my voice quivering. "I do not love him. Love and even imprudent desires have never entered my reckoning, nor will they. Not ever. Not where your master is concerned. Marriage is a call for celebration, not rebuke, nor false fancy." I picked up my goblet and drained it. "Do not concern yourself with my heart or, for that matter, my reputation, Tobias. They're mine to give, mine to make; and I will do so."

Tossing my head, I walked slowly from the solar, proud that I'd shed not one tear.

Not yet.

# THIRTY-THREE

HOLCROFT HOUSE

Midsummer's Eve

*The year of Our Lord 1406 in the seventh*

*year of the reign of Henry IV*

*I* perched on the edge of the bed and stared out the window. As the moon slowly traveled its arc across the sky, the revels next door ceased. The bonfire subsided and the unseasonably cool summer's night wrapped itself around me as the house descended into slumber. The servants had made their weary ways to bed, Adam slipping in through the mews door, Blanche closing the kitchen one below. There was the creak of stairs, followed shortly after by the rustle of the curtain behind me. Saskia entered my room with the familiarity of a servant of long standing, hesitating briefly by the curtained doorway before kneeling and throwing more wood on the fire Iris had lit earlier.

"Are you all right, Mistress Anneke?" she asked.

"Of course. Why wouldn't I be?" I didn't turn around.

She sighed and, boring a hole into my back with that stare

of hers, willing me to meet her gaze, stood to one side of the hearth.

"Because it's not like you to come to bed without bidding us good night."

"It's not, is it? Forgive me. A headache prevented it." My lie was as apparent as the flames licking the wood.

"A headache?" She tutted in false sympathy. "That's too bad. It's no trouble to fix you something. Or"—her tone altered—"I could comb your hair like I used to when you were small and we would chat. You found that soothing."

I twisted and gave her a weak smile. "It's not necessary. I'm hoping it's nothing a good night's sleep won't cure. Good night, Saskia."

Her face revealed how hurt she was by my abrupt dismissal and how unconvinced she was by my words. It didn't make me feel any better.

Waiting till the curtain fell into place and Saskia's soft tread faded, I rose and clambered onto the window seat. The window was open, the shutters flung back. As I inhaled deeply, the tepid scents of evening entered—mostly sweet, tinged with woodsmoke, salt, ale, and the faint ordure of the animals. High in the sky, the moon showed half her face, casting a silvery glow over the garden, forging dark shapes and unmaking others. Stars twinkled, scattered over the blanket of night like tiny treasures. Over the garden wall, a light bobbed within the church; Father Clement preparing for the midnight prayers, matins. I offered my own swift one to the Lord and to Mother Mary, though my heart wasn't really in it.

Despite what I claimed, my heart was with Sir Leander Rainford.

Burying my face in my hands, I resisted the urge to weep, to fling myself upon the pillow and cry the way one does when senseless, shortsighted dreams are dashed. Dreams that, until Tobias announced Sir Leander's forthcoming marriage, I didn't know I'd had—or did I? According to Tobias, they were obvious to everyone.

How could I be so stupid? I cringed with shame.

Resting my chin against my shoulder and wrapping one arm around my belly, I concentrated on quashing the emotions that threatened to overwhelm me. An owl hooted, its movement swift against the starry firmament, making me jump. Releasing a deep shuddering sigh, I let go of my stomach and traced mindless patterns on the sill.

When Father was alive, I'd always hoped that one day a suitable husband would be found for me. Oh, we'd had offers. As soon as I turned sixteen, Father and Hiske were approached by the likes of the cloth merchant's son, Robert Mercer, a cocky, ill-mannered man who spent his father's money faster than he could make it. Father rebuffed him and Robert married Ellen de Lys, daughter of another merchant who specialized in fragrant unguents and oils. They'd taken their business to Saint-Germain. That was four years ago and I hadn't heard anything of them since. Then there was Sir Abel Orped, an old knight who had lost an arm in France and four wives besides and was given land and a small annuity by Lord Rainford for his services. Making no secret that he wanted a wife and sons to farm it for him, I was his third effort at securing a woman in a month. Fortunately, despite Hiske's assertions he'd be a fine husband, Father rejected his offer as well. I wonder if it was because of the man's association with Lord Rainford rather than his violent reputation.

There'd been others too. None had been right, according to Father.

I'd always believed he was waiting for the best offer, the right man, before he gave me away in marriage.

And now? As an orphan and eldest child, I'd no one to speak for me, to tender a dowry that might compensate for my short-comings: namely, two young siblings, brewing, an alehouse, and a blistering reputation.

All that aside, was there ever a time when I could have attracted the legitimate attentions of a nobleman? Once, mayhap . . . But ever since Mother died and Father made the contract with Lord Rainford, the best I could hope for in a husband was a struggling merchant or mayhap a poor knight . . . Never a peer of the realm, not even the youngest son of one . . . Not even a cripple . . .

I sighed. It was long, drawn from the depths of my being. Truth be told, before I decided upon brewing, Sir Leander was unavailable to me no matter what. The son of a lord forming a union with the eldest child of one of his vassals wasn't possible. Though we'd all heard stories of nobles marrying farm girls and kings taking housemaids as mistresses, they belonged in the realm of make-believe, not my reality.

For the time being, marriage to any man was out of the question. And so was Sir Leander Rainford, no matter what my mind tried to whisper. Then why could I not dismiss him? Why was hope, despite my bold denials, still nestling in my breast? Tears welled, burning the hollow my heart had become.

The night was so quiet and still. The distant crash of waves could just be discerned. A dog barked, the leaves rustled, and the faint breeze carried the sounds of Father Clement's novices chanting. The bells of St. Stephen's chimed and St. Bartholomew's began to answer.

It was no good; sleep wasn't going to attend me this evening, not yet.

Staring across the yard, my gaze came to rest on the brewhouse, the place that had given me, in one way, such prospects, and in another, such misery. The place that ensured the family survived and I maintained independence. Yet it was also proving to be a millstone that might yet drown me in good intentions.

Thoughts of drowning led to Father, which then led to Lord Rainford, the house, and what started me brewing in the first place, which led to consideration of wine, ale, and beer. By God, I needed another drink. I needed to drink myself into oblivion and forget the nagging ache lodged beneath my breastbone, and either dam or shed the tears that stoppered up my throat.

Grabbing my shawl, I left the room and crept downstairs, avoiding the spots where the floor protested.

Entering the kitchen, I could hear Blanche's soft snores from her room behind the fireplace. Searching for a cup in the dark wasn't easy; neither was finding a jug of ale. I needed light and to make noise. I couldn't risk drinking in here—not only might I wake Blanche, but I didn't want the servants catching me in my weakness. I yearned for solitude, for the drowsy numbness ale or beer would hasten.

Unlatching the kitchen door, I ran through the garden and into the brewery.

My heart was beating savagely; I felt like a naughty girl or a woman embarking on an illicit liaison. The idea gave me pause and sadness began to crawl through me again. I shut the door, fumbling until I found a candle. The flame spat to life and cast a small halo. I looked around. The kiln and oven were still warm, emanating a faint, comforting glow. Beneath the windows, the cooling ale pooled in the troughs, the moonbeams making the surface sparkle. Singing softly to the ale and the crones as I moved around, I found a tankard, slipped my tunic over my head so as not to stain it, pushed up my elegant sleeves, and recklessly immersed the vessel in the trough, enjoying the mellow feel of the liquid against my flesh. Raising my voice slightly in honor to the goddess of brews, it was as though I drew from the source.

Lifting the tankard, the ale spilled over the sides, down my forearms and back into the trough. Before I lost any more, I slurped the foam and then drank deeply, relishing the way it slid down my throat, appreciating the notes of honey, mint, and even the richness of the mandragora I'd added. On a fancy, I'd paid a goodly sum for it from a hawker who had come to the house, wanting to re-create the draft it was said Circe gave to Odysseus's crew.

Imagining myself to be the goddess Circe, I plunged my tankard into the ale again and drank, opening my throat. After all, I indulged not to quench a thirst but to summon forgetfulness. Even as I filled my cup a third time, I knew I would pay for this folly on the morrow, but as my mind clouded and thoughts became difficult to separate, my heart slowed and the pain afflicting my soul dissolved. Sinking onto the floor, my back to the trough, the agreeable heat of the stove offering solace as well, Leander Rainford, husbands, brewing, and the future became distant winking lands to which I one day might venture.

One day . . . maybe . . . if . . .

They erupted from nowhere, the tears I'd thought banished,

the sorrow I didn't know I carried so very deep within. They fell fast and furiously, for Mother, Father, Will, Patroclus and Achilles, for the cruelty of Hiske, for being thought a whore by a man I knew I could so easily love . . . *but I didn't. Nay. I did not. I do not love you, Leander Rainford. As God is my witness, I do not.* Sobs were torn from my throat and, unable to sit straight any longer, I curled up in a ball on the floor, uncaring that rats scuttled nearby, or that ash from the kiln was my pillow. I wept, hiccuped, and wept some more.

That was how Westel found me, ten minutes or days later, I was uncertain; I didn't care. My pride, my flighty ambitions, my dreams were nothing more than blemishes upon my bodice, runnels of moisture upon my cheeks.

He stood over me, head tilted, those great innocent eyes dark pools that stared and stared. Then, with a sigh I took for tenderness, he knelt down and lifted me into his arms.

At first, I welcomed his embrace. The firmness of his hold, the confidence of his murmuring voice, which didn't seek to question or admonish me, but spoke words I'd longed to hear from other lips. Resting my head against his chest, his fingers wove through my hair, untangling my plaits. The action was soothing, pleasing. One hand stroked my arms, while his lips, whispering, whispering, began to travel from my ear to my neck. I could smell ale on his breath and the reek of old wine. Lost between knowing I had to sit up and extract myself from this comfort, but also wanting to allow the moment to last, to surrender to it for just a little longer and let the pain of remembering fade, I hesitated. A voice inside me was shouting "Move," while another couldn't summon a coherent thought.

Westel's tone changed. The words were hard to distinguish at first, I'd drunk so much ale and so very quickly. As they became clearer, I tensed. He spoke of God, of the first woman Eve, and prayed for the salvation of my soul and his. The words were fast, deep, and wild. When he began to beg forgiveness, for what, I was uncertain, common sense prevailed and, though my limbs didn't want to cooperate, I struggled to extricate myself from his grasp.

He tightened his arms. His hands, at first gentle, clenched firmly. I stiffened.

"Westel. What do you think you're doing? Let me go." I pushed against him.

"Sorry, mistress, but God forgive me, I cannot. I've waited so patiently for this chance." Twining his fingers in my hair as if in a caress, he bundled my thick locks at the nape and pulled hard, forcing me to arch backward. Those long, white fingers I'd once admired easily captured my hands in one of his own, caging them.

He laughed, a sinister snarl I'd never heard from him before. I began to flail and whimper as he brought his face closer. Wrenching my head further back, so my neck was strained and the tears so recently stanched fell again, I'd no recourse but to kick. My first attempt missed, but my second met its mark. With a grunt, he doubled over and then with a strength that defied reason, hauled me off the floor by the roots of my hair and bellowed.

Slamming my head against the trough, he released me briefly. Pain exploded in my forehead. Dazed, blood trickled into my eyes as I rolled onto my back and tried to sit up. Before I could, he straddled me. Seizing control of my hands again with one of his, he fumbled at my bodice.

Bright lights danced before my eyes, bands of torment lanced my head, and hot blood sped down my brow. Above me, in the semi-darkness of the brewery, Westel's angelic face was mottled by light and shadow, his huge eyes reflecting the flame of the candle, and he transformed into something from the abbot's pulpit, an emissary of hell come to take me.

"Slattern! Whore!" His spittle rained upon me. "Weapon of the devil. You tempt all men, but above all, you seek to first tempt and now refuse me."

"Westel, nay, please—" The room spun, and Westel merged with it; a huge black wave was about to swallow everything.

"Shut up!" The slap was vicious, loud, my cries muted. "I'm a mere man, too weak to resist. God knows I've tried. But I'm flesh and blood and why should I be denied what others are not?"

My breathing was labored, my mind in splinters. Agony rode my will, breaking it into submission.

"God will understand. God will forgive. Like all women, you're the temptress, Satan's whore come to seduce mankind."

His mad sermon continued unabated, slaver flew from his mouth. Tearing my dress, he groped my body through the rent fabric, rubbed his hands, his face, his mouth against me. His eyes were fierce; his entire body trembled. I could feel his excitement as he thrust himself against me like a rutting pig.

Twisting and turning, I struggled, but he was stronger and that leaden wave pulled me under. I mustered a cry.

"Whore." He struck me across the face again. "Make another sound and I'll stick you with more than my cock." He leaned over me. "Like I did Will," he whispered.

Bright lights danced before my eyes. I shut them but it was as if the stars spun for me alone. "It was you? *You* hurt Will?" My stomach churned; my mind tried to unravel Westel's words.

"Hurt him? Nay, you stinking rose, I killed him." His tongue, a repulsive slug, traced my neck.

Teeth sank into the soft flesh around my nipple. My wail was collected in his hand as he covered my mouth.

"God, oh, my God," he murmured, his lips suckling, hungry, fevered. Nausea rose, sickness and a terrible fear.

*Will, oh, Will* . . . What monster had I brought into the house?

I gagged, coughed, and tried to draw air, but it was rancid. Who was this man? Holy Mother, help me. I summoned another cry, this time for Adam, for Tobias, for Leander, the good men in my life. Before I could release it, Westel picked up my skirts and threw them over my head, not caring that he blocked my nose and mouth, only that it dampened my cries. He unlaced his breeches, his knees pinning my legs.

"I gave him a chance, you know." He spat and thrust moist fingers inside me, grunting. "Will, who sought to tell tales, turn you against me. Will who thought he was so clever, knew what I was about." He plowed his fingers back and forth. "But he didn't—not even when he died, when he begged me to tell him, I wouldn't. None of you knew. Fools. You still don't."

Cruel fingers gouged the soft flesh of my thighs. My thoughts spiraled and shattered into fragments. This wasn't happening, this wasn't real. I would awake and this would be nothing but a devil-sent dream.

The floor became a vast wheel upon which I was turned and turned, sinking lower and lower, descending into a private hell.

As I felt his manhood against me, hard and slick, I made one last effort to heave him away. With a roar of rage, he grabbed my head in both hands, squeezing it as he might a ball, before dashing it against the floor.

His voice became a rhythmic, brutal accompaniment that pierced the thick fog holding my thoughts captive, my body fast.

"You are the gate of the devil," he chanted. "The traitor of the tree, the first deserter of Divine Law; you are she who enticed the one whom the devil dare not approach, you broke so easily the image of God, you broke this man; on account of the death you deserved, even the Son of God had to die . . . And now, it's your turn . . ."

❧⚜❧

I was choking.

A stream of liquid poured over my face, my exposed chest. I coughed, turned aside to stop the steady flow; swallowed, tasted ale, rolled, and vomited.

"Sit up, slut."

Pulled upright roughly and thrown against a hard surface, I lurched to one side before more ale was thrown in my face. I raised my hand weakly. "Please . . ."

Another slap brought me to my senses. The world compressed until it was just a flickering candle and a ream of paper thrust in my face.

"What's this?" asked Westel, pressing the small book hard into my cheek.

At first, I couldn't make out what he was compressing against me. When he moved it away and made it dance back and forth, my blurry vision solidified.

"My . . . my ale bible."

The next blow was so hard, my head snapped around, my nose striking the trough.

"You cunting whore," he spat in my face. "I know what it is.

What's *this*?" Through half-closed eyes, I saw his finger stabbing the words. "What language is this?"

He grabbed my right nipple and twisted it.

"Please . . ." He twisted harder. "Dutch," I cried. "It's written in Dutch."

He slammed the book against my temple and clambered to his feet. "Of course it is." He began to laugh, the sound making my skin crawl. "And to think I killed her when she could have been of use after all."

"Killed?" My heart almost sprang out of my chest. *Will. Westel killed Will.* "Who else, Westel? Who have you harmed?"

He was beside me again, his face and mouth so very, very close. His hot breath lathed my flesh, fingers cupped my cheek ever so gently. They were wet, sticky. Blood. His fingers were covered in blood.

"Saskia," he purred. "I killed Saskia. She saw what I did to Karel."

*Karel?*

The sound I made was not human.

"He found me in your room fetching this." He thrust the ale bible in my face. "I had to silence the devil's spawn lest he rouse the lot. But I was too late. That cow, Saskia, saw me. Doesn't anyone in this Godforsaken house ever sleep? She'll not tell a soul what she witnessed, not anymore."

*Saskia, my loyal, loving Saskia . . .* My heart was beating so fast. Think. *Think.* "What did you do to Karel?"

"Karel? Just a little shove. He fell, struck his head. I placed him in the chest in your room. God was with me for that's where I finally found this." He held the ale bible aloft. "Do you know how long I've been searching for it? I thought you kept it in the office. But it wasn't there, was it? You'd tease me with it, though, bring it to the brewhouse, talk about your secret little recipes. Then you'd hide it and I couldn't find it. There was only one place left it could be. When I saw you creeping out tonight, I knew my luck had changed." He pushed back his cap and scratched his forehead, chuckling.

I wiped the blood out of my eyes. *Karel. Saskia.* I had to get to Karel. I groaned and retched, the noise loud in the quietness of the brewhouse. "You bastard." I tried to rise. "You'll hang for this—"

His foot shot out, connecting with my ribs, and I fell, panting. I tried to scream, the sound was ragged, pathetic; all the wind had been knocked from my lungs, all the courage, my faith, was leaching from my body.

"Scream all you like; it doesn't matter anymore." He shoved the ale bible down the front of his pants. "They'll not heed you, there's too much else to occupy them."

Pressing my hands against my ribs, I panted. "What do you mean?"

Westel stared out the window above me, and I swear I could see the fires of purgatory dancing in his eyes. "You'll see."

Reaching for his coat, which had been flung across the table, Westel shrugged it on. With all my remaining might, I wished him dead. But death was not something you could will; it came of its own or another's volition. I would be that other. I searched for a weapon, something to wield against him. Around me was a litter of broken tools, an upturned mash tun, bent trays. My hand scrabbled across the floor.

"Why?" I asked him, shuffling forward slightly, trying not to make my actions obvious. "Why, Westel? Why Karel? Why Saskia? Why Will?" I gestured to the remnants of my gown, to my dignity that was spilled on the floor, pressed into the bruises, blood and his seed on my thighs. "Why me?" My voice was tiny.

"Why, why, why?" he mocked me in a mewling tone. "Why not? You deliberately flaunt God's laws and man's and believe there won't be a price to pay? You set out to steal business away from us, from God, and think a cost won't be extracted? Oh, the vanity and evil of women knows no bounds." He crossed himself. "Even now, you don't understand justice when it's been served."

"This is about the ale?" Nothing would come into focus, not properly. Breathing deeply, there was a familiar tang in the air; I couldn't quite identify it, my nose was slightly blocked, the smell of blood and my own fear dominated but they also gave me a sudden clarity. "You're from St. Jude's."

"Aye. I am."

It all made sense now. What I'd always believed to be his growing baldness was actually a tonsure growing out. The constant praying, his ability to read and write, the cap that never came off . . . his endless curiosity and willingness to help with the ale.

"Everything you told me was a lie."

"Not everything. I was raised by monks—that part was true. It's just that, as the son of Abbot Hubbard, I could never be denied a calling. After all, I was born to heed my Lord."

*Abbot Hubbard's son? Oh dear God, help me.*

"I don't understand." I tried to distract him with questions, all the while searching for a weapon, something with which to protect myself. "The alehouse was your idea."

"Aye, it was and you adopted it, just as I hoped."

"You intended me to fail all along."

"Such is your pride and vanity you assumed you were going to succeed."

"I was."

Westel shook his head in disbelief. The light from outside was growing, the smell getting stronger. A steady roar, like the ocean in a storm, grew louder, forcing Westel to raise his voice to be heard.

"You were warned, Anneke Sheldrake; we gave you notice time and time again, but you chose to ignore us. Instead, you sounded the clarion, recruited more soldiers, and marched to meet your destiny. Tonight you face it."

Before I could anticipate him, he lifted the ale-stick away from the wall and in one swift action, raised it above his head. In the undulating light pouring in from outside, Westel was an avenging angel come to wreak a terrible justice.

With all my remaining strength, I screamed, raising my arms above my head. At the same time, I levered myself partly under the trough. The ale-stick swung. It hit the edge of the wood and my shoulder at the same time as my head struck the metal leg. I fell back into blessed shadows and lay completely still.

With a grunt, Westel cast the ale-stick aside and prodded my body with his boot. I fought the blackness creeping into my mind, the agony that roared through my shoulder, head, and heart. Nay, nay. *Karel . . . Betje. Oh sweet Jesù, please don't forsake me . . .*

Conscious of a commotion swelling beyond, of the door to

the brewhouse opening, a blast of smoke-filled air entering, I tried not to let murky relief claim me, but my injuries were too great, my soul and body too sore. I shut my eyes, intending to rise, to run to the house, find Karel, see what caused such smoke and raging light, but before I could, I lost this battle as well.

# THIRTY-FOUR

HOLCROFT HOUSE
Midsummer's Day
*The year of Our Lord 1406 in the seventh
year of the reign of Henry IV*

*E*ventually the blackness receded and, holding what remained of my dress together, I staggered out of the brewhouse, fell onto my hands and knees, and retched. Over and over, I spewed forth nothing but noise, nothing but the empty horror of what Westel had done, had said. Pain cleaved my head, traveled across my breasts, shoulder, arms, and thighs. Doubled over, vile images leaped into my mind, paraded before my eyes until they faded enough to allow me to raise my chin.

Time telescoped until it was nothing more than a raging fire, heat, ash, and smoke engulfing the upper floors of my home. Holcroft House was aflame.

"Nay." Soft black rain fell around me. Timbers cracked and crackled. "Nay, nay. Dear God, nay." I began to crawl forward, one arm held before me, the other protecting my modesty. "Karel! Betje!" I shouted and staggered to my feet.

Outside, Blanche and Iris held each other, wailing and screaming, pointing.

Ignoring them, I stumbled past. "Karel! Betje!"

Bursting through the kitchen door, I collided with Adam. His face was black, his clothes too. Thick gray powder coated his hair, falling in a cascade across his cheeks. "It's no good." He grabbed me around the waist to prevent me from running further into the house. "You'll not get to them that way. The fire's taken the stairs."

"What then?" I found my voice. "*What?*" I screeched. My head was a ball of white-hot agony; terror for the twins overcame my need to stop, to lie down.

"Anneke!" Adam's eyes widened as he took in my appearance. "By God. What happened to you, lass?"

I glanced down. Lord knew what my face must look like, but my dress barely covered me. Spattered with blood, my arms were cut, bruised, my chest as well. "Not now," I said.

Adam removed his coat and wrapped it around me.

"Adam . . ." My teeth were chattering so severely, it was hard to form words. "The children. Karel, he's hurt . . . Westel . . ."

Questions brimming in his eyes, Adam said, "This way."

Grabbing his hand, I started to run, but dizziness overcame me. Adam wrapped an arm about my waist and half-carried me outside and to the other end of the house.

Men poured through the open back gates, the fire drawing people as a candle did moths. They milled in the garden, black silhouettes against the golden fire, wielding hooks with which they pulled down the burning thatch. Others heaved brimming buckets, throwing the contents as high as they could. When the water struck the flames, they fizzled momentarily before flashing to life again. A line ran out the gate, down the lane. Some tended to Shelby, leading the petrified horse from the stables and out into the street. Four men pulled the cart to safety. Neighbors gathered, whether to help, be spectators, or to better gauge the safety of their own property, I was uncertain. I didn't care. I wanted the children.

We staggered toward the mews, pushing anyone foolish enough to hinder us out of the way.

"There. Look!" cried Adam.

Standing at the window of the nursery were Louisa and Betje. I sobbed with relief. Both were crying and coughing, Betje's little arms reaching out through the open space. Thick, angry smoke billowed around them. Betje spotted me.

"Anneke! Anneke! Help!"

I swallowed. Despair tried to take me, but I clamped it down. "I will, sweet one," I called, cupping my mouth in order to be heard. The fire bellowed in an effort to drown out my reassurances.

Beside her, Louisa whimpered, her face dark with soot and heat; only her eyes showed, wide and white and terrified. "Louisa," I yelled. "It will be all right. I promise."

I continued to talk, trying to distract them. Ladders were brought, but they weren't long enough. The drop was dangerously high. The ground hard. They couldn't leap, the risk was too great . . . not unless . . .

I spun around. "Adam, grab a blanket, something Betje can

jump into, quickly!" Adam ran into the stables. He emerged again seconds later with a large blanket—Shelby's—and began organizing men to hold it.

"Louisa!" I stood beneath the window, squinting into the rain of molten ash, ignoring the way it spiraled around me, singed my flesh, my hair, my lungs. The fire growled, the hounds of hell, their fiery jaws snapping, consuming.

"Mistress, oh, mistress, hurry, hurry." Tears fell down her blackened face, causing paler runnels to emerge. "Please, save us."

"Listen. Betje, when I tell you, I want you to stand on the sill and jump, all right? Then you, Louisa, the men will catch you."

"Aye, mistress," said Louisa between sobs. "God help us." She crossed herself. Betje did too, hiccuping, nodding.

The blanket was so small, the men so big, I prayed it would hold, for it was so far to fall. I glanced up again.

"Adam." I grabbed his shirt. "Karel . . . He's . . . in my room. The chest. You must save him."

Pressing his lips together grimly, Adam looked across at my window. Flames danced around the shutters, making the thatch above glow eerily.

"Here, take this." Adam passed his side of the blanket to another burly man; it was Master Blakesmith, the ironmonger. "I'll fetch him, don't you worry." He threw buckets of water over himself then crossed the yard and, ignoring the choking plumes of smoke, ran back in the house. I wanted to follow, but knew if Betje was to be safe, I had to remain where I was.

Standing next to the blanket, beneath the window, I fastened my eyes onto hers. Filled with doubt, scared witless at what I was about to ask her to do, I was more frightened by what would happen if she didn't obey.

"Betje, hold on to Louisa and stand on the sill." My voice barely carried, the noise was so great, the fire so loud and filled with fury. Betje wailed and shook her head. "You must, sweet one." I tried to sound calm, authoritative.

Louisa bent and said something. Betje nodded and, clutching Louisa's hand, oh so slowly climbed onto the sill.

Holding my breath, I watched her clamber onto the narrow strip of wood. It was then I realized she held her doll, Tansy.

"Good girl! Now, stand up."

Betje cried out and shook her head again.

"You must, Betje."

She trembled like a wet cat, locked in fear.

"Betje." I had an idea. "Tansy wants to jump first. All right? Throw Tansy onto the blanket."

Crouched on the sill, Betje looked at me. Holding Louisa tightly, she glanced at her doll then, with a sudden flick of her hand, threw the toy into the air. Against the sparks and whirling ash, the doll descended, limbs splayed, woolen hair flying. She landed in the middle of the blanket. The men cheered as if this rag was a real person.

Fire began to lick the thatch above the window. Betje screamed, so did Louisa. The smoke was like another barrier, a smothering blanket that prepared to engulf them.

"Now! Betje, now." She didn't move. "For Godsakes, Louisa," I cried as there was another explosion and part of the roof collapsed. "Push her!"

A ball of fire erupted through the window, engulfing Louisa and Betje. Screams and yells burst from everyone below.

Falling from the window was a small arrow of flame, a living comet shrieking to the earth.

It tumbled through the night and we all watched in horror until it sizzled onto the blanket where the men, mesmerized, nonetheless still managed to catch it.

They used the wool to swiftly douse the flames. Smoke rose, escaping from the sudden rents, the blackened holes. The smell was sickening, the caterwauling from within worse.

Then, from above us, came a piercing wail.

All eyes flew to the sill. Louisa! Though Betje's fall had been mere seconds, already it was too late for Louisa.

Forever frozen at the window, Louisa became an animated piece of kindling, a Roman candle. We stared helpless, shocked into silence as she was consumed. Her high-pitched screams only ceased when the roof caved, crushing her, silencing her.

I stood immobile, unable to tear my eyes from where she'd last stood until Betje's whimpers alerted me. The men knelt around what remained of the blanket, too scared to look, fearful lest their rescue failed. Ignoring the smoking, charred mass of flesh Betje had become, I pushed through them, knelt, and, keeping the blanket around her, as carefully as I could, scooped her into my arms. Staggering as my own abused body protested her weight, inhaling and gagging as the stench assailed me, I collapsed to the ground.

Some of the men ran forward to help, but I shook my head, sending them away. Relieved of their duty, eager to escape another death they didn't want to witness, the men scattered to pour more water upon the burning remains.

It was futile. Holcroft House would not survive.

Using one arm, I dragged us toward the brewhouse, clutching Betje to my breast, muttering inanities, ignoring the way her little red legs struck the dirt.

Falling against the garden wall, holding Betje, Blanche and Iris joined me, their sobs quieter, their fear transformed into something deeper, darker, as they stared with stricken faces at the bundle in my arms and began to pray.

Together, we watched as men worked to put out the flames, to try and save the adjoining properties. In a parody of the winter snows, soft black and gray flakes, as well as some bright orange ones, fell around us, landing in our hair, on our clothes, settling onto the garden, onto the chickens and pigs, who, roused from their slumber, were making a clamor.

It was some time before I thought to examine Betje. Mayhap, I was afraid of what I would find. Pushing aside the blanket, I sent Blanche for water and gingerly bathed my sister's scorched flesh, made her drink through ravaged swollen lips, lips that had once been such a perfect rose and were now a twisted reddened mass. Blanche found a fresh blanket in the brewhouse with which to wrap her. Pretending the creature in my arms was still Betje as I last saw her, was difficult. Her clothes, like most of her hair, had been burned from her body. Every morsel of flesh that I could see had been colored afresh, the palette either black or shades of carmine. Flensed from her body, it was if her skin could not bear to remain; some stuck to Shelby's blanket. Much came away wherever I touched. It was sickening to see, to hold, and yet I was compelled to do both, to bear witness to my poor little sister's suffering. I'd no doubt whatsoever she was not long for this world and determined she would die in my arms, being cherished, knowing love. Quietly, I prayed to God to please save her, to save Betje, Karel, and, as time went past and he didn't reemerge, Adam as well. I already knew that Saskia was gone. Westel roamed through my mind and I wished him to hell each time he appeared. We prayed, Blanche, Iris, and, before long, Father Clement, who, sweating, soot-streaked, and exhausted, arrived and added his to ours.

God was not with us that night. Not only did a wind arise to blow the ash and cinders north, starting fresh fires that took Master Goldsmith's house and business and the seven properties beyond as well, but the flames devoured all of Holcroft House except, ironically, the brewery. When Adam reappeared, coughing fit to make the earth shudder, and jogged toward us, his singed hair, blackened face, and tragic eyes told their own tale. He fell down beside us and, burying his head in his hands, wept.

I had no more tears. Not that night, not ever again.

When the sun rose, trying to part the clouds of billowing smoke, Holcroft House, its darkened skeleton yearning for the light, was nothing more than charred bones.

# PART TWO
# The Brewer of Southwark

*SOUTHWARK AND LONDON, 1407–1409*

*But first I make a protestation round*
*That I'm quite drunk, I know it by sound:*
*And therefore, if I slander or mis-say*
*Blame it on the ale of Southwark, so I pray.*

—Geoffrey Chaucer, "The Miller's Tale"


*Southwark for the most part pursued its accustomed way,*
*unruly and unruled.*

—David Johnson, *Southwark and the City*

# THIRTY-FIVE

ELMHAM LENN TO DOVER
TO CANTERBURY
After midsummer to end of February
*The year of Our Lord 1406–1407 in the seventh
and eighth years of the reign of Henry IV*

Trapped in a netherworld populated by reassuring whispers interrupted by cruel taunts and roaring flames, it was three weeks before my senses were restored enough to fully grasp what had happened, to understand what I was yet to face.

It was not just the horror and grief of so much death, the final memory of Saskia, Louisa, and my beloved Karel, or Betje's terrible fate, nor the loss of the only home I'd ever known, that I had to reconcile. With my recovery came the painful knowledge that any remaining goodwill I had in Elmham Lenn was irreparably forfeit as well. The fire had unleashed its fury upon my neighbors, destroying other lives and livelihoods. Looking for a scapegoat, people turned against me. Urged on by Hiske, whose capacity for sanctimony grossly exceeded her compassion, the townsfolk affected sought to sue me for restitution. Hurling insults and curses, they haunted the church grounds, waiting for me to emerge from the security of St. Bartholomew's and for their savage justice to be served.

All this I learned from Father Clement, Adam, and Captain Stoyan, who, when I collapsed among the ashes of my former life, had smuggled me and Betje into St. Bartholomew's and declared sanctuary. Keeping us hidden within its stone walls, they ensured we received the best care possible. While my physical wounds were repaired quickly, it was those lodged deep in my heart that festered.

Yet amid the bleakness there was also hope. Despite the dreadful mortification her body had suffered, Betje survived. Told it was God's will, I demurred. Mayhap He did wrap my sister in His tender mercy, but it was also the experienced ministrations of Mother Joanna, the head of St. Hildegarde's, the hospital in town, that kept Betje alive. To this woman of God I owed my sister's life and to Him I was, at first, grateful.

As the days passed and her immolated flesh slowly transformed into raw knots and puckers of red that would disfigure and disable her greatly, I wondered how, having been saved, her life would unfold. How God could be both so cruel and yet so benevolent.

As soon as I was able, I told my saviors what I'd learned that dark night: of Westel Calkin's betrayal; his brutality, to which my own injuries attested; and his ready admission of murder.

Expecting indignation, rage, sworn vengeance, the uncomfortable silence and knowing looks my friends shared as we sat before the fire in Father Clement's rooms knelled a warning. What was being kept from me?

"Mistress Anneke," said Adam, reaching for my trembling

hand. "I'm afraid the justice you seek is not possible . . . that Goddamned blackguard perished in the fire."

I stared at him in disbelief. "For certes?"

"What remained of his belongings was found in the ruins of the hall. His cap, his satchel. There were other things, human . . ." Adam swallowed.

"They could only have been his . . ." finished Father Clement, fingers clutching his beads.

This was the Lord's punishment for the evil Westel wrought? Forgive my blasphemous conceit, but it was not enough. Between him and Betje, I found my faith sorely tested.

Less than a week after I was well enough to roam the church and tend to my sister, Hiske triumphed. We learned the sheriff had been summoned from London. What were my chances—an unmarried woman, a brewster, the keeper of an alehouse—of getting a fair trial?

⌖

Adam and Captain Stoyan arranged our departure—our flight, if I was to call it by its real name—from Elmham Lenn. Our belongings were meager, our fears great. Adam had gone through the debris of Holcroft House and salvaged a few barrels of ale and beer from the brewery and found in the house, beneath collapsed rafters, the tin we used to keep our coin. It was half-full of groats, silver pennies, and some nobles. Not enough to compensate the townspeople, even if they could be persuaded to accept it, but enough to fund our eventual journey to London, where it was decided we could disappear completely. But not yet—London was too obvious a destination. To deter would-be pursuers, we would travel south.

"While Captain Stoyan transports you by ship to a safe house in Dover," said Father Clement, "Adam will take Shelby and the cart and set a false trail north. For as long as I'm able, I'll make folk believe you're still here, in the church. There are many days left before your forty days of sanctuary expire. No one will cross the threshold, not even the city authorities till then, by which time you'll be long gone."

When Mother Joanna offered to come with me and continue caring for Betje, I knew not how to express my gratitude, or the need in me she so readily met. "The dear Lord knows, you've both been punished enough," she said, her eyes alighting upon Betje and then my stomach, before sidling to the bowl into which I'd purged every morning for the past week. In the liquid depths of her lovely brown eyes, I saw that she understood—my silence, my guilt. In that exchange, she became complicit in my wretched condition. I'd not mentioned the rape to anyone. I was ashamed, dirty, soiled to my very core. And, truth be told, I felt somehow to blame. It wasn't only Westel's insults and the stream of invective that had flowed from him that night and lodged in my veins. It was those who, when I first embarked on this venture, and whose opinion I cared about, had warned me of what might happen. They'd possessed a foresight I'd either lacked or willfully ignored. That innocents had paid so dearly for my sin and folly weighed heavily upon my soul . . .

Did we grow complacent in Dover as the months passed and neither the hue and cry nor the county sheriff pounded at our door? Mayhap. Our vigilance, while rigorous when we first arrived, did lessen somewhat. We assumed that we'd slipped into the annals of Elmham Lenn's past, accompanied no doubt by dire warnings of what befell licentious women, and dared to consider safety a possibility. Even to map out a future. What none of us factored in, however, was Sir Leander Rainford.

Learning what had happened at Holcroft House, Sir Leander immediately aborted the trip he'd undertaken with his new bride. What she must have thought, I don't know, but instead of wintering on a sunny coast somewhere in Castile, after merely a few weeks of wedded bliss Lady Cecilia found herself rudely deposited back in London, while her husband, Tobias by his side, made haste to his father's estates. According to Captain Stoyan and intermittent messages I received from Father Clement, Sir Leander was ruthless in his determination to uncover my whereabouts and, may God bless his soul, clear my name. Even now, the thought of him storming through Elmham Lenn, inspecting the remains of Holcroft House, demanding answers from Father Clement, comforting Tobias as they stood over little Karel's grave, is difficult for me to comprehend. Our fate never was and should not be Sir Leander's concern. And yet . . . he chose to make it so. The very notion made my heart accelerate, but also firmed my resolve to exclude him from my life, to protect him from the damage of any association with me. But in those deep, secret places to which I would rarely venture, I felt such warmth and gratitude toward the man. He cared— whether about Tobias's future or mine, I knew not. He cared and it was enough for me. It had to be.

That he continued to intrude upon my thoughts, break down the barriers I so carefully erected, happened when I'd no control or say in the matter. No one is responsible for those who enter their dreams.

For well over a week, Sir Leander remained in Elmham Lenn, questioning the local sheriff, our neighbors, Masters Miller and Proudfellow, and anyone else who might have frequented the Cathaline Alehouse. He even tracked down Blanche and Iris, who had returned to their families after the fire. I thanked Mother Mary over and over that my dear servants could offer him nothing. Their ignorance of my whereabouts was their shield and also mine. For the same reason, after discussion with Father Clement, and with a heavy heart, I'd made the decision not to share my plans, or my grief, with Tobias. It would be as if I too perished in the fire. He was faultless in all this and I would not make him complicit now I was a fugitive.

So why then, as the days passed and Sir Leander's efforts led to naught, did I feel so ambivalent?

Not even Father Clement and Captain Stoyan were spared his angry interrogations, nor, I learned, Abbot Hubbard. Captain Stoyan reported that while Sir Leander hid his evident concern for me beneath resolute looks and terse questions, Tobias did not. Despite his last bitter communication, my heart broke as I thought of him and the losses he had to bear. Being angry with a stubborn older sister is very different to mourning those you believe forever gone.

While grief and self-recrimination occupied my evenings, the days were reserved solely for Betje and the ways in which, first with Mother Joanna's help and, later, Adam's, I could alleviate her suffering. Our first weeks in Dover, settling into the huge house of Captain Stoyan's friends—a wealthy Dutchman and his sister—were mostly a blur. Amid sunshiny days, blustery winds, lashing rain, and the encroaching mellowness of autumn was the relentless insistence of Betje's pain.

Able to cope with the journey to Dover and our first few days in new surroundings, tolerating the unguents and lotions with which Mother Joanna insisted we gently wash and massage her charred and blistered flesh, as well as the potions she was persuaded to drink, it was as if Betje remained unaware of what had befallen her. Or, as I misguidedly believed, that the good Lord had somehow taken pity upon her innocent soul and spared her the suffering that should attend such grievous afflictions. How wrong I was. As the days merged into weeks, it was as if Betje awoke to her state and was tortured anew. The treatments she had tolerated without a murmur, the medicines she had willingly drunk while lodged in St. Bartholomew's, became punishments we cruelly forced upon her. Every wary ministration, every down-soft touch, made her writhe in agony.

Struggling against our attentions, screaming in her strange, hoarse manner, my promise never to shed another tear was sorely tested as I helplessly watched my sister endure. If Mother Joanna hadn't been there, forcing me to hold Betje while she patiently flensed the dead flesh from her arm, legs, head, and cheek, rubbed the oils and sticky lotions into her skin, I would have abandoned the cure long ago. It was all I could do to contain my poor sister, hold her, pray over her, and try to soothe her haunting wails and steady her shaking limbs.

Only guilt and love kept me firm. What right did I have to the relief of weeping? What right did I have to beg Mother Joanna to cease her attempts to help my sister when I'd caused this?

So I bore my sister's agony by never turning from her, by facing every day, every session with Mother Joanna, by her side.

Adam joined us amidst all this, after laying a false trail for those intent on bringing me to justice. Pushing aside his exhaustion, he too did whatever he could to provide succor.

It wasn't until Christmastide that Betje began to bear Mother Joanna's treatments with stoicism. It was also around then that her hand, which had curled into an ugly claw, slowly straightened, the fingers flexing. Likewise her feet, upon which we'd showered so much attention—the toes of one foot had melded into each other, while on the other they'd been reduced to tight little nubs—began to respond. At the same time, the angry red of her flesh faded to the fresh pink of newly grown skin.

Despite the pretty color, suggesting youth and innocence, clear dawn mornings and balmy sunsets, it didn't look new. Shiny and slick, as if it were perpetually wet, Betje's face and one side of her body took on a peculiar sheen. Ridges and runnels meant the skin was never smooth, not like the portion of her features that remained unmarred. Instead, it was as if a crone had shucked off her flesh and passed it to my sister as one does a worn garment. The couple in whose house we dwelled whispered to each other that she looked like a candle that had spent half its wax. The comparison was sadly apt. Whenever I looked at my dear sister, thoughts of Apollo's woman, the oracle who aged and never died, forced their way into my head. She was simultaneously ancient and a child.

Our daily massages, gentle yet firm, continuing till our digits ached and our backs were bent with fatigue, ensured her limbs finally found their old habits again. While her lips would remain twisted in a swollen parody of a smile, the teeth within were white and wholesome. The beautiful gray eye that gazed upon the world, unlike its twin, forever fused beneath a fleshy curtain, began to sparkle with curiosity once more. Denied speech, or perhaps refusing to use words when they might only describe horror, Betje eschewed talk and grunted and pointed to let her needs be known.

Finally, after winter's fury was tamed and the seas began to settle, we were able to introduce her to the streets of Dover, taking her down to the docks to greet Captain Stoyan's ship when he laid anchor in late January. It was during this first foray into the wider world that I learned of its capacity for cruelty once more. Not only was Betje the focus of unwanted attention and comments from passersby, but also exclamations of horror and disgust. How could Christians so condemn one of God's own children? Even with Captain Stoyan, Adam, and Mother Joanna there, and Betje enveloped in my arms and mantle, it was a long walk back to our residence as I seethed at the offense of it. I still recall how, as we sat in silence before the fire in the solar, Betje climbed into my lap and rested her good cheek against my breast. As I swept aside the few locks of hair that fell over her face, I felt wetness and my heart seized.

I would do whatever it took to protect my dear sister from those people and their ready and shallow judgments. I swore it over and over in the depths of my being. As I did so, I knew that in order to keep such a promise, I needed position, money, and the authority that attached itself to both. Only then would no one dare cause my sister injury.

As Betje wept against me, I pledged I would achieve these things, no matter how long it might take, and began to think how I could achieve such a lofty goal.

Perhaps it was fate, perhaps it was something else, but there was only one way I knew to make money and, as my eyes alighted on the old ale-stick that rested in a corner against a chest with some other belongings we'd salvaged from Holcroft House, my plans began to form. A saint I was not and never had been, but for once I wondered what it might be like to embrace the life of a sinner, the life that had once been ascribed to me.

Was I so very wicked that I found the notion appealing?

❧❀❧

It was not intended we'd make the trip to London via Long Southwark Road nor at this time of year. We'd planned that after I'd delivered the baby, which I could no longer deny I was carrying and was due mid-spring, Captain Stoyan would transport us to London by ship and that business acquaintances of his in the Stilliard, the great steel-walled warehouse of the Hanse that lay on the Thames, would harbor us until I could commence brewing again—for that was my means to shore up a life for Betje, Adam, and myself. The child inside me, I didn't consider. Just as we would find our way, it too would have to accept the life into which it was born. If it survived, it would be the son or daughter of a brewer. Bless the captain and Adam that they didn't dissuade me but understood my ambitions.

All our preparations were thrown to the winds the day Sir Leander arrived in Dover. How had he found us? Father Clement must have capitulated and given up our secrets. Nothing else made sense . . .

A torrent of emotions engulfed me. My instinct to flee, to hide my shame, my condition, was paramount. But there was also a strong desire to throw myself into his arms and seek his aid.

I didn't often allow myself to examine how I felt about the child quickening in my body, growing with each passing day until such time as it emerged into the world, a living, breathing reminder of what Westel Calkin had done, the way in which he'd violated my body, my trust . . .

I gripped my stomach, willing the child to cease its movements and, God forgive me, as I had in the many months prior, for it to simply die. I no more wanted this child than I did the memories of its conception or of the man who fathered it. That it would live and thrive when Karel lay rotting in the ground was not something to which even God and my faith in His will could reconcile me.

I could never see Sir Leander or Tobias again. Hesitant fingers followed the curve of my billowing stomach, loathing its strangeness, its roundness. How could I explain . . . this? That I was not complicit in the sowing of this seed? The church preached that a woman was only deemed to have been taken against her will if no child resulted from the union, so my version of events would only ever appear to be a weak attempt to protect my virtue. How was it that I paid with a lifelong sentence for the vile sins of another? Of a man of God, no less? As the weeks passed and my body swelled, it seemed that Eve's curse upon her sex knew no bounds.

Yet, according to Hiske, and even Tobias, virtue and I parted company long before Westel Calkin entered my life.

And so, six months after we left Elmham Lenn, and two days after Sir Leander was reported to be searching the streets, Adam, Betje, and I left the security and comfort of Dover. Mother Joanna retired to the abbey until spring, at which time she would return to Elmham Lenn. Despite it being the last week of winter, despite the sleet, rain, and bitter conditions, and against the advice of Adam and the captain, I insisted we leave. If we didn't, I knew it was only a matter of time before Sir Leander found us.

Some would call it madness to travel when snow and ice carpeted the ground and frosty winds were pitiless and persistent companions, but for us, the February cold quickly became a merciful if not devoted friend. Only the desperate or unbalanced journeyed at this time, and I hoped the conditions deterred anyone inclined to pursuit, including Sir Leander.

We left Dover early, before the birds trilled their morning song or the hearth fires had been banked. Wrapped beneath layers of wool, we headed toward London via Canterbury, a deliberate deception in case we were followed. Traveling cautiously, avoiding company when it appeared, we rested in small lodgings, shunning conversation with patrons and, to the best of our ability, their curious eyes. The days were cold and brief, too often turning into an icy drizzle that blasted us in torn sheets. Not that we had cause to complain, for those very things that made being abroad a trial, also meant the way was mostly devoid of travelers. Unless a market was on in a nearby village or a king's courier or a group of soldiers churned the road, we barely saw a soul. But what protected us also made us vulnerable. Rumors of highwaymen and bandits reached us, and Adam and I determined that, after one close scrape, as soon as possible, we'd reverse our initial intention and seek the company of strangers.

It was our great good fortune that, as we prepared to leave Canterbury, we were able to join a band of pilgrims who had braved the wintry conditions to visit St. Thomas à Becket's shrine and were now returning to London. There was safety even in small numbers and though good King Henry ensured the roads were patrolled, his lands were vast and his eyes and men could not be everywhere.

And so we found ourselves numbered among the pious. If

anyone in this motley band of worshippers wondered why I might take to the roads to seek the solace of shrines and saints, a single servant in tow, one look at Betje's scarred mien silenced them. No one said anything directly, they didn't have to, but even after the initial shock passed of seeing a little one with flesh so mortified you couldn't tell if she was a boy or girl, their interest in me remained. I didn't wear the gray cloak that bespoke a pilgrim, nor did I possess a staff or wear any of the little leaden brooches that denoted other journeys to shrines.

The decision to reveal as little as possible about our past and reasons for braving the roads was taken from me, as it was evident within moments of joining the pilgrims that the price to be extracted for traveling with them would be a tale.

Prior to leaving Dover, Adam, Mother Joanna, and I concocted a story to explain our journey if needed, one that required me to don the mantle of widowhood and a new name. The moment we passed through Dover's high city gates, turning our back on our temporary haven, I was no longer Anneke Sheldrake— that woman was a fugitive, subject to arrest should she be caught. She was also the prey Sir Leander hunted. I was now a Lowlands woman, Mistress Anna de Winter, pregnant widow of a recently deceased (may God assoil him) sea captain, traveling with my servant and grievously injured younger sister to gather what dues my husband's employers, the Hanse, owed, with the intention to resettle in the city.

Alongside a diverse bunch of pilgrims, all of whom shared their stories as we made our way, we swayed atop the cart, loyal Shelby at its head. We were anonymous, protected, and thus we headed to London.

Or, at least that was what we intended.

# THIRTY-SIX

APPROACHING LONDON VIA
LONG SOUTHWARK
February
*The year of Our Lord 1407 in the eighth
year of the reign of Henry IV*

*A*fter days of fog and shivery miles, the clouds parted, allowing beams of golden sunlight to strike the road, illuminating the puddles of water and the thick hedgerows lining the holloway. Enjoying the sudden warmth, Shelby's pace quickened slightly and he raised his head, and I could not help but feel a similar shift in my own mood. Having been denied the sun for so long, it was a welcome companion. Much like the woman sitting beside me.

Adam had surrendered his seat atop the cart to one of the pilgrims, Goodwife Alyson Bookbinder, a much-married wool merchant who, having made her fortune in Bath, relocated to Southwark a few years ago.

Chatting amiably when she first sat up beside me, remarking this was the fourth time she'd traveled this particular route, though never at this time of year, she tried to engage me in conversation, but as the road became treacherous, I had to concentrate and could not respond. Walking in front, Adam took Shelby's head and between us we avoided the worst of the rain-made holes and gullies. After a while, the road improved but by then the goodwife had forgotten her questions and I was preoccupied with a dull ache in my lower back.

We rode in companionable silence, broken only by little grunts from Betje, who had unfurled like a flower at the first touch of the sun before falling asleep against me once more. Chatter from the pilgrims walking or riding flowed around the cart, rising, falling, and melting into the day, becoming a veil that settled over the group. Goodwife Alyson opened a bag on her lap and fished out two apples, passing one to me. I took it gratefully, unaware I was hungry until I caught scent of the fruit.

After a couple of bites, I gave the rest to Betje, who'd stirred, and I listened to her pleasure as she nibbled the tart flesh. Flocks of starlings wheeled above, their song fading, their dark wings silhouetted against the afternoon.

As the sun began its rapid descent, the blue of the sky transforming into blushing pinks and violets, the number of folk heading to the city increased, especially once we left the small town of Deptford. London was almost in our sights. Beside the cart, farriers, blacksmiths, carpenters, clerks, and many other tradesfolk ambled, the manner of their clothing and even their posture revealing their skills. Farmers, keen to sell their livestock in the markets, herded pigs and cattle, while some carried chickens trussed in cages or tied on poles. A noisy choir of baying, clucking, and lowing accompanied our steps. Women, children, drably garbed monks, a couple of jugglers and minstrels, instruments strapped across their backs, also swam in the growing human tide.

As we crested the final hill, I could not prevent the exclamation that escaped my lips. Goodwife Alyson bit back a smile.

Surrounded by a huge angled wall that looked like a frozen wave of stone, sprawled London. According to the goodwife—who now commented loudly on all that lay before us, her gap-toothed grin flashing, her fingers pointing out one landmark after another—the best and worst of the world was contained within those walls, and she should know, she said, having seen enough of it in the last five or so years. From our vantage point, I could perceive the riddle of streets that divided the city, some wide enough to appear more like fields, while others were so narrow they were swallowed by numerous houses. Pockets of green and brown added extra color to a tableau already alive with textures, sights, and possibility. To the right, and seemingly a part of the wall, was a huge stone fortress. This was the Tower, said Goodwife Alyson. A moated castle complemented by smaller edifices, it was the province of all things royal—a symbol of power, untold wealth, cruel justice, and fear. I shuddered. To the left, beyond the city walls, sprawled the other royal residence, Westminster, a grand extravagance befitting the monarch, according to the goodwife.

Between Westminster and an area called Ludgate, new homes and inns were taking shape; jetties the goodwife swore had not been there when she left less than a month ago rose out of the water. Within the walls, plumes of smoke billowed into the air, competing with the steeples of many churches—for, as Goodwife Alyson observed in a strident voice, where there was iniquity there would also be piety and vice versa—and thank the good Lord for that. A few chuckles and some imprecations met her remark. I didn't respond as, by then, the thick, sinuous river had captured my eye. In the dying rays of the afternoon sun it was a shimmering ribbon of gold, wrapping the city. It was simply magnificent.

Coming down the hill, past the taverns, inns, and shops that formed a corridor of bustle between the country and the river, another wonder took its place. Twenty arches and nineteen piers (called "starlings," according to the goodwife) comprised London Bridge, under which flowed the mighty Thames, its waters frothing and surging against the footings; above them, multi-story houses and over one hundred shops bulged. More like a town or suburb, its span was bursting with people, animals, vehicles, color, noise, and, even from a distance, odors.

"I'd never imagined . . ." I said to Goodwife Alyson, struggling to find the words. "I never thought . . ."

"Nay." The goodwife grinned. "No one ever does."

"Betje, Betje, wake, my sweet. You must see this for yourself."

Betje stirred and slowly, painfully, pulled herself into a sitting position, careful not to leave my side entirely.

As Betje's one good eye scanned the horizon, she tilted her chin and pushed back her hood to see the better, and I noted Goodwife Alyson conducting her own examination. It was all I could do not to fling a protective arm over Betje, shield her from the goodwife's study. But I had to allow it, test the waters, so to speak—and the woman.

"Why," said Goodwife Alyson, leaning so her words reached my ears alone, "only one side of the child's face is badly marred. On the other, you can still see the beauty she'd have become and which you, Mistress de Winter, are the realization." Goodwife Alyson sat up and frowned. "I wonder which is crueler? To have it all taken away so there's no echo, or to have something of what you once were to remind others of your loss?"

I regarded her with dismay, but also a modicum of gratitude. She hadn't flinched in revulsion nor ignored the obvious, but sought to discuss Betje's injuries as one might a broken limb or a runny nose. This was easier to deal with than vile observations and abuse.

I pondered her words as we wended our way toward the bridge, the press of people increasing as the sun sank.

With the reins in one hand, my other gently rubbed my spine. Dear Mother Mary, I would be glad to leave this cart. My body was aching.

Outside the Tabard Inn, the place where Goodwife Alyson had started her pilgrimage, the cart all but ground to a halt and Adam leaped onto the tray as those who'd enjoyed a respite from the road thanked me politely and disembarked. Adam assisted the two nuns, a student, and a friar to the ground, warning them to mind the ditch, and I watched them disperse into the crowd. Of the original pilgrims, the only one who remained was the goodwife and she showed no inclination to leave, nodding amiably at me and winking at Adam over her shoulder. He coughed and sat with his back against one of the barrels.

Smoke choked the air, and the stench of tanning hides, blacksmiths' furnaces, and the unmistakable pungency of sour ale competed with the animal and human waste underfoot. Hawkers forced their way through the heaving masses in order to shove wares and greasy food in people's faces while pickpockets and cutpurses worked behind their backs. Using her foot, Goodwife

Alyson kicked the more daring away, while Adam added his own threats. Shelby tossed his head in protest, forcing me to tighten his bit and make reassuring noises. Betje looked about her with interest, thrusting her thumb back in her mouth. I quickly pulled her hood forward, caressing the fabric with gentle fingers. I wanted her introduction to this place to be as kind and welcoming as I could.

There was a light touch upon my sleeve. "You have a place to stay?" asked Goodwife Alyson. "In London?"

Before I could answer, Shelby shied as another horse trod too close. The cart lurched.

"The reason I ask," said Goodwife Alyson as she was flung back into position, "is that it will take some time to traverse the bridge; it's getting late and there's a chill in the air. Rather than entering the city tonight, I wonder if you might consider coming home with me? I live on this side of the bridge, not far from here. There's a warm bed, food, a bath if you like, and, of course, good company." She gave a hearty laugh. "Though, there's some might contest the truth of that statement. For certes, it would give me great pleasure and satisfaction if you'd accept my humble invitation."

I stared at her in disbelief. "You offer me, us"—I gestured to Betje and Adam—"lodgings?"

"Aye. All of you."

"But I barely know you."

"Mayhap, but I've been on God's good earth long enough to know a decent soul when I meet one and, Mistress de Winter, I suspect you're more decent than most." She tipped her head, daring me to contradict her generous assessment. *If only she knew.* Without thinking, my hand rested on my distended stomach. The goodwife's sharp gaze missed nothing. "Since you were so, how do I describe it? Let's say . . . *cautious* with the details of your story and your reasons for coming to London, I can only surmise that there might be more to your tale than you were revealing."

I laughed. I couldn't help it. "Was it so obvious?"

The goodwife shrugged. "To me, but I think the others were happy enough to gaze upon your lovely face; they didn't care what *fabliaux* you wove."

I shook my head, my cheeks growing warm.

"Ah, but don't think for a moment my invitation is a selfless gesture. I tell you frankly, mistress, I'm not partial to that kind of thing. For, while I feel you, Master Barfoot, and the little miss will benefit from a night's rest and all that entails, I also wish to hear your story—the real one—and thus far, that's been denied me. Mayhap, you'll learn to trust me enough to share it." Her grin widened. "Now you've caught glimpse of this city you wish to call home, seen its chaos and glory, inhaled its wondrous scents"—she cackled—"I'm sure you've questions you'd like to ask, and while I don't live in London, I can call it a neighbor and as such know as much about its faults and foibles as one can— possibly more. Perhaps we can serve each other?"

I erred for a moment then opted to continue with the story we'd fabricated so as to maintain our false identities. "While I'm grateful for your generous offer, goodwife, I've a letter of intro- duction to the Stilliard and if they're unable to accommodate us, then I've another. A . . . a friend told me to go to Barking Abbey. She said if for some reason the nuns there refused"— again, I touched my belly—"are unable to help me, then I was to try the Hospital of St. Mary of Bethlehem . . . So, thanking you kindly, I've options aplenty."

"Barking Abbey? St. Mary's?" scoffed the goodwife. "Why, that'll never do."

Adam scrambled to his knees and I felt his fingers gripping the back of my seat.

"Why not?" he asked, his concern ringing in my ears.

"For a start, Barking Abbey is over on Tower Street and, at this rate"—she gestured to the mass of people and animals— "it'll be nightfall before you're on, never mind off, the bridge and wandering through a strange city. The hospital is worse— it's over past Ludgate, out the other side. The gates will be shut before you even get there. As for the Stilliard . . ." She cocked her head and studied me again. "I'm not sure how they'll receive a woman and young 'un, let alone a woman with child. I know, I know, your husband was one of them . . . but this is men we're talking about. You'll not find female company in the Hanse— not in London."

I'd not thought of that. My hand rested upon my belly and a long sigh escaped, ending with a grimace as pain shot along my back and legs.

"What about somewhere closer?" ventured Adam, noting my discomfort. "Not too far from the bridge."

Goodwife Alyson gestured toward the press before us. "The gates'll close soon, but it'll still be dark before the bridge is crossed. The streets of London are no place to be once night falls."

I twisted toward Adam, who looked at me and shrugged. Betje snuggled into my side, lifting her face, and staring with her one glorious eye, as if she were trying to relay something.

I smiled with what I hoped was reassurance and swung to the goodwife, still intending to deny her invitation.

Goodwife Alyson was gazing at Betje as if mesmerized . . . A hand at her side broke the spell and she slapped it away hard. I jumped as an urchin bolted under the legs of a mercer's horse and skidded in mud, his burning fingers in his mouth.

"You little bastard," shouted the goodwife, feeling for her purse with one hand, the other forming a fist that she shook at his retreating back. Turning, she clamped a hand over her lips and stared in wide-eyed horror at us. "My humblest apologies for the language, mistress, Miss Betje dear, Master Barfoot. I don't know what came over me."

A strange noise erupted. Goodwife Alyson started, but not as much as I did. The sounds continued; a type of musical bubbling. It took me a moment to understand it was Betje and she was laughing. Her eye sparkled and the contorted mouth pulled, revealing her teeth.

I gave a gurgle of sheer joy and, holding the reins in one hand, pulled Betje to me. I couldn't credit what I was seeing, what I was hearing, let alone feeling. Joy. Happiness. I tossed my head back and laughter flowed. Adam joined in and so, after a moment, did the goodwife. With my free arm, I dragged Goodwife Alyson closer, dropping a light kiss upon her plump cheek.

"Thank you, goodwife, oh, thank you. You don't know how much I've missed that sound." I planted another kiss upon her brow before pushing aside Betje's hood and depositing the most gentle of all on her shiny scalp. I glanced at Adam, whose face was still crinkled, and then at the crowded road ahead. He shook his head in delighted disbelief before understanding my look and deepening his smile.

"We would be most glad to accept your kind invitation, Goodwife Alyson," I said. "Most glad indeed."

Goodwife Alyson beamed at us. "May God bless you, bless all of us." She didn't conceal her pleasure. "I really do most humbly apologize for my outburst. Mind you, if I'd a groat every time I forgot my manners, then I'd have rooms in old John of Gaunt's Savoy. Well, I would if it wasn't in ruins, as God is my witness, I would."

Adopting a businesslike manner, she directed me toward a lane over which the top stories of houses tilted like old women gossiping, calling out in a penetrating voice for space so I could maneuver through the traffic. In that rather narrow roadway, men loitered in doorways, tankards in their hands, sleeves rolled up to reveal dirty forearms, and caps perched on lank hair. They began to follow us with hard eyes and the growing pains in my back and legs were forgotten. Adam picked up the ale-stick and unlatched his dagger. Goodwife Alyson appeared oblivious to their attentions, but the potential menace of these men was too great for me to ignore. Betje gave a little whimper and withdrew beneath her hood. Goodwife Alyson pointed toward another road leading back toward the river.

"Take that."

A courier dashed by on a small mare, the hooves flinging mud against the cart, scattering the men, who quickly regrouped. "Heed them not, my dears," said Goodwife Alyson in a booming voice. "They wouldn't dare harm me. Or you for that matter. They know to whom they'd have to answer if they did."

"A pretty new goose for the gander, is it, Goody Alyson?" asked a man with a straggly beard upon his chin and very little hair on his head. The other men laughed.

"Or is it a gander you be delivering for your geese?" asked a rather portly man with a wave of white hair, gesturing to Adam.

"I be a gander and like most, ready for a good plucking," said another, thrusting his hips suggestively, and they laughed even harder.

"Be gone with you, Master Black, or I'll make sure your wife knows where you hide your giblets on occasion. You too, Master Cooper."

Their hilarity quickly died and we pressed on.

Adam chuckled quietly, sheathed his dagger, and laid the ale-stick on the floor of the cart once more. "Seems you've a reputation, Goodwife Alyson," he said.

"Aye, that I do. You'll learn what sort and how far it extends soon enough." She began to hum a tune. "What happened back there has little to do with me or how I'm regarded. Expose a man's weakness or threaten his desire and he's softer than eel jelly."

Adam snorted and I grinned.

"Turn right here." She pointed to a wide street. "We're not far away . . ."

We rode beside the river, the wind whipping across the water, jerking Betje's hood from her head. Once again, she gave a burble of laughter and, with a smile that I swear reached to my very toes, I tugged the hood playfully back in place. Rickety wooden jetties propped over the water every few yards, some with punts, wherries, and barges beside them depositing passengers, all men, many of whom wore doublets of velvet, damask, and silk and parti-colored hose; some had fur-lined cloaks or hoods of marten and sable, and appeared very fashionable to my country eyes. Whitewashed buildings squatted on the left, rising to two and three stories. Some displayed a bushel indicating their status as alehouses or taverns, and I began to think of the barrels stored on the tray of the cart and offering some of the contents of one to the goodwife as payment. Smells of cooking wafted over us as we passed places with bold signs swinging in the wind, proclaiming names accompanied by painted symbols. There was the Cardinal's Hatte, the Crane, the Crosse and Keyes, all of which had wide-open doors and windows with seats upon which boldly dressed women lounged. A few were abroad, their mantles trailing in the dirt.

Goodwife Alyson shook her head. "Look at that. A perfectly good piece of clothing ruined in no time because the owners here refuse to take responsibility for keeping their frontages clean." She tut-tutted through a tight smile, waving greetings to those who hailed her.

It wasn't until we passed a sign with what appeared to be a poorly bird on it that Goodwife Alyson ordered me to halt.

"This is it," she said and pointed to a large white house, three stories, with pretty mullioned windows and a red door. Painted upon the sign in dark letters was a white bird with a ridiculously long neck. Underneath was written "The Swanne."

"You live here?" My brows arched. "An inn?"

"I don't just live here, I own it, and it's not an inn. It's a bathhouse. I bought it from a Flemish woman about five years ago, after my last husband, Jenkin, may God assoil him, passed away."

A young boy appeared. "Ah, here's Harry. Give him the reins, Mistress de Winter. He's a marvel with horses. He'll take Shelby around to the mews and ensure he's fed and watered. I'm guessing Master Barfoot might like to accompany him?" At my discreet nod, Adam grunted. "Harry'll look to the cart and your belongings as well. Once the horse is stabled, he'll show you where to come, Master Barfoot. As for you, Mistress de Winter, if you and your sister'll follow me . . ."

No sooner had Goodwife Alyson jumped down than Harry, doffing his cap to Adam and then me, scrambled onto the seat and held out his hands for the reins. "Here, mistress, I'm Harry. Give 'em to me. I'll look after this old beauty. What's he called? Shelby, weren't it?"

Before I could respond, the boy caught sight of Betje, who'd emerged from the cover of my side.

"Gawd Almighty," said Harry, crossing himself. "What happened to you?" Betje took one look at him and with a strangled sound, tried to bury herself in the mantle.

My heart lurched. Angry words pressed against my tongue.

"Harry Frowyk!" cried Goodwife Alyson, and struck the lad sharply upon his legs. He howled in protest. "Watch your mouth. How many times have I told you?" She lifted her arm to land another blow.

"It's all right, goodwife," I said. "Please."

Goodwife Alyson lowered her arm.

"This is something to which we'll have to grow accustomed—the curiosity of strangers. I would rather answer—Harry, isn't it?"—I offered him a sympathetic smile as he rubbed his leg—"as truthfully as I can, than to have rumor and gossip attend us." Cautioning Adam to remain still, I turned my full attention to the boy, pushing back my hood, letting him see my face, and my earnestness.

Harry's eyes widened and his mouth began working.

"My sister"—I touched Betje's arm—"is called Betje. As you

can see, she was badly burned in a fire. She's still very sick and needs a great deal of care. She also needs friends, as do I. I hope I can rely on you, Harry, to be gentle with her and show some understanding. To be our friend?"

Harry tore his eyes from me and looked at Betje. Slowly, Betje crawled from the cocoon of wool, her good eye studying him.

"It ain't so bad once you get used to it, I guess." He cleared his throat and scratched his head with his cap. "You have a nice eye," he said.

It took all my concentration not to let my lips twitch. Adam made a noise of exasperation. For a moment I thought Goodwife Alyson was going to leap onto the cart and box his ears.

"Aye, I'll be your friend, Betty," said Harry finally. "And yours too, mistress, master. You can count on me." With that, he sidled over and took the reins, waiting until, with tight-lipped slowness, I dismounted from the cart and lifted Betje into my arms. Adam clambered over from the back to sit beside him.

Harry ably drove the cart down the side street and through a gate. At the last moment, Adam looked over his shoulder, but by then he was too far away for me to see his expression, but I knew he was anxious.

In the doorway of The Swanne, a crowd of women gathered. Ranging in age from about fourteen into their thirties, they were cleanly attired, their tunics low cut, tightly fitted, and their hair unbound. They all stared agog at me and Betje. I drew her closer. Their looks were not hostile, but neither were they welcoming. A blush began to creep up my cheeks and my eyes narrowed. These women were not decently attired, not by Elmham Lenn standards at least. I glanced up and down the street, taking in the signs, the other loitering women, the expensively dressed men, the horses tethered in specially ordered yards, the punts arriving at the jetties.

"God bid you welcome to The Swanne, Mistress de Winter, Betty," said Goodwife Alyson with a flourish of her hand, adopting Harry's name for my sister.

"What exactly *is* a bathhouse, Goodwife Alyson?" I asked, spinning to face her.

The women chose that moment to run down the steps, surrounding the goodwife, asking questions, touching her arms, shoulders, one even held her briefly and shyly before releasing her. Their voices were excited, warm, happy.

"The good Lord answered my prayers, he brought you back to us safely."

"We've missed you, Goody Alyson."

"There's so much to tell."

"The Bishop of Winchester is threatening to raise the rents."

"Praise Mother Mary you're home."

"Lord James Ashwood visited me three times last week."

"Who's this you've brought?"

"Another sister for the family?"

Introductions were made, names spilling from lips. I tried to acknowledge everyone, but their names blurred. Curtsies were bobbed, there were nods, some whispers behind pale hands. Not one set of eyes failed to lodge upon my belly before flickering away.

I transferred Betje onto my other hip, offering her the protection of my mantle.

"Ladies, let's get inside and have us some wine and supper. I can talk to you better once I'm fed and my guests are as well." I cast her a grateful look. Tiredness was beginning to wash over me and a peculiar heaviness that I attributed to carrying Betje gripped my stomach. A wave of dizziness threatened to undo me.

"Juliana," said Goodwife Alyson. A girl of about fifteen with sandy-colored hair and a dusting of freckles across her nose stepped forward. "Can you make sure there's hot water and fresh sheets in the Lily Room?"

"Oh, but—" Juliana's hazel eyes slid toward me. "That's book—"

"I said, the Lily Room. That's to be Mistress de Winter's and the little miss's while they're with us, is that understood?"

"Aye, Goody Alyson." With one last look in my direction, Juliana scampered away. The others followed at a slower pace, laughing and murmuring, arms around each other's waists. Envy at their sisterhood filled me, and I found myself missing Saskia, Blanche, Iris, and Louisa, but most of all, Betrix. A pang of longing made me catch my breath.

The pain in my lower abdomen grew and spread and I knew it to be sorrow. I shifted Betje again, trying to ease the cramp forming in my thigh. She wriggled and burrowed, making it difficult to hold her.

Unaware of my discomfort, Goodwife Alyson stood back and admired her bathhouse, sighing and running her fingers down her tunic. Church bells began to peal and a herald's trumpet sounded. Laughter floated out into the street.

"Don't worry," said Goodwife Alyson, feeling me stiffen. "They'll be your friends in no time."

"*Friends?* A woman like me doesn't have friends, Goodwife Alyson. Something I learned, much to my chagrin."

There was no self-pity in my voice, just acceptance.

"Well, you do now." Goodwife Alyson faced me, there on

Bankside, the setting sun engulfing her in a last blaze as she folded her arms across her large breasts, daring me to disagree with her. "Like it or not, you have me. I'm your friend."

My eyes became glassy, deep green pools filled with dreams and nightmares. I cleared my throat. "I believe you are, good-wife. And I like it. Very much." I took a deep breath and gave a shaky smile. "Thank you, again."

"For what, pray?"

"For this"—I jerked my head at the vista—"for lodging, but mostly for understanding."

"Ah, Mistress de Winter"—she cocked her head—"mayhap I can call you by that which you're named?"

"Of course. My name is Anna." The new name came easily.

"Anna? Good. And you must call me Alyson. One day, soon I hope, you'll realize it's not such a big stretch—understanding— not for the likes of me. We are women, are we not? Widows." She winked. "Attractive, with assets any man would be glad to lay their hands on." She stuck out her chest and gave her breasts a jiggle, causing my lips to twitch. Betje looked up and regarded her curiously. "We're also businesswomen—a brewer, I heard you say?"

I nodded.

"We're a threat. Threats are abolished, cut down, destroyed, lest they rise and do what everyone fears most."

"What's that?"

"Instigate change, Anna. I'm guessing you wanted something different from what God ordained and for that you've been pun-ished. I don't need to have endured what you have to know what that feels like."

Linking her arm through mine, Alyson began to lead Betje and me toward The Swanne. I paused and put Betje down, waiting till she had found her feet before taking her hand.

"The good news is that here, in The Swanne," continued Alyson as we strolled, "we welcome change. All kinds." She paused. "You see, Anna, change might be unwelcome and it might be unexpected, but it doesn't always have to be adverse-like, does it?"

"I don't know. In my experience . . ." A sharp pain ripped through my torso. I pulled up short, clutching the area near my heart. The breeze made my skirts snap around my ankles.

Alyson went on. "Ah. Well, I think I do. Imagine, my dear, if, using our combined experiences—me as the owner of a successful bathhouse and you as a brewster—we were to work together? Think what changes we might work. Now, that would be something, wouldn't it?"

Alyson spun around. "If you disagree, you can simply say so—" Placing her hands on her hips, she eyed me suspiciously. "Are you all right?"

A giant hand had gripped my lower regions and was squeezing them with all its might, iron fingers wringing the last of my strength, my spirit. I could neither breathe nor speak. I stared at Alyson, willing her to understand, to come to my aid. My legs began to tremble, sweat beaded against my brow, my upper lip, trickled between my heavy breasts. Betje clawed at me, whimpering.

"Anna . . . oh God!" Goodwife Alyson ran toward me, concern writ on her features, her arms outstretched.

Before I could utter a word, wetness splashed down my legs

and collected on the cobbles. I shook my head in disbelief, a wail escaping as I fell to my knees. Betje collapsed beside me, her fingers laced around my arm.

Alyson dropped by my side. "Oh sweet Lord!" she said.

"What's happening?" I gasped and doubled over with a loud groan.

Helping me to my feet slowly, Alyson pulled me against her, taking my weight, uncaring that my gown was stained, that I panted and huffed like an overheated dog.

Dragging me the last steps to the entry, Alyson bellowed in a voice that would wake the dead, calling for Adam, Juliana, and the rest of her women.

The girl named Juliana reappeared, her mouth a circle, her eyes like cartwheels.

"Fetch the Moor's wife," said Goodwife Alyson. "Now."

With a pale-faced nod, Juliana darted away.

Adam emerged from the direction of the mews, running, Harry on his heels. One look and he relieved Alyson of her burden and swung me into his arms.

"What is it?" he asked, his eyes frantic.

"It's the baby. It's coming," said Alyson.

"Nay, nay," I whimpered as another pain seized me. "It can't be, not yet. It's too early."

"Aye, that it is," said Goodwife Alyson, and offered her hand to Betje, who slipped hers in it, her terrified face looking from me to Adam to the goodwife and back again.

I gritted my teeth as another wave of pain swept me. "Better fetch a priest as well," I gasped.

"A priest!" said Alyson, pushing open the door and past the girls who'd flocked to the entrance. "You're healthy, you're young.

Babies come early all the time." She patted my hand and encouraged Adam to follow her and Betje up the stairs. They were narrow and dark and my shoulders and legs struck the walls a few times, despite Adam's best efforts. "You've no reason to fear—no real cause for alarm." I saw her exchange a look with Adam.

Below us, the women talked over one another, and in the snatches I heard the optimism and pessimism that attends every birth.

"I don't fear," I gasped. "I pray."

"We all do, sweet child," said Alyson, swinging open the door to a bedroom on the upper floor, pushing Betje through first before Adam followed with me in his arms. "My girls won't cease to offer prayers until I tell them so."

Holding Adam's shoulder, I heaved myself up in his arms, fixing my gaze upon Alyson, my breathing ragged and shallow. "You don't understand. I don't want the priest for myself. I've no intention of dying. I want it for the child."

Alyson tut-tutted as she pulled back the curtains, threw the rugs from the large bed onto the floor and lifted a clean sheet off a dresser, intending to spread it over the mattress. "The midwife I've sent for, Mistress Verina Vetazes, is the best in Southwark. Your child won't die, Anna, not if God wills and we've any say."

"You misunderstand. There's no question about this. The child will not survive and I want the priest to ensure that when it's born, it is shriven. I don't want it going to its grave in an unholy state."

Alyson stared at me in dismay. "You must not think such things. Don't just stand there, put her down gently," she snapped at Adam.

"Ah, Alyson," I sighed as Adam laid me against the cool, fresh sheet. "You believed me a decent soul, but I tell you for certes, I'm not."

Squeezing a cloth in a bowl of water, Alyson sat on the bed and wiped my brow. The water was scented, warm, and refreshing. I shut my eyes.

"And what makes you so certain?"

"For from the moment I knew this child existed, I've done nothing but pray for its death."

λ

# THIRTY-SEVEN

God forgive you, mistress," said Adam, his face a picture of misery and concern. "You don't mean that." Adam stroked my cheek, brushing aside a tendril of hair.

"I do, Adam. May God forgive me, I do."

Alyson moved aside and began to usher Betje toward the door, calling for boiling water, cloths, and other items on the way. I glared at the offense my body had become.

"I never wanted this." My wild whispers made Adam flinch, but I was uncaring as yet another pain tore through me. When it eased, I continued. "Why would I want it any other way? Why should this . . . this"—I gestured to the swell pushing against my tunic—"being live when my Karel, Louisa, Saskia, and Will do not? Answer me that, Adam." The love and sorrow in Adam's eyes were almost too much. I couldn't hold his gaze. "Even its cursed father is dead. Born of violence, it will do nothing but beget more. It cannot be. It has no right."

"Nay, Anneke. The child has every right. It did not choose the manner of conception any more than you did." I swung my head, my eyes wide, my heart pounding, my discomfort momentarily forgotten. "Love." Adam lowered his voice and once more, caressed my cheek. "The love of a good mother will heal its wretched beginnings, will erase them from its soul . . . And God knows, this child may even ease yours . . ."

Before I could respond, a tide of sheer agony swept over me. Panting and gasping, I grasped the sheet in my fists, lifting it from the mattress, baring my teeth like an animal.

"Childbed is no place for a man." The accent was heavy, odd. Appearing over Adam's shoulder was a woman with skin the color of burnt barley and a voice like hot honey.

Reluctantly, Adam rose, touching my hand lightly. "Think on what I said, mistress, and may Mother Mary and St. Margaret watch over you and your babe. Bless you. I will go to Betje."

Waiting until Adam was escorted from the room by one of Alyson's women, the newcomer sat beside me and began tugging at the laces that held my tunic together.

"You've no need of St. Margaret or Mother Mary. Verina Vetazes is here." The words were molten, glowing, strangely soothing, mesmerizing. She began to pull the garment over my head. Wanting to complain, an invisible vise crushed my womb once more, snatching words away.

"Breathe deeply," said Verina of the Voice. "Here, squeeze my hand."

I did. So tightly, I was certain her fine bones would break.

"She is strong, this one." Mistress Verina nodded confidently at Alyson. "The babe may be early, but it should survive." Before I could ask how she could be so certain, Alyson and two other women were beside me, pulling off the rest of my clothes, wiping my sweating brow and décolletage, putting a wine cup to my lips and parting my legs shamelessly.

Steady, knowing hands felt my stomach. Verina pressed and prodded, spreading the lips of my throbbing cleft and placing fingers deep inside me. I inhaled sharply. It didn't hurt, not really, it was simply the shock of being handled so boldly.

"We have some time yet," said Verina, removing her fingers and wiping them on a cloth. I was horrified to see they were red. "Give her some more wine. Take small sips." I tried to sit up higher in the bed. Pillows were quickly thrust behind me as I was assisted into an upright position. It was then I saw the carmine stains between my legs, upon the sheet.

"This is normal," said Verina as I began to whimper.

"My mother . . . she—she . . ."

"Ah." Verina reached for my hand and placed it firmly between both of hers. Long, tapered fingers curled around mine. "She died in childbed?"

"Aye." I didn't recognize myself in the response. I was twelve years old again, bewildered, scared, expecting golden joy only to discover the blackest grief.

"I will not lie to you, mistress. This will not be easy, but I believe you will endure and so will the life inside you." Her eyes were amber, flecked with the light from the candles. They were kind eyes, wise ones. "The past will not enter this room to make the future. You and I together, along with this child"— she rested a hand on me again—"we will forge our own."

I'd no words left. I was glad this Mistress Verina, with her thrilling voice and confident ways, was beside me, and Alyson and her women, Juliana and Leda. This strange space had become a female haven, where the mysteries of birth and motherhood would unfold.

Alyson sat opposite Mistress Verina, offering me her hand and a jasper stone to ease my birthing pains. Leda and young Juliana, who revealed herself able and shrewd, flitted in the background, tearing cloths, changing the bloodied water, passing lotions that Mistress Verina and Alyson took turns to rub into my flesh, before heaving me to my feet and comforting my groans.

Candles guttered and were replaced; fresh logs were put on the fire. Outside, church bells sounded the hours and I knew when a new day had started. Between each fresh bout of agony, I thought on Adam's words, on the existence inside me struggling to be born, resisting my will that it die. As pain wracked my flesh asunder, guilt tore at my heart. I wasn't sure which was worse.

I came to the awful conclusion that Adam was right. The innocent soul inside me had no more control over its fate than I did mine. Yet I'd held it accountable for not only destiny, but also the sins of its father. Where I was unable to seek retribution from the villain himself, I sought to wreak vengeance upon the one thing I could—his ungodly spawn. Only, it wasn't ungodly. It wasn't culpable. And it wasn't only his. Mistaken in my grief and frustration, I'd allowed hatred to blossom alongside my babe . . . *my babe* . . . How curious and terrifying those words sounded in my heart. I tested them again and again.

My babe . . . my babe . . .

My body was a rag that had been wrung through a laundress's mangle. I couldn't think, couldn't focus. Pain and the constant rush of hot liquid on my thighs, followed by a soothing wetness returned me to the place where hurt ruled. Aware of feather-light caresses upon my sodden brow, of solid fingers against my belly, the hours passed in a fugue of ghastly aches and barely remembered conversations. Trying to distract me, to keep me conscious, Alyson questioned me about my life before Dover. Why had I come to London? Why was I traveling at such a dreadful time of year, and in my condition? Drifting in and out of sense, the waking world and that of my dreams blended, and in my fragile state, I revealed all to the goodwife. After all, was she not owed my tale? There was Mother, Father, Hiske, Karel, Betje before the fire and then after. Louisa laughing, Saskia holding me, Karel jumping up and down on my bed. Tobias stood nearby, shaking his finger, priggish, unforgiving. There was Master Makejoy and a pile of coins, Adam and the great shaggy hounds, Sir Rainford and his astonishing capitulation. Finally, there was Sir Leander, his tender arms, his flashing eyes, his warm lips pressed against mine. I opened myself to the sensations only to find that as I did, the pressure changed and it was no longer Sir Leander, but Westel Calkin who held me, hurt me, thrust into me, forcing me apart . . .

A scream tore from my exhausted body and I grabbed my knees, pulled toward my own center as Alyson and Mistress Verina, helping me squat upon the rushes, supported my back.

"Push!" Verina's melodic incantations became brusque commands.

Unable to do anything else as my entire body metamorphosed into a great maw that would spasm until it had expelled the stranger inside, I focused all my weary willpower on thrusting the little being out, toward the room, the women waiting for it, toward survival. Son or daughter, I willed it to live through this; despite the animosity I had harbored, I wanted it to know that I didn't want it to die. Not anymore.

Tears began to spill down my cheeks, mingling with the sweat. Another cry was wrenched from me and with all my might, I willed my child forth.

There was a moment when I thought I would tear in two, and then, with a rush of heat and blood, I felt it come.

"That's it, once more. Push, push, sweetling," said Alyson, her face beside mine, her voice choked with emotion. "The babe has crowned . . . it's a beauty . . . That's it, that's it, by Mother Mary and all the saints . . ."

There was a tiny cough followed by a small cry. It spewed from the diminutive, ruddy being coated in the fluids that mingled within me and flew straight to my heart.

"It's a girl," said Mistress Verina, and, after holding her aloft for me to see, placed her on the bed, tying the cord that still connected us.

Another spasm rippled through my body, catching me unawares. I gasped and Alyson grabbed my shoulders, holding me steady. "It's simply the afterbirth, Anna, don't you worry."

"Nay," said Mistress Verina, passing my babe, my daughter, to Juliana, who took her as if she were Venetian glass. "Not only the afterbirth. There's another babe yet to come."

Alyson gasped. "Another. Sweet Mother of Jesus!"

I didn't think I'd heard Mistress Verina aright. Unable to speak, my lips opened and shut, my mind dulled for a moment then burst with light, as if the god Apollo had driven his chariot into my head. My thoughts splintered in different directions, into both sadness and elation all at once. It was intoxicating, confusing. They joined again as they headed toward the same destination—my mother's memory.

*There are two. Twins . . .*

Once more I lapsed in and out of consciousness as hours passed and I staggered from floor to bed and back again. The other life inside me, the brother or sister to my daughter, would not or could not leave my womb.

Blood flowed freely. I heard my daughter wailing and another woman enter the room and take her. There were whispers, touches, kisses, soft, urgent prayers, and ghastly potions poured between my lips.

"You can do it, Anneke, you can make it work," said a voice, and I wondered in my delirium if Mother had come from heaven to support me.

Try as I might, this time I could not fulfill my mother's desires and, as the shutters in the room rattled and a weak gray light filtered into the room, the house around us and road and river outside awoke, my remaining babe and I drifted away . . .

❧❀❧

When he asks me in the years to come, I'll have no tale to tell my son about his birth, except that it was almost, as everyone feared, a keening instead of a joyous welcome.

Just as it had with Mother, blood flowed from me in a continuous torrent. With each tightening of my womb and the accompanying pain, it grew worse; neither cloths nor linens nor the actions of the midwife stemmed it. A copper tang caught the back of my throat and filled my lungs. There were whispers, and the looks in my direction were filled with a knowingness I didn't want to acknowledge. Only when Alyson sat by my head and took my limp hand in her own, her face a tired ruin, did I understand that in the hearts of those around me, I was a dead woman.

Light-headed, fading, I nonetheless met Alyson's sad eyes with steely ones.

"Nay."

The word was a weapon of iron, wielded to protect, defend.

"Nay," I repeated. Louder. Firmer. Betje's face swam before me, disconsolate, afraid, her scars apparent on her face; her soul unmarked. Like the babes I was bringing forth, she needed me. I was not going to surrender, not if I had any say in the matter. I heaved myself upright, the room spinning, my equilibrium momentarily scattering.

"Do not look at me as if I've already departed this realm," I snapped at Alyson, squeezing her hand so tightly, she recoiled.

"Anna, forgive me, I . . ."

"I'm not letting death defeat me. But—" A sword of calescent agony lanced my womb. "But," I began again when the pain retreated, "you must fight by my side."

With a trembling smile, she returned my grip. "I'm here."

Letting her go, I pushed aside my sweat-drenched hair and stared at the others. "Doubt has no place in this room. If you remain, you must fight with me. If you cannot, I must bid you leave."

There was a stunned silence before Alyson clapped her hands and the women responded grimly, "We fight." Their words may have been forced but no one left the room. My relief sent me back into the pillows.

"Now," I said, my attention fixed on Mistress Verina, who

knelt at my heels. "Tell me what's happening, what I must do." I coughed and the room dissolved. Despite my bravado, my strength was evaporating, streaming out of me in an ever-widening crimson stain.

With a tilt of her dark head and fire in her eyes, Mistress Verina rested a firm palm upon my rippling stomach. I'd no need to demand her commitment—I could feel it pulsing through me.

"You must use the great courage you have within to anchor you to this life." Her gaze flickered to the first babe before pressing on my abdomen. "To your children."

I nodded once. "Go on."

"The babe is facing the wrong way—it doesn't want to part from you. This is why you're losing so much blood." Another hot gush escaped. "Far too much. The child will kill you and itself if we do not separate you. To do this, I must turn it."

I bit my lip as another wrench took my breath away. Panting, I saw the determination gleaming within the midwife and drew from it.

"Can you?"

"I can . . . but—"

"But?"

"It will . . . hurt you . . ."

I began to laugh but it changed into a wail. "I hurt already, what's a little more?"

"You misunderstand," said Mistress Verina. "The hurt will last a lifetime. If you survive . . . if the babe should, I doubt you'll be able to bear more children."

My head fell back. Alyson wiped my brow, her touch swift, welcome. When she'd finished, I raised my head and stared at Mistress Verina, framed by my bloodied knees.

My constant damning of the children was not to go unpunished after all. "If this is a choice I must make, so be it. Turn the babe. Let God have His justice and decide our fate."

Many weeks later, Adam told me the scream I released, as Mistress Verina twisted the baby in my stomach and I gave one final, inconceivable push, stopped everyone in their tracks. The cats sunning themselves on sills paused amidst their endless grooming. Horses lifted their heads from nosebags; birds ceased their chattering and workers their tasks. The women in The Swanne hesitated in their ablutions and shuddered. Yet, as the bells for none sounded moments after, another sound came— the lusty wails of my newborn son.

Wrenched from my womb, he looked more like a butcher's afterthought than a child. Lifting him toward the ceiling so I could see his small, wrinkled form, the blue and purple cord connecting us throbbing in the suffused light, I knew that God in His wisdom and benevolence *had* forgiven me my evil thoughts, my desire to destroy what He'd created. While the manner of the creation was surely not His intention, the result was. My children had been gifted to me for a reason, and I would do my utmost to understand what that might be. Sending a swift prayer to Him and Mother Mary, it was only then that I allowed myself to truly rest into the pillows and release the jasper stone, which I'd clutched so hard the imprint remained in my palm for hours afterward.

I was dimly aware of Alyson kissing my cheek, her dry lips followed by salty wetness against my mouth, and my heart contracted. This bold and brassy goodwife was made of much softer material. Juliana and Leda brought my babes to me. Struck dumb by their beauty, their innocence, their scent, which was surely of the angels, I marveled that I could ever have believed they carried their father's sins. Worried lest I catch glimpse of him upon their features, I saw nothing but virtue and beauty and fluffy crowns of silvery hues. Who were these beatific beings, filled only with the mystery of life and God's wonder? Reaching out to brush their blessed cheeks, I knew Adam was right. A mother's love—*my love*—would more than compensate for their father's wickedness. I would make sure of that.

*You'll make it work, Anneke, you always do.*

*Aye, Mother. I've been given the chance you were denied. I will make it work.*

# THIRTY-EIGHT

THE SWANNE

Spring

*The year of Our Lord 1407 in the eighth*

*year of the reign of Henry IV*

*I*t was eight days since my babes had entered the world and, though I was ready to leave the bedchamber, Mistress Vetazes insisted I remain confined. Regardless, the twins' baptism could no longer be delayed. Sensing my anxiety, Betje perched next to me as Alyson, Adam, Juliana, and Harry entered and greeted me.

Standing at the foot of the bed, the wet nurses Mistress Vetazes hired, Emma and Constance, held the babes close. Tightly bound beneath delicate white tunics, presents from the women of The Swanne, first my daughter then my son were placed carefully into my arms. I'd not held them both at once, offering my sore and swollen breasts as an excuse, while being more than a little afraid that my initial feelings of love may prove to be temporary.

Trembling with a mixture of emotions, I peered into their tiny faces, and wondered what they saw when they gazed into mine.

Did they feel my awakening love and protectiveness? Or my guilt and horror that I could have ever wished them gone? Or did they sense the new emotion that had crept upon me—the growing fear that they might not live? They were so small and, though thriving, the certainty of their survival was little more than a winking candle. Therefore their baptism must needs proceed.

Tears began to fill my eyes, rising from my heart to stopper my throat. I was a mother. A mother to twins.

"What will we call them?" asked Alyson, stepping forward to take my baby girl and distract me. "Have you decided?"

Clearing my throat, I flashed her a smile of gratitude. "I have." I slid my daughter against Alyson's generous breast. "This is Isabella."

There were sighs of pleasure and approval.

"That be a lovely name, Mistress An . . . Anna," said Adam as we both looked at Betje, who, playing with one of my plaits, gave her equivalent of a smile. "And the boy?"

Passing my son to Juliana, my voice caught. "This—this was more difficult. I decided to call him . . ." My throat seized; the words were stuck; I could not say them. My eyes widened, my chest heaved . . .

"Karel."

I swung in astonishment. "Betje!" I exclaimed, uncertain lest my ears were playing tricks. She released my plait swiftly, her hands pressed to her lips as if to stop herself saying anything further.

"What did you say?" I asked again, quieter this time, taking her ruined hand and stroking the rough skin. "Please, sweetling . . ." A warm tear slid down my cheek. "Say his name again for me."

"Karel." She timidly raised her chin, her eye sparkling. "His name is Karel." Her voice was rough, unused, deep. The tone matched her experience. She gave a crooked smile and dropped her gaze.

I regarded the room then my babes, my body tingling, hoisting Betje's arm aloft, crying freely. "There. You heard it too. His name is Karel. This is our Karel."

Adam fell to his knees by the bed, weeping openly. He cupped Betje's ravaged face in his hands, holding it lightly.

"Oh my. How right and perfect is that?"

Uncertain whether he referred to the name or the fact Betje chose this moment to find her voice, I nodded, my lips trembling as I reached for Betje and pulled her to me. Out of death, came life—in more ways than one.

Adam's face shone as he met my blurry gaze and we exchanged a long, long smile that continued until we caught Alyson, Juliana, Betje, and all those who stood witness, wiping their eyes or, as Harry was wont to do, his nose against his sleeve.

All that was left, when I managed to regain myself, was to announce the twins' godparents. How the others would feel about my choices, I was about to discover.

"Isabella needs two godmothers and one godfather as the church decrees." I turned to Alyson, clearing my throat. "My wish is that you, Alyson, and dear Juliana here will accept that role."

Juliana gasped, her hand flying to her heart. "Me, mistress? Why, I never . . . I mean . . . I am but a servant."

"We're all God's servants, Juliana."

She shook her head in disbelief, her face shining. "That we are." Her beaming smile said it all. "Wait till I tell the others."

I looked meaningfully at Alyson, who regarded me primly.

"If you hadn't asked me, I'd have been mighty offended," she said before bursting into a delighted chortle, flashing her gap-toothed smile, and bent over to plant a wet kiss upon my cheek, making sure no one else saw the swift carriage of handkerchief from décolletage to eyes.

"Furthermore, Alyson," I said, "I wish to celebrate the twins' birth by providing The Swanne with a barrel of beer." Alyson went to object as I knew she would. "Please, Alyson," I said, raising a hand, "I've my pride too. You've done so much for me, for us"—my hand encompassed my family—"let me give a modicum in return."

I'd spent the days since the birth wondering at the events that brought me to The Swanne and into Alyson's world. Fate decreed that Goodwife Alyson and I had not merely crossed paths, but found a burgeoning friendship. Grateful beyond words, I'd discussed with Adam giving Alyson a barrel of beer as payment for our lodging. Considering our initial agreement was to remain but a night, we'd abused her hospitality in ways we hadn't foreseen and received only kindness and generosity in return.

Shaking her head and sighing, she placed a hand on her hip, Isabella resting on the other. "Aye, you've more pride than a king's mistress." She gave a wicked chuckle. "And I can respect that. So instead of objecting, I thank you." She glared at Adam. "No doubt you had something to do with this?"

Adam shrugged and looked to me for support.

"Adam, my dear and most loyal *friend*." I waited for him to note the word; I'd publicly accorded him a status to which, as a servant, he would feel he'd no right. But over and over, Adam had proved himself to be more than a servant. He had remained true for as long as I could remember. "This is what God put me on this good earth to do," he'd say, and indicate that there was to be no further discussion.

Adam Barfoot may be a servant, but he was someone I trusted not only with my own life, but that of my sister and my children.

I looked to him. "Would you do me the honor of being Isabella's godfather?"

Adam colored and shuffled his feet. "I . . . I . . . don't deserve such trust, mistress, such an honor. But," he continued quickly, "as God is my witness, I will do my duty and more besides."

"I know."

His eyes as he turned them upon Isabella were filled with such protectiveness and love, I learned anew I'd chosen well. Alyson slapped his back soundly and gave me a look of approval.

"As for Karel, it's my wish that Captain Stoyan be his godfather." There were more murmurs.

I'd sent a letter to the Hanse three days ago. The captain could be anywhere—the last time I saw him was in Dover, when he was about to head to London. I'd half-expected him to turn up at The Swanne but as yet there'd been no sign. I assumed he was somewhere upon the vast seas.

"Presuming he accepts, and I feel confident he will, I ask that someone stand in for him during the ceremony."

"I could ask Master Godric, my cobbler," said Alyson. "A goodly man who's inclined toward us here."

I smiled. "Give him my thanks. As for the second godfather . . ." I hesitated and pretended to consider deeply a matter I had already decided. My mother and father would turn in their graves at what I was about to do. "I need someone dependable, someone who can be there for Karel when the captain cannot; who can teach him to navigate this world with humor and courage; who can ensure he learns what it means to have God's good grace. I need someone who doesn't judge people by their words or appearance, but by their actions and souls. I need someone he can call a friend."

Adam's face split into a huge grin as he realized to whom I was referring.

"There's one person I know who can do all that."

Looking meaningfully at the young boy leaning on the end of the bed, reaching over Juliana's crooked arm to gently touch Karel's cheek, I waited. All eyes followed mine until Harry, aware of the attention he'd attracted, paused, and glanced around.

"What?" he said, withdrawing his hand quickly. "I wasn't doing nothing wrong."

"Nay, you weren't." I chuckled. "Only right, as you have from the moment we arrived. That's why I would like you, Master Harry Frowyk, to be Karel's second godfather."

Lost for words, the boy simply straightened and stood. It was the only time I was ever to see Harry dumbstruck.

As I announced Betje's role as Karel's godmother, warmth crept through my body and wrapped a comforting cocoon around my heart. Aye, I thought, gazing upon my choices, it was unconventional—a bathhouse owner, an absent sea captain, an urchin, my sister, and servants—all entrusted with the spiritual well-being of my babes. Nothing about this was within the rules. But it felt right.

And so it was, the following morning, I stood at the window as a merry party left The Swanne for St. Saviour's Church near

Pepper Alley in Southwark. The priest, a Father Kenton, had been most glad to receive the twins for blessing. Whether he'd have felt that way knowing the mother's true circumstances was moot. However, donning the mantle of widowhood cast a net of sympathy over my condition and that of my babies.

The festivities that followed their return from church were only matched by the party Alyson threw three weeks later, when I was officially deemed clean by the church and could attend a mass to mark the occasion. I wasn't yet fully healed and still tired easily, but the prayers I offered to my Lord and his Blessed Mother among the many burning candles and smoking incense were heartfelt and grateful, and the ale I downed back at The Swanne was most welcome.

Sitting in a corner of the main hall as evening fell, I watched the dancing. The way in which the young and not so young held each other, clapped, stomped, sang, and drank was a cheerful sight. The twins were safely tucked upstairs with the wet nurses; Betje snuggled upon Adam's lap, a dainty hood disguising the worst of her burns. Dressed in a tunic of burgundy with a neckline so low it was almost indecent, only the frothy lace sewn at the borders protecting what remained of her modesty, Alyson was in her element. Roaming the room, discreetly encouraging her women to absent themselves with a client, and moving from Adam and Betje (and the ever-present Harry) to me, she ensured everyone had drink and food as well as conversation. Amid her attentions, she proffered more toasts than a nobleman's wedding.

The irony of the situation wasn't lost on me. Here I was, a merchant's daughter, destined for an enviable life with a husband of more than average means, a former alehouse owner and brewer, mother of two, living in a brothel. I'd never felt more comfortable anywhere in my life. I could only begin to imagine what Cousin Hiske would say—or Tobias.

What Sir Leander would think was something I didn't want to contemplate. But like a child with the pox, I found myself unable to resist scratching that particular itch. Ofttimes when I'd lain in bed with nothing but my thoughts for company, I relived our moments together, the letters we'd exchanged, and invented fresh scenarios where we weren't beholden to propriety or society or a wife. Foolishly, I relished these imaginings, woven from nothing more than a kiss, a few warm looks, and words upon a page, words that still had the ability to fire my heart and fan my ridiculous longings. Try as I might, I could not forget Sir Leander or the hunger he awoke in me. I would castigate myself and think how appropriate it was that I was living in a brothel, when clearly I was the most immoral of women. At these moments, my thoughts would drift to Mother and her terrible indiscretion, and I wondered if it was the doom of de Winter women to be forever captivated by Rainford men.

Though trepidation that Sir Leander might discover our whereabouts hovered over me, the shadow it cast also made my body grow warm. Was I so very sinful that a small part of me held out hope that Sir Leander might discover our location? That I could see his face, even if it was shaped by scorn or disapproval, just one last time . . .

"A penny for your thoughts," said Adam. Betje leaned against me.

Placing a hand upon her arm, I smiled at them both. "My thoughts are worth more than that, Adam. They're priceless."

Determined to enjoy myself, I banished Sir Leander from my head. This was a night to celebrate. Churched and thus cleansed of the stain of birth, I was on the cusp of fresh horizons.

As I sipped my beer and tapped my foot to the rhythms of tabor and flute, it occurred to me that here in Southwark, among these warm and earthy folk, I'd been given more than a second chance: I'd been granted a new life, and I didn't intend to waste a moment of it.

# THIRTY-NINE

<figure>ornamental divider</figure>

THE SWANNE

Lent

*The year of Our Lord 1407 in the eighth*
*year of the reign of Henry IV*

*A*fter the fear and pain of childbirth, and the circumstances
surrounding my journey from Elmham Lenn, I dwelled for a
time in a fool's paradise and was thus unprepared to receive
my first, and most unwelcome, visitor, who brought with him
a taste of the laws that governed not only the city I wished to
call home, but the Borough of Southwark; a place that, according to this man, was nothing more than a suppurating barnacle
on the backside of the realm. Master Lewis Fynk, Officer of the
Crown, shattered my fantasies and more.

On this particular day, a dull, cold, soggy one where mist
lingered in tattered ribbons, I was in my room enjoying my children, discussing their enchanting habits with the wet nurses.
After an hour, the women returned the babes to the nursery
and, encouraged by Alyson, I took the chance to lay my head

down awhile. I'd burrowed into the feather mattress, pulling the covers around me, chuckling inwardly that I was like an old woman who, nearing the end of her days, reversed the usual patterns of slumber and wakefulness, when the door to my room burst open.

Sitting up as quickly as I was able I lifted the furs more as a reflex than for the purposes of modesty, for I was all but fully clothed, when in stormed four men, followed quickly by Alyson and Adam.

"There she is!" exclaimed a red-faced gentleman, pointing at me with a knobbly finger. He was tall and thin, his cheeks sunken and the hair beneath his cap a thick, chestnut mop. His pale eyes sparkled with triumph and his long, narrow mouth was curved in satisfaction. His clothing denoted him a bailiff; of the three men accompanying him, one was an escheator, the other two constables.

I grew cold. It was difficult to breathe. For certes, I was discovered. Prayers collected in my head and I tried to rise. Alyson pushed past the men and placed a hand on my shoulder, forcing me to remain where I was.

"Master Fynk!" she boomed, causing the other men to stumble over one another. "How dare you. You cannot simply enter the private areas of my residence, let alone this lady's bedroom."

"Lady?" sniggered Master Fynk, standing over us both, looking down his prominent nose at Alyson. "According to the king, if I think you're breaking the law, I may enter wherever I wish. Lady's room or naught." Raising his hand, he flipped it toward me. "Methinks naught."

Narrowing his eyes, Master Fynk smiled. There was no humor in his expression, just righteousness. "And I do dare, Mistress of Disorder and Ill Repute"—he didn't deign to look at Alyson as he spoke—"Widow of Purity and Godliness, by all that is holy and good, I dare."

His words and aggression brought to mind a man I thought banished. The voice, the wild accusations, the violent utterances as he thrust inside me all returned with a blast that took my breath away. I recoiled from Master Fynk and in the flicker of his eyes, I saw the pleasure my reaction gave him.

"And there is my evidence, gentlemen." Master Fynk encouraged his companions forward. "This . . . this . . . *woman.*" All Eve's daughters became something filthy in that single utterance. Anger stirred within me. Alyson drew herself up to her full height and placed herself squarely between the bailiff and me.

"You see. I told you. Goodwife Alyson does keep a pregnant woman beneath her roof." He gave a hollow laugh. "You'll not merely receive a fine for this—the court'll see you cucked and imprisoned, I shouldn't wonder."

For the time it took God's name to form on my tongue, I understood that the presence of the law had nothing to do with the events at Elmham Lenn and everything with my presence in the bathhouse. My initial fear returned one thousandfold: If this man could so threaten a mother, what would he do to innocent children?

The shade in Alyson's cheeks matched her scarlet tunic as she faced him, folding her arms over her bosom.

"Once again, Master Fynk, you have the cock by the comb and the neck does warble and warble without using the sense contained therein." She tapped her temple twice.

Master Fynk turned the color of beet. The other men shifted from foot to foot.

Undaunted, Alyson continued. "You've been listening to tales whispered by a twisted tongue and, if I'm not mistaken, exchanged over a pillow instead of a table, hey? Where was it? The Cardinal's Hatte is your preferred haunt, is it not? Did some wench whisper in your ear? Tempt or taunt you to action? Or could you not perform one duty so sought to try another?"

Drawing back his hand fast, Master Fynk struck her hard across the face. With a small cry, she fell upon me, then rolled onto the floor, her hand covering her cheek. I leaped out of bed and knelt beside her, and gingerly helped her sit up.

"It's all right, Anna. I've been hit by better." She flexed her jaw, staring brazenly at Master Fynk. "And harder." She spat a bloody gobbet into the rushes.

"You will show me the respect I'm due as an officer of the bishop and king," said Master Fynk slowly. "I don't have to answer to the likes of you, good*wife*, but you have to answer to *me*. So, tell me, how do you explain the presence of this one, hey? You know the laws. Pregnant whores are forbidden." Grabbing my shoulder, he hauled me away from Alyson and threw me on the bed.

"Nay, Adam. Don't!" I cried.

Adam stopped mid-stride.

Master Fynk laughed. "*Nay, Adam.*" His imitation was perfect. "You'd do well to listen to her. She's wiser than her years allow. Is she yours?" Before Adam could respond, he continued, his cold eyes sweeping the room, taking in the crackling fire, the drying sheet folded on the chest, the chairs and stools arranged near the window and hearth. The basket of darning, the flickering candles. The shutters rattled in the wind and I felt the frigid fingers of the day.

Master Fynk strode to the window and flung the shutters wide. I took the chance to straighten my tunic and assist Alyson to her feet.

"Watch this one," she whispered. "He be dangerous. Vengeful and treacherous."

I knew the kind too well. I shot Adam a look to remain where he was. The other men stayed mute and, while two appeared uneasy with the proceedings and one gave Alyson continual apologetic glances, the shortest of the men, the escheator, from the insignia on his surcoat, was clearly enjoying the spectacle.

Gazing down upon the river, Master Fynk stood with his back to us. "A whore with child isn't allowed beneath this roof." He flung the words over his shoulder. "Yet, like so many other rules, Goodwife Alyson"—his voice had a singsong quality— "you choose to flout this one and believe you're exempt. For that you'll pay."

Indignation flooded me. "I'm no whore, sir," I exclaimed. Alyson released a sigh. I ignored her. "My name is Anna de Winter from Dover. I'm a respectable woman. A brewster."

He spun around. "A brewster, are we? *Respectable?*" He laughed. "You have an odd understanding of what constitutes respectability." He rubbed his hands together. "I don't care what you are, Mistress de Winter, or what you claim to be. You could be the wife of Satan's brother." He looked me up and down slowly and doubt flickered across his mien. "You're pregnant?"

Lifting my chin and smoothing the tunic over my belly, I waited for his eyes to finish their journey and meet mine. "Nay, sir, I'm not."

Adam cleared his throat, intending, I knew, to support my

claim. I dreaded what he would do or say to protect my name, drawing attention upon himself from this man who wanted nothing more than a confrontation. I continued hastily. "I recently gave birth, aye. But I do not live here. I'm not a slattern, I'm—"

"A dear cousin who has recently lost her husband, you buffoons." Alyson sat wearily on the edge of the bed. "Can you not see?" She waved an arm toward me. "Quality shouts from the roots of her shining hair and those fine green eyes. Look at her hands. Have they seen a day's work?" Brewing hadn't ruined my hands yet, but they no longer possessed the creamy uniformity they once had.

Alyson went on, her voice dull, resigned, and all the more convincing because of that. "I brought her back here with me after I visited St. Thomas à Becket's shrine." She crossed herself and bowed her head. "The grief of losing dear—" She stared at her lap.

"Joseph," I inserted swiftly, silently begging my father's forgiveness.

"Joseph, may God assoil him"—she crossed herself again and the men did as well—"and our terrible journey through driven snow, amid thieves and cutthroats, hastened the arrival of her babes." There were exclamations. "Aye . . . not one, but two." She lifted her head. "Did your information extend to that, Master Fynk? Ask Father Kenton if you doubt. That's right, twins were born beneath this roof you're so ready to curse and fine. If that's not God blessing us, I don't know what is."

"God does not bless the likes of you, Goodwife Alyson." Master Fynk leaned on the sill, unaffected by the cold that stole the warmth from the room. "But He would bless a grieving widow." Turning and standing erect, Master Fynk seemed to reconsider me. A dark look crossed his features.

"When were they born?"

"Over a month ago," I answered.

"Are they baptized?"

"Aye, they're baptized," said Alyson wearily. "And she's been churched as well. Good God, Lewis, can't you accept that your assumptions are wrong this time and leave it be?" She raised her chin, willing him to concede. I held my breath. Flames crackled and a log split. There was a shout from the road and the squeal of pigs. Master Fynk said nothing, only returned Alyson's look with a baleful one of his own.

Slapping her thighs, Alyson finally stood. "I understand you've to keep a check on what happens round here, but I'm telling you God's truth when I say I've done nothing wrong."

"This time," said Master Fynk.

"Aye." She tidied her laces, her lips twitching. "This time."

I coughed. Adam grabbed the poker and stabbed the fire a few times. My, but Alyson was bold. And she seemed to have Master Fynk's measure. Instead of being inflamed by her words, he appeared about to accept them.

"This is accurate?" Master Fynk turned to Adam.

How Adam managed to compose himself to answer was a mystery. "As God is my witness, Master Bailiff."

Adam offered neither respect nor insult.

"If she be no whore, then who might you be?" Master Fynk looked from Adam to me and back again.

"This is my steward, Master Barfoot." I knew what occupied the thoughts of Master Fynk and the other men. If I had a steward in my employ then I was a woman of substance and couldn't possibly be the whore they first believed me to be.

"You not be on the poll tax," said the escheator sharply, lifting his many chins.

"That's because he's not from here. He arrived when his mistress did, Tom Shankle." Alyson shook her head. "He's not been counted yet. Once he is, and if he is still beneath my roof, he'll pay your outrageous sums. In the meantime, he's a guest, like his mistress."

The distant sound of laughter and voices carried. Harry and Betje. She must have run to the front to welcome Harry back from an errand. Master Fynk leaned down and watched a while. No one spoke. I felt the tension that had gripped me since the men first entered start to subside. Alyson winked at me.

"If you be no whore, mistress," said Master Fynk, spinning on one heel, no mean feat among the thick rushes, "and if God blessed you with two children, then how come your other get"—his head jerked toward the window—"looks like the sins of Gomorrah are rendered in her flesh?"

It was a full moment before I understood that he referred to Betje.

"Master Fynk!" Alyson's words bristled with anger. The other men flinched.

"You must take that back, sir," said Adam, and in two paces was standing before the bailiff. The other men grabbed Adam's arms, jerking them behind his back. Struggling, he let fly a string of curses and Master Fynk's long fingers dropped to the sword that dangled from a belt.

"Stop," I shouted. "All of you. Now." The room danced in

my vision for a moment. Ignoring the strange feeling, I stepped past the three men and paused only before Master Fynk. Alyson tugged the men's arms, forcing them to release Adam, which they did begrudgingly after a nod from their master.

Meeting Master Fynk's cold gaze I knew whom I regarded. Here was a man filled to the brim with his own sense of righteousness. It was his moral compass that provided direction to the world. Offense and insult didn't exist when wielded in the name of justice. Cruelty was a means to a lawful end, nothing more.

"The girl you see down there"—I pointed to the street below—"is my sister, sir." I didn't raise my voice, though it was my greatest wish to raise it and have it echo through his every waking moment. I wanted to lift my hand and strike his face until the flesh there was bloodied and jagged. Yet I did neither, for such emotions were wasted on this man.

We both gripped the sill and stared down at Betje, who, unaware of our scrutiny, was walking beside Harry, who was leading a chestnut mare. She was without a cap, which scratched her healing scalp, and the wind lifted the remnants of her hair. From our viewpoint above her, the pink flesh and scars were apparent. Beside me, Master Fynk remained silent, his breathing deep and steady. The dark linen of his surcoat and the fur that lined his cape smelled of woodsmoke and damp days.

Harry threw the animal's halter to Betje and she caught it, giggling with delight that her good hand managed to hold fast. My heart contracted into a knot.

"A man of God, a monk, cast her into flames," I said quietly. "Not because she was sinful, but to hide his own crimes. Thus

God allowed her to live so all who set eyes on her could be reminded of the evil men can do, and that God's justice will prevail."

Considering my words and the weight with which they were delivered, Master Fynk slowly tilted his head. "That is how you judge the story, is it, mistress? I wonder how this bedeviled monk would?"

I gave a hollow laugh. "We'll never know, Master Fynk, because he burned to death in the same fire that seared my sister. One might say that God judged him and decided that hell was to be his abode."

Oh God. Alyson was right; this man was not to be trifled with. There was something about him, a deadly patience, a distorted view of the world, of women, perhaps. It would not matter what we said, or what we did. We were already guilty. Our crime was to exist and he would see us punished for it.

Master Fynk flashed his stained teeth. "Or judged your sister and delivered the same verdict, only this"—his arm described an arc—"is to be her hell."

*Only as long as the evil you embody dwells here . . .*

Alyson stamped her foot. "That's outrageous."

Master Fynk spun around. "The only thing that's outrageous here is your capacity to escape justice."

With one last look at Betje, who disappeared around the side of the bathhouse, I drew the shutters closed and remained by the window, my eyes adjusting to the dimness. I longed to run downstairs and hold Betje in my arms and celebrate her life and soul. I remained mute. I wanted Master Fynk gone before I said something I'd regret.

Alyson was right: *How dare he.*

"Despite what you may believe, Master Fynk," said Alyson, her intonation conciliatory, as if she understood a flag of truce must be raised, "I genuinely follow the laws, unlike some who rely on friends in high places and the exchange of coin to replace obedience." With that last sally, she strolled to the door and called for Juliana. "It's time to leave, gentlemen, Master Fynk. You'll not find whores or devil spawn in *this* room. Even I may wear the apron." She gestured to the one tied over her tunic. Whores were forbidden from donning a garment that denoted domesticity and family. "So can my cousin. Here be only a woman of good birth who calls none other than those at the Stilliard friends."

A fleeting glimmer crossed Master Fynk's face. Assessing me anew while his companions murmured and moved toward the door, he frowned. "Hmm . . . de Winter. It's not a name I'm likely to forget."

Promising he'd be watching The Swanne, and me in particular, Master Fynk and his men finally left. I sank back onto the bed and stared at Alyson and Adam in disbelief.

"I cannot credit that just happened. That they would enter without a by-your-leave, and not only strike you, dear Alyson, but deliver such . . . such insults, say so many terrible things."

Touching her cheek, which still bore the impress of Master Fynk's hand, Alyson sat down. "That's because you're a lady and unaccustomed to such abuse." She wiped her hand across her brow. "For the likes of me and the girls, most men—and especially ones like Fynk—have no such compunction. You heard him—we're whores, we beggar God's will. We deserve no courtesies, only affront, fists, and cock."

"But . . . but . . . the king allows your business, you pay taxes to the bishop, no less—" said Adam.

"Allows? Turns a blind eye more like. But taxes, aye. We pay and more than our fair share." Alyson shrugged. "But I am a woman on my own running a business. You know what that's like, Anna, better than most."

I nodded gravely.

Alyson continued. "The owners of the other bathhouses resent the favor the girls and their customers show me and will use any chance, including a comely and pregnant stranger, to draw the law to our threshold." She gave a dry laugh. "Mainly because it keeps it away from them." Looking every one of her years, she gave a smile that didn't quite make her eyes. "I knew what I be getting into when I came here. What the authorities don't like is that they can't make me something I'm not."

"What's that?" I asked.

"Pliable."

I didn't say anything for a moment. Adam threw some more wood on the fire. Sparks flew into the room and up the chimney, bright stars that dazzled briefly and expired. Rising, I held my cold hands out to the flames. "How did they know I was here? Why should it matter to them?"

Alyson's eyes grew dark. Joining me, she stared at the fire. "Apart from extra money, it don't. Master Fynk likes to remind us every now and again of who and what he is."

"What's that?" asked Adam drily.

"Someone who must be obeyed."

I lifted my face to Adam. Just like the monks of St. Jude's; just like Abbot Hubbard.

Alyson squeezed my shoulder. "Don't you worry any more about none of that. I've been meaning to say, when you're ready, I want to talk to you 'bout something, and I don't mean what

I'm going to charge you for board." At the look on my face, she burst out laughing. "I'm having a jest, my dear. You're my guest. Indeed, you're my cousin, aren't you? It wouldn't be very charitable of me to be taking coin from family, now would it?"

Before I could answer, she left the room.

"Adam," I said once the door shut. "How did they know? About me? About the babes?"

Squatting by the fire, Adam lowered his voice. "It was one of the girls, I think. She wasn't happy we were here, or with the attention you were getting. Saw you as competition; someone who could lure away custom."

I gave him a look of disbelief. "In my state?"

"Ah, Mistress Anneke, in any state, you be a picture worth framing."

I smiled. "What would I do without you, Adam Barfoot?"

"Why, you'd be like a one-legged man, mistress, hopping in a great circle," he said and, using the poker to haul himself upright, proceeded to demonstrate.

He stopped. "And what would I do without you? If you hadn't called us all to sense and Goody Alyson hadn't discouraged those men, I'd be on my way to the stocks or worse." He sat on a stool. "I would have hit him, you know."

"I know. Me too."

Though we both laughed, I couldn't help but feel a dart of concern lodge beneath my breastbone. There'd almost been blows. A tussle that could have resulted in Adam's imprisonment or death. Master Fynk was spoiling for a fight. Confined to the Lily Room, my bedroom, with only my well-being and that of the children to consider, even Betje and Adam hadn't occupied my thoughts the way they once had. Nor had the future, not really. I'd been dwelling in a madman's garden, believing the flowers all lush and fragrant when in reality, weeds grew here too. If one woman complained about my presence to the authorities, when I felt so welcome, what was to stop the others doing the same or worse? And what would happen if my real identity was ever discovered, never mind the accusations from Elmham Lenn that I was positive dogged my every step?

Once Adam closed the door behind him, I clambered back onto the bed. Sleep eluded me. Instead, in the shadows that crept across the walls and over the rushes, every vague shape transformed into a threat. A threat that would, if I wasn't very careful, soon engulf us all.

# FORTY

THE SWANNE

Lent to Hocktide

*The year of Our Lord 1407 in the eighth*
*year of the reign of Henry IV*

Though still cool, the days grew longer and the sun's warmth caressed the walls and shutters, even through the thick cloud that hovered till at least midday. My health returned with each passing day, and the longing to stand upon my own skills and forge a life for myself was becoming more urgent. Alyson encouraged me to stay, to treat this time as a hiatus and find my feet. Apart from Master Fynk's visit, life was good at The Swanne. The babes were thriving; Emma and Constance, whose wages were covered by Alyson until such time as I could repay her, were reliable and kind. But it was Harry who proved as good as his word and became the friend Betje so desperately needed. Although Betje was reticent at first, Harry was patient, and soon she spent her days between the stables and my chamber, grooming the customers' horses, aiding Juliana and the wet nurses as they cared for the twins, or sitting by my side for lessons—something I encouraged Harry to do as well.

Adam also found a purpose at The Swanne. Overcoming his initial aversion for the situation in which we found ourselves, he discovered that many of the girls who lived beneath The Swanne's sprawling roof were not the evil temptresses and slatterns he'd assumed. Many were simple country lasses, or city widows and orphans who, having no way of providing for themselves and nowhere to go, were left with no choice but to either sell their bodies or seek work among those who did. Many had children they'd left with relatives. Ashamed, yet aware that their families must know, it was a dark secret that bound them all.

Only in confession and prayer would they admit to selling their flesh and pay the penance their constant sinning required. Just as she insisted on daily washing of faces and hands, Alyson made sure that every Sunday and many other mornings besides, the girls would stroll to Father Kenton's church and hear the mass—ensuring their souls were as pristine as their bodies.

All those who worked in the bathhouse felt a great deal of loyalty to Alyson.

"We be blessed with Goody Alyson" was a statement Adam heard over and over and which he repeated to me. Whether it was the freckled maid with the crooked nose and huge blue eyes called Yolande, who cleaned the grate each morning and stacked fresh kindling, or the tall, rather morose woman named Oriel, who would take away my chamber pot and ensure there was clean water in my basin, or the lovely Leda with her long, straw-colored hair, all those who dwelled within the bathhouse were steadfast toward the goodwife who gave them shelter, food, and ale and didn't try and cheat them. The same could not be said for others who ran similar businesses in the area.

"I admit, mistress, I had my reservations when we first met," Adam said one night, speaking quietly over an ale in the light of the crackling hearth, "but she be a good woman, Alyson."

From below us came the sounds of music and chatter that were a constant accompaniment to our conversations, to the many plans we assembled for the future. Sometimes there'd be low groans, chuckles, or squeals of delight. I would grow uncomfortably warm and found I was unable to look at Adam. He would simply talk louder. Once, there was an ear-splitting shout followed by a slamming door, running feet, and shrill cries. Adam leaped up and raced from the room, returning shortly to explain that one of the clients tried to leave without paying but was quickly prevented not only by the looming presence of Master atte Place, a general servant and sometime guard, but Alyson herself.

"As God is my witness, Mistress Anna, she stood before this young gentleman, who was still struggling to tie his breeches, her face dark as a storm upon the bay, and insisted he pay. When he swore he couldn't, said his purse had been stolen and accused the young woman he'd been with of taking it, Alyson first scolded him then reached over and grabbed his arm. Before he could snatch it away, she hailed Harry to her side and bid him remove the gentleman's ring." Adam sat on the stool, leaning against the wall, chuckling. "I've never seen the like. Daring as a demon's strut."

"What did he do?"

"What could he do with Master atte Place glowering, Harry and Alyson holding him firm, and those women not . . . er . . .

um . . . occupied blocking his escape. He conceded, apologized as well. Promised he'd be back on the morrow with what he owed, providing his ring is returned."

"You think he'll honor that?"

"Oh, aye. I think his father would be most upset his son lost a ring bearing the Tiptoft seal, don't you?"

"The man was a *Tiptoft*? The royal treasurer's son?"

"More a boy, really. Still had spots." Adam jabbed his chin and forehead a few times. "And a remarkable inability to tie his purse strings properly."

"And those of his breeches, from what you say." We both laughed heartily.

After that, Adam suggested to Alyson that the gentlemen callers to The Swanne be made to pay before they enjoyed the ladies. At first Alyson was resistant, concerned it would drive custom to the other bathhouses, but when Adam explained if the girls asked for the coin once they were alone with the men, then it would be very difficult for the customers to refuse.

Alyson inclined her head and regarded Adam seriously. "Are you sure you've never done this sort of work before?"

Adam grinned. "Nay. But a household is a household and a business"—he shrugged—"is a business, and I understand how best to work both."

After that, Alyson sought Adam's advice on many issues, including one that concerned me. Though I only learned that later.

My family had found a place and purpose here, except for me. I would have to unhouse them once more and take them across the river, to London.

Standing by the window, I gazed across the busy Thames and toward the city. Smoke billowed from crooked chimneys; men pushed carts, loaded and unloaded the punts full of goods while wherries disgorged people, as they moved in and out of the fog. Cogs lay at anchor on the jetties not far to the east, and I could just see pennants flapping atop the Tower. Voices carried across the water, coarse and deep, and I knew without doubt that my purpose lay somewhere in that muddle of misty streets. The time for us to leave was approaching; two evenings ago I'd broached the subject with Alyson and she greeted my announcement with just a resigned look that gave away little. Reassuring her of constant friendship, of the bond created between us when I made her, Harry, and Juliana godparents to my twins, she regarded me with ambivalence. Discussing what we'd do and where we'd go with Adam and Alyson over supper again last night, I was assured of their support and knew the small amount of coin I still carried, plus what Captain Stoyan held in safekeeping for me from sales of my beer in Flanders, would help us to secure a place from which to commence our business.

All I'd brought from Elmham Lenn and Dover, apart from a few clothes that Mother Joanna had given me, Betje, and Adam, were a few remaining barrels of beer, the ale-stick, and some of the instruments that I couldn't bear to leave behind. God knew, it wasn't much, but it was a start. Mother's recipe book may have been no more, but I felt confident I could re-create every single one from memory.

Before we could depart, we needed somewhere to live—a place that could accommodate not just me, Betje, the twins, the wet nurses, Adam, and, in time, additional servants, but also a rudimentary brewery.

Securing premises was something that back in Dover, Captain Stoyan had said he would arrange. However, the lack of contact from the captain had begun to alarm me. Having lost Papa to the might of the sea, I wondered if Captain Stoyan had met the same fate.

I determined to write to Captain Stoyan once more, before we finalized our plans. The next day, Adam delivered the letter to the metal walls of the Hanse, declaring he wouldn't leave until he learned something of Captain Stoyan's whereabouts. Recognizing the stubbornness in his words, the porter disappeared only to return with a large, stocky man of rank in tow.

"*Ja?*" said the man with a booming voice, his beard bristling, his blue eyes cold. Adam described the cut of his dark jacket, the way the seams of the sleeves of his surcoat pulled as if they could barely contain the hard flesh beneath. "I'm Captain Geise," the man said. "I'm told you are seeking information about Captain Stoyan, *ja?*"

Introducing himself, Adam explained what he could. Captain Geise listened, his face revealing nothing. When he'd finished, Adam waited. Behind the captain, the sounds of industry carried. There was the ring of hammers, the clunk and grind of ropes and heavy objects being levered into place. Constant chatter in thick German and the singsong of Flemish formed a counterpoint to the irregular noises. Smoke billowed above the fortified walls, while over the captain's shoulders, Adam could see at least four hulls in dry dock being caulked. The smell of tar infused the air.

Denied an invitation to enter, or to sit upon the bench just inside the confines of the yard, Adam knew what he was about to hear would not bode well.

Captain Geise's heavily hooded eyes narrowed and his arms

folded across his burly chest. "I know who you are and your mistress too. You have not told me everything."

At his tone, Adam's heart sank. Captain Geise did not mince his words.

"Aye," said Adam, "this is true." Like Captain Stoyan, this man would brook no falsehoods.

With a grunt, whether of approval or disdain Adam was unable to fathom, Captain Geise spoke. In short, sharp sentences, liberally littered with German, he told Adam why we hadn't heard from Captain Stoyan and why we wouldn't in the future either.

What happened in Elmham Lenn and the captain's association with me, with my beer, had brought the Hanse into disrepute. The hue and cry sent to capture me had altered the Kontor in Colchester, one of their major centers, and word had spread from there to London. The generous rights the king granted the Hanse meant they earned the wrath and suspicion of my countrymen at the best of times. Captain Geise explained that if it was discovered that Captain Stoyan was helping a felon in any way, that he'd harbored a fugitive aboard his vessel, let alone found her accommodation so she could brew again, the outcome for him, personally, didn't bear thinking about. It would also, potentially, create trouble for the Hanse that they could well do without.

"So, you tell your mistress, if she cares about Hatto as much as I think she does, if she cares about the *Englischer* wool and trade, then she won't try and contact him again."

"What about the letter I left weeks ago? It contained a very personal request." Adam hadn't even bothered to remove my latest one from his surcoat.

"It was never sent."

"Can I ask where Captain Stoyan is now? If he is well?"

"*Ja*. You may."

After a minute of silence, the captain's blue eyes boring into his, Adam lowered his head. The interview was over. There was little point arguing.

"One last thing," said the captain, spinning on the heel of his shiny boots. "Tell your mistress she makes a fine beer. Some was brought to me from Elmham Lenn. Was *gut, ja*."

With that, the porter shut the gate and Adam was left to return to the wherry he'd hired to cross the river.

Knowing Captain Stoyan would not be able to help was a blow from which I thought we'd not recover. I hadn't realized how much I'd counted upon his advice, help, and contacts to make a difficult transition easier. While I knew Alyson would help secure us lodgings over the bridge if I asked, I felt she'd already done so much, I could not impose upon her goodwill any longer.

Realization I was on my own, as I hadn't been before, dawned. I stood staring over the river toward London, understanding, for the first time in weeks, that this was it: all the decisions from here on in were mine to make alone.

I needed to think. To clear my head. Fortify not just plans, but my bruised spirit. Others were depending on me and I swore I wouldn't let them down.

# FORTY-ONE

THE SWANNE

After Hocktide

*The year of Our Lord 1407 in the eighth*
*year of the reign of Henry IV*

*I*t was the first day of spring; the day for me to search for accommodation in London had arrived. Gray and cold with a persistent thick fog low in the sky, it wasn't an auspicious beginning.

Learning that Captain Stoyan was banned from corresponding, let alone associating, with me spurred me to do what I'd delayed for too long. Widowhood, which had lent me an air of respectability and prevented the likes of Master Fynk fining Alyson and administering punishment, might well work against me in the city—especially when it was understood a business was to be part of the leasing arrangement I sought. Dressing slowly, savoring my last minutes in my room, I reflected upon my invented state and how easily I'd adapted to its nuances.

Over the weeks, with all the inquiries and solicitation I'd

received following the twins' birth, my imagined dead spouse had developed a form any real man would be hard-pressed to emulate. From his great height to his broad shoulders, wicked smile, hard work, and determination to succeed, to his utmost consideration and rare temper, he was a paragon of virtue. Until I realized that in many ways, the man I described was Sir Leander. Yet I persisted and trembled lest the original appear and charge me a murderous slattern.

There, I admitted it. Why did I believe so firmly that this would be his response? Why could I not bring myself to imagine a different outcome? Was it because he now possessed a wife? His duty was to her, so he would not, could not, give me a moment of his time. Yet, I would argue with myself, he went to Elmham Lenn, he followed me to Dover, surely that counted for something?

But what?

That Sir Leander would no longer regard me as he once had—with great tenderness—was the real source of my anxiety. I was afraid, above all else, that he would see me once more as a whore. Not so much because I dwelled beneath the roof of a bathhouse (though that would not help), but because I was now a mother without a husband—even a dead one.

How could I explain what had happened without losing his high opinion? My deception, in pretending to be a widow, would simply confirm the worst. At least if I left the confines of the bathhouse, if we did encounter each other and I begged his forgiveness (and that of his father) for the destruction of the property, told him what had eventuated, he might not only absolve me but, as he once did, admire my enterprise as I sought to work and support my family.

On Tobias, I chose not to dwell. I could guess what he would say about my situation. No doubt in his eyes I was responsible for the death of our brother, and for Betje's sorry condition. I had fallen from a respectable woman to an outlaw.

Today, I determined to place this fretting behind me. Today, I would complete the journey started all those months ago in Elmham Lenn. Today, the phoenix would rise from the ashes of Holcroft House and fly to London.

Finishing my toilet and satisfied I was suitably dressed, I closed the shutters against the fetid wind that blew off the river and tossed the mist around, and rearranged my tunic and kirtle, the same ones I'd worn before my burgeoning womb forced me to find more suitable apparel. Surprised to find they hung loosely upon me, I couldn't credit that it had been two months since the twins were born, time I'd spent at unaccustomed leisure. I found it didn't suit me. A piece of polished metal propped against the bureau revealed to me what I'd guessed to be the truth—I'd become gaunt and pale. Not usually vain, I ran my fingers down my rather prominent cheekbones and tucked a strand of hair behind my ear. Well, there was no help for the way I looked. As for the loss of some flesh, it was to be expected. It was nothing a few good meals and some ale wouldn't replace, unlike the other losses that were never far from my thoughts.

Unbidden, an image of Karel replaced my own in the metal. Distorted, stretched slightly, his mouth was twisted in a grimace, his eyes wide with . . . what was it? Fear? Anticipation? I shut my eyes briefly, seeking not so much to banish him but to become accustomed to what now must haunt me. If I'd learned one thing over the last few weeks, it was that the dead didn't depart this world, not really. They were the tears in the well of the heart, drawn in a heavy pail and tipped into the eyes. They were fragments of dreams left upon a pillow; they were the secret ache of which no one spoke, but which remained in the soul.

When I opened my eyes, Karel was gone. But I knew if it wasn't him making an appearance, it would be Saskia, Louisa, Will, or even Westel. I didn't resent their visits. On the contrary, I drew comfort from them—often, a cold comfort. The only exception was Westel, who roused nothing but hatred, guilt, and apprehension . . . but he was my penance; I deserved to feel all those things and, sweet Mother Mary knew, so much more as well. As for the others, there was some succor in knowing they'd not yet abandoned me . . . abandoned us.

The faint wail of a hungry babe disturbed my reverie and, throwing a shawl around my shoulders, I cast a final look around the room that had been my haven. It was the place in which my life had changed in so many ways and I would leave it with no small regret.

But we'd imposed upon Alyson long enough. In order to make any headway, I must move. With a huff of amusement, I took a step toward the door.

"See, that wasn't so hard, was it?" I wrenched it open and strode into the corridor.

⋞⋟⋞⋟

I stood in the solar of The Swanne, a beautifully appointed room on the first floor of the bathhouse where Alyson conducted business and received only her most special and private of guests. Betje was beside me. My heart was heavy as I explained to Alyson I was traveling to London to seek accommodation. She wasn't making it any easier, sitting in a high-backed chair, her face indifferent, her lips pursed. As she turned to regard me, a wicked twinkle gleamed in her eye, as if she carried some secret.

"Alyson"—I reached for her hand, which remained limp and sorry in mine—"you've already been so welcoming, so generous. If not for you, well, I doubt the twins and I would have survived—"

"For God's sake, Anna," she said with a harrumph of disgust, extracting her fingers with force. I backed away. "Don't go maudlin on me. Not you!"

Putting down the mazer from which she'd been enjoying a small ale, Alyson heaved herself out of the chair, walked around the table, and came slowly, inexorably toward me. She wore her favorite scarlet tunic; her kirtle was of the best fabric. Yet, for all her finery, she appeared tired, distracted.

"What if I told you, you don't need to go to London—not today, not any day?"

"Pardon?"

"What if I said, since you be so willing to give it away"—she flung an arm out—"*I'll* take your coin and provide you with what you need."

"Forgive me, Alyson, are you suggesting I remain here?"

Alyson rolled her eyes. Betje giggled. "Aye, she's quick all right, your sister, ain't she?" Lunging forward she grabbed my shoulders and gave them a shake. "Of course that's what I'm suggesting, you daft beauty." Releasing me, she paced across the solar. "I know this is a bathhouse and not the kind of establishment in which you ever thought to be living, or raising children in, but you have called it home the last few weeks, and I thought you might like to continue to do so."

I stared at her in disbelief. "Why didn't you say something

before? Why wait until I'm on the cusp of finding somewhere else?"

The door opened and Adam entered. Alyson shot him a questioning look. Nodding brusquely, he smiled.

A delighted look spread across her features. "Good."

"Adam?" I turned to him, questions brimming.

"It ain't his fault," said Alyson quickly. "If you're going to blame anyone, blame me."

"For what?"

"For waiting till now to let you know that not only can you live here, you can brew as well."

"Brew? But where? How—?"

"That's right, Mistress Anna," said Adam, the words tumbling out of his mouth. "At Goody Alyson's bidding, I've spoken to a miller and he's agreed to supply us with grain, good stock too, and malt the barley as well. His price is reasonable and he's a fine reputation. I've also managed to get two mash tuns—they'll need some work, but Master Batayle of The Star swears by them; said a cooper can repair them in an afternoon." He beamed at me.

Stunned, I sat down quickly. My heart hammered and my knees quivered. "Go on." I knew a business deal being struck when I heard one.

Alyson continued. "Beneath where we are now is a large cellar. It's a cold, old place. Dark with a fair bit of rubbish strewn about—or it did have. Been unused since I bought The Swanne, but, over the last few weeks, I've had cause to reexamine it and I've found it was quite to my liking. It made me think, it did. I've had the girls clean it. The chimney hadn't been cleared since the house was built, by the sweep's reckoning—should have seen the bird carcasses and rat bones." She shuddered. "Of course, I couldn't think to what purpose such a large, cold area with a usable hearth"—she grinned as my eyes widened and mouth dropped—"a dusty old kiln, and a floor so dry Mistress Verina would feel like she was home again could be put, until I tasted your beer. After that, I had a few long conversations with Master Adam here, didn't I?"

Pausing as she strutted about the solar, she smiled at Adam, then me. I couldn't help but return it.

*How had Adam kept such discussions from me? More importantly, why?*

"You've a talent, girl, do you know that?" said Alyson softly.

"I've been told," I said. Betje squeezed beside me onto the chair and sought my hand. In the touch of her fingers and the tautness of her slender frame, I could feel the excitement coursing through her. In many ways, it mirrored my own.

"As for why I haven't said anything before, I wasn't sure how to tell you since you were so determined to walk your own path. I respect that, you know I do. You had your heart set on going to London, doing it all yourself, and while I didn't want to prevent you, I felt I had to warn you . . ."

"About what?"

She held up her hand. "I'll get to that. But what was the point of trying to change your mind if I couldn't offer you an alternative? If I wasn't certain that London would be more trouble than it was worth? Well, Adam and me had some long talks, did some thinking of our own, we did." She flashed him her toothy grin. "I had to have something to tempt you with, something to make it worthwhile staying, other than the pleasure of my company." She winked. "Now he's done what I asked and found you some mash tuns and a supplier for your grain. That means

I can tender you an alternative to London—a good one at that. I can even do better than to offer you a place to live and a place to brew."

"What could be better than that?"

Taking a deep breath, she continued. "I want to offer you a partnership, Anna de Winter. You heard me. A partnership. I'll underwrite your initial costs in return for a small rent and a steady supply of ale and beer. I'll put a roof over your head, your babes, Betje's, and even old Adam's. You can use the girls as hucksters when times are quiet and I'll even throw in Juliana and her wages for good measure. She's yours to train and use in the brewery. As your business grows, we can discuss more servants. Once you start making a profit, then we'll have a natter about sharing it. Think about it, Anna . . . you wouldn't have to move anywhere except from where you're sitting and down some stairs." She pointed to the floor.

My heart fluttered and enthusiasm began to replace the dread that had taken up residence. A cellar would offer perfect conditions. Cold, dry, likely to have an even temperature most of the year. Depending how large the space, I could divide part into a brewery, the other use for storage. And if there was a good supplier who could malt and mill the grain . . .

I was sorely tempted. To be able to remain, to start brewing and with such assistance, my first purchases already covered . . .

"If only it were so simple, Alyson."

With a click of frustration, she moved away. I stood and joined her at the window. Immediately below us was the entrance to The Swanne, the busy street, the slow-moving river. Bells tolled and a flock of pigeons rose in a flurry of feathers, wheeling away to the east.

"It's only difficult if you make it so, Anna. Like anything in this life."

"But over there . . ." I nodded toward London. Spires pushed through the mist, jetties protruded over the water. Patches of sunlight revealed craft being dragged along the river. "There's access to millers, coopers, a reasonable water supply, and everything else I need."

"What? Didn't you hear Adam? Southwark's got these as well."

"It's not just mash tuns, Alyson, or grain. I need suppliers, steady trade, access to boats . . ." My voice petered out. I swallowed. "On a more practical level, I need wood and coal, measures, troughs—"

"Aye, aye. I hear you. Now, tell me, what else are you going to make into a hurdle you won't jump?"

I didn't answer. I didn't know how.

"I know what you need, and what we can't get, well, we can make do until we can." She let out a long sigh. "Anna, I've spoken to a client of mine, Stephen Hamme, who, it happens, owns a couple of successful brewhouses in London. Master Hamme told me some things that have me worried. I wanted to warn you . . ."

"What did Master Hamme tell you?"

"That you wouldn't be welcome over there." She jerked her head toward the city.

I laughed. "Alyson, I'm not that naive. A wise woman once said to me that women like us aren't welcome anywhere. She was right."

Alyson shook her head. "This is more serious than that. Master Hamme said they would hound you out of there faster than the gents here divest their breeches. Oh. My apologies, Miss Betty." Her eyes twinkled. "But you get my point."

"I do." I waited for her to continue.

"In London, the laws are different. I knew that was the case for my type of business, but it's just as bad for brewers. Why do you think there're so many setting up over here? Because it's so scenic? Because it's so clean?"

Behind me, Adam gave a bark of laughter.

Alyson ignored him. "You think you can just stroll over the bridge, move into a suitable house, and brew to your heart's content? I tell you this for naught, Anna, the Mystery of Brewers will see you finished quicker than a pries—" She caught my eye and, looking at Betje, changed her mind. "Damn fast, I tell you."

"How? If I pay my dues, if the ale-conners pass the brew, they'll have no cause for complaint. I'm not seeking to wear the livery, I just want a chance."

"If. If. If." Alyson snorted.

"That's all you wanted in Elmham Lenn too, mistress," said Adam softly.

I winced. "It's not fair." Now I sounded like Tobias, seven years old and being lifted onto a pony and sent to live in another household. I sat back down onto a chair. "I don't understand."

"Nay," said Alyson, "I'm not surprised. But the facts are, despite the friends you have here and what Captain Stoyan once did, you'll find they're not enough. They're never enough. Master Hamme said there's been a terrible lot of cheating going on of late—false measures being used, ale diluted with all manner of stuff, and it's been the women responsible." Alyson pulled a face. "Well, held responsible, methinks. Many from here, from Southwark, as well. Courts are full of brewsters and the coffers full of their fines. A few even get to spend time in the pillory or worse. Ever since His Grace, good King Henry, gave London

charter over Southwark, it's been ruinous for anyone from here—
especially if they go over *there*." She raised a finger to prevent my
interjection.

"I know you're not from here, but in their eyes you will be.
You'll be the Southwark widow, and try telling 'em any different. Think they won't know your story? And I know you don't
engage in such practices as gets those others in trouble. You're
not a cheat, but without a husband to speak for you, or a man
of equal standing"—she cast an apologetic look at Adam, which
went a long way to demonstrating her estimation of him—"you'll
be ripe for accusations and worse. Not just from the ale-conners
and justices, but the other brewers. Imagine how much the
women are going to love having you setting up in their midst?"
She gave a harrumph and looked at the ceiling, cackling.

"Oh, Lord. As for the ale-conners . . . they'll pretend to assess you the same as the rest, but your brews will be scrutinized
in ways others aren't. You'll have fines levied so often and for
no sensible reason; you'll have no money to pay the rent, let
alone the tax. And what about the poll tax once you've become
a citizen? What about that? In other words, anything and everything you do will attract fees and earn scorn and envy. You'll
be regarded as a slattern, dragged before the courts for offenses
that a mummer couldn't invent, and arouse local ire for simply existing. It won't matter what kind of household you run,
what kind of business you build, Anna, you're a woman and a
brewer. You'll be seen as disorderly, as a threat to goodness and
godliness—a sinner—and as such you'll be cast out."

Holding in a sigh, I suddenly felt weary, worn. Echoes of
Westel's cruel words rang in my mind. "I've dealt with worse."

"In Elmham Lenn, aye. But this is London we're talking

about. This is different. You met Master Fynk, yet he can't hold a candle to those over the bridge. Not when it comes to pedantry, cruelty, or the smug self-satisfaction certain men take in wielding authority—particularly over someone like you. Someone young and beautiful. I know."

A tremor ran through me.

She began to stride around the room again. "And you'll not be able to brew both ale and beer, have you thought of that, heh? It'll be one or the other—mark my words."

"And will it be any better here?"

Alyson threw back her head and laughed. "Of course not! In some ways, it'll be worse, because since King Henry changed the charter, the laws of London apply here—well, when they're enforced. But here you'll have friends." She stopped mid-stride. "Here, you'll have us."

In her face it was clear: *You'll have me.*

"You have a choice, Anna, between dealing with corrupt and overzealous tasters, as well as jealous brewsters and guild members who don't give a God's wink about you, Betje, the twins, or anything other than keeping the guild and law courts happy and profiting from you any way they can"—she rubbed her thumb and forefinger together—"all by yourself—*or* you can stay here with me and we'll face 'em together. Brew for The Swanne for starters. Master Hamme reckons if your brew's as good as what he tasted—aye, he was here the night of the babes' christening—then you'll have no trouble selling to the alehouses in Horselydown Lane, or even along the High Street. Happens I know the owner of The Crown, down in Tooley Street, very well." She tapped the side of her nose. "Reckon we might be able to do some business there. Once some of the

nobles or religious houses discover your ale and beer, the orders
will fly in." Unfolding her arms, she came and knelt at my feet.
Taking my hands from my lap, Betje's twined around one, she
held us tightly.

"What do you say, Anna de Winter? How about we go into
business together and show the folk of Southwark, and London
as well, how real ale and beer tastes, hey?"

I could not credit what Alyson was saying, the proposition
she was making. It was beyond what I had ever dreamed . . .
Was it too good? Did disaster loom around the corner? Not just
for me, Betje, the twins, and Adam but, if we joined forces,
for Alyson, Harry, Master atte Place, and The Swanne's girls?
I couldn't bear the thought that somehow I was a harbinger of
doom. Alyson deserved better. They all did.

"Anna," said Alyson in dismay when I didn't answer, letting
go of my hands and pulling herself up with grunts and groans
using the chair next to mine, "why are you being so resistant?
Is it because this is a bathhouse? Or is it that you fear your true
identity will be discovered? That Sir Leander will find you?"

My head, full of ideas, galloping with possibility, was suddenly wiped clean as a child's slate.

The knowledge and understanding in her steady brown gaze
undid me. I glanced at Adam. "Nay," she said, "Adam never
breathed a word. You may not remember, but the day the twins
were born you spoke of him, Anna. A great deal. Him and that
murderous scoundrel, Westel Calkin. Aye, you weren't in your
right mind, you weren't aware. That's why I've kept my mouth
shut—till now."

I nodded, unsurprised that even helpless, my heart had conspired against me.

Alyson cocked her head to one side. "Would it be so bad if he did?"

I shot her a tired look. It was the question I hadn't dared to ask myself.

"I don't know. Sweet Mother Mary, I don't know."

Alyson let out a long sigh. "Mayhap that's as well. I often think if we knew what God intended before it happened, we'd be too afraid to clamber out of bed most mornings."

Collapsing on the chair next to mine, she reached over and gripped my thigh. "Let me put it this way. I've shared my bed with five different men as their wife, but I've never asked anyone to share my business as partner. I'm asking you, Anna de Winter, I'm asking you."

A thousand reasons not to accept Alyson's offer leaped through my head. My ears were filled with "nays" and "naughts." I could see Father's furious visage looming over me, rage burning in his eyes; there was Tobias, shouting; Cousin Hiske and all manner of people from my past letting me know I was finally living up to their low expectations: brewing in a bathhouse. Only Mother's face, as it drifted before me, tears streaming down her cheeks, offered a small smile of hope. *You can make it work, Anneke, you always do.*

*Nay, Moeder, I don't. I didn't.*

*But this time you will.*

I rose, brushing against Alyson as I returned to the window, drawn to gaze across the river toward the bustling city. Watery sunshine struck the gray-brown surface, transforming it into something sparkling and inviting. London too became a patchwork of color and shadow, smoke and greenery, golden opportunity and dark failure.

Below the sill, the cobbles were slick, the ditch that ran down the center of the road a sludge of straw, animal and human refuse, and all manner of rubbish. Dogs and pigs snuffled in the soaking stench, while chickens clucked and squawked like clumsy balls of feathers among the vendors and pedestrians, unlike the urchins who darted about with practiced ease. Hawkers cried their wares and women wearing yellow hoods wandered between them, inviting customers to consider another kind of purchase. Alyson wouldn't be happy that her business was being encroached upon. The smell of a nearby fullers drifted in the open window while to my left, I could just see the edge of one of the watermills churning upstream. I wondered if that was the one Adam had visited.

What if Mother had been right? What if this time I really could make it work? Not over there, in the city, but here? Perhaps here my status wouldn't be such a burden, not with Alyson as my patron; indeed, as my partner. The risk was as much hers as mine.

"The risk is as much mine as yours," said a voice in my ear. I jumped. Alyson had joined me at the window, reading my thoughts. "It's a dirty old place, isn't it? Bankside, Southwark . . . Look at all that shit." She laughed. "But as God is my witness, it's my dirty old place."

"Nay," I said, turning to face her.

Squinting in the sunlight, she raised a brow. "Oh? And why do you say that, you cheeky chick?"

"Because it's *our* dirty old place."

It took her a moment to get my meaning. Then, with a small cry, she pulled me against her. Betje joined us moments later. Adam stood beside us, one hand on Alyson's shoulder, the other upon mine, as together we stared at our grubby demesne.

# FORTY-TWO

THE SWANNE
May Day
*The year of Our Lord 1407 in the eighth
year of the reign of Henry IV*

*I*'d been at The Swanne now for almost three months, yet every time I descended the worn steps to the cellar and entered the brewery, I was newly astonished by what we'd accomplished and the transformation that had been wrought. Tying an apron around my tunic, I wandered between the bubbling mash tuns, nodding God's good day to Juliana and Yolande, who were stirring the contents and inhaling its rich, almost buttery smell. Steam rose to the ceiling before falling like a constant lament down the walls. Nearby, a fire roared in the huge old kiln, trays of grain browning within, Adam keeping a watchful eye.

"How are the twins, mistress?" he asked as I approached.

"Slumbering as only the innocent can," I replied.

Behind one of the columns and on a slightly lower level, Harry, who'd become an apprentice of sorts—at least when he could be spared—was helping Master atte Place shift some barrels. Ofttimes, I would catch Harry out of the corner of my eye and my heart would seize as an unwelcome memory overrode the reality and another taller, older man took his place. As the days passed, this happened less often. Harry was nothing like Westel and, indeed, the brewery we'd created beneath The Swanne was nothing like my small concern at Holcroft House.

What we were building here was a much larger business altogether, one that required me to spend every available moment overseeing every aspect of production as well as training the servants. They were fast learners and keen to earn the extra coin they received for working with me. They deserved it. The cellar wasn't a comfortable place to be—even though the weather outside was warming, it was ofttimes cold below the bathhouse, despite the busy kiln, and quite dark. Only one small window admitted light and the battered door, sitting above the six steps that led into the courtyard, remained closed, except when there were deliveries, as did the other door that led to the kitchen. For now, our brewing wasn't exactly legal—but neither was it against the law. As I was slowly learning, Southwark made its own rules, many in spite of London, and the locals could be both flexible and uncompromising.

Paying poll tax and declaring my occupation as a brewer meant that I incurred not just hefty quarterage for the right, but also the attention of those who were curious as to whether or not I would succeed in my intentions. I wasn't the only female brewer in Southwark, or Bankside for that matter, but I was the only widow and the only woman who was in partnership with a member of my own sex. There were those in authority who watched us with skeptical and ungenerous eyes, finding fault where there was none, attempting to control what I did. I paid my dues without quarrel and gave the appearance of quiet obedience. But, with Alyson's support and encouragement, I continued to make the ale and beer my way—the way Moeder and all the de Winter women before me had.

What I hadn't counted on was what the additional scrutiny of my endeavors meant for Alyson. The Swanne received extra inspections from Master Fynk, who took great delight in ensuring none of the girls were being held against their will (the notorious concubinage), were pregnant, wore the apron, or had the burning sickness. Much to my astonishment, I found out that bathhouses were not supposed to serve food or ale to their customers, but, if Alyson was forced to obey this law, then other establishments would have to acquiesce too, and for all his bombast, Master Fynk knew this would be nigh on impossible. So he tolerated part of the hall being turned into a taproom, and along with visits from the bailiff, constables, watchmen, and other assorted officials, and the subsequent checking of ledgers to ensure charges for rooms and sundries weren't too high, The Swanne became the most well-conducted bathhouse in Bankside.

Alyson shrugged it off with more good humor than I'd expected. "Let them regulate me till their boots get worn marching here and their quills snap with all their damn record keeping. I look after my girls and my servants and they can't help but say so." Only then would her eyes narrow. "If they want corruption, they don't have to look too far to find it."

Alyson was referring to our neighbors, "the Flemish," as she called them, who also ran adjoining bathhouses, ones that had reputations for gambling, violence, and all sorts of wanton behavior. Measuring the worth of one of these kinds of establishments against another wasn't something I ever thought I'd be putting my mind to, but there was a code of honor that was followed at Bankside, and those who flouted it inevitably ended up drawing the wrath of the Bishop of Winchester, and that often meant time in the notorious prison, The Clink.

Pushing these thoughts to the back of my mind, I ran through the list of tasks I'd still to complete. Today was May Day and there were festivities aplenty planned for the evening, and the girls would do a version of the maypole dance, which Betje and I were forbidden to watch. For all that I lived and worked in a bathhouse, Alyson did her utmost to protect us from exposure to its customers and its more scandalous elements, and mostly she was successful. However, I was not completely ignorant. Aware of the occasional brawls, of drunken and sober demands that certain tastes be met, I also stumbled upon semi-clad men and women in the corridors, and had twice now been mistaken for one of the bathhouse girls. I'd quickly corrected that misconception and managed to maintain my dignity. There was an understandable assumption that any woman beneath this roof was there for one purpose only.

Long before the sun set, I would make sure the children and I were in my room. During the day, the twins remained with the wet nurses in the attic room that had now become a permanent nursery, while my sister was, as she insisted, by my side in the brewery.

Squatting at the base of one of the columns, Betje chatted to Harry. With only one good hand, it was difficult for her to hold an ale-stick or a rake, but she'd become adept at knowing just when the grain I still dried for beer was cooked enough to release its flavors. Able to overcome her fear of the flames, she would hover near the kiln and wait for the malted barley to dry. Just then, Adam hailed her. She rose awkwardly and limped to his side, staying out of the way until the hot tray was safely deposited on the table.

Spying me, she waved and popped a piece of hot golden grain between her teeth, biting through the husk. Nodding approvingly at the taste, Betje tried another from a different part to be sure before Adam pushed the tray to one side and replaced another in the stove.

One day, if she chose, Betje would be a fine brewer. Looking at her now, the twisted mass of flesh that cascaded down one side of her face and, I knew all too well, her body, the scant, fair hair that fell in a thin braid beneath her cap, and one functioning eye, I wondered what the future held for her . . . I wondered what it held for us all.

A wave of exhaustion washed over me. I let out a sigh and rested a hand against the trough, glancing at the cooling wort, noting the fine, creamy head that sat upon the ale. I'd sung it to life as the cock crowed this morning, relishing the texture, the taste I'd enjoyed—there was no doubt, it would be a fine batch. But, dear Lord, I couldn't recall ever being so weary.

Still, there was nothing for it but to roll up my sleeves and keep going. Moaning, never mind resting, was reserved for those able to afford such luxuries. God knows, I'd done enough of the latter my first few weeks here to last a lifetime. I'd lost precious weeks and had no choice but to make it up. I grabbed the old ale-stick from where it leaned in the corner hiding the suspicious wet patch beneath, one of my libations to the corner crones (much to my relief, they had heeded my call and joined me the first day I brewed), and relieved Juliana, who, able to work without instruction, went to the troughs to drain the wort. Understanding what needed be done, Adam went to help.

Swirling the mash, pleased with the consistency, I was able to continue my reverie. In the darkness beyond squatted the barrels Master atte Place and Harry had moved. Already passed by the ale-conners, they awaited sale. Most of the contents would be sold in The Swanne. Some of it would rely on those of Alyson's girls willing to be hucksters—selling ale in varying quantities in the street—in their spare time. Already, this had been more successful than we'd hoped, and as soon as one of The Swanne women appeared on Maiden Lane or the High Street with the cart and barrel, so too men and women would queue with their jugs, skins, and even tankards to be filled. Still, it was not enough, not when the girls needed to be paid, and we would have to find other means of distribution if we were to make money. I still lived in hope that one of the religious houses in Southwark or one of the nobles would order their supplies from us, or that the Bishop of Winchester, who'd already praised the drink, would place orders, but none had eventuated. There was something about a brewery and a bathhouse that, while it worked so well for me, was a deterrent to others. After all, what gentleman could hold his head up at table and claim, "This fine brew was bought from the Stews"?

There had be a way to overcome prejudice and, perhaps, I'd already found one.

Six barrels stood aside from the rest. Containing beer I'd brewed with the last of the hops, they'd been left to ferment and were almost ready for sale. With no standing orders, I had to rely on locals to buy it, just like the ale. There were good profits to be made from beer, as it was cheaper to make, but only if drinkers sought it as a preference. Knowing the men of the Stilliard across the river would be our best customers, and possibly also our Flemish neighbors, both of whom preferred beer to English ale, we determined to open a barrel tonight when we knew the Easterlings would sneak into Stew Lane and board wherries to Southwark. If only I still had the contracts to supply the Hanse ships, if only Captain Stoyan was once more able to act as my agent in the Low Countries . . . if only . . . if only . . .

I caught myself.

"If only" was the herald of despondency. But there was something I *had* changed in the hope it would make a difference. There wasn't only the ale-conners' official seal, the three *X*s, emblazoned upon the barrels. I'd added something extra.

It was a fancy, really, one Captain Stoyan inspired a long time ago, when he sat in the solar with me at Holcroft House and drank my first beer.

"This is so good," he'd said, smacking his lips in appreciation, "it deserves its own name." We'd laughed heartily at the absurdity of such a notion.

Since I'd been at The Swanne and used the last of the hops I'd brought from Elmham Lenn, the idea had taken hold. Why not name my beer? My ale for that matter, as well?

I played with names like Anna's Ale and Southwark Superior and laughed at my audacity. For certes, Alyson was having an influence upon me. Weeks went by and while I hadn't decided on a name for the ale or beer, we gradually became referred to as the Bathhouse Brewery. I knew then that a name for my beer and ale would disguise its origins and, perhaps, make purchasing it more palatable for some households. One morning after

I'd served the corner crones, the name came to me. It was so simple and meaningful. I'd heard this name being given to beer by some of the English sailors in Elmham Lenn who'd served abroad in the king's forces. To me, it signified more than simply a point of difference to ale and to The Swanne. In naming the beer, I felt I was also honoring my brother Karel's memory— after all, was he not a son of one of the finest brewers? One to whom I owed my talents?

I found some charcoal and, kneeling before each barrel of beer, inscribed on the wood in neat black letters, SON OF ALE.

Heavy grief but also a sense of wonder tinged with rightness accompanied my naming, my effort to include Karel in our endeavors. I prayed to the Holy Mother and my Savior that what I'd created in my brother's name would indeed pay tribute to his all-too-brief life.

That I also included the goddess Ninkasi in these prayers was between my crones and me. And Mother. Always Moeder.

Westel may have sought to steal her gift, but he'd not succeeded. The de Winter women's traditions were forever emblazoned in my memory. It had not been difficult to re-create the recipes I'd used with such success in Elmham Lenn. I'd even dared to embellish them, sourcing local herbs, spices, and woods for smoking, to add flavor.

Footsteps echoed above me and I cast my eyes in their direction. Alyson was supervising the cleaning and restocking of The Swanne. The muted cries of vendors arriving at the kitchen door occasionally carried, as did tantalizing smells, reminding us that we were soon to break fast. The cook had been particularly busy over the last two days. Juliana cast a longing look toward the stairs and I knew I wasn't the only one feeling the stirrings of hunger. A barrel of small ale had been taken upstairs for the servants.

As I stirred the mash, I ran through the other tasks I had to accomplish today. Betje and Harry must revise their letters. Then there were the little smocks I was sewing for the twins to wear when the weather was warm enough. Keen to see how they measured against their growing bodies, I hoped to be able to spend extra time with them. I also had to ensure the coal and wood merchants delivered, and ask Adam to remind the miller, Master Backster, that we were still waiting on our last batch of ground malt. Charging reasonable prices, Master Backster also had a tendency to preference the orders of other brewers, such as Master Falstof of the Boar's Head on High Street, before mine. Three times already, our brew had been held up because of a late delivery. If this continued, we'd have to seek an alternate miller and that could be hard—they were farther away and the cartage would add another cost I could ill afford. There was also the cooper to see, the ironmonger to pay, Mistress Simister the seamstress to call upon about the new tunic for Betje, and, finally, the farrier to organize.

Wiping a hand across my brow, I grimaced at the thought of what lay ahead with the bells for sext due to sound. Yet, for all my fatigue, my exertions were nothing to what they could have been. Though each brew, the maintenance of the equipment, and the tasks allotted to each servant were my responsibility, I didn't have to concern myself with such mundane tasks as cooking food or finding the money for rent or for the constant supplies required to brew in the quantities I demanded. Here at The Swanne so many of these duties were either shared or taken from me altogether. I'd not appreciated how much easier it would make the whole experience, nor what having a legitimate business partner entailed. Typically generous, Alyson gave me whoever she could spare to help—the only caveat was that I trained them. Juliana and Yolande both showed an interest and were thus assigned to me exclusively, and replacements found to take over their work upstairs. Harry spent at least half his day with us and Leda and Mabel came when we needed extra hands. Even Master atte Place, who usually only appeared sometime between sext and none, started to arrive earlier, his clothes creased, what remained of his hair disheveled, offering to fetch the water, lug sacks of coal and faggots of wood into the cellar, and roll sealed barrels out into the courtyard and into the storage room at the back of The Swanne, ready to be tapped. In fact, any task that required strength, he took over. All he asked was that he be allowed to enjoy a quiet tankard or two of ale as reward.

For all the help I was given, it still wasn't enough.

Aware that this was a huge undertaking, Alyson would visit at least once a day, casting a discerning and generally approving eye over our work. Most evenings, when the shadows grew, the candles were lit, the fires stoked, the children abed, and the girls of The Swanne entertaining their clients, we would sit in her solar, Adam working on the ledgers, and discuss our plans to turn over a profit.

God forgive me, patience was not one of my virtues. I couldn't help but be reminded of how difficult it had been in Elmham Lenn and how, until Captain Stoyan managed to create a network of customers for us overseas, it didn't matter how many patrons we'd attracted or mazers and tankards of ale, let alone barrels and firkins, we filled, we'd floundered.

"If only I could find a market somewhere—someone who'd buy large quantities."

"Aye," said Alyson, frowning as one of the girls let out a playful shriek. "Pity about your captain."

It was. It wasn't just because of the orders he'd found. I missed Captain Stoyan in so many ways. Adam looked up from where he was annotating the books.

"You may not be able to rely on Captain Stoyan, mistress. But don't you worry, someone will come along."

Alyson grunted. "Listen to Master Adam. Do you think some other merchant prepared to take your brew to the Low Countries will just appear like the Holy Grail to a knight? God knows, we get enough of 'em here and all it takes is for one of them to see a sound business proposition . . . but they may as well be blind for all the good it has done us."

Over the last couple of weeks, she'd tried to persuade a few of her more regular clients, successful merchants, to gamble on exporting the beer. Not prepared to buy the brew outright and risk a loss, even when she'd offered to let them take it on credit, they'd balked. Nothing Alyson did or said could move them. What was unsaid was their reluctance to do business with women.

"They'll trust us with their cocks but not their purses," she'd grumbled. "We just have to hope that as word gets around about the quality of your brew, more of the bathhouses will start to buy their supplies from us. Otherwise, we're going to have more barrels than the king's army, only without their thirst to quench." She glared into her mazer a moment before lifting her head and fixing us with a forced smile. "Summer is all but upon us and with the warmer weather and more daylight, what do people find more time to do?"

She looked at Adam and me brightly, but I was too despondent to answer.

"Why, you addle-headed pair. Drink, of course." She rose to her feet and went to watch the moon haul itself over the horizon. "We'll be fine," she mumbled, her back to us. "All we need is a little more time. All we need is one bastard to place his trust in us . . ."

It was the closest Alyson had come to acknowledging she was troubled, which meant we were in a worse state than she was prepared to admit.

Adam met my anxious look with his own. We both knew time was our enemy here—time and the stubborn merchants of London and Southwark who preferred the watery, diluted ale of the other brewers to the richer, tastier, and stronger kind produced by a female brewer.

God knew, if we couldn't find buyers in Southwark, which was filled with alehouses and the homes of nobles that needed stocking, we never would.

⋘⋙

At first I wasn't sure what woke me. A soft tinkle, like a chime in the breeze, that was quickly followed by an explosion of shattering glass, shouts, and shrill cries. Diving out of bed and reaching for a shawl, I ran into the corridor, my first instinct to check on Betje and the twins. The door to the nursery above was shut and I prayed it remained that way. Positioning myself at the foot of the stairs so I might protect them, I tried to discover the source of the growing commotion.

As I leaned over the railing, I was able to see the floor below. Torches blazed in sconces, casting a mottled light onto the wide corridor. All the doors were currently shut. A scream as loud as a smashed plate made me jump, and two half-naked men, who were twined around each other, burst through one of the doors, splintering the wood and tearing it from the frame, their fists flying, arms flailing, legs pumping, teeth bared, and blood flowing. Grunting and swearing fit to rouse the devil, the men punched, kicked, and bit each other. Other doors opened and men in various stages of dress and undress gathered to watch; some tried to separate the brawlers while others urged them to more violence. Not even the fight in the Cathaline Alehouse the day Will was killed compared. Unable to tear myself away, I watched as one man, his breeches falling, his buttocks on display, tried to wrestle a younger, taller one who looked vaguely familiar, back to the floor.

"Don't tell me there's another fight."

Juliana, who'd taken to sleeping in the nursery, joined me on the landing, shaking her head, her hair tousled and eyes heavy.

"Don't these gents have anything better to do?"

"Have the children woken?" I asked.

"Nay, mistress." She grimaced as another blow landed. "Only me. They'd sleep through the king's coronation, your lot."

By this time, quite an audience had gathered, pulling on shirts and surcoats, tugging on breeches—and on the two floors below as well. Craning their necks, men tried to see, while others dared the stairs, some with swords and daggers drawn. Others took the opportunity to leave, scarpering down the stairs and out of sight. There were more shouts and cries as Alyson appeared. Charging up the stairs, a cresset lamp held aloft, her tunic askew, its laces all untied, a young man in tow, she began barking orders, shoving women and men aside with her shoulders and hand. Master atte Place pushed past his mistress, ignoring the half-naked women clutching remnants of clothing and trying to melt into the walls as he barged along. On seeing the tumult was between two of their fellow carousers, men who'd come expecting a fight sheathed their weapons and exchanged them for shouts of encouragement and groans of disbelief as the older man lost his balance and was pushed through a wall. Alyson bellowed, but they ignored her.

Dazed for a moment, the man took the proffered hand of a stranger who pulled him free. With a roar, he threw himself at his adversary, earning cries of approval.

"This happens often?" I asked Juliana.

"Always on May Day and especially throughout summer."

The women certainly didn't look shocked, more amused. Beside me, Juliana tut-tutted but was clearly enjoying the spectacle. Alyson stood at the top of the first flight of stairs, arms folded, a mixture of impatience and fury on her face. Harry appeared and I saw her whisper something to him before, with obvious reluctance, he raced down the stairs, ducking around those who refused to get out of his way.

Just as the brawl looked to cease, the man who'd made the huge hole in the wall used his considerable weight to swing his fist into the side of his rival's head. The slighter man, more a boy really, staggered with the blow and lost his footing. Toppling heavily against the railing, there was a sickening crunch before the banisters gave way and the young man fell.

Juliana and I gasped and followed his descent. It was all over in an instant. The man, arms circling, legs wheeling, dropped two stories onto the rushes below. Mayhap it was God's grace that he struck another gentleman on the way down. Even so, as he landed on his back, limbs akimbo, there was a sickening, dull thud.

All was silent. Only the hiss of Alyson's cresset lamp going out and a small sob could be heard.

The man didn't move. One leg was bent at a peculiar angle, and one arm was twisted behind his back. Gorge rose in my throat.

Juliana crossed herself. I did too and sent a swift prayer to my Lord.

Then, with a clap of her hands, Alyson took control.

"Back to your rooms, girls. Gentlemen, the doctor and the watch are on their way, the sheriff too, no doubt. I suggest you make yourselves scarce." She stared at the culprit, who, pale-faced, with a swollen lip and half-closed eye, scratches and blood upon his frame, stared in disbelief at the body below. From my vantage point, I could see his straw-colored hair, the look of fear that crossed his face. He might have been older than his victim, but he was still young.

"Is he dead?" he asked.

Juliana sucked in her breath.

All eyes turned to Alyson.

Alyson, who'd disappeared into one of the rooms, reappeared and flung a shirt, coat, and boots at him. "Not yet. I suggest you start praying he doesn't die, your lordship. For not even your family'll be able to avoid royal justice."

Scrambling into his clothes, the man made a sound that was part whimper, part agreement.

"Master atte Place," said Alyson. "See his lordship to a wherry, would you?" Returning to her previous position, she pointed toward the way out. Loitering in the corridor, the women whispered as the men left with as much dignity as they could muster. Among them, I recognized a few lords, Master Rodesmith the goldsmith, and from the accents, a number of Lowlanders. Father Kenton and a couple of the acolytes from the abbey scurried down the stairs, pulling up their hoods. Waiting till they'd passed, Master atte Place gestured for the battered nobleman to follow him.

Alyson raised her brow, looking around. "Didn't you hear me, girls? I said, back to your rooms!"

This time, she was obeyed.

I was about to suggest Juliana return to bed, when there was another uproar on the stairs. Ascending against the tide of escapees was Adam. Behind him was another gentleman in a long dark cape. They temporarily barred the way, making it impossible for Master atte Place to fulfill his duty. There was a standoff as no one moved.

The man in the cape gripped the railing and stood on his toes.

"Goodwife Alyson," he cried in a deep, melodic voice. "I must speak with you immediately."

The landing spun and it was only my hold on the banister that prevented my legs buckling. This could not be happening.

"Mistress?" asked Juliana. "Are you all right?" I stared at her, but her features were dusky, blurred. "You're shaking." She touched me gently on the arm.

Catching my breath, I moved out of the dim light and back into the comfort of the shadows. "Juliana, I'm fine. Look to the twins and Betje, please. Keep them safe." I urged her back to the room.

Waiting until the nursery door was shut again, I closed my eyes.

My chest felt as if it was nothing but a vast chamber in which butterflies cavorted and knives were flung. I reeled from exquisite pleasure to extraordinary pain.

*God, Mother Mary, please, let me be wrong.*

*Let me be right.*

The courage it took for me to peer over the railing again could not be measured. I could no longer hear Alyson's words. I was unaware of the women returning to their rooms, of the still-departing men making their way down two flights of stairs, shrugging on surcoats, tying capes and hoods, or of Master atte Place and the injured lord descending. All my focus was on Alyson, Adam, and the man who earnestly spoke to her. I could see the muscle in Adam's jaw ticcing, Alyson's wide eyes as she regarded the gentleman addressing her, then the sly half-smile that twisted her mouth as she listened to him.

I couldn't tear my eyes from the tall, broad-shouldered figure in a woolen cape standing one step below her with his back to me. Willing him to turn around, to confirm or deny my fears, my hopes, I waited. I didn't breathe. I felt sure my heart had seized.

Then, spinning slowly, as if aware of my unrelenting gaze, he turned and raised his face.

The man on the stairs was none other than Leander Rainford. With a cry, I ran back into my room and slammed the door.

# FORTY-THREE

THE SWANNE

After May Day

*The year of Our Lord 1407 in the eighth
year of the reign of Henry IV*

*W*hen the door opened, there he was—my imagination made suddenly manifest. Beyond it, all was cat-quiet, as if the world had fallen into an enchanted slumber. Only we two were awake, aware. The soft light from the landing framed him, a darker version of the man who, ever since he first entered my life, had transformed my dreams, my desires . . .

*God help me.*

Remaining in the doorway, one hand on the frame, the other holding his cane, his eyes covered the distance. I stood, unashamed of my state of undress, of my linen kirtle and shawl, my hair unraveling from its loose plait and spilling over my shoulders. After all, he always undid my best of intentions.

I'd rehearsed this moment so many times over the months

and yet it was nothing like I'd imagined—not the place, nor the time, nor anything else. I had longed for this man. But that was before the fire destroyed everything, before Westel Calkin, the twins . . .

Before his wife . . .

A voice in my head was insisting I order him away, protect my modesty, my reputation. I said not a word. I simply drank in the vision of him, the waking dream to which the noise of his boots and cane against the rushes gave lie. His approach released the sweet scent of lavender, pine, and other wild fragrances. Inhaling, my breath escaped atremble, my fingers sought the solidness of the bedpost. Could he sense the effect he had on me?

He paused little more than an arm's length away. My throat grew dry, words fled. Damn him. In the silvery light, his face was a mixture of dark angles and gray planes, his eyes pools that shone with secret depths. There was a splash outside followed by the caterwaul of a night creature. Dogs began to bark. I twisted toward the sounds, the moonlight capturing me.

Sir Leander hadn't moved, yet his cape was still restless against his boots. Tendrils of black hair brushed against his face in ways I envied. Still I could not read his eyes, his face, while my own, bathed in silver, turned back to him. He had the advantage. How he must feel that after all this time. That he should find me here, in a bathhouse, wearing only a thin shift that did nothing to conceal either my doubts or desire. Was he here to punish? To accuse? God knew, I deserved both.

And yet . . . this was not what I sensed, not what his body, in its unerring stillness, confided to me.

There was so much I wanted to say, to feel, to do. Everything I'd kept buried inside me was poised to escape, buttressed against my lips, hands, and thighs.

Finally, he spoke.

"You look terrible."

I blinked. Mortification heated my face. My hand flew to my cheek, hair, and chest, returning to my hair again. He was right. I was disheveled, unruly; more than that, I was wrong. Sweet Mother Mary, I was in a bathhouse, living in the notorious Stews. I didn't only appear terrible, I was.

The absurdity of my situation, the fires of anticipation being doused so thoroughly and unexpectedly, seemed suddenly comical.

My lips quivered. Clutching the bedpost harder, I threw back my head and laughed. Tears flowed down my cheeks as I raised my eyes and shook my head. How long this went on, I'm not certain.

"Anneke?"

The power of my name upon his lips quieted me. My mirth quickly died and I dashed the tears from my eyes.

"Forgive me, my lord. I'd forgotten the gift you have with words."

A low chuckle issued, turning into a chortle. "I do, don't I. And only you would remind me of my talent." With a smile that caused my heart to flip, he propped his cane against the bed and opened his arms. I hesitated. There would be no going back if I entered them and what was being offered by such an improper embrace, in my bedroom, no less—no standing on virtue or respectability. I would tumble down the social scale even further and become a fallen woman in every respect.

Before I could act, there was the ragged sound of a throat being cleared.

"Mistress?"

Sir Leander's arms dropped.

Loitering in the doorway like a chaperone was Adam. Protective, uncertain, with that one word he told me what was at stake.

With my eyes still fixed upon Sir Leander lest he disappear, I answered, "It's all right, Adam. You may leave us."

"But, mistress—" he began, before a hand gripped his shoulder.

It was Alyson.

"I need you to help me with the lad downstairs, Master Adam."

Good God. Sir Leander's presence made everything else flee my mind. The young man. "Is he . . . is he dead?" I asked.

"Dead drunk," said Alyson. "He's twisted his ankle and hurt his arm along with his pride—nothing that can't be fixed. Master Vetazes, Mistress Vetazes's husband, is with him now, and the sheriff will want a word too, no doubt. The Honorable John Tiptoft doesn't want to make a fuss; he certainly doesn't want his father alerted, so I fancy the sheriff may have to find other things to occupy his time." She shook her head, her eyes narrowing as she regarded Sir Leander, who hadn't moved. "Listen to your mistress. You're not needed here, Master Adam, so how about you come with me."

Alyson led Adam away, casting one last, lingering look at me as she closed the door.

Their footsteps faded. We listened to the house settling, the distant sounds of female voices, the river lapping its banks.

If I lifted my hand, I could have touched his face. Instead, I brushed a stray hair from my cheek. His eyes, which gleamed in the half-light, followed my hand before, stepping closer, his fingers took over from mine, and he cupped my face.

He bent slightly so his eyes met mine. We didn't speak, but drank each other in. Our breath mingled and a soft light twinkled in those midnight eyes. My hand closed over his.

"I've traveled the length and breadth of this country searching for you."

"I know," I whispered.

"I would have searched the world."

"You've found me."

"I have."

He drew me closer.

As his lips met mine, everything that had happened between us, and all that had not, melted into this moment. All the months of grief, anxiety, hardship, and fear slipped away. My shawl slid down my back to curl in a shimmering bundle at my feet.

As I pressed myself to him, wanting to merge with his strength and warmth, something deep inside me unfastened, like a key turned in a lock. Feelings I'd denied flooded my body, expanding me in directions I'd not imagined. I sailed on an ocean of sensation. Waves of longing washed over me, making my fingers tingle and the hot center of my loins ache. The time for pretense was over. Leander was here, holding me and, as his lips left mine to capture my chin, eyelids, temples, and neck, loving me as well.

His hand caressed a trail through my hair, releasing it from its messy confines, before finding my shoulder and tracing the curve of my back with firm but gentle fingers. Pulling me against him, his mouth returned to mine, and his kiss deepened.

My hands did their own exploring. I was bold, eager; a conqueror claiming my territory, staking my claim. I curled the fingers of one hand around the hair at the base of his neck while my other teased the laces at his throat, pulled them apart then found the solidity of his chest. I replaced my fingers with my lips and tongue.

Groaning, he lifted me off my feet, his mouth wild, his fingers touching, probing, caressing. I gasped, threw back my head and arched my back.

As if I were made of gold leaf and might fall apart, he placed me on the bed. I held out my arms to beckon him back. Aware my shift had slipped off one shoulder, the fabric resting precariously on the crest of my bosom, I did nothing to alter my state of déshabillé. Sir Leander's eyes widened, lingering upon my flesh, caressing me with his hot gaze, and I reveled in the ardor my body aroused in him and which matched my own.

"Good God, Anneke," he said, staring. "Don't tempt me." With one knee upon the mattress, he lowered my arms to my sides. With a sigh, he lifted my shift into a more decorous position. His touch left a burning trail that only ceased when he released the fabric.

Moving away to a safe distance, he studied me, and his face softened. "I thought—" he began. "I thought all I wanted, all I needed, was to see you, to reassure myself that you'd survived. That you were unharmed. That what happened at Holcroft House, at Elmham Lenn, hadn't marked you."

He searched my face. I lowered my gaze. I was marked, surely he could see that; marked by the losses I'd suffered and by those who would brand me slattern and murderer. My marks may not be visible but they were no less indelible. I was a changed woman. I would not be here, in Southwark, in The Swanne, welcoming him the way a harlot does her gentleman, except for what happened all those months ago.

The scars I bore were nothing to those Betje carried. I wondered how he'd react when he set eyes upon her.

"You can see for yourself," I said, sitting up, ensuring my shift stayed in place this time. "I am well."

"Are you?" He waited. "Anneke . . . God. I don't know what to say. Sometimes, the only means we have to express how we feel are so inadequate." He took my hand back in his, his thumb stroking my palm. I shivered. "What I'm trying to say, very badly, is now that I've seen you, I can no longer pretend. I want, no, dear God, I need more. I was a fool to think seeing you alone would be enough."

Only in my most private and wicked of longings, did Sir Leander admit to such things. Yet here he was, saying them and so much more. I didn't dare speak.

"My greatest regret is that I wasn't there to protect you, to defend you, Karel, Saskia, and the others. Jesù"—he struck his forehead—"I was not even there to comfort you. Can you ever forgive me?"

"Nay, you were busy exchanging vows, feasting, celebrating your wife. The wife you chose not to tell me about, passing that task to my brother."

"Anneke, it wasn't—"

I didn't let him finish. "You need no forgiveness, my lord. It was not your duty to do any of those things." I winced at how prim I sounded.

So did Sir Leander. "I'm not talking about duty," he snapped. "God, Anneke. I'm talking about what's right." His hand resided briefly over his heart.

I thought about that. What was right. Nothing about what had happened was right—not Will's death, Saskia's, Louisa's, and certainly not Karel's. It wasn't right that Betje was burned or that Westel Calkin unleashed his brutality upon me. It wasn't right that out of such a violent union, two such gentle souls had been produced. It wasn't right that I, Anneke Sheldrake, daughter of a merchant, was reduced to living in a bathhouse in Southwark and forced to make a living from brewing. It wasn't right that the man I wanted and needed was married to another and beyond my reach. Yet all these things had happened.

Right had nothing to do with any of it.

"And it's right that you're here?" I bit back. Sir Leander's whore had grown teeth. "That you abandoned your wife—oh aye, just as you have made a point of learning of my folly, I too have learned of yours—to search for your squire's sister?"

"You're more to me than my squire's sister, Anneke."

"It's Anna now."

"Not to me. Never to me. You'll always be Anneke."

Turning my head aside so he couldn't see the tears that welled, I shut my eyes and took a deep breath. Once, I'd longed to hear those words from his mouth. But that was in a different time, when daydreams were still possible, before a monster had ripped those from me and destroyed my family with the flames of his hatred . . .

But that wasn't true either. I would be the phoenix, the creature who rose from the ashes to soar among the clouds, stronger than before. After all, was I not taking another chance with the brewery? Was I not risking all to make a living? Why not with love as well? After all I'd lost, did I not deserve that?

I no longer had a maidenhead to barter for a title or wealth through marriage. What remained—my body, my love—didn't need to be sold. My brewing and Alyson's support allowed me that choice at least. From here on I could choose to give both to whomever I wanted.

All this raced through my head in the time it took Sir Leander to retie his cape. He picked up his cane again, melancholy etched upon his features, as if he were mourning an end. Before he could step out of reach, I rose to my knees and grabbed the edges of his cape. Was it love he was offering? Did it matter?

Lightning split the sky, followed closely by a long low growl of thunder. Dogs began to howl.

When he turned around, questions on his lips, I let go of his clothes and ever so slowly, my cheeks flaming at my daring, drew my shift over my head and threw it to the floor. I shook out my hair until it draped my body, an unruly veil of russet and red.

Drawing his breath in sharply, Sir Leander took me hostage with his eyes. "Anneke." My name became music, a wild note to which my heart danced.

He stood motionless, only the muscle in his cheek and the throbbing vein in his neck evidence of his perturbation. I willed him to touch me, to ignite the passion bubbling inside us both.

"Do I look so very terrible?" I asked.

Sir Leander gave a bark of laughter, his twinkling eyes capturing every last inch of me, his mouth curving into an appreciative smile.

"Terribly beautiful. Good God, woman. What are you doing to me?"

Unable to wait any longer, I began to undo his laces, pushing the heavy wool cape from his shoulders. It tumbled onto the rushes, followed by his cane, which struck the wood of the bed like a clarion, a call to love.

Clasping my face in his hands, he forced me to look at him. "You're playing with fire, Anneke," he said, unaware of the effect his words had upon me. I was the phoenix, after all. Fire was my element. From its ashes I would rise.

"If I don't leave now, I never will," he said.

Taking his hands, I placed them upon my breasts, gasping as they filled his warm, busy hands, and drew him closer and closer still, falling back onto the bed so he was forced to follow. With a groan that echoed in his chest and in the darkness outside, he bent to kiss me.

Placing my lips softly against his, I murmured.

"Only if that's a promise . . ."

# FORTY-FOUR

THE SWANNE

The next day

*The year of Our Lord 1407 in the eighth*

*year of the reign of Henry IV*

*N*ever before had I so appreciated the artistry of the troubadours and poets, how they could capture an emotion with a mere word or phrase. Pain, sorrow, grief, loss, joy, aye, all these, but the manner in which they described the greatest of sensations— love—made me marvel at their gifts. Had not a thousand ships been launched in love's name? A war of ten years fought for it? Had not Socrates dedicated an entire symposium to defining what this strange and wonderful affliction was? To be able to chronicle the feelings that course through one's heart and head, one's body, the irrational thoughts, the daring and belief in the impossible, was surely indicative of God's grace.

For certes, it was beyond my abilities.

Thus as I lay abed, watching the weak gray light of morning play across the ceiling, although I knew the coming day was likely to be dull and cloudy, I could swear the blessed sun flowed through my window, promising nothing but warmth and luminosity.

I stared at the man who lay sound asleep beside me, his smooth chest rising and falling, his long lashes sweeping his cheeks, the dark bristles of new growth the only shadow on this bright, glorious dawn. It took all my willpower not to rouse him with a kiss or, my cheeks colored as my eyes dropped to the area between his thighs, covered by only a sheet, some other means.

Smiling, I rose quietly, relishing my nakedness for perhaps the first time in my life. Told my body was made for sin, I'd felt ashamed of what I possessed. No more. If what I enjoyed with Leander was a sin, I would embrace it over and over and rename myself Eve.

Or Lilith.

Washing myself quickly with the water from the ewer and basin on the cupboard, my eyes journeyed back toward the bed and my sleeping lover.

Lover. Leander. How beautiful those words sounded together. How right.

I dressed in my kirtle and tunic, binding up my hair, which Leander had so thoroughly tousled. "If you knew how I've longed to do this," he'd said and twined his fingers through it, using my locks to caress my nipples, my thighs, to hold me in place while his lips ventured where I'd ne'er guessed they'd dare . . . I replayed the night—not so much our lovemaking, that was easy, a mere heartbeat or breath away, sending darts of pleasure throughout my sated body—but our conversation.

We'd talked of Elmham Lenn, of what happened after he left—the alehouse, the fire, the deaths. He'd held me close as, for the first time in months, I quietly wept. Tangled in his naked limbs, secure, I found a haven. We spoke of Westel. I didn't need to elaborate. He knew.

"His price was not high enough," he muttered darkly, referring to his death in the fire that consumed the house and so much more. Upon that, we were agreed.

We talked of his marriage, of his wife the Lady Cecilia and, as strange as it sounds, I loved him more that he didn't ignore her. Begging forgiveness that he didn't relay the news of his nuptials to me himself, he admitted that at first he was relieved to pass the task to Tobias.

"As soon as the feeling swept me, I knew I must not shun my duty and told your brother the same. That I would write. But when he suggested you might misconstrue my intentions, I understood it was a test."

"A test? Oh. As to whether or not my feelings were reciprocated."

"Aye. Or mine. You see, I knew my own heart. Of yours, I was less certain. I could not have your brother broker our relations, especially with my wedding imminent, nor did I want him confirming his suspicions. I knew you would bear the brunt of his wrath. Tobias has firm ideas of propriety." He smiled fondly. "Thus, I said nothing. Can you forgive me?"

I did.

Their marriage was one of convenience, and though his wife was not told why he had cut short their honeymoon, she didn't complain either. Ensconced in their London house, Ashlar Place, Lady Cecilia was preoccupied with ordering new furniture and fabrics and ensuring the servants were disciplined and the household efficient. "All that a woman of her station should," I'd muttered, without rancor or envy. Mayhap, there was a little of the latter. How could there not be when my days were spent arranging grain, water, coal, and wood and worrying whether the servants had emptied the mash tuns or the troughs on time, whether the right herbs were added, the water temperature was just so, and the wort boiled for the correct amount of time. If it wasn't these details preoccupying me, it was whether the ale-conners passed a brew or if all our barrels would sell.

Lady Cecilia may be accommodated in Rainford property, have a right to use the family seal and claim the name, and, possibly, bear children (though she wasn't young, I reassured myself on that count, being at least thirty-five), but she did not reside in Leander's heart.

That was mine. All mine.

Around me, the house began to stir. The pitter-patter of feet across rushes, the closing of doors and hushed greetings sounded. From outside came the clomp of hooves and the cries of bakers and other vendors peddling their wares on the way to market.

As I sat to lace my boots, it occurred to me there was only one difficult topic of conversation between Leander and me: Tobias.

After Elmham Lenn, Leander had sent Tobias back to London to join Lady Cecilia and hadn't seen him since. All he could tell me was that dealing with Karel's death, the fire, and Betje's injuries had not been easy for my brother and that he'd spent a great deal of time praying.

"For Karel's soul," I whispered in the dark.

Leander didn't respond immediately. "Nay, my love, for yours."

Tobias wasn't alone in blaming me for what occurred; I couldn't condemn him for that. Then why did I feel . . . betrayed? Abandoned by my own? No matter how I tried to justify his reaction, it rankled.

"You will be reconciled," said Leander. "I will make sure."

Nestled in his arms, it would have been easy to believe, to allow him to order Tobias to behave cordially toward me, but it wouldn't work. Tobias and I had to reach our own accord, not have one negotiated by his master. Otherwise we'd be like England and France, forever snarling across roiling waters, always trying to seize territory from each other or, worse, pretending affection. I couldn't bear that.

I explained this to Leander and he fell silent, stroking my hair, his beating heart offering consolation of one kind while the lingering taste of him on my tongue presented another. There was only one subject we hadn't yet discussed and, as I drifted off to sleep, I knew I would have to broach it soon.

Leaving him to sleep, I closed the bedroom door behind me and hesitated, wondering if there was time to see the twins before I went about my business. The babble of voices from below was the answer. The day had begun without me. Ambivalent about not bidding my babes good morning, as was my custom, but knowing they would be brought to me later, I swiftly ran down the stairs. When I reached the lower floors, servants were sweeping out the large fireplace in the hall; Alyson's voice carried through an open door, Adam answered her with less animation, while in the kitchen and beyond, the oven was stoked, bread was rising on the counter, pails of milk were being slopped over the floor, and a pottage was being nursed back to life. Greetings were exchanged along with a couple of knowing looks. No doubt, the reason for my lateness would be a source of gossip.

Warmth flooded my body, the notion not nearly as disturbing as mayhap it should be.

Opening the cellar door, I descended the stairs to the brewery, praying no one else had yet arrived, for while my babes would forgive my absence this morn, the wort and corner crones would not.

The Lady Fortune was with me. The brewery was deserted. Lighting only one torch and throwing some kindling into the kiln and ensuring it took, I bent over the troughs and, gently parting the foam that had built up overnight, lowered my arm and sang the ale to life. After all the rushing I'd done, peace descended. Here, before the trough, alone with the brew I'd created, I was able to pause, to enjoy the solitariness of the experience, the coolness of the liquid, the way it clung to my arm, like a lover . . . a smile tugged my mouth. *Aye, like a lover.*

Feelings ascended from that secret part of me, the place I'd refused to seek, and filled me with such ecstasy, I was tingling from my head to the soles of my feet, as if I were a fuse about to erupt into a dancing flame. The song deepened, strengthened, each word carrying with it the love I bore for the man lying in my bed.

All this was imparted into the ale and, I swear upon the sacred soul of the Blessed Mother Mary, the brew began to glow.

Withdrawing my arm, I continued to sing, lost in the haunting, joyous melody. Dipping a beaker into the gleaming liquid, I held it aloft before honoring the corner crones. Singing to the wise old women of ale, I knew as they lapped my offering, they also imbibed memories of the evening before and my intense pleasure. That was how Emma and Constance, my children tucked against their sides, found me. Their mouths dropped open, not in wonder, but discomfort. This was an unholy celebration of the kind the church preached against. I saw it in their eyes, their cautious smiles. I didn't care.

A gross error of judgment on my part—but I was not to know that until much later.

Both babes broke into wide smiles as I walked toward them, my arms outstretched, the ale-song only drawing to a close as I took Isabella from Emma and spun her in my arms, kissing her soundly, stroking her face and tickling, before returning her and taking Karel from Constance in her stead. This time, as I embraced my child, I started singing a well-known ditty:

*"Ale makes many a man to stick upon a briar,*
*Ale makes many a man to slumber by the fire,*
*Ale makes many a man to wallow in the mire.*
*So doll, doll, doll thy ale, doll, doll, doll—"*

Each time I sang "doll" I bounced Karel in the air and he giggled; Isabella, seeing her twin so happy, responded with her own. The wet nurses relaxed—who can remain wary around a laughing babe, let alone two? Soon the women joined my song, as did Harry and Adam when they entered. Adam moved in circles around me, lighting the remaining torches and flinging open the window, dodging the mash tuns, table, and barrels, while Harry clapped a rhythm before taking Isabella from Emma in order to caper across the floor. The babes were chuckling, their eyes sparkling. The fire began to crackle and the smell of malted barley and wort filled the cellar.

*"Ale makes many a man to stumble on a stone,*
*Ale makes many a man to stagger drunken home—"*

I froze. Standing on the steps was Leander. Dressed in his surcoat and breeches, his boots shone and the creamy fabric of his shirt rested against the golden skin of his neck. His cape was draped over the arm that held his cane. Beside him was Betje, her hand tucked firmly in his. She was sucking the ends of her plait, a grin on her face.

Panting, I stopped singing but the others continued, their dance only slowing when they realized I'd ceased. Slowly, the song died too, though Harry didn't want to stop.

"Look who's here, Anna," said Betje, tugging at Leander's hand so he might move down the stairs. Juliana must have helped her dress. She wore a brown tunic over a green kirtle, a matching cap on her head. I was nonplussed, as she did nothing to try and hide her face or arm, but Leander did not seem repulsed. I could hear my heart beating in my ears.

"Sir Leander couldn't find you," she said. "But I knew where you'd be. She's always here," she confided to Leander, who nodded solemnly.

"Thank you, sweetling." I smiled at Betje, who, understanding Sir Leander wasn't going to move, shrugged but remained by his side, her wise eyes fixed upon mine, waiting.

"My lord," I began, tucking an objecting Karel under one arm and pushing my hair off my face with another. "You're awake."

"So I am. At least, I think so."

Pretending to be interested in the brewery, he began a slow perusal of it from where he stood on the steps, but the tension in his body shouted it wasn't my brewing that preoccupied him, but the child on my hip and the other in Harry's arms.

Not for the first time, I wished I'd spoken of the babes last night. Whereas discussing what had happened to Betje and

Karel and the others had occupied a great deal of time, the opportunity to tell him about the twins never arose . . . Oh, craven that I was, I never created it and now I was to pay the price. Dread filled my soul. There was no help for it, I approached the stairs, whipping Karel's bonnet from his head so Leander might see his fine head of flaxen hair, the clarity of his green eyes, and know him for what he was—mine.

Drawing closer, Leander stroked Betje's hand with his thumb in a gesture of affection, but sadness emanated from him. My stomach flipped—was it for Betje or someone or something else?

"This is my son, Karel," I said softly, and, with a forced smile, raised him so Sir Leander might see him better.

Sir Leander nodded. "And who is this?" He jerked his head toward Isabella.

"That's my niece," said Betje. "Her name is Isabella. She's not burned."

"Indeed she's not. And she possesses a beautiful name," said Sir Leander. "Almost as lovely as Betje."

Betje's shoulders lifted as she smiled and then studied her boots.

Though I could have kissed him, I frowned. "It's Betty, my lord."

"It's not."

I leaned forward so my words might be for his ears alone. Karel wriggled, forcing me to transfer him to my other hip.

"Aye, Leander, it is. Please, these are the names we go by now. They"—my eyes darted to Harry and the wet nurses—"don't know who we are."

Lifting his eyes from Karel, he regarded me strangely.

Releasing Betje's hand, Leander brought his lips close to my ear. "I knew you were no maiden, my love, but a mother?" He leaned back so he could look into my eyes. "I don't know who you are either," he said with more force.

Before I could respond, he gave Betje a small bow and, without another word, took the stairs two at a time and disappeared.

Once his steps retreated, the steady drip of a pipe, the whinny of a horse, and the snap of wood was all that could be heard.

"For certes, mistress, that's a fine-looking gentleman. Who was he?" said Constance, taking Isabella from Harry and straightening her little bonnet.

"Our brother's master," said Betje, looking toward Adam for confirmation, but he was too busy staring at me. "He's our friend."

"Well, well, well, aren't you the lucky one." Emma laughed and fetched Karel from my inert arms. "That's a mighty fancy friend." She shook her head in disbelief. "Come on then, back to the nursery for you two. Time for your mother to return to work."

I remained where I was as the twins were taken upstairs.

Chatter carried from the kitchen as Emma and Constance regaled the servants with descriptions of the handsome tall gent with the cane. The one clearly smitten with our Anna.

If my heart had not been so leaden, I might have smiled. "Our Anna." Instead, I retraced Leander's rapid exit, recalling the way his surcoat flapped, how his cane struck the steps, and the echoing click of his boots. For someone who last night had been reluctant to leave, this morning he couldn't depart quickly enough. My happiness fled after him, my earlier exuberance replaced by hollowness and dismay.

*Oh, why hadn't I told him about the children?*

Because, if truth be told, I feared exactly what had just happened.

Not only had Sir Leander vanished from The Swanne, it was more than evident he'd forsaken me, a lecherous, untrustworthy whore, as well. Once again, he was gone from my life.

I sank onto the steps and, aware of Betje and Harry, tried not to cry.

# FORTY-FIVE

THE SWANNE
St. John at Port Latin Day
*The year of Our Lord 1407 in the eighth
year of the reign of Henry IV*

Can you blame me that I doubted Sir Leander? Yet four days later, before the bells for tierce had even sounded, he was squatting in the courtyard, not caring that the edges of his embroidered surcoat skimmed the dust, talking to my sister as if nothing was amiss and he hadn't torn my heart from my body and trampled it in the very dirt upon which he knelt. I watched him from the shadows of the mews, holding the sack of hops an Easterling courier had just brought me against my chest.

Seeing him with Betje, listening earnestly to the answer she gave him to his question about the doll she was holding, I was like a wilting flower given moisture. Thirsting for what only he could provide, I unfurled and in doing so, discovered another aspect to him.

Unlike others who encountered Betje and turned away, he was able to see beyond the terrible scars to the person behind them. Taking Tansy when she offered the doll up for closer scrutiny, he smoothed the woolen hair and stroked the wooden face before returning the toy. Betje tucked the doll under one arm, and smiled at Sir Leander, her puckered little mouth curving in a bow. I couldn't hear what they were saying, but when Betje pointed toward the door leading to the brewery, my heart dislodged.

Taking his hand, Betje began to steer him across the courtyard, her limp a minor variation of Sir Leander's own. Seeing them together, so relaxed and natural, quite undid me. I waited till they'd passed then stepped from my hiding place.

"God give you good day, my lord."

Spinning around slowly, Sir Leander waited for me to reach his side.

Betje was not so reticent. She crossed the distance and took my free hand, leading me forward as fast as she was able.

"Anna," she said eagerly, "you have a visitor." Did I? Or was there another reason he was at The Swanne?

For all I tried to pretend to Betje that Sir Leander's sudden departure hadn't affected me badly, I'd failed. My little sister knew; so did Adam, Juliana, Harry, Yolande—in fact everyone at The Swanne. Alyson had made that clear to me.

My plans to remain indifferent came swiftly undone once I saw those eyes. It was as if he plucked my laces and divested me of my garments right there in the courtyard, so bold was his gaze, so full of longing. I stumbled and would have fallen except he released Betje and grabbed my arm, keeping me upright.

His fingers were like a brand upon my flesh.

"You must be more careful, mistress," he said softly. Somehow, he knew what caused my clumsiness. I blushed.

"Aye, I should." Shaking his hand off, I transferred the hops to my other hip. "I cannot tarry. If you wish to see me, you'll have to follow. I must add this to my wort." I kept walking and, to my surprise, unease, and no small degree of pleasure, Sir Leander fell in step beside me. Before I could quiz him further, there was a jangle of harness and a welcome shout behind. Adam and Harry rode Shelby through the gates, the cart stacked with barrels of water filled from beyond the millpond. A wave of relief washed over me. We had quality water for our ale. They waved a greeting.

Betje tugged my tunic.

"Off you go then." She'd been loitering in the courtyard waiting for Harry's return. "But make sure you're both in the brewery by the time the bells sound," I called. She lifted her hand to show she'd heard.

"God's truth, my lord," I said as soon as Betje was out of earshot. "I didn't expect to see you here again."

"And why is that?"

His genuine question took me by surprise. "Not after what you said to me."

Stopping in his tracks, he grabbed my arm, forcing me to halt as well. "I'm afraid my memory isn't serving at present. You'll have to remind me. What ill-mannered words are being attributed to me now?"

"You really don't remember?"

The early sun was in my eyes. It was one of those mornings that promised a warm day to come; the type of day for lovers to linger in shady groves or loll in long grass and share secrets of the heart. It was a good day to barrel beer and start a fresh brew of ale as well. I'd no time for this. With a sigh, I sheltered my face with a hand so I didn't squint.

"I find it hard to believe you can't recall what you said, so clear was your intention." He raised his brows. "You said you didn't know me anymore." I glanced around to make sure no one could hear, then leaned toward him, lowering my voice. "That while you knew I was no maiden, a mother was beyond your ken."

"I said that?"

I extracted my arm from his grip and gave him a level, serious look. "In not so many words."

Genuinely bemused, he scratched his head, his cap sliding back on his dark locks. "Anneke, I'm at a loss. This is the source of your displeasure? Is it not the truth? You're a mother, are you not? Of two lovely children. Unless my brain has been completely addled by the vast amounts of ale we drank that night, you failed to mention Isabella and Karel to me, did you not?"

"Aye, but—"

"I merely pointed out what you omitted. I didn't know you were a mother; therefore, I do not know you anymore. I thought you'd understand, I look forward to the prospect of getting to know the new Anneke, the one who calls herself Anna."

"But you left so abruptly—"

"Waking to find you gone, I came downstairs to bid you farewell . . . and thank you." He cocked his head. "I may have trouble recalling my exact words in the brewery but my memory serves me very well when it comes to the night we shared."

Heat swept my body and I found it hard to remain still.

"You had work to do," he continued. "Aye, I was most surprised to discover you had children, but is it not the common theme of nature when relations are had between a man and a woman, whether those are wanted or not? I was surprised, but no more or less. You are who and what you are, Anneke Sheldrake—Anna de Winter—and I love you for all of that."

I blinked back tears.

His voice softened. "Anneke, your duty called, so did mine. You are a mother and a brewer first. I was required at Westminster—but I'm also a husband. The Lady Cecilia would expect me to break fast with her, so I left. I would only have been in the way . . ."

I hugged the sack to my breast. The stone that had lodged itself in my core ever since I last saw him began to crumble and it was all I could do to remain anchored to the ground. I felt so light I thought I would ascend to the heavens.

"I believed you were seriously offended. That you were shocked to discover I was a mother with no husband." I began to speak quickly, words tripping over themselves. To my chagrin, tears began to spill. "I thought you were disgusted . . . full of regret for what had passed between us—"

"And determined to quit your sight?"

"It's been four days." A single tear traveled down my cheek. I lowered my gaze and turned my head aside. "Nary a word."

Leander's fingers gently captured my chin.

"The longest days of my life thus far." He sighed. "Ah, my love. You think so poorly of me that my love must be conditional? That your experiences cannot alter and shape you, but must leave you untouched, like a statue or religious relic? That is not love. That is possession, or obsession. You have my heart in your keeping, my little brewster—mother or no."

I couldn't respond.

He tilted my face so I was forced to look at him, and continued. "I love you, Anneke Sheldrake—all right, all right, Anna de Winter. That cold glare could dim the sun." He laughed and went to press his lips to my mouth, before remembering himself. For what it was worth, he would protect my reputation, the distinction between me and the other women who inhabited The Swanne—not that many saw a difference. I lived in a bathhouse; that defined me. Not for Sir Leander. Instead, he passed a fleeting finger over my lips and released me, but his gaze kissed not just my mouth but also every part of my flesh.

Adam caught my eye then looked away, shaking his head, a big smile upon his face. Always vigilant, always worrying. Though I knew he wanted so much more for me—marriage to a gentleman, a home to call my own, children with a father—he understood it was not to be my lot and was content if I could at least have love.

And I did. I gazed at Leander. The love of a good man.

The coal merchant, the farrier, and a couple of the maids passing through the courtyard paused to look at the strange tableau we presented, the tall nobleman with his cane, the untidy brewster. Uncomfortable now, I tried to think of what to say, what to do next.

"Back to work, all of you," called a familiar voice, and Alyson arrived, her scarlet tunic flapping around her ankles as she pointed at the offenders. Immediately, everyone scurried back to their tasks, casting last glances over their shoulders to see what she would say to me. When she caught sight of Sir Leander, her step slowed and her hips began to sway. A broad grin split her face.

"God give you good day, Sir Leander." She bobbed her head.

"I'm glad to see you here, milord." She gave me a knowing look. "Glad my summation of you hasn't proved false." Alyson had defended Leander's intentions from the outset. My cheeks grew warm.

Alyson smiled smugly before a frown knitted her brows. "Haven't you got ale to make?" She nodded toward the sack I still carried.

"And beer." I raised the hops. "All the way from Holland."

Alyson screwed up her nose as she leaned in and caught the heady aroma. It wasn't to everyone's taste.

"Well, you'd best get on with it then, hadn't you? Even if customers are harder to come by than that stuff."

It was the first time I'd heard Alyson publicly acknowledge that our ale and beer weren't selling in the quantities we'd hoped. I wished I could reassure her. But everything had already been said, over and over, and nothing altered.

Aware that Leander was listening, I shot her a warning glance. Though I'd told him about some of the problems we were experiencing, I didn't want him to know the extent of them, nor that there wasn't a ready solution in sight. This was something I had to sort for myself.

"Alyson is right, I must get going. The wort will be boiling and this must be added—" I gestured to the hops with my chin. I gazed at Leander, who was deep in thought. I didn't want to leave, yet my brew called. "Was there anything else, my lord?" I asked, keeping my voice level, the hope at bay.

Leander glanced at me, the hops, then Alyson. The bells for tierce pealed, and a flock of doves rose, little gray arrows winging their way east. As the last note faded, it was replaced by the distant cries of vendors making their way to the bridge and London, our everyday choir.

"There was something," said Leander slowly. "I wanted to speak to both of you, as it happens."

"Both of us?" Alyson couldn't disguise her surprise.

"I've come to place an order for ale *and* beer."

"For whom?" I asked, taken aback.

"For Ashlar Place."

I stared at him aghast. That was his house in London, by all accounts a beautiful stone affair, three stories high with moldings, gargoyles, wooden and tiled floors, and glass in every window. It even had a garderobe for each bedroom. It was said to rival The Savoy.

Alyson clapped her hands together in glee. "Ashlar Place! By God, you know how to make a woman happy, milord." She shot Leander a hard look. "How much do you want?"

"Enough to cover the summer months, for now. Beyond that, we'll see, but I hope to supply my ships as well. They'll be leaving for Venice in the next week and I want them well provided."

Alyson's eyes widened as she quickly did the calculations. "My, oh my." She searched for my wrist and gave it a brief squeeze. "This is what we've been waiting for!" She laughed. "A decent order *and* from a nobleman. You wait, once word of this gets out, there'll be no stopping us." She raised her hands to the sky in an attitude of prayer. "Knew You wouldn't let me down, though You had me worried for a while."

Leander grinned. I found it hard to return his smile or share Alyson's joy. It was wonderful we had an order, and from a Rainford, it really was, and Alyson was right, this was the opportunity, the breakthrough we needed. So why then did I feel uneasy? Was it because I could never be sure if it was because my brew deserved such recognition or because it was driven by a sense of obligation? Did it matter?

Silly as it was, to me it did.

Once, I wanted nothing more than to be a maiden from the old tales, rescued from peril at the last moment by a handsome prince. No longer. Oh, I still wanted my prince, who would not? Leander Rainford was the prince of dreams, but was he mine? His heart belonged to me, but in the eyes of the world he belonged to another woman. Was I so very contrary that I wanted to face my perils on my own? Reluctant customers, the Mystery of Brewers, and vindictive officials like Master Fynk— these were *my* hardships to overcome.

Even as ambivalence roiled within me, I loved this man for making such an offer. I had to thank him for his generosity, let him know how much it meant. I also had to tell him that my pride would not allow me to accept. But what about Alyson? We were business partners. I'd no right to let my conceit halt a sale . . . If I spoke to Alyson, she would understand. Had she not made her own way despite five husbands?

Before I could say anything, Alyson had her arm through Leander's and was walking him toward the kitchen door.

"How about you come to my office and we make this official, hey? Master Adam!" she shouted and gestured for him to follow.

Caught in Alyson's enthusiasm, Leander looked back at me and flashed an apologetic smile. When he saw the look on my face he halted. Alyson was brought up short with a great discharge of air.

"Anneke," said Leander, pulling his arm free, "what is this

expression? This frown?" When I did not answer, but lowered my gaze, he sighed. "Ah. I see. Listen, I'm not doing this because I love you—nay, well, that's not true, I am. But I'm also doing it because your ale and beer is the finest I've ever tasted."

I raised my head.

"With all the dinners planned, over summer, the royals we'll be entertaining, I only want the finest served. So does the Lady Cecilia. We also intend to take some to the king's Lancastrian estates for him to enjoy next month."

"The king," whispered Alyson in reverent tones, possibilities mounting in her mind.

I met Leander's steady midnight gaze and saw the truth in his words. "The Lady Brewer makes the finest—and soon everyone will know it."

*The Lady Brewer*, was that what I was called? Or was that how Leander described me? No matter, I liked what it signified.

Not caring that it was broad daylight, or that the laundress and her daughter had come through the gate carrying baskets of linen, or that Betje and Harry were heading in our direction, I reached over and grabbed Leander's shirt and pulled his face down to mine. I kissed him sweetly and for a very long time.

God forgive me, yet again I'd underestimated him. I swore then and there that I would not do so again.

When I drew away, his eyes flickered and darkened. In their sapphire depths, I saw my own desire reflected. I tried to quench the heat rising in my body, to no avail. A spell in the cool cellar would do me good.

Drawing in his breath sharply, Leander grinned. "You don't make it easy for me to offer a persuasive argument when you tender such inducements to give you custom."

Watching us carefully, Alyson began to laugh.

"What's so funny?" I asked.

"That face of yours can't conceal a thing. You may as well just be out with it from the start and save us all the pain."

Tossing my head, I turned on my heel and walked as quickly as I might on trembling legs to the brewery, knowing, despite Alyson's quip, that Leander's dancing, lustful eyes were boring into my back, telling all who saw him that I was indeed *his* lady brewer.

# FORTY-SIX

THE SWANNE
Summer
*The year of Our Lord 1407 in the eighth*
*year of the reign of Henry IV*

By the end of June, we'd sent dozens of barrels to Ashlar
Place. The last delivery accompanied Leander as he left London
and headed north so he and his household, including his wife
and Tobias, could join the king. I would not see Leander again
until after parliament sat at Gloucester in October.

I missed him terribly. Elegant letters, filled with stories of his
travels and the castles in which he stayed and the tournaments
and hunts he participated in, as well as updates of the king's
continuous poor health, did little to compensate for his absence.
Nonetheless, I would lie awake at night and reread them by the
cresset lamp, lingering over the words as memories of our nights
together inserted their way into the accounts.

His absence transformed our lovemaking into sweet recollections that I carefully stowed away like one does precious pieces

of jewelry, taking them out to revel in their sparkle when the household slumbered or during daylight hours to ensure they hadn't tarnished. They served to buttress me against what would be a long summer and filled me with a joy I'd thought would never be mine. Every brew I made, I imagined him drinking it, knowing that each mouthful was born of my passion for him and for what I did.

I tried not to think of him with the Lady Cecilia but ofttimes I would picture the two of them at a magnificent banquet somewhere, sharing the same vessel, he courteously wiping the rim or passing her the most delicate cuts of meat before attending to his own needs. From there my cruel mind would lead me to other intimate moments where they might find themselves together, in her chamber, disrobed, performing those duties that wives and husbands by God's law were obliged.

I'd no right to resent the world in which he was a merchant nobleman, knight of the realm, and husband, with commitments he must meet and burdens he must bear. Yet I did. Now that love had been acknowledged, it flourished in my head, and my heart excused much that, in the depths of my soul, a pardoner would not. How could love be a sin?

But I could not prevent wishing it were different, that the Lady Cecilia didn't exist. Not that it would alter my situation. Leander could no more marry me than move the king's court to Camelot.

I wondered what Lady Cecilia felt when he was with me. Did she know?

Yet I accepted this was the way it must be, for I was a sinner and must serve some penance, even if it was uneasy consideration of Lady Cecelia's sensibilities.

The days rolled into weeks and though I was kept busy, I was also able to enjoy the pleasures that accompanied the growth of my babes. Their tiny bodies fleshed out, their newborn down replaced by cream-colored curls of silkiness. Their noises changed from primitive cries of need to gurgles, squeals, and chuckles of curiosity, happiness, and desire thwarted. When the weather allowed and the brewery permitted a brief respite, I would place either Karel or Isabella in a sling and, with Juliana carrying the other, stroll the streets of Southwark, Harry or Adam providing an escort. We would wander to Moulstrand Dock and along Moss Alley, enjoying Banaster's Garden, catching sight of the jongleurs and jesters performing, or walk along the river toward Winchester Palace, buying a hot pie and some small ale to sustain us and standing aside as a military cavalcade or a group of solemn pilgrims passed by. Roars from the bear garden could be heard and we even encountered the occasional staggering gentleman clutching a bulging purse, eager to spend his winnings from the bear-baiting at one of the gambling dens along Bankside.

A few times we braved the crush of London Bridge with its press of shops and acquisitive vendors. Growing accustomed to the crowds and noise, the combination of wealth and squalor, decency and malevolence, humans and animals, I found each trip became easier and more interesting than the last. Still, I was wary of the oily-voiced vendor or the greasy-haired urchin loitering in my footsteps and would signal to Adam or Harry to make their presence known. From both kind and persnickety hawkers, I purchased everything from ribbons for Alyson and myself and a special gilt-tipped mazer for Adam, to a pretty lace cap for Betje.

Nervous among strangers, Betje chose not to join us, until Harry persuaded me to buy a veil. Finding a piece of fabric among some remnants in a mercer's shop, he lifted it out of the pile, drawing the fine material across the back of his hand. "Mistress! Look. You could sew this onto Betty's cap. Hide her face, like." He held the semi-transparent material over his own. "I can see out, but can you see who's behind?"

I bought the gauze for a price I knew was far too high, but didn't care. That night, I stitched it to a cap for Betje and, the very next day, her features blurred by the pearly veil, she too joined our perambulations.

Growing more confident under Harry's care, Betje's quiet grieving for Karel was slowly exchanged for the comforting presence of her new friend. Watching Harry with my sister, I felt my faith renewed in the goodness of people. He cared for her, without a doubt, and in Harry, Betje found a solace that my presence alone nor the twins could provide.

What I could do was guarantee that Betje, Karel, and Isabella had a secure future. To that end, I continued making ale and beer even though our sales were few and orders, with the exception of that which went to Ashlar Place and Leander, when he was attending the king, nonexistent. This was despite praise for the exceptional quality and fine taste from all who drank it. I despaired. All it would take to alter the situation was for other nobles to place orders for their households, for a few of the borough's many churches to do the same.

Pushing aside my worries, I labored over the mash tuns and the wort and experimented with the beer. With each batch of ale or beer, the ale-conners were summoned. The first few times, the process was smooth. The ale and beer were passed, my measures sealed, and the barrels marked accordingly. I paid the tax and all was well. Relieved, I'd heard of other brewers in Bankside being charged for a range of offenses. Since I scrupulously followed the rules and did nothing to jeopardize my meager sales or the continuance of Leander's order, I believed this wouldn't happen to me.

You would think after my experiences in Elmham Lenn, I wouldn't be so callow.

⋘⋙

Midsummer arrived and quarterage was once more paid to the Borough of Southwark and the bishop's liberty. Whether it was the warmer weather, longer days, or a combination of both, thirsty patrons began to fill the taproom each evening and sales slowly increased. Word spread throughout Bankside and beyond the liberty—the boundaries that denoted where one jurisdiction ended and another's began—and folk we'd not entertained before came to try our ale. Newly arrived Easterlings, learning that beer just like that drunk at home was available, flouted the Stilliard's rules that banned its members from the licentiousness of bathhouses, and became frequent guests. After vespers, when the first stars were twinkling in the firmament, they'd pour into The Swanne, downing tankards and mazers and filling jugs before curfew sent them scuttling back over the river.

Even the hucksters roaming close to the bridge and over by the pillory near Bermondsey Street returned to The Swanne earlier each day, their supplies having been sold. Praise for the ale was plentiful and even the beer was being tasted, though some men swore "it'd ne'er replace our ale."

"Reason you named it 'Son,'" said one patron to Alyson, "is that you know the father is the better man."

Despite the slight resistance to beer, hope that fortune was at last favoring us flowered in our hearts and, as the days passed and we worked hard to replace what was drunk, grew.

Summer's arrival also heralded less propitious experiences—namely, the return of Master Fynk. As a bailiff, he was within his rights to inspect the bathhouse whenever the mood took him or his suspicions were aroused. Since the latter was a constant, he frequently crossed the threshold. Ever since the day he'd accused me of being a pregnant whore and suspected I was not the widow I claimed to be, he'd made a point of observing The Swanne. Forcing Alyson to submit to the thirty-five questions of the ordinances, which meant asking dozens extra of me and the other women as well, he became almost a fixture—an unwelcome one. Ensuring we left the bathhouse for the required hours on holy days and that no woman wore an apron or was kept against her will, Master Fynk hovered over us the way a bat does a belfry.

Disappointed that despite his vigilance, no cucking stool was required or fines could be levied, he would satisfy himself by beating a few of the girls with a stick. While I would be spared this sadistic venting of his frustration, Alyson was not. After he departed, I would find her in the solar and tend to her hurts. Terrible bruises would mar her face, arms, and thighs, and she'd ache and limp about the place for days afterward. The midwife's husband, the Moor and apothecary Marcian Vetazes, was called twice and left potions for her to drink. Refusing to go to the sheriff, she tolerated what a lesser person would not. I feared her fortitude was for my sake.

"Nay, not for you, Anna, though I'd take that and more besides. I tolerate this"—she pushed up her sleeve to expose a violet bruise—"for us all. Master Fynk needs to be the victor. If he can't achieve that one way, he finds another. For the moment, his beatings suffice." She regarded me steadily. "They won't always."

God forgive me, my hatred toward the bailiff built to an impotent fury that I could do nothing except be grateful that, for the time being, I avoided the worst of his retribution. Aye, we endured. Rather than staunching his anger, however, or transforming it to something gentler, our obedience prodded Master Fynk to more pernicious actions.

So it was that finally, as I knew he would, he sought to discredit my brew.

At the height of summer, as two new ale-conners were appointed, Master Fynk chose to accompany them to their first tasting at The Swanne.

Already the bathhouse was filled with customers and while not all were there for drink alone, the ale was flowing freely. The ale-stake had only just been raised when Master Fynk, flanked by four constables and the ale-conners, arrived, ignoring invitations from the women and descending straight to the cellar.

Introducing himself, the chief ale-conner, Master Godfried, a mercer from Churchway by the bishop's palace, was an amiable but serious sort of man. He shucked off his surcoat, quickly donned his leather breeches, and, with nervous glances toward Master Fynk and the constables, accepted a brimming tankard from Adam with a mumbled thank-you. Pouring some of the contents on the bench, he settled himself while his companion checked our measures. Ordering the constables to stay at the foot of the stairs, Master Fynk wandered around the brewery, peering into the tuns, staring at the wort, the crease between his brows deepening. Sniffing, he roamed from station to station, examining everything with a gleam in his eyes. My heart began to sink.

Adam, Juliana, Harry, and Betje kept working, all of them casting anxious looks over their shoulders. Yolande remained by my side, a drying sheet in her arms ready to offer the ale-conners, along with a mazer of good ale.

Nobody spoke. The wort bubbled, the kiln spat, and the mash tuns gurgled. A couple of the constables cleared their throats, one nervously tapping his foot upon the bottommost stair.

I felt confident we'd pass as we'd always done. Drawn from upstream and boiled repeatedly, the quality of the water was without question. The wort had also been boiled, and the ale was not sour, despite the heat. The beer had been in the barrels for almost two weeks and was at its best for drinking. The cellar kept the temperature even, the liquid cool. What was being drunk upstairs and enjoyed was no different to what these men were about to taste.

After the testing period expired, Master Godfried rose with a deep groan, bringing the bench with him.

"Adjudging by my breeches, this be a good brew, mistress."

"Here, Master Godfried," I said, passing him a mazer of ale. I passed another to the other ale-conner. At least one constable licked his lips. "Time to be sure."

Watching the ale-conners' faces as they drank, I was pleased to see their countenances change from wariness to pleasure. Downing his mazer in two gulps, Master Godfried smacked his lips together. "This be—"

"I would like to try some as well." Like a cloud over the sun, Master Fynk drifted across proceedings.

"You'll be trying something worth tasting then," said the other ale-conner, raising his empty mazer to receive more.

"I'll be the judge of that," snapped Master Fynk.

My heart shrank into a hard lump of coal, anger filling the space it had once occupied. It was all I could do not to throw the remainder of the jug in Master Fynk's face. Instead, I bit my tongue, poured him a drink, and waited. Why, I don't know. I knew what was about to unfold. I'd become an actor in a Christmastide farce, doomed to perform my part, say my lines, knowing how the final scene would play.

It was Elmham Lenn all over again.

Only this time, there was no one to whom I could turn. Other brewers would be grateful Master Fynk's attention was not focused upon them. If it meant he would remove me as competition, so much the better. Worse, I was a woman without a man to lend legitimacy to my name and what I did. That I was the business partner of the owner of a bathhouse, another woman besides, undermined everything in Master Fynk's triumphant eyes.

Raising the mazer to his lips, Master Fynk made a show of drinking the ale.

"Faugh!" He spat it onto the floor. "What's this? You're serving pig's piss!" He held the mazer toward the constables, as if it was proof of his outrageous claim.

"Steady now, Master Fynk," began Master Godfried. "This be qual—"

As the mazer was struck from Master Godfried's hand, we watched it hit the floor and the contents stain the stones. "It be piss, I tell you." Master Fynk pushed his face into Master God-fried's. "Piss."

The shorter man recoiled and lowered his eyes. Shaking his head, he didn't dare correct the bailiff. Spinning to face the other ale-conner, Master Fynk applied his glacial gaze until he too looked away, red-faced, placing his mazer upon the table without taking another drink.

Wiping the back of his hand across his mouth, Master Fynk laughed. "You know the penalty for selling watered ale, Mistress de Winter? For adjusting legally tendered measures?" His leg shot out and he kicked the offending barrel. Before I could answer, he did. "Most of it gets tipped into the river." He paused, a huge smile forming as he saw my face pale. I knew what happened to alewives and brewsters accused of fiddling with their brews. "*Most* . . . As for the rest, I cannot tell you what pleasure I'm going to get from tipping it over—"

"Lewis Fynk," boomed a voice. Alyson marched down the steps, her tunic raised to reveal her ankles. "I'll not allow you to do that. You can do what you like to me, but I'll not have you harming a hair on her head."

The marks of Master Fynk's last beating were still evident on Alyson's face as she strode up to him, unafraid, hands on hips, chin raised defiantly.

"Fine," said Master Fynk indifferently, his eyes narrowing slightly. "Then it will be your head that bears the consequences of this cunting whore's deceit." Before anyone could react, he grabbed Alyson by the arms and, twisting them around her back, shoved her toward two of the constables. "Take her to the river. The rest of you, get those barrels down there." His eyes swept the cellar. "All of them."

I cried out. "Nay! Not the beer. You haven't tasted it. It hasn't been assessed, you can't."

"Can't?" Master Fynk grabbed a handful of my hair and snatched me to his chest. I screamed. Betje leaped to my defense but Harry held her fast. Juliana and Yolande had the sense to stop Adam.

Master Fynk drew my face to his. I could smell his breath, see the little red veins in his eyes, the dirt in his pores. I clawed uselessly at his fingers, but they were bands of metal that tightened, no matter how I scratched and pried.

"When are you going to learn, Mistress of Shit and Piss, Lady Liar, I can do whatever I want." Running his nose alongside my neck and cheek, he inhaled loudly then flung me away so hard, I struck the table and tumbled to the floor. Yolande and Juliana couldn't hold Adam. Helping me to my feet, I could feel him shaking with rage.

"You."

It was a moment before we understood Master Fynk was addressing Adam and the ale-conners.

"Help my men get those barrels to the river. You too, you little bastard." This to Harry.

I nodded for them to help. There was no point doing anything else. All I wanted was to reach Alyson.

With one last victorious look, Master Fynk left the cellar.

"Mistress," said Master Godfried, his cap screwed into an unrecognizable shape in his hands. "God knows, I'm so sorry. I don't understand what's happening. Your ale—it was fine. More than fine. I—"

"Can bear no blame for the deeds of others. This has naught to do with you, Master Godfried, or you," I said to the other ale-conner. "I don't think it even has anything to do with my brew. This is about something else altogether." I touched my neck and stared at the spot where Master Fynk last stood.

Waiting until the constables had cleared the barrels away from the door, I scrambled into the courtyard. The women and Betje followed me.

"Juliana, Betje, go to the nursery. Make sure the twins are all right." Betje stared at me. "Please, Betje. I need to know you and the children are safe."

"Don't worry, mistress," said Juliana. "I'll take care of them." Grabbing Betje by the hand, they ran to one of the external staircases.

"Bolt the door behind you," I called. Juliana waved.

Waiting till they were on the first landing, I signaled to Yolande. "Come, let's see to Alyson."

Quite a crowd had gathered by the river: fishmongers; butchers; the farrier; Master Ironside and his son, John; the mercer, Master Cheyner, and his family; the local fuller, wiping his hands upon his stinking apron before pointing to where the barrels sat atop the cart trundling toward the water. Yolande and I forged a path through all these to the river's edge.

There, upon a stool, her hands tied behind her back, her hair falling over her shoulders, sat Alyson, cussing and swearing at those who shouted at her, their fingers jabbing, their tongues wagging, accusing, cursing. I looked around and saw those we called neighbors, some friends even. Whispering behind their hands, shouting insults, indictment was writ on their faces. Even our laundress and her ruddy-cheeked daughters, the tailor, shoemaker, dyer, and many more besides, were not above hurling abuse at a woman they drank with, took coin from, bid

God's good day. The owners of the neighboring bathhouses and alehouses, along with their women, pressed forward, agog, no doubt grateful it wasn't their ale about to be sacrificed to the green waters. While cheating was overlooked in many a craft, a brewer who deceived customers was regarded as the greatest of curs and treated as a pariah. Master Fynk could not have picked a more public way of ensuring Alyson's and my disgrace; from here on in, we would be considered outcasts. The small inroads we'd made with the brew and Alyson with her customers would be meaningless.

The women of The Swanne appeared one by one, emerging under arms, between shoulders, their faces stricken, their mouths downturned. They loved Alyson and to see her brought so low, publicly shamed, wouldn't be easy. Once or two cast looks in my direction, looks laden with significance. This was my fault, and not only in their eyes. I would be held accountable.

Ordering one barrel left on the cart, the rest were swiftly removed and rolled down the muddy banks. Adam and Harry were forced to cooperate, to empty what they'd labored over into the flowing waters. On Master Fynk's command, the bungs were knocked out. Only as the crowd grew and comments began to get louder, did he turn to me, his face lit with that peculiar glow of satisfaction only the self-righteous emit. Upon the river, men poled their barges closer to the banks, wherries drifted upon the outgoing tide, steered within hailing distance so their contempt might be added to the babble of angry voices.

Watching the golden liquid chugging into the river, knowing the ale was good, indeed, better than anything served on the waterfront, that my measures were in order, I didn't let Master Fynk or those now yelling insults see what a terrible blow had been struck. Nor did Alyson. We faced the river, heavy gray clouds threatening overhead, trapping the thick, warm air, and fixed our features so they revealed neither our sorrow nor our anger at this gross unfairness. Inside, I burned with impotence, shame, and no small degree of fear.

A clod of mud struck me on the side of the face. Staggering into Alyson, nearly tipping her over, I cried out, my hand flying to my cheek. I tried to find the offender. Another missile hit, followed by another. Rotten fruit exploded against my tunic, scattered across my chest, caught in my hair and slid down my neck. There were jeers and laughter. I stood in front of Alyson, using my body as a shield, as the air filled with projectiles.

"Slattern!"

"Whore!"

"Cunting bitch!"

"Water my ale, will you?" A man pulled out his cock and began to piss all over the cobbles, his urine splashing Alyson's skirts. There were catcalls, hoots, and cries for others to do the same. Leda, her flaxen hair unbound, went to strike the man, but Adam grabbed her hand and shook his head. Her lovely face contorted into a mask of fury.

More fruit and vegetables were hurled.

I wrapped my arms around Alyson.

"For God's sake. Do something," shouted Master Godfried at Master Fynk.

Signaling the constables, Master Fynk smiled as they abandoned the barrels by the water's edge. At last, we were to be given sanctuary, taken back to the safety of The Swanne until the mob dispersed.

Pulling me away from Alyson, the men were rough, but I

turned toward them eagerly only to find my hands trussed tightly behind my back.

"You're hurting me." My cry was ignored. Dragged to the edge of the crowd, I was turned and held fast.

Standing on a large stone so he could be seen and heard above the crowd, Master Fynk spoke. "For serving improper ale by unapproved measures, Goodwife Alyson Bookbinder, you are sentenced to be doused a dozen times."

The rabble cheered.

*Good God.*

Carrying the last of the barrels on their shoulders, the two constables who'd brought Alyson to the riverbank paused beside her and slowly, chuckling wildly, upturned it over her head as the crowd clapped and whooped.

When I'd last seen this done, the woman choked and vomited, almost drowning in a sea of ale. Not Goodwife Alyson. Like a flower unfolds for the sun, she turned her face and opened her mouth, greeting the golden liquid with glee.

I gasped as she swished some in her mouth, swallowed, and then drank some more as it flattened her hair, blinking furiously as it welled in her eyes, ran in fountains of amber from her shoulders, ears, and hands. Laughing, she shook her head, a wet dog relishing an illicit swim.

"That's it, boys, give me some liquid gold," she cried.

My hands flew to my mouth, stoppering up the laughter I felt building.

The caws and hoots slowly changed as the mob saw Alyson wasn't cowed or frightened by what was being done; on the contrary, she was appreciating every moment.

"By God's good grace," she called in her booming, deep voice, her tongue lathing her mouth. "I am the luckiest goodwife alive. This Son of Ale is the only kind I want rising in me."

There was a great roar of laughter followed by exultant cheers. Adam, who'd been taut as a bow, swung to me and grinned. The women from The Swanne began to applaud, Leda jumping up and down on the spot. Soon, a chant started. "Goody Goody Alyson. Goody Goody Alyson. Son of Ale. Son of Ale."

As the waterfall of liquid became a trickle, the constables eased the barrel down. Only then did I glance at Master Fynk. In the wonder of Alyson's bravura performance, I'd quite forgotten about him. One look now and Alyson's words flew back to me.

*He's a dangerous man.*

In two strides, Master Fynk reached Alyson's side. Raising his hand, his fist curled and, along with a red-faced cry of utter ferocity, dropped.

I ran forward, slapping away Adam's hands. Before I could reach the bailiff someone else did.

"Nay," barked a deep, rough voice. "Your point is made. That is enough now."

It was Leander.

I stopped in my tracks. My heart filled. *Leander.* Why he was here, I cared not. His timing was perfect, his manner imperious. With his embroidered linen surcoat, silky dark hair, shining boots, flashing eyes, and beringed hands, he fairly blazed authority.

"M-my lord," stammered Master Fynk. He tried to pull his hand from Leander's grasp, but could not.

Holding him fast, Leander nodded to the constables.

"See this crowd back to their work." He waved his cane about.

"Aye, sir."

"Milord."

"You"—Leander nodded toward Master Godfried—"untie the goodwife."

"Be my pleasure, me lord."

As he fumbled with the knots, I stepped forward and helped the mercer. I wanted Leander to acknowledge my presence while at the same time I prayed he did not. I didn't want Master Fynk to have yet another reason to dislike me.

It took all my willpower to ignore Leander, but I did, turning my back upon him and the man he held fast, holding the drenched Alyson in a warm hug as she found her feet again.

"You were marvelous," I whispered. "So very brave."

"Bloody foolish."

I held her at arm's length before pressing her back to my bosom. "Aye, that too."

With an arm around her shoulders, I started to walk back toward The Swanne. Leander would see to Master Fynk, of that I was certain. I did not need to see the man browbeaten, as much as I would like to. Alyson had achieved that and so much more.

The scattering crowd parted before us, many going out of their way to pat Alyson on her back, mutter at how unjust Fynk's accusations had been, and congratulate her. Others stood back and shook their heads, mostly in admiration at her daring, but not yet ready to be seen aligning themselves with such scandalous behavior. If Leander hadn't stepped in when he did, Alyson could have been grievously hurt. Time in prison was still not out of the question. There were many charges Master Fynk could lay at her door, scold being the least of them, and much depended on what happened now between him and Leander.

Remaining in Master Fynk's sight would have only served to remind him of his humiliation and weaken Leander's position. Taking Alyson back to The Swanne accomplished many purposes. I could attend to her needs, start another brew, and, between times, make myself presentable. For had not my love returned?

As we reached the path leading to the door, I noted two horses being held by an urchin. There was Leander's black destrier and another, smaller stallion that also bore the Rainford livery.

Before I'd time to fathom to whom the beast belonged, a familiar figure appeared in the doorway, Betje by his side.

My heart lurched and I tripped.

It was Tobias.

# FORTY-SEVEN

THE SWANNE
High summer to early autumn
*The year of Our Lord 1407 in the eighth
year of the reign of Henry IV*

As I lay in bed late that night, sleep was elusive as the events of the day preoccupied me. For certes, Alyson was brave. I marveled at her audacity, her bold defiance, and thanked the good Lord that Leander arrived when he did. If that hadn't been enough to deal with, Tobias and our awkward reunion also kept my thoughts whirling.

Older, taller, possessing the bronzed skin that marked him a sea merchant, he wore a sword at his hip and fine clothes on his back. My throat caught at the sight of him and my heart began to beat fast, as if it wasn't my own flesh and blood upon The Swanne's steps, but a stranger. Betje stood next to him, a bemused expression on her face and I noted that, unlike Leander, Tobias hadn't taken Betje's hand. In fact, the way he fixed his eyes upon me suggested he couldn't bear to look upon her.

In the fleeting time it took for me to leap to that conclusion, anger flooded my body and my steps faltered. Alyson, who I was still supporting, unaware of who waited on the threshold, raised her head.

"God give you good day," she hailed Tobias. "I'll be with you momentarily, fine sir. Please, make yourself comfortable." She waved him back into the bathhouse. "This be a mere setback." Tobias followed the direction of her hand and frowned. "Leda!" she cried, a finger pointing to the heavens. "Leda," she repeated in a quieter tone. "She will do for this handsome one." Pulling me forward, she increased the pace.

Resisting, I dug my heels in, forcing us to pause. "That handsome one is my brother," I murmured.

Alyson looked from me to Tobias. "That's Tobias? The sanctimonious son of a—"

"Tobias," I said loudly, releasing Alyson and striding past before she could make the situation worse. Leda replaced me by Alyson's side and, scrutinizing Tobias as she passed, helped her mistress into The Swanne. Alyson's voice carried as she demanded wine, a footstool, drying sheets, and a blanket. The other women slowly returned to work, all of them casting curious glances at Tobias as they came through the door.

There'd be much to explain . . . if I chose, that was. With his face averted, I couldn't read what Tobias was thinking, but I could imagine. Here was his sister, not only living in a bathhouse and conducting her business on its premises, but she called the owner friend.

Waiting till the last of the women entered, and Betje tactfully closed the door, sealing the women and the few men who'd bounded after them inside, I mounted the steps.

"Are you all right?" I asked Betje, taking her hand.

She squeezed mine back and regarded me steadily. "Aye. Are you?"

I was not. But I summoned a smile. "Of course."

"Tobias is here, Anna," she said, gesturing to him with her disfigured hand, her tone cautious.

*What did my little sister sense? What did she know?*

Without flinching, I swung to Tobias. "God give you good day, brother. I confess I didn't expect to see you, but it does my heart good to see you so well."

Formal, but no less sincere.

Tobias didn't answer immediately and I saw his mouth working strangely. I began to prepare myself for the tirade I assumed must follow, for the accusations, the self-righteous appraisal of my lowly circumstances.

I was about to suggest we retire to the solar so words could be exchanged in private, when Tobias, with a peculiar noise, flung himself in my arms.

"Oh, Anneke, how I've missed you," he said and began to sob.

❖

Only much later, after we were comfortable in the solar, and Tobias and I were able to secrete ourselves in a corner as Leander, Alyson, and Adam made plans, did he explain what had happened since our last correspondence.

Shocked by what he'd seen at Elmham Lenn and by the brutality of Karel's death, and of Louisa's and Saskia's, Tobias's first reaction was to blame me. After all, he reasoned, if I hadn't started the brewery, it wouldn't have attracted the ire of the monks or what followed in Westel Calkin's wake. As he confessed this to me, Tobias had the grace to look shamefaced. But his thoughts were no worse than my own; nothing could punish me more than one glance at Betje or the memory of Karel. It was only once they were back in London that Leander told Tobias the rest of the sorry tale, what Westel Calkin had done to me. When Leander discovered my whereabouts, he learned about my children.

"Anneke . . . I mean, Anna." He gave a tremulous smile and went to reach for my hand but pulled back, uncertain. I took his and held it fast. He nodded and smiled more broadly. "I don't know what to say. There's nothing I can say, is there?"

"Only one thing, Tobias."

His chin flew up, a puzzled expression on his face. "Oh," he said. "Aye, I'm sorry, Anneke. You cannot begin to know how sorry I am."

"That might be true, but you can start by telling me."

And so, over the course of the next hour, Tobias and I were reconciled. Trying to take the blame for what happened, reasoning that if he'd been present, the monks, let alone Westel, wouldn't have dared act, I rid him of that foolish notion.

"Nay, Tobias, Westel was not in his right mind. Your presence at Holcroft House would have made no difference. He believed he had God on his side and therefore nothing he did was sinful or wrong. The monks did not condone his actions. He was set on a course and nothing and no one was going to steer him from what he believed was a righteous path."

Tobias shook his head in sorrow. "If only he'd never darkened your door, you would—"

"Still be brewing in Elmham Lenn, Karel would be alive,

Betje"—I glanced in her direction where she sat playing with Tansy—"would not be so disfigured, and Saskia, Louisa, and Will would still be with us. If you only knew how many times I've thought that, said it, dreamed it. It achieves nothing except to sharpen the wound, color the memories of those I love in malevolent hues. I owe them better than that—we all do. The facts are that Betje is scarred for life and the others are dead. Nothing I do or say, no one I blame, can change that." I took a deep breath. "I'm here now, in Southwark, and a brewer once more. Aye, I've played this game a thousand times and still lose. The only way I can make good of the evil that occurred is to succeed, Tobias, to make my brewing work and ensure a good life for my children. For Betje."

Tobias stared at me. "You'll make it work, Anneke. You always do."

We held each other a long time after that.

Our relationship would never have the warmth and easiness it once possessed; he couldn't reconcile my brewing, or the bathhouse, with his sense of what his sister should be doing, who I should be, but he understood my choices were limited. Unhappy, he nonetheless didn't fault-find as he once would. This was a lesson I believed Leander taught him. What he did to encourage such a transformation, I know not. But it did make the situation easier and meant I could drop my guard.

"Would you like to meet your niece and nephew?" I asked.

Tobias frowned then his face cleared. "I'd not thought of them in that way, but I would like to, very much."

Betje accompanied us up the stairs and, once again, I noticed the difficulty Tobias had looking at her face, how he didn't take her hand or, once beside the crib, encourage her into his lap the way he used to. Betje's shoulders slumped and I saw the hopeful looks she cast in her brother's direction even if he didn't.

Admiring the slumbering babes for a while, we bid Betje good night and left her with Juliana. As we descended back to the solar, I asked about his manner around Betje.

Stopping at the bottom of the stairs, he sighed, locking his eyes onto the torch that burned on the far wall. "I could not credit what I saw when she first emerged from the bathhouse. I thought, who is this little monster leering at me so? Once I understood it was Betje, that my little sister was so transformed, I . . . I didn't know what to do, what to say . . ." He swallowed and it was a moment before he found his voice again. "She is unrecognizable. Her skin, her eye, her beautiful hair . . ." He gripped the railing like a drowning man. In the light of the sconces, his face was pained. "I cannot look at her lest she sees what I do. What future does she have? She cannot hope for a husband, friends, or an ordinary life looking like that. She will endure constant mockery and cruelty. Dear Lord, forgive me, but it would have been kinder if she died."

I drew in a sharp breath and waited till the anger abated. "She's God's creature, Tobias. Her life or death is for Him only to decide, not you."

"Aye, but—"

"You do not know what her life is like. Betje has real friends here—those who love and protect her—apart from me."

He lifted his eyes from the floor.

"Aye, she does. Here, in this bathhouse, this place I know you only tolerate because your master bids you must. Your discomfort is apparent, but hear this—everyone beneath this roof, from servants to owner, has shown her nothing but kindness, and do you know how? By treating her as if she were no different to any other eight-year-old. She works, plays, eats, sleeps, and dreams. Here, she found hope again—so did I." I let that sink in for a moment.

Below us, a young woman scurried out of one of the rooms, laughing, her hair falling down her back, her tunic falling off one shoulder. A portly old monk followed, lifting his robes and skipping along the corridor, giggling.

Tobias pulled a disapproving face.

"Don't be so quick to judge what you think you see, Tobias. Learn to look below the surface, and understand the truth of those you would be so ready to reject, to despise."

"You're not just talking about Betje, are you?"

"That's for you to decide."

Tobias turned to me. "Leander told me much the same thing."

"Then he is wise."

Tobias's eyebrows arched. "Which is the same as saying you are."

"Is it?" I smiled, and we walked back to join the others.

Once I returned to the comfort of the solar I learned the real reason for Leander's timely presence. Oh, I'd caught snatches of conversation, of the excitement in his tone when he spoke to Alyson, and it was evident something had changed Tobias's opinion of my circumstances.

Leander and Alyson were discussing Master Fynk, who, after his mortification at her hands and Leander's intervention, found his pride could only be salved through coin. Leander, after some resistance, harsh words, and warnings, relented, paying him a sum that made my eyes widen.

"But that wasn't what convinced him to capitulate and allow you to brew again," added Leander, shooting me a look that made my heart flip. He parted the rushes with his cane.

"Tell her," said Alyson, rising and pouring another round of ale into everyone's vessels. She was much recovered from her ordeal and earlier that evening had enjoyed keeping clients and the girls spellbound as she recounted her tale over and over. Each new customer insisted on hearing it and Alyson obliged. Thanks to Master Fynk, The Swanne had little to offer except beer (to our good fortune, in his eagerness Master Fynk had overlooked the barrels stored behind the mews). Whereas before the men would have turned up their noses at such a drink, God's grace (and, I liked to believe, sense of irony) smiled upon us, and those who'd once been reluctant to try our beer were keener than ever thanks to Alyson's performance—and Master Fynk.

"I'll have me some of that Son of Ale" was a constant request, according to Adam. "Lords, monks, commoners, didn't matter," he said.

Aware of Alyson hovering over my empty mazer, I snapped back to the present.

"Sir Leander has brought some exciting news."

"My lord." I lifted my brimming mazer. "I would very much like to hear it." My tone was formal. Unspoken between Leander and myself was that our relationship would remain a secret from Tobias. As far as my brother was concerned, it was pure luck that led Leander to The Swanne and my ale some weeks ago—a product his master already knew from drinking it in Elmham Lenn.

"When I heard about a brew of surpassing quality, I had to

go to the source. Much to my surprise, it also led me to your sisters," he'd explained. Tobias appeared happy with that.

Leander put down his drink now and drew himself forward in his chair. "I'm very pleased to be the bearer of excellent tidings. The king has sent me here to place an order on his behalf for your ale and beer."

My mouth dropped open. I stared at Leander. Did he jest? "I'm to trade with the Crown? Is this true?"

Leander gave a laugh. "Aye, mistress, it's true. His Grace wishes to purchase supplies to help quench the thirst of the king's household during the next sitting of parliament. In Gloucester. Tobias has the order in his safekeeping." Tobias promptly patted a pocket in his surcoat. "Three dozen barrels of ale and beer are to be delivered to Gloucester Abbey before the twenty-fourth of October." At the expression on my face, he gave a snort of amusement. "Did you doubt my assurance that the king himself would drink from my supplies? That he would taste your ale and beer?"

"I did." I clasped my hands. "But not now. To think he enjoyed it so much His Grace would like more."

"A great deal more. I should warn you, royal favor is a fickle thing. Once bestowed it can also be swiftly retracted. Despite today's setback, you must reap what you've sown."

My mind reeled. Three dozen barrels.

Leander rose and stood with his back to the open shutters. Strains of music from the street below wafted in on the warm evening air. There were some shouts followed by raucous laughter and a resounding splash.

"Someone's either in the trough or river," sighed Alyson, sitting back down and, despite the heat, pulling a blanket around her legs. She was entitled to play the invalid. For certes, she rejected the role of heroine.

"I've been giving the matter of your induction into royal trade some consideration, mistress," began Leander, glancing into his mazer, swirling the liquid around. "In light of what happened today, I think it would be a good idea if you, Goodwife Alyson, and you, Mistress Anna, accompanied the delivery."

"To Lancashire?" I asked.

"Nay. To Gloucester. I'll arrange a driver, accommodation, and guards to accompany you west. Unfortunately, I have to return to the king's side before you'll be ready to leave." Placing an elbow on the sill, he leaned back, his cane dangling from his forearm. "I don't trust Fynk not to act against you as soon as my back is turned or, worse, when I'm out of the city. If you absent yourself for a while and leave the running of the brewery and the bathhouse to others for a few weeks, it will give him time to recover his injured pride and for the people here to forget what happened. It might also force him to focus his attentions elsewhere."

I flashed a look at Alyson. She was seriously considering the proposition.

"There's another reason. I think the king would very much like to meet the woman who, of his own admission, brews the finest drop he's tasted."

"His Grace said that?"

"He did."

Tobias nodded. "He did, Anneke, he really did."

I couldn't help it. I began to laugh. From having my brew tipped into the Thames and all over Alyson, being shamed and discredited before the folk of Bankside, Southwark, this morning, here I was, hours later, being told that the greatest man in the land rated my brew the best.

Sometimes more happened in a day than in a lifetime.

Hence, my thoughts refused to settle as I lay down to sleep. Through the open window, clouds glided across the moon, stealing its silvery light and plunging the room into darkness before, like a curtain before a performing troupe, parting and spreading a lunar glow across the bed.

Understanding the sense in Leander's proposal, my only concerns were leaving Betje, the babes, and the brewery—in that order. A few weeks was not long, but as I knew all too well, so much could happen even in a short time. Fate oft possessed a peculiar sense of humor that meant you could not place too much trust in well-laid plans, or reassurances that things would run smoothly—destiny would likely intervene to prick such conceit.

Presenting my worries to the group, I was reassured that Betje would be cared for by Adam, Harry, and Juliana. The twins had Emma and Constance and, as for the brewery, had I not been training apprentices these last months?

Alyson looked at me wryly. "Do you doubt those you taught yourself?"

"Nay," I said slowly. How could I explain that there was more to my brewing than malt, water, and hops?

It was only as Leander departed (much to my disappointment, but he could hardly send Tobias back to Ashlar Place while he remained), his hands lingering daringly on mine, sending shafts of pleasure along my arms to congregate in my center, that he added a caveat. "I'll be heading north in two weeks," he said. "The Lady Cecilia will remain in London. I should warn you, until I leave, I will be a regular presence." A smile drifted across his mouth. "The king has asked I report on your progress."

From the look Tobias flashed him, it was evident that wasn't quite true. But I understood the private message behind his words. He would ensure we had time together, even if it was to be brief.

It would have to be—a month was not much time to make the quantities the king required, especially since Master Fynk, and the thirsty patrons that evening, so kindly depleted our stores. But if we worked hard and employed some extra staff, it was enough. Concern about funds for purchasing the extra barley, water, wood, and coal, never mind the additional barrels that would be needed, was allayed when Leander gave Alyson a heavy purse. Only later did I learn the coins were Leander's own. This didn't detract from my excitement at the opportunity being offered, nor did it still the strange sense of foreboding that accompanied such good news.

Tossing and turning, running over everything I had to do, the moon waned and the sky transformed to an ashen cupola before sleep finally claimed me. Dreams crammed one on top of the other, populated by crowds of Master Fynks leering, jeering, and pulling my hair until it came out in long, ruby clumps. There were numerous Alysons, tossing back their heads and opening wide, gap-toothed mouths to drink fountains of golden ale. They disappeared to be replaced by Tobias, solitary, atop a branded barrel, weeping, burying his face in his elbow before, with a look of sheer horror, he pushed away Betje, who reached for him with scarred arms. They were replaced by a faceless king, regal, tall, dispensing justice and coin with a long, sparkling scepter that spat the latter out one end and had a cruel, shining blade fixed upon the other. The scepter twirled above me as I knelt before his majesty. I didn't know which end I was to receive.

Leander appeared and approached the king. As he did so, the scepter stopped turning and the king pushed Leander aside and stepped down from his dais to stand over me, the scepter hovering above my head. His bejeweled hand disguised which fate was to be mine—coin or blade.

As I raised my head, Leander cried out, his voice far away, beyond reach. "Nay!" he screamed, as a bright piece of metal arced above me and descended.

I woke with a sickening lurch.

# FORTY-EIGHT

THE LONDON ROAD AND GLOUCESTER

Autumn

*The year of Our Lord 1407 in the eighth*

*year of the reign of Henry IV*

*A*lyson and I left Southwark one cool day in October, just over a month after we received the king's order. Forlorn, Betje stood on the steps of The Swanne flanked by Adam and Juliana, Harry behind her. The hand Adam rested lightly on her shoulder did more to reassure me than Juliana's common sense and the babes' rosy cheeks. Smiling bravely, Betje waved a kerchief and asked that God watch over us and grant us good fortune. Emma and Constance lifted the twins' arms and waved them back and forth as if they were rag dolls doing their owner's bidding. There my family stood, a picture of sentimental leave-taking, as we trotted off down Bankside and toward London Bridge to join the laden cart awaiting us in Cheapside.

Four burly, armed outriders dressed in Rainford livery and a taciturn driver, enough to deter any brigands, escorted us as we negotiated London, swathed in our woolen cloaks, marveling at the sight presented by St. Paul's towering over the magnates' houses before we exited through Ludgate and crossed the refuse-filled River Fleet. The only spectacle that upset an otherwise uneventful trip across London was a large group of mourners gathered in a churchyard where it seemed a number of people were being buried. Bells tolled and my heart grew heavy with remembered sorrow.

Alyson crossed herself as we passed and murmured a prayer. Mine were silent and addressed not only to the dead but also to the pain of those who survived.

Death had attended Bankside over the last few days as well. Church bells had tolled the news and we'd all paused in our duties to offer prayers for the deceased. More than usual seemed to be ascending to meet their Maker of late.

At the time, I thought little of it. It was only as we passed the funeral that I recalled the bells pealing throughout the days leading up to our departure. Pushing my harried thoughts to the back of my mind, I tried to concentrate on where we were going rather than what we were leaving behind.

The countryside opened before us and, upon a road that grew progressively worse the farther we rode, we joined the stream of other travelers. Our cargo drew stares and comments. After all, it wasn't every day two well-dressed women were seen transporting three dozen barrels with the royal seal, bound with ropes and partially covered with canvas, riding west.

Tugging at my new tunic and kirtle, enjoying the downy feel of the marten lining of the cloak against my cheek, I was grateful to Alyson for the gift of my clothes.

"We are off on king's business, so we need to look the part.

I don't care what people think of me, but I do care what they make of you. We're going to dress like ladies and cast doubt upon those who believe us to be otherwise."

Alyson's tunic was dyed in her favorite color—scarlet—the stitching so fine it could barely be discerned; her surcoat was lavishly embroidered with peacocks, falcons, and, as a nod to her business, long-necked swans. She certainly appeared a lady. Her silver-streaked brown hair had been styled and pinned beneath an elegant cap and the gloves that hid her reddened hands were of the finest leather. In my emerald tunic with an equally magnificent surcoat of topaz and ruby, my hair dressed, my hands warm, it was easy to feel like one as well. Gentlemen took a second, polite look and even doffed their hats respectfully. The farther from London we ventured, the more often peasants stopped and gawped or even curtsied and bowed as we passed.

Alyson would raise a hand and wave, chuckling quietly at their courtesy. "If only they knew," she'd whisper under her breath. I wondered what our driver thought, but he barely said a word and kept his eyes fixed on the road. The escort occasionally drew level with us, but if they spoke, it was only to inquire as to our well-being or inform us the next stop wasn't far away. Though the conversation between Alyson and myself was filled with the possibilities of what lay ahead, my mind was with who and what I'd left behind.

It wasn't easy to leave Betje or the babes, but I understood that necessity; securing the present in order to shore up the days ahead meant I'd no choice. What I hadn't considered when we made our plans that warm night in September was that absenting myself for a few weeks meant I had to pass to Betje the last of my brewing secrets, held by the women of my family for generations. Not that I didn't trust her; after all, she was a de Winter. Brewing was in her blood. On the contrary, my reticence was because once I revealed them, I could no longer pretend that she was still a child, still dependent upon me to make her way in the world. At eight years of age, her entry into the adult world had already been delayed as I persuaded myself that her injuries meant she required more time. I couldn't fool myself or anyone else on that score any longer; disfigured or not, she was more than ready and able to embrace the work of a brewer. It was me who was unprepared. I'd underestimated my sister. In lecturing Tobias, I'd failed to heed my own advice to look beyond the facade.

I had confessed some of my ambivalence about leaving to Alyson one evening as we sat companionably in the solar; filling the number of orders that had arrived in the wake of our royal favor was a real concern.

Suddenly, all the custom I'd longed for arrived within a matter of hours. The old and ailing Bishop of Winchester placed an order, the Bishop of Rochester as well. The abbot of St. Augustine, and the friars at St. Thomas's hospital, swiftly followed. Every day orders were delivered—from the gentry, lawyers, knights, inns, hostels, private homes, and more besides. From Southwark, London, and beyond, couriers and servants arrived with orders.

"Tell your master we'll send word when the order is ready."

"Come back in a week and the ale will be here."

"If you return at month's end, there'll be a brew for you."

Over and over, these phrases rang in my head as I calculated how we'd manage.

After two weeks of this, it was evident that on top of the

king's order, we'd be unable to produce so much with the limited equipment we had.

"We need help, Adam," I said with resignation. Until we were paid, I wasn't quite sure how we'd afford it, but it was clear we couldn't continue with the few hands we had, let alone when I was in Gloucester.

"We do," agreed Adam. "And extra mash tuns and troughs."

Using much of the coin Leander provided, we purchased the necessary equipment and supplies. Alyson found me additional servants. Along with an extra trough from a farm in Surrey, Adam and Harry also brought back Thomas, a broad-shouldered, shy young man keen to help in the brewery. I was too tired to argue and set him to work straightaway. I barely remember hiring two girls, Milda and Rose. At nineteen, barely younger than me, Milda felt the urge to provide constant commentary on everything as a way of asserting authority. If she hadn't been so good at what she did, having brewed since she was five, I may have let her go. Chatter aside, she was an asset. With Harry taking more responsibility in the brewery, another lad, Walter, was brought in to take over his duties. All I can recall is that he had dark eyes and a mop of brown hair out of which his ears jutted like the handles of a mazer.

It was Alyson who convinced me to only have Betje brew ale in my absence. "The beer, that Son of Ale, well, I don't care what young Harry thinks, only you can make that."

"Harry thinks he has what it takes to make beer, does he?" I swirled my drink in the goblet, watching the way the dense liquid and frothy head mingled.

"He does. Just ask him." Alyson laughed. There was no malice in her statement, only great fondness and a pride she disguised with harsh discipline. Responsible for him since his mother, who had been one of her workers, died, she'd kept him under her roof. Harry also wriggled his way into her heart.

Hers wasn't the only one.

Rising before dawn the morning after my conversation with Alyson, I crept downstairs while the house was still quiet. I wasn't certain when I would find the time to initiate Betje into the rites of the brew but knew, as the day for departure grew closer, it couldn't be delayed too much longer. Cool and dark apart from the cresset lamp I held and the rosy light leaking through the window, the cellar was filled with the sharp aroma of hops and the malty one of ale. I wove my way between the additional tuns to the troughs beneath the window. Three now sat where one had once sufficed. Foaming wort bobbed inside and, putting down my light, I pushed up my sleeve and slowly lowered my arm into it.

Cool, the wort was a lover's caress, sweet and enveloping. My arm slid through the liquid and song burst from me. Louder than I intended, it was both lament and celebration. Borne on every note was my fear of what might happen in the future and my rejoicing in what had. I sang for the ale, the beer, for Betje, Harry, Alyson, Adam, the twins . . . but most of all, I sang for Leander. Leander, who, through his belief and love for me, had made this brewery viable.

In many ways, leaving for Gloucester at this time was utter madness, but it was essential to ensure continuity of Crown trade. It was also important that I trust my sister and servants to do what I'd been training them for these last months.

And yet . . . I was anxious about placing trust in anyone other than myself.

*Betje is ready. This is her inheritance as much as it is yours—
as one day it will be Karel's and Isabella's . . .*

And so I sang my song in a way I never had before and felt
the ale respond.

About to lift my arm, another voice joined mine. I swung
around, my hand still in the wort, to see Betje descending into
the cellar. One hand on the wooden railing, she raised her head,
smiling, her song continuing as mine briefly faltered. An image
of the corner crones cackling and performing a jig danced across
my vision.

Fate, my old women, the goddess Ninkasi, Mother Mary, or
the good Lord Himself (or perhaps all of them) decreed the time
was ripe.

With one arm tranquil in the wort, I held out the other to
Betje. Moving as fast as she was able, her eye shining, her face
too, she folded herself against me, her tune uninterrupted, eager. Together, we turned to the trough and sliding my arm free
from the wort, I twined my fingers around Betje's and lowered
our arms into the ale. She gave a small gasp that became part
of the song. Swirling the mixture gently, working in a rhythm,
we sang.

Memories of the first time my mother introduced me to the
ale, to this wondrous ceremony of transformation and thanks,
overlaid themselves upon our ritual.

Whispering to her the same words Mother had to me all
those years ago, I encouraged her to keep singing as I spoke.

"In touching the ale and singing of its goodness and richness, my sweetling, we bring it to life. The ale is alive in ways
we don't understand. It's one of the great mysteries of existence,
a gift given to us by the ancient gods and which the good Lord

welcomes. The brew lives so we may be nourished and find pleasure in imbibing, so we may honor the heavens. So we sing to awaken it to life, to give our thanks and love for what it adds to our days. For though we are mortal and our time here fleeting, ale and beer are of the immortals. When we drink their gift, for a brief moment we become one with them."

Indicating she should keep her arm immersed, I reached for a tankard and filled it. "It's time to thank those who keep constant watch, who dwell within all breweries whether the maker is aware of them or not. They ensure we respect this gift, this bit of immortal magic, and pay our proper dues. Ignore them at your peril. The corner crones are the gods' emissaries, and we must acknowledge them and what they do." Taking Betje's other hand, I drew her away from the wort and moved from one corner of the cellar to the other, bending and offering the crones their daily libation.

As we finished, we emptied the tankard, our faces aglow. Betje threw her arms around me. We held each other tightly and I could feel her little body trembling.

"Oh, Anneke, I've touched the stars and seen heaven."

"Aye, my love. That you have." I dropped to one knee and took her chin in my hand. "You must remember to do this each day, sweetling. No one must know. Do you understand? It's our secret."

She nodded, tears welling in her eye.

About to release her, I saw something move on the stairs.

It was Harry.

Crouched down, he didn't know I'd seen him.

He'd witnessed the forbidden, the pagan rites that gave my ale and beer its quality, its "magic." Mother had warned me that if it was discovered, what we did would be considered an act of heresy that would attract the most brutal punishment.

"People fear what they don't understand," she'd explained and told me I must tell no one. "They would believe it devil's work. Yet it's most godly; it's of the divine."

Harry's spying on us didn't disturb me as it would have only months ago. I'd changed, our circumstances had as well, and, if we were to succeed, if the wheel of fortune should turn in our favor, if I was to go to Gloucester, the time for secrets was over. The gods and corner crones had spoken. It was time to trust those beyond the family, those I knew would protect the de Winter traditions and those responsible for carrying them out.

"Harry," I called.

Betje exclaimed, spinning out of my arms, her hands flying to cover her mouth. She gazed from me to Harry and back again, fear on her face.

"It's all right, sweetling." I held out a hand. "Come here, Harry. There's some folk I would like you to meet."

And so, on what became a bright summer's day, Betje and Harry not only met the crones, but sang the ale to life. Together.

All this coursed through my head as Alyson and I journeyed along the bumpy road to Gloucester. Birds swooped and warbled, gliding on the air; in the hedgerows, fat bees purred, supping on the late-blooming flowers.

This was only the third time in my life I'd traveled anywhere, and I confess that I was captivated by the sights, from towering trees resplendent in their cloaks of umber, claret, and jade to small churches, great estates, thatched cottages with wheezing chimneys and freshly plowed fields. A noble lady's box-like carriage rumbled past, replete with at least thirty outriders and dozens of carts laden with chests and servants for which we had to pull off the road, as did pilgrims and priests, knights and peasants. Concerned for our comfort, Leander intended we would be five days on the road with accommodation organized at inns, a private home, a priory, and a wealthy merchant's house in Oxford.

Overwhelmed by the chivalry we were shown, Alyson kept sending prayers of thanks to Mother Mary and Leander, all the while smoothing the fabric of her new tunic or twirling the laces on her surcoat.

Dispatching letters from each of our stops, I wrote to Betje, describing what we'd seen that day, what we'd eaten, and resisted the urge to send reminders to care for herself, the babes, and the brew. Instead, I sent instructions to Adam, who I knew would understand that my intention was not to harangue but to reassure myself. It was testimony to Alyson's trust in Adam that she left the day-to-day running of the bathhouse to him as well.

"He's a Godsend, that man. Kind and clever, decent, he is. You're blessed to know one such as him. I'm blessed . . ." Hesitating, she pulled her lip. "Pity 'bout . . ." Her voice trailed off and she found something else to distract her. She never did explain what was such a pity and I never thought to ask.

Finally, on the twenty-second of October, after a wet, gloomy day on the road, we arrived in Gloucester.

❦

A light rain fell as we passed beneath the city walls. The outriders showed our papers to the porters, paid our fees, and with a bow and lingering stares, we were admitted. Gloucester itself was a large city, best known for being the place where King

William ordered the *Domesday Book* written, and as the resting place of King Edward (which Alyson determined to visit—"I must have that badge to add to my collection"). It was also renowned for the number of wool merchants and drapers who dwelled within the walls. The enormous spire of Gloucester Abbey loomed large, dwarfing the many other churches competing for God's attention and ours. Parliament would sit within the high Abbey walls the day after the morrow, when His Grace King Henry would meet the commons and make the laws that governed our land. However, I was more interested in ensuring the ale and beer I'd made was available and fit to drink. In order to do that, I had to unload the cart and check the contents. The beer would be better for having been left, but if the ale had soured, then the entire trip would have been for naught. We were staying at Master John Banbury's house, a well-known merchant who was acquainted with Leander and who, we were reassured, would care for our cargo and us.

We rolled along Northgate Street, passing by an open market in the middle of which was a huge cross. Turning right, we entered Westgate Bridge Street, one of the main thoroughfares. Crowding the street were numerous inns, cottages, and multistory houses, many with shops. The familiar stench of slaughtered animals greeted us as we passed the butchers' stalls. Side by side in their aprons, the butchers hacked, plucked, and blooded the carcasses, all the while shouting to attract customers. On the opposite side of the street, more genteel operations were underway in the mercers' shops. I drank in the sights, the crowded houses, the occasional crofts, the Boothall, and, through a gap in the buildings, the wide, flowing Severn River. Barges, some larger craft, and punts idled by the docks. Mid-river, boats lay at anchor. Swans and ducks clustered fore and aft, drifting in the dark shadows of the vessels.

It wasn't until we passed St. Nicholas's Church that we came to Master Banbury's house. It was a huge, imposing place of three stories, and though it was made of wood, the roof was tiled. A wool merchant, Master Banbury was also the bailiff of Gloucester. We rode through wide-open gates, past the large shop with its milling customers, into an enormous galleried courtyard where chickens, pigs, and horses roamed, and servants carried buckets and baskets. In one corner, a smithy worked a forge, while in another, two boys fought with wooden swords. Shouts issued as we appeared and servants ran forward to grasp the reins, one leaping on the back of the cart, startling Alyson, to instruct the driver.

The horses were brought to a halt and the outriders dismounted, stamping their feet and exchanging loud greetings with Banbury's constables, who came forth when they saw who'd arrived. Two beautifully dressed older servants stepped forward carrying small wooden steps that they promptly placed on the ground for me and Alyson. Their forearms hovered at just the right height for our fingers to grasp as we alighted.

Nodding thanks, I stifled a groan as my feet hit the dirt. Though we'd taken our time reaching Gloucester, enjoying four changes of horses and a slow journey, the trip had still taken its toll and I was grateful to be off the cart, even if I'd sat upon a plush cushion for the duration. From Alyson's muttering and moans, she felt the same.

A man wearing a velvet surcoat appeared.

"God give you good day, ladies," he said, and bowed. "I'm Master Edulf Hardsted, Master Banbury's steward. If you would follow me."

Ushered past the kitchens and through a side entrance, we followed Master Hardsted's stockinged calves up some stairs, along a well-lit corridor, to a burnished wooden door, which he opened, gesturing with a sweep of his hand that we should step through. Announcing our presence in dramatic tones, he closed the door behind us, abandoning us in what was evidently the solar. From a chair by the large window, a man of medium build with light brown hair and dancing dark eyes rose.

"God give you good day, Mistress Anna, Goodwife Alyson. I am Master John Banbury and I do most humbly welcome you to Gloucester and my home."

Master Banbury was a congenial man who quickly offered us refreshments. Sipping a Bordeaux wine, no less, from a fine goblet, I studied the room, noting the large crackling hearth, the number of chairs, the tapestries, swords, shields, chests, and tables displaying plate and other fine objects. Master Edulf reappeared and whispered something to his master.

"Excuse me," he said. "What with guests arriving hourly, the king imminent, and business making demands, I am a poor host."

We reassured him this was not the case, and he advised that our barrels were being taken to the abbey where, once they were stored, we'd be able to inspect them.

Master Banbury escorted us back downstairs, where we were given further refreshments in the great hall. Around us, servants worked, preparing the room for what looked to be a feast. Additional trestles were erected, rushes replaced, silver shone, candles renewed, and extra wood for the fireplace brought in. We learned from one of the knights seated by us that a special supper was being held tonight, hence the preparations.

"Are we invited?" asked Alyson.

"I'd have thought Master Banbury would have made mention." Alyson scowled. "Aye, you'd have thought."

While we may have fooled others with our fine garments, Master Banbury knew what we were and evidently didn't want us gracing his tables that evening. Though I felt embarrassed, I couldn't blame him. The king's retinue was in town; Gloucester was filled with nobles, merchants, and the highest church officials as well. This was his chance to make an impression, just as it was mine, and there was no place for brewsters and bathhouse owners in his hall tonight, even if they were acquainted with the Rainfords and on the king's business.

Clearly I hadn't made a very good impression on Master Banbury, despite my fine clothes and manners.

Some people looked through facades and still didn't see.

Finally, we were taken upstairs to our room. The housekeeper, a stout but surprisingly young woman, advised us that a tray would be delivered at suppertime. Until then, we were at liberty to explore or rest at our leisure.

"The master apologizes for not inviting you to dine in the hall tonight, but he said it's not a place for ladies. He's hosting the Worshipful Company of Mercers, you see, and Master Thomas Chaucer—he's likely to become Speaker for the Commons, you know—and a few others. He said it could become rowdy."

After that, my impression of Master Banbury underwent an immediate reassessment.

As we settled ourselves into the room, with its generous pile of furs on the bed and a window opening onto an expansive view of the town, Alyson pulled her boots off and asked, "How are you s'posed to meet the king if he's not here yet? My understanding was we deliver the brew, stay a couple of days, then return, hopefully with the king's blessing in our ears and a contract for more ale in our hands."

I sat on the bed. The mattress was soft, the furs quality. My hand stroked them absentmindedly.

"That was my assumption as well. I'm sure His Grace can't be far away—the town is bursting with folk expecting him. Not all of them will be able to wait upon His Grace's leisure."

Alyson leaned back in her chair. "Neither can we. I was happy enough to place some distance between myself and Master Fynk for a few weeks, but king's decree or naught, I'll be heading back within a day or two. Some of us have to work."

"Aye." I flung myself back on the bed, my arms describing arcs in the fur as my head sank into the soft pillows. Sunlight dappled the ceiling, making the panels between the dark beams writhe. "Some of us do. But thank the dear Lord, not right this moment."

Intending to rest my eyes but briefly, I drifted into the deepest of slumbers.

⋘⋙

It was not yet vespers when we took advantage of the late sunshine and wandered through the town. Master Banbury may not have desired us in his hall (with good reason), but he showed us hospitality in other ways, sending an escort for us when he learned we'd like a stroll before supper. Master Gervase Fuller

was a newly appointed constable, the youngest son of a successful fuller who lived by the quay. Having grown up in Gloucester, he was able to show us the best streets and take us to shops
where the owners were less likely to swindle visitors. We wandered along the main road, back past the large cross to Oxbode
Lane, which was bursting with shops selling everything from
beads and spices to knives, candles, and laces. Bartering with
the shopkeepers, Alyson purchased some gloves for Betje and
Juliana, a necktie each for Adam and Harry, and other trinkets
for the girls. Near the Church of the Holy Trinity, I bought
some lovely fabric for a new tunic for Betje and some dresses
for the twins. Like Alyson, I spent my coin on baubles to amuse
Betje and Harry as well as something for Juliana, Constance,
and Emma. For Adam, I bought a beautiful quill made from a
dark wood that had an elegant peacock feather attached.

The afternoon sunshine quickly faded to the soft hues of
gold, rose, and duck-egg blue. The first stars twinkled in the
firmament, and a flock of starlings rose to swerve one way, then
another, before disappearing to the west. As we passed by a tavern and some alehouses, talk was loud and much of it about the
king. He'd arrived at the abbey only hours before, whilst we
slumbered, with his vast entourage, including his sons. My ears
pricked for news of Leander, but with so many by the king's
side, the chances of even a whisper were unrealistic. Nonetheless, I hoped.

What we did hear were rumors about the king's health. Unable to ride the distances to which he'd once been accustomed,
his river journey from his estates in Lancaster had been slow. He
was afflicted with a skin complaint that rendered him very ill;
no doctor or apothecary had been able to fathom the source of

it, though many had tried. Doctors in Gloucester were poised to come to his aid if necessary.

King Henry had assured the Lancastrian succession with so many sons, but that didn't stop the Ricardians, who either still believed King Richard was alive or that his blood should inherit, stirring up old enmities. Even here in Gloucester, I'd heard the king referred to as the usurper—a name that could land the person uttering it in a great deal of trouble. All I could think was that the king's health must be a great deal worse than I'd suspected if that sort of talk was about.

Alyson pulled her cloak more tightly around her as a cool breeze ushered in nightfall and we prepared to head back to Master Banbury's residence. "Since it's in the same direction, how 'bout we walk past the abbey walls," she suggested. "It'll get us out of this wind and we get a chance to see where the king is staying."

And Leander. I smiled at her gratefully.

With seeming goodwill, Master Gervase steered us into Grace Lane and along the street that ran by the abbey walls. Almost immediately the wind dropped. The abbey dwarfed the entire area. The main spire soared into the violet heavens and, over the walls and hedges, I caught glimpses of the chapel, its arches with their saints, gargoyles, and twinkling glass. As we approached the gates, the cloisters' rows of elegant columns came into view. A monument to faith and godliness, the abbey was truly re-markable; a place both fit for a king and his dear Lord. My eyes were so busy scanning the towers and spires that I failed to notice two monks deep in discussion with the guards by the wooden gates.

Dressed in the king's livery, with pikes in their hands and

swords at their hips, the soldiers stepped in front of the monks, whether to protect them or ask our business, I was uncertain. It was only when I heard the ring of a sword being drawn that I gasped and halted abruptly. When they saw we were but two women and a gentleman, they relaxed and waved us on.

Holding each other tightly, Alyson and I scurried past. At the last moment, I looked through the open gates in the foolish hope that Leander might be loitering in the gardens beyond. As I did, my eyes alighted on the monks. These were no ordinary men of God, but from their habits and bearing, bore high rank within the church.

The taller of the two glanced my way and, as his pale eyes met mine, I staggered. Only Alyson's firm grip prevented me from falling as everything before me darkened and my heart pounded in my ears. Recovering, I loosened my hold upon Alyson and looked over my shoulder, but the monk had turned his back to us.

My head spun. My thoughts whirled.

I barely remember the rest of our walk, arriving at Master Banbury's, passing through the gates, Alyson giving the porter a groat and thanking Master Gervase for his excellent company. Music and the sounds of merrymaking drifted from the hall. Ascending to our chamber, Alyson prattled on, telling the waiting maidservant where we'd been and what we'd seen. I barely registered any of it. Undoing my cloak, I let it fall upon the bed and drifted to the window. Though it was dusk and the silhouette of Gloucester's buildings and crofts spread before me, the abbey foremost, I saw none of it. All I could see was a pair of pale blue eyes, so like those that haunted my nightmares.

"What is it?" asked Alyson after the maid had left. "You

haven't said a word since we passed the abbey. Pining for Sir Leander, are you? You didn't really expect to spy him, did you? You'll see him soon enough, sweetling."

"Nay," I said finally, facing her. "It's not Sir Leander I'm thinking about."

There must have been something in my tone, for Alyson cupped my chin in her hand, concern on her face. "Tell me, chick, who is it who's stolen your tongue and invaded that pretty head of yours? You've not been the same since we saw those monks."

A quiver ran through me and I folded my arms around my body. "Alyson, I can barely breathe, barely think." My eyes darted to the window. "I know this sounds impossible, that it defies sense, but I swear to you, as we passed the abbey, I saw someone I thought never to see again."

"Who?"

"I saw Westel Calkin."

# FORTY-NINE

THE HOUSE OF JOHN BANBURY
AND GLOUCESTER ABBEY
Twenty-fourth of October
*The year of Our Lord 1407 in the eighth
year of the reign of Henry IV*

*S*haring fears with loved ones does much to reduce them. Rather than dismissing worries, they try to make sense of them while also offering consolation. So it was as I sat and talked with Alyson and, later, after the bells for compline sounded and the remnants of supper were taken away, Leander and Tobias as well.

When the knock on the door sounded, I believed it to be the maidservant come to collect our trays. Distracted as I bade her enter, it was only when I heard Alyson exclaim that I turned around and saw Leander and Tobias on the threshold.

I wanted nothing more than to fly into Leander's arms and shower him with kisses, but, containing my feelings, I dropped a curtsy and offered him my hands instead of my mouth. My

brother I embraced warmly, admiring the cut of his new surcoat and breeches, both, he informed me, in honor of his first
parliament; he would accompany his master to each sitting.
We summoned the maid and requested additional cups to be
brought and more wine. With Alyson and Tobias as my chaper-
ones, Leander's presence could not damage my reputation and
so we were able to converse easily and exchange stories about our
respective travels.

Relieved to know we'd encountered no troubles on our trip,
Leander inquired as to the health of everyone in Southwark.
Much to my chagrin, I hadn't heard and was only able to inform
him that when we parted, all was well.

The frown that marred his brow did not concern me, though
I caught Tobias casting his master an uneasy look. Before I
could question the source of this discomfort, the maid entered
with a tray. Drinks were poured and a platter of pork dumplings
provided for the men, who ate with relish.

"We had supper hours ago," explained Tobias, with the hunger one expects of a man of eighteen. "Since then, we've had
to endure endless introductions to knights, lord this and lady
that, and so many monks. I'd not thought to see that number of churchmen gathered in the one spot until I ascended to
God's side."

Leander spluttered his drink. "In my experience, by God's
side is not where you'd find them, Tobias."

"Amen to that." Alyson chuckled.

Mention of the monks recalled my earlier sighting. I could
not join the laughter but found myself wrapped in a mantle of
worry once more.

"What is it, Mistress Anna?" asked Leander, putting his

goblet down. "From your expression, it's evident something is bothering you."

Cursing myself that I could not dissemble, I tried to smile. "'Tis nothing, my lord, but a foolish woman seeing ghosts where there be none."

"What ghosts?" Leander looked from me to Alyson.

Quickly, so Alyson didn't embellish, I told Leander and Tobias what had happened and who I believed I saw.

"I know it's irrational, imprudent even, but this monk had the same almost silver-blue eyes and wore the robes of a Benedictine, and . . ." My voice petered out. Articulating what had happened hours after the event greatly lessened its power to disturb me. I shrugged.

"For certes, eyes like that are not common, but they're not uncommon either," said Leander softly, his words the caress he could not extend physically. "Rest assured, mistress, I will make some inquiries and see if I can discover who this monk might be. Let us see if we cannot end your perturbation. I only vaguely recall Calkin myself, but enough to recognize him if, like the good Lord, he's been resurrected."

"You mock me, my lord."

He shook his head. "I seek, mayhap poorly, to reassure you."

This time the smile reached my eyes and showed my gratitude.

"The rogue Calkin is dead, Anneke," said Tobias. "Leander and I searched the remains of Holcroft House thoroughly—no one could have survived such a terrible blaze. We . . . er . . . spoke to the monks of St. Jude's, Abbot Hubbard as well, though he was replaced not long after what happened."

My eyebrows shot up. I'd not known that.

"Aye," said Tobias, "he became very ill. Calkin never returned.

Abbot Hubbard denied any knowledge of him, admitted to having only one son and that was not his name. Claimed he would abjure such behavior in a monk, let alone a child of his. No matter who we asked or how hard we probed, we found no proof of a Calkin ever having existed—except in Holcroft House."

"But he did."

"Indeed, we met him, though I have trouble recalling him, so little did he draw attention to himself. Rest assured, dear sister, God has punished him for his vile sins."

The fire crackled, a candle went out, its dark smoke an ethereal finger that pointed heavenward. For all that I should forgive, I could not. I hoped Westel's soul resided far below. Merry voices carried along the corridor along with faint strains of music. No one spoke.

Tobias was right. Leander and Alyson too. Westel was dead, and every time I thought about him, or believed I saw him, I was merely bringing him and his wicked deeds to life again, punishing others and myself over and over. It did no one any good, least of all me. I had to bury him once and for all.

"You're right," I said finally. "It was just a trick of my mind. God has punished him and for His eternal justice I am grateful." I clapped my hands together. "Now, my lord"—I twisted toward Leander—"tell me, when do I get to meet His Grace? After all, is that not the purpose of this journey?"

Leander gave a look that melted my heart and tested my resolve not to throw my arms around him and beg him to carry me into the shadows then and there. I half rose and then sat again.

"My, you are excited, Anneke." There was a note of disapproval in Tobias's voice.

I bit back a laugh. Oh, I was.

"Well," said Leander, rubbing his chin. I noticed then how tired he looked, the shadows under his eyes, the way the muscle in his jaw throbbed when he moved his leg. Here I was, anxious about phantoms when real pain wracked my beloved. "Tomorrow will be a busy day for His Grace, but I'm hoping that once the commons choose their Speaker, and discussion starts, Arundel will ensure the sittings are not too onerous for the king. He's not enjoyed the best of health lately."

"So we'd heard," said Alyson. "What ails His Grace?"

"No physician has yet been able to uncover the problem, despite taking samples of royal piss almost every other day and consulting the stars." Leander shook his head. "It matters naught what they give him—potions, unguents—his skin burns, and he is afflicted with angry pustules over his body. He suffers great lethargy from time to time, hence the slow trip to Gloucester, eschewing the road for the river."

"He needs Marcian Vetazes, does His Grace. Works marvels, that man." Alyson folded her arms and nodded sagely.

"Our apothecary," I explained.

Leander seemed to consider the possibility before continuing. "I'm hoping, however, that His Grace will see you the day after the morrow. If I've any influence, it will be by week's end."

I wasn't sure how to respond. What I really wanted to know was when I would see Leander again. "And you, my lord, will it be busy for you as well?"

"Parliament always is. That's why, now that I'm assured my friend Banbury has made you comfortable and that you and the brew have arrived safely, I must depart." He sighed and heaved himself to his feet. Relying on his cane to keep him steady, he went to the door and paused.

I rose, smoothing my tunic. "My lord, forgive my fuss, but I must inspect the brew before the king tastes it. It wouldn't do for him to be served an ale that has soured or a beer that does not froth into a tankard, now would it?"

Leander smiled. "I doubt your brew would ever suffer the faults that afflict others. But you have a point. Tobias will escort you to the abbey's cellars after tierce tomorrow. You won't be the only brewer wanting to ensure the king's supplies made it here intact, so it would be good to arrive early."

Tobias frowned. He didn't like the idea of my needs taking priority over his. Leander clapped him on the back. "I've recommended your sister's brew to the king; if there's something wrong with it, I want to know before His Grace. Parliament can be a dull affair. You'll thank me for this distraction. Wait and see."

Tobias appeared dubious but resigned. I flashed Leander a grateful look.

"Come, Tobias, I promised John we'd join him for a drink in the hall. I just hope he's able to remember I kept my word."

Bidding adieu, I remained at the door as the men descended and, with a last look and wave back up the stairs, retreated into the hall. Shortly after, the maid came and helped us undress. Alyson wasted no time clambering beneath the furs, muttering her prayers as swiftly as she was able. Within minutes, gentle snores wafted the curtains.

Drawing a chair up to the window, I rested my elbows upon the sill and stared into the night. The moon glimmered on the river and the crenellated towers of the castle. Below, night watchmen, lamps held aloft, patrolled the streets; and within the dark, figures darted around corners and into doorways just ahead of their radiant path, those few folk brave or foolish enough to defy curfew and wander without light.

Though I'd made a commitment to bury Westel, it was moments like these, when I was left with no company but my straying thoughts, that he returned from the grave, larger than life and with a malice that made me tremble. Leander might think eyes that color weren't uncommon, but it wasn't just the color that made them different; it was what I saw reflected in those opaque orbs that made me quake in the depths of my very soul. For what I hadn't told anyone was that in that brief moment when our eyes locked I saw not evil or a gaze of longing or lust, which even monks were capable of giving. Nay. What I saw was fear. Fear and disbelief. And, in that, the monk's eyes echoed mine.

⊰≫×≪⊱

"That's ours, over there," I said, raising the cresset lamp high so it illuminated the corner of the cellar.

"Where?" asked Tobias, lifting the light he carried and almost bumping the monk Brother David, who had led us down here, in the face with his elbow.

"See? It says Son of Ale, there, beneath the band." I pointed to a stack of barrels.

"Son of Ale?"

"It's what your sister calls her beer," said Alyson, squeezing past. "Just as well or we'd be here all day trying to find the bloody barrels. Oh, excuse me, brother," she said, trying to swing around, but colliding with Tobias. "I'd not expected so many."

The black-garbed monk merely raised his eyes to the ceiling and crossed himself.

Forcing my way between the hundreds of barrels bearing

the brands of other brewers, I reached my own. When I entered the cellar and saw how many were stored in neat rows beneath the abbey—and these just for the king's and parliament's consumption—any fancy I had about being given Crown trade on the basis of this delivery dried quicker than a spilled ale in summer. Why, there was beer from Flanders, Belgium, Norwich, Chester, Brigstock, Tewksbury, Surrey, Kent, London, and many more places besides. Local brewers had also provided ale. Brother David explained how suppliers were sourced from everywhere and only the best were selected for the king's table.

"His taster and possibly one of his lords will be down shortly to try a couple of the brews. This occurs daily. Those approved end up at the high table."

"What about those that aren't?" asked Alyson.

"Why, they're for the commons to drink, or the monks."

"But how does the taster get through all these?" I looked around the cellar, trying to take in the vast number of barrels and skins.

"He doesn't. It's simply not possible." Brother David's voice was sympathetic.

"So mine might not get tasted at all."

Alyson huffed. Tobias shifted uncomfortably from foot to foot. Trying not to become despondent, I thought about those other brewers who didn't even get this opportunity. There was no point worrying about what might not happen. What if the king did try my brew? It was important that, just in case this should occur, I knew what he would experience. Taking a deep breath and trying not to cough as the cold air entered my lungs, I indicated two barrels. One bore the name Son of Ale, the other the three Xs branded in the manner of Southwark ale-conners and which denoted my ale. "Knock the bungs out of those, Tobias. Alyson, do you have the tankards?"

"Aye," said Alyson, sliding one expertly beneath the spot where Tobias struck and caught the little wooden plug. Ale chugged into one then another. Tobias quickly pushed the bung back in, hammering it sealed. Only a little liquid spilled onto the floor.

Putting my lamp on top of a neighboring barrel, I reached for the tankards. Passing one to Father David, I raised the other and, swirling it a few times, smelled the contents, capturing the earthy, rich odor of the malt, the smoky scent of the moss I'd burned with the wood and the herbs I'd added to impart flavor. But the proof was in the tasting.

Brother David was about to take a drink when a noise at the other end of the cellar made him pause. Voices followed by laughter and leisurely footsteps. A light bobbed. People approaching quickly, no doubt other brewers come to do exactly that which we were about.

I took a quick sip and was most pleased with the result. I lifted my tankard for Brother David to do the same.

"If you would just come this way, Your Grace," said a rough voice. "You'll find some of the lesser-known brews."

*Your Grace?* I shot a puzzled look at Alyson, who was staring wide-eyed at the approaching figures. She jerked her head furiously in their direction.

Turning, I watched a short but very wide monk holding a lamp aloft draw nearer. Behind him, three dark figures could just be discerned. The tallest had a graying, forked beard, a fine mustache, and his high forehead glinted, as if it were embedded with jewels . . .

"Your Grace," whispered Brother David in shocked tones

and dropped to his knees. Tobias and Alyson followed suit. If Alyson hadn't tugged my tunic, pulling me down beside her, I think I still would have been gawping, a brimming tankard in my hand as the king drew level. As it was, I fell into a deep curtsy, my chin tucked to my chest, one arm across my middle, the other still holding the ale.

Though I'd not yet offered proper thanks to them, I believe the gods and crones were looking out for me in that very moment.

"What's this?" said His Grace, laughter in his voice. "A monk, Brother David if I'm not mistaken, a squire, and two comely wenches waiting here to serve me?"

Before I could rise or explain our presence, the tankard was lifted from my fingers. I followed its journey from my hand to the king's mouth, and for the first (but not the last) time met the dark, weary eyes of my liege.

Only later was I to learn that, exhausted from his journey downriver from Evesham, the king had foregone the first day of parliament, much to the chagrin of the commons and lords, and left proceedings in the hands of Archbishop Arundel.

That was why, instead of listening to his cardinal virtues being sung by the holder of the church's highest office in the land, my king was in the cellars drinking ale.

My ale.

"Well, may the Lord shine blessings upon me," he said, smacking his lips together and then taking another swallow. "This be very fine. Who be responsible for this?"

"That would be me, Your Grace." Thanks to Ninkasi and sweet Mother Mary, I found my voice.

Turning to the monk beside him, the king lifted the tankard and studied the metal, as if the vessel were somehow responsible for producing what sat inside. "Uncommonly fine. Ensure this is served tonight." Draining his drink, he stared for a moment into its emptiness before realizing his subjects still knelt upon the cold dirt floor of the cellar.

Indicating we should rise, he smiled at me. "Is your ale always so fine?"

"Not as much as her beer," said Alyson before I could answer. "Would you like some of that too, Your Grace?"

Much to my delight, the king would not be satisfied until he tried that as well. While it was poured, I took a moment to study him. In the lamplight, I could see the skin affliction that Leander had mentioned. Pustules marred one side of his face; angry, red, and suppurating, they traveled over his temple and beneath his fair bonnet. Not even the bold ruby of the liripipe that trailed over his shoulders could disguise the marks on his neck. Beads of sweat dotted his forehead, despite the chill, and dark crescents underlined his inquisitive eyes. Even his hands suffered from the disease; they appeared scalded and sore and, though he tried to hide it, a slight quiver troubled them. None of this detracted from his magnificence. His height was mighty, and his chest and shoulders those of a warrior. The fine fabric of his embroidered surcoat gleamed in the flames, and the milky quality of the shirt that frothed at his wrist and neck was apparent. The fragrance of pine and cloves floated from his clothes and, I was certain, his forked beard as well. He spoke easily with us, his lords, Brother David, Alyson, and Tobias, reserving most of his conversation for me, taking great interest in my responses.

I'm not sure how long we spent in the bowels of Gloucester Abbey with the king, but it's a time I won't forget in a hurry. After trying the beer and questioning me thoroughly about where I learned to brew such quality, the king insisted we follow him from the cellar and make arrangements with his steward for more stock immediately.

"This reminds me of what I drank in my youth, in Prussia. God's truth, yours is among the best. It even surpasses that which the Hanse has supplied me with over the years. You have a magic touch, mistress."

His words made me glow. It wasn't the first time that had been said, but hearing it from King Henry endowed the words with a particular significance.

Exiting the cellar in the king's wake, we received astonished looks from the many monks, knights, merchants, and others who hovered around the chapels and cloisters, waiting to do the king's bidding, report a grievance, or merely witness parliament.

Outside the royal chambers on the first floor, the king bade us farewell. "I will leave you in the capable hands of my Lord Neville. He will see to it that you have a charter to provision us with ale and beer. I want a goodly supply sent to Eltham for Christmas, Thomas." He shook a finger at the broad-shouldered man with dark hair beside him. "I hope that is in your capacity to achieve, Mistress Anna de Winter? Certainly, your champion, Sir Leander—your master, I believe?" The king turned his intelligent eyes upon Tobias, who promptly blushed to the roots. "He speaks most highly of you and your accomplishments."

"He has great faith in Mistress Anna, Your Grace," said Tobias, executing a smart bow.

His Grace spun back to me, brows raised, waiting for my response.

"Indeed, Your Grace. It's well within my capacity to accomplish."

"Why did I not doubt that for a minute?" The king smiled. It was a sad, gentle smile, as if he'd almost forgotten how. "You're a rare one, mistress, that I can see. An exceptional flower in a field of chaff. Sir Leander is most fortunate to have found you. So, God be praised, am I." He took my hand. The skin was coarse, irregular. "Not that I imagine someone like you would be lost for long."

Raising my hand to his mouth, his lips were warm and firm, but his look was not the sort to which I'd grown accustomed. It wasn't lascivious but respectful; he gazed upon me as a crafts-woman first. The twinkle in his eye that followed his kiss, however, was not that of a king, but a man. "I will enjoy recalling your face while I drink your ale and beer, Mistress de Winter. More than you will know."

Curtsying deeply, when I straightened once more he was gone.

"Wait here," said Lord Neville. "I will have the agreement drawn immediately." We watched him leave, excitement burst-ing forth only once he was gone.

"God's goodwill and that of all the saints and angels was upon you today, Anna." Alyson threw her arms around me. "I cannot credit what happened. Fancy that. There we were, about to test the brew and who comes upon us but King Henry, may God bless and keep him for ever and ever." She grabbed my hands and spun me around. We giggled like little girls.

"Hush," said Tobias, waving us to silence as we drew stares from some monks and pilgrims. But he too wore a grin.

When the bells for sext sounded, Brother David bade us adieu and God's grace. "Though I believe you've had your fair share today." He patted my hand kindly.

Standing in the outer chamber of the king's suites, we were

brought refreshment and invited to sit on the benches that lined the walls. While I sipped a mazer of ale, I could not eat the trencher of bread or the cheese that was offered. My stomach churned and my mind was filled with plans. The sooner I returned to Southwark, the better. Now I was to be accorded the status of royal brewer, a title Alyson could not recall being given in Southwark and certainly not to a woman, the orders I already thought plentiful would increase at least tenfold.

"A hundredfold," corrected Alyson. "Sweet Jesù, we're going to have to hire extra hands and fast. We can write to Adam and have him start looking for suitable lads and lasses. We've no time to waste." I agreed.

Yet while we waited for Lord Neville to summon us, I barely noticed the time passing. Tobias came and went, Alyson found the wife of a mercer and their acolyte son to chat with, but I simply sat in silence, making lists in my head, working out how I would fill the king's and others' orders. I was also considering how I could get word to Leander. Oh, I knew Tobias would be sure to tell him of our good fortune as soon as parliament finished sitting for the day, but I wanted to thank him myself. Without his recommendation, without his suggestion that we come to Gloucester, none of this would have happened. Now, not only were my future and Alyson's assured, but those of Betje and the twins as well. I could see when Tobias looked at me that he understood and accepted that while this may not have been what Father or Mother had planned for us, or what he desired, and while much pain and suffering, loss and misunderstanding had led to this moment, we'd arrived nonetheless.

The de Winter and Sheldrake fortunes were on the rise.

Just as the bells for sext rang we were summoned; the doors

opened wide, a servant in royal livery, with a large quivering nose and eyes that alighted upon us before fixing on a point above our heads, led us into a small study with a large desk. Behind it sat a thin gentleman in dark robes. The insignia on his surcoat revealed he was a lawyer. Indicating I should sit on the stool before the desk, and Alyson and Tobias remain standing, he pushed a piece of parchment in front of me and quickly ran through what was written upon it. I should have had a lawyer present or someone with more knowledge of these kinds of things, but I was no fool; though I confess seeing the king's coat of arms with its three fleurs-de-lis and lion and unicorn holding the shield did dazzle me and mayhap made me cast sense aside.

Taking the quill from the lawyer, I signed the designated portion, the lavish ostrich feather tickling my nose and making me to sneeze. Emboldened, I laughed, as did Alyson, who also squeezed my shoulders and dropped a light kiss on top of my head. At that, even the lawyer raised his head and grinned.

"We must needs return to Southwark as fast as possible and secure this order," I said, clutching the copy of the royal agreement while trying to slide my fingers into gloves.

"Southwark?" Raising his chin momentarily, his brow furrowed, the lawyer lifted a few papers from one pile and, glancing casually at their contents, shifted them to another. "You'd be better off tarrying here awhile."

"Oh, why is that?" said Alyson in a haughty tone, assuming he was casting aspersions on her home.

The lawyer dropped the last of the papers on top of a growing mound and straightened the edges. "Have you not heard?"

"Heard what, sir?" I asked.

The lawyer glanced at Tobias. "Have you not told them?"

"What?"

"We received notice that pestilence has once again marred our shores. London, Southwark, Bishop's Lynn, even York. People are dying by the hundreds. You'd be wise to avoid returning until it's safe."

Horrified, I leapt to my feet, the stool rocking on its legs.

*Betje. The twins.*

"Forgive me, sir, then it's more imperative than ever that we leave at once." I spun to Alyson, who was wringing her hands, her mouth working but no words escaping.

Tobias looked at me in pity, shaking his head. "Anna, are you sure that's wise?"

The lawyer regarded me over steepled fingers. "I fear your ale has gone to your head, mistress. You're safe here."

"But my babes are not, and they need me. May God give you good day, sir." With more force than I intended, I pushed past Tobias, Alyson in my wake, and marched out of the abbey, blind to the looks my swift passage attracted.

"Why didn't you tell me?" I snapped at Tobias.

"It had not yet been confirmed and we didn't want to alarm you."

*We?* I recalled the looks my brother and his master had exchanged. "You'd no right to keep this from me."

"Or me," added Alyson, fury coating her words with a fine spray. "We're not children to be shielded from bad tidings, but women who have responsibilities, a duty of care to others."

Abashed, Tobias's mouth folded into a grim line. "I must tell Sir Leander." Excusing himself, we parted company. I barely gave him a thought.

All I could think was that the bells, the people dying in Southwark, in London, all made terrible sense.

Pestilence, the murrain.

Once again, Death was knocking on my door, only this time, I wasn't there to ensure it remained closed to him. I wasn't there to protect my babes.

"Oh, Anna," said Alyson, her voice a lament as we all but ran back to Master Banbury's. "Why did we ever come?"

For once, I'd no answer.

# FIFTY

SOUTHWARK, THE SWANNE
Late October
*The year of Our Lord 1407 in the eighth and
ninth years of the reign of Henry IV*

A journey that should take four days took us less, thanks to Sir Leander and the horses and escort he placed at our disposal. Unable to accompany us, he sent Tobias and the guards who'd originally brought us to Gloucester in his stead. Mounted upon two fine destriers, we left as dawn broke on the twenty-fifth of October and passed through Ludgate before curfew on the twenty-eighth.

The entire way, rain and sleet lashed our bodies; icy gales transformed our cloaks into giant wings as we rode like the hounds of hell were snapping at our heels. Truth be told, I felt little. Barely recalling where we stayed or what we ate, my one purpose, my consummate focus, was on getting back to The Swanne—to Betje and the twins. Rumors of the pestilence were rife and each time we changed horses, the number of dead and the areas afflicted grew. The closer we drew to the city walls, the more evidence of the horror presented itself. There were mass graves, houses set to flame, weeping children, women, and stoic men grieving over freshly dug mounds. Hovering above it all was the stench of death.

Filled with trepidation and urgency, scarves covering our noses and mouths so we didn't breath the foul odors, we rode through London, crossing a much subdued and fogbound bridge. Suspicious faces peered at us from cracked shutters, limpid voices called for help, God, their mothers, from murky corners. People scurried out of sight to avoid contact. In London and Southwark fires burned, the gray smoke rising and blending, joining the city and its poorer cousin together in a way they never would be upon the earth before merging with the leaden clouds that slumped over all. Church bells rang; hollow, discordant voices tolling dirges for the dead and dying.

Evening was upon us by the time we trotted past the darkened doors of inns, taverns, shops, and the infamous bathhouses of Bankside. Apart from a cart covered with a sodden piece of canvas and two men, their faces wrapped in filthy linen, walking solemnly on either side of the poor beast dragging it, while the lamps attached to the cart spluttered their protest, it was deserted. Only as we drew level with the cart did I see the stiffened limbs jutting out of the corners, the swollen, putrid flesh gleaming ghostly in the fragmented light, and caught the overpowering stench. After that, I could smell nothing else.

Without speaking we rode, choosing not to look at each other lest we see our own trepidation confirmed. Anxious faces pressed to windows and peeling back pigskin to spy our passing meant our arrival was noted.

Knocking at The Swanne, it took Alyson's shouted threat and Tobias's demands before the gates were reluctantly opened. Snapping shut behind us, lads I'd never seen before secured the bolts then ran forward, their eyes assessing our state before helping us to dismount.

"Who might you be?" Alyson turned upon the youths, taking in their slovenly appearance, their dirty faces and filthy hands, slapping a proffered arm out of the way and sliding off her mount unaided. Tired, afraid, she bristled with fury.

The poor boy she addressed trembled. "I be Hodge, mistress, Hodge le Dun, assistant to the ostler." He jerked his chin toward the older boy waiting to help me. "That be me brother, Ralph le Dun."

Alyson grunted and spun around, her eyes grazing the shuttered windows, the stable door ajar, the overturned barrel in the mud.

One of the guards helped me off the horse. Smoke was thick in the air, but it failed to disguise the sweet, ripe smell that only death conveys: the pungent miasma of sickness. Screwing up my nose, I looked at the barren spaces where less than two weeks ago, womenfolk bustled along corridors and up and down the stairs, tradespeople entered and exited, shouting for assistance or payment, deliveries arrived and customers were entertained. Banished into the halls of memory, there was only silence. Silence filled with foreboding.

Rain began to fall. Light at first, collecting in opaque pools at our feet. Still, we didn't move and no one came. My throat burned. None of this augured well. I tried to find some courage, the strength to face what we would find, but it was in short supply. All the prayers I'd sent to the good Lord, to Mother

Mary, the desperate, belated bargains I'd struck from the time we left Gloucester to this moment—anything to prevent or reverse what I feared—seemed futile. It was evident they hadn't been answered. God was not in the mood to trade.

Alyson took a deep breath, but before she could shout or I could offer caution, we heard voices. First Harry then Betje stumbled out of the kitchen door, Harry holding a cresset lamp and a dagger.

With a wail of relief, Betje limped over, while Harry, much to my surprise, let alone Alyson's, cast aside his weapon and flung himself into her arms, rendering her speechless.

At the sight of Betje, the guards exclaimed, one crossed himself and turned away. Anger swelled, and Tobias went to admonish them, but paused. They took her scars for the pestilence and were anxious for their safety. Seeing me clasp her, they were shamefaced. Give them a battlefield, a foe with a sword, and they would fight to the death. But a disease that works in stealth and attacks with no warning, which wields an invisible and corrupt weapon? Who creeps into homes and businesses, lurks upon the streets and river? That's an enemy worth fearing, and on spying Betje, they confronted their own weakness.

"Betje, my sweetling. Are you all right?" I showered kisses upon her head, dismayed by the greasy tangles, the filth that matted her gown and cheeks.

"I am," sobbed Betje. "Isabella and Karel too. They're safe."

The twins lived. *Thank you, Blessed Mary, oh my sweet Lord Jesus Christ, thank you.*

"But . . . but Anna . . ." She hiccuped, unable to speak for her tears. I held her close, looking over her head toward Alyson, who stood with her arms around Harry, her eyes glassy.

"Hush, sweetling, all in good time." Tobias came to my side, dropping to one knee beside Betje, stroking her hair, ignoring the knots, the dirt.

Around us, Hodge and Ralph tended the horses in the growing dark, the guards helping them. The rain was steadier now, steady and ice cold, frozen pinches to the flesh. There was no sign of Adam. The knot of wire that had sat in my stomach since we left Gloucester tightened, lancing my rib cage and finding its way into my throat.

Holding Harry tightly for a moment longer, Alyson then held him at arm's length, blinking the water out of her eyes. "Pull yourself together, me lad. I need you to be a man and tell us what's happened." She led him under the eaves and we followed.

Swiping the back of his hand across his nose, Harry shivered and nodded. Passing the lamp that had been doused by the rain to Alyson, he lifted the ends of his coat and wiped his eyes.

"We learned of the pestilence the day after you left. 'Twas a foreign man brought the news, said he used to be a captain with the Hanse."

My heart flipped. "Captain Stoyan? He was here?"

"That's him. Told us to make preparations. Him and Master Adam, they did what they could but they was too late." Harry dropped his eyes and swallowed.

"Go on, lad." Alyson's voice was thick, tight.

"It was already 'ere, Goody Alyson." Harry raised his hands in a helpless gesture. "Must have been a customer who was infected. He passed it to Bertha, for we found her two days later." He held the bridge of his nose as if to restrict or contain the recollection. "It was awful. She had these big, black boils oozing yellow, and was coughing fit to burst. Juliana tended her first. I went and fetched Master Adam and the captain. When they saw her, they ordered us to close the doors, not to allow anyone to enter. After that, the carters came for the body . . ." He gave a small sob. "Then, others fell ill as well. It was so fast, we couldn't do nothing, though we tried . . ."

Betje gave a cry of remembrance; I drew her closer.

"Where are Captain Stoyan and Adam now, lad?" asked Tobias.

Harry pointed toward the house, but before he could answer, a voice rang out in the dark.

"I be here." Holding a torch above his head, a familiar and welcome form approached, one I'd thought never to see again. Older, more creased but still possessed of those clear gray eyes, Captain Hatto Stoyan strode across the yard, his boots splattering the mud, plunging into the puddles.

Stopping short, he lifted the torch. "Now here's a sight to mend a fractured heart," he said. "*Liebchen.*" His eyes softened as he regarded me. Turning, he raised the torch higher and examined Alyson, Tobias, and the guards. With a grunt, he lowered it.

I stepped forward, intending to hold him before sense found me and I lowered my arms. "What are you doing here? I thought the Hanse forbade you from—"

"I resigned my commission. My God, child, you needed me here."

"Captain, how can I—"

"There will be time for *danke schön* and stories later," he said. "*Gott* be willing."

I quickly introduced the captain and Alyson. The captain gave Alyson a courteous bow. She bobbed a curtsy. Tobias gave a brusque nod that the captain returned.

"Goodwife Alyson," said the captain gravely. "I've some very bad news."

Raising her chin, Alyson pressed her lips together, her expression grim. "Tell me, how many of my chicks have I lost?"

Captain Stoyan hesitated. "Why don't we go into the house? It's warmer there and we'll be out of the rain."

Tobias put a hand up to prevent me moving. "Wait." We all stopped. "How do we know the pestilence won't take us if we go in there?" He nodded toward the door.

"We don't," said Captain Stoyan, and wrenched it open.

Leaving Hodge, Ralph, and the guards in the courtyard, we entered through the kitchen. There was a crackling fire in the hearth. The table was laden with bowls of eggs and ladles coated with a fine, milky slurry; a slumping sack of flour and a heel of old bread had been pushed to one side. On the benches, jugs of water and clean cloths were laid out, drying for reuse. A truckle bed and two makeshift mattresses took up the rest of the floor.

"We've been sleeping here," explained Betje, pointing to the truckle bed. Tansy lay, doll's limbs akimbo, upon the fur.

Unclasping our cloaks and laying them over stools near the fire, we sat on the edge of the bench.

"Very well," said Alyson. "We're out of the rain now. You can tell me."

With a deep breath, Captain Stoyan did. "So far, seven have died—" Alyson bit back a sob. "And two are not long for this world."

Dear Lord. Nearly all the girls.

I reached for Alyson, but she held a hand up to keep me at bay. "Who?"

Captain Stoyan looked at Harry. Crossing himself, mouth

atremble, Harry tugged his coat and, like a sentinel at a gate, stared into a dark corner and, in an expressionless voice, began. "Bertha, Leda, Juliana—"

I quickly stifled a cry as Harry continued. If he allowed himself to think of the life contained in the names, of the memories shared, the hopes and dreams snuffed out, he wouldn't be able to go on. He was being the man Alyson required and, in doing so, was the bravest among us.

Alyson collapsed to the floor, her tunic billowing, her head sinking to her chest. Her fingers scrabbled against the stones, helpless, hopeless. When I sank down and put my arms around her, she didn't resist, but pressed her wet cheeks to my bosom and opened her mouth in a silent cry.

Dear God. Juliana, bless her sweet soul. Bless them all. The weight in my chest became unbearable. Soundless tears coursed down my cheeks. Betje leaned against me, her arms looping my shoulders. Harry ceased talking, and, with the last name, the valor that had sustained him fled and he was as a marooned vessel. Captain Stoyan took over, continuing to count the toll. There was the laundress and her daughters and some men besides—customers, tradespeople who frequented the bathhouse; it wasn't only the girls who died. Neighboring establishments had fared worse. Tobias asked questions and it became apparent that it was only Captain Stoyan's warning, his courage in ignoring Hanse orders to cut all ties with me and to never come to The Swanne, along with Adam's foresight in closing it to further business, that had kept the casualties low. *Dear God.* Low. Even one life was too many. And it wasn't over yet.

With one hand upon Alyson, I held Betje as close as I could. What had my poor sweetling suffered in my absence? How frightened she must have been with all that death and illness around her, the randomness with which people were chosen. And yet, she'd been spared, my babes and Harry too. That was something for which I must be grateful.

Pushing Betje's lank hair from her face, I tried to study it by the light of the fire. Her features were inscribed with experiences no child should have to endure, and yet God in His wisdom had sought to test her further. Anger at our Lord diminished the gratitude I'd felt only moments earlier. Punish me, by all means, she who has sinned and sinned again, but Betje? Juliana? Could *she* not be spared? Was Betje's suffering and all this death my punishment? Alyson's too? But the twins, they'd been kept safe from this horror—so far.

Alyson dried her eyes and raised her face to Captain Stoyan. "And what about now? Is the pestilence still in the house? Still affecting my girls?"

"Some. They . . . linger. We tend to their needs. Sometimes, the passing is swift. Other times, not so."

Alyson nodded. "But you, you've survived."

"Aye. And more besides. Once we understood most of the girls were infected and some of their clients, we moved down here, away from the . . . from them. We left the upper rooms to the ill," said the captain. "We opened the windows to rid the place of the miasma, kept other doors shut. Locked the twins"—he looked to me—"along with their nurses and trusted servants, in the brewery. It was the best place for them. There's plenty of food and water. We communicate through the door. They are all well." He swung an arm toward the short passage that led to the cellar. "For some reason, the pestilence isn't here on the lower floors. We exit and enter the top floors from outside."

"Why are you not down there?" I asked Betje softly, nodding toward the cellar. "Why is Harry not?"

Betje chewed her mouth, the new front teeth pressing upon her lower lip making it protrude further. "We're s'posed to be. We were." Captain Stoyan made a clicking sound. I could barely hear her words. "But we wanted to help, so one night, Harry and I snuck out the other door, into the courtyard." I stared at her in horror. She didn't understand what she'd risked, what was at stake.

*"Help?"*

"I tried to talk her out of it, mistress, as God is me Lord, I did," said Harry. "But she wouldn't listen, would she? So, I came with her."

I looked from one to the other, shaking my head.

"It's what you would have done, Anna," said Betje. "The captain and Adam needed us—God protected us as I knew He would."

Searching for a response that wouldn't express only antagonism and confusion, I sat back on the bench and simply held Betje tighter. Her faith was greater than mine—in God and me. Dear sweet Lord, that she sought to render aid.

What Adam must have thought . . .

My thoughts froze. Adam. Where was he? Alyson appeared to arrive at the same question. Using the bench for leverage, she struggled to her feet and glanced around.

"Where is Adam, Captain Stoyan?" I asked, afraid of the answer.

Breaking off his conversation with Tobias and the guards, Captain Stoyan turned slowly. "You'd better follow me."

With one arm around Alyson, I took Betje's hand and once more we followed the captain.

"Tell the men they can come and sit in here," said Tobias to Harry, who, with a glance at Alyson—who gave her consent—raced back outside. Captain Stoyan led us down the main corridor, toward the hall. "We locked the front door and, during the day, when Adam and I weren't tending to the sick, we kept guard. The lads you met, they manned the gates."

"Stop people getting in?" asked Alyson.

"*Nein*. Stop the infected getting out." Captain Stoyan's brow furrowed. "There were some of your clients who were most unhappy they were being forced to remain. In my experience, nobles and monks are very good at giving orders but not so at following them." He touched the top of his scabbard. "We found ways of making them obey. Five died within days. Their bodies, along with the girls, were given to the cart, may God assoil them. We'd no choice, you understand." Captain Stoyan put a comforting hand on Alyson's shoulder. She didn't shrug it off but dabbed her eyes. "Of those who may yet survive, there'll be trouble for our pains."

Alyson's brows shot up and she snapped her kerchief like a whip. "Ungrateful bastards. Don't they know you likely saved their lives?"

"And that of their families."

Stopping before the door that led to the front chamber, Captain Stoyan appeared about to say something, and then changed his mind. With a long, tired sigh, he pushed against it.

The door swung open and, in the light of the fireplace and burning candles, another truckle bed could be seen; erected down one end of the room, chairs and stools had been pushed against walls, the rushes forming hillocks around the legs. Facing the fire were three chairs and a small table upon which sat two thick candles, a book, a mazer, and a jug. Cloths hung near the hearth, as did a clean shirt. Extra blankets were folded at the end of the bed. Adam lay beneath the covers, his eyes shut, his breathing hoarse. Approaching cautiously, there were no black buboes, no open sores or yellow fluid upon his flesh. Aye, he was pale and shrunken, but he didn't have the pestilence. Stuffy, the room didn't carry the pungent odor of sickness, just the stale smell of unwashed flesh and sweat.

I looked over my shoulder at first Alyson, then Captain Stoyan. "What's wrong with him?"

Indicating I should sit, Captain Stoyan squatted beside my chair and in a low voice explained. "I don't know; only that, one morning, I awoke in the kitchen and found him thus. He has all but lost the power of speech. The right-hand side of his body is limp, useless. He cannot walk, feed himself, or anything else." He stared at me meaningfully. "When I understood it was not the pox, I carried him here, mainly so he wouldn't disturb the children." He flashed Betje the warmest of smiles. "Your sister has taken it upon herself to care for him. She feeds him, reads to him, washes his face and hands, rubs them. Harry and I, between us, attend to his other needs."

Turning to examine Adam, I wondered when had he grown so old. Somehow, I'd thought of him as ageless, almost immortal, and yet here he was, a withered man of many years. His eyelids were so fine, I could see the network of veins upon them and the movement of his eyes behind them. What was he seeing as he slumbered? Lines crisscrossed his cheeks, from the corner of his eyes, fanning toward his temples. They ran in lines from his nose to edges of his mouth. Even his neck, once so firm and upright, had collapsed into a concertina of flesh, as if his spine had melted. His right arm lay upon the bed, the hand curled into a claw.

"I've been rubbing the ointment Mother Joanna taught us to make into it," said Betje, her small fingers twining through Adam's, demonstrating.

My voice caught in my throat. Sitting opposite, Alyson's face crumpled.

Captain Stoyan stood, his knees creaking, his hand upon the back of my chair. "I've seen this before, men who, after surviving a storm at sea, pitting themselves against great odds, find their body betrays them when they need it most. Some recover. Most are never the same again."

"Has the doctor been? The apothecary?"

"*Ja*, the apothecary, but there was naught he could do and there were others to tend. He gave us valerian, said to keep him warm, allow him to sleep. When he wakes, to encourage movement. Read to him. All is being done."

A small amount of spittle had collected in the corner of Adam's mouth. I leaned over to dab it away. As my kerchief touched his lips, his eyelids flew open. Blinking back the tears, I gave a watery smile. "God give you good day, Adam Barfoot."

The spark behind the eyes was still the same, but the noise that came from his mouth was not. Lips and tongue refused to cooperate, the sounds issuing being more animal than human. Nodding and taking his other hand into mine, I kissed the back of it. When I drew away, a salty wetness coated the skin; I brushed it away gently.

"Dear Adam. I'm back, Alyson too—"

Alyson rose slightly so her face was in his line of vision. His eyes took a little while longer to slide to her face but, when they did, the sounds increased.

"And Tobias. He's here." I beckoned him forward, moving aside so Adam could see him.

Tobias's mouth twisted awkwardly and, backing away from the bed, he shook his head, his eyes glassy.

I took pity on him and, turning to Adam, spoke softly. "We've come to relieve you of the burden of care. You have looked after Betty and Harry so well. You saved the twins—you and the captain. I do not know how to thank you. We want you to rest, Adam." I choked and had to pause and contain myself before continuing. "We will take over now. It's our turn." I wanted to say everything would be all right, that he would be fine, nothing further would happen. But who was I to offer such platitudes? Predict what God would see fit to throw at us next? I could not give Adam false hope; I knew he would expect nothing but the truth from me.

Understanding more than he was able to convey, Adam ceased trying to speak and relaxed into the bed. Betje continued to massage his hands and, after a while, Captain Stoyan disappeared, returning with mazers of ale and some bread for us to eat. I'd had nothing since before Ludgate and, much to my surprise, was famished. I watched as Betje patiently broke the bread and fed it to Adam, dipping it in the ale to soften it before squeezing it between his teeth. Harry, who'd rejoined us at some point, stoked the fire. Captain Stoyan and Harry absented themselves, the captain telling Betje to remain with us. I only discovered later that they went to tend the sick upstairs.

Alyson, Tobias, and I spoke for a long time, discussing what had happened here in Southwark and at Gloucester, and what we were to do, pausing occasionally as our emotions and the enormity of what we faced almost overwhelmed us. When the candles finally burned out and Adam, with the help of some valerian, slept once more, we left him in peace, Harry by his side.

We retreated to the kitchen where the guards sat down one side of the table, Hodge and Ralph with them, ale in their hands, the remnants of bread before them.

"What are you going to do?" I asked Tobias.

With his back to the hearth, Tobias's face was cast in shadows and only the outline of his body was distinct. It could have been Leander standing there, only it wasn't. "I was to see you safe and then return to Ashlar Place and look to the Lady Cecilia. It's too late to leave now. I'll have to go first thing in the morning—only . . . Anna . . ."

"Only what?"

"Are you *safe*? I mean, there are people dying above us." His eyes flicked to the ceiling. "Around—" His arm swung out to take in all of Bankside.

I gave a dry laugh. "As safe as anywhere else here. Or there," I said, jerking my head toward London. "I could ask you the same question. Has the pestilence reached Ashlar Place?"

"Not that I'm aware. What I do know, however, is it's here and so are you."

I went to his side. "Your duty is to your master and his wife, Tobias. I will be all right. Betty has survived thus far. The twins too. Sir Leander entrusted you with a task—you have completed a portion, now you must see it through. Whether you remain here or not will make no difference to God's plans."

"I know. It's just . . ."

His dark eyes met mine.

"Aye." I whispered and rested my forehead against his. We stood like that for some time.

One of the guards belched, and another slapped him on the back. Alyson said something caustic and ordered them outside to the mews, shoving some bedding in their arms. Grumbling, they rose. It was getting late or, rather, early. A new day was due to dawn.

Fumbling for my hand, Tobias held it tight then released it. "It's time for you to go now, too. Knowing you will be in the cellar goes some way to easing our parting."

While sitting around Adam's bed, we'd reached some hard decisions. Desperate to see my babes, certain I was not infected, my only choice was to remain in the cellar until such time as it was safe to reemerge. Alyson would stay in The Swanne too.

"As you must see to your babes, I must see to my mine," she said. "What's left of them, may God assoil them."

Captain Stoyan and Harry would continue what they'd been doing. With a sigh, I first wrote to Leander, a note I entrusted to Tobias, and then followed the small, narrow hallway that led to the cellar stairs. Assuming Betje would accompany me, I was soon disabused of that notion.

"Not me, Anna," she said in her soft, throaty voice as we reached the door. "I must be here for Adam. You go to my niece and nephew. I will be here when this is over."

When had my little sister grown the head and heart of her elders? Struck dumb, I simply nodded.

And so, before the cock crowed and the sad bells of St. Mary's chimed daybreak, Captain Stoyan lifted the heavy bar off the cellar door and undid the latch. And with a farewell that refused to acknowledge how dire the circumstances—clutching first the captain, then Alyson, Tobias, and Betje to my breast, trying not to think about the possible consequences of our decisions—I descended into the cellar.

The bar slid into place behind me with a dull thud and the clang of the latch echoed. I paused on the dark steps. Sorrow, regret, and a terrible, aching fear anchored me to the spot.

It was sometime before I was able to move again. And though my babes awaited me below, the devil's dark humor afflicted my every step, making my descent one from which all light and hope had fled.

# FIFTY-ONE

THE SWANNE
Late October to Christmastide
*The year of Our Lord 1407 in the ninth
year of the reign of Henry IV*

*O*ne person's calamity is another's fortune, I'd heard say, and that was certainly the case with the pestilence. The day we emerged from the cellar after it had passed, having ravaged the population like a fire through a field, we were fearful of what we'd find. Clinging to faith and the power of our prayers, despite evidence to the contrary, we entered the world with fresh eyes and renewed hope and vigor. For though we'd lost a great many to its deadly grip, we'd not suffered the losses of our neighbors who'd lacked Adam and Captain Stoyan's foresight and had instead seen The Swanne's closing as an opportunity to take custom. All the women of the Cardinal's Hatte had perished along with their master, as had the folk who owned and worked at the Boar's Head. Seven alehouses in the area would never reopen their doors, nor would two large taverns.

One of the first things we did was go to church, braving the snow and gusts of ice-driven wind. Father Kenton, who had also survived, said it was the freezing conditions that had driven the pestilence from our shores and, while it would produce its own kind of hardship, God was benevolent. In the candles we lit for the souls of the dead and the prayers whispered heavenward, we gave our shivering thanks.

It was only once that initial wondrous rush of relief passed that we understood what the loss of so many signified. Of the women of The Swanne, only three girls survived: Rose, Golda, and Mary, and that was due to the tireless ministrations of Alyson, Captain Stoyan, Harry, and Betje. The only customers to endure were a brother from St. Thomas (who sang the praises of Alyson and Captain Stoyan) and the son of Lord Chester: the latter, very badly scarred, swore that his father would seek vengeance upon Adam and the captain for forcing him to remain.

Ever with an eye to business, Alyson chose to cease trading as a bathhouse for the time being and turn everyone to helping in the brewery. After all, she reasoned, we had the king's order to fulfill. Captain Stoyan was sent to buy another mash tun and a trough, as well as barrels, butts, measures, bungs, and any other equipment I needed from premises whose owners would never again craft a brew. Guilt-ridden that we could purchase the extra equipment we needed so cheaply and swiftly, I was also grateful that we could offer coin and even work to some of those who were left with nothing.

Not even those who lived on the river escaped the pestilence. Not wanting to profit from others' misery, but needing to do something useful and wanting to remain on the water, with the money he'd saved, Captain Stoyan bought a barge from a widow who'd lost her husband and baby. Ferrying cargo and passengers across the Thames, giving priority to The Swanne's brewing business, he became a regular sight on the cold waters.

Alyson predicted our orders would increase once word of the Crown trade got around, and she was right. What augmented this was the shortage of other brewers to meet the needs of common folk and richer ones. Once again, local brewsters run out of business by the bigger alehouses and taverns (and the machinations of Master Fynk) were able not only to reenter the market but yield coin from trading. On market days, hucksters and brewsters started parading around the square and up and down the side streets, along London Bridge, selling jugs and skins of their home brews. Whereas once they would have been competition, they were welcome as they enabled us to focus on the larger orders. Some of the alehouses on St. Margaret's Hill and along the High Street that had lost their brewers also placed orders with us.

Travelers and troubadours would often call by and, for an ale or two, exchange tales and poems, songs and music. Thus we learned that the pestilence had mainly stayed within London and Southwark, though the port towns of Bishop's Lynn, Dover, and even Norwich and York had experienced losses as well. Itinerant workers, who had waited out the worst in Rochester, Canterbury, and other towns, made their way through Southwark en route to London in search of employment. The need for able men and trades had increased. Some called and requested work from us, especially young women who were orphaned by the plague and without a roof or skills. We took on a few, the cleaner and better spoken among them. Over time, The Swanne family was slowly restored to its former numbers and Alyson prepared to open for regular business after the Feast of the Epiphany.

Working from dawn to dusk, we filled our barrels, hogsheads, kilderkins, firkins, jugs, and skins. Every day, Master atte Place and Harry would load up either Shelby or the larger cart we'd taken to Gloucester and which Leander had generously sent back to us with barrels to be filled for the monks of St. Thomas, Winchester Palace, and even the great houses of West London, though Captain Stoyan transported these. Every day, we added more barrels of beer to the king's order, stacking them one atop the other in the mews, where they would await the approval and branding of the ale-conners. As November segued into December and Christmastide approached, we began to brew the king's ale as well.

⟨⟨⟨⟩⟩⟩

Since the pestilence vanished much in the manner it appeared, quietly, without fanfare or warning, leaving us humbled but not broken in its wake, I'd written to Leander several times and received correspondence in return—letters that lifted my spirits and did much to revive me when the magnitude of our losses and the number of orders overwhelmed me.

My earlier missives had been full of death and sorrow, but of late I'd been able to write in a more positive vein, about the growth of the twins, improvements in Adam's speech and movement, and Betje's remarkable abilities as both healer and brewer. Displaying gifts that were not apparent when I was her age, I was excited by the promise she showed. With each response I received, his concern for me and the well-being of my family leaped off the paper, even though he did his best to dis-

guise this with amusing tales of parliament and the great debate
concerning the Thirty-One Articles, to which the council, tired
of the commons and the debts they never met, objected. He
reported the goings-on at the abbey, and the gossip at the king's
table. Of his wife, he made no mention. His words, whatever
their subject, never failed to make my heart stop and my breath
quicken. Giddy as a girl around a maypole, I would hear the
cry of the courier and the stamp of hooves and wait with barely
suppressed excitement for Ralph or Hodge to call out that there
was a letter.

There were two communiqués, however, only days apart
and just before Christmastide, that upset the stability Leander's words generally restored. The first arrived on the Feast of
St. Nicholas, just as Harry came into the cellar to show us the
bishop's costume he would be wearing that evening when he
presided over our merrymaking. Gathering around him in excitement, there were oohs, ahhs, and laughter aplenty. Thus I
missed the sounds of the courier and knew nothing of his arrival
until Hodge came downstairs and placed a missive in my hand.
Slipping away from the group, I sat atop a barrel and read what
Leander had written.

Whether it was serendipity or some perverse Godly quirk,
Leander's note was also about bishops—a bishop and a monk.

*My well-beloved Anneke, I do commend myself to you, wish-*
*ing with all my heart that you are as well as your last letter*
*described.*

Writing that he would be spending Christmastide at Eltham
Palace, he also made mention that he hoped to be in London

before then, as the king had spoken of how much he was anticipating more of my ale and beer over Christmas. Leander offered
to accompany the order to Eltham and was granted permission.
The sole reason for his proposal, he confessed, was to see me. I
paused and held the letter against my heart.

It then went on to describe the closing stages of parliament
and the shocking news of the murder of King Henry's sworn
enemy, the Duke of Orléans. While this was most unsettling to
read, how such a great man could be so brutally dispatched, it
was the last part of his letter that disturbed me the most.

*Since you departed Gloucester with such haste and without the
prospect of discovering the identity of the monk who bore an
uncanny resemblance to the rogue Westel Calkin, I have, as
promised, sought to discover who this man might be. Upon describing his eyes and the color of his hair to the prior of Gloucester Abbey, he was able to identify the man immediately.*

My stomach did a somersault.

*Rest assured, my well-beloved, the man you saw is not Westel
Calkin, who, as we confirmed, perished in the flames of Holcroft House well over twelve months ago.*

I paused. Was it really so long ago that we fled Elmham
Lenn? That it was. So much had happened . . . The past had become like a vague dream or an opaque curtain that I sometimes
had to push aside to glimpse what lay behind it, only to find the
borders had become indistinct, the colors muted. The capac-

ity it had to throw me into despair or melancholy had lessened somewhat. Recognizing this had a peculiar effect. Ambivalence warred within me—relief the power that thoughts of Westel and his wicked deeds had to upset me was no longer so immediate, but also sadness that Karel's sweet face could no longer be recalled with the ease and passion it once could. Indeed, my Karel, as he grew and changed, was beginning not to replace my brother, but to merge with memories of him. With a sigh, I understood that the passage of time was a one-way journey and, while we could look back over our shoulders and reckon where we'd been and what we'd achieved, we could no more return to that place or change the impression we left than prevent the sun from rising.

Time could be both a cruel mistress and kind. Today, her torments were many as I could recall Westel and his actions far more readily than I could the visages of those I loved. Though I didn't want to, I'd no choice but to continue reading, my throat constricted with the dry dust of unshed tears.

*This monk is the recently appointed prior of St. Jude's, and is known as Roland le Bold . . .*

I frowned. Roland le Bold. Where had I heard that name?

*Though I did not spy nor speak to the man directly and thus was unable to satisfy myself as he had recently (for reasons not known to me) quit Gloucester, he is regarded as clever and Godly. The talk is that the king intends to confer upon him the Bishopric of Winchester.*

Dear God. If this was so, Roland le Bold would one day soon be our neighbor.

*My greatest hope is that these tidings do not cause you grief, my well-beloved, though a man who does so resemble your tormentor, your evil adversary, may shortly be dwelling in Southwark. I believe your great good sense will allow you to understand that a physical likeness to a dead enemy does not a living character define. Le Bold is not Westel Calkin and, from discussions I've had with those who know him well, seems a fit and worthy successor to the current bishop. Rumors do surround this man and what they claim is that in the short time since he replaced the rogue Abbot Hubbard, he has made St. Jude's prosper even further and overturned its sullied reputation. The wealth they accrue, mostly from brewing, is shared with Elmham Lenn and surrounding villages, making le Bold a figure of regard both among common folk and the church. For certes, his name was oft-mentioned.*

*My intention here is to allay your fears and I hope with all my heart this is what I have achieved. I will send you further news from this part of the world as soon as I am able. Unless, God willing, I may deliver it myself. May the Holy Trinity have you in its keeping.*

*Written on the second day of December.*

He signed with his usual flourish.

It may have been Leander's intention to reassure me, but my inability to place the name Roland le Bold troubled me deeply. So did the news that St. Jude's was doing well from brewing. Was that because they'd removed the competition? That evening, I read the letter to Alyson, Betje, Harry, Adam, and Captain Stoyan.

"There," said Alyson, clapping her hands together, "you've nothing to worry 'bout, as we said all along."

"Betty"—I turned to my sister, who was rubbing Adam's hand with a special liniment Mother Joanna had taught us to make—"does that name mean anything to you?"

Betje paused and screwed up her brow. "Not le Bold." The look she gave me finished her thought. *Only Calkin.*

With a sigh, I folded the letter, noting Adam in a state of great agitation. "What is it?" His arm flailed and he thumped the chair. Betje was forced to drop his other hand and to lean out of the way.

Adam stared at me, blinking rapidly.

"You know the name?"

Adam made a noise that we knew to mean "aye," and, though I pressed and asked all manner of questions, no further information could be gleaned. Frustrated, we ceased trying. Adam slumped in his chair and refused to look at me.

My sleep was interrupted that night, filled with flames and vile words delivered on sprays of spit. I tossed and turned, listening to the wind for what seemed like hours before finally drifting off into a broken slumber.

Two days later, a letter arrived that cast other thoughts aside—this time delivered by special courier.

It was Tobias.

❖

Called into the yard, I first thought my brother had come in Leander's stead to accompany the king's order to Eltham, but when I saw the look on his face, I froze mid-stride and my heart, which clamored to see him, beat ferociously. Pain flowered in my neck, pricked the back of my eyes, and stopped any words leaving my mouth.

Dressed in fine livery, with a heavy, ermine-lined cape, he dismounted from his horse and in four steps was by my side.

"Anna . . ." No longer did Tobias stammer over my new name. We were slates wiped clean and wrote our own stories now. Tobias was about to deliver the next chapter.

"Sir Leander?" The name was but a whimper on my trembling mouth.

"He's in good health." Frowning, Tobias handed me a scroll sealed with wax and bearing the Rainford mark. "He bade me give you this."

I stared at the roll in my hand, featherlight by any standard but weighted with portent nonetheless. Why did I not want to open it? Why was I filled with foreboding?

Shaking, I broke the wax, which fell like symmetrical drops of blood onto the snow, and unrolled the parchment.

*Mistress Anna . . .*

What? Not well-beloved?

*I greet you well and send you God's blessing and mine. I write to you now to inform you of the sad and terrible passing of the Lady Cecilia, my wife.*

My hand rushed to cover my mouth. I raised my face to Tobias. He nodded grimly.

*I wanted you to learn of this from me first and no other. For the time being, I am at Ashlar Place where I am making arrangements for her burial and mourning. After the period is over, I know not where I will find myself.*

 *Written on the Feast of the Conception of Our Lady, Leander.*

"How?"

Tobias stamped his feet and slapped his hands together a few times. His escort had not yet dismounted and their breath parted the air in frosty plumes.

"Don't answer. Come inside and get warm. Tell your men to go to the kitchen. Cook will provide for them."

Tobias followed me upstairs and into the solar where, before a blazing fire and with some mulled wine, he told me about the Lady Cecilia. How, even before Tobias left for Gloucester back in October, she had been possessed of a dreadful cough that was hidden from Leander lest it cause him concern. Blood would stain her kerchief with growing regularity. Upon learning of her affliction, Leander sent the best doctors to tend her. Despite the bloodlettings, the star charts that were read, and the potions drunk, she grew progressively weaker, her breathing more difficult until, finally, Leander was summoned home. He arrived just yesterday.

"He was too late, Anna. Though she received Extreme Unction, she passed into the Lord's arms only an hour before he arrived, Leander's name on her lips."

Bowing my head, I sent a prayer to sweet Jesù for her soul. "May God assoil her," I murmured, and was surprised at the deep sadness I felt for this woman I had never known but who

I'd wronged so markedly and who occupied a great deal of my thoughts. After all, we loved the same man.

"My master grieves, Anna, and it is difficult for me to leave him at such a time, but he insisted."

I barely heard Tobias; all I could think about was Lady Cecilia dying alone, without her husband, without the comfort of his presence. The poor woman. She deserved better.

"Anna, Anneke." Tobias stepped closer. Troubled, his brow was drawn and a tic worked in his cheek. "There's something I must ask you and, if I'm wrong, I beg your forgiveness now."

"What is it, Tobias?" Birds took wing in my chest. From the look on his face, the distant manner in which he had given me the letter, I knew what he was going to ask and I feared the question. Would I have the courage to answer him truthfully?

"Sir Leander . . . Leander was most insistent that I deliver that." He pointed at the scroll curled on Alyson's desk. He shook his head slowly. "I find it strange that of all those he must tell, of all those he reaches out to at a time of such grief, it is you. It puzzled me, as a great many things have over the last year: his desperate need to find you, his desire for your ale and even your beer over other perfectly fine alternatives. The way he ensured your brew was offered to the king, how he would describe your talent. How he used Lady Cecilia's dowry to repay his father the debt *you* owed for the loss of the house when it burned down."

I stumbled into a chair.

"Did you not know that?"

With my hand upon my breast, a poor attempt to still the moths that fluttered within, I answered, "I did not."

"Perhaps I should not be telling you, but he did. It seems he can forgive you anything, even the veneer of respectability you lost when you left Elmham Lenn in the manner you did."

"Tobias—" I began to rise.

"Let me finish."

I sank back onto the cushion again.

"For months, I tried to persuade myself that Sir Leander did it out of the kindness of his heart, took pity on my family when circumstances were so dire. That he didn't want your foolish preferences—"

"Please, Tobias—"

"Let me finish!" he shouted so loud the words propelled him forward, hands clenched by his side. I shrank back.

Lowering his voice, he continued. "Making my way here today, the reason for this forgiveness, generosity, and, frankly, absurd patronage occurred to me. I hesitate to ask lest I be wrong and grossly offend you and the memories of loved ones."

"What do you wish to ask, Tobias?"

Inhaling deeply, his eyes fixed on mine, he took a step closer. "Am I a bastard?"

Elevating his chin, there was high color on his cheeks that threw into contrast the mauve shadows beneath his eyes. I'd failed to see them before, being so caught up in the news he delivered.

"You see, I know Leander has a great fondness for you, one would have to be blind to not. The actions he takes on your behalf are more akin to those of a lover." His eyes flickered; I looked down. "Or what one would do to protect the interest of familial relations. Lover, I discredited at first but, mayhap, I'm wrong?"

I didn't respond.

"I see." His lips thinned. "Which led me to consider family. At once, so much made sense. Thus, I'm compelled to ask, am I a *Rainford* bastard?" The air escaped his lungs.

A falsehood teetered on the tip of my tongue. It would have been so easy; it would have spared so much heartache.

My response was whisper-quiet. "You are a Rainford, Tobias." His chin fell to his chest. "How long have you known?"

"Since Mother died. How long have you?"

His head flew up. His eyes were metal. "Lady Cecilia told me—not directly. She made mention of how fortunate I was that my father saw fit to bestow, if not his name upon me, then to at least ensure I reaped its benefits. She assumed I knew. I didn't understand at first, not until I took Leander's behavior into consideration." His fists were white-knuckled balls at his side. "I didn't believe it at first. I thought it a cruel jape. Why didn't you tell me?"

"Because it made no difference which side of the bed you were made upon or whose blood flowed in your veins. It still makes no difference. You are Tobias Sheldrake, my brother."

He began to laugh. It was forced, brutal. "But I'm not, Anna, don't you see? All this time I've operated under the delusion that though Father never appeared to care for me, he at least secured me an honorable position in the Rainford household, and as a squire, no less. I told myself that though he never showed affection, he must be invested in my future, otherwise why go to the trouble of procuring such a posting? Giving me to the Rainfords, I believed, was an act of fatherly care of the kind I'd been lacking. I did feel gratitude toward him, while laboring to find the feelings befitting a son toward a father—pride, a desire to emulate him, fondness. They never came. I felt only anger, fear, and loathing, and thus I felt guilty and disappointed in myself that I was such an ungrateful wretch. Discovering I was given to the Rainfords not out of paternal duty but as part of a business deal struck years earlier, both liberated and crushed me. For all that Father or Lord Rainford cared, I was a bale of wool, wine, or livestock to be traded and exchanged over a handshake and signature."

"Tobias—"

He continued as if I hadn't spoken. "In the end, Father didn't even profit from the agreement, nor did you and the twins. I've gained and you have lost everything, because of Father, because of me." His voice became thick. "Here I was, accusing you of damaging the Sheldrake reputation, when all along I've been the blight on the name—a name I've no right to bear." He flung his arms out and gave a bark of laughter. "The irony, Anna, the irony."

He crossed the room and gripped me by the forearm, his fingers digging into my flesh. "And you knew and never said a word."

"I . . . I . . ."

"Don't say anything." He let go of my arm and, in one swift action, collected his hood and cloak. "Truth is, I don't know whether to thank or curse you for not disclosing the truth. Knowledge can be a terrible thing—especially when you don't know what to do with it."

"What do you mean?"

"Now I know *what* I am, I need to work out *who* I am. Who I want to be. I also have to make amends for the losses I've caused."

"There is no compensation to be had, Tobias, not by me. You

didn't cause any of this." I tried to hold him, but he threw off my hand. "It was God's will."

"What? Father's bargain? The loss of our fortune? You being forced to brew—"

"That was a choice."

"Was it? Do you really believe that, Anna?" He made a grunting sound. "And what of Karel's death? The evil Calkin wrought? Was that God's will? Do you believe that?" He waited. I didn't reply. "I didn't think so."

"You're my brother, Tobias, regardless of what's happened."

"Am I?"

His eyes bore into mine until I was forced to look away. Hadn't I thought to use his birth against him, to fling the truth like mud when he sought to denigrate and control me? Hadn't I used knowledge of his true father to further my cause and that of the family of which Tobias no longer believed himself a part?

It was not Tobias who finally destroyed what we'd once been, that blame was mine alone to bear. Shame rose inside me. I was no better than Father, or Lord Rainford. It was not for Tobias to make amends, but me.

As these thoughts circled in my head, crows picking at memories, Tobias donned his cloak.

"Exactly," he said when still no answer was forthcoming. And before I could reassure him, ask that we talk further so I could beg forgiveness for my part, he left the room without another word.

# FIFTY-TWO

THE SWANNE

The cruelest winter: Christmastide to February

*The years of Our Lord 1407–1408 in the*

*ninth year of the reign of Henry IV*

*N*either Leander nor Tobias arrived to accompany the brew to Eltham. In the end, four days before Christmas, Captain Stoyan, Harry, and Master atte Place delivered the cargo. They returned the following day brimming with excitement; our ale and beer had been well received by the official taster, His Grace, and the peers of the realm sharing Christmastide at Eltham. This alone should have made the time of year special, as should the additional orders that came via the royal bottler, the man in charge of all the king's drink, and which were delivered by courier before the year was even over. Yet they failed to do so. Consumed by pity and guilt toward Tobias, sympathy and yearning for Leander, wanting to comfort both, I was forced to work.

In many ways, the demands of the brewery were a blessing as they distracted me from what I couldn't change.

Tobias departed before I'd time to write a response to Leander's tragic news. Quickly putting quill to paper after he left, I pushed our conversation to the back of my mind and wrote what needed to be said at such a time. I made no mention of what had passed between Tobias and myself, but offered my prayers and sympathy for his grave loss, and entrusted my heart into his keeping. I asked Hodge to deliver it.

As the weeks passed and there was no reply, I tried to ignore my growing concern.

Having kept the secret of Tobias's birth for so long, I saw no point in revealing it now. If he chose to tell others, I would support him—likewise if he did not. This didn't stop me worrying about the way we had parted, the doubts he'd expressed and the blame he was so ready to wear like a hairshirt. I wrote a long missive to him, absolving him of all responsibility for what had happened to us and confirming what I hoped he knew he always had—my love.

I prayed for him and his heart, hoping that in Leander's company, returned to his duties at court, he would find some solace and, most of all, what he wanted. His words rang: *I need to work out who I am. Who I want to be.*

Understanding that desire only too well, my subsequent letters contained no advice or warnings. I recounted simple events, like caroling around the fire, feasting upon goose and venison, baking eel pies. I told of Isabella's and Karel's growth and changes, teeth acquired, curls cascading, bruises obtained through curious explorations. I spoke of Betje, and of my efforts both inside the brewery and without. By concentrating on the activities of family members from whom he was ready to divorce himself, I hoped he would recognize the love and inclusion extended to him.

Christmastide came in a blend of holly, mistletoe, and fragrant smoke from the enormous yule log salvaged by Captain Stoyan, who on the Feast of St. Thomas the Apostle moved into The Swanne, renting a room from Alyson and thus becoming part of our ever-growing concern. Snow fell thick and fast for days on end and the howling winds found every crack and crevice and set us shivering even as we sat before blazing hearths, wrapped in blankets and sipping mulled wine. Still, no letters delighted my day; no words from Leander or Tobias to provide Christmas cheer or much-desired reassurances. I began to wear glumness like a tunic, as anxiety slowly eroded my joy in the season.

January made way for February and the winter grew colder and more savage until, one day, when the clouds slumbered over Southwark and a chill wind blew along the river, a longed-for courier finally arrived.

Unable to wait until I was on my own to read the letter pressed into my hand by an excited Hodge, I opened it in the brewery, eager to learn of Leander's well-being, of Tobias's as well.

I'd only to read the first line to have my heart put at ease before, in the next few, it was set bouncing around my chest again.

*My well-beloved Anneke.*

*I apologize with all my heart for my lengthy silence and want you to know that my lack of communication in no way reflects my deep and abiding concern for your well-being and that of your family.*

I paused. Alyson manifested before me.

"If you think you're keeping that to yourself, chick, you're wrong. Not after the agonies of wondering we've all endured and all your moping. Come, read it to us."

I stared at her.

"Speak up," she said.

Much to the chagrin of Alyson, Betje, and the girls who gathered at my feet, I skipped a few lines.

Clearing my throat and raising my voice slightly, I continued.

*There has been a bloody uprising in the north. Seeking to take advantage of the king's ongoing illness that has become a daily struggle he bravely endures, and this wretched weather, Lords Bardolph and Northumberland have seen fit to put into motion their planned treachery—a rebellion. Though King Richard passed many years ago, they refuse to recognize His Grace's sovereignty and call him the usurper.*

*Wanting to end this sedition once and for all, Henry has ordered his armies into the north as fast as possible. By the time you read this, I will be leading the good men of Elmham Lenn and Suffolk to the border where we will conclude these treasonous plots once and for all.*

*Rest assured, I will care for your brother as I would my own.*

Quietly, I sent blessings to him on wings of love that he saw fit to write and tell me, that encoded within his letter were reassurances and so much more.

"Well?" said Alyson.

I'd paused too long.

"Is there more?"

I glanced back at the worn paper.

*Excuse the brevity, my well-beloved, but know as we go into this final battle, it is with the strength of your love and my every hope for your good health and eternal prosperity.*

Ending my reading on a whisper, I did not share the way he closed this correspondence, nor was it demanded of me. But it made ribbons flutter in my chest and warmth invade my throat. *Oh, my beloved, stay safe. Dear, sweet Lord, keep him safe. Keep them both safe.*

"There's to be another battle then," said Master atte Place grimly.

"If it hasn't already been fought," said Alyson. "It explains why you've heard nothing these last weeks. King's had him all over the country, rallying troops in secret."

"Aye, the letter was written nigh on two weeks ago. He could not risk the information falling into the wrong hands." I folded it slowly, emotions tumbling over each other as I tried to reconcile my relief that Leander and Tobias were well with my fear that their circumstances may have altered.

"Please, God," I said softly, "let them be alive."

"Try not to dwell on any other possibility, chick." Aware that work in the brewery had stopped, Alyson glanced over her shoulder, put her hands on her hips, and glared. "Come on, I don't pay you to sit on your arses and rest your feet." She stamped her foot. "Back to work."

Mumbling, everyone slowly returned to the tasks at hand. Putting down the scoop she'd been holding, Betje came to my side.

"What will you do?" asked Alyson.

"What all women must do in this situation"—absentmindedly, I stroked Betje's hair—"wait. Though waiting does not sit well with me, Alyson." She nodded. "But I will see to it that a letter is sent in return and that whosoever delivers it waits for a response. I would know how my lord and my brother fare—for good or ill."

"What about the courier who brought this one? Can you not use him?"

"He's a king's messenger. Hodge said he downed a small ale and left. Even if I could, I wouldn't ask him to tarry while I put quill to paper."

"You'll be hard-pressed to find anyone to go north," said Alyson. She enfolded me in a brief hug before releasing me. "Not if there's to be fighting."

We looked at each other.

"It's likely over by now. But I will find someone."

"I've no doubt," she said and went back up the stairs.

Before the light failed, I'd read the letter twice again. Deciding Adam should share in the news, I went to the solar.

He nodded as I read it. His movements were improving daily, his face did not appear so lopsided, and his speech was becoming clearer; it no longer sounded as if he swallowed words before they were formed. Captain Stoyan called it a miracle. I preferred to call it Betje. Persistent and constant, my sister tended to Adam's needs, which were not simply physical, but of the heart and soul as well, talking to him, waiting patiently while he exerted himself to find the words, reading to him, massaging his limbs back to life.

Alyson declared her a saint, Harry boring, for he lost his companion during this time. I knew why Betje did it and marveled at her compassion, her understanding that yet again demonstrated a wisdom beyond her years.

Adam listened, and when I told him I wished to send word to

glean some news of Leander and Tobias, but was uncertain who could be relied upon to deliver it, he smiled.

"Captain Stoyan. Give him something to do instead of f . . . f . . . freezing . . . on his barge. That way, you get a r . . . report from someone you trust."

I stared at Adam in consternation. "Can I ask such a thing? Do you think he would?"

Adam tried to smile. "Well, you won't know unless you t . . . try."

Leaning over, I planted a kiss on his cheek. "You're right. Thank you, Adam. I will ask him and pray he agrees."

"He will," said Adam, with the confidence only a close acquaintance can muster.

Seated at Alyson's desk, I wrote Leander a brief but loving note, informing him that all was well in Southwark and we prayed for his and Tobias's safe return. And that I, particularly, longed for this to happen. Lest it be read by other eyes, I couched my love in terms that only he would understand.

Sealing the note with both wax and a kiss that conveyed all that my words could not, I bade Adam farewell and went downstairs.

"Where is Goody Alyson?" I asked Cook and Eve.

"Are you all right, mistress?" asked Eve, earning a scalding look from Cook.

"Never better."

"She's in the courtyard, mistress," answered Cook.

I flung my cloak over my shoulders and tied my hood into place. Pulling on gloves, I looked around. "Betty?"

"Waiting in the stables for Harry to return."

"God give you good day!" With a wave, I all but skipped out the door.

Alyson was in the courtyard supervising a coal delivery, her scarlet tunic bold against the newly fallen snow.

"Where are you off to, chick?" she asked as I waded through the snow, a big smile on my face.

"To hire a courier."

I enveloped her in a huge hug, trying but failing to lift her off her feet. "Put me down, you goose." She began to chuckle. "Who might that be?"

Hearing the commotion, Betje came running over. "Anna, are you all right?"

"Why does everyone keep asking me that?" I stroked her cheek. "I am better than all right. And when I return we will celebrate."

"Return from where?" asked Betje.

Alyson cocked her head. "Celebrate what?"

"I feel as if Christmastide has passed me by and I should make belated amends."

Alyson folded her arms and nodded approvingly. "It's never too late for amends."

"Indeed, that's what I think. I won't be long—back before curfew for certes and"—I squatted beside Betje, tugging at her hood—"then we'll rejoice." Retying my cape that had come loose when I attempted to pick up Alyson, I began to stride toward the gates, making way for Harry returning with a cart full of milled grain.

"Where are you going, Mistress Anna?" cried out Harry.

"To see Captain Stoyan," I answered. "My German Mercury." With a laugh, I disappeared out the gates as if there were wings on my feet.

While I'd been aware of the constant snow and strong winds and the frost that coated the windows, making them appear as if they were made of pigskin and not glass, I'd been confined indoors for weeks. Stories of ink freezing in inkwells, animals dying of cold, and the river ceasing to flow washed over me as I stepped into the day and spied the thick white coats on every building, the dead animals in ditches, their thin, craggy limbs encrusted by winter's breath. An abandoned well, too frigid to draw from, had broken buckets buried in hillocks of white powder at its base. The wind bit my exposed cheeks. The tales I'd heard but dismissed as fancy were both real and cruel.

But it wasn't until I stood upon the dock where Captain Stoyan moored his barge that I could no longer ignore the great and terrible effects of winter.

Adam had been serious when he spoke of the captain freezing. I thought he'd meant physical discomfort, something the captain would complain of nightly when he returned to The Swanne, when what he actually referred to was nature's course.

The wide, shifting river, once a seething, ceaseless rush of water that bubbled and frothed against the footings of the bridge and swirled in mighty currents as it sped toward the sea, was a solid mass. Boats were stuck in its midst, their ropes and sails garlanded with frost and ice. Children and adults slipped and slid across the glassy surface, shrieking with laughter, holding hands. Women and men hauled great sacks across, their backs bent, panting. Some risked weighty carts, their oxen and horses ignoring the slow-moving waters beneath them. Dogs scrambled to find purchase as they chased each other along the slippery edges, barking and growling. On the riverbanks, canny vendors lit fires, roasting chestnuts and other fare for purchase. Hawkers roamed back and forth, selling hot drinks.

It was like a fresh world had been created, one populated by the brave and foolhardy.

Even the docks, manacled in icy gauntlets, gave an air of industry to the scene. So did the boats and barges trapped in a glacial clinch. Among them was Captain Stoyan's barge, *The Lady Swanne*, upon which my gaze came to rest.

Smoke escaped from a vent in the small aft cabin, but not a soul appeared to be on board. Barrels were lashed down one end, along with bales of wool and sacks of barley, rye, or some other grain, which were covered with a flapping canvas. Wooden crates were stacked neatly toward the other end, their contents a mystery. Spending each day upon the barge, the captain both guarded his goods and—I now understood—waited with a mighty impatience for the ice to melt so he could resume work.

My steps faltered and I drew my cloak around me tight, the wind lifting the ends and lashing my ankles.

"Captain?" I cried out, a gust snatching my voice and hurling it against the ice. Perhaps he was upon the river? I covered my brow and peered.

"*Liebchen!* Mistress Anna." I spun around. "What are you doing out in such weather? Are you mad?"

Ducking out of the cabin, a cloud of smoke following, was Captain Stoyan. Snow began to fall, timid flakes that melted on contact. He strode across the deck, slipped and quickly regained his balance, chuckling at his near tumble, and leaped onto the wooden planks of the dock. The captain took my hand and gave a curt bow.

"What are you doing here? You'll freeze if you don't keep

moving." He indicated those on the river, most of whom were abandoning the ice, desperate to reach shore as the snow began to fall faster.

"I can see that," I said, nodding to his barge.

"*Ja*. It's been like this for days now. It will be longer yet, I fear." Screwing up his eyes, he raised his face, snowflakes catching on his eyelashes and beard.

"I've come to ask a favor."

Captain Stoyan raised his brows. "Then ask—consider it granted if it's in my compass to do so."

I grinned, my eyes softening. God had been kind indeed to bring this man back into my life.

"I was wondering if you would deliver a letter for me? It's for Sir Leander." I gestured to the barge. "I thought it could be delivered by river, but I was foolish to think that possible."

"Anything is possible and water is not the only mode of travel available." He gave me a warm smile and flicked the snow out of his thick hair. "Of course I will. It will give me something to do until the frost melts and I may once again ply my new trade upon the water."

"Before you so readily agree, you need to understand where I'm asking you to go." I quickly explained what I required and that a horse would be made available to him.

"This is not hardship but an adventure, something I've been sorely lacking of late. I will welcome it after being ground to a halt because of this." He gestured to the ice. "It will do my heart good to see Sir Leander and Tobias again and to know that in doing so, I will ease yours."

"Thank you, Captain. Thank you."

He waved his hands dismissively. "I will leave now, today,"

he said, examining the sky. "But before I go anywhere, I must secure the barge." He frowned at the goods on the deck. "I will ask Master atte Place to retrieve those and secure them at The Swanne until I return. Wait here. I'll be but a moment."

Walking as fast as the snow and ice would allow, he crossed the dock, leaped onto the deck, and disappeared inside the little cabin. Moments later, the smoke issuing from the small chimney ceased and he reemerged wearing a thick woolen cape with a hood, gloves, and with the sword he wore during the pestilence strapped to his side.

My eyes widened. I'd not considered he'd need a weapon. I began to protest, to retract my request.

The captain heard me out then smiled. "*Liebchen.* I'm grateful for the chance to serve—to see for myself what is happening beyond Southwark and London. Hopefully, I bring home good tidings, *ja?*"

"*Ja,*" I said, and spared the captain further protests. There was no more left to say. He'd made up his mind and had my eternal gratitude.

Linking his arm through mine, the captain didn't so much escort as helped me keep my feet as we walked along the river, into the wind and back to The Swanne. Ice-laden blasts pummeled my chest, taking my breath away, trying to rip the hood from my hair.

The farther we walked, the more the gasp-worthy blusters made it impossible to speak. My insides lurched at the thought of Leander and Tobias and the threats they faced, not simply from the rebels, but from this bitter, bitter cold. And now I had asked the captain to endure it as well.

Holding tight to each other, Captain Stoyan and I skidded

on the frozen ground, pushed through fresh piles of snow. Shops had closed their shutters, as had many houses. The few vendors I'd seen as I walked to the dock had already packed up and gone home. Skinny dogs lay curled, shivering, in doorways, while a few fluffy pigeons roosted in the eaves of the church, their feathers ruffled, their little heads crooked beneath their wings. Though it was barely none, lights flickered in houses, while plumes of gray smoke were ripped from chimneys and scattered to the sky. Drifts of snow formed lopsided mountains against doors and on stoops, sealing the occupants within white cocoons. Captain Stoyan was right—what possessed me to venture out this day? The answer was simple. I rested my glove against my breasts.

It took us almost an hour to cover a distance that would normally take much less time. Entering the kitchen, we divested ourselves of wet cloaks and gloves, and crowded at the fire. Trying to shoo us out of the way, Cook pushed steaming mugs of spiced wine into our hands. Flecks swirled on top and we sipped the contents gratefully. Finishing quickly, the captain excused himself and went to his room to pack some belongings.

When he reappeared a few minutes later, I gave him the letter, and watched as he carefully stowed it in the pocket of his surcoat. I also gave him a message to pass to both Leander and Tobias, whispering it to him. Captain Stoyan smiled and patted the place where the letter rested against his broad chest. "Both shall reach their destination, *liebchen*, which means I will too. Do not worry." He glanced out the window. "If I leave now, I may make it to Ludgate before curfew."

Laughter carried down the stairs along with a familiar voice.

"Do we have visitors, Cook?" I asked, lifting the captain's cloak from the stool near the fire and helping him back into it.

"Aye, important ones. Though what they are doing about in this weather I don't know. Sometimes you have to wonder about these men of God." She rolled her eyes. "They might have His ear, but I think they be selective sometimes 'bout what it is they be a-hearing, for surely our dear Lord would tell 'em not to step abroad today but gather in prayer and the warmth of community?"

"Men of God, women who brew, neither listen," said Captain Stoyan under his breath. "Nor does this captain." He pulled his gloves on. "I will not interrupt Goody Alyson and Adam with farewells then, but ask you do this on my behalf, *ja*?"

I agreed and tried to pass him a purse, but he would not take it. "You requested a favor and I accepted. Coin does not pass between friends."

I shook my head. "You don't believe that for a moment."

"*Nein.* But it sounded good, did it not?" he winked. "Seriously, I do not want or need your coin. Not since you repaid my investment in your first brewery."

I was yet to pay the captain for what he'd contributed since the pestilence as well—in kind and with hops. Once the king's treasury paid for the ale and beer we'd supplied, we would all be in profit.

So it was, with prayers for his safety and a long embrace, I bade the captain goodbye.

I waved from the kitchen door and watched the way the horse churned the snow as it trotted out the gate, then I went back inside and straight to the hearth. Cook and Eve were busy making pottage and bread. The voices upstairs became louder. Cook's words came back to me.

"Men of God, you say, Cook?" My stomach fluttered. "Who are they?"

"From the palace." She jerked her thumb over her shoulder in the direction of Bankend and Winchester. "Goody Alyson said you were to go up to the solar when you came home." She slipped my half-drunk mug from my hands. "Only, with the captain here, and taking his leave, I didn't want to be rude. There are drinks and food upstairs," she reassured when I didn't move immediately.

Thanking her, I left the kitchen with reluctance.

At the door to the solar, which was slightly ajar, I eavesdropped on the conversation taking place inside.

"Do they resemble their mother?" asked a familiar tone that set my teeth on edge and my heart racing.

"Oh, indeed, your grace, that they do."

"What about the father?"

There was an uncomfortable gap, which was my cue to enter.

Pushing the door wide open, I was greeted by a strange scene. Sitting by the fire were Alyson, Betje, and Adam. Adam was propped in a different chair than usual, while behind him stood Emma and Constance, wringing their hands and scrunching their aprons nervously. In the middle of this group, comfortably ensconced in Alyson's favorite chair, sat a man in the black robes of a monk. His head was bowed as he cooed at Karel and Isabella wriggling on his lap, his jeweled cap gleaming in the firelight. His pale white hands confidently held one on each knee. As I stared at those long beringed fingers, their exquisite shape, my heart stopped.

I knew who owned those hands.

Stepping forward, everything I'd tried to repress, all that I'd convinced myself I hadn't seen, hadn't felt, didn't know, rushed back to the surface. My knees began to tremble, my palms to sweat. It was as if I'd swallowed a melting candle and my throat was stoppered up with wax. Sensing, or perhaps hearing me, Betje turned, and I saw in her stricken look and in the noises that now began to issue from Adam and the shaking which beset his body, that they also knew who it was sitting in Alyson's solar, holding my sweet babes.

Before I could snatch the children away, Alyson jumped to her feet. "Anna!" she exclaimed, tripping toward me across the rushes, flashing me a look of warning. "Look who's come to visit, God be praised. The honor we've been granted." One arm swept wide to indicate the man on her chair and the two monks standing behind him. She gave a forced smile and wrapped her fingers tightly around my forearm, her meaning clear. "May I introduce Bishop Roland le Bold, the new landlord of Winchester Palace and an eager customer who has just placed a very generous order for your ale."

Leander may have tried to offer reassurance that the man I spied in Gloucester, the man I believed to be my nemesis, was only a harmless monk named Roland le Bold, but as Bishop le Bold passed first Karel then Isabella back to their wet nurses, and the twins held out their chubby little arms toward me and began to cry, I knew I had not been wrong.

Whatever he called himself, whoever he pretended to be, Roland le Bold, the freshly appointed Bishop of Winchester, now rising to his feet to greet me, his bleached eyes gleaming strangely, was none other than Westel Calkin.

Murderer, liar, rapist, and, God help me, father of my children.

# FIFTY-THREE

THE SWANNE
Mid-February
*The year of Our Lord 1408 in the ninth
year of the reign of Henry IV*

*I* wanted to denounce him then and there, but Alyson's counterfeit delight, Betje's palpable fear, and Adam's vulnerable state, as well as my instincts, screamed caution. Pretending he didn't have my acquaintance, he expressed pleasure in the babes, and sorrow at the various tragedies that had befallen my family. Well versed in my faux history, he spoke of the loss of my husband, how resourceful I was to brew and to do it so well. Staggered by his boldness, I could barely respond. Casting a look of sympathy toward Betje, which alighted not on her face but somewhere over her shoulder, Westel said he would pray for her and Adam. Sincerity dripped from him like honey from a comb and though I felt sickened by this mummery, I sustained my performance. Westel was no longer a servant or a mere monk—the quality of his robe, the sparkling rings on his fingers, the leather of his boots, the cap upon his head—all declared his high office, the resources upon which he could draw. Greatness attended him as did menace and, for the time being, I must be obedient to his whims.

Unnerved, and understanding something was greatly amiss, Alyson was louder than usual and she filled any silences with mindless chatter, which Westel responded to with grace and an amity I never recalled him possessing before—or had he? Perhaps, at first, it had been there.

Aware of his glance falling upon me, I could scarcely think. If I'd not been so eager to send Captain Stoyan upon his way, I could have sent word to Leander of our visitor, confirming I had not been mistaken. Alas, it was too late and now I had to endure his company and fret about his intentions. Westel had crossed this threshold for a reason, and it did not bode well for any of us. I didn't have to wait long to find out.

All gallantry and affability, he demanded a tour of the brewery, arranging it so that I alone would escort him. In itself this was not unusual, and caused no comment among the servants, though Alyson did offer a meek protest and Betje clung to my side.

"It is all right, sweetling, I will show his grace the brewery and be back before you can say ten paternosters." It was what Adam used to say to comfort me as a child and I saw in his eyes he understood. Betje did as well and released me with reluctance, joining the wet nurses and taking Isabella.

Aware of Westel upon my heels, his hot breath against my neck, I was at first relieved to see the brewery all hustle and bustle. A combination of steam and smoke filled the air. Rose and Golda stood over the mash tuns, the new girl, Margaret, keeping a firm eye on them while tasting some freshly cooked grain.

Master atte Place hoisted another huge tray into the oven. Beyond them, Rupert sorted barrels, rolling some, hefting others. Whistling a well-known air, he was lost in daydreams. Over by the troughs, Harry was tapping ale into a barrel, while Thomas was poised to lend a hand.

Before I could say anything, offer introductions or any kind of explanation as to what was going on, Westel called out from the stairs.

"Begone, all of you."

Glancing up, amusement on their faces, it took the servants only a moment to understand this was no prank, that a high-ranking churchman was in their midst. I nodded curtly.

"Leave your tools. Master atte Place, I will look to the grain. Go and enjoy the fire and a small ale." Warily, the girls put down their mash sticks; Ralph righted a barrel with a thud and stomped past, crossing himself, while Thomas came forward and bowed to Westel before dashing up the stairs. One by one, they ascended. Only Harry remained, defiant, pretending not to notice us, that he didn't hear.

Touching him upon the shoulder, I whispered. "Go, Harry, please."

"But mistress." He flashed a look at Westel over my shoulder. The bishop had left the stairs and was staring into a mash tun. "I don't like the look of him."

Bless him.

"Looks can be deceiving."

"Only sometimes," said Harry, and, unhappy at my insistence, pushed out his chest and, giving a small huff in Westel's direction, left.

Once the door had shut, Westel lifted his face. Even through the curtain of steam, it was apparent he hadn't changed that much. Still pale, a little fuller around the cheeks, a neatly trimmed fringe of hair revealed it was still that wondrous silver color that reminded me so much of Mother's, Karel's, and Betje's too. Now my babes possessed it, but I could reassure myself that the legacy was not Westel's alone. Returning my gaze, his mouth turned up at the ends. Not for me the huge smiles and repetitive flashing of teeth that I once mistook as an obsequious desire to please. This was a triumphant leer. A man who oozed self-possession and the arrogance of achieving goals at any cost had replaced the old Westel. Godliness was not a part of his mien and I marveled that I'd ever likened it to that of angels. As I'd told Harry, looks could be deceiving.

I'd no doubt my Godsent retribution, that I'd spent almost a year anticipating, was before me.

"Well," said Westel, coming around the tun, closing the space between us, "here we are, God be praised."

He paused on one side of the table. I circled until I was directly opposite. Pushing a bung out of the way, I placed my hands, palms flat, on the top, relieved they weren't shaking.

"What do you want, Westel?" I asked.

"I am 'your grace' now."

I didn't respond. Westel gave a bark of laughter. "Still stubborn, I see."

"Haven't you taken enough? Aren't you satisfied? Did you see what you did to Betje? You murdered my brother, you murdered Will, Saskia, and Louisa." The names struck with all the force of a feather. He did not even blink. "People who trusted you, welcomed you into their lives."

"You blame *me* for their deaths?" He gave a hollow laugh.

"Why, you've created a monster, haven't you? How convenient. A novel way to salve a pricking conscience." Picking up a measure and turning it in those long fingers, he continued. "Nay, Anneke Sheldrake, *I* didn't murder your brother or your servants. They were, sadly, tragically, killed by fire. It was, may God assoil them, a terrible accident. Or, as some might argue, God's will. What have you done to incur such wrath? Such a burning lesson?" He gave a harrumph of delight at his wit.

"Will was no accident. That was not the Lord's decree, but yours."

He put down the measure carefully. "Your family doesn't do well among the elements, does it? First your father drowns, then your so-called husband, while the rest perish in flames."

"What do you want, Westel?"

His laugh was genuine now. "It's not Westel. Westel never existed. I am and always have been Roland le Bold."

It struck me then where I knew the name. Westel had claimed him as his mentor. It was le Bold who wrote the glowing reference, the papers Westel presented me that day at Holcroft House and upon which I'd based his employment. I bowed my head and shook it slowly.

"I see you've worked it out."

I gulped. "Are you also Abbot Hubbard's son?"

"Aye, but he too is dead." He feigned being crestfallen. "Something he drank didn't agree with him."

"That doesn't explain why you're here."

Roland let out a long, deep sigh and, flicking the measure one last time, began to strut around the brewery. "Why do you think, Anneke?"

"It's Anna now, Roland."

Halting for a moment, he cocked a brow before continuing his study of the room. "So I've heard—from every cursed mouth since I arrived in this Godforsaken place. *Anna* de Winter this, *Anna* de Winter that. You've developed quite a reputation . . ." His eyes scoured my body, slowly, menacingly, as if he were touching me. I remained still, though the urge to recoil was almost more than I could bear. He moistened his lips. ". . . for brewing. Even the king sings your praises." He chuckled. "It never occurred to me that the woman from Southwark who brewed fit for the king's table was none other than my obstinate little brewer from Elmham Lenn—the one who wouldn't surrender her recipes. The one who would not die. I thought you gone from my life for good. When I saw you in Gloucester, I could scarce believe my eyes."

He wasn't the only one.

"I tried to persuade myself it wasn't so, that you were a spirit come to haunt me just when I was on the cusp of achieving what I've worked so hard for."

"Mayhap it was God's will?"

"Mayhap it was." Roland's eyes narrowed to slits, protecting a secret. "It took only a few discreet questions, some stories over wine, for your history to come out." He began to laugh. "You are quite the inventor, are you not? A dead husband, a new family and name—very clever."

"Not clever enough. You found me."

"And with a word here or there, the right ones in the right ears, so can others."

My body became numb. *Here it comes.* "What do you mean?"

"There was quite a hue and cry raised over you; over the destruction at Elmham Lenn."

"Only because *you* were believed dead."

"Oh, but, Anneke . . . Anna"—he gave a sly smile and held out his arms—"I still am. You see, as far as anyone but a few of your servants and family are concerned, Westel Calkin never existed. Even my own father denied me."

I took a deep breath. "It would not take much to prove you did exist—that you still do."

He shrugged. "But it will take a good deal more to convince anyone that Roland le Bold, the man who, God be praised, transformed brewing at St. Jude's, who through trial and error, through creativity and talent, making an ordinary drink a remarkable one, was anything but a humble, selfless monk. I made St. Jude's both solvent and wealthy, Elmham Lenn as well, Anna. Aye, me—your monster. Using your mother's marvelous recipes, I am a hero of the church. The Archbishop cannot do enough; after all, it was under my patronage that St. Jude's was able to enhance the king's purse, fund his relentless wars and skirmishes, and prevent the treasury becoming bankrupt. Being given this bishopric and carte blanche to transform it is my reward. Imagine, if I could turn a place like St. Jude's into a growing concern, what I can do here. Especially with the Lady Brewer—isn't that what they call you?—upon my doorstep, the first woman to receive Crown trade, and for her beer as well as ale. What is it you call that foreign drink?" He glanced around, his gaze alighting on the barrels. "That's it. Son of Ale."

He cast a critical eye over my equipment. The smile left his face. "You want to know why I'm here? I'll tell you. You stood in my way once. I won't allow you to again. This is my stepping-stone to the court, to Rome. I'm not going to let some brewster, a cunting whore like you, ruin my chances."

This time, I laughed. "You? Rome? What, as a cardinal or are you aiming higher? The bastard son of an abbot?" His face began to redden, but I didn't care. "A man who murders at whim, who rapes women, deceives, lies, corrupts? Who fathers children—"

"I was right. They're mine then? Those two whelps upstairs?"

My heart pounded. There was no point lying. He would learn the truth soon enough if he didn't already possess it. "They are yours."

He stared at me, then nodded slowly. "I wouldn't be the first monk to father children, nor the last."

"It's *how* you fathered them that might be of interest—to the court, to Rome."

Westel . . . Roland's eyes turned into agate slits in his face. Then he threw back his head and guffawed. "You really think to use *that* against me? You think anyone cares what a whore like you says? Don't feign surprise. I know of Sir Leander. If you spread your legs for him, it's not a stretch"—he chuckled—"for anyone to assume you'd do the same for someone else. After all, you're a very beautiful woman, Anna." He glided toward me, his fingers outstretched. Lifting a lock of hair from my breast, he slowly twined it around his finger. "A very, very beautiful woman. Beauty such as yours is only good for one thing—a man's delectation, in whatever way he chooses. How could any-one, let alone a naive young monk, resist you?"

Tugging my hair hard, he released it. I didn't give him the sat-isfaction of crying out, though tears sprang to my eyes. I forced them back as he strode past the mash tuns, striking one with his fist. "For Godsakes, you live in a whorehouse, you're only doing what your kind are born to—tempt better men to sin, poison hearts and souls with your body and lascivious ways." He spun around. "Even now, you're thinking about it, aren't you? Ways of seducing me. What for? My silence? My cooperation?"

I stared at him. By God, the man belonged in Bedlam.

"Even if I confessed to everything, Anna, do you think I'd be denied a papal indulgence? Me, who is now regarded as a master craftsman, whose gift from God he shares with all? A favorite of the church, of court?" He strode back to the table and, leaning across, lifted my hands, studying them, running his thumbs over the back. "They're not as lovely as they once were. Reddened, calloused, like a washerwoman's. You work hard, don't you? You've achieved so much with so little and against such odds. Your deformed sister, your servant little more than an animated vegetable, and yet, here you are, the toast of King Henry's dinners, lover of one his finest merchant-knights, and a woman of means."

"Indeed, Roland. We've both accomplished much since Elmham Lenn. But you still haven't told me why you're here. If I cannot harm you by revealing the truth about the twins, about what you did to me, to the others, why do you see me as a threat? Surely, I am the least of your concerns."

"God's truth, this is so. But even the least of them deserves attention lest they grow into bigger ones. I'm a great believer in excising the poison, removing the rot, stamping out a problem before it's beyond my control." Behind him, the kiln began to smoke and the odor of charcoal filled the air. Screwing up his nose, Roland continued. "You know what it's like to lose everything, the lengths you'd go to keep hold of what you have, don't you?"

I tried to pull my hands away, but he wouldn't release them. I'd forgotten that strength. A metallic taste filled my mouth;

huge birds flapped their wings inside my chest, making breathing difficult.

"Then we have something in common." Dropping my hands, he folded his arms. "Understand this, Anneke Sheldrake, Anna de Winter. It matters not what you call yourself because the consequences if you do not heed my words will be the same." He pointed his finger at me, a dagger ready to strike. "If you should reveal who I am to anyone, mention that we once worked together . . . If you breathe a word about your mother's recipes—"

*They were still in his possession.*

"—then I will not only reveal who you are and from whence you came, I will ruin everything you've built for yourself here. I will destroy this brewery and the bathhouse. I will see your children sent to a nunnery, your sister—Betty, you call her now?—on the streets. Imagine what life would be like for her the way she looks? Imagine your beloved Adam without a roof, or patron." He walked around the table until he was so close, I could smell his cassock, feel the ermine that lined the edges against my arm, see the sheen on his ashen flesh, the way the light from the kiln made his hair glint and gave life to his colorless eyes. "Imagine what I could to your lover, Leander Rainford." I stepped back. "Imagine what I could do to your brother . . . though I'd heard tell he's only half yours."

I bit my lip to stop a cry escaping. *How did he know that?*

Running his hand down my face, he gave a soft smile. "Talk is cheap in Elmham Lenn and there was much of it at Holcroft House. Will, whom you believe to be some saint, and Louisa, who did nothing but gossip, were eager to share the stories and rumors that beset the house of Sheldrake. I might have doubted them once, but seeing your brother with Sir Leander, his paternity was obvious. He's a Rainford through and through." His fingers dropped from my face to trail down my neck and zigzag across my chest until they rested atop my breast. Drumming them gently over my flesh, he watched them a while. "What do you pay Father Kenton to absolve your sins? Or do you prefer a pardoner? For God does not take kindly to consanguinity, yet you perform it over and over." Capturing my breast in his hand, he grasped the nipple between two fingers, twisting it through my tunic.

"Enough." I struck his hand and backed away, once again putting the table between us. "Enough, Westel, Roland—"

"Your grace. I will settle for nothing less than your grace."

Bile rose. "Your grace."

Roland flashed those even teeth.

Raising my palm to prevent him coming closer, I was panting. The air was close, thick. "I understand what you're saying."

"Saying?" He came closer. "Anna, I'm not *saying* anything. I'm not even threatening. I'm telling you what *will* happen should you speak one word about the past, of what's been said down here today; if you should reveal the truth of my brewing success—" He lunged and grabbed my hair, using it like a rope to bind me to him.

Refusing to cry out, to give him the satisfaction, I gritted my teeth.

Twining the thick strands around my neck, he brought my face to his. His lips were almost upon mine. The cellar disappeared to be replaced by the brewery at Elmham Lenn. It was nighttime; I was reeling against a table, blood pouring from a wound on my head.

Snatches of conversation came back to me. *You are the gate of the devil. Traitor of the tree.* There was pain, terrible pain, and knowledge of imminent death, of life ending, brutality. Shadows filled my head, clouded my vision. I began to shake; my will to defy deserted me.

"As God is my witness and Savior," he growled in my ear, "I will crush you and everyone and everything you love. Do you understand?"

I couldn't speak; the hair was so tight around my neck. I half-nodded.

"Good. Now, on your knees." With brute force, he pushed me to the floor. Whimpering, I didn't resist. Terror had me in its clutches and would not let go.

"Let us seal our deal with a blessing, shall we?"

Crowning my head with his hand, he held me fast. His manhood strained against the fabric of his cassock. Swallowing, I raised my face, my eyes burning. "A blessing?"

"Believe me, the seed of a holy man is indeed blessed. You will imbibe, my poisonous rose, my sweet harlot and, together, we will both feel God."

Sending prayers to Mother Mary, the crones, Ninkasi, anyone who would listen, I shut my eyes and opened them again. Roland was hoisting his cassock, gathering it in the crook of an arm. His white knees were exposed, his milky thighs with the dusting of fine hair. I could smell urine and sweat.

Pulling me toward him, toward the weeping, stiff paleness that filled my vision, he began to pray.

*"Pater noster qui es in caelis sanctificetur nomen tuum . . ."*

The door at the top of the steps burst open. Roland dropped his cassock and turned around, rearranging himself.

Thanks be to sweet Mother Mary, the crones, Ninkasi, and all the female saints that they answered my prayers. Harry, Betje, Alyson, and Master atte Place came tumbling into the cellar, the other two monks in their wake.

I hauled myself up by the table, hoping no one had seen my humiliation.

"Anna!" said Alyson, beaming with such ferocity she was fit to burst. "Your grace." She gave Roland a small nod. "We were worried. You were down here quite some time and we couldn't risk the mash becoming spoiled or the grains burning. Appears we were just in time." She fixed Roland with a look.

The grain! I'd quite forgotten. Master atte Place pulled the smoking tray of dark brown husks from the kiln. It hissed as it touched the cooler, damp wood. The barley was ruined.

Rushing to their posts, Betje, Harry, and the other servants who'd waited timidly at the top of the stairs curtsied and bowed to Roland, who stood, indifferent to their presence. I knew we'd pay for this interruption, for the manner in which everyone made it clear their loyalties were with me.

Bishop Roland made as dignified an exit as possible, waving the monks at the top of the stairs out of the brewery.

No one heard his last words as he brushed past me, as our bodies connected. "*Everyone* you love," he murmured.

I didn't know I was holding my breath until the sound of hooves in the courtyard released me.

# FIFTY-FOUR

THE SWANNE
Late February to late March
*The year of Our Lord 1408 in the ninth*
*year of the reign of Henry IV*

*T*hough Roland le Bold threatened to destroy me if I made mention of our shared history and the recipes he stole, and I didn't doubt he meant every word, I knew I had to divulge, at least in part, what had passed between us. Alyson was no fool and Adam knew the sins this man carried; it would be an insult to pretend nothing had occurred, especially after we had spent so much time alone. Nonetheless, I didn't concede everything. The shame I felt at what he wanted me to do, at what had almost happened, was too much.

Ensuring the brewery was back to normal and Betje remained to supervise, I followed Alyson upstairs to where Adam, greatly agitated, waited. Asking for ale and wine to be brought to the solar, I shared the bulk of what happened: that he was indeed Westel Calkin—a false name created solely for the purposes of inveigling himself in our midst—that he had survived the fire, and had gone on to use my mother's recipes to make St. Jude's prosper. So much so, he'd been rewarded with an elevation in rank and the promise of more seniority to come; brewing became the means of his rise within the church. I explained that if I mentioned anything of this to the authorities, he would simply invoke a higher one.

"God?" spat Alyson.

"In some measure. He would use the church against us, and God knows"—I gave an apologetic smile for my poor pun— "as His voice on earth, that's powerful enough."

"A voice that speaks in whispers with a forked tongue." Alyson came to my side and wrapped her arms around me, holding me close and stroking my hair. "Ah, my chick. This visitation from the past will sorely test you. For that I'm sorry." We stood like that for some time, the snow striking the mullioned glass, the wind whistling under the door and between the cracks, causing candles to flutter and the fire in the hearth to dim before roaring to life again. "What do you wish to do, Anna?" she asked finally. "Ignore, obey, or defy him?"

I held Alyson close, grateful for her warmth, her affection. Resting my cheek on her shoulder, I glanced over at Adam, who had not taken his eyes from me.

"Above all, I want to defy the bastard. Even ignoring his threats would make me feel slightly better. But . . ."

"But?" Extracting me from her arms, Alyson regarded me gently.

"For the time being, I will obey him."

Alyson made a noise of disgust.

"You have to understand, it's not only me Roland will hurt.

I have to think of Betje, the twins"—I twisted toward Adam—
"and others as well."

"I do understand and I think you be wise. Only, I hope
you're not including me in that list of yours," said Alyson, letting me go and sitting down. "I'm perfectly capable of handling
one cocky monk, Bishop of Winchester or not."

I couldn't help smiling. So did Adam. "I will handle him my
way—by pretending I never discovered Westel survived, that
the Bishop of Winchester is just that, the lord of our manor, and
no one who would concern me, unless it's to make ale for him."

"Well, he's made sure you'll be doing that. Wants no less than
ten hogshead of ale."

"I wonder why? The bishops have a brewery and he admitted
he has my mother's recipes. He could make it himself."

"Not in those quantities he couldn't. I suspect he wants to do
business with the Crown's brewer. Mark my words, that's what
he's about. He wants to be able to boast that the king's brewer
supplies him as well. He also wants an excuse to keep an eye on
you—both of 'em. This is all about him, Anna, not you, never
you fear."

Easy to say, much more difficult to do. For all that I made
bold statements of denial, I would never know peace again.
Westel-Roland would leap into my mind when the cock crowed
the dawn and when the sun sank beyond the horizon in the
evening. He would arise as soon as my thoughts stilled and sleep
tried to claim me.

I would obey Roland and I would be filled with despair at the
price my obedience would exact: fear had come home to roost,
not just in The Swanne, but in my very soul.

�‹⋙⋘›⋗

At the end of the week, notice was given that the Bishop of Winchester intended to raise the rents. As of Hocktide, they would be more than double. The reason given was the pestilence and loss of income from empty houses and businesses.

I knew the real reason. We all did.

Upon receiving the news, Alyson slumped heavily in her chair in the solar, trying to accommodate how she would manage the new charges, especially since business in the bathhouse had not yet recovered.

"Simple," said Adam after listening to her curse the bishop, God, and everyone else besides. Alyson and I turned toward him. Trying to speak, every word was an effort. "C . . . charge more for beer."

"What?" said Alyson.

"I can't, Adam." I pulled the blanket over his knees and tucked it down the side of the chair. "You know that. There are laws against such practices. The ale-conners, or worse, Master Fynk, would charge me. The tax is fixed."

Adam gave a peculiar grimace that was meant to be a smile. "In L . . . L . . . London, aye. In S . . . S . . . South . . . South . . . S . . . Here. Nay."

"He's right, you know." Alyson sat back and rubbed her chin. "Adam"—she pointed at him—"no doubting you're a smart one, aren't you." She clambered to her feet and slapped Adam's shoulder on her way to the window. "The ale we can't touch but the beer, well, that's already sold cheaper, I don't think anyone would notice if we raised the price a little. Such a pity more don't drink it. If only those bloody Londoners would develop a taste for it . . . we'd be making more than we could spend, double rents or not. The only one who buys any sufficient quantities to make it worthwhile raising the bloody price is—" She lifted glittering eyes to mine.

"The king," I finished.

"All we need do is raise the price of the king's order and it will help cover the extra costs the bishop is charging." Alyson rubbed her hands together in glee. "In fact, it won't be us the bishop's robbing blind, it will be His Grace. Seems fitting that, don't you think?"

My brows drew together. I didn't like the idea of cheating the king, especially after what I'd been granted in his name, and said so.

"Cheating? Why, his liege hasn't seen fit to pay us for the first few lots he's received, so I would hardly worry about cheating His Grace."

"What if we chase the treasury for payment?"

"We'll do that and all as well. We may even charge our new prices for the last order when we send the bill." Alyson shrugged at the shocked expression on my face. "Why not? We've got nothing to lose."

*Oh, Alyson, you're wrong*, I thought. *We've everything to lose, which is exactly what Roland intends.*

❖❖❖

Winter gradually released its stranglehold on the land, surrendering most ungraciously to spring. The snows melted, the river, with a great groan and a crack that sounded as if the devil himself had opened a doorway to hell, started to flow once more. Busy in the brewery, we worked before dawn until well after night fell, mashing, singing the wort to life, adding hops, but also honey, wormwood, and a wonderful herb called eyebright, which I put in for both flavor and as a panacea to reduce the chills and coughs that beset so many in the house over winter.

During this time, and much to my consolation, a letter arrived from Captain Stoyan. From the beautiful handwriting, it was evident he'd hired a scribe to do what he could not. Paying the courier, I told him to go to the kitchen while I went to my bedroom to read the contents in private and form a response. The rebellion had been averted and the king was riding to Yorkshire via Nottingham with the intention of serving justice upon those involved in the plans to dethrone him. Captain Stoyan, understanding that Sir Leander was with the king, was riding north.

All being well, he predicted he would be back in Southwark by the beginning of April. He prayed that the river had seen fit to cast aside her wintry mantle so he might return to his preferred state, upon the water instead of horseback. Guilt lanced me as I thought of the hardship the captain was enduring on my behalf. He finished by asking that God and the Holy Trinity keep me and guide me, and had signed the letter himself.

Offering a swift prayer to the captain and thanks for such loyalty and thoughtfulness, I remained in my bedroom longer than intended, lost in thought. Knowing where I might find Leander, or at least his destination, did I dare write to him about Roland and confess what I'd promised I would not? I would not risk such a rash move—for the same reasons Leander had maintained silence while the rebels plotted, I would as well.

The bells for none disturbed me and, with a rush of remorse at the time I'd wasted, I tucked the letter under my pillow. I paid the courier and raced back to the brewery.

The following day brought more tidings and unexpected guests to The Swanne. Arriving midmorning, two men asked Alyson if they might meet with me. A maidservant, Sophie, hired to take on Juliana's duties upstairs, fetched me from the brewery. Whipping off my apron, I quickly tidied my hair and was escorted to the solar, where Alyson was entertaining the guests. Concerned as to who would want to see me, my first thought was Roland was behind their arrival. As I hovered at the threshold, however, I wondered if they'd been sent by Master Fynk.

On spying the men sitting opposite Alyson, enjoying a mazer of ale, my mind was immediately laid to rest. These men were neither from the law or church. Their insignia declared them to be from the Mystery of Brewers, a London guild lacking a royal grant of incorporation, but able to wield much authority nonetheless.

What was their purpose in coming here, to Southwark? To see me? Could it be they'd caught wind of the additional charges we'd put on the beer? Even so, I wasn't under their authority, being neither a member of the Mystery nor paying them quarterage.

Intrigued and even a little alarmed, it wasn't till I caught Adam's steady look and calm nod that my nerves settled. Rising when I entered, Alyson introduced Master William Porlond and Master Stephen Hamme. Bowing low, they studied me with curiosity before retaking their seats. I wasn't able to drink the ale offered or keep my hands still. Why were they here?

"Mistress Anna, I hope I may call you that?" asked Master Porlond, the younger, and more rotund, of the two. He was an official of the Mystery. His companion, Master Hamme, was both a member and a brewer of some repute. Friends with Alyson, he'd been the one to sell us equipment and proffer advice when we first started. Smiling at him warmly, I turned my attention to Master Porlond.

"You may, good sir."

"We've been keeping a close eye on you, specially since you earned the honor of Crown trade. May we offer congratulations. I have to say"—he held his mazer away from his body and examined it—"this is a mighty fine brew."

"Thank you."

"Do I detect some oak?" asked Master Hamme.

"Aye, and hyssop," I added.

Smacking his lips together, Master Hamme nodded appreciatively and took another swig. "Told you she was good."

Alyson raised her brows but chose to remain quiet.

I turned expectantly to Master Porlond.

"I won't keep you waiting any longer, mistress. The reason we are here is twofold. We want to extend an invitation to you to join the Mystery of Brewers—"

"Oh—" Of all the things I'd thought to hear, it was not those words.

"In London," finished Master Porlond.

"Oh." Strange how the same word or sound could convey two entirely different meanings. *The Mystery of Brewers.* Sweet Jesù, this was not expected either. But in London . . .

Master Porlond looked to Master Hamme, who nodded encouragement. "You may not be aware, mistress, but in light of recent events—"

I frowned. To what did he refer? For a moment, panic set my features as I thought of first Roland le Bold, then the rebellion, before I finally understood he meant the pestilence.

"—positions have become available."

"Not merely positions," added Master Hamme. "Though it's true, London is dangerously short of decent brewers at present and the mayor is most unhappy. What we want to offer you, mistress, is an altogether different and, we hope, pleasing proposition. We have a brewery for lease. God in His wisdom has seen fit to allow me to own two. Unfortunately, the family leasing my second one was afflicted with the pestilence. No one was spared, not even their servants, may God assoil them. It's empty. It's also fully equipped. Even has leaden pipes and copper tubs and a millstone so you can take care of your own milling if you should choose to do so. There's easy access to a good water supply. And living accommodation above—enough for your servants and children. I understand you have three?"

"Two. My younger sister lives with me as well."

"Ah, she be the crip—oof."

Master Hamme doubled over as Master Porlond's elbow connected with his side.

"Anyhow"—Master Hamme coughed, casting a dour look at his companion—"we understand that living in London was something, mayhap, you once considered—and what with the bishop doubling the rents, we thought you might like to give it more thought. I'd lower the rent for the first year, until you're settled."

The men stared at me. I glanced at Alyson who was no longer smiling, but concentrating on a spot on the floor. I knew that look.

I'd not really considered London again, not since the king ordered my brew and certainly not since the murrain, and yet . . . it made sense. With Roland le Bold returned, and as lord of the manor, moving out from under his watchful eyes—away from his threats—might be a solution. London was bigger. For me, for us, it could be safer. I would be one of many brewers, protected by the Mystery no less—or forced to concede to their rules. If the Mystery admitted me, there was no reason for the Hanse to refuse to trade. What if I could reestablish the connections I'd made in the Low Countries? Export again? Captain Stoyan would give me advice there, help too, I'd no doubt . . .

Plucking at my lower lip, my eyes now trained upon the rushes as my thoughts danced in circles, it took me a moment to realize the men were waiting for an answer.

"You do know what an honor it is to be asked to join the Mystery, don't you, Mistress Anna?" said Master Porlond.

"I don't think a woman has ever been invited before." Master Hamme scratched his head. "I mean, we have quite a few women in the Mystery, but most are wives of brewers or inherited the position when their husbands died. You are the only one we've approached whose husband wasn't a member first."

"Then it's indeed an honor that you bestow upon me, gentlemen." I smiled. Master Hamme colored while Master Porlond smoothed what remained of his hair across his scalp and nodded.

Standing, I ran a slow hand down the front of my tunic, which the men's eyes followed. "Aware of the privilege *and* the honor you accord me with such a generous proposition, can I ask your indulgence a little further, gentlemen?"

Without even conferring, they both said, "Aye."

"If I could but have a little more time to consider this—more for the sake of my family, my servants, my friends, and my business partner." I gestured to Alyson.

"Oh, of course, of course," they chorused.

"Take as much time as you like," said Master Hamme.

"Till Hocktide," added Master Porlond darting a firm look at his associate.

I curtsied to indicate I accepted their terms, and the two men leaped to their feet.

"Thank you," I said warmly, first to one then the other. "Thank you. Hocktide it is. I confess, you've given me much to consider. I'm sorely tempted by what you offer."

"You're meant to be," said Alyson quietly. The men spun toward her. Standing, she considered them, her arms crossed under her breasts, thrusting them forward. "And, should you accept, Anna, they be getting a prize indeed. A woman who has not only Crown trade, but who is, of His Grace's own admission, the king's preferred brewer."

The men muttered and nodded. Alyson dared a wink. Adam tried to smile.

"If you would excuse me, I must return to the brewery."

The men bowed and asked that God give me good day. On the way out, I stopped by Adam's chair and took his hand. He squeezed my fingers and pulled me closer.

"You'll make it work, Anneke," he whispered hoarsely. "You always do."

With tears burning my eyes, I left the room.

⋘⋙

I believed Alyson would be resistant to the idea of me joining the Mystery, let alone uprooting all and sundry and shifting my life and business to London. As such, I didn't give the offer, as flattering and, indeed, tempting as it was, too much consideration.

Alyson and I had been through much together and, in the time I'd known her, she'd proven a loyal and wonderful friend. I didn't intend to act in any way that might cause her upset or undermine our relations, but Alyson had other ideas.

Waiting until Betje and Harry had gone to bed, when only Adam, Alyson, and I were in the solar, accompanied by strains of music from downstairs and the occasional squeals and laughter of the girls, she pushed aside the paperwork she'd been doing and let out a long, tired sigh. Stretching her arms before her, she rotated her shoulder. "Adam, some days I miss your nimble fingers and quick mind more than most. Today is one of those days."

"It's n . . . not those you miss," said Adam slowly. "It's m . . . my way with figures."

Giving him a strange look, she grinned. "Not mine, more's the pity."

Adam's cheeks reddened.

"You're right, Adam. It's your ability to transpose these sums that I wished I possessed." Picking up her goblet, Alyson drank her wine, then lost herself in its depths. "So," she said, as her head shot up, her eyes locked on me. "Have you thought much more about what them Mystery men said?"

In the middle of darning Betje's tunic, I didn't answer immediately. "I've thought about it," I said, lowering the needlework. "I've thought about it and dismissed it."

"*Dismissed?* Are you daft?"

I looked at Alyson in wonder. "*Daft?* But I thought you would object."

"*Object?*" she screeched. I began to laugh.

"What's so funny?" she grumbled.

"We keep repeating each other."

I could see Alyson going over our conversation, then she chuckled. Adam, too. "That we do. But I'm serious. Why would I object when it's what you've been wanting since before you got here? It was your dream, to go to London."

"It was W . . . Will, wasn't it, Anna," said Adam, "who predicted you'd be the finest brewer in all England? If you go to L . . . London, perhaps that can happen."

His words took me back to that joyous evening, so long ago now, when Adam and I returned from Lord Rainford's and I laid out our plans to brew to everyone. I remembered the toasts we'd drunk, the excitement and hope that had filled the house. And Will, eyes shining, his face flushed with the ale, making his wild declaration. Dear God, we were all daft back then, when anything seemed possible.

"He did, Adam," I said quietly. "He did. But, Alyson, I am more than happy with being the finest in Southwark."

She snorted. "This seedy old borough? When you have London at your feet? What you're worried about is upsetting me, hurting me feelings, aren't you?"

I opened my mouth to argue but closed it again.

"See," she said to Adam. "I was right."

"It's not only you," I added. "It's me, Betje, Adam, and the twins as well."

Alyson arched a brow.

"We have a home here, a life—a good one."

"For how long now that Roland le Bold is here?"

I couldn't answer.

"What if I told you that I'd come with you? That we'd all come across the river and start over? Would that persuade you to take this chance, grab this opportunity with both hands, before it's too late?"

I sat forward on my chair, not crediting what I heard. "Are you saying you'd leave The Swanne?"

"I'm saying I'd bring it with me, and on me bloody back too." She threw up her hands. "Of course I'm saying that." Leaving the table, she came and sat beside me, taking my hand and placing it between hers in her lap. "The Swanne has been very good to me and, I hope, I've been good to it." She looked around the room. "But, like a marriage, sometimes you have to know when to walk away."

"I thought all your husbands died?"

"Did you now? Same thing, isn't it? If they're dead to me, they're as good as in the ground." She fanned the air before her face, as if ridding it of foul humors. "Anyhow, it's time for me to walk away from here. I've felt that way a while. I think that's why I kept going on all those pilgrimages; I wanted to ask God and the saints what I should do. I wasn't content. Then, what happens? You come a-walking into my life. Your sweet sister, Master Adam over there, and yourself—one of the most beautiful, smartest chicks I've met and with enough pluck to outdo the king's best.

"I'm not letting you turn down an offer that will be the making of you, Anna, but nor am I letting you walk out of my life. So, I'm coming with you. Actually, I don't know why I'm bothering asking. You've naught to say in the matter. We are London bound—all of us. You will join the Mystery so you can become what young Will always predicted you'd be."

"The finest brewer in all of England," said Adam again and with a trembling hand, raised his mazer.

Hesitating only a moment, I threw my arms around Alyson and hugged her as tightly as I was able.

"I don't deserve you. I don't deserve this." Tears began to flow, stoppering my throat and making speech difficult.

"What rot. I don't know anyone who deserves it more and the sooner you start thinking like that instead of listening to the likes of that mad bishop, the better off everyone'll be." Helping me to my feet, Alyson led me to where a jug of ale and an ewer of wine stood.

"This isn't good enough," she said, peering into the ewer. "We need beer if this is to be a real celebration."

"Thought it wasn't to your taste?"

"That can change."

Letting me go, she went to call for the maid.

Adam sniffled quietly. I dropped a kiss on his withered cheek.

"She's r . . . r . . . right, you know."

Wrenching open the door, Alyson let out a small scream. Spinning around, I saw what startled her.

Standing in the doorway was a tall, dark-haired man leaning on a cane.

"And what are we celebrating?" asked Leander. "Because for certes, I could do with a drink."

I'd always been taught that ladies do not shout, run, or pick up their tunics in order to hasten movement, or forget themselves with ungainly displays of affection.

I'm sorry to say, Cousin Hiske was right all along.

I am no lady.

# FIFTY-FIVE

THE SWANNE

Late March to June

*The year of Our Lord 1408 in the ninth*

*year of the reign of Henry IV*

*W*hen you find the person who is the half that makes you whole and complete again, as Aristophanes describes, there's sometimes no need for words. Just the presence of the beloved has the capacity to renew the world and make it dawn afresh. So it was with Leander. Banishing the demons that Roland's threats had aroused, the nightmares his touch had invoked, I sailed into Leander's arms and was returned to a safe harbor.

Tempered by the presence of not just Alyson and Adam but Captain Stoyan as well, our initial embrace was joyous, but restrained. Not that it would appear that way to those who witnessed my ebullience. I still smile when I recall it.

Almost immediately, as Leander saw for himself Adam's condition, our mutual joy was dampened. Seated beside Adam, Leander patiently waited for answers to his questions. Watching them out of the corner of my eye as Alyson and I gathered near Captain Stoyan so he could recount his adventures, I was filled with love and pride. For all the Rolands and Master Fynks of this world, it was good to be reminded that there were also Leanders, Adams, and Hatto Stoyans.

Riding north, the captain saw the aftermath of the triumphant battle at Bramham Moor where the rebels had been defeated (as this was related, I closely studied Leander for signs of injury and much to my relief could detect none), and finally caught up with Leander in Nottingham toward the end of March.

From there, having delivered my letters and ascertained that both Leander and Tobias were in fine spirits, the captain elected to journey on with the king's company to Wheel Hall in the very north. It was here that the king meted out both punishment to his enemies and rewards to his supporters.

Leander picked up the tale. "The Earl of Northumberland met a traitor's death."

"What's that?" asked Alyson.

Leander hesitated.

"Do not concern yourself with my sensibilities," said Alyson scornfully.

"Madam, I was not." Leander gave Alyson a grin, and then looked to me.

Alyson gave a bark of laughter. "You cheeky cock."

"Pray, continue." I smiled. I also desired to know, as chilling as the answer would be.

"A deserving and vicious one, Goody Alyson. His body was hacked to pieces and parts sent to Newcastle, York, Lincoln, Berwick, and London. That's how I come to be here. I offered to bring his head. The graybeard sits on a pike atop London Bridge as we speak, a reminder to those who seek to betray the throne."

Shuddering, I glanced toward the window, imagining the rotting face of the king's seditious earl. Indigo darkness scattered with jewels lay beyond the thick glass.

"The nature of our task meant we were able to cross into Southwark, despite curfew and the closing of the gates, the guards being sympathetic to our cause. Thus our late arrival. I'm most pleased to see we haven't disturbed your slumber, as I feared, but a celebration. What is it you celebrate?"

In a babble of enthusiasm, Alyson and I told him and the captain about the offer from the Mystery, looking to Adam on occasion for confirmation.

"Mistress Anna." Captain Stoyan offered his hand and pulled me to my feet, kissing first one cheek and then the other. "This news is *gut, ja*? You will accept?"

"She's accepting," drawled Alyson, "we all are. And none too soon, not now Bishop Roland le Bold holds the power and purse strings of this part of Bankside."

"Le Bold?" said Leander, his brow furrowing. "He's taken up residence already? You've seen him?"

I nodded.

Leander started. "He wasted no time since Gloucester."

A stygian cloud descended. I didn't want to discuss Roland and the long shadows he cast. There was much to be glad about and I wished to concentrate on that. I would tell Leander Roland's real identity in good time. But Alyson had other ideas.

"She was right all along, you know," said Alyson. "Roland le Bold is the blackguard Westel Calkin."

Captain Stoyan spluttered his drink. Leander rose to his feet, his hand on his sword.

"Please, Alyson"—I placed a hand on hers and gripped it— "not now." I went to Leander, put my palm on his chest, and met those oceanic eyes. "There is no mistaking him, he is Westel Calkin."

"Anna, I am so sorry." Leander cupped my face. I placed a hand over his.

"You have nothing to be sorry about. It is Wes . . . Roland, who should be sorry."

"I will make him."

It was an oath, solemn and true.

Why then did it scare me so?

Spinning out of Leander's orbit, I tried to make my voice sound light. Bringing the jug around to top up mazers, I attempted a laugh. "Oh, he offered me threats to guarantee my silence. In this, I've chosen to disobey him, not with the intention to report him to authorities, but so I can inform those I trust about his machinations." Holding the jug in both hands, I paused by Leander's chair. "Le Bold has made it more than clear that not only would his past sins be pardoned should I seek justice, but that he would ensure everything we've achieved here, and not just the brewery, is ruined. He's not only threatened me, my lord, but all those who have aided and, as he sees it, abetted me in my endeavors."

"And what of those who aided and abetted him?" Leander growled.

"*Ja*," said Captain Stoyan. "What of the prior of St. Jude's, the sub-priors, and those who endorsed all that le Bold did?"

"At the least," said Adam, "they h . . . harbored a criminal."

"The old abbot is dead. I've no proof, don't you see?" I turned to Leander. "You said yourself that the abbot denied any knowledge of Westel Calkin. They even seemed shocked to learn he'd been accused of such a thing. And that's all it is. Accusation with no foundation—being able to identify him achieves little. He could claim a conspiracy and convince a jury it's mere resemblance. That he's Westel Calkin's distant relation. He would say it's nothing but a jealous brewster's malice."

I sank into a chair.

The fire crackled. A light breeze blew through the room causing the flames on the candles to sway. Aware of eyes upon me, I couldn't raise my head. Tears blinded me and I didn't want them to be mistaken for weakness, not when they were born of frustration.

"There are other ways of ensuring justice is served," said Leander quietly.

"That there are," I agreed. "And I know the types of which you speak. All of which place you in grave danger, and that I cannot bear."

"And I cannot bear the thought of doing nothing," snapped Leander. "Of allowing that rogue the upper hand. He must be made to pay for what he's done." He ground his fist into his thigh.

"At what cost?"

Leander glared at me, his early warmth replaced by a deadly solemnity.

"But would it be worth it?" suggested Alyson.

"Worth the twins? Betje? Adam? Worth what I've worked so hard to achieve, and against the odds?" Rising, I went to the hearth and stared into the flames. "Don't you think I haven't dreamed of vengeance? Of punishing the man who tore apart my family and brought so much evil into the world?" I half-turned. "I did little else for months and all it brought me was misery. I thought it was because he was dead and there was no recourse, no matter my dark desires or wishes, that I wallowed in anguish. I was wrong. Finding him alive made me understand that revenge is not what I want. It won't bring back Karel, Saskia, Will, or Louisa. It won't rebuild houses or transport us back to Elmham Lenn. It won't change the fact I brew for a living." I turned to face them, uncaring that tears streamed down my cheeks.

"If I seek justice—of any kind"—I looked pointedly at Leander—"then I risk losing all that I've gained since Westel . . . Roland. I risk losing the twins, Betje, you"—I gestured to Adam—"you as well," I said to Alyson. "And, my lord, I risk losing *you*." My eyes softened and I choked back a sob. Leander began to rise, but I gently pushed him back in his seat. "If I don't lose you and all the good that has come from evil Roland le Bold and his plots, then I will lose everything by corrupting my soul in enacting a revenge that's not my right. As God is my Lord and master, I refuse to be molded by retaliation. That is not justice, that is self-destruction. I would rather flee again and start afresh.

"That such opportunity, to join the Mystery, to live in London, is placed before me now when the situation is so dire shows the hand of God, does it not? I did not see it that way until you declared you would join me, Alyson." Putting the jug on the mantelpiece, I knelt before Leander. I tentatively took his hands. "That is God-given justice, my lord. If I'm to be punished, if Roland is, let it come from Him. Not me, not you.

Didn't Socrates say, 'The secret of change is to focus all of your energy not on fighting the old, but on building the new.' This is what I choose."

I levered myself upright again and finished pouring the drinks.

Leander's frown deepened. "You make it impossible to argue."

It was not a compliment.

Sitting back down, I tried to turn our thoughts to other matters, knowing the subject was by no means closed. "Where's Tobias? Is he here, or does he remain in the north?"

Captain Stoyan's head snapped toward Leander and, from the expression on his face, he was curious how Leander was going to answer the question.

Prevaricating, still disturbed by my attitude, Leander sipped his drink.

"Your brother sends a reply to your many letters that I swore on the Good Book you would receive." From out of his dusty surcoat, he pulled a rolled piece of paper and passed it to me. I took it somewhat reluctantly.

"I'll read it later," I said.

"Then, we will talk further," said Leander. He didn't only mean about Tobias either.

We made light conversation before Adam, aided by the captain and Alyson, made his way to bed. Bidding us good night, the captain and Alyson didn't return.

Taking me in his arms, Leander held me tightly. For the first time in weeks, in spite of our differences earlier, I felt myself relaxing. The shards of steel that had dwelt in my stomach, spine, and throat became malleable. Running my hands over his surcoat, enjoying the feel of the velvet, the whiff of spice and pine that clung to him, as well as the faint odor of horseflesh, I fitted my body to his and nuzzled his neck.

How long we stood like that I could not say, but when he finally raised his head, it was with that determined gaze I knew too well. I'd barely time to register, to ask about his well-being, when, steadying himself against the chair, he scooped me off my feet and into his arms.

"Hold fast," he ordered, picking up his cane. I locked my hands behind his neck.

"You don't have to carry me, Leander, I'm more than capable of walking by myself."

"I know. Some would argue that for a woman, you're far too capable."

Understanding he intended to debate me further, I gave a sigh of resignation.

"That's why you bring the devil out in me, frustrate me beyond reason, and it's why I love you. It's also why you will allow me, at the very least, this indulgence."

⋞⋟⋟⋞⋞

Much later, when the moon was a silver crescent high in the sky, and a parliament of owls had taken wing, their haunting cries echoing in the still night, I lay in Leander's arms. We hadn't made love; what had been discussed quenched passion, though not our love. Lying back against the covers, my head pillowed on his chest where the steady beat of his heart was like a lullaby, we talked long into the night. Sometimes our words were heated and strained, but more often, they were frank and reasoned.

Leander insisted that I tell him everything Roland had said, a full accounting. Of what he did, what he tried to force me to

do, I remained mute. Not because I wished to protect Roland,
or even my own modesty, but because I knew that any restraint
I asked of Leander would become impossible. He would charge
down to Winchester Palace and demand a reckoning regardless of who witnessed it or how his role would be perceived.
Leander's desire to strike Roland down, run him through with
a sword was already palpable. Anger heated his body, made him
restless. Rising from the bed as reason battled with instinct, he
strode around the room, his limp more apparent tonight than it
had been for a while. He wanted, needed, vengeance. Knowing
Westel was alive, that he lived not far away, was almost more
than he could bear. I understood that.

But bear it he must. For me.

This, I told him. What I did not share was my fear that
despite Leander's strength, connections, and titles, his revenge
would fail and Roland would triumph. He would use Leander
and my love for him to wound me more grievously. I could not,
would not allow that to happen. So, I advocated, I beseeched.
Using my own womanly arsenal, I even wept.

Though he comforted me and made vague promises that left
me uneasy, he continued to envisage a revenge befitting a man
such as le Bold. His silences, his tense limbs and shallow breathing revealed much to me.

Trying to divert his thoughts, I asked about the battles, the
king's health (which was very poor), and even, with the gentlest
of questions, about his late wife. Answers, though given, were
superficial and distracted. As he spoke of Bramham Moor,
the place where the final skirmish against the rebels took place,
he described the endless cold, the dreadful, chilling winds that
froze the rivers and hardened the ground, making it impossible

to bury the dead. He told me how, at Wheel Hall, an abbot was put to death and the Bishop of Bangor imprisoned at Windsor. This last was to remind me that King Henry was not above meting out justice to clergy and was meant to allay my fears. In that, my beloved failed.

Finally, as the moon disappeared and the stars dissolved, we fell asleep, dreams of Roland le Bold churning and churning like the Thames as it beat against the footings of London Bridge.

⋘⋙

Leander left early the following morning to return to Ashlar Place and his own affairs. He was tired, disgruntled, and more than a little moody. Anger that I had made him promise not to act formed a black impenetrable cloud over him. Captain Stoyan returned to his barge, a cartload of barrels accompanying him to be delivered upriver to Westminster. The captain was eager to resume business and sail the green waters once more.

Bidding Leander adieu, acutely aware of the strain that had developed between us, I saw the barrels safely onto the cart and into Captain Stoyan's care before returning to the brewery. I'd already sung the ale to life and honored my crones and there was great comfort in resuming familiar patterns.

I was struck by the beauty of this workshop of mash tuns, troughs, gleaming copper, burning wood, rising steam, puffs of gray smoke, and abundant goodwill. The air was filled with the heady, rich scent of hops and mash. Lifting a beaker from where it hung by a nail on the wall, I went to the trough and sank it deep into the wort. Glancing up, Harry smiled.

"That'll have no trouble passing, mistress. That's a mighty fine brew, even if I do say so myself. Fit for a king."

Rose cuffed him good-naturedly across the head.

Raising the beaker to him, I drank. Harry was right. It was smooth, with an aftertaste of honey, a hint of pine, and the tang of woodsmoke. In many ways, it reminded me of Leander and for a moment, I felt a twinge of sorrow.

I made up my mind there and then that, come tonight, if he should return, I would seek to mend our rift. I could not bear that we were at odds, not when a much greater adversary loomed.

❦

Putting an end to the minor discord between Leander and myself proved unnecessary. From the moment I saw him again, he was in much better humor—indeed, he didn't mention Roland le Bold and I determined to avoid the subject unless the need arose. Set to join the king at Pontefract for Easter and then journey to Leicester, Leander and I spent every night till then in mutual embrace.

The day he departed for Pontefract, I made certain he also had a letter for Tobias, who, Leander had told me vaguely, was occupied attending his affairs elsewhere. My brother's missive to me had been brief but loving. He refused to allow me to bear responsibility for what had befallen the family, swearing he would yet make amends for the ignominy of his birth, promising to restore the Sheldrake name and our relations in the process. How he thought to accomplish such an unnecessary task, I knew not. What I did know was that I could never use the name Sheldrake again and, even if Tobias was successful in his mission, wasn't certain I wanted to—I was a de Winter now and content to be so.

Over the next few weeks, we worked hard to meet the king's orders and those from the Duke of Clarence, the brethren of St. Mary's and St. Thomas's, as well as the large order from Roland. Hocktide came and went and we managed to pay the rent, Harry and Master atte Place delivering it to Winchester Palace on Alyson's behalf, thanks to the increased price of the beer which the king's purse bore without complaint or, God is good, knowledge.

It came as no surprise when the day after the rent was paid, Master Fynk darkened our door. On the pretext of accompanying the ale-conners, he made much fuss. In a repeat performance of his last visit, he declared our ale sour and the beer unfit to drink. Alyson's threats of summoning Sir Leander didn't sway him, neither did Adam's demands for the sheriff to act as mediator.

"The ale-conners declare this brew unfit. Not even I would dare contest their findings," he replied calmly and ordered one third of all we made, whether it had passed previously or not, be tipped into the Thames.

Alyson began to argue, but I grabbed her arm. "Don't. This man is not above cucking you in the Thames, or worse, sewerage, and this time, he'll see it done properly."

Alyson shut her mouth, but she was seething.

However, not even the bribed ale-conners would condone having the king's beer tipped into the dirt. Acceding to my argument that the beer was unfit because it required at least another week in the barrels, Master Fynk nevertheless insisted that the ale made for the king be destroyed and said the conners would return in a week to test the beer. By the time the bells for vespers rang, almost half our brew had been drunk by the river.

It was a huge blow and set us back enormously. I wouldn't let it defeat me. Working till the lack of decent light made it impossible, we doubled the amount we put in the tuns. Alyson and Captain Stoyan helped every moment they could spare. My greatest asset, though, was Adam. Slower, still finding long speeches difficult and not quite able to find enough dexterity in his hand to hold a quill, Adam could stir a mash paddle, load kindling, and test wort. Able to instruct and supervise, having him working again not only gave me a chance to make the king's order and Roland le Bold's (I wanted him to have no cause to complain), but it restored Adam's confidence.

Easter celebrations were subdued, though the church was once again full as spring brought visitors to Southwark by river and road, many of whom would require lodging, ale and food for their bodies, as well as nourishment for their souls. Sales of ale and beer were, perforce, limited, due to Master Fynk's interference, so Alyson hired more girls for the summer. What she lost in beverage sales was made up for by other, less tiring, means.

The extra work required to make orders meant less time to think about le Bold, but also set in motion plans to move. Though I'd written to Masters Hamme and Porlond stating I would accept their offer, it had not yet been made official. Receiving two gentle nudges from them by letter already, I didn't want to wait for a third. I had to make the time.

One sunny afternoon in May, after Master Fynk had paid another visit and ordered fourteen barrels emptied and leveled a hefty fine, with Alyson by my side and a more able-bodied Adam as chaperone, I arranged to visit the premises Master Hamme offered to lease me. Captain Stoyan took us across the river so we didn't have to endure the crowds on London Bridge.

A pleasant wind wafted about our faces as we stood on deck and watched London draw nearer. Brief though the journey was, escaping the brewery and Southwark, the fear of Roland and the machinations of Master Fynk did me much good. I pushed my concerns aside and soaked up the atmosphere. There were many craft upon the river, taking advantage of the temperate conditions to fish, carry cargo and passengers, or simply take to the waters to be seen. Decorative punts, lavishly curtained and with elegant lamps fore and aft swinging with each stroke of the oars, glided past, the coats of arms of noble houses on display, their women passengers decked in sumptuous silks and embroidered linens, their hair coiled and plaited and crowned by the finest gauzes. Troubadours strummed their instruments and the voices of poets drifted across the waters.

As we poled alongside London Bridge, far enough away to resist the currents and eddies that tested the hardiest of sailors, we caught sight of the teeming crowds on the Bridge, heard the cacophony of voices competing for custom. Buckets were emptied out of the windows of teetering houses, offal and bloodied bones were tipped surreptitiously from a handcart, all swallowed by the waters. Children and some men cast lines from the footings, birds flapped overhead. The smells of life and death clung to this part of the river and we raised our kerchiefs and scarves to cover our noses and mouths lest we inhale the filthy miasma.

We came ashore at Dowgate close to the Stilliard and, from there, followed Wall Brook, which, though containing much refuse, maintained a steady flow. On we walked, past the church of St. Mary Bothaw, inns, taverns, private residences both well-kept and poor, passing Old Fish Street and understanding why it bore that name, before reaching Cornhill Street. At the corner, near the water conduit known as the Tun (and the adjacent cage, stocks, and a pillory, the latter miserably inhabited by a baker), we met with Master Hamme, who escorted us to the brewery.

Imagine our astonishment when we saw the name on the building—it too was called The Swanne. Alyson beamed.

"I asked my Lord for a sign. I didn't think he'd be so bloody obvious about it though." This Swanne, while a large building of three wooden stories, nevertheless differed from its counterpart in Southwark. Darker but with bigger rooms, it had a small courtyard and a tiny mews. Close to St. Michael's Church (but not too close, as Alyson was swift to note), a tavern named The Pope was two doors down, while on either side were residences, one belonging to a German mercer, the other a baker. Inside was mostly clean, though the walls had smoke stains, and the kitchen was possessed of only a makeshift oven. Apart from these, the downstairs was shared with a large hall, buttery, stables, and storage rooms. Upstairs, there were two reception rooms, although the smaller one could be used for an office, as well as five bedrooms. The attic held more. There was even a garderobe that emptied into the ditch.

Downstairs, the brewery exceeded my imaginings. Running the length of the house, it had four long narrow windows, allowing light to stream in. It had two doors, one internal and one external that led to the courtyard and mews. Inside was everything Master Hamme promised—two large mash tuns, leaden troughs and pipes, and a big kiln. There were two quern stones, one too big for an individual to operate, and there was also space that could be used for malting if we chose. Altogether, it was a pleasant surprise.

Most importantly, it had access to a clean water supply. There was also a nearby market and it was not too far from the river and a number of docks. My intention to petition the king for a license to export to Flanders and other parts of Europe would be a priority.

Its position, within London's walls, meant I'd have to adhere strictly to the laws that bound those inside. Now I understood why Master Hamme was offering it to me, and so cheaply. Would I have to make a choice between ale and beer? Would the Mystery allow me to brew both? Apart from the ale-conners and the tax, I'd managed to make my own rules so far. Living and working in London would change that. Having Roland le Bold as our bishop did as well. It was a case of the lesser of two evils.

When I broached my concerns about brewing ale and beer, which broke the rules of the Mystery, Master Hamme didn't contradict me. "Aye, mistress, but those who make these rules be a-changing annually. Furthermore, you're only breaking rules if you get caught. I won't be a-telling if you don't." He winked. "You'll find the outbreak of pestilence changed many things."

With a discretion I hadn't expected from him, Master Hamme left us alone for a while. After wandering through the building again, we gathered in the brewery.

"Well?" I asked.

Alyson, Captain Stoyan, and Adam looked at each other. Adam was pale and tired. It was his first big outing since his illness, and though he was enjoying himself immensely, it was evident he needed to sit down.

"Adam?" I asked when no one spoke.

"I've looked at the ledgers, Anna, and if they are true, this brewery did well. Not as well as you're doing now, but it didn't have C . . . Crown trade." His lips twisted, and though he tried to continue, no sound came. Raising his withered arm as high as he could, he gave the equivalent of a shrug. "If you leave The Sw . . . Swanne, you could not do better than here."

I turned to Alyson. "I agree," she said. With hands on hips, she gazed around. "There's potential here, Anna, and not just for a brewery, but to offer accommodation, food as well, attract good-quality clients. I like it." She jerked her chin toward the stairs. "I like him."

"And, Captain, what do you think?"

"If they won't say it, I will. I think anything that gets you out from under le Bold's nose is good. I also think it will be easy to export from here. The docks are solid, the water deep, the storage excellent. *Ja*. It's good."

Everything they said confirmed my feelings.

"Very well, let's begin negotiations."

It didn't take long to settle on a price and conditions. Once I started production, I would be invited to join the Mystery. Making arrangements to sign a lease and to begin moving in July, we said farewell to Master Hamme and rowed back to Bankside.

Alyson and the captain chattered excitedly, while I sat with Adam, watching the river slide beneath us, enjoying the roll of the water, the spray that occasionally struck our warm faces. Above us, gulls soared on the thermals, cawing to each other, their white plumage gleaming in the rose-gold of the sky, turning them into giant butterflies.

I thought back over the afternoon, and though I sent prayers to the Lord and His Mother, I also sent some to the crones. For what I didn't tell the others was that as I entered the brewery, I spied my old women squatting in the corners as if they'd spent their entire existence there. Grinning wickedly, they licked their parched lips, letting me know that they were thirsty and it was my brew they were waiting for.

I could not wait to get back to The Swanne, to share the news with Betje, Harry, and the twins. I would write to Leander and Tobias as well. Knowing I'd be leaving Southwark and the sphere of Roland le Bold would, I prayed, offer the peace of mind we all deserved.

❖〰❖

Do not the church fathers warn of invoking the devil's name lest you summon him? Though I didn't utter it, my thoughts appeared to beckon the one person I least wanted to set eyes upon. The person whose presence still had the power to make me tremble, to doubt my resolutions and those of others. As we pulled into the dock and Captain Stoyan and Alyson tied off the barge and anchored her, there he was, Bishop Roland le Bold. Surrounded by cronies, including Master Fynk, he halted at the end of the dock and watched us disembark.

Noting the swagger in Master Fynk's steps, the arrogant set of his chin, everything became clear. I had believed he was acting of his own volition, to punish Alyson and me for our defiance and Sir Leander's intervention, but now I understood he was simply following orders. Those of Roland le Bold.

Why? Hadn't Roland said he would only seek to ruin me if I revealed the truth? How could he possibly know of my conversations with my friends at The Swanne, with Leander? He didn't. They made no difference.

Alyson linked her arm through mine. Clutching his walking stick tightly, Adam took my other arm while Captain Stoyan led our group. Courageous, we crossed the dock as if we had not a care in the world.

Pausing where the bishop stood, giving blessings and receiving them in return, we waited our turn to offer obeisance. To do otherwise would be ill-mannered and almost heretical. I would give him no cause for complaint.

Accepting our reverence, he retracted his hand and smiled.

"God give you good day, Mistress Anna," he said unctuously.

"And you too, your grace."

"Pleasant day for the river, is it not?"

"Most pleasant." I gave a curtsy and sought to pass. His hand flashed out and held my forearm. Alyson was rudely shoved out of the way. She made a noise of protest but fell silent when a guard lowered his pike in her direction and snarled.

"You wouldn't be seeking to leave, would you?" said Roland, so softly only Adam and I could hear.

My eyes widened. *How did he know?*

"Because in order to leave my manor, my jurisdiction, you must seek permission. Mine. Failing to do so incurs penalties, harsh ones, and steep fines—enough to make most people paupers. I'm sure you wouldn't want that, would you?"

"Nay, your grace. I would not."

Roland offered another smile and nodded benignly. "You see, it's my responsibility to make Southwark strong by enhancing the trades we offer, the skills folk can rely upon, bolster its reputation, especially since licentiousness and ungodliness has stained it so. The pestilence has offered an opportunity for renewal that I will not let slip past. A brewer who has Crown trade is a blessing, is it not? And did not the good Lord say we should share our blessings? If, God forbid, you were to take your talent away, then my manor, my liberty, would be denied and our reputation suffer. I cannot allow that. I will not." Flashing those perfect teeth, he gave a wave of dismissal, turning and throwing coins toward a gaggle of urchins who leaped upon them. Bowing his head, he continued walking along the river. "God give you a good night," he called over his silk-clad shoulder.

It was like a blow to the stomach and I doubled over. Adam strove to hold me upright and Alyson ran to my side. They helped me to a rock, where I slumped. "Is what he said true? Do I need *his* permission to leave?"

Shielding her eyes with her hand, Alyson watched the bishop greeting locals. Captain Stoyan and Adam followed her gaze. I did not.

"If it's not true today, there'll be notice it's so by the end of the week. If there's one thing I've learned about your bishop, Anna, he won't be thwarted. And if he thinks he has been, his punishment is swift."

"And he gets others to mete it out," said Adam.

"Master Fynk?"

"Exactly."

Alyson lowered her hand. "You need to watch yourself, chick."

I held my emotions in check. "Aye. We all do."

# FIFTY-SIX

THE SWANNE
Late June
*The year of Our Lord 1408 in the ninth
year of the reign of Henry IV*

*P*erhaps I was a fool to ignore Roland's warning, but I did. Without flaunting it, plans to move to Cornhill Street proceeded apace. We told only Betje, Harry, Emma, and Constance, the latter two being sworn to secrecy. The remainder of the women, Master atte Place, Ralph, Thomas, Golda, and Rose and the tradesmen and -women with whom we dealt regularly knew nothing of our intentions. Nor did the clients.

Or so we thought.

In the meantime, we continued to brew, despite Roland's efforts through Master Fynk to prevent us meeting our orders and being blacklisted as a consequence. Two more brews were tipped into the Thames, and Alyson, who protested loudly and scornfully and accused Master Fynk of being a puppet who merely let a bishop pull his strings, was heavily fined and sentenced to being shackled in the pillory on the High Street for being a scold.

Master Fynk had underestimated her popularity. Though he ordered a full kilderkin of ale to be tipped over her, it was a very warm day and Alyson thanked good Master Fynk for cooling her passions. A crowd gathered, most clutching rotting fruit, eggs, and dung. Listening to Master Fynk list Alyson's crimes, there was some discontented mumbling and glances at Bishop le Bold, who sat upon a chair watching proceedings. It was one thing to make mockery of a baker who put ground stone in his bread, or a regrateresse who bought up ale and waited until it was in such short supply she could sell it on at inflated prices, but this was different. Alyson was regarded as an honest woman—both in her dealings in the bathhouse and in the brewery. None among those present had cause to complain about what she served. Why, hadn't her brewer earned Crown trade? Reluctant to hurl objects let alone abuse, people muttered and hovered. Master Fynk soon tired of waiting and, after flinging some mud and insults of his own, sensed the temper of the crowd didn't favor him. As soon as he saw the languid wave of the bishop's wrist, he ordered her released. By the time Captain Stoyan, Adam, and I helped Alyson from the pillory, the constable whispering apologies, the bishop and Master Fynk had gone.

Regardless of the obstacles thrown our way—including the news that Master Fynk had been appointed sheriff of our borough—we climbed them. Exhausted, burning at the injustices inflicted upon us, we suffered it all quietly because we knew we wouldn't have to endure much longer. Once the king's order for summer was complete, we would begin to pack and then, in the last week of July, move across the river.

I wrote to Leander every other day as he'd requested, keeping him informed of what was happening, though I spared him some of the more unjust and mortifying details. There was little point angering him when there was nothing he could do.

Much to my surprise, Leander's letters weren't full of admonition and advice as I half-anticipated. On the contrary, they reinforced that soon le Bold would no longer concern me. Leander wrote mostly about the king's failing health and how even a proposed journey to Windsor by horseback had tired him so much, he opted to repair to his barge for most of the trip. Queen Joan was concerned and remained by his side as, for the time being, Leander would as well. The good news was that the king intended a visit to his trusted confidant and friend Archbishop Arundel, who lived upriver in Mortlake Manor.

*Once His Grace is settled, my beloved, I will come to you. The distance is negligible, thus I can fulfill my official duties with a clear conscience, as well as those, despite sound arguments to the contrary, my heart needs.*

I clung to those words as I did to the hopes the end of next month held. It was only later I placed another interpretation upon them.

On June fifteenth, after many setbacks, the king's order was loaded onto Captain Stoyan's barge to be delivered to both Mortlake Manor and Eltham Palace. At the same time, Harry and Master atte Place transported Roland le Bold's order to Winchester Palace. Produced from the same batches, I was determined that le Bold would not have cause for complaint if the king was content.

Though there were still more brews to make before I ceased production in Bankside, I was persuaded the quality of what I'd made for the king would ensure Crown trade continued.

The ale and beer I'd sent passed both my taste test and that of the ale-conners. Adding some efficacious herbs to the ale, I hoped that they would facilitate a speedy recovery for the king. If one thing was assured, they could do no harm.

❖

Uncertain what woke me, I lay on the bed, stripes of sunlight banding my legs through the shutters where my shift had ridden up. I yawned, sat up, and stretched my arms above my head. Distant thuds, almost musical in their depth, became louder and the buzz of voices and frantic shouts brought me rapidly to my senses. Leaping out of bed, I grabbed my shawl from the chair and wrapped it around my shoulders, threw open the shutters, and pushed out the window.

A fine mist augured a warm day ahead. The bells for lauds chimed as I gazed on the river and the wraithlike city on the other side which, this time of the morning, appeared to float upon the waters.

Below, a crowd strode the cobbles. Talking excitedly, they wandered from bathhouse to inn to home, knocking on doors, talking, gesticulating, frowning, and shaking their heads at whoever answered. The Swanne was next to receive the news. Adam wrenched open the door before anyone could pound upon the wood. I leaned out and tried to hear what was being said. I caught the words "His Grace," "death," "gravely ill." Adam's responses were lost to me, but soon the mob left, eager to pass the bad tidings along.

I left the shutters ajar as I withdrew from the window. Piecing together what I thought I heard, I was saddened beyond measure. To think that the man I'd met in Gloucester, my king, the man who blessed me with his trade and thus altered my fortunes, was finally succumbing to the terrible illness that, according to Leander, had afflicted him for such a long period.

Quickly I washed, dressed, and went to the brewery, determined that my ale song would be as much for the king as my brew. As I had been tardy to rise, Betje and Harry were already there and together we serenaded the brew. While they attended to the tuns and the kiln, I gave my offering to the corner crones, whispering that it would not be too much longer before we removed to our new lodgings. Disgruntled that so much of what they'd overseen had been lost to the river, I persuaded myself that they were also looking forward to our relocation. I was literally counting the days. Imagine, we would start brewing afresh—in London. The very notion made my flesh tingle.

Breaking our fast after tierce, I was sitting in the kitchen, intending to take small ale to Alyson and Adam, who I knew were in the solar tending the books ready to pass to the next owner (who was yet to be found), when the clatter of hooves and the cry of a courier forced me to put down the mazers I'd filled and follow Sophie out into the yard.

Mounted upon a sweating horse was a rider I knew well as he'd delivered many letters to me of late. Reaching in my apron for a coin, I passed it to him in exchange for a sealed scroll.

"God give you good day, Nab. There's small ale and bread in the kitchen."

"May the Holy Trinity bless you and keep you, mistress, I thank you but I mustn't tarry. I'm to continue to Elmham Lenn, my lord's orders."

"Elmham Lenn?" The name still had the ability to conjure so many conflicting memories. Hearing it from Nab's mouth made it even more confronting. "Why?"

Nab shrugged. "Don't know, only that it's urgent and Master Tobias is expecting me."

*Tobias? He was in Elmham Lenn? I'd assumed him back by Leander's side . . .*

Before I could ask another question, the courier wheeled his horse and, kicking up dust and debris, cantered out the gates.

I was still in the courtyard when Alyson found me, staring at the open letter in my hand.

"There you are. I wondered . . . Anna, what is it? Why are you so pale? Is it Leander? Is it Tobias?"

Raising my head, I gazed at her blankly.

Grabbing me by the shoulders, she shook me hard. "Anna, you're frightening me. What is it?"

I held out the paper, my hands shaking. "It's the king. He's fallen into a sleep from which no one can awake him."

"May God help him," said Alyson crossing herself. "Didn't you hear the fuss earlier? This is known throughout the land."

"You don't understand. They're saying it's not natural, that it's the devil's work. There are some claiming he's been poisoned."

"God help us." Alyson crossed herself again.

I found breathing difficult. Holding out the letter, I shook it in Alyson's face.

"Alyson, Leander writes that His Grace was drinking my ale

when he collapsed. It was the batch I added the myrica gale into. I thought it would help . . . I . . . I . . ."

Alyson snatched the letter from me and read it through quickly.

"God help you, lass."

"It's said to be good for stomach upsets and can even be used as a powder to ease skin complaints. I thought since His Grace suffered from both . . . Alyson"—I raised wide disbelieving eyes to hers—"what if I caused this? What if it's me who has poisoned the king?"

"Hush, hush, my chick." Alyson wrapped her arms around me and pulled me close, pushing my head into the crook of her neck, dropping her lips to my ear. "Be silent. Do not think such things and, dear Lord, do not say them. Not to anyone. Listen. It's not you. It cannot be. We all tasted the ale, even Roland le Bold has ale from the same batch and we've heard nothing. Do you think that if it was poisoned, the bishop would let it pass? Leander is simply informing, not warning you." She scanned the letter over my shoulder. "He writes he'll be here tonight. Till then, you must not make mention of this. You must continue as normal. And it is, do you hear me?" She thrust me at arm's length, waiting till I met her eyes.

"I do, I do. I hear you."

But I did not. All I heard was the sound of fate rushing forward with black wings to finally claim me.

◆≈≈◆

The day passed slowly. Every sound, every hoof on the cobbles, every shout from the courtyard, I would jump to my feet and run to the door or look out the window. I'd long given up on the brewery. I was of no use in there, and I didn't want my nerves to affect the brew or alarm Betje. Visiting the nursery was a disaster. Wanting to climb over me, the twins, who were now fleet of foot and endlessly curious, weren't interested in the cuddles I offered and needed in return. When Emma and Constance said they would take them for a walk before supper, we were all relieved.

Staring out the solar window, my arms resting on the ledge, I tried to enjoy the sunset, the way cushions of gilt-edged pink merged with ribbons of copper before melting into the beginnings of the violet evening. Spires soared into the air, piercing the firmament as if to insist that Heaven pay attention. Seagulls and doves wheeled against the sky, wherries dotted the river, and the cobbles below thronged with folk coming and going on their business.

Every time someone entered The Swanne, the bell above the door sounded. Voices traveled up the staircase, all discussing the same thing: the king. News spread fast, but bad news infected everyone who heard it. But, as Alyson wryly noted, bad news was also good for business.

"Come away from the window, Anna. He will be here soon, you know he will."

I spun around reluctantly. "Why am I not as assured as you, Alyson? Why is my heart a-quiver?"

"For no reason I can fathom, sweetling. Sit down, I will ask Sophie to fetch you a small ale—nay, some of my Bordeaux wine."

Her footsteps sounded in the corridor and I could hear her calling for Sophie. I turned back to the window. "Where are

you, Leander?" I looked at where the river met the sky for so
long, remembering the afternoon we spent in Cornhill Street
and the promise of the new venture, I forgot the ground.

"There she is," shouted a deep voice. "Don't let her escape."

Startled, I looked down. Marching toward The Swanne, surrounded by soldiers armed with pikes, their swords drawn, was
Master Fynk. Pointing straight at me, he led half the men to the
entrance and signaled for the remainder to go to the back gates.
Shoving people aside, the men, led by Master Fynk, ran into the
bathhouse.

I stood frozen to the spot. There were screams followed by
angry calls. I could hear the tramp of boots on the stairs; doors
opening and shutting; more cries. My heart pounded, my body
flamed with heat before becoming colder than the Thames in
winter. I had to get away.

Before I could act, the door flew open. Standing on the
threshold was Alyson, a cape in her hands. "Quickly, quickly."
She ran toward me and threw the cape over my shoulders. I felt
strangely comforted as it enfolded me. Alyson tied the laces and
pulled the hood down to hide my hair and face. "Dear God,
Anna. I'm sorry, I should have listened, acted faster, hidden
you away. But who would have thought . . ." Placing an arm
about my shoulders, she spun me around, ready to leave.

"Mistress Anna de Winter," purred a voice.

Our heads shot up. Leaning against the doorframe, a long
dagger in one hand, a piece of paper in the other, was Master
Fynk. "And I thought you'd be the type to surrender without
trying to fight or seek flight. How easy it is to assume honor
when everyone knows women of your ilk have none. Guards,"
he barked over his shoulder, "seize her."

Stepping out of the way, he admitted four huge men into the room. Shoving Alyson aside, one of them twisted my arms and tied my hands behind my back. Another held me by the shoulders, shaking me roughly, though there was no need. I'd not had time to gather my wits to resist.

Alyson found her feet and unleashed a tirade.

"Leave her go. Do you know who this is? This is the king's brewer. You've no right—"

The biggest of the guards swung his arm backward, collecting Alyson on the jaw and sending her hurtling into the table. She fell heavily. Her lip was split, her eyes unfocused. Master Fynk threw the paper on her breast. It landed like a drunken bird. "I've every right as this warrant will attest."

"Please, don't—" I began, before Master Fynk struck me across the face. My head snapped back, my cheek flamed. My mouth filled with a coppery taste.

"You will say nothing till I tell you to. Guards"—he leered one last time—"take her to The Clink."

*The Clink. The bishop's prison. Sweet Mother Mary, help me.*

Ignoring his threat, as they pulled me forward, I cried out. "Pray, what have I done?" I knew. I knew. I'd never been so afraid in my life.

The blow came swiftly and the force of it made my ears ring. One eye began to swell.

Reeling, my head swam, my knees buckled, but the guards held me upright and dragged me out of the solar.

"Do? What did you do?" Master Fynk imitated my voice, capturing the terror, the disbelief perfectly. "As if you didn't know." Changing tone, he waited until we were on the stairs. In the doorways were the women and some of their clients. The girls stared at me in shock and sympathy. A couple dared to reach out, only to have their arms knocked brutally away. Clearing his throat, Master Fynk answered my plaintive question.

"Mistress Anna de Winter, I'm arresting you for the most heinous crime there is." He paused, enjoying the sudden silence.

A clatter on the stairs broke it. I looked down and saw Betje and Harry peering up. A groan escaped me.

Following my gaze, Master Fynk leered. Louder than a town crier, he continued. "I'm arresting you for murder."

There were gasps, denials.

*Oh, God and all the angels help me.*

The king was dead.

Amidst tears and protests, shouts and jeers, I was hauled from The Swanne.

# FIFTY-SEVEN

THE CLINK, SOUTHWARK
Late June
*The year of Our Lord 1408 in the ninth
year of the reign of Henry IV*

*T*hough it was the Southwark sheriff who arrested me, the seriousness of the charge should have warranted my incarceration in London: Newgate at least, but the Tower most likely for a crime against the king's person. I would face the authority and discipline of the King's Bench. Instead, I was neither marched nor rowed across the river to London; I wasn't handed over to the king's men, but rudely paraded through the streets of Southwark and thrown in The Clink.

A crowd followed, mocking and heckling, their numbers increasing with each step until the guards were forced to clear a passage. Barely aware of them, all I could think of was Betje and the twins. Betje's stricken face staring up at mine as she understood the seriousness of the charge. And poor, brave Alyson. That guard was vicious. Her hurts would be significant. I prayed they would care for one another and that when Leander arrived, they would convey the urgency of my situation. Leander would know what to do, how to secure my release from this dreadful place.

The Clink was part of the Bishop of Winchester's liberty, which meant Roland le Bold could hold me until the royal court was ready to deal with the charges. That could take days, weeks . . . dear God, it could take months . . .

What he could do to me in that time did not bear thinking about. *I will destroy everything and everyone you love.*

*Oh God, Leander, help me.*

Thrust in a dark stinking cell, I was manacled to the wall and left to sit on urine-soaked straw. If I ever wondered about the origins of the prison's name, the sound of the door clanging shut left no doubt. The sound echoed throughout the vast chambers, final, deadly. Cackles and hoots resounded from cells I could not see, but whose inhabitants had rushed to the bars to study the new arrival. Toothless, dirty women crowed, their lean, scratched arms reaching through the bars. Children younger than Betje, their faces streaked with grime, their eyes lumps of unforgiving coal, took note of my fine tunic, my clean hair, before spitting in my direction. Whores, wretched orphans, thieves, heretics—they were all here. And now I was one of their number. I was the worst kind of villain—a traitor.

Unable to move too far before the chains pulled me back, I sat on the straw. Piercing through my tunic, it clawed my thighs. I tried to flatten some, disturbing the creatures that lurked beneath it: lice, vermin, and God knows what else. Three large rats poked their noses through before disappearing. Gray shapes scurried into the corners. The floor was not much better.

Slimy, dank, and filthy, it exuded its own foul odor. A small grated window to my right admitted a faint strip of light and I could hear the sounds of passersby going about the afternoon's business, unaware of the women trapped below or, more likely, indifferent to their fate.

As the cell slowly darkened, I pondered my own and prayed fervently for a sign, for hope . . . for a miracle.

Sound carried down the corridors, mostly the wails and derision of the other women. Gruff male voices could also be heard as well as grunts and giggles. Curling against the wall, I tried to block them. Water dripped from somewhere above—at least I hoped it was water—forcing me to find an alternate place to sit.

What I couldn't comprehend was, if the king was dead, why were the church bells not sounding? Why were there no laments? No crying? Even when King Richard died, there'd been those who'd walked the streets of Elmham Lenn weeping and wailing.

I didn't have to wait long to discover the reason.

The jangle of keys and the dull, heavy steps of the gaoler were accompanied by a lighter tread.

It was difficult to discern who it was until a cresset lamp illuminated his face. Roland le Bold. No longer in his robes of office, he wore a simple surcoat and breeches. This was how I remembered him: not as a man of God. It was Westel Calkin restored to life.

I tried to stand but was forced to bend slightly because of the shackles on my hands. Ordering the gaoler to leave, Roland waited till his steps faded then moved closer, the lamp held high in one hand, the other pressing a kerchief to his nose.

Ignoring the stench, the dirt, he squatted at my feet, peering into my face. Barely able to determine his features, I focused on the liquid gleam of his eyes.

"I warned you, Anneke. I told you what would happen if you revealed our past."

I shook my head. Tears I didn't know I'd harbored began to stream down my cheeks.

"Nay, don't deny it," he said softly, sweetly. "I have it on good authority that you've been bleating to everyone. Well, not you, exactly, but your lover. He's been asking questions, paying for answers, visiting people I hoped to forget and inviting them to remember what they should not. And, tell me, how would he know with whom to speak, where to go, if you hadn't told him?"

"Sir Leander would never—"

"Oh, come now, Anneke." His voice was wheedling. "Of course you've told him. Whispered your pain across the pillow." He collected one of my tears on the tip of a finger, holding it toward the lamp and examining it as if it was an exquisite jewel. "How could you resist eliciting sympathy from such a one? How could you not appeal to the warrior in him by playing the suffering damsel?" He flicked the tear into the shadows and rose. "You're all the same, wanton whores who'll deploy any trickery to get your own way. I cannot blame him. God knows what you've told him, what lusty rewards you've promised, but he is prying and I don't like that, Anneke. You broke our deal and now you will pay, just as I promised."

"I've done nothing wrong."

"You always were a fool, Anneke. When are you going to understand, it doesn't matter what you *have* done, it's what people *believe* you have done for which I seek recompense." He laughed, and his eyes glinted in the flame.

"I didn't poison the king . . . I did not." My nose was running and I was unable to wipe it.

"Oh, I know that."

I stared at him in disbelief. "Then—then why am I here?" The sob I released became a cough.

"Because you're responsible for the death of two of my monks. Did Master Fynk not tell you? After a mere sip of their drinks, they fell to the floor, dead. Your ale on their lips and in their throats. They were the only two to try it, Anneke, the only ones."

"There was nothing wrong with my ale."

"Not when it left The Swanne, perhaps. But by the time it reached the monks' mazers, something terrible had happened to it."

My eyes widened. "You . . . you . . ."

Roland laughed again. "Perhaps you're not so great a fool."

Wincing as the flesh on my injured eye pulled, I tried to touch it, only the manacle cutting into my wrist prevented me. Roland began to laugh harder.

"And to think, when the king is dead, you'll be blamed for that too. It won't take much for a jury to find you guilty. Already, those summoned to do their duty descend upon the palace, eager to see justice done in my court."

He reached over, his hand brushing my hair, lifting a tangle from my shoulder.

"Roland, don't. Please."

"I do like it when you plead. Do you remember?"

I recoiled, my hair pulled taut in his grip.

He held the strand, tightening it so pain lanced my scalp. I refused to respond even though it smarted terribly.

Eventually, he tired and released my hair. "I should keep you here longer, just for the pleasure of seeing you . . . like this. Bent, broken, ready to do my whim—if not now, then soon, very soon." He swung and grabbed the back of my neck, forcing my face into his crotch. I twisted away, shut my eyes, but he pushed harder, thrust his thighs. I couldn't breathe, but I could feel him stiffen. I went limp. Ceased to struggle. I even managed to stop crying. It's not so difficult when rage replaces sorrow.

He flung me away from him with a grunt, and I fell hard upon one knee.

"Perhaps not." He turned his back.

"Wait. At least leave me the light. Some water?"

Without answering, he walked out of the cell and didn't look back. A short time later, the gaoler returned to lock me in.

Engulfed by shadows, the rats became bolder, leaving the corners to stare at me, their eyes gleaming in the faint bands of light from the window. After a time, I no longer saw them. All I saw was Roland le Bold's pale face and colorless eyes; his perfect mouth and perfect teeth locked in an eternal smile that expressed not humor or joy but, like a herald with a trumpet, announced my eternal damnation.

⊰≫⤫≪⊱

"Mistress Anna? Anna? Be you there?"

It took an instant to gauge where I was, why the room was so dark, why it smelled so foul. Everything came back to me and I sat up, forgetting the manacles, which pulled so fiercely I cried out.

"Are you all right?" hissed the voice.

It was coming from the window.

It wasn't so much light as a lessening of the shadows that enabled me to discern a face pressed against the bars.

"Harry?"

"The same, mistress. I've food and drink for you, and blessings and prayers from everyone. And a message from Sir Leander."

My heart felt too big for my chest. "Praise be to God. Give me a moment." I tried to get as close to the window as possible. Even though he whispered, Harry's voice was unnaturally loud in the dark silence and I feared we'd be heard.

Managing to stand beneath the window, I tried to straighten, but it was impossible. A rat scurried across my feet, making me jump.

"You there, mistress?"

"Aye, Harry. But I can't stand. Not properly. They have me in chains."

A series of curses were unleashed. "Forgive me, mistress."

"You're forgiven, if I had but the strength, I would say the same. Tell me, what message from Sir Leander?"

"My lord says the first thing I was to tell you was, you're not to lose heart."

I choked back a sob. "Go on."

"He says the king still lives and his condition hasn't changed. That's good, mistress, right?"

"As good as it can be."

"He said he knows about the monks, that le Bold, curse the bastard"—Harry spat—"be assembling jurors whom he's bribed to stand in judgment of you." My heart sank. "But he, Sir Leander, will do everything in his power to stop this happening. He said to tell you that he's summoned a . . . whatcha call it? A Corner to come."

"Coroner."

"That be it. He's also been sending couriers out all night.

Doesn't care 'bout curfew or nothing." Harry paused. "Mistress, I'm not s'posed to tell you this, but Sir Leander came here, to The Clink. Demanded to see you. The bastard bishop wouldn't let him. Said it's against the rules. Rules be damned. They let whores into the men's prison and men into the women's. Le Bold makes his own."

"That he does, Harry."

I couldn't help it, I began to weep.

"Aw, don't cry, mistress, please don't cry." He placed his arm between the bars and tried to reach me. I raised my hand as far as I could. Our fingertips just touched. "Sir Leander will make it right, he will, I knows it. And, if he can't, then I dare the church to take on Goody Alyson."

"Is she all right, Harry?"

"She is sore and marked but this is Goody Alyson we're talking 'bout, course she's all right."

Funny how even in the darkest times, a smile will still find you.

"And Betje?"

"She's crushed, mistress, God's truth. But she's staying strong—for you. She worked in the brewery till late. We both did. Till Sir Leander arrived, anyhow. He is looking after her, me and Adam too. And, before you ask, Adam and the twins are fine. The twins know nothing, which is the way you'd want it."

"It is, Harry, it is."

"Everyone is praying, mistress, and those who can are writing too. What they're doing that for, God knows, but if it'll help . . ."

"Aye."

"You're also to let me know if there's anything you need. Goody Alyson, Betje, and Cook sent these for you." Retracting his arm, he began to push a skin of ale through the bars. I caught it in my cupped hands. Next, he shoved through a linen napkin tied with string. I could smell the bread and chicken. It made my mouth water.

"Thank you, Harry. Bless you. Please, tell Sir Leander, I won't—" Damn my tears. "I won't lose heart. And tell Betje and everyone else, I'm fine. I am well. I'm not harmed." *Not yet.*

Harry pushed his face close, trying to look down and see me. "It's dark in there, mistress."

"That's what I'd like, Harry, some light."

"I'll bring it tomorrow."

"Is it safe for you?"

"For now. Sir Leander said no one pays attention to lads on the street. He's right."

Reaching down to me, he waggled his fingers. I stroked the tips.

"Bless you, Harry Frowyk, bless you."

There was a loud sniff, then Harry pulled his arm away. The gray light brightened before I heard a faint "God bless you," and he was gone.

I sat down heavily, my back against the wall, my treasure trove of fare in my lap. So, Roland had summoned a court to convict me. The penalty for murder was swift and harsh—death by hanging. But if the coroner could arrive in time and prove my innocence, I might yet be spared the noose. Leander made sure I knew the king was still alive so I'd understand the weakness of le Bold's case against me. Though not if he could prove my ale killed those monks.

Whether I was accused of killing king or pauper, death was death; the one great leveler regardless of birth or wealth.

Movement to my left reminded me of the rats, who had caught the scent of food, and I remembered how hungry I was. Pulling the stopper out of the skin, I drank. This was no small ale, but a full-tasting brew. How ironic if it was the same that killed the monks. Though I knew it wasn't my drink that ended the monks' lives, but Roland's callous intervention. That such hate could lie in the soul of a man of God unnerved me.

Unwrapping the linen, I picked up the bread and chicken and began to nibble. There was a lump of cheese as well, which I first thought to save till morning but, hearing the scratching of the rats and their chittering, I changed my mind and, casting crumbs to the other side of the chamber, finished everything I'd been given. Turning the linen inside out, I spread it on the straw and, exhausted and overwhelmed by the events of the last hours, lay down. It would be for but a moment . . .

<del>≪≳⟩×⟨≲≫</del>

Eight days later, I was taken from the cell. Every night since I'd been incarcerated, Harry and, one time, Betje and Alyson, had come to the window and given me news and provisions. The day after I was interred, they'd bribed the gaoler to give me a chamber pot, light, food, water, and other essentials, but while he'd taken the money, nothing manifested. That Betje braved the streets, albeit with Alyson and Harry, despite my reassurances, revealed that Harry's reports must have failed to proffer sufficient reassurance. Upon peeking into the cell, lit as it was by the weak glow of a cresset lamp and inhaling its pungent smell, she'd cried. She tried to reach me by putting her arm between the bars like Harry, but she wasn't tall enough.

For the first few days, Leander tried to use coin to gain access to me, but it had been refused. Alyson said the only reason for that was because the bishop was paying the gaoler more.

"Or threatening him," I added.

"Or both."

From Alyson I learned that Master Fynk and his constables had questioned every single person at The Swanne. "They got nothing out of me, mind, nor Adam or Master atte Place, but some of the girls and young Ralph and Hodge came back mighty sore. They broke Emma's arm . . ." Her voice petered out. "Threatened to hurt the twins."

"Oh God. Alyson . . ."

"Captain Stoyan has taken them and Constance to the Stilliard, to Captain Geise."

*Thank God.*

Alyson squeezed her plump arm through the bars with much difficulty. Twining my fingers through hers gave me such comfort as I'd not believed possible. Resting my head against my arm, I too cried.

"Sir Leander got word from your brother, chick, and I'm to tell you he's left Southwark. Adam is with him."

My heart plummeted and my tears fell faster. "Sir Leander has gone? Adam too? Why?"

"He wouldn't say lest he gives us false hope. But he has a plan. He says when he returns, he'll have the key to your freedom."

I prayed he was right. We all did.

So when they came for me, I left the cell without protest, escorted by two guards, the old gaoler locking the door behind me.

Taken from The Clink, I was led through a passage and into Winchester Palace next door. Conscious of the state of my clothes, how matted and dirty my hair had become, I would appear a right and proper slattern. The men escorting me remained silent, though the guard on my left shot me glances—whether hostile or sympathetic, I was uncertain. I tried to keep my chin up, my eyes focused only on what lay ahead, but as each step brought me closer to the jury that would try me, my mind and eyes wandered into some dark spaces.

I was ordered to wait before a pair of large wooden doors, polished to a high sheen that complemented the gleaming metal of the pikes of the soldiers standing on either side of them, and took some deep breaths to try to steady my racing heart. A lump blocked my throat, as if I'd swallowed something solid. Perhaps that's what it was, my fears all bundled together in a sphere, which I must consume lest it consume me.

Finally, after a considerable length of time, the doors opened and a short man dressed in the bishop's livery commanded me to enter.

Sitting on a dais were a great many men, decked out in their finest garments, their brows beetling, their eyes narrowing as they watched me approach. In their middle was Bishop Roland le Bold.

Adorned with the accoutrements of his office, he looked the part of a bishop. The expression of triumph on his face was only matched by the features of the man standing at the end of the table, Master Lewis Fynk. To my left were benches for ordinary folk. Seated in the front row were Alyson, Betje (God help me), Harry, Captain Stoyan, and at least half the girls from The

Swanne. All of them nodded and smiled, but their eyes widened as they regarded my state. Only the look on Betje's face revealed how pathetic, how doomed, I must appear.

Behind them was Father Kenton and some of his parishioners whom I knew well enough to greet at mass. There was the miller, the water carter, some of the mercers who patronized The Swanne, our local fishmonger, his wife and son, as well as many of our neighbors. At the back stood Captain Geise from the Stilliard, along with four Flemish sailors. But where were the Southwark nobles? Surely, for such a serious offense, the murder trial of a local woman would have had them filling the seats? And yet nobody represented the peers of the realm.

Returning the nods and smiles of those I knew, my gaze lingered upon first Betje, then my other companions, trying to tell them without words that I wasn't beaten, despite my appearance. That there was fight and faith within me yet.

I glanced to my right and the benches there held a strange assortment of folk. Some I recognized. There was Emma, her arm bandaged, her face puffy and bruised, and next to her were Rose and Golda, both staring despondently at the floor. Golda's lovely brown locks had been shorn and Rose wore a swollen lip. The rest I didn't know, but an aura of hostility and guilt surrounded all of them. Were they here to witness the trial as well, or for another purpose?

I glanced back toward my friends, my brows raised in a question.

Recognizing that a communion of sorts was taking place, Bishop le Bold barked an order. Stepping forward, Master Fynk unlocked my chains, though the manacles remained around my wrists. As the sluggish, heavy coils slithered to the floor, I shook my head, flexed my hands, and then tidied my tunic to the best of my ability, locating grit and straw that I slowly removed and allowed to fall to the floor. It was all I could think to do that would not make me appear like a cornered animal, a trembling quarry. Pretending an indifference I by no means felt, I raised my head and, as a lawyer rose from a desk in the corner and began to read the charges, met the eyes of every man who sat facing me. Some had the grace to look sorrowful, others guilty. Most, however, appeared irate and restless. At first I thought it was because they felt there were better things to be done with their time but, as the trial began and they rested their forearms on the table and whispered and grinned among themselves, I understood they were here not to see justice served but a woman they already assumed to be guilty, punished.

Finished, the lawyer scuttled back to the desk that he shared with one other of his profession and three scribes.

Rising to his feet, Roland smoothed his robes then twisted the ring on his right hand, never taking his eyes from mine. Nodding gravely, he glanced at the papers spread out before him.

"Murder," he began in his deep melodious voice, "is the most serious of offenses. But, to murder, in cold blood, two men of God and in their house, is the most heinous sin on God's earth. You brazen hussy, you viper within the Godly breast of Southwark—"

There were a few sniggers.

"—within the liberty of my manor, did strike down two good men, my men, God's men as well, and by the most invidious means possible. You did it by poisoning their ale."

The public benches released a roar at this and there was much muttering and some shouts for justice. I remained silent, still.

Each breath was an ocean in my ears; my heart an instrument playing a discordant tune.

Roland went on to summarize the rest of my crimes. According to him, I was a murderer, a harlot, a false brewer, and a felon of the highest order.

Commencing with a list of the fines leveled against me and the number of times I'd been forced to tip out my brew (which was met with protests so loud from the benches, Master Fynk shouted them to be quiet or they'd be ejected), he went on to explain my living situation, how while I brewed during the day, I lay with men at night.

"That's a lie," shouted Alyson. "Does she not wear the apron?" She gestured to the soiled one over my tunic.

"Merely another ploy," said the bishop, "to fool those who do deal with her. The evidence is clear; this is not a respectable woman. After all, what respectable woman would lie with not only her brother's master, but"—he paused and his eyes scoured the room—"her brother's father."

There were gasps of horror and shock. Clutching my heart, I stared at Roland in disgust and disbelief.

"You lie."

"Nay, mistress, you do—with a member of your own family."

I stumbled as my head filled with wild thoughts that careered into each other before exploding into fragments that cohered into one solid image—Leander and Tobias side by side.

Dear God. How could I have been so blind? All along, the truth was before me. The resemblance between them was uncanny, but assuming them half-brothers, I'd been able to dismiss it as part of their shared paternity. And it was—though not in ways I'd ever imagined, ever foreseen. Why did Sir Rainford allow me to assume he was Tobias's father? Why did Leander?

Sweet Mother Mary. The church judged Leander's and my relationship harshly, for certes, but believing that the consanguinity went only so far as Leander being Tobias's uncle, I was able to receive pardons from Father Kenton. I glanced at where he sat behind Alyson. Clutching his cross, his lips moved. I willed him to look at me, wanting to convey that I knew naught of this. If I had . . . oh dear Lord, if I had, then I never would have allowed myself to love in the first place.

Leander was Tobias's *father*? Could it be true? It would explain the strange way Lord Rainford had responded to me when I said my mother had confessed. Disingenuous, there had been something he was hiding, but I dismissed it, believing the worst was revealed. God forgive me that I hadn't insisted on a full explanation. Of course, that was why Tobias was squired to Leander, his father, a role well beyond what our station deserved.

I felt sick.

Betje buried her face in her hands; Harry tried to comfort her. Alyson was pale. Only Captain Stoyan met my gaze. His strong face and steely eyes displayed only contempt—not for me, but for the bishop.

"*Nein.*" He mouthed. "*Nein.*" He shook his head.

If only that were true. Why would le Bold say such a thing if it were not?

I shut my eyes and tipped my head back till I faced the ceiling before opening them again. An enormous iron candelabrum was suspended above, the fat pillar candles spluttering and flickering though the light in the room was bright.

*Because he would say anything to cause you pain.*

Waiting till the shock of his announcement had died, Roland continued. I lowered my chin and prepared myself for what was to come next. I pressed one hand against my stomach that roiled and gurgled. Beads of sweat formed upon my upper lip. My back was sticky, my décolletage as well.

Worst of all, if it were true, if Leander was my brother's father, it didn't change my affection for him. I could no more stop loving him than I could cut out my heart.

"Good gentlemen, before you deliver sentence, there's something else I ask you to consider which bears upon these grim proceedings." Roland paused and crossed himself, his ring catching the light of the torches burning in the walls. "Just when you thought her catalogue of sins, that her wantonness, her disregard for the laws of God could not be worse, she defies the laws of king and country as well."

The murmurs were not so loud this time lest they miss hearing what I was to be charged with next.

"This vicious viper, suckled on the bosom of Eve, the greatest sinner the world has known and who caused us to be exiled from the arms of our loving Father, served the same ale that murdered my monks to the king."

There was uproar. The men of the jury turned to each other, some started screaming across the floor at me, shaking their fists, throwing quills, slates, paper, to the floor. Some drew their daggers and drove them into the table.

"That must be why the king fell into a sleep from which he does not wake."

"You cunting whore!"

"You devil's bitch."

"His Grace will surely die."

"Traitor."

Staggering backward, I raised my arms as if to ward off their verbal blows, and I struck one of the guards, who shoved me violently. I fell to my knees. Unable to bear it any longer, Betje leaped from the bench, dropping to my side, her arms around me, her face buried in my breast. Harry followed, wrapping his arms around her, trying to haul her back, terrified she'd be punished for such insubordination.

"If you needed further proof, then you've only to look to her sister—her full-blood sister, to see God's wrath, his attempt at justice, etched upon this spawn's face." He strode around the table and with a malicious tug, ripped the veil from Betje.

There were screams. One of the women on my right fainted. The jurors who weren't already standing leaped to their feet, yelling.

"Stop." My throat was tight, the words too soft. "Stop." It was louder but not enough.

Rising to my feet, Betje's bemused expression following me, I shook my head, raised my chin, and shouted, "Stop!"

The crowd fell silent. Betje's sniffles and Harry's quiet words of comfort the only sounds.

"Accuse me all you like, say what you will of my character, but do not malign my sister."

I glared at Roland, willing him to challenge me, dare me to reveal how she came to be so disfigured. As much as I wanted to, I knew that way lay even greater danger.

With deliberate slowness, I took the veil from Roland's fingers and reattached it. One of the guards tried to stop me, but Roland waved him back.

"All who come within your sweet-scented orbit do surrender their innocence," said Roland finally, almost sadly. Tapping Harry on the shoulder, he jerked his chin.

"Return her to her seat and keep her there and naught will be said of this."

I nodded. "Do it, Harry, Betje."

One last hug and Betje went unwillingly, her head bowed.

Bishop le Bold also sat, as did the jurors.

"In case my evidence is not enough, Master Fynk has assembled those who will support my claims and testify against the offender." He gestured to those on my right.

Not Emma! Not Rose! But of course these two, and more. Their injuries suddenly took on a more sinister cast. What had he threatened to do to them that hadn't already been done?

Each person was made to stand and answer questions from the jurors and Roland. Most of the responses were delivered in a monotone, rehearsed and devoid of emotion. Others were more impassioned, either from vindictive streaks or the desire for a purse they'd no doubt been promised. However they were coerced, every word condemned me further. Hoisted me upon the rope I knew awaited me at the Tower.

*Leander, where are you?*

From the number of looks Alyson cast toward the door, I wasn't the only one concerned on that score.

The sun rolled across the sky. People came and went, even some of the jurors, sating thirst, hunger, and other needs. Neither invited to sit nor offered refreshment, I stood until I swayed with fatigue. Not once did Alyson or Captain Stoyan leave the chamber. Harry and Betje did, but briefly.

It wasn't until the last rays of sunshine feebly struck the wall behind the jurors that the testimonies drew to a halt. Added to my transgressions was witchcraft. Emma, with a stricken look, delivered a damning account of the ale song and the one rite I thought unobserved—my libation to the corner crones.

"And does she curse God and the Holy Mother when worshipping these pagan effigies?"

"Aye, she does."

"And does she divest herself of her clothes and dance naked before their shrine, decrying the birth of the baby Jesus and the sanctity and purity of all saints?"

"Aye."

My confidence that Leander would arrive at the last moment, that this trial would be exposed as the sham it was and the real criminal unmasked, ebbed away.

When the verdict was finally delivered, no one was surprised.

"Guilty," said the first juror, and his decision was repeated a dozen times, each one a death knell that brought my hanging closer. My only hope now lay in a law that, in any other situation, may have raised a chuckle or at least a witty observation. The law that decreed the church could not put anyone to death.

It was the only respite I was likely to receive.

Unless Leander appeared and overturned this verdict or could arrange some impossible marvel, the outcome once the King's Bench heard the evidence would be identical. They were not known for disregarding the church in matters of law. If anything, they generally imposed a more serious sentence.

Trying not to reveal my fear, my utter despondency that Leander hadn't arrived, I faced the bishop.

Once again forced to wait while those in the chamber quietened, Roland regarded me steadily, a small smile fluttering about the corners of his mouth.

"Under usual circumstances, the Bishop's Court cannot sentence a felon to death, no matter how grievous the crime. However, considering the serious nature of these offenses, their duration, the impact they've had upon the good folk of Southwark and Bankside, never mind that two of our beloved brethren have been cruelly murdered, may God assoil them, I do believe we have grounds for modifying the laws slightly. As she took the life of those in the church, is it not right the church should take hers? An eye for an eye, et cetera?"

There was a rumble among those present. Looks were exchanged: horror, consideration, frowns, cautious nods.

I let out a gasp. I swear, it was as if Roland had reached into my chest and wrenched the hope from it. My ribs contracted, my legs began to shake.

The jurors looked at each other, eyebrows raised. "This is most unusual, your grace," said one.

"But there are precedents, if not here, then on the Continent," said another.

"What I propose," said Roland, "is to follow the statutes closely in but one regard."

"Your grace?"

"On no account must blood be shed. So the manner of her death must be such that this does not occur."

"How do you propose to do that? Even hanging, the usual death for a traitor, often draws blood."

They began to speak as if I was not quivering before them. I shot a look at Alyson, who understood and whispered to Harry, who led Betje from the room. Casting a lingering look in my direction, she didn't even object. She knew we were beaten.

How long the conversation went on, I do not know. I do know that when they'd reached agreement, there were a few minutes of silence while the scribes finished recording the punishment. When they had done so, Bishop le Bold signaled for Master Fynk to bring forth the document that sealed my fate.

Unfurling it with great drama, Roland cast his eyes over it before passing it to Master Fynk with a nod of approval.

"Read it," ordered Roland.

It wasn't until he reached the part where the details of my death were outlined, that I really listened.

"She is to be sealed in an empty ale barrel which will be set atop lighted faggots where she will burn until nothing remains but ashes."

Alyson and Captain Stoyan jumped to their feet. Captain Stoyan threw himself at Master Fynk and was restrained. Alyson tried to reach out to me, but before she could, my mind went blank.

Unable to stand, think, or breathe, I toppled to the floor.

# FIFTY-EIGHT

THE CLINK

The following day

*The year of Our Lord 1408 in the ninth*

*year of the reign of Henry IV*

*I* woke before cock crow. Clambering to my knees, I prayed to my Lord Jesus Christ, Mother Mary, and, because I must, to the Goddess of Brewing and the corner crones. I didn't pray for my salvation, it was too late for that, but for the lives and souls of those I loved and would leave behind. Most of all, I asked that Leander be able to forgive himself. My death would haunt him, though I was the one who had convinced him not to seek his version of justice, but to allow it to be the Almighty's. God had chosen to punish me when, if I'd allowed Leander his way, I might have been saved. Leander understood that though God might see His will be done, when it came to vengeance, man would always surpass Him.

Only then did I pray for my soul, and that, if what le Bold

said about Tobias's paternity was true, I might be forgiven for sinning where I sought only to love.

I did not regret what I had shared with Leander. I could not. Mayhap, this was to be our punishment.

I prayed for Tobias and thanked my dear Lord that we were, in our way, reconciled before my death.

Visitors hadn't interrupted my last night; there'd been no whispers in the dark, no nourishment offered. The gaoler, perhaps feeling sorry for a condemned woman, explained that the bishop had ordered the street outside my cell to be guarded, and had forbidden any communication. What he did allow was a basin of water and a cloth. Water and food, if you could call food bread so hard I could not pry even a crumb loose with my teeth and a pottage so watery I drank instead of sipped it, he also arranged.

Unable to sleep at first, I had sat with my knees against my chest and revisited everything that had been said and done that day. It would not have mattered what statements I'd made, how much I'd denied the charges or what proof of innocence my friends and family offered—I was condemned before I entered the room and le Bold knew it. He'd been planning this for a long time. Implying he would leave me undisturbed if I did not mention the past was merely a ruse so he could ensure my downfall was complete.

After everything that had happened, after everything I'd been through because of him, he had his final victory. Not only did he have a position of respect and power in the church, upon my death he would be able to seize all my property. I didn't own much, only the barrels of ale and beer that had not yet been sold or delivered and the equipment in the brewery. He already possessed Mother's recipes. But that was not enough; not the recipes, nor the losses entailed in acquiring them. It had never been enough. He wanted, as he said, to destroy me utterly and, if it meant crushing others, including Betje and the twins, he didn't care. It made his victory sweeter.

I wept then, not for me, but for my sister and my poor babes. Alyson, Adam, and Captain Stoyan wouldn't escape his justice either. I wept for Leander, that I would not see him again, would never feel his loving embrace, his midnight gaze, experience one last time the passion he brought into my life. Know again his trust in me, his faith.

I had cried myself to sleep and, when dawn arrived, found a peculiar quiet, almost as if contentment had found me. Perhaps it was resignation. I couldn't alter what had happened, or what was to be, but I could ensure that le Bold's last memories of me would be unforgettable.

As I washed myself carefully, removing tunic and kirtle and scrubbing the grime of the last few days away, I was also cleansing my spirit.

When Master Fynk and the guards came to lead me away, I was standing beneath the window, listening to the sounds of Southwark, the borough that had offered me sanctuary, success, friends, and love. For that and so much more, I was grateful.

The cockiness that defined Master Fynk wasn't so pronounced as he walked ahead, leading us through gloom-soaked passages and into the harsh daylight. Blinking after the dimness of the prison, it wasn't a bright day and, as my eyes grew accustomed, I was able to see the heavy gray clouds that clustered overhead.

Our footsteps resounded on the cobbles. Guards wearing the bishop's livery stood to attention as we passed, then fell in behind us. Was I so dangerous that I must be accompanied by so many fearsome men?

As we rounded the corner and entered the huge courtyard of Winchester Palace, the reason for the guards became apparent. Hundreds of people were crowded into the space, all facing toward a small dais in the center. Once I was spotted, the crowd, who'd been relatively quiet, began to murmur, quickly swelling to a roar as they pointed, shouted, and tried to draw near, only to be deterred by a pike or sword.

We plowed our way through to the clear space in front of the dais. Keeping my head bowed, I focused upon my boots, scuffed, the toes dirty with whatever lay upon my cell's floor, kicking my tunic about. It too was soiled, a band of scum weighing it down.

It wasn't till we drew to a halt that I raised my head and the roar of the people dimmed, like the sounds of the sea trapped forever within a shell. Straight in front of me, a small pyramid of faggots flamed. Next to them, an empty barrel lay on its side, the lid on the ground next to it. A cooper in an apron stood nearby, his hammer in one hand, the other crooked behind his back. He glanced at me before his eyes slid away.

On the platform above stood Bishop le Bold and some of the jurors. Members of the senior clergy were also there. I was so close, I could see their cassocks were stained, their fingernails dirty. One belched and thumped his chest, another yawned. The oldest stared at me with a look of such compassion it took my breath away. Of Alyson, Captain Stoyan, Betje, and Harry, there was no sign. I was glad. I wanted them to remember my life, not the nightmare of my death.

For just a moment, sadness enveloped me as I realized there

would be no Leander, no last-minute rescue, no hero to alter events and change destiny.

Leaving me amidst the guards, Master Fynk ascended the platform and, calling for quiet by raising his hands, read from a scroll he pulled from his belt.

Hearing my list of misdemeanors and sins again, I almost laughed. They were absurd, except nothing about this was funny. And hadn't I always anticipated this? That someday the transgressions I'd committed, big and small, would have to be paid for? Aye, I had. But in all my imaginings, I'd not foreseen my trial or reparation being delivered by le Bold. This was the cruelest of jests and a small part of me could not credit it to my God, even though His goodwill had been wanting of late.

With every sin read, the shouts and noise of the mob grew. I dared not turn around, though part of me wanted nothing more than to declare the entire catalogue a lie and a conspiracy and a twisting of the truth. Only . . . I couldn't. Most bore some element of veracity that rendered outright denial of even the most outrageous claims impossible.

The last crime was heresy. Courtesy of my ale song and the corner crones, the elements that had helped make my ale so popular made me a heretic. I was now a traitor and heretic. The greatest sins according to God, king, and fellow man.

Hisses and cries flew around me as the guards grabbed my arms and forced me to my knees in front of the barrel.

"Get in," snarled one of them, landing a kick to my side.

I tried to obey, but every time I placed my head in the barrel and inhaled the scent of wort, hyssop, barley, and woodsmoke, I withdrew it. This was one of my barrels. I could not, would not comply. This was a most wicked injustice.

The bishop yelled an order and while one guard held me fast, the other righted the barrel. Lifted off my feet, I was shoved inside and held down.

"Nay, nay," I screamed, my earlier resolve to be dignified gone. "These are unjust accusations, they're contrived, they're—"

The lid shut off my last words. Slammed against my head and driven down until I was forced to bow my neck, I tried to push, to throw it off, but squeezed into the small space, my arms lacked mobility. Nails were hammered in, one by one. I shouted, I slammed one fist against the wood, kicked the sides, but my efforts were feeble, ineffectual.

Dear Lord, this was really happening.

Spears of ice shot through my body, my heart pounded so fast and hard it should have exploded from my chest. Tears flowed down my cheeks, the words I tried to say drowning in my sorrow, my terror.

"Nay, nay," I sobbed, pummeling the wood.

Outside, all fell quiet. My own whimpers stilled. I heard them. Muffled at first, coming closer, growing louder.

"Stop this at once!"

"It's unlawful."

"In the name of Mayor Drugo Barentyn, halt the punishment."

My spirits soared. There was to be a last-minute reprieve; rescue was nigh.

The crowd began to chant, "Stop the execution, stop the execution."

Sounds of scuffle, of restraint carried. Urgent conversations took place.

I pressed my ear to the wood. Though the voices were close, I couldn't make out what was being said, only the insistence behind them. Once more, silence was called for and eventually granted.

This time, Roland le Bold spoke.

"Masters Porlond and Hamme from the Mystery of Brewers . . ."

*Good God. What were they doing here?*

". . . would declare this execution unlawful due to the criminal being a resident of London and therefore under the jurisdiction of that borough and bound by its laws. They declare this in the name of the mayor, Drugo Barentyn." There was a pause and rustle. "They cite this deed as their evidence, signed by the guilty woman, Anna de Winter, on the sixteenth of June, which indicates she paid a six-month lease on a property in Cornhill Street, thereby making her, officially, a resident of London."

Could this be true? Would I be spared le Bold's form of justice yet?

There were cheers as well as disgruntled noises. Some were more bloodthirsty than others.

"But I say, and the jurors agree that, despite these orders from the Sheriffs of London, Master Thomas Duke and Master William Norton"—there was the sound of paper being unfurled—"and the pleas of the mayor, because the brew that killed the monks of Winchester and which rendered the king unto death was made here in Southwark *before* the lease was signed, in premises rented from this manor, Mistress de Winter can be rightfully tried and punished by our laws, Southwark laws."

The shouts almost drowned out his next words. "A decent attempt, gentlemen, but a failed one. No more delays, place the barrel on the fire."

Unprepared, when they lifted me, my chin struck the wood

hard and I bit my tongue. Unable to place me, the guards threw the barrel upon the flames. Jolted, my head hit the lid and, for a moment, spots swam in front of my eyes.

Though I could hear the crackling of the fire, the heat was not immediate.

"This is barbaric," shouted Master Porlond.

"Are you mad?" yelled Master Hamme. "This is not lawful. It cannot be. Rescind this punishment immediately. If she is guilty, let the King's Bench try her."

"I'm afraid it's far too late for that. Look to the barrel."

Whether they did or not, I don't know, for the terrible heat had finally penetrated, scorching the wood, creating smoke that filled the little space and made me cough, my eyes and nose streaming even as I tried to recoil from the blackening wood. It seared my skin, branded me with fiery fury.

"Lord in heaven, save me," I gasped, as my throat filled with deadly hot fumes.

# FIFTY-NINE

The barrel rolled, fast, flinging me against the hell-fired wood. Unable to breathe, to speak, it was only when it violently stopped and the lid was wrenched off, that I was able to gulp air and dared to believe, thank the crones, my ordeal was over. A wall of noise, shouting, the clashing swords, and the clamor of battle surrounded me.

"Anneke, oh, Anneke."

Were my ears deceiving me? For certes, my eyes were not capable of sight while they burned with tears, smoke, and the rain of falling ashes. Lifted from the barrel by strong arms, the press of firm fingers, I staggered. Prevented from falling, soothing words of comfort were given before a hand swept my hair from my face.

"Leander?"

There was a choke of laughter and a blanket was thrown about my shoulders, making me wince. "Aye, aye. It is me, my love. Almost too late."

Dashing the back of my hand across my eyes, Leander's face swam, but I could see the doubt there, the crippling guilt, the tightness in his jaw.

"Nay," I croaked, suppressing the cough that rose, "God have mercy. Just in time."

Ignoring the pain in my limbs, allowing the coughs that wracked my body to escape, I nestled into his arms, only partly attuned to the tumult. Leander half carried me away from the platform until we were beneath some battlements. He waited until I found my feet then let me go.

A small cry of protest turned into a croup-like bark.

"Look to her," he said. "There is justice to be served." And, with a tender kiss, did leave.

I cried out as he departed, sword drawn, when another set of hands claimed me.

"Anna, my chick."

"Mistress."

"Alyson. Adam." Relief made my knees go weak. I found the wall and held fast until Alyson and Adam, cautious of my hurts, lowered me to the ground.

A wet cloth pressed against my eyes and the blanket was flung from my shoulders. With much tut-tutting, Alyson ordered me to keep the cloth in place as she examined the injuries I'd sustained. Down on one knee, Adam spoke quickly into my ear so that I could hear him despite the commotion.

Betje was safe, the twins and Harry too. Leander had wrought a miracle and brought justice to Southwark.

Before I could ask how, the mighty clang of swords, bellows of rage, and the stomp of boots grew. Bloodcurdling screams rent the air and panic as well as a sense of jubilation was tangible. Unable to hold the cloth in place any longer, needing to know what was happening, I pulled it from my face. Slowly, the scene before me came into focus.

The fire had been extinguished; the barrel shattered. Men in Rainford livery and royal livery fought alongside Archbishop Arundel's soldiers, hacking and slicing the bishop's men. I couldn't see Leander, but I did spy Captain Stoyan, wielding a sword with an agility to which no seaman has the right.

The crowd assembled to witness my fate were not fleeing as I first thought. Women, children, and the elderly were trying to exit the courtyard but were being prevented by the bishop's men who were forcing them to remain. Instead of obeying, the mob turned upon them, clinging to their arms, their knees, toppling them, stealing their weapons and running them through. Indifferent to their fate, the commons fought back.

I watched in wonder as the men, ignoring the weapons threatening them, joined the melee, throwing themselves at the guards, dragging them down with sheer force of numbers.

"They fight for justice, Anna. For you," said Alyson. "They've been railing against le Bold and Fynk for some time, at the ad hoc and cruel way laws were enforced. What they tried to do to you, well, if they'd succeeded, life in the Stews and the Liberty would have been nigh on unbearable. You became a rallying point and the final straw."

"I thought they were here to bear witness to my death. They called for it."

"On the contrary, chick, they roared for your life."

A trembling hand found my mouth as I tried to make sense of what was happening. Fists flew, bones crunched, and daggers and swords found their targets. Fast and full of fury, pent-up emotions, and fear were released in sheer, bloody folly, the madness of berserkers. The fight shifted as the number of fallen mounted, and those left standing tried to find spaces to continue.

Not far away, lying facedown, his head twisted to one side, was Lewis Fynk. His skull had been cleaved and blood poured over his cheeks and ran in rivulets along the lines of his face and into his mouth. The sneer he wore in life had, in death, become a mask he would display unto heaven or, if God willed, hell.

For that was where he belonged.

The bishop's soldiers, unable to comprehend that their armor and swords did not incite fear or submission, that the enemy was everywhere, were crawling on their hands and knees in an effort to escape. Helped by the commons and his allies, Leander's men made a quick finish, the last of the bishop's men surrendering.

The monks atop the platform were taken into custody. I didn't see Roland.

Unable to believe I was free, that Leander had come as promised and with a small army, that Roland had not had his victory, I couldn't move. There were so many questions, so much I wanted to know.

Alyson understood. First stroking my hair, she then stood, wiping her hands upon her apron. It was dirty and rent. "It will all be explained. You've endured more than anyone has a right. We're to get you back to The Swanne, fed, cleaned, and rested. We'll send for the apothecary. Sir Leander's orders. He will meet you there as soon as he can."

Taking an arm each, Alyson and Adam helped me to my feet,

and then began to lead me toward a door. The noise was more subdued, the fighting all but over. Those of the bishop's guards not disarmed and standing in a disorderly gaggle with swords pointed at them were either dead or fled. The common men, so brave and quick, had dispersed. It was fine to get caught up in the heat of battle, but wounding a bishop's soldier carried severe penalties and absence was a surer bet than a possible reward for aiding a rout. Only the brave or foolish remained to search the dead for plunder. Leander's soldiers chased them away. Of Leander, the jurors, of Roland, there was no sign.

"Wait." I stopped at the door. "What's happening? Where is Leander? The bishop?"

Alyson cocked a brow at Adam.

"There's to be another trial. This time the real criminal will face his accusers."

"Le Bold? I don't understand, how is this possible?"

"Sir Leander is how," answered Adam.

"When, when will this trial be?"

"It's to happen immediately, mistress. Le Bold was captured by Arundel's men and taken inside. There, a different set of jurors awaits. Sir Leander made sure of that."

"Take me there, Adam. Now."

"But mistress, you heard Goody Alyson, you're to rest."

I gave Adam a look I usually reserved for Harry when he said something that both displeased and amused me. He turned to Goody Alyson for support.

"There's no arguing with her once she has her mind set. We'll take her to see justice done."

"She's in no fit state—" began Adam.

"Don't talk about me as if I'm not present. If I could but have some water, or ale, I will be fine. I hurt, but I will heal. Believe me, Adam, I need this more than I require food, salves for my wounds, or rest. I cannot rest while I know le Bold is free. I cannot."

Without further argument, they led me back across the court-yard, past the prisoners, and through the door that less than an hour earlier, I'd exited.

Sneaking into the back of the chamber, Adam found me a seat and, between the heads of nobles, men of the church, lead-ing merchants, Masters Hamme and Porlond and many others besides, I watched the trial of Roland le Bold.

Presiding over it was Archbishop Arundel. How Leander persuaded such a man to attend, let alone lead the trial wasn't at first evident. Having him there rendered Roland's complaint that he must be tried by church laws redundant.

Ordered to silence, Roland stood where I had only yesterday, as Leander, his surcoat torn, blood staining his shirtsleeves, read a catalogue of wrongdoing, starting with everything at Elmham Lenn.

Accused of murder, arson, and theft, his crimes did not elicit the gasps of disapprobation mine had. Everyone in the room knew what was being ascribed to Roland, but still many wore expressions of disbelief, especially the monks, as if one of their brethren could not be capable of such mortal sins.

They didn't know Roland le Bold.

Standing tall, Roland didn't look defeated or even concerned. Donning the arrogance I'd lately observed, he appeared confi-dent that he would be absolved.

That was until Leander began to call witnesses.

Much to my astonishment, familiar faces emerged from the

sea of people on the other side of the room. There was Brother Osbert from St. Jude's, bowed in misery, his hands buried in the sleeves of his cassock. Thinner than I remembered, the once-haughty features had been humbled. Rubbing his face in an effort to shed the fatigue that clearly gripped him, he answered the questions put to him. He told the jurors that Roland was not only Abbot Hubbard's bastard son, but that the prior had endorsed his insinuation into the Sheldrake household under a false name so he could learn what he could of brewing techniques with the intention of replicating them. Once the brewery began to impact on St. Jude's profits, he was ordered to steal the coveted recipe book and put an end to my brewing enterprise. Asked if they had offered payment for the book, Brother Osbert nodded.

"On two occasions. But the wench would not agree." He hesitated. "We threatened her, and for that I do beg the Lord's forgiveness." He raised his eyes to the ceiling.

"It is not only the Lord's you should ask," said Archbishop Arundel quietly.

While Brother Osbert didn't believe the abbot intended everything that occurred, he possessed knowledge of it and, once le Bold returned to the priory and modified the way brews were made and sold, and profits soared, he rewarded the perpetrator with rank and privileges far beyond the usual.

When asked why he chose to come forward, Brother Osbert hesitated. It was then the resentment and jealousy he felt at being overlooked in favor of le Bold became apparent. Dissembling, he spoke of how what occurred didn't fit with the church's teaching or his conscience; he could no longer hold his silence. When Tobias Sheldrake appeared at the gates of St. Jude's seeking answers, he took it as a sign from God.

I shook my head in disgust. His confession was as much about revenge as it was a burdened soul.

"What name did Bishop le Bold use while he lived in Elmham Lenn?" asked the Archbishop.

"Westel Calkin."

"And it's Westel Calkin who set fire to Holcroft House, the property of Lord Hardred Rainford, leased by Mistress Anneke Sheldrake, now known as Mistress Anna de Winter?"

"Aye, your grace."

"Is Westel Calkin present among us?"

Brother Osbert raised his head and pointed directly at Roland. "As God is my Lord and Savior, that is him."

There were murmurs and Alyson rested a light hand upon my shoulder. Motivated by revenge or scruples? Did it matter if the felon was caught?

I was uncertain.

After that, the trial moved swiftly. Witness after witness, most from Elmham Lenn, came forward. There was Father Clement, bless his soul, and, much to my astonishment, Master Perkyn, Blanche, and Iris as well.

Adam leaned forward and whispered in my ear, "Sir Leander asked me and Tobias to convince them to come." He sniffed and wiped his eyes. "When they knew it was for your sake, Anna, they needed no such prompt."

Timid at first, trembling as they stood before the might of the Archbishop, they answered questions without any guile or venom and thus condemned le Bold further.

It was then I noticed Master Makejoy, more rotund, older, but no less industrious, sitting at the end of the table, passing pieces of paper, whispering explanations to the Archbishop and the other jurors. Catching my eye, he bowed his head and smiled.

My heart filled. What was that old proverb Captain Stoyan used to quote? One he heard from sailors in the ports of Venice? "The enemy of my enemy is my friend."

Even Tobias, initially obscured among the other witnesses, came forward to give evidence. As he spoke, I learned where he'd been the last weeks, and the tasks Leander had assigned him. Wanting more than anything to rush to his side, I hoped that whatever residue of friction existed between us, it was now forever extinguished. What faith in me his ruthless quest to uncover the truth revealed. It was beyond my comprehension.

Likewise, as I glanced around the chamber—at those giving evidence, the paperwork littering the long table, the serious faces of the officials and the sullen ones of the witnesses—the scope of what Leander sought to accomplish for my sake became apparent.

As Roland had planned to eliminate me, so had Leander silently and diligently worked to thwart him. And had done so for some time; from the moment I identified le Bold as Westel Calkin, Leander had set his wheels in motion. And to think I'd lectured him on restraint. Watching Leander smoothly control the trial, moving from one witness to the next, encouraging further questions, demanding answers, I marveled at this man who called me beloved. As he strode around the chamber, using his cane for emphasis as he spoke, I saw the warrior, the man who refused to allow his deformity, his twisted foot, to dictate his life. Replacing the cane with a sword, I could imagine it bearing down on his enemies, and see them trembling before his wrath. Adam once spoke of how folk tended to underestimate Leander.

I'd been guilty of doing the same. Never again. To do so was to invite peril.

From the expression on Roland's face, it was evident he felt the same. He also understood that convicting me of charges that were false had merely brought his fate forward, and Leander and everyone knew this to be so. I was going to be exonerated and, after all this time, after so much death, loss, and grief, Roland was going to get what he deserved—God willing.

The trial continued well into the afternoon, by which time Roland le Bold's future was sealed. With each testimony, each remembrance of what he'd done at Elmham Lenn, even those who had believed his protestations of innocence were beginning to doubt. Still, there was reluctance to pass a severe sentence upon a man of God, especially one in such a prestigious office, appointed by the Archbishop, no less. That was, until the final piece of evidence was given.

Leander called Sir Gilbert Woodley, the coroner. At the mention of his name, Roland visibly paled. An imposing man with dark hair and bristling brows, from the moment he began to speak, his voice like dark velvet, he captured the entire room.

"Having examined the bodies of the deceased monks and the mazers from which they imbibed the drink, it's clear their deaths were not caused by the ale alone."

"It was poisoned," shouted Roland, imploring the jurors. "Of course, it wasn't the ale alone. That slattern brewster infected the entire barrel. She was out to murder me. She knew I could identify her as the felon who destroyed Lord Rainford's property and murdered her own brother and servants in the process."

There were dark mutters and knitted brows.

"Nay, your grace," said Sir Gilbert calmly. "Your grace"—he

turned to the Archbishop—"the barrel was not poisoned, merely the mazers."

"How can you be certain?" spluttered Roland. "We tipped the barrel into the Thames immediately."

"Mayhap you did," said Sir Gilbert, "but the king's steward did not get rid of His Grace's ale. As a consequence, I've been able to test the king's brew, which was branded and marked with the same seals as yours, by Southwark ale-conners, and find it clear of any questionable ingredients. The brew was not poisonous—not the contents of the barrels, at any rate. In fact, it's an uncommonly fine brew." He gave a small bow in my direction.

Unaware I was present till this moment, heads turned toward me, and I saw Leander frown and then shake his head, a small smile on his lips. I returned the coroner's courtesy with a dip of my chin.

"Examining the monks' bodies knowing the ale was clear, however, did lead me to form other conclusions."

"Share them if you please, Sir Gilbert," said Leander.

"From the discoloration upon the monks' lips and from reports of the smell that hovered about the corpses' mouths, and the manner of their death, which was described as swift, preceded by tremors, vomiting, and extreme pallor, it's clear that the deadly herb hellebore was used. It's my belief that Bishop le Bold, seeking to implicate Mistress de Winter, added hellebore to the monks' mazers in order to make it appear as if the brew itself was poisoned."

Exclamations were followed by loud whispering.

"Hellebore? Where would I attain such an herb?" Roland had to raise his voice to be heard.

Leander waved forward someone from the crowd on the other side of the room. It was an officer of the Hanse.

"Captain Geise," whispered Adam.

"Captain?" Leander flipped his hand in the man's direction. "Mayhap you can answer."

Removing his cap, Captain Geise bowed to the jurors before answering. "*Ja*, my lord. One of my men was tasked with purchasing the exact same herb for the bishop last month."

"Prove it," snapped Roland, all efforts to remain calm forgotten.

"You requested there be no bill of sale, so I cannot."

Roland turned to Leander, a smirk upon his features.

"Which doesn't explain how this was found in your quarters," cried a voice from the back. Captain Stoyan pushed his way to the front holding aloft a small bag. Before the room, he opened and tipped some of the contents into his palm, holding it out so Sir Gilbert could identify the plant. A number of stringy, dark brown stalks were visible.

"That is hellebore," said Sir Gilbert.

"This is preposterous. Your grace," Roland beseeched the Archbishop, "this could have been acquired anywhere and be said to have come from my rooms."

"True," said the Archbishop. "Do you have proof this is indeed the property of the bishop?"

Captain Stoyan turned and beckoned to someone else. A young acolyte reluctantly made his way to the edge of the crowd. One side of his face was bruised and he walked favoring his right foot.

"This is Bishop Roland's servant, your grace," said Leander. "He will swear that this bag was in a chest in the bishop's rooms."

"What is your name, lad?" asked the Archbishop softly.

"Payn, your grace."

"Payn who?"

Payn shot a look at Roland, who glared at the boy with such ferocity, I felt sure it would render him mute.

"Le Bold, your grace. I am Payn le Bold."

The room erupted.

"And," he said, shouting to be heard, "I also have this." From beneath his shirt, he held up a tattered old book bound in leather and tied with string.

Mother's recipes, my ale bible.

Above the din, Roland shouted, "Sir Leander has bribed these witnesses. Every testimony has been paid for."

"Aye," called a voice, "a darn sight more than you paid, you tight-arsed bastard."

There were hoots and cackles.

After that, the verdict was swift and final.

"Bishop Roland le Bold—" Archbishop Arundel asked everyone to stand. Waiting until the room fell quiet, he continued. "On the morrow, you will be put to death according to the laws of both church and king. Our laws decree that such a sentence cannot be carried out on church property, therefore, you will be transported to the Tower, whereupon, as the sun rises, you will hang by the neck until you are dead."

Roland turned white. His eyes widened and a harsh, terrible scream issued from his throat. Guards descended upon him, hauling him out of the room, trying to prevent him from injuring himself as he pulled at his chains, swung his body side to side. "Nay! It's she who must die! The viper, the poison rose of Satan!"

I didn't hear what was said after that; I no longer cared.

Justice was served. Because of my beloved, Leander, I was a free woman.

As Roland le Bold, formerly Westel Calkin, was led into the bowels of the Palace and The Clink, I was taken out another door, into light and liberty.

The liberty to finally be who I was, love whom I chose, leave Southwark and, with my family and friends, establish my brewery in London.

# SIXTY

THE SWANNE

July

*The year of Our Lord 1408 in the ninth*

*year of the reign of Henry IV*

*E*xhaustion battled with exhilaration as celebrations at The Swanne continued long into the night. Though I'd had the bath and rest I'd delayed in order to bear witness to Roland's trial, and eaten fit to burst, part of me was still trapped in the barrel. Trying to repress the flashes of memory that insisted on conjuring the full horror of it, I determined to focus on the good as I sat in Alyson's solar drinking ale and beer with my family and friends. Huddled next to me was Betje, Harry by her side, their faces glowing with quiet disbelief, words tripping over each other in an effort to leave nothing unsaid, as only those who have escaped tragedy are sometimes wont to do. Others prefer quietude—not without, but within. It was the latter I sought, even amid the gaiety and abandon.

Allowing the twins to remain in the solar, I held them to my breast and, possibly sensing the peace their mother radiated (a great deal due to their presence), they snuggled into my bosom contentedly, gently tugging my hair, giggling and clapping, so that Constance and Emma (who could not cease apologizing) could enjoy a dance and some drinks.

Adam played his pipe and Master atte Place a drum. Captain Geise, the man who surprised us all with his unexpected aid and generosity in caring for the twins and Constance (since I had become a Crown trader, the Hanse's reputation was no longer under threat if members associated with me), plucked a gittern. They played a bawdy song about a knight and his mistress.

To be in the company of Blanche, Iris, Father Clement, Master Perkyn, and Master Makejoy brought me much happiness. When Tobias and Adam had ridden into Elmham Lenn and sought them out, they were first surprised and delighted to see them. Shocked to discover I was in such dire trouble, upon learning they could help, they made swift arrangements and left for Southwark immediately. Leander organized horses, an escort, and accommodation.

"Grand it were too," said Blanche.

"Oh aye," agreed Iris, watching the dancers with such longing I bade her join them.

Father Clement gave me messages from Mother Joanna, and Master Perkyn from Olive and many more besides. When Master Makejoy joined us, a mazer of ale in his hand, I asked after my cousin's health only to see a look of sadness cross his face.

"You wouldn't have heard, would you, mistress? We'd no way to find you. Hiske died of the plague not these few months past." He lowered his head and I expressed my sympathy discovering, much to my surprise, that I meant it. I'd always known, deep down, that the discordant relations I'd shared with my cousin had little to do with me, despite appearances.

"I know you and she didn't always see eye to eye," said Master Makejoy, pulling a kerchief from his surcoat and blowing his nose loudly, "but she gave me some very joyful times and I'll be hard-pressed to replace her. Nonetheless, she believed in family and I know she would have wanted me to come here to your aid, mistress. She bore a terrible guilt over what happened betwixt you. I hope, may God assoil her, that she can rest easy now."

I wasn't quite sure how to respond, so I patted his hand.

It was Leander who, upon returning to The Swanne with Captain Stoyan, took me from the festivities and up to my room, offering neither apologies nor explanation. Some ribald comments accompanied our departure, but I simply laughed. All I wanted was to be alone with my beloved.

Shutting the door, he leaned against it. I sank onto the bed with a groan. The unguents Alyson had rubbed into my burns may have alleviated much of the pain, but they also made my tunic and kirtle stick to my flesh and I longed to divest myself of them. I began to tug at my laces.

"Are you going to stand there all night, my lord, or join me?"

Leander chuckled and pried himself from the door. Watching him approach, his rolling gait and what it signified, I almost pitied those who failed to recognize the strength, the dexterity that emanated from him, despite the affliction. There were those, as I'd learned, who never looked beneath the surface, preferring to remain in the shallows.

He propped his cane against the chair and sat beside me. Placing a hand over mine, he stilled my fingers. "I want nothing more than to stay, if you're sure."

"Quite sure."

"Isn't there something you want to ask me first?"

I shrugged. "Is there?"

Leander lifted my hand and kissed my fingers one by one. "Alyson told me—"

"That never bodes well."

He didn't smile. "Alyson said that during your trial, le Bold mentioned consanguinity. That he said Tobias was *my* son."

"He did . . ."

Leander nodded. "Well then. Do you want the truth?"

I pulled my hand away and walked to the window, treasuring the places upon my hand where his kisses had fallen. The shutters were open and the warm, gray day had turned into a balmy night. The clouds that had slunk over the city remained, swallowing the moon and stars.

"I'm afraid of the truth." I spun around. "I would rather love in ignorance than feel guilty every time you touched me, every time I had lustful thoughts or desired you as, even though I wilt from tiredness and injury, I do now."

A flicker of a smile crossed his face.

"Anneke. It's not true. Le Bold presented a falsehood, mayhap to enhance your wickedness."

My hands reached behind to grab the ledge as my body slumped and my head bowed. "Thank God." Steadying my thoughts, I raised my face. "So Lord Rainford is Tobias's father?"

"Nay. It's Symond. Symond is his father. Tobias is my nephew."

"Your *brother*?" Repelled by the thought of my sweet, gentle mother with that brute, I was at first lost for words. "Sir Symond? I never knew, would never have thought . . ." I shook my head. "Why then did your father make Tobias *your* squire? Why did he place *my* father in so much debt? Punish him for the sins of my mother and your brother? Why did he let me believe it was him?"

Leander sighed and patted the bed beside him. When I sat, he took my hand in his again. "Do you remember the day, when you were a little girl, that you and your mother came to Scales Hall?"

"I do. You were most discourteous to me and, if I recall, when we met again at Holcroft House, you claimed not to remember our first meeting."

"Well, that wasn't true. I was simply being contrary." He stroked my palm. "When I was young, I was boorish to all outsiders, most of whom, because of my leg"—he looked at it, turning it slightly—"would treat me as if I was in need of a mind as well." He sighed. "You may recall that what I lacked in courtesy that day, Symond more than made up for."

"Indeed. He was very kind. Kept me amused the entire time my mother was with your stepmother."

"He did. But, like anything Symond does, it was with a purpose. Keeping you entertained was a way to ingratiate himself with your mother. She was very beautiful, you know."

"Oh, I know."

"Your mother felt indebted to Symond for what he did and, the next time she came to Scales Hall, she brought him a small gift. Finding him in the stables, she tried to give it to him. Symond refused, said there was only one gift he wanted from her and if she wouldn't give it freely, he would take it."

"You're not saying . . ."

"I am. Symond raped your mother."

I exhaled, a long, sad note of despair. Mother never intimated, never said. I'd assumed so much, misjudged so badly. *Moeder, forgive me.* That I too had suffered such a fate, what did that mean? Was there a purpose? To teach me a lesson for being judgmental when compassion was needed? *Dear God.*

Extracting my hands from Leander's, I lowered my head into them. "All along, I thought, I believed— Mother encouraged me to . . . I thought she'd given herself freely."

"Not freely. Though it was what I understood for years as well. That she'd seduced Symond. I only learned the truth from my father recently. She was forced, and most violently by all accounts."

It was some time before I could raise my head. I inhaled and let the breath out slowly. "Tell me, why was my father punished for your brother's sin?"

Leander straightened his leg with a grimace. "Once your mother admitted to your father she was with child, he knew it couldn't be his. He'd been away for months and the timing was wrong. Only then did your mother confess what happened. In a rage, your father rode to Scales Hall. He confronted Symond, who didn't deny what had happened, but the great, arrogant fool, instead of offering apologies, compensation, contrition, anything, chose to cast aspersions upon your mother's character, called her whore and other such names." Leander had the grace to look abashed. "Your father, forgetting he was dealing with such a young man and someone—forgive me, Anneke—above his station"—I waved a hand; it was but the truth—"demanded a reckoning. Already angry, he lost his temper. He gave Symond such a beating. When Symond drew his sword, your father unsheathed his dagger. He was swift, too fast for Symond. He slashed his face from here to there." Leander drew a line that mimicked the scar upon his brother's face. The one I had thought earned in battle. "I think he would have finished him if one of the stable boys hadn't fetched Master Evan, who told Father. Had they not pulled *your* father from Symond, well . . .

"Finding his eldest son in a bloody heap, unconscious, Father would have demanded justice then and there, and been in the right to take it, had he not known instinctively that Symond was responsible for what had befallen him. Even at fifteen, Symond was crafty, underhanded, spoiled. Learning the truth, my father struck a deal with yours. While Symond was carried to his room and doctors sent for, father promised to provide for the child in your mother's womb and, once he came of age, to take him into his own household. For his silence and cooperation, he promised your father recompense in the form of material comfort. But he also intended your father to be punished. The doctors didn't think Symond would make a full recovery; they thought he would suffer permanent injury." Gesturing to his leg, he scowled. "I don't think Father could cope with the notion of having two sons maimed. My father concluded that it was only just that *your* father suffer as well, and decided to hurt him where it would matter."

"Money."

Leander nodded. "He ordered Master Makejoy to draw up a contract. I'm not convinced your father read it properly before he signed. Realization of what he had agreed to only came later. I believe he simply wanted to put the entire episode behind him. Hence, your father settled upon an arrangement that saw your family economically secure, but only while he remained alive.

Upon his death, as you know, everything reverted back to the Rainford estates."

I held Leander's hand tightly. "Father never did put what happened to Mother behind him. He wasn't able . . ."

"Tobias."

"He always treated him . . . differently. When I learned from Mother a version of what happened, I believed it was because Father was a cuckold and Tobias was a reminder of it that he divorced himself from the family and appeared indifferent to our fates. But it was so much more . . . Tobias was also a reminder of a poor business deal, of revenge failed. Of temper lost." I examined our entwined hands. How strange that from such hate, such bitterness, blossomed our love. "Didn't your father think of the innocent in all this? After all, Mother did not ask for such violence. Neither did Tobias. The twins . . . me." My voice grew smaller.

Leander stroked my hair. "Truth be told, I don't know his exact reasons, but I've had cause to try and reconcile them lately." He kissed my hand. "Your father threatened the Rainford family. He nearly killed the heir. He marked him for life. Father is nothing but patient. He kept his end of the bargain, gained your father's collaboration and, when the time was right, welcomed his bastard grandson into the Rainford fold. Once your father died, there was no one left who knew the whole story except my father and Symond—and what version were they to tell? As far as Father was concerned, his liability and the threat your father posed finished upon his death. He could wipe his hands of the Sheldrakes forever, his fiscal responsibilities were concluded. That was, until you came along and offered to continue the arrangement."

"I didn't know . . ."

"I thought you did. I thought that, like your mother, you were offering yourself to a Rainford."

"In exchange for the house. You believed I was selling my morals, selling my family to yours . . ."

"Can you forgive me?"

I twisted slightly so I faced him.

"All is forgiven. This had naught to do with you, with us. Dear God, what our families did to appease damaged esteem, to prevent God's justice taking its course. If only the truth had been told in the first place."

"Sometimes, a lie serves everyone better, beloved. You know that more than most."

He was right. I did.

"Can you forgive *me* that I doubted you? Not once, but many times over the last months."

Leander took me in his arms and lowered me to the bed. "I will tell you the answer to that in the morning . . ."

# SIXTY-ONE

THE SWANNE, SOUTHWARK, AND THE
SWANNE, CORNHILL STREET, LONDON
July
*The year of Our Lord 1408 in the ninth*
*year of the reign of Henry IV*

We woke to shocking news. As he was being transported across the Thames to the Tower the previous evening, Roland le Bold had escaped. Seemed he had friends after all and, where he lacked them, he had the funds to purchase allegiance. Archbishop Arundel's men delivered the tidings, along with orders for Leander and Tobias to join the search. A hue and cry had been raised and, as I watched Leander dress, I could hear the sound of horses corralling in the street, shouts and whistles, soldiers going from bathhouse to bathhouse, inn to inn.

The poise I'd so recently reclaimed dissolved in an instant.

"Must you go?"

"I must." Holding my shoulders, careful not to press the parts where the skin was reddened or blistered, he kissed me with such love and gentleness that in spite of my fear, my body responded. As he drew away and I looked in those eyes, a premonition grabbed hold of me, stealing my breath away.

"What it is, Anneke?"

"Nothing, nothing," I gasped, not wanting to release him. "You'll be careful, won't you? Roland is dangerous, cunning. If he can have his revenge, he will."

"He'll not get far, Anneke. Of that you have my word."

How could I explain what crept into my head and compressed my heart? I remained motionless as he left the room, weighed with the burden of prescient knowledge. When Tobias knocked and entered to say farewell, I was still in the same spot.

"Take care, Tobias, of yourself, of Leander," I whispered as I held him close.

"Always." With a grin, Tobias left as well.

I knew without a modicum of doubt that I was never going to see either of them again.

◸⧓⧓⧓⧓⧓⧓⧓⧓⧓⧓⧓⧓⧓⧓⧓⧓⧓⧓⧓⧓⧓⧓⧓⧓⧓⧓⧓⧓⧓⧓⧓⧓⧓⧓⧓⧓⧓⧓⧓⧓⧓⧓⧓⧓⧓⧓⧓⧓

Bidding Blanche, Iris, Master Perkyn, and Father Kenton goodbye late that morning, giving them a letter for Mother Joanna and promising to write to them all, a shadow was cast over our farewell. Once more, Roland le Bold hovered over my days, coloring all that I did and thought. His phantom presence was a leech I couldn't pry loose no matter what.

During the evening, a message came from Leander. He and Tobias were ordered to remain at Ashlar Place and resume the search the following day. The Archbishop and Duke of Clarence were there as well. There had been initial sightings and, Leander assured me, Roland would be found and the sentence carried out.

God's truth.

The next day was our last in Southwark. While I'd been in The Clink, Betje and Harry, along with Thomas and the girls, had barreled the remaining brew, sending the bulk across the river and only keeping enough for household consumption. The rest of the equipment was stowed and ready for transport. Alyson suggested delaying our move until le Bold was caught, but after all we'd been through, I didn't want to remain in The Swanne a day longer than we must. Though I loved the old building, and I was very fond of Southwark and its loyal folk and the support they'd given me, the notion of starting afresh appealed very strongly.

And I refused to let Roland le Bold interfere with my life again. We would go ahead and move to London as planned.

Mayhap, I felt I had to maintain a brave face for Betje and the twins, for Harry, Alyson, and Adam as well, but as the afternoon wore on and there was still no news of Roland or any sign of Leander, I took the twins for a walk along the river. Since the girls who wanted to continue working in a bathhouse had left, finding employ elsewhere, and the brewery and bathhouse were all but packed away, there wasn't much for Alyson, Betje, or Harry to do. Along with Emma and Constance, they accompanied me.

When we commenced our walk, moving in the direction of Moulstrand Dock, from where, if there was no mist, we could see Westminster, the weather was mild. Weak sunlight pierced the clouds, throwing shafts of pastel light upon the river and warming our bodies. Westminster was a large, golden building in the distance, surrounded by forests at the rear and a large dock at the front. More buildings were being erected along the banks between London's walls and the king's residence, the city expanding almost daily. I should have been excited by the business prospects more noble and wealthy merchant houses presented, but I was too caught up with other matters.

By the time we headed back to The Swanne over an hour later, gray clouds had replaced their paler cousins and a light rain began to fall that quickly became heavier. Running ahead, Emma and Constance promised to have hot sheets and ale ready. The twins pleaded to remain with us. Karel walked between Alyson and me; Isabella between me and Harry. We held hands, a garland of humans. The twins would point excitedly at dogs, cats, boats, and people, giving them names—not always the right ones—trying to outdo each other in speed and volume. When they grew bored with that, they insisted on being swung over rapidly filling puddles and the ditch. Their giggles were infectious, so even though we were soaked and tired once we reached The Swanne, we were prepared to enjoy last drinks and a small celebration as well.

Retiring to the solar after donning a clean tunic (the one I'd put aside for tomorrow, when I'd take possession of the other Swanne), I sank into a chair and sipped my ale. I'd overestimated my strength and found exhaustion settling over me.

A few drinks and much reminiscing later, weariness was forgotten and we were a rowdy bunch, the twins adding to the noise with their squeals as Betje coaxed them onto Harry's back for rides. Outside, a storm raged, the rain lashing the shutters, thunder growling between flashes of white lightning. Even nature expressed both its fury and its desire to cleanse and renew. Enjoying my family and friends, it was easy to forget Roland le Bold, though every sound I heard through the wind and rain made my heart leap lest it was Leander returning.

It was well after vespers before the twins went to bed. Carrying a sleepy Isabella upstairs, followed by Constance with Karel, I tucked them in and said prayers, asking that God bless them and our venture and keep them safer in London than they'd been here.

Returning downstairs I was about to open the door to the solar when I hesitated. The music had started once more and everyone was enjoying themselves. I would not be missed a short while and there was something I wanted to do. Solicitous of my well-being and fearful that le Bold remained at large, since I'd been rescued there was always someone by my side and I'd not a moment to myself. I would take one now and do what was needed.

Lighting a cresset, I opened the brewery door and descended like a queen at a coronation, slowly, with dignity, inhaling the lingering scent of hops, barley, and the comforting smell of burned wood. Pausing a few steps from the bottom, I surveyed my domain and liked what I saw. Little more than silhouettes, the tuns, troughs, and even the kiln that was now emptied of its ashes, were a busy landscape of soft curves and sharp angles. Reaching the floor, I wandered between the tuns, around the table adorned with neatly tied packages containing measures, weights, bungs, and mallets. As I roamed, I began to sing. Though there was no ale to pour, my final song was one of thanks—to the ale and beer that had been born here and to the corner crones for making it possible.

Finding the last remaining barrel, still quite full and its lid askew, I searched for a tankard. Finding one on the hook above, I scooped it in the ale. Moving from corner to corner, I offered the crones my final libation. In my mind's eye, I saw them, with their bent backs; long noses; kind, wise faces; the wrinkles fanning from their eyes as they smiled and cackled at this last offering, knowing the best was yet to come. Then, their expressions changed. Without finishing what I'd poured, they retreated back into the shadows, melted into the walls, muttering ominously.

Unsettled, I looked over my shoulder, frowning when only the darkness greeted me. Mayhap they didn't want to leave yet and were showing their displeasure. God and Ninkasi knew, the crones could be mercurial creatures. I retraced my steps, the cresset in one hand, tankard in the other. I lifted the tankard to drain the dregs and join the crones when something struck me on the back of the head.

I fell forward, only narrowly missing the table, dropping the cresset, the breath knocked out of my lungs. Rolling over onto my back, I saw the light wink dimly, revealing a dark figure who, before I could cry out, leaped astride me and covered my mouth.

"God give you good death, Anneke Sheldrake."

Roland le Bold.

The crones knew. They'd tried to warn me.

With a strength born of the malevolence I knew he possessed, and which froze me into submission, Roland hauled me to my feet, covering my mouth again once I was upright. My inertness lasted only till then. I thought of the fight I'd witnessed in the courtyard at Winchester Palace, of the lives that had been risked and lost. I thought of my friends who'd traveled across the country to ensure my freedom, to ensure justice was served. I thought of all Leander had done, Tobias as well. They hadn't failed me. I would not fail them.

*Damn you, Roland le Bold.*

He would not cow me again. If I was to die this night, I would resist with my last breath. Biting his hand till I drew blood, his hold only firmed.

He laughed. I kicked him, drew the tankard I still clutched and struck him in the temple. His grip loosened and I took the chance to flee.

Catching my hair, he yanked me back into his arms; vise-like, they banded my torso, squashing my breasts, pulling my arms into my sides. I threw my head back and heard something crack. There was a loud groan and then the smell of blood.

"You devil's bitch, you cunting slattern." His tone was different, muffled. "Did you think I'd go quietly, that your lover would triumph? Nay. Nay. Nay." With each nay, he slammed my head into the barrel.

Dizzy, I became limp in his arms.

"That's the way, my hellish rose, my perfume of hell."

Bending me over the barrel, he pushed my face into the ale, his hand holding the back of my head down. At first, I gulped and gagged, but the ale refreshed me, cast off the light-headedness. I bucked and stamped, but he thrust me deeper into the barrel. Ale bubbled around me. I tried to hold my breath, to fend him off, but the ale, my own brew, recognizing its mother, its creator, sought to envelop me. It entered my nose, my ears, and all the time, it gurgled into my mouth.

I would not end this way. I would not. Ale was my life. Not my death.

There was a loosening, the hands upon me were gone. My head flew up and I gasped for air, my hair arcing like a whip to slap my back, before I was thrown to one side.

"I said, get off her, you dirty bastard."

Alyson stood, broken jugs in her hands, ale dripping from the shards.

I scrambled to my feet, panting, wiping my face, my heart pounding.

Looking up at us from the floor, Roland grinned through bloodied teeth. His temples streamed blood, his nose was bent at an odd angle, his upper lip engorged. "You'll not escape justice this time," said Alyson, and before Roland could move, broke the remainder of the jugs over his head.

Roland slumped to one side.

"Quick, Anna, help," she said, grabbing him under the arms, nodding for me to take his feet.

God forgive me, I hesitated only a second before lifting him by the ankles. He was heavy, but so was the burden he'd forced me to carry, the fear he'd instilled since I first set eyes upon him.

"Into the barrel with him," barked Alyson, and heaved him to the edge.

With a roar, I lifted him higher, rolling him into the amber liquid headfirst.

At first, Roland didn't react; he didn't move and I thought perhaps he was already dead. Then, like a fish fighting its hook, he thrashed and kicked, dislodging one of my hands, his foot striking the floor before trying to connect with my hips, chest, head. He pulled himself up, took a huge lungful of air before Alyson struck him with the lamp and he fell forward once more.

I grabbed his legs, my fingers digging into his flesh, forcing him down, down.

One of his hands managed to grab the edges of the barrel, trying to raise himself back to the surface. Another hand appeared, the fingers curling around the lip. He freed his hips and began to drag the barrel toward him. He was going to tip it over. I let go of his legs and, leaning heavily on the barrel to prevent it inclining further, began to prise his fingers loose.

I managed to get one hand free. Alyson worked upon the other. "Get his feet," she roared. "Push him back in."

Sinking her teeth into his fingers, Alyson held one arm above her head, an ankle clutched in her hand. Finally, with a last violent jerk of his leg, his hand let go. We held him fast, pushing him deeper into the ale.

God forgive me, I didn't let go of his feet; Alyson, her hands submerged, pushed down on his back.

Whether it was the struggle he'd already put up or he just resigned himself to fate, it didn't take long for Roland le Bold to die.

Feeling his body go flaccid, I released him slowly, carefully. In silence, we watched him sink, face-first, his legs twisted above the water. The ale gurgled and belched. Bubbles exploded on the surface before it grew still.

"Wait. Not good enough," said Alyson. Lifting the lid off the ground, she poked and shoved Roland's legs, bending them, forcing them into the ale. I helped.

When the barrel contained him, Alyson tried to put the lid in place. It didn't matter what she did, it wouldn't seal and slid off, clattering to the floor. Breathless, we stared at the lid then each other, unable to believe what we'd just done, what we'd survived.

Another noise alerted us. There was the stamp of booted feet above, cries and shouts. The door opened and we spun toward the stairs. Coming down them was Leander.

Holding a torch aloft, he took in my wet hair, bloody forehead, and torn tunic, Alyson's wild countenance, and called over his shoulder: "She is safe. They both are. Check upstairs." There was a reply and a stampede of feet.

Turning back to us, Leander approached as fast as he was able. Holding out his arms, I fell into them, placing my ear against the reassuring beat of his heart. "God be praised, you are safe—but not by my hand," he said with such sadness and guilt that I held him as tightly as I was able.

"Alyson saved me," I whispered.

"We saved each other," said Alyson.

Kissing the top of my wet head, he held out his other arm and invited her to share the embrace. She did most gratefully.

"This lifetime isn't enough to repay you, Alyson, or to make up for not being here when you needed me, Anneke. Where is the bastard? What's happened to him?"

Withdrawing slightly from his arms, Alyson and I faced what we'd done.

Lifting the torch higher, Leander gazed at the barrel and let out a long whistle. He squeezed us tighter. After a moment, he began talking softly.

"He never left Southwark. Under cover of darkness, the guards loaded him onto a boat to transport him across the river, when they were attacked—from the water. It was a clever ruse. Assuming he'd been transferred to the other barge, they scoured the banks of London and found it moored near Dowgate. A search began in earnest from there. But he never boarded. When I discovered the truth, I came straight back. There were sightings, by the millponds, by Smith's rents. It was then I understood what he intended and came to warn you. I was too late."

"Not too late." I bent and picked up the lid and, with a straight face, passed it to him. "We can't get this to stay in place."

Passing the torch to Alyson, Leander regarded me wryly. "I'm happy to be of service, my lady."

Ramming the lid into position, he grabbed one of the wrapped tools from the table and hammered it shut. Ale leaked out the barrel, staining the outside of the wood, forming tears, runnels of blood, wet scars. Trapped inside was the man who had caused all these things and more.

"Tomorrow," Leander began softly when he'd finished, leaning upon the top, "I will ask Captain Stoyan to arrange to have this barrel taken out to sea."

"Aye," said Alyson, one hand upon Leander's chest, the other on my arm. "Far out."

"Will God forgive us for what we did?" I asked.

"I believe God may not forgive," said Leander cautiously, "but He will understand. Le Bold abused his power, the trust others bestowed. He committed terrible crimes and all the while professed to be doing our Lord's work."

"I think that's one worker God won't miss," said Alyson.

"All the same," said Leander, "I'm glad he wasn't wearing the cassock when you killed him. For you may console yourselves that you killed an evil man, not a monk."

"Makes no difference to me," said Alyson. "Either way, as man or monk, he was wickedness itself."

I didn't want to say it, but I felt the same.

We stared at the barrel, the torch crackling. Footsteps resounded above. Leander glanced up. "I'll tell my men the search is over. Get a message to Tobias." He glanced at me. "He swore he would not rest till le Bold was found. Unless we tell him the truth, he'll never know peace again."

"Can we afford to tell the truth to anyone?" I asked, worrying my lower lip.

"Come," said Alyson, "let's discuss this over a drink, shall we? Not in the solar, not yet. I want to celebrate and if that makes me a sinful woman, then give me a badge and I'll wear it with pride."

"Shouldn't we also pray for his soul? Pray that he finds the peace in the hereafter he never found on earth."

"Peace?" said Alyson. "Get away with you, I hope he rots in hell and never knows anything but torment." She gave the wood a sharp kick. "It's no more than the prick deserves. That's what I'm drinking to."

I couldn't help it, I laughed. My body was humming as the song of ale stirred within me, as relief replaced the fear.

Following Alyson, Leander and I walked back to the stairs. "Are you all right, my love? Did he . . . did he hurt you greatly?"

"Not greatly. Alyson prevented that and I am so very thankful."

"He'll never hurt you again."

"Aye, he won't. And I know I should feel guilty, that I should seek penance for what we did, pray for *our* souls and suffer remorse, but I don't want to do any of those things. He killed my brother, he killed Saskia, Will, and Louisa and others besides. Alyson's right. He deserved what happened. Only, I don't feel like celebrating either. It's wrong to seek vengeance, I know, but if the opportunity is offered and we take it upon such a deserving villain, is that a mortal sin?"

"Mayhap." Alyson paused on the steps and turned to look down upon us. "But answer me this. Is it a sin if anyone other than God—and we three here—knows? Is it a sin if your conscience is clear? That's what we need to talk about."

With a wink and a laugh, she continued. I could not.

"Is your conscience clear, my love?" asked Leander.

"For now, but I will still confess."

"Who would absolve you of such a sin?" asked Leander. "Better to hold your peace."

"I was thinking of confessing to Father Clement."

"You are intending to return to Elmham Lenn sometime soon?"

"Nay," I said, and walked up the remaining stairs, Leander's chuckles in my ears.

As Leander went upstairs to notify his men and send them home, Alyson and I latched the brewery door and locked it, Alyson pocketing the key. Voices in the courtyard followed by the jingle of tack and whinny of horses drifted in not long after. By the time we'd stoked the fire, Leander rejoined us. "I told the others that you were refilling the jugs and would be up soon. They're relieved to find le Bold is not here and are continuing their search. We'll have to come up with a story or it could go on for days. Only"—his eyes rested on the brewery door—"I'm not sure what to tell them."

"Easy. Nothing. When Captain Stoyan takes the barrel, tell him not to go out to sea, but to open it and pour the contents in the river. The body will wash ashore as night follows day or the moon chases the sun. When it's discovered, everyone will have their answers; they'll assume God saw fit to punish the bishop. Tobias will know peace and so will we."

"That means we'll have to tell the captain what happened," said Leander.

"Aye," said Alyson.

"A version, mayhap?" I said.

Leander gave me a small smile. "Mayhap."

"Hatto can be trusted," said Alyson, misinterpreting the look that passed between Leander and me.

I agreed.

"Before we drink," said Leander, "can we agree never to speak a word of what happened in there again?"

"Not a word," said Alyson, hand atop the stopper on the skin.

"Not a word," I agreed.

Leander leaned in. "Alyson I believe, but as for you, Mistress Anneke, any time you give your word you're apt to break it."

Pretending an affront I didn't feel, I put distance between us. "It's not always of my choosing."

"Nonetheless, I think I've a solution."

"Well, that can wait till after we down something, for God-sakes!" said Alyson, placing mazers before Leander and indicating he should pour. While he did that, she sat me closer to the fire, throwing me a sheet so I might dry my hair and tunic. Lifting my hand, I gently touched the tender flesh of my forehead. There would be bruising—le Bold's final mark.

"To life," said Alyson, and lifted her drink.

"To new beginnings," I said.

We looked at Leander. "There's only one thing I want to toast. Rather, one person."

I tilted my head. "Oh?"

His smile broadened and those eyes did twinkle. "To the Brewer of London."

"To the Brewer of London," said Alyson, standing, raising her mazer, and downing it in one gulp.

"But I'm not—not yet."

"You soon will be, my chick. The finest in the land. I know it. I feel it here." Alyson slapped her midriff. Walking around the table, she gave me a resounding kiss on the mouth. "Now, let's return to the festivities upstairs before we arouse more suspicion." She lifted the heavy damp curtain of my head and winced when she saw my forehead. "We'll have to think of something to explain these as well. Oh, the stories we'll be telling." And her eyes gleamed at the notion.

Turning our backs on the kitchen and brewery, taking fresh jugs of beer and some wine with us, we returned to the solar and the friends and family who awaited us there.

# SIXTY-TWO

Late July
*The year of Our Lord 1408 in the ninth
year of the reign of Henry IV*

*T*wo weeks later, as I observed Leander standing by the window, enjoying the warm London breeze, I thought of all we'd achieved.

The move had gone smoothly, with the brewery fittings and our furniture and household goods transported across the river by Captain Stoyan. While the servants and additional help we'd hired arranged everything upstairs under Alyson's watchful eye, I supervised the placement of equipment downstairs.

The copper pipes fascinated Betje, Harry, and Yolande, while Thomas and Master atte Place could not cease examining the slotted tuns that came with the premises. Reminding them that there was work to do, I had to prevent them exploring until everything was in place.

Excited by the change and by their new nursery, which was a

larger room on the second story, the twins walked up and down the stairs, grabbing the railings, crawling and running through rooms, hiding beneath tables and in chests, getting under everyone's feet, and generally exhausting Constance and Emma, who found even their endless reservoir of patience drained.

Each night I fell into bed, pleased with how The Swanne was taking shape. From the second day, using supplies we'd brought from Southwark, Alyson opened the taproom and began to sell our ale and beer. Already, we had additional orders to meet, on top of our regular customers. Masters Porlond and Hamme had visited and declared themselves pleased and arranged a date for me to be invested into the Mystery of Brewers.

Leander organized for Captain Stoyan to take the remaining sealed barrel from The Swanne down the river.

"What's wrong with it?" asked the captain as they maneuvered it up the stairs.

"It's soured," said Leander, and quickly explained.

"Ah. It's a monk's pissy brew then," said Captain Stoyan.

Leander's lips twitched. "Aye, one of a kind."

As Leander sat on the chair near the bed and pulled off his boots, rubbing his twisted foot before undoing the laces of his shirt, I put down my mother's recipe book, pulled myself to the edge of the mattress, and touched his thigh.

"Thank you," I said.

"What for?"

"So much, so much." I found my voice becoming thick. "You saved me, you know. Not only my life, but *me*."

Leander gave a dry laugh. "You save yourself so often, Anneke, I sometimes wonder if you need me at all."

Rising, I stood in front of him and waited until he shifted

position so I might sit in his lap. "My lord," I began, linking my arms around his neck, "whatever else you think of me, whatever else you might say—" He opened his mouth, but I placed my fingers against it. "Shh, let me finish. However it might seem, know I *always* need you—more than that, I *want* you."

He gazed into my eyes, his face softening, his eyes glistening. "Now may I speak?"

I nodded solemnly.

"I want *you*. God, Anneke, from the moment I first saw you, I wanted you. What I never anticipated, what has delighted me to my very soul, is that I *need* you too." I went to say something, but this time, he stopped me with a kiss. "Not yet. I'm not finished." He paused and his sapphire eyes looked deep into mine. His warm breath was on my cheek, his hair beneath my fingers. "I love you, Anna de Winter, Anneke Sheldrake, in whatever your next incarnation will be. Know this, I will always love you."

I bent my head and silenced him for a long time.

Nestled in his arms, watching the stars twinkle and listening to the unfamiliar night sounds of Cornhill Street, something occurred to me. "My lord, on our last night at The Swanne, you said you didn't believe I could keep my word and that you had a solution. While I chose not to be offended by such an outrageous suggestion"—I smiled—"I'm curious to know. What was it?"

"Simple," said Leander, untangling my braid. "You must marry me."

I placed my hands on his shoulders and leaned away so he was forced to drop his fingers. "*Marry* you?"

"That way, you must promise before the Holy Church and in

the sight of God to obey me, so when I ask for your word, you've no choice but to abide."

I burst out laughing. "My lord, that is the funniest of proposals. I don't need marriage to obey you—or not."

When he didn't chuckle or smile in return, I stroked his face. "Sweet Mother Mary, you're serious."

"Most."

"But, Leander, you're a knight of the realm, the son of a lord, a king's man, and I'm . . . I'm . . ."

"The most remarkable woman I've ever known."

"I'm a brewer, Leander. Your mistress, a murderer . . ." I arched a brow and looked at him out of the corner of my eye. "You can stop me whenever you wish, my lord."

"You're all those things. But you're also my brewer, and I wouldn't have you any other way."

"What would your father say?"

Leander's brow furrowed. "Frankly, I don't care. But you might be surprised. I don't think he'd object, at least, not too hard." He gave a half-grin. "I'm the youngest son and a cripple—"

I made a noise of objection. I barely noticed his infirmity; like Betje's scars, like our histories and memories, it was a part of who he was.

"For all that you may think poorly of him because of what he did to your family, he perceived himself as putting a terrible wrong right. That he lacked judgment, that he did not consider the future for all concerned, I think are points he would concede. I, however, want to consider the future—our future. In taking my name, not only is yours assured, my love, but so is Betje's and the twins."

"Is that why you ask, my lord? To put a terrible wrong right? You did not rape my mother, Leander, you did not sign a devil's deal that rendered my family destitute; you're not responsible for what Roland did to me either." I stared past his left shoulder, at the lamp flickering by the bed. "I know you feel great affection for Betje, but how . . . how could you love Karel and Isabella knowing who . . . knowing their father?"

"The same way I love Tobias, knowing how he came into this world. Tobias is a good man, a decent man. Are you worried the twins will be tainted by their father's blood? Not if I've any say, Anneke, not if you do either. Just as Symond has had no say in Tobias's upbringing—that was one thing my father did do right." He took my chin in between his fingers and forced me to meet his eyes.

"What do you say? Do we create a new, unconventional family from our band of misfits and cripples? A brewer and a knight, adorable giddy twins, and sweet little Betje?"

"Don't forget Tobias."

"Never."

"Nor Adam and Alyson—"

"Aye . . ."

"And Captain Stoyan."

"Well . . . I jest my love, I do but jest. Of course."

"And dear Harry."

"And dear Harry." Leander sighed and raised a finger. "I will draw the line at any of the girls—not even my father at his most agreeable would concede their inclusion."

I laughed and kissed his finger.

Lost for words, my thoughts spiraled to the heavens. Wasn't this what I'd always dreamed of, wasn't this what, in the secret depths of my soul, I'd always wanted? A husband, a family? It had been, once. But if the events of the last couple of years taught me anything, it was that I didn't *need* that anymore. I'd the love of a good man, husband or not; I'd my sister, my beautiful children, and such dear, dear friends. I had the type of family of which I'd always dreamed—bound by love, not blood; by experience, not rank or status; and not even the Rainford name could change that. I'd an occupation I loved and a successful trade. Being the best brewer in London, or England as Will had once declared, was no longer an impossible dream but an attainable goal. It wouldn't be easy; I'd be a fool to imagine otherwise. There were more battles to fight, arguments to win or lose and more injustice to overcome. But I could do it—together, we all could. Was I so very wrong to *need* to achieve that as well?

It was who I was.

But what Leander asked of me, it wasn't about need. It was about want. And God and the crones and Mother Mary and Ninkasi knew I wanted him. More than I'd wanted anything in my life. But still . . .

Taking Leander's face in mine, I held it firmly, studying the firm mouth, the dark bristles, the little dimples that resided in his cheeks, before locking onto his eyes once more and seeing the hope, the want, residing there. "I love you almost too much to become your wife, Leander. You have so much to lose by tying your name to mine, to my reputation."

"Your answer is nay, then?" He tried to pull away, not in anger, but disappointment. I wouldn't release him.

"I didn't say that, did I?"

"Nay."

"If you recall, I said 'almost.' You see, my lord, I too can be selfish." A light began to dance in those eyes. "Leander, can you wait until I'm settled here in Cornhill Street, till the brewery is solvent and established? Can you wait till I'm secure in the trade and have trained new journeymen to assist Betje, Harry, and Adam?"

"Why?"

"Because then I want you to ask me again."

Understanding dawned and his face transformed. His mouth twitched.

"I can, beloved. I can."

I leaned my forehead against his, lowering it till our noses, then our lips, just touched. His heart drummed beneath my palm, vibrating along my arm and answering the rapid beating of my own.

"What will your answer be then?"

"If I tell you now, then I spoil our tale."

"Not for me. Never for me."

"Then, my answer will be aye, beloved," I whispered against his mouth, breathed into his very soul. "It is aye."

# AUTHOR'S NOTE

*L*ike most historical novels, *The Lady Brewer of London* draws upon real places, events, records, and people, as well as a documented political and cultural backdrop—including all aspects of beer and ale production, and the laws and punishments described—to enrich and add veracity to a work of fiction. What I'd like to do here is explain where I've either followed or veered from fact to create the tale you've just completed.

The book opens in the bustling port town of Elmham Lenn, which is an invention. Though a fictitious place, it's loosely based on medieval Bishop's Lynn (now King's Lynn) and Cromer, both port towns on the east coast of England.

The second half of the novel is set variously in medieval Southwark (mainly Bankside) and London, as well as Gloucester, and in terms of setting is as close to accurate as possible. Using original maps from the era and a slightly later period, historical records, and the work of so many wonderful and erudite historians, I've tried to re-create the sense of what it would have been like to live and brew in those times. While I've aimed for authenticity, I've chosen to modernize the spelling of some genuine locales in Southwark and London (for example, St. Saviour's Church instead of Sint Savyors and Pepper Alley in lieu of Peper, etc., though some others maintain the original, such as the Tabard Inn and the Cardinal's Hatte) in case keen readers wish to track these places down. I have, however, taken mild liberties as to the exact location and names of certain streets, churches, and conduits (for the sake of the story) around Southwark and London, though most are precise.

The references to King Henry IV, or Henry Bolingbroke as he is also known, and his whereabouts at different times throughout the novel are faithful, including physical descriptions and those of his ailments. The skin affliction he suffered is documented fact. It's also fact that the king slipped into a temporary coma on the date described, many believing that he was at death's door. He made a recovery, but his health before and after was never very good. It's also true that, much to the chagrin of the nobles, officials, and merchants who'd descended on Gloucester for the sitting of parliament on October 24, 1407, Henry didn't make an appearance, leaving Archbishop Arundel to officiate instead. The reason for his failure to attend is not known, but probably had something to do with his recuperation from the long river journey, even though this would not have been arduous. He did attend parliament on the second day but kept silent.

It's also true that King Henry developed a taste for beer, something historian Ian Mortimer, in his excellent biography *The Fears of Henry IV*, attributes to his time in Lithuania as a young man. This worked very well for the novel and it was not too great a stretch (I hope) to have him ordering Anneke's beer, let alone ale, for his own table.

The plague that strikes London and Southwark in 1407 is

based on an obscure record, and I thank my dear friend historian Dr. Frances Thiele for uncovering that and other facts for me. There were many outbreaks over this period, some worse than others and none as great as the plague the century before (1348–1350) or the Great Plague that decimated London in 1665–1666.

The Thames famously froze in the winter of 1407–1408, and various entertainments occurred on the thick ice of the river, including Frost Fairs. Likewise, the descriptions of crops thriving or failing, wars, allegiances, and the ports owned and operated by the Hanse or Hanseatic League, and various trade and pilgrim routes are all based on actuality.

As for the ale, beer, and other alcoholic beverages that feature in the book, references to the methods used in brewing, the levels of consumption, as well as the taxes and laws, are historically correct. In medieval times people didn't have the choices, knowledge, or understanding of health that we do now. Water, which was often polluted and brackish, was considered dangerous—and it was. While other alcoholic and nonalcoholic drinks were available in England before the 1400s, the main beverage consumed by the young and not so young, particularly in the lower classes and religious houses, was a home-brewed ale. In the 1400s, people drank on average between one and a half to five liters (the latter in extreme circumstances) of ale a day (often on top of wine, sack, cider, and mead). While A. Lynn Martin, in his scholarly book *Alcohol, Sex and Gender in Late Medieval and Early Modern Europe*, explains this consumption by analyzing the figures and proposing when and where these amounts were downed, taking into account the food eaten while drinking, as well as the strength of the beer and wine (which was reasonably heady), it still leaves us with the undeniable truth that a great deal of alcohol was consumed every day. That meant that most people were at least a little inebriated much of the time.

Ale was regarded as a safe and relatively cheap means of quenching thirst and providing much-needed dietary nourishment. It was drunk on rising, given to children, downed regularly by paupers and princes, nuns and priests, sailors and soldiers. People went to battle, farmed, birthed children, treated illnesses and injuries, made important policy and diplomatic decisions, married, died, cooked, cleaned, sewed, and accomplished a range of tasks affected by the drink they consumed all day every day. It's a scary thought!

Ale-making was a domestic industry or a by-product of other cottage-type businesses, like baking or milling, and was mostly (but not exclusively) undertaken by women. The ale was flavored with various spices and herbs, as well as the woodsmoke used to cook the grain, and was often sickly sweet. There was great variety in quality and taste. In this book, Anneke uses barley exclusively to make her ale, but other crops were used depending on availability and region. As a consequence, rye, oat, and other grain-based ales or a mixture of these were also made.

Quantities made differed, but whatever was produced had to be drunk very quickly before it soured, so it was sold or shared with neighbors (bartering likely happened in exchange for a brew) and impromptu parties erupted with the attendant fun, violence, and propensity for accidents they still engender.

People appreciated that a kind of magic occurred when water, grain, and yeast came together. Though the term "yeast" was yet to be used, it was understood that the frothy head that was produced must be preserved and transferred to each new brew. They called this "godisgoode." It's likely that the combination of dosing a fresh batch from the previous brew, as well as the yeast build-up on equipment and in the air in the brewing space, would have contributed to the maintenance of yeast as well.

While almost anyone could brew, evidence suggests few were *consistently* good at it. Woe betide the person who sold sour, watery, or tasteless ale. They not only attracted the wrath of the authorities and fines, but worse, the fury of the village and townsfolk. Pillorying, dunking (called "cucking"—there was even a special "cucking stool" designed for this purpose), and all sorts of punishments were regularly meted out—mostly to women—sometimes even to those who produced a fine ale or sold one. What happens to Alyson when she incurs the wrath of the Southwark bailiff Lewis Fynk was not uncommon. This was because women's role in brewing was regarded with suspicion. It was a double-edged sword. Women associated with brewing provided something necessary to everyday life, yet were often resented and perceived as "disorderly" troublemakers who were licentious, dishonest, and needed to be reminded of (male) authority, God, and the law. That taverns, inns, and, in the novel's case, bathhouses often went hand in hand with ale consumption compounded perceptions.

While some monasteries (and thus monks) were involved in large-scale production (relative to the era) and often sold their ale for a profit, brewsters and alewives played a really important role in the manufacturing and local distribution of ale up until around the 1500s, when men slowly took over. Historian Judith Bennett, in her marvelous book *Ale, Beer and Brewsters: Women's Work in a Changing World, 1300–1600*, attributes this to an interesting and quite complex notion. She argues (and I use this as an epigraph in the novel), "When a venture prospers, women fade from the scene." That is, once decent profits could be made from brewing and the scale of production grew, it became a male-dominated and very lucrative (despite taxes and government controls, which were strict) business. Men stepped in and women were eased out as more intensive labor and greater capital were required to maintain a brewing business at this level. The only exceptions were a few widows and resourceful wives and daughters—most of whom inherited their businesses, which eventually passed into male hands either through marriage or sale.

Another reason women left brewing was because of the additive, hops. Before roughly 1420 in England, with few exceptions (Anneke being one), the ale the women made contained no hops (imported beer, which contained hops, was drunk but not favored as a beverage). This herb—from the same family as marijuana—came from Europe and when placed in a brew made the ale quite bitter, but also preserved it. Preservation, via hops, was what changed the face of the brewing industry forever.

Once hops were introduced as a regular part of brewing, the product had a longer shelf life. The new drink, called beer to distinguish it from ale, could be made in larger quantities, exported around the country and overseas. It was also cheaper to make, requiring less grain, so the overheads were fewer and the profits greater. Regarded with distaste and as "un-English" by many at first, beer was gradually adopted as the preferred beverage. Initially, even the laws reflected the negative attitude toward the hopped ale, as those who made ale were forbidden from making beer and vice versa. (It's important to note that "ale," as a description of a type of beer, didn't come into use until the 1800s.)

It was the ambivalent role of women in brewing, as makers of something essential to the diet of medieval folk, as bitches and "witches," and the constant assertion of authority and control over them and their product through the presence of ale-tasters and taxes and guilds (the latter virtually excluded them) that inspired me to write *The Lady Brewer of London* and explore, through fiction melded with fact, what it might have been like to brew in these times. You may have noticed that I've used the terms "brewer" and "brewster" interchangeably throughout the tale. While "brewer" mainly applied to a man and "brewster" to a woman, men could, in certain regions of England and in Scotland, be called brewsters. While the scholars I used mostly differentiated between the sexes, I wanted to acknowledge that both sexes could be called either by referring to Anneke as both a brewer and brewster.

Many of the alehouses and taverns mentioned are authentic to the era and, while I'm on the subject of actual personages and places, the mayor of London, as named in part two, was a real person as well. There are others scattered throughout.

Ale-conners or ale-tasters must have been the bane of brewers' lives, dependent as they were on their goodwill and permission to sell their brew. The scenes with Anneke early in the novel (and later, in Southwark) are drawn from facts as presented in H. A. Monckton's *A History of English Ale & Beer*. Contested by other sources as to its accuracy, Monckton's notion of an ale-taster wearing leather breeches and sitting in spilled ale was just too good not to use. Admittedly, I took liberties with the other formalities, though the marking of barrels and the taxes set, as well as the notion of an ale-stake, and a bushel, are accurate and were drawn from numerous other sources, such as H. S. Corran's *A History of Brewing*, Richard W. Unger's *Beer in the Middle Ages and the Renaissance*, Iain Gately's *Drink: A Cultural History of Alcohol*, Peter Clark's *The English Alehouse: A Social History 1200–1830*, Patrick E. McGovern's *Uncorking the Past: The Quest for Wine, Beer, and Other Alcoholic Beverages*, Ian S. Hornsey's *A History of Beer and Brewing*, and Judith M. Bennett's "Women and Men in the Brewers' Gild of London, ca. 1420" in *The Salt of Common Life*, edited by Edwin Brezette DeWindt, as well as many more books besides.

The characters William Porlond and Stephen Hamme are based on real people. William Porlond was appointed clerk of the Brewers' Guild of London in 1418 and managed to keep detailed records until his death around 1438–1439. It's also recorded that in 1407 one Stephen Hamme owned a brewhouse that was exceptionally well equipped. Using their relationship to brewing and the Mystery of Brewers, I plucked these men from history's pages and gave them a place in Anneke's tale. I hope they don't mind.

The laws of London and Southwark did differ, and despite King Henry granting London authorities charter over Southwark during this period, little changed and Southwark maintained its reputation as an area rife with criminals, lowlifes, gamblers, prostitutes, animal sports, and those who flouted the law—including the laws around brewing. That it would have been a colorful group of manors and liberties in which to dwell, I've no doubt, and it's no surprise that many immigrants set up businesses there (including bathhouses, most of which were run by Flemish) and that over a century later, theaters also found a home in and near the Stews. I'd also like to acknowledge Martha Carlin's marvelous book *Medieval Southwark*, which so vividly brought to life the area, its rich history, and the folk and laws within it.

The basic laws as related in the final court cases follow the procedures laid out for trials of women, murderers, and members of the clergy, with modifications and deviations to suit the story. The laws mentioned in relation to prostitutes and bathhouses, and which Lewis Fynk accuses characters of breaking, are also accurate—there were many more besides, and the poor women who either chose (if you can call it that) or had no other option but to enter prostitution had a harsh life. If they found a good master and mistress, they were indeed blessed. Alyson Bookbinder, owner of The Swanne, is not only a good mistress, but as many of you will have realized, she's Geoffrey Chaucer's Wife of Bath as I envisage her in the next stage of her life, beyond what we know of her from *The Canterbury Tales*. Having exhausted (some to the grave) five husbands and being full of life and bountiful in character, I started to imagine what she did with herself beyond the pages of her prologue and tale in Chaucer's *Tales*, and so Alyson, proprietor of The Swanne in Bankside, was born. The title of the novel also gestures to these wonderful, bawdy, and heartfelt narratives, and I hope Chaucer forgives me such audacity with one of the richest characters and most marvelous stories in English literature. I will be returning to Alyson's story, pre–*The Lady Brewer of London*, very soon.

I've also denoted the passing of the years through the novel in accordance with medieval tradition, which was to use the day the king ascended to the throne as the beginning of the first year of his reign, not as a modern reader might expect, from the first day of the new year. So, Henry IV, for example, was crowned on October 29. Accordingly, the year of his reign changes each October 30.

Speaking of "New Year's Day": in medieval times, this was generally regarded as falling on Lady's Day, March 25, though some records also recognize January 1. I have used the latter.

During the period in which the novel is set, the papacy was based in Avignon and Rome due to a schism in the church. Benedict XIII was expelled from Avignon in 1403; however, he was succeeded, after a Council was held in Pisa to resolve the issue (but made it worse), by three "antipopes," none of whom resided at Avignon and who weren't recognized by the English, who supported the Roman papacy and Pope Gregory XII. Captain Stoyan threatens to close off the Benedictines' access to the pilgrim trails to Rome, but later there's a reference to Avignon as well, so I thought I should explain.

As is usual with historical fiction, I have also played with facts to suit the narrative, and I hope that the marvelous scholars, journalists, and beer academics, and the many writers whose work I have drawn upon and to whom I'm indebted, the websites that I've pored over, and any history buffs will forgive me this imaginative play and understand that I had to change the ingredients in order to brew to my own recipe. Any mistakes are completely my own and I do humbly ask your forgiveness.

# ACKNOWLEDGMENTS

$\mathcal{T}$he three years I spent researching, writing, and rewriting this novel have brought so many wonderful, knowledgeable, and generous people into my life. Finally I get to publicly thank them here.

First, my dear friends who, when I said to them, "My next novel is going to be about a medieval brewer," didn't fall about laughing, but showed (or feigned!) real interest. Only my husband, Stephen; my son, Adam; and my daughter, Caragh, understood the irony—that someone who doesn't drink beer had made the decision to craft a novel about, and thus devote a few years of her life to, the amber liquid. And you know what? They didn't doubt for a second I would do it—now that's a loving family!

To my fabulous friend Kerry Doyle, who, along with Stephen, read an early draft and offered kind and sage feedback—you're a rock. Kerry and I go back a long way; through some very bad times, her enthusiasm, care for others, and bright shiny spirit have never dimmed—thank you. Also to Jim McKay, who, after reading a few chapters, encouraged me to please continue—

I did, Jim, and here it is, in no small part due to you. Thanks must go as well to Joanna Lindsay. Beside me through writing this book, she was happy to share a w(h)ine or three whenever either of us needed it and listen to me ramble on about all things medieval and brewing.

Katherine Howell, author extraordinaire, is the best writing buddy one could wish for. If it wasn't for the hours we spent on email and phone, supporting each other through conception, drafting, and editing, these last three years would have been a poorer experience indeed. Thank you so much, Katherine.

Huge thanks must also go to my beloved friend Dr. Frances Thiele, whose harp music not only soothes and inspires me as I write, but who is also my go-to person for historical conundrums. Franny, you're a wonder. Thank you to my gorgeous and dearest of friends, Dr. Lesley Roberts, who traveled throughout the UK with me on a fact-checking and creative mission—not just for this novel, but my next two as well. We shared a room in some strange and marvelous places, numerous adventures, so many laughs, and discovered extraordinary people and places that will weave their way into future books. Thank you for being beside me in every sense of the word, Lesley. I love you dearly.

Thank you also to my sister, Jenny (who was by my side the day the idea for the story was born); my uncle Peter; my aunt Helen; Peter Goddard; Sheryl Gwyther; Alison and Greg Hall; Dr. Anthony Eaton; Margaret Wenham; Dr. Lisa Hill; Dr. Malcolm Maclean; Jason Russell; Danny Matheson and Kazuo Ikeda at Jam Jar in Battery Point (where I spent many hours thinking and researching); and the Prince of Wales and Shippies (my fabulous and fun local drinking holes where I could witness liters of beer being consumed in a convivial atmosphere and among friends, such as Christina Schulthess, Peter Jenkins, and Ali Gay). Klaus Stroehl and Sandra Poth for ensuring my German was accurate: *Danke Schön alles Liebe*. Thanks also to my wonderful mum, Moira Adams, and mother-in-law, Pat Brooks, both of whom always asked how the writing was going, even when I know they didn't really want to hear the answer— love you both very much.

Brewers are such generous people. I'd only ever met one, my friend Nick Cleave (and thank you, Nick, for your help as well), until I embarked on this novel and, since then, I am fortunate to call more of them mates. Those brewers and distillers I contacted were unstinting with their time, knowledge, and, frankly, their support of my idea—this woman they didn't know then and may yet regret they ever met. Over a dram or a drink or two, they would discuss, demonstrate, and answer my endless questions about brewing, opening their minds and hearts. My gratitude to Bill and Lyn Lark from Lark in Hobart, the place where the idea for *The Lady Brewer of London* was born, cannot be expressed enough. They have since become dear friends and thanking them here is only a small part of what I owe for the love and care they've extended to Stephen and me since we moved to Hobart, let alone their interest in this novel. I also want to thank their fantastic staff, from the erudite and kind Mark Nicholson to head distiller Chris Thomson, and Becs the barmaid, who, unbeknownst to her, with her husky voice and tales of whisky, sent me on this journey in the first place.

I also want to thank Ash Huntingdon of Two Metres Tall, and Owen Johnson—then of Moo Brew—who was fantastic. Likewise, Scot Wilson-Browne of Red Duck Brewery, Alfredton, Victoria—thank you. The passionate and intelligent work of some fabulous beer historians, beer aficionados, journalists, and medieval historians whose work on brewing, craft brews, the Middle Ages, England, London, Southwark, women, and the history of beer and other alcohol has been utterly invaluable throughout the writing process.

I also want to thank my publisher, Harlequin. From the moment Sue Brockhoff read my manuscript, her boundless enthusiasm for Anneke's story has been infectious and quite incredible to experience. Likewise, my brilliant editors, Linda Funnell and Stephanie Smith. Linda and Stephanie, you are both a writer's gift and I am eternally grateful that you were given to me.

I want to thank the magnificent management, sales, and marketing team at Harlequin, especially Michelle Laforest, Cristina Lee, Adam Van Rooijen, Adrian Kaleel, Camille Poshoglian, Lauren Roberts, Annabel Blay, Calla MacGregor, Emma Noble, and all the fabulous others who helped bring my novel to life.

This book would never have seen the light of publishing day had it not been for the commitment and belief of my extraordinary agent, Selwa Anthony. When I first explained my idea, she offered nothing but encouragement, even cracking her velvet whip when I started to take a bit too long to complete it. I feel so blessed to be part of her writing family and don't tell her enough how much it means to me—hence *The Lady Brewer of London* is dedicated to her, again as a part thanks for believing in what I love doing and being there for me.

The support and love of my children keeps me going and while I know they're proud of me, it's only a fraction of the pride I feel in them—thank you Adam and Caragh.

I want to thank my readers—without you, this book would

not live beyond these pages or my imagination. This is for you as well.

I wish to acknowledge my beloved friend Sara Douglass (Warneke), who, though she is no longer here for me to laugh, chat, and *sláinte* with, still sustains me when I recall her marvelous wit, wisdom, and generosity. I miss her every day.

Always last and never least, I want to thank my beloved Stephen. Inspired by my research and my growing devotion to, if not the drink, beer, then certainly the process and the magic brewers achieve, he has started his own craft brewery, Captain Bligh's Ale and Cider, in an old brewery in the heart of Hobart. Encouraging my writing, listening to me opine about medieval techniques (even as he was trying to master his own contemporary ones), Stephen as always has been unflinching in his support, energy, and commitment to what I do. Certainly, he loved being my research assistant, and we had so many fun times arguing about and tasting different brews as well as making many of our own. We're a good recipe, my love. This, like all my books, is for you.

# GLOSSARY

*My* intention was to make most of the unfamiliar medieval terms clear by creating context throughout the novel, but sometimes this hasn't been possible, especially regarding the use of festivals and religious feasts to mark the passage of time as well as some of the dates used.

Below is a small glossary I have compiled.

### *Holidays and Festivals*

**Michaelmas:** September 30. This was the day upon which the last of the harvest was gathered. It was when rents were due and a time of feasting as folk prepared for winter.

**St. Martin's Day or Martinmas:** November 11, and traditionally the day for slaughtering livestock.

**St. Catherine's Day:** November 25. St. Catherine was the patron saint of lawyers, wheelwrights, rope makers, carpenters, lace makers, and spinners. She was also the guardian of single women who, on this day, would often pray for a husband. Catherine wheels were lit, special cakes (cattern cakes) made, and feasts held. This day was more popular on the continent and slowly fell out of favor in England.

**Feast of St. Nicholas:** December 6.

**Conception of the Blessed Virgin:** December 8.

**Feast of St. Thomas the Apostle:** December 21.

**Adam and Eve's Day:** December 24—Christmas Eve.

**St. Stephen's Day:** December 26.

**Twelfth Night or Epiphany:** January 6. Marks the end of the twelve days of Christmas celebrations and is said to be the day God revealed Jesus Christ was his son.

**Feast of the Epiphany:** The last of the Christmas feasts.

**Hocktide:** The second Monday or Tuesday after Easter. Rents were due on this day.

**St. John at Port Latin Day:** May 6.

## Dates

I use the terms "kalends," "nones," and "ides" to mark days of the month as was done in the medieval period.

**Kalends:** Fell on the first day of the month.

**Nones:** Fell on the seventh of months with thirty-one days—namely January, March, May, July, August, October, and December—and on the fifth of other months.

**Ides:** Fell on the fifteenth day of months with thirty-one days—namely January, March, May, July, August, October, and December—and the thirteenth of other months.

## Time

The passage of time followed in the novel is that used by the church and translates loosely as follows:

**Lauds** was at dawn or even earlier.

**Prime** was around six o'clock in the morning.

**Tierce** was approximately nine o'clock in the morning.

**Sext** represented midday.

**None** was around three o'clock in the afternoon.

**Vespers** was at six o'clock in the evening or dinnertime.

**Compline** was approximately nine o'clock at night or bedtime.

### General terms

**Escheator:** Someone who dealt with "escheats," property, that's not entailed by a will and is ceded to the Crown. The role of the medieval escheator was varied, but he most often was someone who dealt with lands and acquisitions involving a royal license (or those who attempted to evade one) and/or authority or with someone who committed a felony. In the case of felony or fraud, the property could be seized. The escheator was often assisted by a bailiff and clerks.

**Cucked/cucking:** A popular punishment meted out to those who broke the law. It involved being dunked in or doused with water or, as in the novel, ale.

# ABOUT THE AUTHOR

KAREN BROOKS is the author of twelve books. She is an associate professor and honorary senior research consultant at the University of Queensland, and an honorary senior fellow at the University of the Sunshine Coast. A newspaper columnist with Brisbane's *Courier Mail*, she's also a social commentator who has appeared regularly on national TV and radio (including a four-year stint on *The Einstein Factor* as part of the Brains Trust). Karen has a PhD in English/cultural studies and has published internationally on all things popular culture, education, and social psychology. An award-winning lecturer, she's taught throughout Australia and in the Netherlands, and keynoted at many education conferences around the country. Before turning to academia and writing, she was an army officer for five years, and prior to that dabbled in acting. For some reason, all her career choices start with A: acting, army, academic, and author! Nowadays she has slowed down somewhat and finds her greatest contentment in studying history and writing—both historical fiction and serious social commentary.

When not writing, she loves being with her family (husband

Stephen and two adult children, Adam and Caragh) and her "fur kids"—the dogs, Tallow and Dante, and four crazy cats: Claude, (Thomas) Cromwell, Jack Cade, and Baroque—and spending time with friends, cooking, traveling, reading, and dreaming.

Karen currently lives in Hobart, Tasmania, in a beautiful Georgian house built in 1868, which has its own wonderful stories to tell.